KATIE

Liverpool Taffy

*The Girl from
Seaforth Sands*

arrow books

This edition published by Arrow Books in 2005

First published in the United Kingdom in 2000 by Heinemann

Arrow Books
The Random House Group Limited
20 Vauxhall Bridge Road, London SW1V 2SA

Random House Australia (Pty) Limited
20 Alfred Street, Milsons Point, Sydney,
New South Wales 2061, Australia

Random House New Zealand Limited
18 Poland Road, Glenfield,
Auckland 10, New Zealand

Random House (Pty) Limited
Isle of Houghton, Corner of Boundary Road & Carse O'Gowrie,
Houghton 2198, South Africa

The Random House Group Limited Reg. No. 954009

www.randomhouse.co.uk

A CIP catalogue record for this book is available from the British Library

Papers used by Random House are natural,
recyclable products made from wood grown in
sustainable forests. The manufacturing processes conform to
the environmental regulations of the country of origin

Printed and bound in Great Britain by
Cox & Wyman Ltd, Reading, Berkshire

ISBN 0099499673

KATIE FLYNN

Liverpool Taffy

arrow books

For Margaret Campbell of Eastham,
who understands better than most why I write
these books;
thanks, Margaret

'It's right here. Can you stand some of those packages on the paving stones, now? It'll give your arms a rest till the tram comes by.'

Oh happiness, Biddy thought as she began to stand her burdens down and rub her aching arms. It was good to be out in the bright, crisp morning suddenly, good to be about to ride on a tram, even if the company of a nun did rather damp down the excitement of the occasion. We used to ride trams all the time and I never thought twice about it, Biddy told herself, standing guard over the parcels and gazing dreamily up the road towards the Gaiety Cinema, with its pictures of the stars and the posters proclaiming what was on unfortunately not clearly visible from this distance. We used to go to the cinema and eat a meal at a restaurant . . . we had our days out, to the seaside, picnics in the country . . . but they'll come again, the good times. Mam says she's resting well now, with no job. She'll probably be fit as a flea by Christmas.

'Ah, this looks like our tram. No dear, don't try to pick up all the parcels, it's a quiet time of day, the conductor will carry them aboard for us.'

A nun, Biddy knew, was unlikely to have to carry anything much for herself in a city like Liverpool, where a religious order got the respect it deserved from the largely Catholic inhabitants, but Sister Eustacia's order being less well known than some, she occasionally had to draw attention to herself with a discreet downward jerk of the head to her flowing black habit and the beads which hung at her waist.

'All right, Sister, but there's a powerful number of parcels; I'd best give him a hand.'

Biddy began to load herself up and as the tram stopped beside her, its bell giving one last clang as it did so, she hopped aboard, leaving the conductor to get out,

9

pick up the rest of the parcels, and give Sister Eustacia his hand.

'Mornin', Sister,' he said affably. 'Where's you goin' dis fine mornin'?'

'To the Wellington Rooms on Mount Pleasant, please,' Sister Eustacia said with all her customary politeness. 'Me and me little helper, here.' The long, chilly fingers touched Biddy's cheek. 'How much would you be wantin' from us?'

'I'll not charge for a parcel-carrier,' the conductor said, grinning at Biddy. 'Sure an' she's doin' you one favour, I'll do you another. If an inspector comes on board I'll run up and give her a ticket at once, mind.'

'That's uncommon good of you – bless you, my son,' Sister Eustacia said, making a small sign of the cross with her two fingers. 'Sit by me, Bridget, but keep an eye on me parcels.'

Isn't it an odd world, now, Biddy mused, sitting beside the nun on the wooden slatted seat and dragging the biggest parcel to rest against her skinny calves. Here's nuns at school telling us not to lie or cheat, yet Ma Kettle tells everyone who'll listen that she's poor but honest when she's neither, and Sister Eustacia lets the tram conductor give me a free ride, when if I hopped on board and then off again without paying, like the bad boys do, she'd go all po-faced and talk about sin, and the bible, and how hot the flames of hell burn.

She glanced sideways at her companion, but Sister Eustacia was examining the big brown paper bag of peppermints. She was not counting them exactly – more gloating, Biddy thought suddenly. Eh, there's not much fun for a load of holy women shut up in a convent all day; this shopping trip once a month is the poor soul's payment for an awful lot of kneeling on hard floors and saying prayers for people who can't be bothered to pray for themselves. And not a peppermint would she touch until she was given leave, even though there was a free bag in there, a little extra, handed out by Ma Kettle probably in much the same spirit as that of the bus conductor when he had refused to accept a fare for Biddy. There's a lot of good in people, Biddy concluded, wriggling round so that she could look out of the window as the tram joggled along down Byrom Street and swerved left around the Technical College. What's a free ride for me and a few parcels, after all?

If the journey to Mount Pleasant was completed in record time, the journey back to the Scottie was not. To say that Biddy loitered would not have been fair, but she certainly did not hurry. It was a clean, crisp sort of day, especially welcome after so much rain and cold, and for some reason Biddy felt happy, as though the free ride was just the beginning of the good times which she was so sure would soon come back.

What was more, as the tiny little door in the great big gate creaked open to Sister Eustacia's knock, the nun turned to Biddy and pressed something into her hand.

'Here, Bridget . . . you're a good girl. Buy yourself a bun, or a ride home in another tram.' She turned unhurriedly back to the little door and to the squat, bespectacled nun peering out. 'Ah, Sister, can you send for someone to help me with my shopping?'

Biddy had thought about another tram ride, but the truth was, it would only get her back to Kettle's Confectionery sooner and when she got there it would undoubtedly be time for toffee-making, which would be enjoyable enough on a cold day but which did not appeal when the sun was out – and Biddy was on borrowed time thanks to Sister Eustacia.

If we had walked we wouldn't have reached here for

another forty or fifty minutes; perhaps not for a whole hour, Biddy reminded herself, wandering slowly along the sunny pavement. So there's no way I could be back in work yet. And I'm not wasting money on a tram fare. I'll buy myself a big currant bun and an apple; I just fancy an apple.

She had her currant bun and her apple, ambling along as she ate, and then decided to have a sit-down for ten minutes in St John's gardens. But there, belatedly, conscience pricked. She was being paid, this really was Ma Kettle's time, and though she had a cast-iron reason for not getting back exactly early, she did not feel it would do to turn up late. Sure as a clock ticks I'll be seen by some interfering old busybody who'll tell Ma Kettle I was spotted on the tram, she thought bitterly. And then I'll lose the job and Mam and me'll never get out from under.

From under precisely what she did not explain, even to herself. She just chucked her applecore into a bed of roses, still blooming as gaily as though the month was June and not September, and set off at a smart pace for the Scotland Road and Kettle's Confectionery.

'Ah, 'ere she is! I've got the toffee boilin', chuck, but it'll be ready for pourin' in ten minutes. I couldn't save you but a morsel o' bread an' jam, but there's tea in the pot. Get there awright? Sister pleased wi' you?'

Biddy sidled round the counter and headed for the back room. She felt as though there was a sign on her forehead with *big currant bun and an apple ate in your time* emblazoned upon it, but when she saw the size of the piece of bread and the thin smear of jam she was quite glad she had been deceitful. It was just about enough to fill a tooth cavity, and she'd been slogging all that way on foot with enough weight in her arms to break 'em . . . or at least, that was what old Ma Kettle thought.

'Sister was pleased,' she called back, however. Remember how hard you had to search to find this job, she commanded herself. When you're a bit older, a bit more ladyfied, when you talk in a 'shop voice' all the time an' not just sometimes, Mam says you'll get decent work in Blacklers or George Henry Lee's, but until then take what you can get and be grateful.

'Good, good. You won't let that toffee overboil, chuck?'

'I'm taking it off the stove now,' Biddy said, adding beneath her breath, 'If I've got the strength to lift the pan after having nothing to eat since tea last night.'

'What? What was that? Leave the bread 'n' jam till the toffee's coolin', there's a good girl.'

'Right,' Biddy said, thinking that in the time it would have taken her to swallow the bread and jam she would have lost less than half a second. She heaved at the blackened pan, staggering as it left the stove-top with a decided squelsh and she felt its full weight. 'Got it, Mrs Kettle. . . . Cor, it's no light weight this lot.'

'It's coconut toffee,' Mrs Kettle said, appearing in the doorway. 'Ah, you ate the bread an' jam first, I see. Well, no matter . . . pour careful, girl, I don't want toffee all over me decent scrubbed table-top.'

'I didn't . . . eat . . . it,' Biddy panted, muscles cracking as she strove to tip the pan gently into the first of the half-dozen tin cooling trays. 'It's still there, missus, on the wall-table. It's just rather little.'

'Steady, steady!' Mrs Kettle said anxiously as the flow began and the sweet brown stuff began to run steadily into the tray. 'That's right, that's right . . . not too full now, or you'll never 'ammer it up into small enough bits. My lor, that stuff cost enough . . . steady I say!'

'The pan's so heavy,' Biddy wheezed, shifting it along to the second tray. 'I'm not Samson you know, Mrs Kettle.'

'You eat like 'im,' Mrs Kettle said, not nastily but just as one stating a fact. 'All that bread an' jam gone in a coupla o' minutes! Ah no, I see you've left a tat.'

Biddy finished pouring toffee and stood the pan back on the stove top, sweat running down the sides of her face. She glanced across at the disputed piece of bread and jam.

'I haven't had time to eat anything, Mrs Kettle,' she pointed out. 'I got the toffee straight off the stove – isn't that what you left me, then?'

'No it is not,' Mrs Kettle said, sounding injured. 'You'd run an errand for me, Bid . . . is it likely I'd cut you down to that? Bread's a price, I grant you, but I declare no one's ever called me stingy.'

Not to your face, Biddy's mind said, whilst her mouth, much the more tactful member, agreed that she had never heard anyone be so rude.

'No, nor you should,' Ma Kettle said huffily. 'I left you the best part of 'alf a loaf . . . well, three decent slices,' she added. 'Now where . . . ah!'

She had opened the door leading to her own private quarters as she spoke and there, on the back of the door, hung a navy donkey jacket and a navy cap. Mrs Kettle leaned through the doorway. 'Ja-ack! Come down 'ere this minute, you bleedin' rascal! Wha' did you go an' tek the bread 'n' jam for, eh? Don't I feed you? That was for me assistant!'

A muffled roar came from beyond the doorway. It sounded like a denial, interspersed with some laughter, and an explanation, but with the doorway filled by Ma Kettle and Jack being in the flat upstairs, Biddy could not hear what he said.

'Jack says it were Maisie, then, greedy great gannet,' Ma Kettle muttered, having obviously interpreted the roar without any difficulty. 'That girl! I pays 'er to keep me place clean and she sneaks orf into me boilin' kitchen an prigs bread an' jam what's meant for me bleedin' shop assistant! I'll clack 'er bleedin' lug for er!'

Biddy, who had seen a stout, cross-looking girl poke her head round the door occasionally with a message for Ma Kettle, grinned to herself. She knew nothing about Maisie save for her appearance, but it occurred to her that anyone who worked for Ma would have to learn to look after themselves. Obviously it applied whether you cleaned her flat or sold her sweets, because Maisie must have been hungry to have taken the bread and jam.

Ma Kettle withdrew from the doorway and slammed the door. Crossly. Then she waddled across to the small cupboard to the left of the stove. Bending down she withdrew a loaf and a pot of jam, three-quarters used. 'Jack's sorry, 'e'd 'ave stopped 'er, only 'e didn't know it were yourn,' she explained, beginning to hack another slice off the loaf. 'None of me lads would tek what waren't theirs . . . poor but honest, that's us Kettles; well known fact.'

It was very late and very dark before the toffee was all made and cooled, hammered into sufficiently small pieces to please Ma Kettle, clattered into the big sweet jars and placed high on the shelves. And it was not as though the toffee was her only job. There was cleaning the sweet-making pans, which could take a couple of hours if Ma Kettle had forgotten to leave them in hot water, and scrubbing the worn lino in the back room and the boards in the little shop. The big window had to be cleaned, the display dusted and any flies which hovered must be pursued with the fly-swat, this being a much more acceptable method of fly-slaying – to the customers, at least – than hanging fly-papers or setting wasp-traps. When you were not serving customers you were always busy, so that by eight o'clock, when Kettle's Confectionery closed at last, Biddy was always so tired that she walked home in a daze, often arriving so weary that it was all she could do to cut herself and her mother bread and cheese for their supper.

But tonight, perhaps because of her little trip out and the two meals she had enjoyed, Biddy found the walk home less tiring than usual. She and her mother now had a room in a house in Virginia Street, just behind St Paul's church which, in its turn, was behind Exchange Station. It was quite near the docks, which Biddy liked, and handy for work, though you couldn't say it was the healthiest spot in the city. All day and for quite a bit of the night the racket of the trains – and the filth from their engines – befouled the air and though their landlady constantly reminded them how fortunate they were, Biddy sometimes had her doubts.

When Mam's cough got worse she had tried to move, but it wasn't easy. Mrs Edith Kilbride's rent was possible because Mam kept an eye on their landlady's four small children whilst she went off to work at the nearby station as a cleaner. Kath O'Shaughnessy and Edith had lived on the same street in Dublin, years ago, and had remained good friends, which would have made leaving difficult. Besides which, paying a normal rent, until Kath was back in work once more, was next to impossible.

Despite the lateness of the hour there were plenty of people around in the streets and quite a crowd were coming out of Exchange Station. Biddy dodged round them and dived down the subway which came out in St Paul's Square. From there it was a short walk along Earle Street and into the narrow house in Virginia Street.

Biddy was humming a tune as she ran up the stairs, for their room was on the first floor. She hoped her mother had managed to get something for their tea – for some reason she thought it might be fish – and was already anticipating a nice bit of cod with a pile of boiled potatoes and maybe even a bit of cake for a pudding. The tiny widow's pension which the O'Shaughnessys drew had been due this morning, which usually meant something substantial for tea. Biddy's own wage, though useful, was too small to provide anything hot and the savings which Kath O'Shaughnessy was carefully husbanding were used to pay the rent.

Biddy stopped outside their room to get her breath, then tapped on the door and opened it. She always tapped as though it was a real front door, though of course it was only one room, and her mother usually called out cheerfully, then came across to give her daughter a kiss. But today, as Biddy entered the room, everything was different. For one thing her mother was in bed, not up, and for another, she was not alone. A tall, worried-looking man was sitting on the edge of the bed writing something in a book and Edie Kilbride was standing by the mantel, her face very pale. She turned as Biddy entered the room, looking stricken.

'Oh, Biddy, dear . . . oh Biddy, I don't know how to tell you . . . sure an' 'tis the last t'ing either of us expected . . . oh Biddy, this is Dr Godber, who has somet'ing to say to ye.'

The man on the bed turned towards her. His face was solemn but as he turned he had glanced down at his watch and Biddy could tell that he was longing to be on his way.

'Ah, Bridget! I'm afraid I have sad news for you, my child. Very sad news.'

'She's been took bad, hasn't she?' Biddy quavered, moving towards the bed. 'Poor Mam, she's been getting better slowly, but now she's been took bad. What must I do, sir?'

As she spoke she glanced towards the pillows – and stopped short, a hand flying to her mouth. There lay her mother's shape, but it was covered completely by a sheet, pulled up to hide her face.

The doctor followed her glance.

'She's . . . she's gone to her reward,' he said awkwardly. 'I'm afraid, Bridget, that your mother haemorrhaged about an hour ago. She lost a great deal of blood and died soon afterwards.'

'Died?' Biddy could see the man's mouth moving, she could hear his words, but somehow they had no meaning. A great sheet of glass had been interposed between them and she felt as though someone had stuffed her mouth with cotton wool and her ears, too. Was that why the doctor's voice was so small, so insignificant? And what had they done to Mam, why had they pulled the sheet right over her face? She would have difficulty breathing, he really ought to be more careful of a patient, even if she was neither rich nor important.

She leaned forward and twitched the sheet down before anyone had divined her intention or could stop her.

There lay the mortal remains of Kathleen O'Shaughnessy, her face glassily pale, her eyes closed. The pillow on which her head lay was dark with blood, her hair, loose for once, matted with it. And horrifyingly, even as Biddy watched, her mother's jaw dropped slowly open and her head rolled a little on the blotched and bloodstained pillow.

Biddy screamed, as shrill as one of the trains drawing out of Exchange Station, and jumped back, then as swiftly moved forward, to fall on her knees by the bed.

'Mam, are you all right? You aren't dead, you aren't, you aren't! Oh, Mam, say something!'

A pair of hands caught her shoulders, pulling her

upright, then turning her so that she faced away from the carnage on the sheets.

'It's awright, Bridget, it's awright, she's gone luv, she's gone where no one can't 'urt her no more. Come on, come on, you don't want to stay 'ere, because your Mam ain't 'ere no more, she's left, that ain't your Mam, that's just an empty shell, a body what she don't want no more. She were a good soul, your Mam, a good friend and a good little fighter, but she's gone from 'ere, now, and you must be gone too. Come down wi' me an' the kids, we'll get a meal, talk about what's to be done. Come on, come downstairs wi' your Aunt Edie.'

Biddy had never called Mrs Kilbride anything but Mrs Kilbride, but now she sobbed in the woman's arms, clutching her desperately, hanging onto the only solid thing in the suddenly tippling world, Edith Kilbride's plump, motherly arms.

'Is . . . is she really dead?' she asked fearfully. 'Really gone for good? Won't there be no more laughs, no more good times?'

Mrs Kilbride did not answer at once but Biddy heard her swallow convulsively and felt the plump little hand pat her back.

'Sure there'll be laughs an' good times, chuck, but it'll be up to you to make 'em, now. Your Mam can't help you there. Ah, she were a good Mam to you an' a good pal to me. . . . Come on, come downstairs, I'll 'ave the kettle on and we'll wet our t'rottles an' 'ave a bit of a chat, like. Come on, leave the doctor to see to things here.'

Biddy heaved a deep, tremulous sigh and glanced once more towards the bed. Dimly, she realised that there was truth in what Mrs Kilbride had said. That thing lying on the pillow wasn't really her mother, it was just a cast-off shell which had been left behind when her mother's soul had fled.

Slowly, but without a backward glance, she allowed herself to be led from the room.

'It's ever so good of you, Mrs Kilbride, to suggest that I stay wi' you and keep an eye on the kids, like my Mam used to do,' Biddy said wearily, when the funeral was over and she was packing her pathetically few possessions into the old carpet bag her mother had once used for her heavy shopping. 'I'm not ungrateful, honest, but it wouldn't be fair on you, not in the long run. Mrs Kettle's said I can move in wi' them, she doesn't have a daughter, only sons, so I'll be useful. And it'll be a roof over my head and a job, for a while at least.'

She had been very surprised when Mrs Kettle had not only come to the funeral but had made the offer

'You come along o' me and live over the shop, same as all us Kettles do,' she had urged. 'I'll feed you, dress you, see you right. What d'you say?'

She had to say she would, of course. Mrs Kilbride couldn't afford to feed another mouth unless that other mouth could bring in a wage, and since Biddy couldn't be in two places at once she could not envisage herself working for Ma Kettle and taking her money home to the Kilbrides, whilst also staying at home all day to look after the kids.

'There's a truckle bed you can use,' Ma Kettle planned busily. 'Being as 'ow I been a widder-woman these fifteen years, you can share my room. Of course I shan't pay you a wage, like, seeing as 'ow I'll be treatin' you like me own flesh an' blood, but I'll see you right, no need to worry about that.'

'Thanks,' Biddy said dully. 'Thanks very much, Mrs Kettle.'

She was too shocked still to do more than think, fleetingly, that at least the food would probably be better than she and Mam had managed out of their small resources. Often there were quite appetising smells floating down from the flat above the shop; she had sat at the counter minding the shop and eating bread and jam and her mouth had downright watered at times.

'You fetch your gear, then,' Mrs Kettle said. 'What about your Mam's things? You're welcome to bring any furniture, fittings, stuff like that. And if you want me to dispose of anything . . .' she paused delicately, her bushy little caterpillar eyebrows twitching interrogatively, '. . . we might mek a few bob, between us,' she finished.

'It's all right, thanks,' Biddy said. 'Aunt Edie was good to Mam because they were pals as girls, in Dublin. They were the same build, so she's having Mam's skirts and jumpers and that, and there wasn't much in the way of furniture. The bed was ruined . . . so I'm lettin' Aunt Edie have what's good there, to make up.'

'Aunt Edie?' It seemed to Biddy that Ma Kettle drew back a little when she said the words. 'I never knowed you'd got an aunt in the Pool. I daresay she'll want you when you're big enough to earn a decent wage. Perhaps I'm wrong to offer, and you with a relative actually on the spot.'

'She's got a lot of kids,' Biddy said tiredly. 'She can't afford to keep me. But if you've changed your mind, Mrs Kettle . . .'

'Me, change me mind? Bridget O'Shaughnessy – dear me, what a mouthful! – Bridget O'Shaughnessy, the day I withdraw a kindness may I be roast on a spit! She ain't your real aunt, I daresay?'

'No, not my real aunt. Just a friend of Mam's,' Biddy admitted. 'When shall I fetch my stuff over, Mrs Kettle?'

'Why, tomorrer, if not sooner! And just you call me Ma, same's the boys does. Want a hand wi' your gear?'

Since Biddy's gear consisted of a spare skirt and

blouse, a cloth-bodied doll called, rather unoriginally, Dolly, who was too shabby and dirty to be worth selling, the carpet bag and her mother's wedding ring, Biddy told her benefactress that she could manage, thank you. She went back to the house in Virginia Street, said good-bye to everyone – the kids cried – and picked up her bag. Then she trudged slowly round to the shop, suddenly feeling as though the world had slid away from beneath her feet, leaving her spinning uneasily in space.

Three days ago, she thought wonderingly as she walked, three days ago I was Somebody. I was daughter to Kath O'Shaughnessy, lodger to Mrs Kilbride, shop assistant at Kettle's Confectionery shop. And now what am I? I'm nobody's daughter, nobody's lodger even, certainly nobody's shop assistant, because a shop assistant is paid a wage and Mrs Kettle had made it clear that she would not be paid. Now I'm just Biddy O'Shaughnessy, an orphan who Ma Kettle is about to befriend. Or take advantage of. We'll see.

And she trudged on along the dusky pavements, heading for whatever fate had in store. As she passed the shop windows she saw her reflection, saw one small, skinny fourteen year old, with dark curls, blue eyes, and a pointed chin. Once someone said my chin was obstinate and when I wouldn't eat my greens Da called me a fuss-pot, she recalled, thinking back to those long-ago, happy days. Once I would have looked very carefully at Ma Kettle's proposal and probably turned it down. But that was when I knew where I was going and what I wanted, Biddy told herself ruefully, changing the carpet bag from her left hand to her right, for though not particularly full, it soon began to feel extremely heavy. Yes, that was before Mam went and left me. Now I've got to fend for myself and I'd rather a roof over my head than a gutter and yesterday's *Echo*.

Well, her thoughts continued, I'm down now, flat as a ha'penny on a tramline, but I'll recover myself, given time. I'll lie low for a bit and see what's best, but for now, it's Ma Kettle's and like it. Otherwise they'll slam me into an orphanage or the workhouse or something, and I wouldn't like *that* at all.

Ma Kettle was waiting for her. The shop was closed but the door hung open and there she was, boiling toffee in the back room and keeping a weather eye open, she explained, for Biddy.

'Normally, I'd tell you to finish this boilin' off for me,' she said, ushering the girl into the back room and through the doorway which, until this minute, had been forbidden territory for a mere Kettle employee. 'But seein' as you're goin' to live in, you'd best come up and meet the rest o' the fambly.'

Carpet bag in hand, Biddy followed Ma Kettle up a flight of stairs and into a large, rather dismal living-room. It should not have been dismal, for there were dark red curtains pulled across the window, a deep, comfortable-looking sofa and number of saggy arm-chairs with faded, dark red upholstery – Biddy shuddered – the colour of dried blood, and the only light came from a dim little bulb with a red shade which robbed it of any brilliance it might once have possessed. It shone down on a large table covered with a maroon chenille cloth and on four upright wooden chairs with carved backs and tight leather seats. Even the walls were dark, the paper having lost any colour it might have possessed in favour of a uniform brown years ago. In fact, the only bright part of the room was the fire which roared up the chimney and the brass fire-irons which twinkled in the grate.

There were three young men disposed about the room

in various poses and Ma Kettle introduced them to Biddy in an undertone, so as not to disturb them.

One was at the table directly beneath the red-shaded light. He was probably seventeen or eighteen and was poring over a book through a pair of small, wire-rimmed spectacles balanced on his oddly upturned nose. He was pudgy, with light brown hair, and took no notice whatsoever of either his mother or her companion. Biddy was informed in an awed whisper that this was Ma Kettle's youngest, her beloved Kenny.

Jack came next. He sat by the fire, elbows on knees, a slice of bread on a toasting fork held out to the flames. He was in his early twenties, tall, well-built, dark-haired, and wearing a seaman's brief white shirt and blue trousers. He looked round and grinned as his mother said his name, white teeth flashing in his tanned face. Jack, Biddy remembered, was a sailor and not home often. He was the one who had allowed the maid to prig her bread and jam though, so her answering smile was tepid.

The third man sat opposite Kenny at the table eating a plate of what looked like scouse. Biddy knew this must be Luke, the eldest son, but Ma Kettle told her so anyway. Luke reminded Biddy sharply of Ma Kettle for he was stout and had little grey eyes which met her own shrewdly, calculatingly. He was twenty-five, she knew that much about him from idly listening to Ma Kettle boasting in the shop, and worked at Tate's. He was, naturally, the source of the cheap sugar which Ma used in her home-made sweets.

'And this is Biddy O'Shaughnessy,' Ma Kettle said, once she had named each of her sons. 'Biddy's comin' to live 'ere for a bit, boys. She'll give an 'and in the shop, in the 'ouse. . . . You want anything doin', just 'ave a word wi' me and I'll see she sets to and does it. You 'ad your dinner yet, Biddy?'

'No, not yet,' Biddy said, thinking again that the scouse smelled good. 'I left Virginia Street before Aunt Edie got round to thinking about a meal.'

'Right. Just for tonight you might as well eat in 'ere, wi' us.'

She waddled out of the room and Biddy followed her into a tiny, dark little kitchen with a knee-high sink in one corner and a smelly, coke-burning stove in the other. There was a broken-down chair, a bare electric light bulb overhead and a large table. It was warm because of the stove, but cheerless, unfriendly. All the rooms are the same, they none of them want me, any more than Ma Kettle or her boys do, Biddy thought despairingly. Oh, how will I live in this horrible house with all these horrible people?

But it was not a question to which she could give an answer. Instead, she watched as Ma ladled a very small helping of scouse and a couple of boiled potatoes onto a plate and handed it, rather grudgingly, to her.

'There y'are; same as us,' she said, as though Biddy suspected that Kettles ate something far more glamorous than mere scouse. 'You'll be like a daughter to me, you shan't go short.'

Sitting down at the table and devouring the scouse in a couple of minutes, Biddy looked up hopefully as she scraped the spoon round the now-empty plate. And how had Ma managed to ladle out the stew without getting a single piece of meat in her spoon? There had been meat in Luke's portion, lots of meat, she had noted it specially.

'Done? Well, then, we'll go through together and see about the toffee,' Ma Kettle said, whisking the plate from under Biddy's nose. 'I won't get you to wash up yet, since Luke's still eating.'

Biddy took a deep breath. It was now or never; she sensed it.

'Mrs Kettle, I've not eaten since last night and I'm – I'm still hungry. Is there any scouse left?'

The boys had all been busy with their own affairs, but now Biddy was painfully aware of three pairs of eyes fixed on her, as well as of Ma Kettle's incredulous, beady gaze.

'You're still *hungry*? After a plateful of me good stew, what's full o'meat an' luv'ly fresh veggies? Can I believe what I'm hearin'?'

'Yes, I'm afraid you can,' Biddy said clearly, using her very best 'shop' voice. 'I'm *extremely* hungry and though I'm sure it was a mistake, there was no meat in my helping. However, if there's none left, perhaps you could give me some money to get some chips? You did say you'd feed me instead of wages, and . . .'

She shot a quick glance at Luke, opposite. His little eyes were like marbles, hard and glassy, and his small mouth was tight. Beside her, Kenny continued to ignore her, apart from giving her one incredulous glance from behind his spectacles, though whether he approved or disapproved of the stand she was taking, Biddy had no idea. Over by the fire, Jack was grinning, taking his toasted bread carefully off the fork, though he said nothing.

'Ah . . . well, if you've 'ad no brekfuss, nor nothin' else all day . . . I know, you can fill up on bread 'n' jam,' Ma Kettle said triumphantly. 'There's enough o' that stew left for the boys' dinners tomorrer, if I does extry spuds. Or rather, you can do 'em,' she added, quite unable to keep a trace of sheer malice out of her tone. 'Seein' as 'ow you're goin' to gi' me an 'and about the place.'

'I don't work so well on bread and jam,' Biddy said demurely. 'I need a decent dinner, Ma.'

It was the first time she had omitted to call her employer Mrs Kettle and the shot went home. Ma looked uneasily at her boys, now all three of them studiously avoiding her glance, then heaved a great sigh. 'Scouse it is, then,' she said heavily. 'Someone told me girls couldn't put away their food the way lads do, but I see 'twas just one of them tales folk tell. Come through to the kitchen, chuck.'

Much later that night, when she was curled up in the tiny truckle bed with Dolly clasped to her bosom and Ma Kettle snoring like an elephant in the big brass bedstead not more than a foot away, Biddy went over her day. It had been painful beyond measure to watch her mother's coffin being slowly lowered into the impersonal earth at Toxteth Park cemetery. Then it had hurt to say goodbye to Mrs Kilbride and the kids. She had never been particularly happy in the scruffy, down-at-heel little house on Virginia Street, but at least Mam had been there and they had enjoyed some pleasant times, especially when Mam felt well and they had talked about her starting work again, moving to a better neighbourhood, training Biddy up so she could be a saleslady in one of the big clothing shops.

Still, girls do leave home at fourteen and go into service, Biddy told herself. Probably, if Mam hadn't met my Da and fallen in love with him and fled over here to Liverpool, I'd have gone into service in Dublin round about now. And I'd have felt pretty lonely and lost in someone else's house, too.

But in service you had other servants. In service you were paid a wage, got time off, could go home sometimes, perhaps as often as once a week. You could save up, buy yourself the occasional treat, have a best friend to giggle with. Since her mother's illness and her own employment by Ma Kettle, even friends from school had called less often, busy with their own lives and unable to spend their time waiting for Biddy either to finish work or finish nursing her Mam.

If things were different I could get back with Kezzie and Maude and Ellen, Biddy thought hopelessly. But things aren't different, and I'll just have to put up with what I have got, for the time being. And besides, I did all right today, didn't I? Old Ma Kettle was rocked back on her heels by me asking for more scouse, just like Oliver Twist in that book me and Mam read last year, but she gave me some, she shelled out. Perhaps, if I can keep it up, she won't use me too badly, and I'll like living here. Perhaps even the boys might not be too horrible, once I get to know them.

One thing, you've got to stand up for yourself in the Kettle household, because if you don't no one will, she thought, just before she went to sleep. I've got to be tough, like them, or they'll flatten me.

And presently she slept, to dream of putting a ha'penny on the tramlines so that it might be squashed penny-sized, only to find that the ha'penny had turned into Sister Eustacia, who had reproached her for doubling her income in so sneaky a fashion. And she had stood up to Sister Eustacia and told her about Ma weighing her thumbs and doing the kids out of the odd sweetie, and Ma had come surging out of the back room, saying, 'No scouse for you, amn't I goin' to treat you like me own daughter, you serpent's tooth?'

After that, the dreams got odder and odder. Ma made her wear a pair of boy's trousers and a boy's shirt because she said clothes were always handed down in good, close, Catholic families and the trousers tripped her up when she was serving people and the shirt sleeves dangled in the toffee and got disgustingly sticky. And at intervals throughout the night the dream-Ma would shout, 'No scouse for you, madam – amn't I goin' to treat you like me own daughter, you serpent's tooth?' and poor Biddy would think up clever arguments to get herself fed properly but they never worked. Either the table would turn into an elephant, trumpeting loudly, or it would tip over and run out of the room, or the food would simply disappear whilst Ma, with a big smile on her face, advised Biddy to fill up with bread 'n' jam and whisked the bread into the fire and the jam into her apron pocket.

When Biddy woke it was still dark, and the trumpeting elephant table was standing by her truckle bed. She gave a little squeak of fright and the table turned into Ma Kettle, huge in a white petticoat, man's socks and a long grey shawl.

'Come on, child,' Ma Kettle said, not unkindly. 'Jack's off back to sea this mornin' so you must be down early to mash the tea. Then you can start off the brekfuss . . . the boys 'ave bacon, a couple of eggs each, a pile of bread wi' margarine on . . . but us wimmin, we'll mek do wi' bread 'n' scrape an' a nice pot of tea, shall us?'

Biddy was tired after a restless night and confused to find herself in Ma Kettle's frowsty little bedroom, but one thought came clear to the front of her mind as she climbed stiffly out of bed and reached for her clothes. Don't let her push you around, the thought said. Stand up for yourself!

'Bacon and egg,' she said therefore, with all the firmness she could muster. 'I work best after bacon and egg.'

'Ah,' Ma Kettle said, after a pause so long that Biddy began to wonder whether the older woman had gone back to sleep. 'Oh ah. Bacon an' egg, eh?'

'Bacon an' egg at breakfast,' Biddy said hastily. It was years since she'd tasted bacon and egg, but she did see that if Ma Kettle chose to take her literally she might well find the rest of the family eating roast chicken whilst she dined – lightly – on a tiny piece of bacon and a pullet's egg. 'Girls need something more for dinner, of course.'

'Of course,' Ma Kettle said. She sighed. 'Better get a

move on; Jack's fond of an early cuppa. And he'll want his brekfuss betimes, too. Better shift yourself, chuck.'

Biddy, throwing her clothes on, said meekly that she would do her best to hurry. She realised that, having got her own way, she must be careful not to provoke Ma Kettle by being cocky. So she did not wash and Ma Kettle did not suggest that she should, she just hurried downstairs and began to hunt out the ingredients for the boys' breakfast.

At least she isn't going to try to starve me, she told herself as she got the huge frying pan out of the cupboard and put it carefully on top of the stove. As the fat began to hiss and spit she broke the first egg into it and stood the bacon ready. A real breakfast, and as soon as the boys were fed she, too, could eat this wonderful food! It was worth getting up early, worth slaving for Ma Kettle all day in the shop and half the night in the house, if she, Biddy, ate as well as the boys!

Chapter Two

In January no beach is at its best, but Richart David Evans,
Dai to his friends, sitting on the little cliff above the beach
at Moelfre, looking down on the grey shingle, the black
fanged rocks, the slow inward saunter of the silvery
winter waves, was not seeing the scene before him. His
mind was closed to the beauty, as it was to the cry of the
gulls, and the salty, exciting, indefinable smell of the dark
green weed and the wooden fishing boats, pulled up
above the tideline.

His Mam was dead. After weeks of suffering she had
died first thing in the morning four months ago, when
Da had been out in the long garden at the back of the tall
house on Stryd Pen, hoping to find that one of the hens
had laid an egg with which he might tempt his heart's
darling, for there was no doubt in Dai's mind that Davy
had loved his Bethan true.

Davy had been devastated by her death, unmanned
by it you could say. For weeks he had been inconsolable
and Dai and his sister Sîan had done their best to comfcrt
him, to see that he ate, slept, even mourned, with some
degree of self-control. But a month ago Sîan, who had
been engaged to be married for over a year but had
delayed the wedding first because of her mother's illness
and then her death, had wed her Gareth and moved into
his cottage in the nearby village of Benllech. And Da, Dai
brooded darkly, had done the unforgivable.

He had brought another woman into Mam's home.

'Fond of the girls is your Da,' Mam had whispered to

her son just before she died. 'Marry again he will, love –
marry again he must, for that's your Da for you. Don't
resent the girl of his choice, Dai, my dear, but if you need
a home while you come to terms with what's happened,
don't forget my old friend, Nellie McDowell that was.
She's Nellie Gallagher now and if you need help, or . . .
or anything . . . the sort of thing you'd have turned to me
for . . . then Nellie will do what she can. Her address is in
my little bureau. We still exchange letters from time to
time. If you hurt, love, you must go to her. There isn't a
better woman living.'

'Mam, Da wouldn't . . . but I don't want to talk about
it. And if it pleases you, I'll see this woman some time.
Oh Mam, we love you so much, I don't know what we'll
do without you.'

Bethan had smiled, the thin face suddenly bright with
real amusement. 'I know well what your Da will do! Now
give me a kiss and go about your business; I just wanted
one quiet word.'

Two days later she was dead and now . . . Dai gritted
his teeth and thumped his knee with a clenched fist. Now
his father had brought Menna from Amlwch into the
house because he said it needed a woman's touch – and
it didn't take any particular effort to realise three things.
First, that Davy had known Menna for some time, and
known her quite well what was more. Second, that he had
not brought her in to act as his housekeeper but for a far
more intimate purpose. Third, that Menna, whilst delighted to be living with Davy, had no desire whatsoever
to share a house with his son.

Oh Mam, Mam, how well you knew my Da and how
foolish I was not to see that his weakness for a pretty face
was stronger even than his love for you, Dai mourned
now, staring blackly out over the sea. And what do I do
now? Stay here, to keep at bay at least some of the scandal

that will soon be rife? Or go? It will mean leaving the *Sweetbriar*, and the fishing, and my nice little attic room and pretty Rhona from the Post Office, but then a man has to leave his Mam's home one day and make a home for himself. My time to leave has come sooner than I expected, because I've been so content here, but I can't stay. Not when Da installs her as his wife, which he will do. It's the only way; the villagers won't have him living shamelessly in sin with a little town hussy who doesn't know our ways.

But what to do? The *Sweetbriar* was his own craft and he and his friend Meirion worked her together; they could find the fish when others searched in vain, they were a good team and made money, quite a lot of money at times when fish was short and others could not find.

There was the lifeboat, too. He had just been taken on as a deckhand and loved it, was almost looking forward to the heavy seas of winter as a chance to prove himself. If he left . . .

The village had been his life for twenty years, he knew nothing else. Every man, woman and child here was his friend, would stand by him, agree with him if he told Da . . .

But Mam had known this would happen and had warned him that it was no use resisting. She knew Davy well, his charm, the way his dark eyes warmed and softened when they fell on a loved one. She understood completely that Da couldn't go on without a woman, and had urged her son to accept Da's choice – but Menna! Brassy-haired, shrill-voiced, she was the kind of woman that Dai liked least, the sort he avoided when he took a boatful of fish round to Arnlwch and popped into the pub afterwards to wet his whistle before turning for home.

So leave then. No option, no choice. Just leave. Meirion would continue to fish the boat, give Dai a share of his profit if his friend was in need. So far as Dai was concerned Meirion could have the *Sweetbriar* and welcome; better him than Davy Evans, who would probably sell it to buy Menna a gold anklet chain or a locket or whatever silly frippery such a flibbertigibbet might desire.

But go where? He did not intend to run to Liverpool, with his tail between his legs, to this woman friend of Mam's – what was her name? Gallagher, that was it. A Scottish-sounding name, or an Irish one, he wasn't sure which, he just knew it wasn't a good Welsh name. And anyway, what could a motherly woman do for him? He had lost the only mother he wanted, now he must take the man's path.

As he sat on the cliff edge and glowered, unseeing, at the sea, a man walked across the beach below him, then looked up and shouted.

'Dai, bach, what's up wi' you, mun? I'm baitin' lobster pots; goin' to give me a hand?'

It was Meirion.

Meirion stood on the shingle with the bag of fish pieces swinging from one hand and watched Dai scramble down the cliff towards him. Dai came down with his black curls bobbing on his head, his strong legs carrying him easily and swiftly over the rough going, his eyes intent on the ground at his feet. Like his Da, Dai Evans was good to look upon and the girls vied for his favours, but to Meirion, Dai was special. Fond of Dai he was, like brothers they had been all their lives, and worried he was at the way Dai had taken Bethan's death.

Darkly. That was how he had taken it. Meirion was used to his friend's eloquent eyes reflecting his moods, but of late those eyes had seldom sparkled and had looked opaque, angry. Then there was the girl Menna. No one approved, but there were those who understood, though Meirion was not one of them. How Davy Evans could take a brassy piece like her into his home, with Dai still so hurt by his loss, Meirion could not understand, and there was talk amongst the women – who knew everything – that Davy had always been a one for the girls, that having a bedridden wife for fifteen months before her death had tried him more than it would have done some men, that he had been visiting Menna in her father's public house in Amlwch for more than a twelvemonth. . . .

Dai crashed down the last few feet of cliff and crunched across the shingle towards Meirion. He looked better, less haunted, Meirion decided, considerably relieved. The curly grin which revealed the white, even teeth was splitting Dai's tanned face and his eyes warmed when they met Meirion's in much their old way. 'Aye, I'll give you a hand with the pots, bach. Meirion, my mind is made up. I'll be leavin' Moelfre as soon as I can get a berth on a ship out of Amlwch. I'll ride over tomorrow – want to come?'

Dai had an old motorbike, his pride and joy after the *Sweetbriar*. He and Meirion had taken it to pieces and then put it together again half a hundred times; they knew it as they knew the palms of their own hands, and loved it, too. They both rode it, sometimes one in the driver's seat whilst the other rode pillion, sometimes the other. For years and years everything they did they had done together – taking the *Sweetbriar* to sea, bringing in the catch, selling it, lowering each other down the cliffs on a rope to rob seabirds' nests, digging for cockles, chasing the giggling holidaymaking girls in the summer, flirting with them, teasing them . . . then turning back to the local girls for real companionship, to sensible Rhona and sweet Wanda . . . even their girlfriends were friends.

'Goin', Dai? What for? Why, in God's sweet name?'

Meirion's voice was shocked, he couldn't help himself. If Dai went, how on earth would he go on? His instinct would have been to go too, to set off for Amlwch the following day and never return if that was what Dai wanted, but it was impossible. His Mam needed him, he had been the man of the house since his Da had been lost at sea. They had a good garden, good crops, but times was hard, they needed him, and not on some little coaster miles from here, either. He must be here, on the Isle of Anglesey, looking out for them, guarding them.

'Why?' Dai sighed, picked up a lobster pot and began to insert the bait. 'Oh, Meirion, bach, you must know as well as I do that I can't stay here and see that woman take my Mam's place! What's more, she do hate me very heartily, and though I'm angry with him, I want my Da to be happy. He won't be happy with me disapproving of his woman and his woman searching her mind for ways to discredit me with my Da. So what better than a berth on a ship heading for anywhere but here? What better than a complete break?'

'But . . . but the *Sweetbriar*, your place on the lifeboat . . . even the old bike, damn it! Dai, you can't go, this is our place, where we belong! You can't let her push you out!'

'She's not pushing me out, I'm going before she starts,' Dai said crossly. 'She'd try, I don't deny it, but she won't have the trouble. As for the *Sweetbriar*, she's yours until I come back, or decide not to, or whatever. And yes, miss the lifeboat I will, but if I sign on aboard a coaster in Amlwch then no time would I have for the lifeboat, anyway.'

'Where'll you live when you come ashore?' Meirion asked plaintively. He brightened. 'Or will you come home, then? Back here, to us?'

'I don't know, I've not made up my mind yet,' Dai said

guardedly. 'I'd like to, but . . . well, there's no gettin' away from it, mun, Menna hates me right well.'

'She won't mind you in small doses,' Meirion said with surprising shrewdness. 'It's only twenty-four hours a day, seven days a week, that she finds difficult, I guess. Right. I'll come over to the port with you. What time are you leaving?'

Biddy gradually settled down in the Kettle household. She was startled and a little upset to find that Maisie had been sacked, but as Ma quickly pointed out, with two of them at it the work of keeping the flat clean and the boys neat shouldn't be too difficult. And Ma Kettle could have been worse, for all she was tightfisted and dishonest. She had at first ordered and then tried to wheedle Biddy into giving short weight but in this Biddy proved adamant. 'I'd burn in hell if they didn't catch me and spend me life in prison if they did,' was her stoutly repeated excuse, and when Ma Kettle explained that it was not so much dishonest as good business practice, that in fact her sweets were worth a great deal more than she charged for 'em, only folk were so mean they wouldn't give her a decent price, Biddy just sniffed and began to clean down.

'Then you'd best not serve customers; you'll cost me too much,' Ma grumbled but Biddy, who believed in speaking her mind, pointed out that at least an assistant who was too honest to cheat the customers was also too honest to cheat her employer, which meant that the little wooden till with its tiny compartments for farthings, ha'pennies, pennies and so on was safe from the threat of thieving fingers.

This caused Ma Kettle to look thoughtful and afterwards Kenny told Biddy that she had taken exactly the right stand. "Cos we 'ad a gel afore you, Trix 'er name was, an' she took from the till, nicked sweets, gave 'er mates special prices, walked off 'ome one night wi' a bag o' sugar in 'er bloomers . . . Ma prizes honesty after that.'

Oddly enough, Kenny, who looked such unlikely friendship material, was becoming a good friend to Biddy. His appearance was against him, of course, the hard little eyes behind the spectacles seeming to look accusingly out on the world, but that was just short-sightedness. Kenny was bright at his books and enjoyed being tested on his recently acquired knowledge and Biddy liked to help, and he saw his parent rather more clearly than she saw herself.

'Stand up to 'er,' he continually advised Biddy. 'She'll like you for it in the end. 'Sides, you works 'arder than most, it wouldn't do to let 'er keep you short o' grub. Think what she saves on Maisie's wages, let alone on yours. You want to see her wi' Aunt Olliphant; Aunt won't stand none o' Ma's bossin' – she's the younger sister – but Ma respecks her for it. So if you want seconds of puddin', say so.'

'I don't see why she grudges me,' Biddy had said once, in the early days. 'I swear she counts up every cabbage leaf that passes my lips to see whether she'd be better paying me a wage instead of giving me my meals.'

Kenny chuckled. The two of them were sitting on the hard bench in the shop kitchen, ostensibly studying. Kenny worked for a firm of chartered accountants and was going to take exams to better himself and he had told his mother that Biddy was a big help to him since she understood the work and could ask him the sort of questions he would get in his exams.

Mrs Kettle didn't grumble, because they only worked after the shop was closed, and with Christmas over there wasn't the call for the extra slabs of toffee, bags of fudge, candy walking sticks and sugar mice which sold so readily over the holiday season.

'Now's the lean months,' Ma Kettle had said as February came in with a cold wind and snow in bursts. 'We should tighten our belts, eat less, not more. We won't 'ave to work so 'ard because we don't sell so much. Think on, young Biddy.'

Biddy, however, decided that the cold made her hungrier than ever and several times sharp words were exchanged over her ability to look such a skinny little thing but to eat like Jack, Luke and Kenny.

'Stick to your guns; you eat wharrever you need,' Kenny urged whenever his mother was out of hearing. 'Remind the old gal that at least you doesn't nick 'er perishin' toffee. Even Mais nicked 'er toffee.'

Spring came, but despite the milder weather and longer days it was difficult to rejoice over much, since the shop kitchen was mostly too hot anyway and of course with the approach of Easter the Kettle establishment started on Easter treats – chocolate eggs, marzipan fruit and flowers – which meant that Biddy was busy from morning till night, and often too tired to sleep soundly either, what with the stuffiness of the small room and Ma Kettle's reverberating snores.

'I'll have to get out of it by the time summer comes,' Biddy told herself desperately, as she fell into her truckle bed each night. 'I remember last summer – swatting flies, chasing bees, sweating till I was hollow and dried out – I don't know as I can stand that again.'

The trouble was that Ma Kettle was determined to have her money's worth out of Biddy. I'm sure she jots down all food costs, my share of the fire – not that I ever see it – wear and tear of chairs, tables, knives and forks, and then thinks she ought to work me harder, Biddy thought desperately, as she mixed icing sugar, almond flavouring and egg yolk in a huge bowl. Other people get Sundays off, I know they do, but Sundays is housework day and all I seem to do is scrub floors, make beds, wash the linen, peg it on the line, run out and get it in if rain threatens, put it out again, fetch it back and iron it, fold huge sheets and then carry them up to make the beds up again, starch Luke's shirts, mend his frayed collars . . . the list went on and on.

'Tell the old gal you're 'titled to a day off, same as the rest of the world,' Kenny advised. 'You could come wi' me on the ferry over to Birkenhead, and then by bus out into the country. Go on, tell Ma you need a bit of a rest. She goes off to see Aunt Olliphant, we fellers go off to see a bit o' life, why shouldn't you?'

'I will,' Biddy decided. 'She can only sack me, after all.'

And in a way it worked.

'A day off? Lor, chuck, what next, I asks meself? I treat you like me own daughter an' you want a day off?'

'If you had a daughter, Ma, and made her work seven days a week, the priest would be after you,' Biddy pointed out. 'You aren't too keen on me goin' along to mass either, are you?'

'May you be forgiven,' Ma said piously, going through the shirts that Biddy has just ironed to make sure there wasn't a crease on any of them. 'As if I'd let a member of the Kettle 'ousehold miss mass! It's only that you will loiter goin' and comin', when there's a hot dinner to prepare, that's the only reason I just occasionally asks if you wouldn't rather stay at 'ome.'

'I'd rather stay at home and rest, but you wouldn't want me to do that,' Biddy said, as near to tears as she had ever come whilst under Ma's roof. 'I'm that weary, Miz Kettle, that I hardly know how to go on. It's just work, work, work, from mornin' till night, and never an hour to myself.'

'Then you go to mass, dearie,' Ma Kettle said expansively. 'Don't you worry about me, stuck 'ere at 'ome wi' a thousand and one things to do. Just you go off and enjoy yourself.'

'I will, then. Thanks very much, Ma. Kenny's going to take me on the ferry to Birkenhead, and then into the country! We'll be home for tea, though.'

'Now wait on,' Ma Kettle said anxiously, putting down the last shirt. 'I didn't say . . . what I said was you might go to mass, I didn't say . . .'

'Kenny said you weren't mean enough to try to stop all my fun,' Biddy continued as though she hadn't heard. 'I'll work all the better for the break, I'm sure of it.'

She told Kenny later and the two of them giggled over Mrs Kettle's protestations, and Biddy waited to be hauled from her bed on Sunday morning and informed that her mentor had changed her mind. But although Ma Kettle was quieter than usual, Biddy went downstairs, got breakfast, washed up and cleared away and then announced that she would see everyone later that evening.

'If I had any money of my own I'd bring you home a bit of a present, but since I've not had a penny since my Mam died you'll have to forgive me if I come home empty-handed,' she said to Mrs Kettle as she and Kenny stood by the back door. 'Tara, then.'

Ma Kettle sniffed and when they were half-way down the road she called them back. 'There,' she said, pressing a few small coins into Biddy's hand. 'Enjoy your holiday and don't bother wi' presents; them shirts was ironed a treat.'

Wide-eyed, Biddy rejoined Kenny and opened her palm, to show him a whole sixpenny piece and six farthings.

'Mean ole bag; but at least she give you summat to spend.'

'So long as she doesn't sack me when we get home,' Biddy said, though not as though it was something she feared. She gave a little skip. 'Wish I had a best dress. . . . Oh Kenny, it's good to be outside without an errand to run!'

'You want to say "no", more often,' Kenny grumbled. 'She can't be led, the old woman, but she can be pushed. We all found that out years ago, or we'd be nothin' but slaves, like you.'

'It's different for you,' Biddy reminded him, slowing to a saunter and sticking the money in the pocket of her tatty skirt, for even with weekly washing one skirt will not last for ever and Ma Kettle had showed no inclination to buy her a new one, or even a new-second-hand one, which would have done admirably. 'You are her own son; how you look reflects on her. And she's fond of the three of you, you know that. Besides, you're earning good money. If she chucked you out you could afford lodgings. What would I do, Kenny? Someone of my age can't earn enough for digs, I'd be chucked in the workhouse and I really am scared of that.'

'Yeah, it's 'ard for you,' Kenny agreed. They were on the sloping road which led down to the landing stage now and Biddy sighed ecstatically and felt the little coins in her pocket with something approaching bliss. A whole day off, the sun shining, and money to spend! If only today could last for ever. But it couldn't, of course. Tomorrow was Monday; she would be busy in the shop from eight in the morning until eight at night, so she must make the most of today.

It was a wonderful day out, there was no doubt about it. After serious consideration, Kenny advised Biddy to put her money away somewhere safe and forget about it. 'Keep it for emergencies, a rainy day,' he urged her. 'Today's my treat. How'd you like a bus ride? That way we can get into real country.'

They rode the bus into green fields, got off and

climbed over a mossy gate. The grass in the meadow beyond was tall and starred with wild flowers, to none of which Biddy could put a name.

'Ain't it just lovely?' Kenny said. 'I brung a picnic – me Mam said I could but she were too lazy to cut it for me, so I done it big enough for two of us. I know how you can eat, young Biddy, so there's all sorts . . . fruit, too. Even a chunk of stickjaw.'

'She never gave you her toffee?' Biddy gasped. 'I'm sure she'd cut my hands off at the wrist if I so much as licked me finger after hammering a slab in bits. Oh Kenny, you didn't prig it, did you?'

'She moaned and groaned, but she said I could 'ave some if I 'ammered it small,' Kenny said cheerfully. 'Stop worryin', young Bid, an' enjoy the day. There's a stream over there, under them trees – ever dammed a stream, 'ave you?'

When they had cleared up a slight misunderstanding over the word 'dam', they went over to the stream. It chuckled along over its pebbly bed, with trees hanging over it and little fish playing in the brown pools. It was the most beautiful thing Biddy had ever seen and she knelt on the bank, dabbling her fingers in the clear water for ages, before the serious work of damming began.

It was such fun! She had made sandcastles at New Brighton years ago, laboriously filling her bucket and then carefully upending it so that the contents stayed firm and formed the castle's battlements. She had walked down country lanes between her parents and seen the patchwork cows, the pink pigs, the rosy apples on the trees. But this – this was even better! She and Kenny scooped clay and pebbles, formed a deep ridge, shouted to one another . . . you would never have known that Kenny was a young man of seventeen, gainfully employed at the offices of Burke, Burke & Titchworth, or that

Biddy was an orphan with no real home to call her own. For the whole of that sunny day they were just a couple of kids, playing a wonderful, messy game and enjoying every minute.

'Look at me skirt,' Biddy gasped, when they had made the dam, watched a huge pool gradually form, and then broken down the dam to let the water swirl back into the main stream once again. 'The earth here is yellowy, I'm sure it's stained this skirt for ever.'

'It's clay and a good job, too,' Kenny said roundly. 'You was beginnin' to look a right mess, our Biddy. Time Mam bought you some gear, if only from Paddy's Market. One of these days you'll be a young lady, you're quite pretty already when you laugh and aren't tired out. Now shall we 'ave our picnic?'

They ate their food, then lay down on the mossy bank, though Kenny refused to let Biddy lie in the sun as she would have liked to do.

'You'll get sunburned an' you won't be able to work tomorrer, you'll be in pain, too,' he told her. 'Best lie in the shade, chuck.'

Biddy agreed, meaning to move out into the sun for a little, but as soon as she closed her eyes she slept.

Kenny's mouth descending on hers woke her in a complete state of panic so that she was struggling already as consciousness returned and began at once to try to speak, to push at his shoulders. She had been dreaming pleasantly that they were still eating their picnic, but just at the moment when he started kissing her she assumed, the dream had changed; she was a sandwich and Kenny was about to eat her, was actually sinking his teeth into her bread and lettuce! When she woke to find it was really happening, he really did seem about to devour her, panic gripped her. He was no longer Kenny Kettle but a dangerous stranger who could mean her harm. She brought her knees up and felt them sink into his stomach and as he moved back a little she screamed and hit out. He gave a pained grunt and sat back, looking guiltily down at her, one hand going defensively to his middle, the other stroking his scratched chin. 'What d'you want to do that for? Shovin' me off like that? I wouldn't 'urt you, you know that!'

'It was the shock,' Biddy said, scrambling into a kneeling position and glaring at him. 'I was asleep . . . it's horrible to be woken up by someone suffocating you.'

'Suffocatin' you?' Kenny laughed. 'By God, no wonder you 'it out! That, you silly kid, were a kiss . . . 'cos you looked so pretty, lyin' there.'

'You should kiss cheeks, not mouths,' Biddy said definitely. 'My Mam always kissed me cheek. Mouths are for eating with . . . oh Kenny, I dreamed I was a sandwich and you were eating me!'

He had been frowning down at her, clearly both perplexed and annoyed, but at her words his face cleared and he laughed out loud, throwing his head back to do so. He no longer looked threatening or different, he just looked like Kenny, who had been kind to her, who had brought her out for a picnic despite his mother's disapproval.

'There, ain't you jest like the silly kid I called you? You kiss kids on the cheek and young ladies on the mouth, you 'alf-wit.'

'If I'm a silly kid, then treat me like one,' Biddy said with some sharpness. 'Don't you go doin' that again, I didn't like it, Kenny.'

'You screamed so sudden an' whacked me so 'ard you didn't get it,' Kenny said in a grumbling tone. 'Just when I was about to do me Valentino on you, up comes you bleedin' knee an' 'its me right in the essentials . . .'

'All right, I'm sorry,' Biddy allowed. 'But no more of that sort of nonsense, eh, Kenny?'

'But I liked it,' Kenny pointed out, scrabbling their things together. 'Biddy, you never give it a chanst, honest. You'll like it awright when you put your mind to it.'

'No I shan't,' Biddy insisted. 'But you're packing up – is it time for the bus?'

'Very near,' Kenny said. 'Umm . . . Biddy?'

'Yes, Kenny?'

'Per'aps you're right, per'aps you're a bit young for that kissin' lark. What say we forget it, for now?'

'Good idea,' said Biddy, considerably relieved. She liked Kenny and enjoyed his company but something told her, in no uncertain terms, that if she started all that kissing business it wouldn't be long before Kenny wanted other favours. Mam had said, before she died, that Biddy didn't ought to go getting involved with lads until she'd sorted out her future and that suited Biddy just fine. Besides, she had a very strong feeling that if Ma Kettle ever found out that Kenny had taken to kissing her little skivvy, she would be out on her ear without a character, regardless of who was at fault.

The bus arrived and they climbed aboard. Kenny kept shooting little sideways glances at her; he reminded Biddy strongly of a puppy who is hovering outside a butcher's shop with intent. Every time you catch the puppy's eye he thinks you can read his mind and acts ashamed.

So because she was a kind-hearted girl she reached over and gave his hand a squeeze. 'It's all right you know, Kenny,' she said hearteningly. 'We've had a really lovely day and everything's been fine. Perhaps we'll do it again one day, eh? Come over here and dam a stream and have a picnic and that. Perhaps next time we could bring your Ma, if you'd like that.'

Kenny laughed, but he squeezed her hand back and the naughty puppy look disappeared from his eyes. 'Eh, you're a nice kid, our Biddy! I wonder what Ma's got us for us teas?'

Biddy was trotting down the Scotland Road on her way to buy Ma Kettle some strawberries for frosting when she saw Ellen Bradley walking along the opposite pavement. She immediately hollered and waved. 'Hey . . . Ellen! Come over here a minute!'

Ellen glanced around to see who had called her and spotted Biddy. Despite the fact that the two girls had not met for a year she crossed the road at once. 'Bridget O'Shaughnessy, if it isn't yourself,' she gasped. 'I thought you'd gone back to Ireland wi' your Mam, cos we've not seen hide nor hair of you down our way for so long. What's been 'appenin' to you?'

'A lot,' Biddy admitted, linking her arm with Ellen's. 'Have you got a minute, Ellen? Because it's a long story and right now I'm in a bit of a pickle and I'd appreciate some advice.'

'Advice? I'm your gal for advice,' Ellen said. 'Ask away, queen.'

Biddy noticed that her old friend looked very smart and had grown beautiful since they had last met. She must be well over sixteen, Biddy calculated, since Ellen had been a class above her in school, and she looked very self-assured. Her smooth yellow hair was fashionably short, her lips looked a good deal redder than Biddy remembered them, and her brows and lashes had been darkened. Biddy glanced at the brown and cream two-piece suit and the high-heeled brown shoes on Ellen's feet, then wished fervently that she had not been sent out in her boil-ups – the sugar-stained white apron, the draggly skirt, the blouse spotted and scarred with the making of a thousand sweetmeats. But having called to her friend, she had best explain herself.

'Well, first off, my Mam died a year ago next September. They sacked her from her job six months before she died and we had nowhere nice to go, but we'd have managed if she'd stayed well. After she died I couldn't afford to stay on in our room so I agreed to move in with the Kettles; I was working at Kettle's Confectionery, still am, and that's all part of my problem.'

'Change your job, then,' Ellen said, without waiting for Biddy to finish speaking. She led the way to a pile of empty crates outside a butcher's shop and perched on one, patting the space beside her to indicate that Biddy should join her. Biddy did so and the two of them sat there in the morning sunshine, watching the passers-by with unheeding eyes whilst they talked. 'Don't tell me Ma Kettle pays you enough to keep yourself ... *We're poor but honest, us Kettles; ask anyone,*' she mimicked. 'I've not been in there for years, but when we were kids we reckoned she give short weight, the old devil.'

'Well, that was a long time ago,' Biddy said tactfully. She did not intend to get involved in a discussion of her employer's morals. 'The thing is, Ellen, she gives me bed and board but she don't pay me. Well, think about it – where could I afford to live on the sort of money I could earn? I'm younger than you, too, I'm only just fifteen. So as far as I can make out, Ma Kettle's got me for another year or so.'

'Yeah ... don't you have no relatives, though, Bid? Usually, when someone's Mam dies, relatives take you in.'

'Well, I've *got* relatives, of course, but they're all in Ireland,' Biddy said. 'I've never met them. My Mam ran away with my Da, you see, and they came to Liverpool. Her sisters and brother, and my Gran and Grandad, must be there still. Mam tried to write when she first married, but not even her sisters bothered to reply. Then she wrote again when Da was killed, and never had so much as a word of sympathy, let alone an offer of help. So I couldn't expect them to do anything for me, could I?'

'Well, I don't know; it isn't you they were annoyed with,' Ellen began, then shrugged and sighed. 'But if Ma Kettle don't pay you much – sorry, if she don't pay you anything – then you wouldn't be able to afford the ferry across the Irish sea, so that knocks that idea on the 'ead. So is that your problem? Gettin' in touch wi' your relatives?'

'Oh Ellen, of course it isn't,' Biddy said, exasperated with her friend's butterfly mind. If that was what growing beautiful did to you, she herself had better stay plain. 'I told you it had to do with the Kettles. It's Ma Kettle's son, Kenny.'

'Kenny Kettle!' Ellen giggled. 'What a name, eh?'

'He can't help his name,' Biddy said defensively. 'But last spring he took me out for a picnic . . . we crossed over to Birkenhead on the ferry and caught a bus right out into the country. We had a lovely time, I really enjoyed meself, but then, just before we got on the bus to come home . . .'

'He kissed you?' Ellen hazarded.

Biddy stared at her. Ellen looked such a fluffy little thing with that bouncy yellow hair and her big, blue eyes, but she was shrewd, for all that.

'You're a mind reader,' she said accusingly. 'How did you know, Ellen?'

'Because that's what nine boys outer ten would ha' done,' Ellen said promptly. 'You're young an' pretty – what else did you expect?'

'Oh! But I didn't want him to kiss me, Ellen.'

'Ah well, he weren't to know that, were 'e?' Ellen asked wisely. 'Not till 'e'd tried and been told to keep 'is kisses to 'isself.'

'Oh, I see. Well, if only he'd listened it would have

been all right, but now if I so much as pass him in the back kitchen he sort of grabs at me. And it isn't only that I don't like it, but if she caught us Ma Kettle would tell me to sling me hook and then what 'ud I do?'

'Ah, I see your problem. No money, a feller what's got 'ands like a octypus an' 'is Mam jealous as a cat. Hmm.'

'I don't think Ma Kettle's at all jealous,' Biddy said fairly. 'But she wouldn't want Kenny getting mixed up wi' me, it stands to reason. She wants him to pass his exams and be a credit to her.'

'Same thing; she disapproves,' Ellen said. 'What you want, queen, is out; right?'

'Oh, yes! But how, Ellen?'

'We-ell, I do 'ave an idea, but we'd best meet again, talk it over. When are you off?'

'Off?'

'Free from work, Bid,' Ellen said impatiently. 'Do you 'ave Sundays? What time do you finish? Six? 'Alf past?'

'Oh . . . well, I don't get much time off . . . oh Ellen, I don't get *any* time off, not really, because Ma Kettle has me clean the house, do the washing and so on, on a Sunday, we work all day Saturday until ten at night because people going to the cinema shows want sweets when they come out. . . . I might get away later on Friday . . . say nine?'

'Too late. What about first thing in the mornin' on a Sun . . . oh 'eck, you work then. Tell you what, make th'old bag gi' you a day free. Say you must 'ave it, chuck. This Sunday an all. An' come along to Shaw's Alley, up the back o' the King's Dock. We'll 'ave a bit of a clack an' a cuppa an' see what we can sort out.'

'Shaw's Alley? But you lived quite near us, on Paul Street,' Biddy said, about to slide off the crate but arresting herself to unhook her apron from an upstanding nail. 'How come you've moved?'

'Honest to God, Biddy, you ain't the only one what's done a bunk! Me family live at Paul Street still, it's just me what's in the Alley. Are you comin' or not?'

'Next Sunday morning? At about tennish? That'll be all right, because she'll think I'm in Mass. I'll be there. Where's it near?'

'It's on the corner o' Sparling Street . . . don't tell me, you won't know it, not down there. Well if you catch a tram . . . no, a leckie's out o' the question, no dosh . Gawd . . d'you know Park Lane, chuck?'

'Of course,' Biddy lied haughtily.

'That's awright, then. Mek your way there, keep to the right 'and side till you come to Sparly, then it's the first proper turnin' off on your right and I'm second from the corner. Me name's writ on the door, jest knock an' come up.'

She had jumped down off the crate as she spoke, smoothed a hand over her bouncy yellow bob, and was hurrying up the road again. Biddy ran after her and grabbed her elbow.

'Ellen . . . don't go yet! Where's your job? You haven't told me a thing, I did all the talking!'

'Oh! Well, no time now, queen. I'll tell you all about it Sunday mornin', tennish. Tara for now.'

Biddy, abruptly remembering her errand, stood staring after her friend for a moment, then, with a shrug, retraced her steps to the greengrocer's shop she had been about to enter when Ellen's familiar figure had crossed her vision. Mrs Ruby Hitchcot was lovingly setting out her strawberries in a glistening mound under a notice which read 'Fresh today! Straight from the Wirral!'. She turned and smiled at Biddy. 'Mornin', queen. What can I do for you this bright mornin'?'

Biddy had met Ellen on the Thursday and by Sunday she

was in a rare state of excitement. She thought about telling Kenny, which would mean he might well walk up with her at least as far as Sparly, but decided against it. The fewer people who got wind of the fact that she had met up with an old friend, and guessed that the old friend might help her to escape from the Kettle ménage, the better.

On the other hand though, Kenny always went to the same Mass as she did, because then they walked up and back together, shared a pew, sometimes shared a hymn-book, and talked softly whilst waiting for the service to start. It made the service more amusing, Biddy acknowledged that, but now it also raised a considerable problem. If she told Kenny, then he might want to accompany her, which could be awkward, or he might want to stop her seeing Ellen, which would be worse. She absolved him of being a tale bearer and wanting to tell his mother, but if she did manage to get away he would come searching for her at Ellen's . . . and might even put his Ma onto her if Mrs Kettle demanded her address from him.

Sunday dawned warm and sunny. Kenny suggested that she might get another day off and go along to Seaforth with him. 'We could bathe,' he said hopefully. 'We could paddle, anyroad. Why not, our Biddy? It's time you 'ad some fun.'

'Look, I'm going to Mass,' Biddy said patiently. 'We'll talk about it after dinner, eh?'

He scowled. 'I'm not goin' to Mass, not on a day like this. I'm not goin' to miss this sunshine even if you wanna 'ang around the 'ouse all day. I'll meet you out and I'll have a word wi' me Mam.'

'All right, if that's what you want,' Biddy said. 'See you later, then, Kenny.'

After the day out with Kenny, Ma Kettle had been prevailed upon to buy Biddy a best coat and skirt and a pair of decent shoes. The shoes had cardboard soles and were made of thin, cheap leather and the coat and skirt came from one of the stalls on Paddy's Market, but they seemed very fine indeed to Biddy. So on Sunday morning she donned the blue coat and skirt, the striped blouse and the navy shoes, perched a straw hat on her curls, and set off for Mass.

The Kettles attended St Anthony's at the top of the Scotland Road so Biddy turned in that direction, walked a hundred yards or so and then crossed over the road and retraced her steps, feeling excitingly wicked as she did so. It was risky but after all, what could old Ma Kettle do to her? Slinging her out on her ear seemed less likely now, for it had gradually been borne in upon Biddy that she was a very useful person indeed in the Kettle household. Where else would Ma Kettle get someone who could help Kenny with his studying, cook meals, clean, launder, make sweets . . . and best of all, do it without a wage and without ever dipping her fingers into the till?

So she could perfectly well have asked for at least half a day off, but in fact that would have complicated things still further. Mrs Kettle would have grudgingly acceded to her request and Kenny, ears pricking, would have stuck to her side closer than glue. All would have been spoiled, so though this way she was deceiving Ma Kettle, Biddy did not let this affect her enjoyment of the day.

If Ellen asks me I'll stay to dinner, she planned, hurrying along the pavement in the sunshine. And when we've had our talk perhaps I can walk down by the docks . . . I wonder what it costs to use the overhead railway? She could still remember how thrilled she had been as a child when her Da had taken her for a ride on it, all the way from the Pierhead to Seaforth and back, feeling like a proper princess as she peered into the docks, whilst her knowledgeable father told her all about the shipping that swung at anchor there.

But she would not part with her hard-won money on a treat, even if it was within her means. And that was not impossible, because Biddy had discovered that she could earn a little money from time to time, though if Ma Kettle had known, Biddy imagined she would have put a stop to it at once, on the grounds that Biddy's time and talents were hers, bought and paid for by the roof over her head and her meals. Because Kenny had insisted, Ma Kettle always gave Biddy at least a penny and sometimes more for the church collection each Sunday, but Biddy would not have dreamed of pocketing money meant for such a purpose. Her money, unlike Ma Kettle's, was made by fair means only.

It was Biddy's neat handwriting which was in demand. Ma Kettle had soon discovered that a notice written out in Biddy's hand was clear and legible as well as better spelt than anything she herself could produce. And then the grocer down the road, when Biddy had popped in on an errand, had asked if she could do some notices for his window.

Biddy complied and was grateful for the pence which found their way into her pocket as a result. She refused to allow herself to spend them, however, no matter how desperately she might long to buy something, and as a result she had several shillings, all in pence, ha'pence and farthings, salted away inside her pillow, a small, hard lump amongst the feathers.

She had transferred six pennies and four ha'pennies to her coat pocket earlier in the morning and now she jingled them thoughtfully as she walked. A ride on a leckie would be nice, but she grudged spending the money, especially on such a sunny day, when walking would be a pleasure. If she wasn't asked to dinner she could always buy herself fish and chips . . . her mouth watered at the prospect . . . that was, if she decided not to go home to Ma Kettle's until really late, though that would mean her deceit in not going to Mass might be discovered, which could have unpleasant consequences.

Biddy had just decided to tell a few lies for once – enough were told in the Kettle emporium each day to make her ears burn – when she realised that she had been so busy thinking and walking that she was actually on Old Haymarket, where the trams lined up when waiting for passengers.

'You want to go straight down Whitechapel, along Paradise Street and then turn left into Park Lane,' Mrs Ruby had advised her when she asked the best way to Sparling Street. 'Best tek care, though, chuck. It's rough down by the docks.'

So now Biddy crossed over the road junction with its mass of tramlines and started off along Whitechapel. She felt light and airy, pleased with herself. She was not running away, nothing so daring, but she did feel she was paving the way for a change in her circumstances.

And a change was overdue. It isn't that the work is so terribly hard, it's just hot, monotonous and constant, Biddy thought now, wondering whether it would be all right to take off her blue coat and allow the sunshine to warm her arms, for the blouse had short sleeves. Wasn't Ma Kettle ever young herself? Doesn't she remember that finishing work, having a break, is what it's all about? She does know, because look how she spoils the boys! Luke's shirts must always be immaculate, his food always on the table, she doesn't take money for his keep the way any other mother would, so he's not thinking of marriage, he's far too comfortable. And then Jack, though he's away most of the time, gets spoiled rotten when he does come home. Breakfast in bed, his favourite grub always on tap, friends home for tea, money for the cinema or the theatre slipped into his hand as he scans the pages of the *Echo* for entertainment. Even Kenny gets what he wants . . . which is why he can ask for time off for me and get it without an argument.

A tramp with his greatcoat over one arm passed her, grinning to himself in the sunshine. He had no teeth and he was filthy but he did look happy, Biddy reflected. Perhaps teeth and cleanliness weren't everything, then. She turned to watch him for a moment; he was free in a way she could never imagine herself being. He went where he fancied, begged for food or stole it, slept under hedges in good weather and in barns in bad. She supposed, vaguely, that he must sleep in workhouses in the city since barns and hedges were both rare . . . and saw that the road had changed. She was now on Paradise Street and must start keeping her eyes peeled for Sparling Street.

'Well, Ellen, you're very comfortably settled here. It's a lovely flat, it must cost you quite a bit, so you've done well for yourself.'

The two girls were seated on a comfortable blue plush sofa in Ellen's living-room. She had already shown Biddy round the flat, which was on the first floor and consisted of the living-room in which they sat, a very fancy bedroom, all pink rugs and cream curtaining, with a very large crucifix on one wall and a rather improper picture on the other, and a tiny kitchen.

Ellen, in a pink silk dress with a dropped waist and with pink plush slippers on her small feet, was sitting on the sofa beside Biddy. She was smoking a cigarette rather inexpertly, and at her friend's words she nodded and looked pleased.

'Yes, it's awright, this. It's a pity there's only the one bedroom, but I get by.'

'I don't see why anyone should want more than one

bedroom,' Biddy said frankly. 'Ellen, what is your job? It must be an awfully good one for you to live here – you don't even share!'

Ellen blushed. Biddy watched the pink creep up her friend's neck and flood across her small, fair face.

'I do share in a way, from time to time. And as for me job, I'm a saleslady in Gowns in a big department store. The feller that's got all the power, my floor manager, is a Mr Bowker. He's trainin' me to do the buyin' for Gowns so sometimes I go up to London with 'im. In fact 'e's promised to take me to Paris next spring. Yes, it's norra bad job.'

'I wish I could get a job like that,' Biddy said wistfully. 'You are so lucky, Ellen! If I could just get a little job, perhaps even a live-in job, then I might be able to save up for a room somewhere. But I'd never run to anything like this.'

Ellen got up off the sofa and went over to the window. Without looking at Biddy she spoke slowly. 'Biddy . . . what about if we shared this place, you an' me? Only you'd 'ave to – to pay in other ways, per'aps.'

'What ways?' Biddy asked, immediately suspicious. 'I'd do the housework and the cooking willingly, if that's what you mean.'

'No, though you'd 'ave to do your share. No . . . it's – it's me voice, me accent, like. They say you won't get no further in Gowns unless you learn to talk proper, and you . . . you can do it awready, like. So would you teach me? Show me 'ow it's done, like?'

'And if I do, you'll let me live here with you? What rent would you want as well? And where can I find a job, Ellen? Because you'd want rent, and anyhow; I'd have to eat.'

'I don't want no rent. To tell you the truth, Biddy, it ain't me what pays the rent, norrin the way you mean. Me – me friend pays it.'

'Your boyfriend? Does he live here with you, then? What'll he think if I move in? You'd have to ask him first, Ellen.'

'Well, that's the other side to it, chuck. If you'd just clear off out when 'e comes over, 'e need never know. 'E don't come over all that often, per'aps twice a week, an' 'e never stays the night, 'cos . . . well, 'e never does, I swear it.'

Biddy frowned. There was something funny going on here! Now that she thought about it, girls of sixteen just didn't get to be buyers for big department stores, let alone live in the style to which Ellen had obviously become accustomed. Mam and I lived comfortably enough, but we didn't have silk dresses, Biddy remembered. Mam often said that she didn't allow her soft Irish brogue to be heard by customers, but even without a scouse accent she had never risen to be a buyer! And a boyfriend who paid the rent but didn't live in the flat and never stayed over, a job which paid Ellen, at sixteen years old, well enough to wear pink silk dresses and to have a wardrobe stuffed with expensive garments . . . what *was* going on?

'Look, Ellen, what you do is your business, but I must know what's up if I'm going to share with you,' she said as firmly as she could. 'Who is this boyfriend who's so generous . . . is he – is he *married*?'

'Oh 'eck, I knew you wouldn't jest . . .' Ellen turned away from the window, crossed the room and sat down on the sofa beside her friend. Then she turned her head and looked Biddy straight in the eye. 'Awright, the whole truth, eh? 'Ere goes, then.'

The sad little story was soon told. A child of a large family, Ellen had desperately wanted what she called 'a nice life'. She got a job as a waitress in a big café not far from the pierhead and, following the example set by the prettiest, cheekiest member of staff, she began to flirt with any male customer who seemed interested.

A great many seamen were not only interested, they wanted to get on even closer terms with pretty little Ellen Bradley, who made eyes at them and agreed to meet anyone after work who would spend a few bob on her.

Then Ellen discovered that Mr Bowker, who was middle-aged, with false teeth and a thickening waistline, was watching her as he ate his chops. He was important, he rarely came into the café, and now, when he came, he liked to be served by Ellen.

'So young, so fresh,' he murmured to one of the other waitresses. 'She's wasted in this place . . . I'd like to see her in Gowns.'

'He meant out of gowns,' Mabel told her, giggling. 'A rare one for the girls is Mr Bowker, though he does his pinching in private, like.'

Ellen hadn't known what Mabel meant, not at first, but after her very first outing with Mr Bowker she understood. She could have nice things, if she would let her elderly admirer have certain privileges.

'Mr Bowker was ever so nice, 'e took me to the flicks, bought me a box o' chocolates, drove me 'ome in 'is big motor car . . .'

She made light of the clammy caresses, the persistent hand at her stocking top, though Biddy could tell from her expression that she had been shocked by his behaviour at first. The thing was, she told Biddy, that a boy's hand could be – and often was – slapped away, but she had hesitated to give a man old enough to be her father so much as a quick shove. Not exactly a shy or retiring girl, nevertheless by the time she had finished her story her face was crimson.

The upshot of those first tentative meetings had been that Mr B was very quickly enthralled by her, and terribly jealous of the fact that in her present job other men could look at her, flirt with her – might even have the success with her so far denied him. He tried hard to get her alone, to take advantage of her, but Ellen said proudly that she'd more sense than to let him carry on the way he wanted without any strings. And the depth and degree of his jealousy, when you realised that he was not himself free to marry her, carried a price.

'A good job at the store and a place of me own, that was what I wanted in exchange for – for not lookin' at other fellers no more,' she said. ''E was all for givin' me a job in Gowns – all women customers, you see – and I said if 'e coughed up a flat an' all, 'e could come round whenever 'e wanted, but 'is ole woman, she won't stand for 'im pissin' off when 'e should be at 'ome, so it's daytimes only, thank Gawd.'

'And you let him do – do *that* to you?' Biddy asked incredulously. Ill-informed as she was, she could still see that doing 'that' with a rich old man could not be to everyone's taste.

'Oh aye, whiles 'e pays me price. Now, chuck; are you on?'

'Wait a moment. Ellen, it isn't just so's I can teach you to speak properly, is it? You're lonely, aren't you? Why don't you ask one of your sisters to share?'

'Honest to God, Biddy, you want your 'ead lookin' at! If me Mam found out I were livin' tally wi' a feller old enough to be me Da she'd tear me 'air out be the roots an' t'row me body in the Mersey!'

'Yes, I suppose... but you are lonely, aren't you, Nell?'

Surprisingly, the use of her old baby-name brought tears to Ellen's big blue eyes, though she snatched out a hanky and wiped them away as quickly and unobtrusively as she could.

'Well, aye, in a way. All the wimmin at work's years older'n me, an' the folk round 'ere turns up their snitches at me. They think I tek sailors, but I don't, I wouldn't, that's a sin . . . it's just Mr Bowker.'

'Do you call him Mr Bowker still?' Biddy asked, amused. 'After all, you're living tally with him . . . or that's what you said.'

'I call him Bunny Big Bum when we're in bed,' Ellen said, giving a snuffle of laughter. ''E's a funny feller, but 'e means well. Now will you share or won't you?'

'I'd love to share,' Biddy said recklessly. 'What'll I tell old Kettle, though? And Kenny, I suppose.'

'Tell 'em lies, real good ones,' Ellen said at once. 'After what old Ma Kettle's took from you you don't owe 'em nothin'. Say you met your Mam's sister an' she's goin' to tek you in. And 'ear the old devil wail', she added gleefully, 'when she realises she's gonna have to pay someone to skivvy for 'er in future!'

Chapter Three

Biddy walked home in a very thoughtful mood after her visit to Ellen Bradley. She had been offered an escape route though she was quite shrewd enough to realise that it was not, perhaps, going to be an ideal arrangement. She would have to keep out of Mr Bowker's way, which would mean that any personal possessions she might amass – she had few things to take with her – would have to be kept hidden away at all times, and because Ellen did not want anyone to get to know anything about the way she lived, she would almost certainly involve Biddy in her web of deceit.

But how else was she to escape from the Kettles, without becoming a vagrant in the process? Jobs in service were possible, she supposed, but when could she apply for such a job? Scarcely in what little free time she managed to scrape. And in this venture, she realised that Kenny would not stand her friend. He was always after her to better her lot, told her constantly to stand up for herself, fight back, but he would not want her to move out. He must know that if she did so, his chances of a quick kiss and a cuddle would be cut down dramatically – cut out, in fact, Biddy told herself darkly. She liked Kenny all right, but not like that.

Ellen had invited her to dinner, so she had helped to cook a meal, helped to eat it, helped to clear away afterwards. She was glad to find that Ellen was a good cook and clearly managed her little love-nest well. She commented on this and Ellen said tartly that anyone brought up as a third child in a family of a dozen had to be handy, else they'd go under.

So along Sparling Street, up Paradise Street and into Whitechapel Biddy pondered her next move. Tell a big, beautiful whopper and claim she'd met a long-lost relative who needed Biddy's help about her own home and was willing to take her in? Or tell the truth and put up with the calumny of being ungrateful and selfish – or just walk out, leaving a note behind, and spend the rest of her life hiding from vengeful Kettles?

She was still pondering when she reached the Scottie, still wondering what to do for the best. Because of something Kenny had let drop she had realised a couple of days earlier that before she moved in, Ma Kettle had not only employed Maisie, she had had another girl in on Sundays and Wednesdays to do the laundering and ironing, to mend anything that needed mending and to do any marketing which Maisie and she herself had not done.

So when I moved in a couple of girls lost their jobs, not just Maisie, Biddy told herself. The money I've saved the old skinflint! But it'll really go against the grain to have to pay out money for three girls. . . . Lord, whatever shall I do? Perhaps it really might be better to say nothing and wait my opportunity – something must turn up.

Keeping her visit to Ellen entirely dark would not be possible, she realised, because Kenny had said he would meet her out of church after Mass. But she didn't think he would split on her because he was still her friend, though less so with every time she repulsed his advances. She wished she did not have to do so, wished she found him attractive and wanted his kisses, but the truth was he was too much his mother's son. Every time she saw his bunchy face near her own she was sharply reminded of Ma Kettle – and the last person whose kisses she would welcome would have been that lady's.

Still, she had enjoyed a day out and now she had hope. The spectre of being stuck as Ma Kettle's slave until the day one of them died had actually receded . . . and it was a stupid fear anyway, Biddy told herself. She would have got out sooner or later, now it seemed it was to be sooner.

She reached the shop and went round the side as she always did when it was shut. There was a tiny yard which stank of cats and dustbins and was looped across and across with greenish washing lines, and facing her was the back door, a great block of tarry wood with a high latch. With a sigh, Biddy crossed the yard, ducking under the sagging lines as she did so and reflecting a trifle bitterly that since usually on a Sunday afternoon the lines were laden with sheets, Ma Kettle had obviously decided to save them for Biddy to do as a treat. She reached the door and lifted the latch, heaving at the weight of it. It swung outwards, creaking, and a huge bluebottle, which must have been lured in by the Saturday smell of boiling treacle, lurched drunkenly past Biddy's right ear.

'Damned old fly,' Biddy muttered. 'I hope someone covered everything last thing Saturday or I'll be scooping fly-blow off every sweet in the place.'

The back door gave onto the boiling kitchen, which one crossed to enter a tiny, dark passageway from which the linoleumed stairs ascended to the flat above. Outside, it was still a sunny afternoon but in here it was cool and quiet. Which was odd, Biddy reflected, tiptoeing up the stairs, because usually on a Sunday afternoon the house resounded with the noise of cleaning, laundering, ironing . . . only of course since she was responsible for most of those noises, it would be quiet without her.

She reached the landing and opened the kitchen door. Someone had put the sheets to soak in the upstairs sink, which was unusual and would mean she would have to carry them downstairs wet, weighing half a ton, to wash them in the little back scullery as she always did. She sniffed the air; dinner had not been cooked today – mercy, don't say the old devil had put off having dinner just because there was no Biddy to cook it for her!

Biddy left the kitchen and stood looking thoughtfully at the two remaining doors which led off this landing. One was the living-room, the other the bedroom which she shared with Ma Kettle. The boys had the attic bedrooms above, as she well knew, since as soon as Luke and Kenny were in the kitchen having their breakfast she was supposed to rush up the stairs and make their beds. Kenny had lately taken to making his own, presumably hoping to get round her, but Luke probably didn't know how, certainly he had never so much as plumped a pillow in the nine months that Biddy had been working here.

Better try the living-room first. She opened the door, and knew before it creaked back that the room would be empty. She stood back, her heart beginning to pound; this was definitely odd. She had never known Ma Kettle go out on a Sunday afternoon without very good reason and the church service she attended was long over. Jack was home, to be sure, but he went out with his mates, not with his Mam, and Luke had recently met a young lady – not that Ma referred to her as such, she was *that nasty, scheming hussy* so far as Ma was concerned – and liked to visit her home on a Sunday afternoon.

Best look in the bedroom, then. No doubt Ma was laid down on her bed for half an hour. . . . Biddy opened the door and stuck her head round it. The big brass bedstead was empty, her own small truckle bed pushed almost out of sight beneath it. Biddy could just see her rag doll's small, round head lying on the pillow.

With a frustrated sigh, Biddy closed the door and went downstairs. Was Ma Kettle in the shop, going over her accounts or checking stock? Or in the tiny scullery beyond the boiling kitchen, perhaps pouring water into the big copper so that Biddy could start on the sheets as soon as she returned? But the shop was deserted so Biddy went through into the scullery and looked rather helplessly about her.

The little room was dark and dank and at first Biddy could make out very little in the gloom, then she spotted the note. It was propped up on the copper as though Ma assumed she would go there as soon as she got back from church. The message on it was simple.

'*Do laundry*,' it said. '*Cook dinner*.'

Biddy stood looking at the note for a long time. Ma Kettle had not bothered to say where she had gone or why, nor for whom the note was intended. She had expected Biddy back after Mass, of course, so if she had left quite early she might have reasoned that Biddy would get the sheets on the line in plenty of time to get them dry. Or she might simply have thought to herself that Biddy must not begin to believe she might enjoy a few hours off without paying the penalty.

Finally, Biddy left the scullery. She went up to her room and rooted around under the bed. The old carpet bag was still there. She took off the blue coat and skirt, the cheap shoes, the little straw hat with the ribbon round the crown, and put on her working clothes and the cracked old shoes she had worn when she first came to Kettle's Confectionery. Then she checked her change of underwear, which had lived in the carpet bag ever since she moved in because Ma Kettle had never suggested she might have the use of a drawer or two. Next she picked up her pillow and thrust her hand through the hole in one end and deep into the feathers, withdrawing the lumpy little scrap of torn linen which contained all her worldly wealth.

Then she picked Dolly off the bed and put her in the

carpet bag on top of the underwear, and after that she turned and looked around the small room. She felt a little pang, but only a little one: it had been, after all, a refuge of sorts.

Downstairs, she went back into the shop and found her lettering pen and the big bottle of blackish ink. She fetched the note from the scullery and sat down at the table. She read Ma Kettle's words again, then smiled and bent her head, beginning to write.

Presently she stood up and propped the note against the ink bottle in the middle of the table, where no one coming into the room could fail to see it. It now read, in Ma Kettle's spidery hand, *Do laundary, cook dinner*, and under that, in Biddy's neat script, *Do it yourself*.

'I don't know what came over me,' she told Ellen later that day, when the two of them were settled down over a bread and cheese supper, with the windows open to let in the breeze from the river and a glass of stout beside each plate. 'It's the worm turning, I guess. And do you know where she'd gone?'

'Can't imagine,' Ellen said, sipping stout. 'How d'you find out, anyroad?'

'Well, I was going off down the road, feeling a bit scared in case she turned up and got really nasty, when someone called me. It was Maisie, the one who used to work in the flat.'

'I didn't know you knew her,' Ellen said. 'Or that she knew you, for that matter. What did she want?'

'She wanted to know if I was slingin' me 'ook, as she put it. She grinned like a Cheshire cat when I said I was, and then she told me Ma Kettle had been invited to her sister Olliphant's for tea . . . but listen to this, Ellen, she'd been invited last week but hadn't said a word to me, in case I thought I ought to go too! As if I would, as if I cared a fig for her old sister, who's probably just as horrible as her. But wasn't that mean? To go out just leaving me that message, when she could have told me before I went to Mass that she'd be out when I got back.'

'Not that you went to Mass,' Ellen said, spearing a pickled onion and popping it into her mouth. She crunched and then swallowed before she spoke. 'Still, I know what you mean; she's norra nice woman, that one. But it gave you all the excuse you wanted to scarper, didn't it?'

'Yes, it did. And all the reason I needed not to tell her where I was goin' or anything. And if Kenny gets in first, which he probably will, he'll read the note and under-stand that things had just got beyond bearing.' Biddy leaned back in her chair and gave a sigh of pure content-ment. 'Oh Ellen, just to be able to go to bed early, for once! Just to know I shan't be heaved out to wait on those boys . . . it's heaven, honest to God.'

'Yes, I wouldn't mind if I didn't 'ave go to in to the shop tomorrer,' Ellen admitted. 'Still, it's awright when I'm there, specially if I gets a customer early. The custom-ers like me,' she added, 'It's Miss Elsegood and Miss Nixon what don't.'

'They're just jealous because you're young and pretty, and probably they'd like Mr Bowker to spend money on them instead of you,' Biddy said generously, for the more she thought about it the less she liked the thought of an old man pulling her about. But Ellen, though she smiled, shook her head.

'Nah, it's not that because they don't know about me an' Mr B. Well, I don't think they does, anyroad. But they know a waitress shouldn't 'ave 'ad a good job in Gowns first go off, they know there's something fishy goin' on.' She hesitated. 'What you goin' to do tomorrer, Bid?'

'Dunno. Take a look around, maybe. It seems a long

time since I went into a nice shop and browsed a bit. Why?'

'We-ell, your money won't last for ever, and . . .'

'Oh, I'll look for a job first go off,' Biddy said, conscience stricken. 'Sorry, for a moment I quite forgot I needed to earn. What pays best, would you say? Waitressing, shop work, that sort of thing?'

'Factory work's best,' Ellen said authoritatively. 'You wouldn't get taken on in a shop in them clo'es – why didn't you keep them nice things you 'ad on, earlier?'

'She bought 'em,' Biddy said briefly. 'I know I earned 'em, but I didn't want her saying I'd left with property belonging to her. She could have put the scuffers on me.'

'What, the way she treated you, chuck? She wou'n't dare! There's a law in this country 'ginst slavery, you know!'

'Yes, but it's provin' it,' Biddy pointed out, ever practical. 'It would be her word against mine, because I didn't go shouting it from the rooftops, exactly. Still, I'll look for a job first thing.'

'I only said it because it's a deal more difficult to find a job than to look,' Ellen said rather gloomily. 'Tell you what, we're much the same size, how about if I lend you somethin' to wear, eh? Somethin' decent? Jest till you're in work, like.'

'Oh, Ellen, you are kind . . . but don't lend me anything too good,' Biddy urged. 'Just a plain dress and some shoes. I know what you mean, I wouldn't give me a job myself in this old gear.'

'Right. Now if you've done wi' them onions, what about a spot o' kip? We've both gorra long day tomorrer.'

Biddy very soon realised that Ellen was right; jobs were hard to come by in the city, with a good many girls chasing every one. But she did have an advantage; she was able to accept a very small wage and she was experienced at shop work.

69

Against that experience, however, was set the fact that jobs on the Scottie and in that general area were out, for fear of meeting a Kettle face to face and having to put up with at worst outright abuse and false accusations, and at best coldness. But the weather was fine, Biddy's little store of money meant that she could keep going for a week or two before the situation became desperate, provided she was content to eat cheaply, and for the first time since her mother had died she knew what it was to have time to herself.

Being just fifteen, there was enough of the child in Biddy to enjoy watching the trains steaming in and out of Lime Street, walking down to the pierhead to see the ferries come and go, sauntering along Sefton Street and watching the overhead railway chugging noisily along above her head whilst the masts and funnels of the big ships were easily visible in the nearby docks.

And neatly dressed in borrowed pink cotton with her curls tied in a knot on top of her head she looked sufficiently respectable to browse for hours in Lewises, George Henry Lee's and Blacklers, dreaming of the day when she would be able to shop here, to ascend to the restaurants on the top floor and eat delicious food, to buy a straw hat with a field of daisies and poppies strewn across the brim, to try on elegant ankle-length skirts and to tittup around in patent leather shoes with heels three inches high.

But of course jobs do not just materialise, so towards the end of her first week Biddy began to search for employment. She bought the *Echo* each evening and scanned the advertisements, she looked in all the shop windows as she passed to see if anyone was after a shop assistant, and she hovered outside a small factory which made leather handbags in the hope that someone might come and put a 'wanted' notice on the big wooden gates. She had decided to leave Tate's for the time being at least. Luke worked there, in a managerial capacity admittedly, but with my luck, Biddy concluded gloomily, he'd be the one to interview me for the job, or I'd walk slap into him in the corridor, and that 'ud be me scuppered.

The two girls were sitting in the living-room of the flat one evening, companionably sharing a fish-and-chip supper whilst Ellen soaked her feet in a bath of cold water and scanned the paper, when there was a knock on the door. It was the first time such a thing had happened since Biddy moved in and both girls panicked at once, Biddy flying across the room and trying to hide behind the sofa whilst Ellen, going very pale, whisked the paper out of sight beneath the cushions, tried to do the same with Biddy's fish and chips, with disastrous results to the upholstery, they discovered later, and adjured Biddy, in a piercing whisper, to shut up and stay still or they would both be out on their ears.

It was Biddy who came to her senses first.

She emerged from behind the sofa and grabbed Ellen's arm. 'Say I've just popped in to share your supper,' she hissed. 'He won't suspect a thing... act natural, for God's sake, or a babe in arms would know we were up to something!'

'Oh yes... oh Bid, you're a bright 'un... you've come to 'ave your supper wi' me, you're an ole friend from me schooldays,' Ellen muttered, mopping her brow. 'Oh bugger me backwards, 'e's ringin' agin... talk about impatient!'

'Your language!' Biddy said, giggling. 'Go and let him in, and act cool, will you?'

Ellen disappeared and Biddy, sitting demurely on the sofa with her plate and its damaged food on her knee, listened. She heard Ellen's high voice, a laugh, a masculine burr of speech, and then Ellen said, 'Come along in then, for a moment,' and her feet pattered back across the linoleum with a man's heavier tread sounding behind her.

The footsteps drew nearer and Biddy had picked up the newspaper and was scanning the job advertisements when the door opened. Ellen came in, and one look at her face showed Biddy that whoever had been at the door, he or she represented no threat.

'Biddy, meet me friend Mr Alton,' she said gaily. 'George, this is Biddy O'Shaughnessy, what's stayin' wi' me for a while. We was at school together . . . George was one of me pals before . . . well, we got to know one another whilst I worked at Cottle's, on Ranelagh Street. 'E's an assistant at the Sterling Boot.' She turned to her guest. 'Sit down, do, George, an' I'll get you a glass of stout.'

George was a pleasant-looking young man with short, fair hair, a tiny moustache and blue eyes. He grinned at Biddy and sat down beside her, carefully catching his trousers above the knee and pulling them up a bit as he took his place on the sofa.

''Ello, Miss O'Shaughnessy,' he said genially. 'Nice to meet you. Nice to meet any friend of Ellen's, come to that. You in Gowns?'

'Hello, Mr Alton, nice to meet you. No, I'm . . . '

'No, she worked at a confectioner's,' Ellen said, bustling out of the room in the direction of the kitchen. She came back with the jug of stout and an extra glass. 'She's not workin' right now, more's the pity.'

'A confectioner's? I seem to recall . . . but I daresay you're huntin' for somethin' different, or d'you want another job in that line?' Mr Alton asked genially. 'Can't wait on, I s'pose? There's a waitress wanted at Fuller's, next door to the old Boot.'

'No experience,' Ellen said, answering for her. 'But you could try for it, couldn't you, Bid?'

'I wouldn't mind, but most places seem to want experience,' Biddy said. 'Ranelagh Street? That's quite near Lewises, isn't it?'

'Aye, that's right. Nobbut two minutes walk away . . . well, if you walk the way I do in me dinner-break it's two minutes, anyway. Now let me see, someone was talkin' the other day . . . people do chat while they try on boots an' shoes, some customers get real friendly, but this was a feller what lodges not far from me on Chaucer Street . . . that were about a job vacancy . . . let me think.'

He thought, frowning, whilst Ellen poured the stout, then as he accepted the glass his brow cleared. 'Got it!' he said triumphantly. 'D'you know Cazneau Street, Miss O'Shaughnessy?'

'Yes, quite well, it's quite near the Scottie . . . ' Biddy was beginning when the incorrigible Ellen broke in.

'Let 'im finish, queen. George is a right good 'un for knowin' today what the rest o' the world knows tomorrer. Tell 'er, Georgie boy.'

'Well, there's a confectioner's on the corner o' Rose Place an' they're wantin' a young lady what knows a t'ing or two about confectionery. I walk past the shop of an evenin', it's a nice enough place. Cleaner than Kettle's, on the Scottie, but old Mr James meks 'is own taffy an' that.'

'Well, thank you very much, Mr Alton,' Biddy said. 'I'll try there and Fuller's, as well.'

She told herself she had no intention of applying for the job on Cazzy, it was far too close to the Scottie, but at least she knew about it; if she got desperate she could try there. And Ma Kettle didn't go out much, she was too fat to enjoy exercise, so the chances of her actually walking into another confectionery shop and spotting Biddy behind the counter were pretty remote.

Ellen seemed to guess what she was thinking.

'She wouldn't 'ave a clue you was there,' she said cheerfully. 'Nor would them Kettle boys. When you can get taffy 'alf price or free you doesn't go an' pay for it, not unless you're light in the 'ead. Nah, you'd be safe as 'ouses in another sweet-shop.' She turned back to George. 'She used to work at Kettle's but she left,' she explained. 'Would you like a cheese sarney, George? We've got pickled onions, too.'

Upon George admitting that a cheese sarney with pickled onions would go down a treat she trotted out of the room, leaving Mr Alton and Miss O'Shaughnessy eyeing one another somewhat awkwardly.

'Umm . . . so you're jest a pal, Miss O'Shaughnessy, an old school friend, like?' George said at last. 'An' you're stayin' 'ere a while?'

'That's right,' Biddy said. 'It's ever so good of Ellen to let me, especially when I've got no job, but I'll remedy that as soon as possible, of course.'

'Course you will,' George said heartily. 'Well, me an' Ellen's old friends ourselves, I enjoy comin' here from time to time. Usually I nips into Gowns to tell 'er I'm comin', but today I jest popped up on the off-chance.'

'That's nice,' Biddy said awkwardly. 'It's nice to have friends to visit.'

'Very nice,' George agreed. 'D'you get out much, Miss O'Shaughnessy?'

'Yes, quite a bit. Especially now I'm searching for work.'

'An' what about evenin's? The flickers? The the-aytre? A bit of a knees up at the local . . . ' he broke off, the ready colour rising to his cheeks. 'Oh no, you're a bit gre . . . young, I mean for public 'ouses. Still, I guess you like a good cinema show, eh?'

'I haven't been to the cinema for ages, but I used to enjoy seeing films,' Biddy was beginning, when George leaned across and pressed something into her hand. She glanced down at it; it was a round silver shilling.

'Go an' enjoy yourself,' George said earnestly. 'Get out

and about while you're young, Miss O'Shaughnessy. See a fillum, or 'ave a spot of supper . . . jest so's me an' Ellen can 'ave a couple o' hours to ourselves, eh?'

'Oh, but . . . It's awfully kind of you, Mr Alton, but I don't know whether I ought . . . Ellen never said . . .'

'She wouldn't, would she?' George said. 'Bit awkward, what? She never knew I were comin' over tonight, for starters. But she'll be pleased as punch to know you're 'avin' a good time, and . . . ' he broke off as Ellen entered the room and turned to his old friend. 'Ellen, I give your pal a bob for the flickers; what d'you say?'

'Well, George, that's very generous of you, but you don't 'ave to go, Biddy, if you don't fancy the cinema,' Ellen said, looking almost as pink-cheeked as her guest. 'Still, if you'd like a bit of an outing . . .'

Biddy stood up and crossed the room. 'I'll be back tennish,' she said, trying not to sound as shocked as she felt. She had managed to make herself accept the presence of Mr Bowker, though she knew she would always think of him as Bunny Big Bum and dreaded their eventual meeting, but she definitely did not approve of her friend living tally with one fellow and having another visit her in the first one's expensive little flat.

'Thanks, luv,' Ellen said. 'We'll talk after.'

She must have read the coolness in Biddy's eyes and the slight stiffness in her friend's attitude – and so she should, Biddy told herself furiously, clattering down the stairs. So she jolly well should, taking Mr Bowker's money the way she does and then playing fast and loose with his affections! Still, at least George Alton was a shop assistant, not a sailor. If Ellen started bringing sailors in she, Biddy, would definitely move out!

The *Jenny Bowdler* was a coaster, carrying any cargo it could get up and down and around the coast of Britain.

She was Dai's first choice simply because she was needing a deckhand the day that he and Meirion visited the port of Amlwch, simply because he had applied to the Skipper and got the job, but he was not sorry. It was a good life, though the work was hard and time ashore brief.

And right now the *Jenny* was nosing her way into a small port on the west coast of Ireland. They had a load of timber to take ashore here and they would probably pick up bricks, or dressed stone, or – or cabbages and kings, Dai thought ruefully. And once they had exchanged cargoes they would be off again, with very little opportunity to take a look around, or do more than go into the village to send a postcard home, buy some fresh fruit or vegetables, and get back on board.

It was a fine, chilly morning, and very early. Mist curled round the hills, hiding their tops from inquisitive eyes, and on the long meadow which sloped down to the right of the harbour the dew, Dai knew from his own experience, would hang heavy. He sighed again; he liked the sea, he enjoyed the comradeship and the hard work aboard the *Jenny*, but he missed his own place, his friends, the exhausting, muscle-straining work on the fishing boats and then the pleasure to be had from tending your garden, watching the crops grow, the beasts begin to thrive.

'Wharra you thinkin' about, you dozy 'aporth?' A hand, large and square, smote Dai right between the shoulder blades, making him choke like a cat with a fur-ball. 'Are ya comin' ashore, wack?'

Greasy O'Reilly was immediately identifiable by his nasal Liverpool accent. Dai swung his fist around his back and hit something softish; no part of Greasy was actually soft. He was a square, pugnacious young man of about Dai's own age but he had been reared in a far rougher school.

'Wait'll we see dem Liver bairds come into view,' he would say to Dai whenever home was mentioned. 'Eh, Taff, dere's no more beautiful sight I'm tellin' yiz.'

'Everyone's home is special, see, Greasy,' Dai assured him. 'Amlwch isn't my home, but it's near enough for me. Tell you what, bach, when we get back to Anglesey you can come an' stay wi' me for a day or two. Then when we reach Heaven – Liverpool to the uninitiated – I'll come home wi' you.'

'You're on! We lives in a real posh slum, us O'Reillys do,' Greasy said with relish. 'An' I gorra sister, she's a smart judy, what'll do anyt'ing for a mate o' mine. 'Ave you gorra sister, la?'

'Yes; she's married to a very strong man who ties seamen in knots and chucks 'em into the 'oggin at the least suspicion of a smile in my sister's direction,' Dai had said. 'Nice try though, Greasy.'

But now, holding the stern rope and waiting to jump ashore and tie it round the nearest bollard, Dai had no time for chit-chat.

'Yes, I'm coming ashore, if you haven't split my adam's apple in two, thumping me like that,' he said. 'Ah . . . she's closing!'

He crouched on the rail, then sprang over the narrowing line of dark water and onto the cobbles below and in a couple of seconds the *Jenny*'s stern was secured, whilst ahead of him Mal Stretson followed suit with the bow rope.

The fenders bumped gently and the small ship cuddled up to the jetty like a lamb to the mother sheep. Men appeared on deck, the Skipper came down from the bridge and everyone began to scurry. They all knew that the sooner the cargo went ashore the sooner they would be able to follow suit, and the port was an attractive little place.

'Irish gairls is gorgeous,' Greasy said as he heaved at

the first bulk of timber. 'Gorgeous an' willin'. Oh, will ye look at that little darlin'.'

Dai raised his eyes and looked. The 'little darling' was a strapping wench of no more than thirteen or so, standing on the cobbles with a small sister hanging onto her hand and a basket on one plump hip. She saw Dai looking at her and smiled.

'You'd better ask her if she's got an older sister,' Dai muttered as Greasy began to heave on the timber. 'I'm not cradle-snatching, boyo, not for you or anyone else!'

'She's older 'n she looks,' Greasy said confidently. 'See the kid wi' 'er? That'll be 'er sprog.'

Dai grinned. 'Stupid you are, mun. Them's little girls both; but never mind, we'll find ourselves something nice for a night in port – where's the pub?'

'It's in the Post Office and General Store,' another man said, overhearing. 'Haven't you been to Ireland before, Taffy? Oh ah, a bit be'ind the times is Ireland.'

Dai shrugged and came staggering out onto the cobbles with his load. 'Anglesey's the same, so I should feel at home. Come on, Greasy, move yourself, we want to get off before dark, don't we?'

They found two girls, gentle, lovely girls who laughed with them, walked with them and refused to do anything more with them, greatly to Greasy's disgust. 'But we're just poor sailors, starved of love,' he pointed out pathetically. 'We've been at sea months . . . we're only askin' for some kissin' an' cuddlin', dat's all we want. Well, all we reckon we'll get,' he added conscientiously.

'You're two lovely fellers,' Rose said, smiling at him. 'But isn't this a small community, now? And how would we face people if they t'ought we were easy? No, no, to walk and talk is fine fun, but to go wit' the pair of you to the woods would be dangerous.'

'Woods? Who said woods? But a stroll in the sand'ills now...'

'Sandhills are worse; sure an' sand is soft as sin,' the other girl, Iris, said. She was walking beside Dai, smiling teasingly up at him with her soft pink mouth curved delightfully and her head tilted. 'What 'ud the Father say if he t'ought we were that sort of gorl?'

'Oh, well,' Dai said, smiling back. 'We'll never know, will we? And now how about a drink before we go back to the *Jenny*?'

They slept on board, of course, and next morning Dai rolled out of his bunk early, before they were due to take on their new cargo, and went out into the misty pearl of dawn. He walked until he found a pebbly beach and then took off his shoes and socks and waded into the slow-moving sea, bending down now and again to pick out a smooth pebble and skim it over the little waves as they hissed gently inshore.

He was so homesick! Moelfre was like this in the early dawn, when the fishing boats were putting to sea. You looked inland and saw the cows up to their bellies in the milk of the mist, you looked at the rocks out to sea and saw them monstrous, rearing out of the sea half seen, half invisible, seeming to undulate slowly as the mist began to dissipate.

And the smells here were not so different either. Seaweed, sand, the smell of wet rocks, the softer scents of grass and leaf which came to you in wafts as you left the sea and began to climb up the beach.

He found a little lane wandering between the lush meadows and followed it a short way. He leaned on a mossy gate and considered the cows beyond, a long stem of grass sweet between his teeth. Higher up the lane trees leaned, forming a green tunnel. There would be wild raspberries in the woods, he had already sampled some of the sweet, sharp little wild strawberries from the banks of the lane.

He turned to retrace his steps. They would eat, then begin to load the cargo. Best get back before he was missed.

Get back! If only he could go back home, but there had been a fierce and terrible row between him and his father before he left and there had been deep bad feeling on both sides.

'The girl is a good girl,' Davy had shouted at him. 'No word against Menna will I hear! She is a good girl and willing to be your friend, rascal that you are, boy. You will treat her with respect while you are under my roof and no more dirty talk will there be about Menna taking your Mam's place . . . she knows she can't do that, she seeks only to comfort me, to make my hard lot easier . . .'

'Then you won't marry her? There's nothing between you?'

The silence that followed went on several seconds too long. Davy and Dai were in the meadow above the house, out on the brow of the hill which nosed down, eventually, into the sea. Behind them was the monument to those who had lost their lives aboard the *Royal Charter*, when she sank within sight of land in the worst gale any man had known. Before them was the sea which had swallowed her up – her and many another vessel, all carrying good men who did not deserve such a death.

'Marry? Ah well, now . . . that's to say . . . she is a good girl, I'm telling you, Dai bach, and your Mam would think scorn on you to say otherwise . . . if my Bethan were here . . .'

'You make me sick, mun!' The words had burst from Dai even as he bit his lip to try to prevent them. 'If Mam were here she'd have your Menna out from under her roof before the cat could lick its ear! No place for two women in one house, she'd say, and Menna would be back behind the bloody bar of the Crown, where she belongs!'

Davy was not as tall as Dai, but he drew himself up to his full height and glared at his son with something very like hatred in his dark eyes. 'Faithful to your Mam I have been for thirty year, since the day we wed! A good Da to you and Sîan, too. But talk like this I will not take, d'you hear me, boy? Menna is here to stay and you are out . . . d'you hear me? Out! You shall not sully Mam's memory or Menna's good sweetness to me in my hour of need with your dirty tongue. Out! Out! OUT!'

'I'll go, and willing,' Dai had said quietly. 'And never darken my doors again, Da, as they say in the old melodramas? Is that what you want? Because I tell you straight, I won't come back here whilst you and Menna are sharing a roof and neither wed to the other. That isn't how Mam brought me up to behave, and I thought better of you. Sîan and Gareth don't say much, but they're of my mind. So it's no children you'll have if you . . .'

Davy screamed 'Out, I said!' and turned on his heel. He almost ran down the long meadow, leaving his son standing at the brow of the hill, with the bitter taste of defeat in his mouth.

His father was in the wrong and would never admit it; he was behaving in a way which would have Mam turning in her grave if she knew of it, which Dai prayed was not the case. Well, it was the end, then. The end of happiness, contentment, the end of his closeness with his father, his pleasure in the home they had shared for so many years.

He knew he could take a ship out of Amlwch because he and Metrion had ridden the motorbike over there a week since, and there had been jobs, then, for someone with his experience of small boats. But then he had hesitated, not wanting to burn his boats, to close the door on Moelfre, his home, his entire life.

He would hesitate no longer, however. He would go as his father bade him and never come back. Never, not even if the old man married the bitch and gave her his name. Never, not if the sweet sky rained blood and the sea turned to boiling oil.

Never. Never. Never.

But now, sauntering along the little Irish lane and reliving that terrible day, Dai told himself that never was a long time; too long. His father would marry Menna no matter how often he said he would do no such thing, because the village would not let him keep her living there as his mistress. Davy was obstinate, but once his son had gone he would do the decent thing by the brassy little bitch.

So I could go home . . . well, I could go and stay with Sîan at first, I suppose, make sure of my welcome, Dai told himself, turning to blink full into the rising sun so that the tears in his eyes were, naturally, just the tears that rise to anyone's eyes when you stare straight into that red-gold brilliance. Besides, what a fool I am to feel like this after only a few months away! In a couple of years when I go back Da will kill the fatted calf for me; that's his way. He can't hold a grudge, never could. Any more than I can.

Only I'm holding out now, Dai reminded himself, slowing his pace even further as he reached the village green and began to cross it. I'm hugging my grudge against my Da and his fancy woman close to my heart and feeding it and seeing it swell and grow huge out of all proportion, and why? Because I'm desperate for the sight and sound of my own place and someone's got to be blamed for my not going back and I can't blame myself. Oh, Dai Evans, you're a poor feller if you can't forgive a man's foolish passion and a girl's weakness, he told himself. Perhaps Greasy's right; when I find someone myself and love them deep and true then I'll understand what's come over my Da and . . . and that woman.

Because Davy was very lovable – to himself Dai could admit that. Women always did like Davy, and obviously Menna was no exception, even though Davy was old enough to be her father. So Menna could no more help being attracted to Davy than the moth can deny the flame, and if she felt – rightly – that Dai was a threat to her spending the rest of her life with the man she loved . . .

Oh shut your trap, mun, you are sounding like a talking picture or a wireless play, Dai told himself gruffly. It's going to take time before you can look either of them in the eye – and them you, for that matter. Give yourself time. Stop tilting at windmills and gnawing your fingernails to the bone, let things slide a little.

He reached the end of the village green and dropped onto the quay. Greasy was sitting on the ship's rail, eating a bacon sandwich. He saw Dai and waved.

'Where you been, tatty'ead?' he said thickly. 'You'd berrer 'urry or you won't get no bacon abnabs, I've et most of 'em awready.'

The job in Fuller's would have done Biddy a treat, but as she guessed, they really wanted a girl who had had waiting on experience.

'But we'll be starting a beginner before Christmas, so you come back, dear, in a few weeks an' mebbe we'll start you on then,' the lady who interviewed her said with a friendly smile. 'You've got a good appearance and a nice, bright way with you. Don't forget, if you don't get anything else, come back.'

'I will,' Biddy said, trying to smile to hide her sinking heart as she turned away from the shop and began to walk home. Christmas! What on earth should she do if she couldn't get work well before then?

Ellen had an answer to that, of course, and had told Biddy about it the night after she had 'entertained' George for the first time.

'Look chuck, beggars can't afford to be choosers; if you can't get nothin' what pays enough then you 'ave to supplement your income, like. That's why George visits me . . . see?'

'No, I don't,' Biddy had said, after a confused pause during which she tried to sort the sentence out. 'Why should George supplement your income? I mean you're well paid and you've got Mr Bowker. What else do you need?'

'Oh, this an' that,' Ellen said airily. 'Norra lot, just a bit more dosh than I've got, now an' then. An' you're a pretty judy. George said . . .'

'I don't want to know what George said – or not until I understand you properly,' Biddy said slowly. 'George came for a couple of hours with you, he sent me off to the cinema . . .'

'Which were a kindness, 'cos 'e could 'ave just telled you to sling your 'ook,' Ellen reminded her. 'But 'e give you money for the flickers.'

'Yes. Oh, Ellen, did he – does he – give you money for – for being with you?'

'Norra lot,' Ellen said quickly. 'But yes, 'e does. Why not? Mr Bowker pays for the flat, why should George get 'arry Freemans?'

'But . . . but you said Mr Bowker was jealous, so he got you the flat and the job so's he could have you all to himself,' Biddy said, having given it some thought. 'So if you're seeing George on the side you're cheating on Mr Bowker.'

'Oh, yeah? An' what about Mrs Bowker, eh? Ain't the ole feller cheatin' on 'er with me an' on me with 'er?'

'I don't think that's quite the point. But if you're saying that I ought to go with a feller and charge him money, that's not on, Ellen. My Mam's dead so she can't kill me, like yours would, but . . . but it 'ud break her heart and I don't intend to do that. I'd sooner go to the workhouse, I tell you straight.'

'Oh!' Ellen said, clearly abashed by the vehemence in her friend's tone. 'Oh well, it were only a suggestion, like. Anyroad, you'll gerra job. Course you will.'

At that stage, Biddy had believed she would indeed get a job and probably a good one, too. But the trouble was that most people had taken on all the staff they needed at the start of the summer and did not want to take on anyone else until the Christmas rush started. Biddy tramped the streets and got kindness from some, cold indifference from others, but she did not get a job.

So now she was putting on Ellen's pink cotton dress, a white straw hat and her own black shoes. Ellen had told her she might wear her new straw hat with the daisies round the brim, her navy sailor suit and matching cotton gloves, but it seemed rather too dressy for an ordinary July day. Besides, Ellen wanted to wear it the next time Mr Bowker took her out since he had not seen it yet, and it would not be the same if Biddy had to wash it after a wearing. All I want is to get a job, and the pink dress is respectable and clean, Biddy reminded herself. It goes better with my colouring than navy, too. So I'll rub my shoes over and then . . . then I'll go round to Cazneau Street and just take a look at the confectioner's on the corner of Rose Place. The job is bound to be gone by now, it's days since George came, but there's no harm in looking.

She was in fact beginning to realise that it was point-less avoiding the Scottie for the rest of her life. If you were poor you needed shops like Ma Kettle's and Paddy's Market and it looked as though she were destined to be poor for a good long time to come.

So she cleaned the flat, prepared food for an evening meal, and then set out, grimly determined not to come back until she had a job. She would try everywhere . . . up and down the Scottie if necessary but definitely in that area since it was the only part of the city she had not tried.

Human nature being what it is, the nearer Biddy got to the Scotland Road, the more curious she became. She had heard nothing of any of the Kettles since she left and did not expect to do so, but she was absolutely longing to know who Ma Kettle had got to replace her and how the shop was being managed in her absence. In nine months she had done so much – all the notices were now written in ink, on stiff white card, the window display was changed at least once a week, she had been a demon on flies – her prowess with a swat had called forth much laughter and not a little admiration as she zoomed round, swiping vengefully.

I wonder would it hurt just to take a peep? she asked herself, as she walked demurely along Cazneau. Well, I'll visit James's Confectionery first, just see if the job's still in the window.

She reached the corner where Rose Place met Cazneau Street and suddenly got nervous. She walked straight past the corner shop without even glancing in the window, and then stopped, pretending to look at next door's display – and then looked in earnest. LAWRENCE MEEHAN, BOOKSELLER read the sign over the door, and the place was crammed with books.

Books! At school, Biddy had been a great reader, devouring everything the nuns had put within her reach. At home, her father had encouraged her love of books, though of late years she and her mother had simply not been able to afford it. But now, all her interest was aroused over again and she went slowly along, examining every title on every spine, wishing she could go inside, turn books over, touch them, read a few words . . . if she had a job, of course . . .

She turned on the thought and retraced her steps, peering in the window of the small shop next door. There was a bright display of jars full of tempting-looking sweets, an enormous stone jar packed with the paper windmills dear to little children's hearts, and a pyramid of small stone bottles of ginger beer. But no card advertising a job as a shop assistant.

There, you left it too late, Biddy scolded herself, her heart sinking down into her boots. What an idiot you were . . . what a coward! You were too afraid of the Kettles to come back here, and look how you are rewarded! A job in a confectioner's would not be particularly well paid but at least it would have meant she was earning money and now she had lost even that hope.

But having come so far it seemed downright stupid to turn meekly on her heel and go back so she continued to walk up Cazneau, and when she reached the junction with Juvenal Street she hesitated for a moment and then turned left onto it. When she reached the Scottie all she had to do was turn right, walk a couple of hundred yards, and she would be outside Kettle's Confectionery.

And when it came right down to it, what had she to lose? She might as well pretend she had never worked there, because she never would again, but it would be interesting to see what had happened since she left.

She walked on, turning the corner, walked on again. Probably Ma Kettle wouldn't even recognise her in the pink dress and white straw hat, she reminded herself. She had never worn anything half so fine at the Kettle establishment. So she continued on her way with a certain confidence in her step. The boys would be at work, Ma would be busy . . . what a fool she had been not to do this before, it would have saved her a few sleepless nights if she had resolutely returned to the Scotland Road and faced what was just a silly fear of being embarrassed.

She reached the familiar shop front and stopped dead, her heart jumping into her mouth.

The shop was closed, the window draped with what looked like white sheets, and instead of sweets, flowers crowded against the glass. There were more flowers piled against the door . . . no, not flowers as such, wreaths.

The shock held her spellbound for moments and she was still standing there, a hand to her throat, when someone bustling along the pavement stopped in front of her.

'Well, if it isn't Biddy! The funeral's in an hour or so, love . . . will you look at all them flowers!'

It was old Mrs Hackett, a regular customer at Kettle's Confectionery. She was smiling, nodding her head at the wreaths, the white-draped window, the white card edged in black, all of which were blurring before Biddy's vision.

She was dead! The old battleaxe was dead, and all Biddy could feel was the most appalling guilt. I bobbied off and the ol' skinflint tried to manage alone and it killed her, she thought dazedly. Oh my Gawd, there was me telling Ellen that I'd not bring men in, when I've as good as killed an old lady who never did me any harm . . . well, not lasting harm, anyway, she amended. Oh *poor* old Ma Kettle, what'll the boys do without Ma to boss them and slip them money and look after them?

But Mrs Hackett was still standing there, smiling up at her, only the smile was beginning to look a little fixed. 'Didn't you know, queen? Well, I'm that sorry . . . 'twas a shock to us all, a turble shock. But life must go on, as they say.'

With a great effort Biddy concentrated on Mrs Hackett and the scene before her. 'No, I didn't know, and I'm very sorry,' she murmured. 'What – what a sad loss, Mrs H.'

The old lady nodded and muttered and Biddy smiled down at her and shook her own head but her mind was in a turmoil and as soon as she could decently do so she left Mrs Hackett and turned to make her way back along the Scottie and Juvenal Street. She felt she could not possibly go in and offer condolences to the boys, particularly as Kenny would undoubtedly try to persuade her to return and Luke would blame her for his mother's sad demise. She found she had no desire to go up and down the Scottie, pop into Paddy's Market, have a clat with old customers or neighbours. Even her curiosity over the sweet shop had vanished like frost in June. With Ma Kettle gone it no longer mattered who was in charge – perhaps Luke would leave work and take over, or perhaps his young lady would be behind the counter in a week or so. Whatever happened, people must know she had left the old girl in the lurch, they would put two and two together . . . oh Gawd, wherever she worked in future it wouldn't be on the Scottie, where Ma Kettle's death would be a nine days wonder for a lot longer than nine days!

At the end of Juvenal Street she turned back onto Cazneau and it was only then that something occurred to her. That bookshop had looked so nice, why not just pop in for a moment and see if the bookseller knew of any jobs going? Tradesmen and local folk often did know such things and although she had avoided this area in her previous searchings she now realised there had been no real need. Even now, though she would not work on the Scottie itself if she could avoid it, she could see how foolish she had been to ignore the busiest part of the city in her job search. And as she was here, right on the spot, she must do what she could to help herself.

She retraced her steps but instead of going into the confectionery shop she went into Meehan's. An elderly gentleman sat behind the counter reading a very large book through equally large spectacles perched on the end of his nose. When he saw her he put a finger in the book to keep his place and gave her a pleasant smile.

'Can I help you, madam?'

Madam! I am going up in the world, Biddy thought, trying to push back the thought that, if he knew she had as good as murdered Ma Kettle, he would not have spoken to her at all, let alone so kindly. She cleared her throat nervously.

'I wonder if you could tell me whether there are any shops in the area needing staff? I came up this way because I understood that the shop next door, the confectionery, needed an assistant, but the job is taken, and since I do love books I thought I'd take a look at your stock and ask you, if you don't mind, whether you know of anyone needing an employee with previous experience in the retail trade?'

The old bookseller smiled.

'I don't think you'll find a lot around just at present, and I think I can guess why. The schools are all in, there aren't any public holidays coming up . . . shopkeepers tend to wait for the children just leaving school in the summer so they can pay less, rather than having to pay for someone who's been in work for a bit. Sad, but there you are. And rich folk are saving up for their summer holidays . . . if I were you I'd leave it for a few weeks. Ah . . . wait a moment, there was something I noticed earlier, when I was having a quiet read . . .'

He reached under the counter and came up with a copy of the *Echo*.

'I contribute the odd review to the paper,' he explained, 'and one of my pieces is in tonight's issue, so the editor very kindly sent me round the first edition off the presses. I did notice something . . .'

His gnarled finger ran down the column, then he cleared his throat and looked at her over the top of his spectacles.

'Here it is; I thought I'd seen something. Shall I read it to you?'

'Oh, please,' Biddy said fervently. She was all too aware that it is usually the early bird which catches the worm and knew that buying the paper off the street vendors meant that she was seldom the first to reach a prospective employer. 'What do they want?'

'It's one of the big shops on Ranelagh Street; they're looking for a young person, it says, to do deliveries. Could you manage that, do you think? I imagine it would mean carrying heavy parcels for long distances, but you seem strong enough and often these places provide a bicycle. Ah, since it's a large clothing emporium perhaps the parcels would not be so very heavy.'

'Which . . . which shop is it?' Biddy stammered. 'I'll go round there at once – as it says "young person" they might look on a girl as favourably as on a boy, don't you think?'

'I do. You must ask for a Mrs Mottishead and the shop is called Millicent's Modes.'

'Thank you very much; I'll go round at once,' Biddy said. She glanced around her. 'And I'll spend my first wages in here,' she added spontaneously. 'It's such a lovely shop!'

'Thank you again, madam,' the man replied. 'And if you do obtain the position you can tell me all about it when you buy your first book; good afternoon . . . Ah, one small thing.'

Biddy paused in her flight.

'Yes, sir?'

He was fumbling under the counter and presently held out his hand to her. 'I wonder if you have money for a tram? Consider this a loan, if you like, but a tram would considerably speed your arrival at Ranelagh Street.'

'Oh, sir!' Biddy gasped, taking the money. 'I'll pay you back as soon as ever I can – this is so kind of you!'

'Nonsense, my dear. I know a prospective customer when I see one! Now be on your way – and good luck!'

When Ellen came home that evening, Biddy met her at the door. Her whole face was alight and a marvellous smell of cooking came from the kitchen behind her.

'Biddy! Don't tell me you've gorra job at last!' Ellen squeaked. 'Well, I'm that pleased . . . where are you workin'?'

'At Millicent's Modes, half-way up Ranelagh Street,' Biddy said proudly. 'The money is nothing compared to what you earn, but it'll do me until I can get something better. Everyone's rather standoffish but it won't make any difference to me, because I'm the delivery girl. They're going to get me a bicycle and I'm to go all over the place, mostly between the shop and the lady who does their alterations, who is a gem, a positive gem, Miss Whitney told me. Apparently this woman used to live in Renshaw Street, but she's not been well so she's gone to live with her daughter, in a back-to-back on Great Richmond Street, and Miss Whitney says she keeps having to send staff panting off up there when they could be more gainfully employed doing their proper jobs. I was lucky really, since they'd both thought of employing a boy, but having seen me, both Miss Whitney and Miss Harborough agreed that girls were, in general, more careful and that when I wasn't delivering, I could serve customers. What do you think of that? And they're going to pay me five bob to start and seven and six if I suit. That's ever so much more than Ma paid me, when she paid me anything, that is. So . . . oh, Ellen, do you know, I'd clear forgot?'

'Forgot what?' Ellen said, squeezing past her and going into the kitchen. 'Wharra you gorrin the oven, chuck? It smells that good!'

'Roast mutton with onions and potatoes cooked in the gravy,' Biddy said. 'But Ellen, I went down the Scottie, and the most awful thing has happened. When I got to Kettle's it was shut, and the window was all draped in white. Old Mrs Hackett said the funeral was in an hour and I came out of a shop and saw the hearse go past – ever so posh it was, with the huge coffin an' black horses . . . I felt ever so bad about it.'

'Oh, Bid!' Ellen gasped, genuinely shocked. 'Whatever 'appened?'

'I dunno. I suppose . . . well, she wasn't used to doing the hard work herself, I suppose she overdid it. She was always tight-fisted – I don't mean to speak ill of the dead but everyone knew she'd never spend a ha'penny if she could get away wi' spending a farthing – so I daresay she couldn't bring herself to pay someone to do all my work. I feel so guilty, Ellen, as if I'd killed her myself.'

'Aye, you would, but you shouldn't,' Ellen said after a moment's thought. 'I don't want to speak ill of the dead either, in case someone's listening, but she were a right old bitch to you, queen, and you no more killed 'er than I did. In fact you probably give 'er a new lease o' life, slavin' for 'er the way you did. If it 'adn't been for you she could 'ave popped off even earlier. I'm sorry she's snuffed it – well, fairly sorry – but she didn't do nothin' for nobody, so I shan't lose no sleep over 'er. And now just answer me this, afore I forget. Can you ride a bicycle? I don't remember ever seeing you aboard one?'

'Well, strictly speaking I can't, but I had a go on one the year before my Da died and I think I had the hang of it then. Da borrowed me one from a kid up the road and said if I could keep upright for the length of our street he'd buy me a bicycle of my own for Christmas. Only he died before he could. Does that count, d'you think?'

'Don't really marrer, I guess,' Ellen said, putting her nose up and sniffing the rich scent of cooking just like the kids in the Bisto advert. 'You'd learn quick enough when you 'ad to . . . an' now let's gerrat that grub before it overcooks on us.'

Chapter Four

Biddy soon began to enjoy working at Millie's, as the staff called it. She wobbled a good deal on the elderly bicycle at first and rammed the pavement edge several times, causing herself to suffer abrupt descents, but she soon got the hang of it, though of course with the big black iron carrier on the front piled with boxes, the balance was very different from the neat little machine she had learned to ride ten years before.

Miss Whitney and Miss Harborough were a couple of cold fishes though, and preferred to say nothing when she limped in with skinned knees, apart from a sharp 'And what 'appened to that silk gown, Miss?' before turning back to their own affairs once more.

But on the whole, Biddy decided she preferred it that way. The Kettles had taught her that, for good or bad, interference was not to be welcomed. Ma Kettle had tutted and got upset when Biddy burned her fingers by snatching hot tins out of the oven or inadvertantly pouring hot toffee too fast so that she splashed herself, but her concern had been in case Biddy was less quick next time, so it could scarcely count as genuine interest.

'It's ever such fun,' she said blissfully to Ellen after a couple of days during which she had delivered a great many boxes to various addresses, all to her employer's entire satisfaction. One of these deliveries had been a box containing a gown, a hat and some elbow-length gloves to a Mrs Isabella Purgold at No. 19 Grove Park. It was an enormous old house in Toxteth and the Purgold cook had given Biddy a cup of tea and a Welsh cake hot from the oven, and this and other kindnesses had undoubtedly coloured Biddy's view of her new job. 'You're out in the open air, cycling around, you visit posh houses which means you can have a good old squint at their lovely gardens and sometimes a close look at kitchens and hallways, too. Do you know, even in this day and age some of our customers employ butlers!'

'I'll 'ave a butler one of these days,' Ellen said. The two of them were eating buttered toast before leaving for the day's work. 'Come on, let's shift . . . at least you've got your old bike, I've gorra catch a leckie.'

'You can come on my carrier if you like,' Biddy offered, ducking to avoid the swipe her friend aimed at her. Ellen was very much the young lady in her tight skirts and frilly blouses; you wouldn't catch her riding pillion on a bicycle, particularly if another girl were steering it.

'Gerron wi' you,' Ellen said, snatching her coat off its peg and slinging it round her shoulders. She perched a small hat on her yellow hair and thundered down the stairs, shrieking over her shoulder as she went, 'don't forget to fetch me 'ome some chops, it's my turn to cook tonight!'

When Biddy got back to the flat that evening, with the chops and a nice big cabbage, Ellen was already home and in a high state of excitement. 'You know you've been teachin' me to speak posh, Bid?' was her first remark as Biddy entered the kitchen. 'Well, I been doin' it at work for weeks an' weeks . . . well, ever since you come to live, anyroad . . . an' when I'm with Mr Bowker, acourse. An' it's paid off. He's takin' me to London to look at autumn fashions, we're leavin' tomorrer mornin' fust thing!'

'Well, that's wonderful,' Biddy said rather doubtfully. 'I'll miss you ever so much, Ellen, but I'm glad for you.

Where will you stay? Not together, will you, in case it gets back?'

'Course together, an' how can it possibly get back? We're goin' as Mr and Mrs Smith,' Ellen said triumphantly. 'We're goin' to ever such a posh 'otel, we're 'avin' a suite o' rooms, an' all, wi' a proper tiled bathroom, fluffy carpets, a great big double divan bed . . . ooh, it's goin' to be ever so romantic.' She hugged herself tightly, beaming at Biddy . 'We'll see the King an' Queen, we'll go to the the-aytre, we'll 'ave us dinners at posh restaurants . . . no expense spared, Mr Bowker said.'

'I've seen the Queen back in '34 when she came to the "pool,"' Biddy said complacently. Inside her head she thought, *and without having to put up with some old man fumbling at my stocking tops, either*, but she said nothing aloud. Ellen had mentioned the fumbling at her stocking tops the first time she had told Biddy about Mr Bowker and though Biddy was quite shrewd enough to realise that the stocking tops had been but the beginning of Mr Bowker's explorations, she found that her mind refused to go beyond that, and was thankful to find it so.

'You're a poet and didn't know it – *I seen the Queen*,' Ellen giggled, obviously so excited over the prospect of the London trip that anything would have amused her. 'Oh Bid, I can't wait! We'll 'ave a chauffeur-driven car when we wanna see the sights. Mr Bowker says the bath's as big as me bed 'ere, very near . . . gold taps, 'e says, an' bathtowels what two could share they're so 'uge.'

'You make it sound like the Giant's castle in *Jack and the Beanstalk*,' Biddy said, smiling at her friend's pink, excited face. 'Oh go and start packing, I know you're longing to, I'll cook tonight.'

'Oh Bid, I love you!' Ellen squeaked, rushing out of the kitchen without delay. Her voice echoed through the doorway. 'Shall I wear me cream linen, or d'you think it'll gerrall mucky in the train?'

It had never occurred to Biddy for one moment that she might have any sort of difficulty due to Ellen being away, but she did. She waved her friend off at an early hour in the morning then cycled off to work as she did each day.

She worked hard, and it was hot, so by six o'clock she was longing for a rest and a cool drink but she still had one more parcel to deliver before she could make her way home. And that, naturally, was at Mrs Bland's, on Great Richy.

Biddy was rather looking forward to having the flat to herself, so she cycled off good-temperedly enough, weaving through the traffic and trying to avoid both the potholes – caused by motor vehicles – and the dung-piles – caused by dray-horses – so that she could keep both her person and her parcel clean and unrattled. She reached Mrs Bland's daughter's small house, delivered her box, refused an offer of a cup of tea and a cheese sarney with mixed regret, and turned once more for home and the flat on Shaw's Alley.

She arrived there late, hot and rather cross, to find George on the doorstep, looking every bit as hot, though the crossness faded when he saw her pushing her bicycle wearily along the pavement.

'Ello, Miss O'Shaughn . . . I mean Biddy; where's Ellen?' he greeted her. They had agreed that it was foolish for him to call her Miss O'Shaughnessy and that Biddy would do very well some weeks before. 'I went into Gowns in me lunch break but she weren't there, an' that sharp Nixon woman told me Ellen 'ad gone 'ome early.'

'Oh dear, how horrid of her, because she must have known perfectly well that Ellen wasn't at work today,' Biddy said, getting out her key and inserting it in the lock.

She dared not leave the bicycle out in the Alley but always took it into the tiny, square hallway which they shared with the occupants of the ground-floor flat. 'In fact she's not here at all, she's got a few days off and is staying with . . . with friends.'

She pushed the bicycle ahead of her into the hallway and propped it against the stairs. The ground-floor flat had a front entrance, she and Ellen the side, so she always left her bicycle down here, where she and Ellen – and any guests they might have – were the only people likely to go near it. Having stowed her bicycle, Biddy turned to George. He had come into the hall and was standing watching her, his expression enquiring, but as she spoke he heaved a sigh and turned towards the outside door.

'She's with 'im, you mean,' he said resignedly. 'Oh well, can't blame 'er, I suppose. No point in me waitin', then?'

'No point at all, she won't be home until the end of the week,' Biddy assured him. She hesitated. He was a close friend of Ellen's and he did look awfully hot. What was more, he would now have to turn round and walk all the way to Chaucer Street, and though the sun wasn't as hot as it had been at noon, the streets were like echoing, airless canyons and would continue to be extremely stuffy until darkness fell. 'D'you want to come up for a quick drink? There's some lemonade on the cold slab.'

'That 'ud be prime,' George said gratefully, standing aside to let her lock the outside door. 'It's a long way back to Chaucer Street in this 'eat, though I could stop off at the Eagle, on Parry, for a quick bevvy, I suppose.'

'Yes, I suppose you could,' Biddy echoed guardedly. She knew that the Eagle was one of the public houses on Paradise Street but had no idea what sort of a reputation it had. 'Come in, George.'

George followed her into the kitchen, where she hung

her jacket on the hook behind the door and then went over to the cold slab to fetch the lemonade. She had made it herself, buying and squeezing the lemons, boiling them up with sugar and pearl barley and finally putting the lot through a fine hair sieve. Now she poured some into a glass, added water, and then turned to George. 'I'd quite forgot, there's a bottle of that stuff Mr Bowker drinks – sherry wine I think it is. He gave it to Ellen. Would you like to try some?'

George said he wouldn't mind so Biddy poured him a tumblerful and pressed it into his hand.

'Go and drink it in the living-room,' she urged hospitably. 'I'll make a couple of rounds of sandwiches and then come through and join you. I really don't think I could bear a cooked meal, not with the heat being what it is.'

George carried her lemonade and his tumbler of sherry through to the living-room and Biddy followed after about ten minutes with a big plate of cheese, lettuce and cold roast pork sandwiches, garnished with various pickles. She and Ellen were very fond of pickles.

'There you go,' she said, setting the plate down on the low table between them. 'Dig in, George.'

'Ta, Biddy. It'll be a pleasure. My goodness, you cook the best bloomin' sangwidges in the 'ole of Liverpool so you do!'

They laughed together at his small joke, then set to and demolished sandwiches, pickles and yet more lemonade and sherry wine.

'That were grand,' George said at last, leaning back in his chair. His voice sounded deeper than it usually did – slower, too. 'Well, what 'ud you like to do now, chuck?'

Biddy shrugged. 'I don't have a lot of choice so I expect I'll wash my hair, iron my blouse and skirt for the morning, and go to bed. How about you, George? I suppose you'll be wanting to get back?'

She was too polite to indicate that he had been in the flat quite long enough, but she hoped, nevertheless, that he would take the hint and leave quite soon. So she was rather disappointed when he smiled and shook his head.

'No 'urry, no 'urry,' he said genially. 'What about six pennorth o' dark?'

'What's that?' Biddy asked.

'I meant would madam like to accompany me to a moving picture? There's quite a variety to choose from . . . did you get the *Echo*? If so, read 'em out and choose the one you'd most like to see.'

'Oh . . . no thanks, George. I don't think Ellen would be too pleased to find I'd gone off to the cinema with you,' Biddy said, having realised that he was asking her out. 'Anyway, it's too hot.'

'Not in the cinema it ain't,' George said at once. 'Honest, Bid, it's ever so dark and cool in the big picture 'ouses. Come on, be a sport . . . Ellen won't mind, not you an' me she won't. Why, I don't mind 'er goin' off wi' 'er old feller, do I?'

'It wouldn't make any difference if you minded like anything,' Biddy reminded him sadly. 'Still . . . what's on at the Forum? Or the Futurist?'

'That's a fair way to walk, though,' George pointed out fairly. 'What about the one on St James Street? What's it called?'

'The Picturedrome. But George, if we go up to one of the cinemas on Lime Street it's halfway back to yours and about the same for me. So that would be fairer.'

'D'you think I'm the sort o' feller what don't walk a girl 'ome after a visit to the flickers?' George said indignantly. 'No, I wouldn't dream of lettin' you go off alone after dark. We could go back to Ranny to the Regal . . . but let's make it the Picturedrome, shall us?'

Biddy frowned, but having examined the various

attractions they chose the picture showing at the Picturedrome, mainly because it starred Mae West, about whom both had heard intriguing stories.

'We can go in now, chuck, and you can still be in bed by soon after ten,' George said, helping Biddy on her with her jacket. 'Are you sure you wanna wear this? It's awful 'ot still.'

'You can't go out without a coat of some sort, not at night,' Biddy said, rather shocked. She decided not to bother with a hat, though, and put her hair up on her head with a length of pink ribbon to match Ellen's pink cotton. Good thing I was wearing it when she packed, she thought, having examined her friend's empty wardrobe, or I'd be going to the pictures in my working clothes!

She and George went down the street, joined the queue, and went into the more expensive seats. They settled themselves, George produced the humbugs he had bought on the way in, and they leaned back in their chairs just as the magic curtains parted to reveal the opening credits.

And that, Biddy thought afterwards, was just about the only enjoyable moment she spent in that cinema until the interval.

George, who had seemed so nice and sensible when Ellen was in the flat, became horribly active as soon as the main feature started and darkness fell. First he put his arm round her; then he tried to squeeze her breast. Shocked, Biddy discouraged this by elbowing him in the stomach and pinching the back of his hand, aiding her efforts by telling him to 'stop that' in no uncertain terms.

The trouble was, George did not seem to understand that she meant what she said and only desisted, in the end, when she informed him, in a furious under-voice, that if he touched her once more she was going to walk out and go straight home.

'I were only bein' friendly, like,' George muttered, shrinking down into his seat. 'Dere's no need to t'ump a feller!'

A hoarse laugh from someone in the seat behind cut him off short. 'Dat's ri', gairl, you tell 'im! The cinema's for watching de bleedin' screen, not for pushin' your luck wi' your young lady,' the hoarse voice commented. 'Give 'im pepper, the 'ard-faced get!'

This caused Biddy almost as much embarrassment as George's groping fingers and she dug him crossly in the side. 'Now see what you've done, we'll be a laughing stock. Just shut up and sit still.'

George morosely obeyed, but during the interval he bought her an ice cream and apologised. The hoarse-voiced one had either forgotten them or left the cinema, at any rate he didn't comment again, and for the rest of the programme George behaved himself pretty well, though he did hold her hand. But Biddy, faced with either holding his hot and sweaty palm or letting that palm stray where it willed, decided that hand-holding was the lesser of two evils and grasped him firmly, her grip more constabular than fond, though George seemed unaware of it.

When the film ended George apologised again as he was walking her the short distance home. 'I thought I were bein' polite, see?' he said miserably. 'Ellen, she'd be mortal offended if I didn't give 'er a cuggle an' a few squeezes in the flicks. Honest to God, I were just bein' polite, Biddy.'

'I accept your apology so long as you don't do it again,' Biddy said resignedly. 'Lor', it's quite lively round here despite it being so late – I suppose it's because it's been such a hot day and no one can sleep.'

It was true that on every doorstep men and women stood or sat, chatting, calling out in soft voices, eating fish and chips. Indeed, the smell of the vinegary fish and chips was so delicious that when George suggested he might buy them some, she was easily coerced into agreeing. With Ellen away she was too afraid of an unexpected expense to throw her own money about, but throwing George's was a different matter. Besides, she thought rebelliously, he owed her something for all that wrestling in the cinema, which had quite spoiled her enjoyment of the main feature.

'But you aren't coming up to the flat unless you swear on your mother's life that you won't start any of that nonsense again,' Biddy said severely. 'What about it, George?'

'I swear on me Mam's life that I'll be a good lickle boy,' George said, putting on a squeaky, childlike voice. 'Oh Miss O'Shaughnessy, I'll be good, I'll be good, I'll be good!'

Biddy laughed, but unlocked the door and ushered him into the flat. 'There's plenty of that sherry still . . . or there's a couple of bottles of stout left, if you'd prefer it,' she said, peering under the sink where they kept their drinks. 'Or I could make you a cup of tea if you'd rather.'

George opted for the stout so Biddy poured his drink and her own lemonade and carried the two thick, straight-sided glasses and the second bottle of stout through into the living-room. George was sitting on the couch, with the two newspaper-wrapped parcels before him on the small table. Biddy eyed him, but decided it was safe enough to sit beside him on the couch provided a good foot of cushion separated them. After all, he had sworn on his mother's life, what more could she ask of him?

All through the fish and chips and the drinks they chatted amicably, and then Biddy stood up. 'I've got to turn you out now, George,' she said half-apologetically.

'But it's work tomorrow for both of us. Good night, and thank you for a very pleasant evening.'

She held out her hand. George took it – and pulled with a fierceness and abruptness which had Biddy catapulting forward with a gasp, to find herself neatly fielded by George's arms.

'Hey! This is just what . . .'

'Every decent feller kisses a girl good night,' George said smugly. He was holding her pressed so tightly to his chest that she had no room for manoeuvre, scarcely room to breathe. 'Come on, be a – be a li'l sport.'

The little sport tried to kick and found herself suddenly sitting down hard on the couch, then being pressed back into the cushions by George's weight. Then his mouth came down on hers – and it was absolutely horrible, even worse than being kissed by Kenny. Fumes of stout and sherry mixed were bad enough, but George seemed to have some mad idea that kisses were accompanied by *licking*, and by a spirited attempt on his tongue's part to get into her . . . ugh ugh! . . . mouth!

At first Biddy fought with clenched teeth, but then she tore herself free for a moment and spoke. 'George, I said . . .'

It was enough. Before she knew it he was on her again and this time, having opened her mouth, she found it horribly full of George, who was being quite disgusting and accompanying all this tongue business with hands which did not merely explore but pillaged. She heard the buttons on her – Ellen's – pink cotton pop and scatter, felt cool air for a moment on her flesh, tried to get her hands up to drag the sides of her dress together, got them trapped somehow . . . tried to scream . . . but he was almost suffocating her, she could not breathe, she must breathe . . .

She bit. It was not easy because the weight of his jaw

was holding her mouth open, but she managed it. She bit hard, what was more, and viciously. George squawked – lovely sound – and began to pull back. But it might be just a trick to calm her fears, so Biddy brought both knees up into his crotch and had the immense satisfaction of hearing him give an almost feminine screech, at the same moment rolling off her and onto the floor with a heavy thud.

Biddy rolled off the sofa after him, got to her feet and bolted. George was moaning, trying to speak . . . she had bitten his lip, there was blood on his chin . . . but she did not wait to listen. She simply flew out of the living-room and into the kitchen, where she dragged open the cutlery drawer, fumbled for a weapon, and waited, a carving knife in one hand and the sharpening steel in the other.

Presently George's head poked round the door. His mouth had stopped bleeding but it had swollen and gone all puffy and one eye was darkening; it was already little more than a slit.

'Wharra you wanna do 'at for?' he enquired thickly. 'I worren' goin' to 'urt 'oo.'

'Well, I intend to hurt you,' Biddy said quiveringly. 'If you come one step further into this room I mean to hurt you very badly. I – I shall beat your head in with this . . .' she flourished the steel, ' . . . and cut your heart out with this,' she added poking the carving knife in his direction.

'Oh,' George said doubtfully. 'You're a bloody 'ickle vixen, d'you know 'at?'

'I may be a vixen, but you're a ravening beast, George Alton, and you shan't mess me about ever again,' Biddy said roundly. 'I mean it; I'll carve your bleeding face off your neck if you don't go home and let me go to bed.'

'I'm goin', I'm goin'.' George said sulkily. 'When she comes back I'm goin' to tell Ellen o' you.'

'You won't need to, because I shall tell her on you first,'

Biddy said triumphantly. She flourished her weapons. 'Out, George. Now!'

She followed George as he shambled across the hall and out and down the stairs, waited until she heard the front door slam, then went quickly down to lock up.

The first thing she noticed was that her bicycle was missing.

It was positively the last straw. Biddy shot out of the doorway and into the road and there, trying to pedal defiantly off, was George. Only he wasn't used to her bike with its big iron carrier, and was making heavy weather of it.

'Stop, thief!' Biddy shrieked. 'Stop that man, he's stealing my delivery bicycle!'

She did not just shriek, either. She ran, knife in one hand, sharpening steel in the other, and caught him up as he was trying, very inexpertly, to turn left into Park Lane. A number of men, lounging outside the pub on the corner, were just beginning to stir themselves, having obviously heard her shouts without altogether understanding them, when Biddy caught up with the erring George. She grabbed the bike by the back mudguard and pulled with all her strength.

As the bike shot backwards George gave a terrible howl and clutched himself, doubling over, then collapsed sideways into a heap.

'Eh, chuck, you've done 'im a mischief I wouldn't mind bettin',' an elderly man said, giving the writhing figure on the pavement a disparaging kick. 'Drunk, is 'e?'

'I don't know and I don't care. He stole my bicycle,' Biddy said. She could feel the curls on top of her head standing up like a dog's hackles with rage and indignation. 'I'm off back to my bed. Good-night, all.'

There was a chorus of good-nights from the men, some ribald remarks which Biddy completely ignored, and a moan from George. Then Biddy hopped onto her bicycle and cycled home, sore, stiff and aching, but with laughter beginning to bubble to the surface.

By golly, but George had got his comeuppance this evening! One way and another, he'd think twice before treating a young lady like a common prostitute again!

She went into the entrance hall of the flat, carefully locking the door behind her in case a vengeful George tried to burglarise her again for making him look such a fool, and propped her bicycle up in its usual spot. Then she climbed the stairs, let herself into the flat, locked up . . . and simply fell on the bed, fully dressed, and giggled weakly for a few moments, until she found that she was crying as well. Tears coursed down her face, ran into her mouth, down the sides of her neck . . . because it had been a really horrible evening and she never wanted to set eyes on George Alton again.

She boiled a kettle so that she could wash in hot water, remembering as she did so that George had sworn on his mother's life that he would leave her alone. His poor mother -- I do hope I haven't condemned her to death, so to speak, Biddy thought. Oh, wouldn't it be awful if he got home and found his Mam dead? She suppressed the horrid thought that it would certainly teach him a lesson and began to wonder, instead, what she would say to George the next time she met him, because since she and Ellen shared the flat, she could scarcely hope to avoid him for the rest of her life.

But it was no use worrying; ten to one George's Mam would remain hale and hearty for another twenty years, and ten to one Ellen would sympathise with her plight and condemn George as no gentleman.

With this heartening thought, Biddy scrubbed herself clean, slipped into her nightdress and went off to bed, where she cuddled Dolly close and told her she much preferred her to a horrid young man, much. And presently slept the sleep of the righteous, despite her aches and pains, which were extensive enough to make her moan softly whenever she turned over.

'Well, so you whacked George in the gob an' locked 'im out – serve 'im right for muckin' you about,' Ellen said, when she got back and was told the saga of the cinema visit. 'Wharra puddin' 'ead! 'E needn't come round 'ere tryin' to mek up to me after that. No sir!'

'I'm glad you aren't annoyed with me, but I couldn't think what else to do,' Biddy explained. 'I didn't want to hurt George, but it was him or me. If only he'd not drunk all that stout . . .'

'It'll 'ave been the sherry; 'e ain't used to sherry,' Ellen said wisely. 'An' as for you bein' responsible if 'is Mam dropped dead then you'd best start prayin', since she died when George were three years old an' 'e's twenty-five if 'e's a day. Now stop chewin' over what's done, 'cos it can't be undone, an' let me tell you *my* news. Bid, we 'ad a great time, it all went like a dream, and Mr Bowker says when 'e goes to Paris in the spring . . .'

'Oh, the swine, no wonder he was willing to swear on her life that he'd be good! Still, I do feel relieved to know I've done no harm there. But wait on, Ellen! Tell me about the London trip first, so I can be properly envious.'

In fact, Ellen told Biddy about her London trip many times over the course of the next few days. The only part of it she had not enjoyed was the first night, when Mr Bowker had snored horribly loudly and kept her awake for hours, and just when it seemed that sleep was about to overtake her the traffic had started up and the hotel staff had begun to clatter.

'And I didn't much enjoy talkin' posh all day and night,' she admitted as the two girls made themselves a meal a few nights after her return. 'Me jaw ached and me eyes watered wi' so much squeezin' of me vocal chords. But it were worth it – we never 'ad a cross word.'

'That's lovely,' Biddy said absently. 'Ellen, do you mean you won't be seeing George again?'

Ellen shook her smooth blonde head. 'No, I don't suppose I will! 'E wouldn't dare come crawlin' round me, not after what 'e done.' she sighed. 'We've seen the last o' Master George Alton.'

'Good,' Biddy said decidedly. 'You don't need him, anyway, Ellen. Not now you've got my money coming in. I'm on six shillings a week now, you know.'

'You did mention it,' Ellen said dryly. She looked sideways at her friend, who was chopping onions at the kitchen sink. 'Biddy . . . don't you want a feller?'

'No,' Biddy said shortly. 'No time. Cor, these onions are strong, my eyes are running.'

'When I asked you to share, I thought you'd be good fun, though,' Ellen said thoughtfully, after a moment. 'I thought we could go around together, meet fellers, go dancin' . . . all you ever want to do is eat an' sleep.'

She sounded so injured that Biddy bit back the laugh which threatened.

'I'm awful sorry, Ellen, but my job's really tiring,' she said. 'But if you want to go dancing on a Saturday night I wouldn't mind going with you. It would be fun, and though I don't exactly want a feller, I wouldn't mind a very quiet one, just someone to go around with a bit. But I'm still a bit young for all that . . . that . . .'

'Oh, that! I din't mean that, exac'ly. But a girl can't go dancin' without a feller . . . that's to say you go in without 'em, then they come over to you and bob's your uncle!'

'Ye-es. Only don't you think . . . I mean if Mr Bowker got to hear of it . . .'

'That's the trouble,' Ellen said. 'Mr Bowker sometimes

don't get the chanst to see me for a week, ten days. I gets awfu' lonely then, Bid. It's different for you, what you've never 'ad you never miss, but . . . well, I gets lonely.'

It would have been rude to say, in an astonished voice, 'Do you *like* all that nasty business, then?' so Biddy wisely kept her mouth shut, and after a moment or two Ellen said, 'Then we'll go dancin' next week, eh? On Sat'day? There's quite good places to go – the Acacia, up on Everton Brow, that's good, the best one for us, I'd say. We can catch a leckie, they run 'em late on Sat'days.'

'Well, so long as you realise I can't actually dance a step,' Biddy said somewhat anxiously. 'They won't try to make me dance, will they?'

Ellen laughed. She was looking sleeker, more contented than ever since her London trip, Biddy thought. Wouldn't it be odd if Ellen really was in love with Bunny Big Bum, and eventually got him to the altar? Though divorce was dreadfully wicked, but if Mrs Bowker was quietly to pass away, and she was old and ailing, Ellen often said so . . .

'No one will make you dance, goose,' Ellen said bracingly. 'Besides, it's called the Acacia Dancing Academy, which means they do lessons, too. Only I'll teach you . . . here!' She began to shove and push at the kitchen table. 'Give me an 'and wi' this, then we'll 'ave room for a practice session.'

The port of Grimsby, on the east coast of Lincolnshire, was as good a place as any to have engine trouble, probably better than most since it was a large and thriving port. And at least, as the Skipper said, they had managed to get the old *Jenny Bowdler* safe in harbour before the engine gave one last wheezing cough and packed it in.

'It'll be the best part o' two weeks, lads, afore we sail

again,' the Skipper told his crew. 'Anyone want to sign off?'

Dai hadn't spent his wages, they were all tucked away, a nice little amount. He looked at Greasy, who was in a similar position, except that Greasy helped to support his mother and the kids, and raised his eyebrows. Greasy gave him a bit of a nod; go ahead, the nod said, if you make the move I'll back you up.

'I'd like to sign off, Skip, and Greasy O'Reilly would, too,' Dai said. 'It isn't that we're discontented, but we'd like to see more o' the world, see? And there's big sea-going vessels, fishing boats, all sorts, eager to sign experienced hands. We'd relish a change, like.'

Seamen, when they're young, go from ship to ship all the time. It's the best way to gain different experience, to fit you to take your ticket, if you've a mind to do well in the merchant service, the Skipper knew it as well as Dai and Greasy. So he just grinned at them, wished them luck and paid them off. The other men on board would probably stay for a while at any rate, then they, too, would change ships.

'Where'll we go, Taff?' Greasy asked after the two of them had arranged a cheap bed in a communal lodging house for seamen on the waterfront and were returning to the *Jenny* to pack up their gear. 'What'll we do, eh, la?'

'Shall we have a go at trawling, mun?' Dai asked innocently. 'Nothing quite as good as a fishing trip, there is. It's nearly October and up in the north the fishing boats will be making their way along the coast, following the herring shoals, and the Scottish fishergirls follow the boats. They sweep down from John o'Groats to Land's End, bringing their catches ashore at each port for the girls to clean and process. Why, those girls can gut the herring quicker than you can swallow a mouthful of ale, and they swear better than a Liverpool navvy – if we sail from here you'll have all the female company you want, come October.'

'You want to fish for herring, then? That's orright by me, la! But they shoot their roes in October, November, you say, and then what'll we catch? An' I've never caught a fish in me life, though I don't mind eatin' 'em when the chance comes.'

'Oh later, I want to go distant-water trawling,' Dai said dreamily. They reached the *Jenny* and went on board, clattering noisily down the companionway to their quarters. 'No use going home until spring, by then my Da will have had a chance to miss me, see? Sian writes regular, bless her, and a batch of letters I've had; they caught up with me here. My Da married his little brass barmaid and is beginning to miss the homemaking he had with my Mam, see? I'll give him the winter to knock Menna into shape, then I'll go home.'

'What's this distant-water trawling?' Greasy asked, suspicion in every tone of his voice. He took an untidy and probably dirty pile of clothes and crammed them into his filthy holdall. 'I don't like the sound o' it an' that's a fac'.'

'It's catching the great Icelandic cod and the real big 'uns, right up in the north. It's seeing polar bears an' penguins, and the air so cold it's a danger to breathe in without a warm scarf round your face, mun,' Dai told him, rolling his clothing neatly and stowing it in his own bag. Working on small fishing boats teaches you tidiness the hard way. 'It's icebergs bigger than the biggest sky-scraper in New York and snow wherever you touch land and the blown spume freezing before it clatters on deck in foul weather. It's wicked hard, wicked cold . . . but exciting, dangerous, all the *interesting* things,' Dai said with deep conviction. 'You'll not be interested, I suppose?'

'Whassa money like?'

'If you survive, it's the best. They call distant-water trawlermen two-day millionaires because they make it and spend it fast. But I don't suppose . . .'

'Now you're talkin', Taffy; I'm on.' Greasy's voice was laconic, but Dai saw the sparkle in his friend's small grey eyes, the grin twitching at Greasy's long, mobile mouth. 'No need to talk like a ha'penny book, I got your drift and I'll come wit' you. Awright? Got the message?'

'Aye, you'll come distant-water trawling, but we'll start with the herring first. Well, the *Girl Sally* will be taking on at the end o' the week which gives us long enough to get geared up an' let our folks know.' Dai, standing by his stripped bunk, hesitated. His bag was packed, his only decent pair of shoes were slung by their laces round his neck . . . but was it fair to involve Greasy in something like distant-water trawling? It was the most dangerous way to go to sea, and all ways were pretty dangerous. He himself was all right, he knew what he was doing, longed for the challenge, and besides, no one was waiting for him, no one would shed more than the odd tear if he went down out there, amongst the ice-floes. But Greasy was one of a big family, they needed him – and the money he earned.

'Eh, la, you've got a face like an empty beer glass – I can see right through it,' Greasy remarked with a sigh, then leaned across and punched Dai's shoulder. 'I'm tough, remember? Eldest of 'leven kids, brung up to fight me way outa any paper bag what stands in me way, that's Greasy O'Reilly. There's only two t'ings I want from me life, Taff – wimmin an' 'ard cash. I 'aven't done too good wi' the first lately, but the second makes up for a lot. So I'm goin' distant-water trawlin' now even if you back down, me fine bucko – got it?' He pushed his unshaven face close to Dai's. ''Ave I got t'rough to you, son?'

'Yes, just about,' Dai said equably, slinging his bag up

across his shoulder and padding across their sleeping quarters. 'And don't blame me, mun, if you come back wi' frostbite in all your extremities; things can fall off in the ice an' cold you know.'

'Extremities? Does that mean wharr I think it means? Brass monkey weather, eh?' Greasy chuckled and followed Dai up on deck. 'Oh well, la, we'd best find ourselve a coupla judies before we sign on and lose our big attractions, eh?'

It was a very cold day. Biddy was cycling along, head down, nose buried in the scarf she had acquired, thanking the lord – and Ellen – both for the warm woollen scarf and her decent pair of gloves. Biddy was no hand with her needles but Ellen was not only an excellent knitter, she loved doing it. So Biddy bought her the wool and the pattern and Ellen sat there, evenings, and knitted away, and first the thick and comforting scarf and then the lovely little navy blue gloves grew like miracles on the end of her needles.

Biddy was better paid than she had been, because her wages had risen to seven shillings and sixpence a week in September and now, in early December, she was beginning to reap the reward for punctuality and her cheerful disposition.

Tips! At first Biddy had simply done as Miss Whitney or Miss Harborough told her; she had taken boxes all over the area, had handed them in and gone back for more. But gradually, as she became a familiar sight pedalling along on her old black bicycle with the laden carrier, she was hailed by customers, servants from the big houses, and even by other traders.

'Biddy love, are you goin' past the Post Office? 'Ere's a bob – get these stamped for me an' stick 'em in the box . . . keep the change.'

There was no harm in it, it did not hold her up, or if it did she pushed a little harder at her pedals, did not dismount at the foot of steep hills, coasted down at reckless speed. And after a time even Miss Whitney and Miss Harborough began to ask for favours and pay her the odd pence.

'Take this parcel to No. 3 Shawcross Road, there's a Mrs Mablethorpe waiting for it. Oh, and Biddy, on your way back would you pick up some cornplasters from Boots, on Ranelagh Place? My mother likes the ones they sell, she thinks they're bigger than the ones I got her from Banner's, on North John Street. I'll give you ten pence, though I believe they're only eightpence ha'penny. Oh . . . keep the change.'

And no sooner had she grown used to the size and type of corn plasters preferred by old Mrs Whitney than Miss Harborough would start.

'Biddy, the hem shortening and the relining should be ready by now and we've a batch of darts to be let out, take them up to Mrs Bland and tell her we want them as soon as possible. And whilst you're that way you might nip into Leigh's, on Scotland Road, and fetch me a pound of their best butter. My brother Sidney and his family are coming over on Sunday and Mother does like me to provide a good tea for them. Oh, and if you're anywhere near Chiappe, the confectioner, you might get me some Fishermen's Friend throat lozenges and a quarter of a pound of those special Italian chocolates he sells. They make a lovely present – tell him it's a present and he'll wrap the box in pretty gold paper and put a piece of ribbon round it.' Miss Harborough counted out the money slowly. 'That should be plenty; keep the change, if there is any.'

So the little hoard, this time tucked away in another pillow, though still with Dolly on guard, gradually grew and as Christmas approached, pleasant thoughts of presents, jollity and two whole days off from work began to take possession of Biddy's mind. Last Christmas had been grim, with Ma Kettle still bent on instilling the spirit of slavery into her new possession's mind and Biddy's loss too raw and recent to allow her to enjoy the festivities, but this year would be different. She and Ellen were going regularly to dances at the Acacia and meeting lots of new friends. They were much sought after and though Biddy still held back from meeting any young men apart from actually on the dance floor, she was easier with them and enjoyed their company.

But now she was cycling along in the late afternoon dusk, having been all the way out to Brompton Avenue to deliver a party dress. Today's errand was for Mr Smythe from the shoe shop, who was a keen horse rider and had ordered a new saddle for his mare from Benjamin Holland, the saddler on Mount Pleasant, and wanted to know whether Mr Benjamin would deliver the saddle by the following Friday.

Biddy had ridden energetically on the way out, but it was a long way. She had already travelled along Croxteth Road, into the Boulevarde, through Catherine Street and left into Hardman Street. Mount Pleasant was out of her way, but the tip – given in advance – had been generous so she took the necessary turnings and arrived on Mount Pleasant as dusk was definitely falling and the street lights were being lit. She hailed the lamplighter cheerfully and he directed her to Mr Holland's premises, where she found Mr Holland sitting on a tall stool mending a harness which had come unstitched.

'Afternoon,' Mr Holland said, and Biddy speedily explained her errand.

'Oh, the Smythe saddle . . . yes, I'll deliver it Friday morning,' Mr Holland said, smiling comfortably. 'Tell Mr

Smythe ten o'clock Friday.' And as Biddy was turning away he added, 'It's gettin' dark, lass. Time you was tucked up in your own 'ome, not bicycling around the icy streets, runnin' errands for young fellers what ought to do their own work.' He ferreted in his pocket and pulled out tuppence. 'Here . . . Buy yourself some 'ot chestnuts, I heard the seller callin' them not ten minutes gone.'

'Thank you very much,' Biddy said sincerely, pocketing the coins – this was her lucky day! 'I'll tell Mr Smythe Friday, then.'

Once outside the shop she mounted her bicycle once more, extremely glad that a good deal of her journey would now be downhill, and set off. She skimmed along, the icy wind nipping at her nose and bringing tears to her eyes, but the thought of the warm shop and the cup of hot tea which Miss Whitney or Miss Harborough would undoubtedly make her when they saw how ice-cold she was, cheered her on.

She came past the Adelphi at a cracking pace and swerved into Ranelagh Place. A tram was thundering down on her so she steered into the side, away from the tramlines, glancing at the tram incuriously as it passed.

She had brought the bicycle almost to a halt as she did so and as she balanced there, half on the saddle, with one foot firmly on the road surface and the other on the pedal, she caught the eye of someone staring out of the window of the tram . . . and for one startled moment she thought it was Ma Kettle, come back to haunt her. But only for a moment. Then she remembered Kenny's Aunt Olliphant and realised she must have seen that lady. How odd that she should have met, by proxy, a woman she had never actually clapped eyes on but had recognised just from a strong likeness to her dead sister!

For a moment, Biddy stayed where she was, then someone hooted at her and the driver of a horse and cart, which had also stopped to let the tram go past, shouted at her to 'Gerra move on, gairl!'

Biddy obediently pushed her bicycle out of the stream of traffic and over to Ranelagh Street. Normally, she would have mounted and ridden the rest of the way home, but because she had got off the bicycle she saw it would be just as easy to walk and not to try to re-enter the busy stream of traffic. And because she was on foot, she glanced, as she passed him, at the newspaper seller on the corner, and at the fly-sheet – then stopped, staring open-mouthed.

'Abdication! Prince of Wales to go!' the fly-sheet read. And now that Biddy really looked, she realised that despite the bitter weather people were actually queueing up to buy a paper and were standing about in the cold reading, instead of hurrying back to their shops, offices and homes.

Biddy joined the queue, her money in her hand. She would buy a paper and see what was happening – the last time she had thought about the monarchy was when she and Ellen had been discussing whether or not they would get a day off for the Coronation; now, it seemed, there might not *be* a Coronation! It was that woman, of course, that Mrs Simpson person, who had wanted to marry the beautiful Prince of Wales and had expected to be accepted, despite the fact that she had been married before. Oh, what a lot she and Ellen would have to talk about when she got home tonight! And what a topic of conversation it would provide with customers, too . . . I bet the royal family have a funny sort of Christmas, after this, Biddy told herself, turning into the entry beside the shop.

She wheeled the bicycle round to the back door of the shop and went in. She had not given Mrs Olliphant another thought since reading the fly-sheet and now it did not seem a particularly odd coincidence, though before she had been looking forward to telling Ellen. Now, it was the Abdication which would be on everyone's lips. Everyone would want to have a read of her paper, that was for sure. Biddy took off her gloves, scarf and tam o'shanter and hung them near the small gas fire, then went through into the front of the shop.

'I'm back, and freezing,' she told Miss Whitney, who had just finished serving a customer and was moving behind the counter looking rather pleased with herself. 'In fact I'm so cold I haven't even opened my *Echo*, yet. Can I make myself a hot drink before I go and tell Mr Smythe his saddle will be delivered on Friday?'

'I'll make us all some tea whilst you run round to the shoe shop,' Miss Whitney said brightly. 'Why on earth are you wasting money on a newspaper, Bridget? I thought your friend Ellen usually picked one up on her way home from work.'

'She does, usually. But today, what with the Abdication and everything, I thought I'd like to have an earlier look,' Biddy said with studied casualness. 'I must say I'd like to know who'll be King instead of the Prince . . . and whether there will still be a Coronation in the New Year.'

'Abdication? Then 'e's done it, has he?' Miss Whitney said eagerly, coming through into the back room and holding out a hand. 'Let's have a quick peep, there's a good girl. I'll make you a cup of tea whilst you go and see Mr Smythe and by the time you get back I'll have got the gist of what's happening to the Royals. Oh, by the way, was Mrs Shawcross pleased with the dress?'

'I don't know; a maid took the box in,' Biddy said briefly, lingering in the doorway. Not only would the short run down to the shoe shop turn her into a moving icicle all over again, it would mean a decided delay in finding out about the Coronation. Would it be the Duke of York and his Duchess who became King and Queen, she wondered hopefully? Ellen adored the Duchess and collected all the press photographs of her that she could find. 'The saddler was awfully kind, though. He said it was dangerous out on the dark streets for a girl like me.'

'Old fool,' Miss Whitney said unkindly. 'Off you go, Biddy, get it over with. The tea'll be mashed by the time you're back.'

Not daring to continue to make excuses, Biddy ran down to the shoe shop, delivered her message and ran back again. She thought it was mean of Miss Whitney simply to take over her paper, but that was typical of the older woman. I've a good mind to charge her for it, Biddy thought rebelliously, hurrying along the icy pavement. After all, she earns an awful lot more than I do, she could well afford it.

But she knew she would not, not really. Miss Whitney could be unpredictable and Biddy really did like her job. She had no desire to find herself back on the job market.

So she joined Miss Whitney and Miss Harborough in the back room, since the hour was late and few customers visited the shop after five, and they all read the paper, discussed every possibility, and decided that, on the whole, they were pleased that the Prince of Wales was going to live for love and the Duke and Duchess of York, such lovely people, would be crowned King and Queen.

By the time she got back to the flat that evening Biddy felt she knew every tiny detail of the life the royal family would be living over the next few months, and she and Ellen were able to pore over the story a second time, for Ellen, foiled of an *Echo*, since they had sold out by the time she got out of work, had picked up another paper and they were able to compare reports.

It was not until just before bedtime that Biddy remembered seeing Mrs Olliphant on the tram, and then she and

Ellen decided that Ma Kettle's long-suffering sister must have moved into the shop in Scotland Road, to keep it running for the boys.

'There you are, girl, now you don't 'ave to worry that the shop'll go to rack and ruin wi' them lads in charge,' Ellen said cheerfully. 'Now chuck us somethin' to get eggs out of a fry-pan an' we'll eat.'

They had trawled the North Sea for herring and taken a liking to a couple of the local lasses with their fresh complexions and broad Lincolnshire accents. He and Greasy had been contented enough with their fat, Grimsby landlady in her crowded boarding house on Victoria Street, within shouting distance of the Alexandra Dock. They found the Scots fishergirls rough company, but liked them, too, for the way they could drink, swear and kiss.

But Dai's intention to sign on a distant-water trawler never wavered and Greasy, though he never said much, felt the same. It was time they got away from the shores of Britain, saw other seas, experienced other climes. And the Arctic attracted them both as being sufficiently dangerous – and the work sufficiently well-paid – for a first step to their exploration of the sea.

So the beginning of January saw them aboard the trawler *Greenland Bess* as she nosed her way carefully from her berth out into the tide-race. Dai went about his work, but he could not resist a quick glance behind them as they slipped out into the open sea . . . at Grimsby, the gaslights showing as circles of gold in the blue-black, pre-dawn dark of mid-winter, at the roof tops, red and black, at the narrow, shadowy streets which, in daytime, resounded to all the noise and bustle of any busy port.

He would miss Grimsby, and Susie Lawler, and his mates off the *Girl Sally*, but he would soon make friends with his present shipmates, and anyway Greasy was aboard.

The gulls were aboard too, standing along the ship's rail with their feathers ruffling as she came head to wind. The sea was nothing much yet, they were still sheltered by land on both sides, for Grimsby lies snug against the Lincolnshire coast with the Yorkshire coast throwing a protective arm around the mouth of the Humber, with the Spurn Head lighthouse on its final extremity, winking away cheerfully in the darkness. But with a freshening wind and the *Bess* already butting her way through the increasing swell, they would soon begin to feel the motion.

Dai stared out at the sea for a while longer, then he turned and went down the companionway to the fo'c'sle. He was not on watch for another three and a half hours, he might as well get a meal and some rest. The ship's cook was an unknown quantity, he would test him out, and besides, he would be on watch quite soon enough.

Below, men lounged on the hard benches, some with plates before them laden with bacon, eggs and fried potatoes, whilst thick white mugs of strong tea waited for their attention. Others had eaten and leaned back, reading books, playing cards, talking idly about anything but the work on hand.

Dai went over to the galley and announced his presence and watched as the galley boy slapped bacon, eggs and potatoes onto a chipped plate. He took the plate and waited for his tea, then walked back to the mess table.

Greasy ducked his head as he came into the lamplit room. He grinned across at Dai; they were on the same watch, so they were both free for a bit. 'Gerrin' your grub in, Taff? Looks good! I'll 'ave some o' that.'

In his turn he went over to the galley whilst Dai sat down and reached for the sauce bottle.

This, he knew, was just the beginning. The journey out to the fishing grounds was mostly boring, rarely either particularly exciting or particularly dangerous. And it tooks days to reach Arctic waters, where the big fish could be found. But it would give him and Greasy time to sort themselves out, to get used to the different types of work they would be expected to tackle. He grinned to himself. He'd have something to put in his next letter to Sîan, that was for sure!

Chapter Five

With Christmas over and the new year celebrations only a memory, Biddy and Ellen settled down to the serious business of earning their living. Biddy, it is true, was more serious about it than Ellen, since she knew herself to be entirely alone, without the support of parents or family. Ellen, though she did not often visit her mother's home, did go there from time to time. She had spent Christmas there, taking Biddy with her despite her friend's strenuous objections, and they had a real family day, with lots to eat, a few small presents, and plenty of good company as more and more members of the Bradley family returned to spend at least part of the day with 'Mam an' the littl' uns'.

No one asked difficult questions about Ellen's flat, so Biddy surmised that, though they might not approve, they most certainly understood. And seeing the cheerful poverty of the tiny house, crammed to the eyebrows with people and very short on possessions, she could understand both Mrs Bradley's silence and Ellen's absence.

In addition to the Bradley family themselves, all eleven of them, there lived in the small house both grandmothers and a grandfather, Ellen's Auntie Edie, a cousin of five whose mother had died and whose father was mostly at sea, and a couple of well-fed cats.

'We used to 'ave rats,' Ellen said briefly, when Biddy commented on the cats' gleaming coats and well-rounded sides. 'Mam gives 'em a lick o' milk now an' then, but not much else. They keep us clear o' vermin, an' the neighbours don't 'ave no more trouble either.'

Biddy looked at the cats with more respect after that.

January, however, seemed like the longest month in the history of the world. Biddy continued with her deliveries, but tips were rarer now, in what Ma Kettle had called the hungry months. And it snowed – how it snowed! It wasn't too bad in the city centre, where traffic and the feet of those working and shopping there kept the carriageways clear and the pavements at least passable. The street sweepers did a good job too, but once you got out a bit, then Biddy soon discovered it was not always possible to use the bicycle.

'I'm scared of comin' a cropper and ruining a parcel,' she explained nervously to Miss Whitney, one morning when the snow was blowing horizontal and piling up by the roadside, as the traffic crept slowly through the white streets. 'What's more, I can't get along at any sort of speed on the old bike while the snow's so thick. I was wonderin' whether it might be better if I caught a tram?'

'You'd best walk,' Miss Whitney said crossly. She had come back to work after Christmas very sharp and critical. Miss Harborough said it was because her mother was ill again, and cranky with the cold, but Biddy, who bore the brunt of the other woman's displeasure, felt this was no excuse.

Now, she looked resignedly at Miss Whitney. 'I don't mind walking, but it's going to take me all my time just to get to Mrs Bland's place and back again. And there are three customer deliveries to be done, all in different parts of the city; shall I start by going to Richy and then come back here and see how I've got on?'

Miss Whitney pulled a sour face and rolled her eyes ceilingwards. 'As if I've not got enough to do,' she said crossly. 'I suppose you'd best catch a tram. But don't linger, if you please.'

'I never linger,' Biddy said rather sharply. She was absolutely sick of being found fault with and thought Miss Whitney was being very unfair. 'Apart from anything else I'm too cold to hang about.'

Miss Whitney pulled a disbelieving face but she got some money out of the till, counted it, and then handed it to Biddy. 'There you are, that should be sufficient for all the deliveries, if you walk between the last two. In fact there should be no need for you to come back here until you've finished, so you can do all four.'

'Oh! Well, I suppose I can eat my carry-out in the tram,' Biddy said, rather dismayed. After tramping the snowy streets all morning she would be aching for a sit-down and something hot, but she did not like to say so to an obviously bad-tempered Miss Whitney. Instead, she put her coat, scarf and gloves on, shoved her carry-out into the deep pocket of her coat, and headed for the doorway into the shop.

Miss Harborough was sitting behind the counter filling in the stock book. She was writing very slowly and carefully, with the tip of her tongue protruding from the side of her mouth, but she made a face and jerked a thumb at the back room when she saw Biddy glancing in her direction. 'Disappointed in love,' she hissed, with a quick glance over her shoulder to the back room, where the senior sales lady hovered. 'That nice Mr Mickleburgh has got tired of waiting; he took a younger lady to the Temperence meeting, I believe.'

'Oh, no wonder she's ratty; I'm sorry I didn't sympathise more,' said the soft-hearted Biddy, hurrying towards the outer door. 'But she shouldn't take it out on us, should she?'

'No, but who else is there?' Miss Harborough said simply. 'You can't altogether blame her; she can scarcely get nasty with her Mam, she's well into her eighties.'

Biddy murmured something and slid through the door into the storm. It was blowing a hurricane and snowing like fury. When she looked up, the flakes whirled down so fast that they made her dizzy, grey goose-feathers against the lowering white clouds. But you've got a good coat, Biddy, and your lovely warm scarf and gloves, she reminded herself. She was wearing rubber boots, too, and though her feet got cold, at least they were unlikely to get wet as well. The rubber boots had been Ellen's Christmas present, and she valued her friend's good sense more every time she put them on.

At first, her journeying went well. Mrs Bland asked her in for a cup of tea, and though Biddy had to gulp it down so hot that she scalded her tongue, at least it gave her courage to go out into the storm once more and battle her way back to the main road and the tram stop. She walked on top of the snow down Great Richmond Street, turned into Cazneau Street and walked down it as far as Richmond Row, where there was a tram-stop at which several damp, cross-looking people already stood.

'Have we got long to wait?' Biddy asked her neighbour, a spotty girl of about her own age carrying an armful of what looked like legal documents. The girl sighed and shrugged.

'Oo knows? I been waitin' twenty minutes . . . one should be along any time now.'

'They'll come in a bunch when they does come, like bleedin' sheep,' a fat little man with a pipe and a filthy black coat remarked. He sucked vigorously at his pipe, making horrible gurglings. 'Aw, it's gone an' died on me – anyone got a light?'

Someone had and presently, when the trams did indeed come sheepishly along in line astern, everyone in the queue joined in an ironical cheer.

'Mine's second in line,' the girl with the legal documents said. 'Which one's yours, chuck?'

'Any. I'm going to Old Haymarket, I'll change there,' Biddy said, getting aboard the same tram as the spotty girl since the one in front fairly bulged with passengers. 'If this snow goes on it'll be over my boots before evening.'

'At least you've got boots,' the spotty one said as they sat down on the nearest wooden seat. 'My boss sends me miles, knowin' full well I'm delicate, in these 'ere papery shoes. Still an' all, it's nobbut a step from the tram stop now.'

'I'm a delivery girl,' Biddy explained, indicating the increasingly soggy parcels in her arms. 'I'm off out to Brownlow Hill next, then over to Canning Street, and since the senior sales lady said I wasn't to go back to the shop I suppose I'll have to eat my carry-out as I leg it over to Hartington Road.'

'I dunno where 'alf of them are,' the spotty one said gloomily. 'Still, you've got the boots for it.'

'That's true,' Biddy agreed, and they both lapsed into silence until the Haymarket was reached, when Biddy jumped down, waved to her new acquaintance and set off, crossly it must be admitted, to find the tram which would take her to the bottom of Brownlow Hill.

Despite the weather, though, she did well enough, doing the delivery in Brownlow Hill in good time and apologising in such heartfelt tones for the soggy state of the parcel that a kind-hearted housekeeper gave her a sixpence and sent her on her way with a screw of blue paper containing sultanas. 'The scones ain't ready yet, queen, but you mi' as well suck on these,' she said, handing them over. 'What a day, eh? Real brass monkey weather.'

Biddy smiled and agreed, then set off to walk through to Canning Street.

It was a long, wet trek and by the time she delivered the third parcel the fourth was looking very poorly indeed and in her pocket her carry-out was oozing all over the place, bread and jam having become almost a part of the paper they were wrapped in.

'Well I declare!' Biddy said aloud, almost in tears as she contemplated the ruin of the only meal she would get until six or seven that evening. 'I can't eat this, and I'm freezing cold and terribly hungry. Shall I spend that sixpence on chips? Oh no, I've a *much* better idea!'

For it had occurred to her that she was not all that far from the flat in Shaw's Alley, and no one would blame her – indeed, no one would know – if she nipped back there now, changed out of her wet things, dried them out before the gas fire and got herself a cup of tea and a bun.

As well as that, she could dry out the brown paper of her final parcel, which might mean that at least the garment within would arrive at its destination not actually soaked.

So Biddy trudged past St James's cemetery and the new cathedral, along Upper Duke Street, and turned down Cornwallis Street. Once there, it was straight onto St James's until she reached Sparling Street. And then it was no time at all before she was fumbling for her key, inserting it in the lock, and letting herself into the flat, almost sobbing from cold and looking like a snowman, for she was caked in the stuff from head to foot.

She went up the stairs wearily, leaving a mixture of mud and snow on every step, and unlocked the door to the flat itself. No fire had been lit but even so it felt gloriously warm to Biddy.

I'll put on the gas fire and hang my wet things in front of it, and then I'll boil a kettle and have a hot wash, she promised herself gleefully. It would serve Miss Whitney right if I didn't go out at all any more today, but just stayed here, in the warm. She would get really worried around five and serve her right, miserable old slave-driver.

But she would not do it, of course, because she liked her job, though she could not wait for spring to arrive.

Biddy bustled round the kitchen, preparing herself some dry sandwiches – she threw the soggy ones out of the window for the birds, poor things – and getting a drink of hot cocoa, a real luxury in the middle of the day. She spooned conny onny into her cup, added cocoa powder from the tin, and when the kettle boiled she poured the water carefully on top of the milk and powder, stirring fast as she did so to prevent lumps forming.

She had taken her coat, scarf and gloves off, and her boots, too, and now, whilst she waited for the cocoa to be cool enough to drink, she examined the rest of her garments. Her brown cardigan was soaked – she slipped it off – and so was her skirt. Best change that, too. She thought stockings a waste of money but was wearing an old lisle pair of Ellen's, much darned, and some thick fishermen's socks over them, to try to combat the cold from the rubber boots. The stockings were soaked from boot-top to welt, but the socks were dry.

She was sitting on the kitchen stool, sipping her drink and taking ravenous bites from her jam sandwich, when she heard a noise in the hallway below, or thought she did. Gracious, suppose someone came visiting and there was she, sitting on the stool in her knickers and patched, shrunken vest and nothing much else! I'd best get some dry things out, Biddy told herself, conscience-stricken, though she heard no more sounds from the hallway. Better safe than sorry, anyroad.

She slid off the stool and padded barefoot across the kitchen. She stopped for a moment on the tiny landing, then opened the bedroom door. She had a clean grey skirt in her half of the wardrobe. . . .

But something was happening amongst the pink blankets and crisp white sheets of the big double bed. There was a heaving and a grunting, much movement, little cries. . . .

Was Ellen ill? Had she not gone to work after all this morning, or had she been sent home? Biddy took an incautious step into the room and suddenly realised that there was a face she didn't know staring, round-eyed and incredulously, up at her. Hair stood up, thick and grey, streaked with white, on the stranger's head and just under his chin was a yellow thatch topping a small, cheeky face which she knew well. Ellen was in bed with . . . oh God, it was Mr Bowker, Bunny Big Bum himself!

To say that Biddy was dumbstruck was putting it mildly, but at least she acted in the best way possible. She simply turned on her heel, closing the door gently behind her, and fled. Back in the kitchen, she rearranged her coat, scarf, tammy and gloves so that the side which was dry was turned away from the heat and the side which was still wet towards it, and then she got herself hastily into her still-damp skirt and blouse. She left her cardigan to drip, but she put on the fishermen's socks. Then she sat down on the stool again, her heart thumping and her cheeks burning, and waited for retribution.

It was not long in coming. Presently the door opened cautiously and Ellen came into the room, closing the door gently behind her. Her face was scarlet.

'Oh, Bid . . . I told 'im you was a sister, just popped in to see me, like, an' 'e said what about the lock, 'e'd locked it 'isself an' 'e wasn't about to believe you was able to get through a locked door. 'E's ever so angry wi' me, 'e went on at me ever so. Can you think of anythin' to calm 'im down?'

'I think the only thing to do is tell . . .' Biddy was beginning, when the door opened again and Mr Bowker came, with calm and deliberate steps, fully into the room.

He looked steadily at Biddy and it occurred to her that he had quite a strong face, and was not at all the foolish old man she had imagined. He had flattened his thick grey-and-white-streaked hair and his roundish, pinkish face no longer looked flustered or embarrassed, but rather accusing instead. He addressed her at once, without preamble.

'Were you about to say the only thing to do was to tell the truth? Because I do commend that attitude most earnestly.'

'Yes, I was,' Biddy said. She could feel Ellen's anxiety and her own bright colour had fled, she knew, leaving her white as milk. She was so happy here and through her own foolish forgetfulness she had mucked the whole thing up. Mr Bowker would send Ellen away and naturally that would mean that she, Biddy, would be homeless once more. Why oh why had she not remembered that Mr Bowker often came back with Ellen in their dinner break? Why oh why was she such a selfish idiot?

'Good. Truth may avail you something, though I've no idea what. Fire ahead then.'

There was a pause whilst Biddy collected her thoughts, then she began to speak. She spoke slowly and clearly and did not once look at Ellen but kept her eyes fixed on Mr Bowker's chilly grey gaze.

'Ellen and I are old friends. We were at school together and we lived near, too. When my mother died, though, I had nowhere to go, and Ellen offered to take me in.'

Ellen gave a low moan. She obviously thought that Biddy had not really intended to tell the truth, but what else could I do, Biddy thought miserably. Lies were far too complex – too late, as well.

'She offered to let you live here?'

'Yes, she did. On condition that I understood it was

not her property and behaved myself properly, and was never here when you wanted to call. She – she was lonely when you weren't able to be with her, and with me here as well there could be no – no misunderstandings over – over her position.' Beside her, Biddy felt Ellen relax a little. 'She thought it was better, safer, all round, if there were two of us, rather than her living here alone,' she finished.

Mr Bowker frowned. 'Two of you would be safer than one?'

Ellen clearly thought it was time she took a hand. 'Mr Bowker, you know I'd 'ad fellers before I met you. Well, some of 'em were . . . were persistent, like. They saw me with a neat 'ome – home – of my own and I couldn't tell 'em about you, could I? It were – was – difficult for me to keep 'em at bay until Biddy here moved in.'

Mr Bowker nodded slowly, but his eyes never left Biddy's. 'And you are a good girl? I'm afraid I don't know your name, apart from Biddy, that is.'

'I'm Bridget O'Shaughnessy, sir,' Biddy said breathlessly. 'And I'm a good girl . . . well, I'm not yet sixteen, so young gentlemen don't consider me old enough to be interesting, I don't think.'

Mr Bowker gave a short bark of amusement. 'No? Are the young men of Liverpool blind, Miss O'Shaughnessy? However, I take your word for it because I can see you're not a liar. And I do believe you've got a point. You can keep little Ellie here on the straight and narrow far more easily than I can, because I have – commitments – which make it difficult for me to visit her as often as I should wish. Do you pay rent?'

'Not very much. Two shillings a month.'

Mr Bowker's eyebrows rose. 'Ellen is very generous with my property, two shillings a month is a small rent indeed! Very well then, Miss O'Shaughnessy! I am prepared to let you remain here, paying your present rent, whilst you can tell me with your hand on your heart that Ellen doesn't bring gentlemen back to the flat. I don't believe she does, but I'd like to be certain.'

Biddy, guiltily remembering the late-lamented George, nodded her head vehemently.

'Indeed I'm sure Ellen wouldn't bring gentlemen back here, Mr Bowker, but you have my word that if she did such a thing, I would move out at once. I can't say fairer than that, can I?'

He nodded curtly, then glanced across at Ellen, his eyes softening. He's mad for her, Biddy thought, he really adores her and believes every word she tells him! And he's rather nice, she must settle for what she's got, though to do Ellen justice since George had disappeared she had never once brought anyone back to the flat, and though she enjoyed flirting with her dancing partners she was as reluctant as Biddy to meet them outside the Acacia dance hall.

'Agreed, Ellen darling? You wouldn't deceive me?'

Scarlet-faced, Ellen threw herself across the kitchen and into Mr Bowker's arms, causing him to stagger and go almost as red as she.

'As if I would, Mr Bowker!' she said rapturously. 'Oh, I hated deceiving you over Biddy, now everything will be so nice and straightforward. But Bid, whatever are you doing here in the middle of the day?'

'I got soaked through doin' my deliveries,' Biddy admitted. 'My carry-out was all soggy as well, so I came back for a warm and some dry clothes. Only I never thought . . .'

'We must go,' Mr Bowker said, cutting across Biddy's explanation. 'Come along, my dear, we'll leave Miss O'Shaughnessy in peace to finish her meal and dress in dry clothing.' He turned to Biddy, starting to smile.

'Good afternoon, Miss O'Shaughnessy, it's been a pleasure meeting you.'

They reached their fishing ground on the eighth day out and began their search. Already ice was building up everywhere, so that very soon the Bess would not look like a ship at all, but just a roughly made chunk of ice. Dai and Greasy were old hands now, this was their third trip and they knew exactly what they were doing. They fought the encroaching ice without being told to do so because they knew that if the ice built up too much then the sheer weight of it could force the vessel to turn turtle, and if that happened there would be no survivors. In the extreme cold, men would be dead moments after touching the water.

Everything was different out here, even the compass could lie as it swung wildly, searching for magnetic north. The sea seemed always rough, the breakers coming at you from all angles, and because of their nearness to the pole the earth's rotation deflected their little cockleshell craft from their planned path.

But below decks it was as warm and pleasant as the crew and the officers could make it. Above, it was a white hell of ice, with everything hidden a few yards from the ship's side by the persistent, drifting fog.

Dai knew better than to lean on the rail because anything you touched out here would freeze you into position like a fly in amber, but he stood near it, staring. He wore a woollen hat beneath his sou'wester, a scarf wrapped around his nose and mouth, two thick jerseys under the waterproof smock, but he was still cold. His breath had frozen on the scarf and when he breathed out it semi-melted, then froze again. The only thing that thrived in these conditions were the fish, and there were fish down there, big 'uns, but you didn't shoot your trawl until you were right on top of them, and the skipper would choose the right moment.

Presently the bell for watch change sounded and Dai turned and made his way to the bridge; he was on bridge watch for the next four hours and that meant spending an awful lot of time keeping your eyes peeled . . . not for other shipping but for icebergs.

They were beautiful, there was no doubt about that, but deadly, too. They swung along as though they knew where they were going, performing their cumbersome dance of curtsies and dips as they went, great mountains of azure and emerald ice, carved by the rough seas into peaks and turrets, castles and canyons. The bit you saw seemed vast, but you soon learned that beneath the 'berg on the surface wallowed ice seven times as large again. If you went too close – or if she veered in your direction before you could take evasive action – you could be sucked under by the currents she caused, or holed on her hidden ice.

Dai entered the bridge and the warmth enfolded him like a blessing. Behind the wheel the Mate turned and grinned at him.

'Taking over from me? Keep her on slow ahead . . . there's pack-ice around as well as the 'bergs. But we'll see Bear Island soon, and that's where the best fish lie. No use trawling until you've sounded the sea-bed, ask anyone. Well, ask the old man, he's the one who'll give the order to shoot the trawl. All right?'

'Fine,' Dai said, slipping into the place the Mate had just vacated and putting his hands to the smooth wood of the wheel. 'Col will be along quite soon, he'll see I don't do nothing stupid.'

'I'm staying until Col gets here,' the Mate said with a dry chuckle. 'One stupid move by you, boy, and we could all be dead. Look at that one, on your port bow!'

The iceberg was another castle in the air, fretted turrets reaching up towards the sky, delicate sea-green ribs flanked by misty blue shadows which deepened to indigo. And against it the sea sucked and swirled, now green, now grey, now whiter than snow as a big wave crested and crashed against the ice. It gives you something to remember, the strangeness, the beauty, Dai told himself, glancing at the 'berg and then back to the *Bess*'s intended path. But it didn't do to forget what you were doing and let yourself marvel at it; you wouldn't last long if you did that.

They had found bottom, which meant they had found fish, or thought they had, and were about to shoot the trawl. All hands were on deck, except firemen and the chief engineer of course. The firemen never stopped stoking their boilers, the engineer watched his dials and corrected them, tuning the engine's note until it sounded just right. It was important not to lose power in these tricky, unpredictable seas.

It was near midnight, the sky clear for once and streaked and coloured by the Northern Lights, which would have illumined every face aboard, only the oil lamps were lit for shooting the trawl. The men lined the rail, watching the sea's surface but with one eye on the old man, standing on the bridge, watching them, the sea, the sky . . . his eyes everywhere.

Two men went to the winch, two more manned the door. The others took up their appointed places, Dai and Greasy amidships on the port side. Everyone poised, waiting.

The Skipper had his hands on the wheel; they called him the old man when he wasn't listening but he was no more than twenty-eight or nine. You needed to be young and strong out here. Slowly, the Skipper brought the *Greenland Bess* broadside to the wind. The sea surged inboard as the engines slowed to a mutter, holding the little ship steady.

The Cod End was swinging out now, the Skipper leaning out of the bridge window, staring about him, judging, waiting. The trawl was unlashed and Dai found he was tense as a bow-string, eager for the command which must come any moment now.

'Cod End outboard! Let go!'

There was a flurry of activity as the trawl shot into the sea. The Skipper had withdrawn into the bridge again and was once more giving orders down the voice pipe to the engine room. Dai watched as the trawl began to float free, the floats pulling against the swell. The order for 'Slow Ahead' had been given but the Chief knew his job; the *Bess* wallowed and went astern for a few seconds to allow the trawl to spread across the water before it sank.

The deck hummed with activity now. The winchmen released the brakes, the fore door and after door were released and crashed into the sea with a tremendous roar.

The deck hands cleared the deck; they were not wanted now, but as soon as the *Bess* stopped again the hands rushed out into the cold once more to do their appointed tasks and presently the Mate leaned over the rail and examined the trawl, now held in position, sunk to the right depth, and trawling everything which came within its maw.

'All square, and level aft!'

Up on the bridge the Skipper nodded, spoke to the crew member on the bridge with him, and turned away from the window.

On the deck, Greasy and Dick nodded to each other and headed for the companionway. Below, they lit cigarettes with freezing, trembling hands and took deep, nerve-calming drags.

'In three hours she'll be bulgin' an' we'll haul,' Abe Brown said, squeezing past them. 'Better get some rest as you aren't on watch.'

They nodded, every muscle aching from the recent strain. Three hours and it would all happen again, only this time the trawl, with luck, would be full . . . considerably heavier. But they had a vested interest in the catch . . . every man aboard would be watching eagerly, praying for a good haul. Bonuses were paid on fish caught.

'C'mon, let's see if anyone's got a card game going; it's scarcely worth going to bed for three hours.'

Greasy nodded. The two of them walked along to the mess deck.

'I'm gonna write to me Mam,' Greasy said, as they settled on the wooden bench. 'I'll post it soon's we git ashore. You join the card school if you like, Taff.'

'Can't be bothered,' Dai said lazily. 'I'll write to my sister.'

But they had both drifted into an uneasy sleep by the time the bell sounded for the haul to commence.

Spring came at last, a long, sweet spring to make up, Ellen said, for the worst winter for years and years.

'I don't think it was a particularly bad winter,' Biddy protested, but Ellen said waspishly that she had thought it was pretty bad when she was trying to bicycle up Mount Pleasant in a blizzard and since that was true, Biddy stopped arguing.

The two girls were getting on as well as ever, but Biddy had noticed that Ellen was nervy, edgy. Her friend had made no attempt to bring anyone back to the flat since the awful day when Biddy had met Mr Bowker for the first time, but though they still went dancing and enjoyed young men's company, it was gradually borne in upon

Biddy that Ellen, who had so loved to flirt, seemed to have lost all interest in such frivolous pastimes.

Instead, she spent a great deal of time doing things to her hair, trying new cosmetics and buying pretty clothes. She even began to do a little dressmaking, and one day she came home with a pad of thick, interesting looking paper and a box of colours and announced that she wanted to go on the ferry over to Woodside and paint the scenery.

'Can you paint?' Biddy asked tactlessly.

Ellen narrowed her eyes at her friend. 'Anyone can paint,' she said firmly. 'Are you comin' or not?'

'Well, what'll I do while you paint?' Biddy said. 'What if it rains?'

'If it rains we shan't go,' Ellen said firmly. 'Don't be stupid, Bid, no one paints in the rain.'

'Well, I'll see what it's like next Sunday,' Biddy said cautiously. 'One day a week off isn't much. I don't want to waste it sittin' on a river bank watching you dabble.'

'Well, I'm sick o' hangin' round the flat all day Sunday, waitin' for somethin' to 'appen,' Ellen said pettishly. 'If only Mr Bowker wasn't so scared of 'is wife 'e could take me trips on a Sunday. I'm goin' to tell 'im if 'e don't watch out I'll get meself a seven-day-a-week feller.'

'Then you'd lose your nice flat – and so would I,' Biddy said, trying to jolly Ellen out of her glooms. 'We'd neither of us like that much, would we?'

Ellen shrugged. 'Oh, I dunno. Mebbe I wouldn't an' mebbe I would. I'm fed up wi' t'ings the way they are an' that's the truth. Straight up!'

'It's the spring,' Biddy said wisely. 'Everything's all new and flowery and that, but life goes on just the same, only duller. But things will brighten up; Mr Bowker will take you to Paris, like he said, and . . .'

'Yeah, there's that,' Ellen said, brightening. 'I'll ask 'im when we're goin' tomorrer, first thing.'

Mr Bowker told Ellen that they would leave in a fortnight and stay in Paris five days, and though she pouted at him and said it wasn't long enough and what was wrong with a week, she came home much more contented with her lot and drove Biddy mad for days and days by insisting that they talk nothing but French in the flat.

'But we can't speak French, we weren't taught,' Biddy protested, only to have a penny primer shoved into her hand.

'I bought us books, one each,' Ellen said triumphantly. 'Parlez-vous Français, mademoiselle? An' now you say you can speak a little . . . it's on the next page, I think.'

Biddy had interesting plans for her friend's absence. She intended to spring-clean the flat, colour wash the walls in all three rooms and get some new curtains. Instead of dancing on a Saturday night she would go to the cinema – alone – which would be a rare treat and she would also look seriously in the *Echo* for another job. She was extremely fond of Ellen, loved her in fact, but more and more lately she got the feeling that, if it was possible, Ellen would like to move in with Mr Bowker on a full-time basis. I must be prepared, she told herself desperately, I must try for a better paid job so that if we ever lose the flat I can support myself.

She had one other plan which she intended to put into practice during Ellen's absence. She intended to make toffee.

Biddy hated waste and it had occurred to her some time before that all the knowledge that she had amassed of the sweet-making industry was being totally wasted. It wasn't difficult to make really delicious sweets and people liked them – why should she not spend some of her savings on sugar, margarine and milk, on flavourings and cocoa powder, on peppermint essence and icing sugar, and see if she could sell what she made? Of course she realised that to turn Ellen's little flat into a sweet factory would be very unfair, but whilst Ellen was away she could see no harm in a little experiment. If the sweets did not sell, or if they came out wrong, then she would have lost some money and gained some knowledge – the knowledge that she was not cut out to run her own business. But if, on the other hand, the sweets were delicious and sold well ... it was at the very least another string to her rather meagre bow.

On the day that Ellen and Mr Bowker departed, Biddy did her work as usual, but she took the opportunity of nipping into one of the cheap grocery shops on the Scottie and buying up a large quantity of loose sugar. Ellen had left on a Wednesday and would return quite early the following Monday morning, so on Thursday Biddy completed her purchasing and then waited, in an agony of impatience, for Friday. She had told her employer, firmly though with an inward quake, that she needed an afternoon off to decorate the flat whilst her friend was away. Christmas was over, Easter had not yet arrived, and Miss Whitney seemed to have got over her wintry temper; at any rate she said that it would be all right so Biddy hurried home at noon, parked her bicycle at the foot of the stairs, and went into the kitchen. She had actually decorated the flat already, working during the evenings until past midnight, and now she looked round with considerable satisfaction. She had the whole afternoon to make her sweets; she had better start right away!

Biddy's experiment was successful. The sweets were delicous and she really enjoyed using her skills in this direction after so long away from sweet-making, and on the Saturday she got her delivery bicycle out and crammed the sweets, neatly packed in conical paper bags, inside the carrier. She arrived at Millie's and picked up her deliveries and then began her rounds. But at every house she visited she mentioned that she had made a few sweets . . . and at almost every door she sold at least one bag and usually more.

'They're real tasty,' a gardener said, with a mint humbug in one cheek. He looked at her list and pointed to chocolate fudge. 'That sounds good; give me a pennyworth, would you?'

Well, Biddy told herself that evening, sitting by the fire in the kitchen and sewing the last hem on the living-room curtains, if I am ever homeless, there is one thing I can do.

But happily, Ellen's gloomy mood seemed to have left her in Paris, never, Biddy hoped, to return. She came home bubbling with enthusiasm for all things French and vowing undying love for Mr Bowker who, she said, had been a good 'un from start to finish.

'We seen the Eiffel Tower, the Madeline or whatever it's called, we took a cab out to that Versailles place . . . it were grand, Bid, grand! Oh, I'll never moan at 'im again, even if 'e can't come to the flat as often as I'd like 'im to. We never mentioned 'is wife once, oh Bid, we were so very 'appy!'

'That's wonderful,' Biddy said. 'What d'you think of the flat?'

Ellen glanced round her, then hugged her friend exuberantly. 'It looks prime,' she declared. 'Ted will be so pleased, 'e likes to think we're tekin' good care o' the place. Oh Biddy, you are good to spend time on our little 'ouse. I love you better'n I love any of me sisters!'

'Ted! When did you decide to call him by his first name?'

'He told me to use it,' Ellen said almost shyly. 'Oh Biddy, I've always liked 'im, but after those five days I love 'im, I really do. I – I want to please 'im, not just because of the things 'e gives me, I want to please 'im all through, if you know what I mean.'

'I know what you mean,' Biddy said, but she was secretly surprised. She had liked Mr Bowker, thought him pleasant – but for pretty, frivolous Ellen to say she loved him like that – well, it was a surprise.

'You don't know, not really,' Ellen sighed. 'I didn't know meself . . . but I do now. I don't mind any more that 'e can't be with me all the time; if 'e could, 'e would. I'll be 'appy wi' what I can get.'

This was so unlike Ellen that she reduced Biddy to staring dumbly, but then Ellen started to unpack and to show Biddy all the wonderful things she had bought in Paris and Biddy exclaimed and admired and went and made a supper for them both and finally the two girls went to bed, only to chatter half the night as Biddy told Ellen about the sweets and Ellen told Biddy all the things she had forgotten to tell her already about Paris.

They were about to haul and Greasy and Dai had been roused from their berths, to tumble out of them, half-asleep still, and struggle into their foul-weather gear.

If this catch was good they would head for home, so everyone wanted to see the trawl bulging with fish, even though that meant more work as the fish were gutted and packed into the holds and ice, cut from the deck each day, was thrown down to keep them fresh.

Dai glanced around him as he took up his position. The familiar sight of the other crew members was reas-suring, though it had been a devil of a voyage this far. They'd found three times at the start of the fishing, only to haul an empty trawl aboard. Then they'd snagged the trawl, the winch had stuck, and Bobby had fallen on the ice and broken his wrist.

But now all seemed well. Dai was gently swinging the

enormous hammer with which he would strike the pin out of the towing block to release the trawl. He waited, poised, ready. He heard the Skipper faintly from the bridge, giving the order which would bring the *Bess* broadside to the wind. They all felt the engines slow, shudder and the Skipper shouted out through the window, 'Let her go, Taff!'

Immediately Dai swung the hammer and smote the towing block. The warps left the block, the bridge telegraph rang for stop . . . and the winch began to heave in the trawl.

Dai's hands were frozen, his jaw ached with the cold, but he moved forward to take up his position as the winch continued to turn and the doors came up, then the trawl, the floats breaking surface first.

The men leaned over to the side to heave the net aboard and suddenly everyone was dodging out of the way, as the Cod End was jerked aloft. If something went wrong now a man could be killed by the weight of fish in the net, for it was bulging, heaving, wriggling with the size of their catch.

The Mate gripped the knot of the Cod End with both hands and tore it undone. The fish crashed onto the deck and slithered and slipped and slid into the pounds. A huge haul, the faces looking down on the fish beamed. A couple of tons? Dai couldn't judge, wasn't sufficiently experienced, but beside him Col was grinning, the Mate smiled, up on the bridge he could see the Skipper's satisfied face.

That was it, then; the last haul had been worth all the sweat. They were homeward bound!

It was a bright April day with a sweet breeze blowing off the Mersey and the spring flowers in the gardens and squares in full bloom. Biddy worked hard all morning, delivering summer dresses all over the city and now she was cycling slowly back to Ranelagh Street, hoping that Miss Whitney and Miss Harborough would have some more deliveries for her, or at least some alterations which she could take round to Mrs Bland. During the winter she was quite pleased when she was asked to work in the shop but on a day like today she wanted to be outside.

Turning into Ranelagh Street, she got down off her bike and wheeled it across the pavement down the entry. Because the weather was fine she left it outside the back door and popped into the shop. She had cheese and beetroot sarnies today, her mouth watered at the thought of them. And if Miss Whitney would let her, she would take her food down to the pierhead and sit on the wooden seat along with all the old sailors and watch the shipping and think about the coming weekend, when she and Ellen had quite made up their minds to catch the ferry over to Woodside and have a picnic and paint and mess about all Sunday.

We'll go to Mass first, both of us, she was thinking, for Ellen was not by any means a regular churchgoer. Then we'll go off on the spree . . . it'll be fun to have a day out for a change. Ellen was right, the winter was a long one, now spring's here we should make the most of it.

She was in the shop, waiting for Miss Whitney to finish serving a customer, when the door burst open and a figure flew in. Miss Whitney glared, the customer swung round and stared, and Biddy was about to step forward and say, in the approved fashion, 'Can I help you, modom?' when she recognised the intruder.

'Ellen! What's wrong?'

Ellen looked ghastly. White as a sheet, her striped blouse was done up on the wrong buttons and bunched up under one ear and her coat was cock-eyed. She wore no hat and her yellow hair was wildly windswept, and to Biddy's horror she saw her friend was wearing slippers; slippers, in the city centre and on a weekday! But Ellen was plainly in a terrible state.

'Biddy! Oh thank God . . . can you come? The most awful thing . . . I can't explain here . . . Biddy . . . can you come – now this minute?'

Miss Whitney's eyes were like saucers and her mouth had dropped open. She did not speak as Biddy ran out from behind the counter and took her friend in her arms.

'Calm down, Ellen, just calm down. I'll come with you, everything will be all right, now we'll walk quietly down to the river, it's my dinner-break now anyway . . . come with me, we'll sort it all out.'

'I'm so sorry, madam,' Miss Whitney was saying to her customer. 'I don't know what all that was about but my assistant is a sensible young thing, she'll calm the gel down. And now, if you would like to try . . .'

The glass door shut behind them and Ellen began to moan. Tears welled up in her eyes and ran down her ashen cheeks.

'Ellen, what *is* it? Can't you tell me? How can I help you? Is Mr Bowker ill?'

'I'm not sure. But I think he is. When I run out 'e was mekin' the most awful snorin' noise, 'e didn't seem to hear me when I asked what were wrong . . . Bid, you must come back to the flat, if 'e's ill then I'm in terrible trouble.'

'All right, though it isn't your fault if he's ill,' Biddy said, submitting to the urgent tugging on her arm. 'How did you get here?'

'By taxi. It's waiting. Do come on!'

'I'm coming as fast as I can,' Biddy said patiently. 'Ah, I can see the taxi . . . what a good job he waited. We'll be back there in no time now.' The girls climbed into the back of the taxi and Ellen said, 'Shaw's Alley!' so briskly and with such decision that Biddy began to hope her friend was coming out of her terrified state, but Ellen would only shake her head and look nervously at the back of the driver's head when asked questions, so Biddy sat back and waited. They would be at the flat soon enough.

'Oh, don't ask questions, Bid, just come an' tek a look! Tell me 'e's awright an' I'll stop cryin', you can be sure o' that. Come on, tek a look.'

Mr Bowker was in the bedroom. He was lying on his back, his grey head on the pillow, his naked body half-covered by the sheet. He looked almost well, almost ordinary, though his expression was stern.

Biddy touched him gently. His flesh was cool, but what else should she expect? He was naked and it was a chilly day. She leaned over him. He did not move and she realised, with a chill, that his chest was not moving either. He did not appear to be breathing.

Beside her, Ellen put a quivering hand on her lover's shoulder. 'Ted? Ted, love, it's Ellie. Are you all right? Oh Ted, I do love you so much, but you mustn't be ill, you really mustn't. Tell me you're all right really . . . just sleepin'!'

'Get me the round mirror off your dressing-table,' Biddy said suddenly. 'Hurry, Ellen.'

Uncomprehending, Ellen fetched the mirror and handed it to her friend. Biddy took it and held it to Mr Bowker's lips. After a couple of minutes she looked hard at the mirror. Its bright surface was undimmed.

'What did you do that for?' Ellen said, her voice shaking. 'Oh, Bid, I'm bleedin' terrified!'

'You must pull yourself together, dear,' Biddy said. Her own voice was none too steady. 'I'm afraid Mr Bowker . . . oh Ellie, I'm almost certain he's dead!'

The two girls stared at each other in consternation. What on earth were they going to do? Mr Bowker and

Ellen should both have been back at work by now and wherever he had died, he must not be discovered in the flat of one of his employees. Biddy was quite calm enough to realise it, but Ellen suddenly began to weep, tears pouring down her face. She threw herself on the bed, clasping Mr Bowker's dead body in her arms, smothering his face with kisses.

'Oh Ted, Ted, don't leave me, I can't face it,' she sobbed. 'You know 'ow I loved you . . . you was all I wanted, the money an' the trips away an' the pretty clothes didn't marrer a damn. Come back to your Ellie, don't leave me!'

'Darling Ellen, he's gone and he can't come back,' Biddy said, her own eyes filling with tears. 'But we must be sensible – you must be more than sensible, you must be very brave. Go and get dressed properly, dress slowly and carefully, Ellen, brush your hair, wash your face, and put some make-up on. Don't you see, we can't let him be found here, and you've got to go back to work and act absolutely normally or we're lost.'

'Act normally? *Normally*? When Ted's dead, when he won't come 'ome to me no more . . .'

'Yes, normally. Unless you want the police, and the most dreadful scandal – why, you might even find yourself in the dock! We don't know why he died yet, though I'd guess it was a stroke or a heart attack, but whatever it was, love, we can't let him be found here. Particularly not like this.'

'Oh, Bid, I'll do me best but I'm not meself,' Ellen said helplessly, the tears still raining down her face. 'What must I do? Say it agin.'

'You must go into the kitchen, boil some water, have a good wash and get dressed slowly,' Biddy said clearly. 'Dear Ellen, I'm going to dress Mr Bowker whilst you do that, and then you must go to work. No, don't shake your head at me, I said you'd have to be awfully brave and I meant it. But think of poor Mr Bowker, the scandal, Ellie dear. You wouldn't want that for him, would you?'

'There'll be a scandal when 'is wife finds out 'e owns the flat what I live in,' Ellen said mournfully, but she wiped her eyes with the heels of her hands and gave Biddy a watery smile. 'I'm ashamed that I can't 'elp you wi' Ted, but I'd only break down. I'll go an' wash now.'

She left the room. Biddy collected Mr Bowker's clothes from the chair on which he had laid them and began to dress him. It was unbelievably difficult and several times she was tempted to call Ellen through to help, but each time she resisted the temptation. Hard though it was to push the inanimate limbs into sleeves and trousers, it was better to struggle on alone, and get the job done before Mr Bowker's limbs began to stiffen, rather than have a hysterical Ellen on her hands.

It was tempting to tell oneself that it would be all right to leave off the underpants, or the front buttoning vest, but Biddy knew they must get everything right so that no one suspected. His sock suspenders and armbands, both objects which Biddy had never come across before, baffled her completely until it occurred to her to ask Ellen what they were. They were diligently put in their right places and then Biddy, who had done most of the task without once fully opening her eyes, looked down at Mr Bowker as he lay, neatly on his back once more, on the bed.

Poor chap! He had been a good husband to a very difficult woman, a good lover and provider to Ellen . . . he had even been good to Biddy in her way, since he had not turned her out and had always spoken nicely to her. And now he had been mauled about by her inexpert hands – the sock suspenders had been tried, doubtfully, in some unusual spots before it occurred to her to get

Ellen's advice – and would, she supposed vaguely, presently be transported somewhere distant at the dead of night, where he could be respectably discovered in the morning.

'You 'aven't 'alf made a mess of 'is 'air,' an accusing voice behind her said, causing Biddy to jump almost out of her skin. 'Gimme a comb, for God's sake.'

It was Ellen, washed, dressed and tidy. Even her eyes looked less swollen, though there was a tell-tale redness about them if anyone had looked closely. Ellen snatched a comb off the dressing-table and tidied Mr Bowker's hair, then smoothed a small hand down his cheek and round his chin. It was, Biddy thought, the sweetest and gentlest of farewells and it carried with it all the meaning and the love which had been missing when Ellen had cast herself so tempestuously upon her lover's body earlier.

'There, my darlin',' Ellen said softly. 'Thank you, dear Father, for the good times, an' take good care o' my Ted, 'oo never 'urt nobody.' She turned away from the bed. Tears glittered in her eyes once more but she smiled resolutely at Biddy. 'All over now, Bid. What's to do next, then?'

'Oh, Ellie, you're wonderful,' Biddy said warmly. 'Go off to work and forget everything. We can't do much else anyway until . . . until much later. I'll finish tidying up here and then I'll go back to work as well. We'll come home at the usual time – I'll tell Miss Whitney and Miss Harborough that you'd gone home and found – found someone had picked the lock and got into the flat. You'd come to get me so's I could see if anything of mine was missing.'

'Will that do?' Ellen asked fearfully. 'They won't send for the scuffers or nothin', will they?'

'No, because I'll say that when I got back I realised I must have left the door on the latch and no one had been in at all,' Biddy said, improvising rapidly and quite astounded by her own capacity to lie at a moment's notice. 'I'll say I flew out in a great rush and left things in a mess, having overslept. Don't worry, Ellen, that side of it's easy. Now just you go back to work, there's a dear.'

'All right, if you're sure you can manage,' Ellen said. 'I'll be a bit late, but all they can do is dock me pay. What'll I say when Mr Bowker doesn't come back, though?'

'No one will ask you to say anything, not if he's been as careful as you say he has,' Biddy said shrewdly. 'If they ask you, just shrug and say something a bit cheeky . . . you know the sort of thing.'

'Right.' Ellen was still very pale, but Biddy saw, with considerable relief, that her friend was calm and collected. 'I'll go now, then. An' . . . thanks, Bid. I'll never forget what you done for me today.'

Alone in the flat, Biddy tidied up. She was loth to move Mr Bowker but she had said Ellen was to tell people she thought they'd had a break-in. Suppose the lie came true? Suppose someone really did break in, or suppose the window-cleaner came? And looked through the window and saw a fully-dressed corpse lying on the bed?

'I'm sorry, Mr Bowker, but it's for the best,' Biddy said apologetically, pulling him into what looked like a comfortable sleeping position, on his side. She thought about curling him up which would look more natural, but when she tried there was resistance and she realised he was already stiffening. Best not, then. He would be easier to move straight up than curled over like a dried-up railway sandwich.

Presently, having done everything she felt she should, she locked the flat and hurried back to work. She told Miss Whitney and Miss Harborough the story she had concocted for Ellen and was gratified at the ease with which they swallowed it, Miss Whitney even going so far as to tell her to buy a Yale lock for the door, so that it would automatically lock when shut.

'It would be worth the money for the peace of mind, Biddy,' she said rather severely. 'You lost a good hour's pay, running off like that.'

'Sorry, Miss Whitney,' Biddy said meekly. 'I'll mebbe do that – buy a Yale.'

And with the words, the enormity of it all hit her like a blow to the stomach. She had no idea how long it would take, but soon enough the flat would be closed to them and she and Ellen would be homeless. All the months of saving and scheming, all their sweet-making, for she had shown Ellen how to make sweets too, and they had produced quite a lot, was going to be needed at last. Total independance, which she had dreaded, was just around the corner.

'Come along, Biddy, don't stand there dreaming; Miss Ryder came in this morning and bought a tea-gown, only it's a little long in the skirt; she wants four inches off it. And Mrs Bland will have let out those darts for Miss Hetherington of Randolph Street, so if you take the skirt and pick up Miss Hetherington's dress . . . you can kill two birds with one stone.'

Shuddering slightly at the thought of killing birds, Biddy took the proffered parcel and set off. It took her most of the afternoon to complete her errands, for Mrs Bland had a gown finished for another customer on the Boulevarde, so one way and another Biddy was kept busy until it was finally time to go home.

She arrived back as dusk was falling and the lamplighter was doing his rounds. She climbed the stairs and entered the flat, feeling her heart sink as she did so. She went into the kitchen, put the kettle on, crossed the hall and opened the bedroom door. For some reason she was deeply disappointed to find that Mr Bowker's body was still there, though since only she and Ellen knew what had happened, and since Mr Bowker was in no state to walk out on them, heaven knew what she had expected to find.

So. There was to be no miracle, neither had it been a dream or a nightmare and no one had come along and stolen Mr Bowker, or seen him through the window and caused an outcry. Now he was once again her problem. Biddy stood staring down at the bed for a long time, then went back into the kitchen, made the tea, and was drinking her first cup when Ellen clattered up the stairs and into the room. She looked almost her usual self and smiled quite brightly at Biddy.

'Tea? Lovely. Bid, is 'e ... is it ...'

'I haven't moved him, so he's still there,' Biddy said, trying not to sound impatient. After all, Ellen had as much right as she to pray for a miracle. 'Hush a moment though, Ellen; I'm trying to think of a plan.'

Moments passed. Ellen poured herself a cup of tea and stared into it like a fortune teller into a crystal ball. Biddy continued to think.

At last she heaved a sigh and sat back in her chair. 'Look, Ellen, they're going to start wondering as soon as Mr Bowker doesn't turn up at home tonight; right?'

'Yeah, I reckon so.'

'But they won't start searching, because all men stay out late sometimes, or have appointments, or work over. Would you say that was right too?'

'I dunno,' Ellen said doubtfully. 'I think 'e usually went 'ome straight after work. 'Is wife weren't a well woman, and she 'ad a bitter tongue.'

'Well, there you are, then. If he doesn't turn up at his usual time everyone will think to themselves, *the poor feller's got his leg loose and isn't likely to come running back with his tail down for a few hours*, and they won't give the matter another thought. Right?'

'Mebbe,' Ellen said, still cautiously. 'It's difficult to know, 'cos I don't know 'oo she'd tell.'

'It doesn't matter,' Biddy said patiently. 'What does matter is that we've probably got twelve hours' grace before the police and so on start searching. Because someone must know he owns this flat and I suppose it's an obvious place to look. Only not at once.'

'My Gawd, d'you think the scuffers will come 'ere?' Ellen said fearfully, standing her cup back on its saucer with a clatter. 'Oh Bid, we've gorra gerrim out of 'ere by then!'

'Yes. And we can't take him far because it'll be a carrying job and we're neither of us that strong, but if we use my bicycle . . .'

'Your *bike*? Biddy, 'ow are you goin' to get 'im to stay on?'

'We're going to have to pretend he's drunk and sort of lie him across the seat and the handlebars,' Biddy said, having made up her mind. 'Then we can push him into the Wapping Goods station which is only a stone's throw away, and somehow get him aboard a goods waggon. Then when he's found he'll be miles from here and it'll probably take them ages to identify him. What about that, eh?'

'It sounds all right,' Ellen said, cheering up. 'Oh Bid, it sounds foolproof! When do we start?'

'When the pubs have closed,' Biddy said. 'Once the pubs close the streets are quiet and then is the sort of time a couple of girls might be pushing their drunken feller back to his own home. Yes, we'll leave it until the pubs close.'

It had sounded easy enough in the well-lit kitchen, but the fact proved to be very much more difficult. Just getting Mr Bowker out of bed was awful and took their combined efforts, and getting him downstairs was worse.

'Don't bump him on the bannisters,' Biddy implored her friend in a hissing whisper as they strove to line Mr

Bowker up with the staircase. 'If he's bruised they'll suspect foul play.'

'Oh God . . . look, Biddy, let's wrap 'im in somethin', 'is poor fingers keep stickin' out.'

They wrapped him in a blanket and this considerably eased their descent, though Biddy pointed out that there was no way they could push him through the streets disguised as an extremely large papoose.

'Wharron earth's a papoose?' Ellen asked, pushing her hair off her hot, damp forehead.

'It's a Red Indian baby. They swaddle them up in blankets. Here, prop the bike up against the wall whilst I . . .'

They struggled silently for five minutes, sweat running down their faces, then Ellen leaned Mr Bowker against the banisters and scowled across at her friend.

'He's too stiff,' she whispered. 'He won't bend, not natural, like.'

'Don't moan, get him on the bleedin' bike,' Biddy hissed back in a furious undertone. 'It's late, and dark, and there's not likely to be many about, put your arms round him and hold him up whilst I move the bike.'

It took them twenty minutes to get Mr Bowker aboard and then they discovered other snags; his feet, for one. They would not stay on the pedals, but they kept getting thumped by them as the pedals revolved, and Biddy was deathly afraid of bruising. In the end they took the chain off – a black and messy business – and with Mr Bowker balanced stiffly and awkwardly between saddle and handlebars they unlocked the door and pushed the bicycle and its grisly burden into Shaw's Alley and round the corner into Sparling Street.

There was, as Biddy had predicted, no one about, but to their dismay a considerable amount of sound was still coming from the direction of the goods station.

'They must work all bloomin' night,' Ellen moaned. 'What'll we do now, our Biddy?'

She was clutching the corpse whilst Biddy handled the bicycle, which was acting rather like a horse would in similar circumstances, except, of course, that the bicycle had no excuse since it could not sense the nature of its burden the way a horse would. But perhaps because of Mr Bowker's unnatural stiffness, or the height of him, or the weight, the bicycle veered from left to right and from right to left, looking far more drunk than either the girls or its passenger.

'The dock . . . I'll turn in a big circle and we'll go over to Wapping Dock,' Biddy gasped breathlessly. 'Hang on, both of you.'

She managed to turn the bicycle rather neatly and then headed grimly down Sparling Road towards the brightly lit dock area. A quick glance at Mr Bowker did not exactly convince her that he looked like a live drunk, but she had often stepped over a man lying comatose in the gutter, drunk as a lord, and knew that drunkenness had many faces.

'What'll we do? Tip 'im in the 'oggin?' Ellen wheezed. Being a shop assistant was not a good training for lugging corpses, Biddy realised. She herself, used to hefting heavy parcels and riding an elderly bicycle for hours at a time, was taking it far more in her stride.

'No. We'll prop him in a corner, a dark corner, and leave him,' Biddy whispered. 'Look, under the docker's umbrella, that will be fine. Come on, not far now.'

It was not far. As they emerged from Sparling Street, however, they saw that they were not the only people abroad at this hour. A figure was huddled on the steps of the public house on the corner, singing softly in a cracked old voice.

'Another bleedin' drunk,' Ellen hissed, as venomously

as though poor Mr Bowker was indeed a drunken friend. 'Just let's 'ope 'e isn't noticin' us, that's all.'

'He's not noticing anyone,' Biddy said, as they passed the blackened, tramplike figure. 'He's too busy feeling sorry for himself.'

It was true that the tramp kept moaning beneath his breath whenever he stopped singing and as they passed, keeping well clear, it was obvious why.

'Filthy ole bugger's been sick as a dawg,' Ellen said. 'Ah, nearly there, queen.'

They pushed the bike the last couple of yards and collapsed against one of the pillars which supported the overhead railway. Biddy looked around, selected an appropriate spot, and pointed. Together, they heaved their passenger off the bicycle – which fell over with a clatter so loud that both girls froze where they stood, convinced that it would bring the Law down upon them – and somehow managed to drag him to the spot they had chosen against the pillar but out of the light of the gas lamps.

'Prop him up,' Biddy hissed. 'That's it . . . now scarper!'

She nearly forgot the bicycle, but remembered it in time and jumped aboard, forgetting they had disconnected the chain until her foot, on the pedal, went crashing to the ground.

'Doesn't matter, I can push it,' she said, but she was speaking to empty air. Ellen was already across the road and turning into Sparling Street.

Pushing the bicycle, bruised and aching all over after that short but terrible journey, Biddy limped home.

To face, she thought grimly, whatever the morrow might bring.

Chapter Six

For two whole days Biddy and Ellen waited to hear what would happen to them. At work, Ellen said there were grumbles about Mr Bowker not putting in an appearance but nothing more interesting was said. No one made any bones about assuming that his wife was ill again, and one or two said he was a 'poor feller, wi' a woman like that holdin' the purse strings', though so far as Ellen knew Mrs Bowker was not a rich woman. And if his wife telephoned to speak to other heads of department about her missing husband the information was not passed on to the staff.

By dinner-time on the second day, when Ellen had nipped out in her break to tell Biddy, just with a look, that nothing had happened, Biddy became secretly convinced that no one had noticed Mr Bowker and that, if she should chance to pass along Wapping later that day, she would see him, still propped against the pillar, gazing sightlessly ahead of him.

She voiced the thought to Ellen, who said she was a fool, and then said that she herself had wondered about body snatchers . . .

'We've got to keep our nerve and wait it out,' Biddy said that evening, as they prepared their meal. 'Remember, there are heaps of drunks in Liverpool. Until they find out, he's just another one.'

'I keep tellin' meself that,' Ellen said miserably. 'But if we don't 'ear somethin' soon I won't 'ave any nerve to keep. I'm a nervous wreck, honest to God.'

'Yes, I'm not what I was,' Biddy agreed gloomily. 'Did you bring the *Echo* in? Let's have a read whilst the potatoes cook.'

She skimmed through the paper – then stopped, a finger marking her place. 'Ellen,' she said slowly. 'It's in here! I don't know why I didn't think of it, but it is in here, in the stop press. Shall I read it to you?'

'No . . . let me look.' Ellen grabbed the paper and the two heads, the fair and the dark, bent over it.

'Man collapsed on Wapping Dock. A man aged between fifty and sixty was found dead on Wapping Dock earlier in the day by a docker on his way to work. He is believed to be Edward Alexander Bowker of Upper Hope Place. Mr Bowker is believed to have suffered a heart attack; foul play is not suspected. Mr Bowker leaves a wife but the couple were childless.'

'We-ell!' Biddy laid the paper down and blew out her cheeks in a long whistle. 'It's all right, Ellen, we're going to be all right!'

'We're off the bleedin' 'ook,' Ellen said joyfully. 'Oh Bid, I'm that glad, 'cos it were none of it nothin' to do wi' you. You were a real brick to me and I won't ever forget. Gawd, let's get our suppers on the go, I'm that starvin'!'

The next day at work there was a certain amount of oohing and aahing, but the fact that Mr Bowker had been well-liked actually cut down the discussion. Though the senior staff were all interested in who would take over his job, the junior staff had their own lives to lead.

'It isn't even a nine days wonder,' Ellen said rather sadly to Biddy when she got home that night. 'Most of 'em haven't even mentioned it. 'Eads of Department don't interest 'em unless the feller's a real stinker, then they'd put the flags out. As it is, they're just carryin' on as usual.'

'I wonder how long it'll be before they twig that the rent isn't being paid for this place? Or did he own it?' Biddy said. She was making peppermint creams and the rather sickly smell pervaded every corner of the flat. 'Either way, we'll be kicked out soon enough.'

'At least it's summer; we can kip down in St John's gardens or catch the over'ead railway out to Seaforth an' sleep on the sands,' Ellen said with a giggle. 'We ought to start huntin' for a place, though, Bid. Somewhere we can share.'

They knew they should search, but somehow they did not. Instead they continued to live in the flat and to go to the Acacia each Saturday night. Ellen flirted desultorily with the young men she danced with, but it seemed to Biddy that all the pleasure had gone out of it with Mr Bowker's death. It was not that Ellen was sad any more, because she had got over that stage. She was just idly going through the days, seemingly content enough but not wanting another friendship to take the place of the first.

'We're marking time,' Biddy said one fine evening in July, when they had walked down to the pierhead to watch the big ships steaming up the Mersey whilst they enjoyed the breeze and the sunshine. 'It's as though we can't really get on with our lives until we know what's going to happen about the flat. Still, it can't be long now.'

It was not. They got back to the flat with fish and chips which they had bought from a shop on Park Lane and found a thin-faced gentleman waiting on the doorstep.

'Mr Bowker? Is 'e in? Rent was due a fortnight since. 'E's always been a regular payer, but . . .'

'He had a heart-attack some while ago,' Biddy said

when Ellen seemed disinclined to answer. 'Who paid the rent last month?'

'Quarterly; it's due quarterly,' the man said. 'Dead, you say?'

'Yes, he's dead. But in the past we paid our rent to him each week,' Biddy said, thinking on her feet so to speak. 'Will it be in order if we pay you direct in future?'

The man had been looking annoyed and aggressive, but he nodded quite pleasantly at her words, visibly relaxing.

'Aye, that'll suit. Can you pay me now?'

'How much do you want?' Ellen asked, speaking for the first time. 'We don't keep cash in the house, but I'm sure we can withdraw some money tomorrow.'

She was using her 'posh' voice, to Biddy's amusement, but it seemed to do the trick.

'I'll want six pun' ten shillin',' the man said in a businesslike voice. 'It's a good flat – self-contained.'

'Right,' Ellen said, as though pound notes grew on trees and she had a flourishing orchard. 'What's your address, Mr er . . .? I don't think I caught the name?'

'Mr Alderson. And your name, Miss? For me books, like.'

'Oh . . . I'm . . . I'm Miss Sandwich and this is Miss . . . Miss Fisher,' Ellen gabbled, clearly unprepared for the question. 'Where's your office, Mr Alderson? We'll pop in tomorrow, if we may.'

'I lives at Barter Street, not far from Prince's Park,' Mr Alderson said. He gave them a sharp look. 'If me rent's not paid by midday tomorrer, mind, I'll re-let and you're out.'

Ellen drew herself up and gave him a glare of well-simulated fury. 'Mr Alderson, I've said we'll see you tomorrow. Come, Miss Fish.'

She unlocked the door and pushed Biddy inside, then

slammed and locked the door behind them. Biddy, gig-gling wildly, sank down upon the bottom stair.

'Oh Ellen, you said I was Miss Fisher, not Miss Fish,' she gasped out at last. 'And . . . and why did you call yourself Miss Sandwich, for heaven's sake? I don't think it is a name at all!'

'It is! Anyway, it don't matter 'cos we'll never see 'im again. Oh Biddy, gerroff them stairs an' let's go up and eat us chips! I'm always 'ungry these days.'

'It's because you're still unhappy,' Biddy said wisely, getting to her feet. 'All right, we'll go and eat.'

Later however, when the fish and chips had been washed down by a cup of good, hot tea, she returned to the subject. 'Ellen, I know we couldn't possibly afford six pounds a quarter, but there are other flats. Your sister Polly's in work, if she came in with us, and one or two more, wouldn't we be able to afford something? You don't want to live at home with your Mam again, do you?'

'No, I don't. But . . . oh, Biddy, I may 'ave to! I 'aven't said nothin' before, but I think . . . I think . . .'

'You think what? Don't say they're going to sack you from your lovely job!'

It was the worst disaster Biddy could imagine, since it would mean that Ellen would not be earning, but it turned out that there was another disaster which had not even crossed her mind.

'No, they've said nothin' at work, but they soon will; Biddy, I think I'm in the family way!'

'The f-*family* way?' Biddy stammered. 'What do you mean? You don't mean you're going to have a baby? But how can you, when Mr Bowker's been dead almost three months?'

'I reckon I'm more'n four months gone,' Ellen said miserably. 'You said yourself I ate a lot; I'm eatin' for two,

I guess. So it's either go in one of them places for bad girls or go 'ome, and if me Mam'll tek me in . . .'

'Oh, Ellen, of course she will, your Mam's ever so kind,' Biddy said, hugging her friend. 'But I thought you were careful, or Mr Bowker was, anyway. I thought you said . . .'

'It were a mistake,' Ellen said drearily. 'Anyone can mek a mistake. And now I've told you I've gorra admit it's real, see? Before, I told meself it weren't goin' to 'appen, even though I knew it were.'

'And you've not told your Mam yet, nor your sisters?'

'I've not even told meself I said,' Ellen pointed out rather sharply. 'So much 'as 'appened, chuck, that it were easy to push it to the back of me mind. But now I've gorra face up to it. I'll tek a day off work – can you tell 'em I'm sick? – an' go down an' see me Mam.'

'Right,' Biddy said. 'I'll see if I can get a place somewhere . . . there must be somewhere . . .'

'Come wi' me, back to me Mam's,' Ellen suggested, but though Biddy thanked her and hugged her once more, she refused.

'Your Mam will have enough on her plate with you and a new baby,' she said shrewdly. 'Your house bulges at the seams already. But I'll manage, never you fear. Us O'Shaughnessys are a tough lot, my Mam told me so.'

It was easy to talk about lodgings but not so easy to get something even half-way decent, as Biddy discovered next day. She carried her trusty carpet bag in to work with her, stowing it away in the back room, and told Miss Whitney that the rent of the flat which she and Ellen shared had been put beyond their means by a new landlord and asked for a couple of hours off to search for new accommodation.

After two hours she returned to the shop. 'It'll have to

be the day off, or I'll be sleeping in Millie's doorway,' she told Miss Harborough despairingly. 'I never thought a place would be so hard to find, never! And some of 'em's not rooms, they're just a bit partitioned off, and the bugs . . . well, it's not what I'm used to.'

But desperation began to set in as six o'clock got nearer. She returned to the shop and reclaimed her carpet bag, then trudged off again. And before night fell she found a room, of sorts.

The house itself was situated in a court off the Scotland Road, too far from Millicent's Modes to be truly practical. The room on offer, to a single young lady or gentleman, had been the property of a daughter of the house, and she bitterly resented being pushed out and incarcerated with half a dozen smaller sisters, particularly by a girl of her own age. She said quite audibly, whilst Mrs Tebbit, the landlady, showed Biddy the room, that 'Mam really wanted a feller – we all does', which did little to reassure Biddy as to her welcome here.

But it was a roof, somewhere to put her carpet bag and Dolly. Biddy had brought her own pillow, complete with the little lump of savings buried deep in the feathers, and the woollen blanket which Ellen had knitted out of bits and bobs of leftover wool.

'You'll bring your own beddin', o' course,' Mrs Tebbit snapped, when she saw Biddy staring, appalled, at the dirty, stained mattress with the stuffing oozing out from one end. 'I never provide no beddin'.'

Biddy was grateful she had brought her own bedding. The house was terribly overcrowded with a couple of seedy-looking middle-aged females whom Mrs Tebbit had referred to, collectively, as 'Auntie,' an ancient grandfather who had glared at Biddy with pointless senile fury as she was taken through the back kitchen, and an old grandmother with a flourishing beard and moustache who reeked of liniment. And of course there were eight or nine assorted children and presumably a Mr Tebbit somewhere in the offing, since the youngest child was still a babe in arms.

But at least I've got a room of my own, Biddy thought thankfully. At least I shan't have to share anything but the stairs and hallway.

Something of this may have shown in her expression, however, for Miss Jane Tebbit, the injured daughter, who appeared to be about Biddy's age and was already beginning to look and sound like her mother, put her oar in as Biddy stood silently surveying the small room.

'We don't carry up your washin' water, neither,' she said aggressively. 'There's a tap in the yard, you 'elps yourself.'

Biddy thanked them both, tongue in cheek, and proffered the first week's rent, which was received with a sniff.

'My ladies usually pay a month ahead,' Mrs Tebbit said, taking the money with assumed reluctance. 'Or two weeks?'

'A week is what I'm used to paying,' Biddy said calmly, but with a deep shake of fear inside her in case the woman called her bluff. She was afraid of sleeping rough, and equally afraid of having to go to a boarding house or small hotel and pay their exorbitant prices if this place fell through.

However, despite the sniff, Mrs Tebbit obviously felt that half a crown in the hand was a good deal better than waiting for another desperate person to appear, and she and her daughter disappeared down the rickety stairs, leaving Biddy to 'make yourself at 'ome,' as Mrs Tebbit put it.

Alone, Biddy sat down on the bed, then sprang up again and examined the surface of the mattress uneasily.

Bed bugs! She might have known, and they were dreadfully difficult to get rid of. What was more, the bites the disgusting insects made on their victims were easily identifiable; employers did not like those who worked for them to show the marks of poverty and deprivation too clearly. They found it easier to say that Miss so-and-so was dirty and didn't wash, though God knew if washing cured bed-bugs there wouldn't be one alive in most of the houses along the Scottie Road.

Paraffin? Was it that which killed them? You could catch them on a wet bar of soap and put them out of the window, or set fire to them with a lighted match, or squash them . . .

Biddy shook the mattress vigorously, then propped it up against the wall and pulled the rickety iron bedstead into the middle of the room. She put her pillow on it, then laid her blanket out and put Dolly down on the bed. She would rather sleep on bare springs than share her bed with the fat grey bugs which needed her blood to live.

The next few weeks were miserable ones for Biddy. She and Ellen had planned to go up to London to watch the Coronation but Ellen was in no condition to travel and Biddy didn't have the heart to go alone. She went to the cinema and watched it there, and fell in love with the whole family – the pretty little Duchess who was now Queen Elizabeth, her handsome husband and their two beautiful, curly-headed little daughters. But somehow it all fell a bit flat after the lovely plans she and Ellen had made together. No one, as yet, had taken the place of her friend.

So Biddy continued to work as hard as ever, handed over the rent to Mrs Tebbit each Friday, and searched for decent accommodation which she could afford whenever she got the opportunity. But when she found a nice little room the price was beyond her, and often to her horror she found even worse conditions than those under which the Tebbits lived.

Once she went round and visited Ellen, to find her friend almost as miserable as she.

'They sacked me from Gowns when they saw me stomach sideways,' Ellen said. 'I spent me savin's on a sewin' machine, though, so I'm takin' in curtains, alterations, stuff like that. It makes me a bob or two.' She smiled at Biddy. 'Makin' sweets, are you? To 'elp out, like?'

'If you could see where I live you wouldn't ask,' Biddy said, pulling a face. 'It's not a nice place, Ellie, and they aren't nice people. I try to eat away from the house because it's so dirty, so I couldn't possibly make sweets there. Still, as soon as I find somewhere decent I'll be out, you may be sure.'

'I'm thinkin' of havin' the kid adopted,' Ellen put in. 'What do you think, Biddy? There's no Da for it, so I might as well, hey?'

'What does your Mam think?' Biddy asked guardedly. She could quite see the advantages of adoption, but parents could be funny about such things she had heard.

'She says it's my life and my soul that'll be at risk if the Lord don't approve,' Ellen said rather uneasily. 'I'll wait till its born . . . but I might let someone 'ave it who can give it a chance. I can't, God knows. But in a way, I want the kid.'

'You'll marry, though, Ellie, one of these days,' Biddy said. 'Then you're bound to have other children.'

'Oh aye? Oo'll marry a judy what's got another feller's kid?' She flapped a hand at Biddy as her friend began to answer. 'Ne'er mind, lerrit rest, time will tell.'

Summer turned to autumn, and with the colder weather, Biddy was forced to spend money she could ill afford on an extra blanket. She went up to Paddy's Market though, and bought second hand, which was a help, and could not resist taking a quick look at Ma Kettle's emporium as she went past; even her life there seemed bearable when she was lying in her narrow bed at the Tebbits', listening to them quarrelling and swearing at one another downstairs, or hitting the kids or each other when tempers really rose.

Not that I'd go back, she reminded herself sometimes. At least here I'm all right during the daytime. I've got a nice job which I enjoy and I'm earning my independance slowly but surely.

As the weather got steadily colder, living with the Tebbits became easier in some ways and more difficult in others. The bed-bugs disappeared, and since the fleas could be kept at bay with liberal doses of Keatings powder, Biddy felt she could stand them. But the paraffin stove in her room, on which she was supposed to cook her meals leaked, which meant fumes forced her to open the window whilst using it. So any warmth from the little stove was lost through the open window, and anyway she was becoming increasingly suspicious over her can of paraffin, which seemed to become empty, in some mysterious fashion, whether Biddy lit her stove or not.

Someone's nicking my paraffin, Biddy told herself, and decided to save up for a lock. She did mention the strange way her paraffin disappeared to her landlady, but Mrs Tebbit drew herself up, sucking in her stomach and pushing out her very large chest, and announced that there were no thieves in her house, a remark so reminiscent of Ma Kettle that Biddy had hard work not to laugh.

She did not laugh a week or so later, though, when December brought the first snow-storm of the season. Biddy had had a hard day bicycling through the newly laid snow, and though it was pretty and she enjoyed the freshness and sparkle which it added to the dingy, early-morning streets, she remembered all too clearly the difficulties it had made for her the previous winter and dreaded a repetition. What was more, Ellen's baby had been born a fortnight earlier and she had gone round to the Bradley home and taken some clothing for the child, only to realise that, though Ellen adored her son, things were going to be hard for her. The baby seemed to drain her of energy and even her sewing did not bring in enough money to support them both. Biddy had willingly handed over a bob as well as the clothes, but she could see that her friend would have her work cut out to manage and intended to do her best to help out. Cold weather, therefore, was very unwelcome on several counts.

However, she cycled up the Scottie Road and turned off into John Comrade Court, known locally simply as Commie, actually anticipating her return to the Tebbit household with something akin to pleasure. She had a couple of eggs up in her room and half a loaf of bread, so she had splashed out on a pint of fresh milk when she had seen a milkman earlier, and intended to make herself French toast, a delicacy of which her mother had been inordinately fond.

The milk was in a ginger-beer bottle, nestling in the pocket of her warm duffle-coat and she had some bull's-eyes which a customer had given her. Quite a feast – and best of all, a new book!

Living so near to the shop now, she often popped in on Mr Meehan, the bookseller on Cazneau Street, and picked something to read out of his tuppenny tray, for Mr Meehan did not just sell smart new books, but some older ones as well.

Biddy had gone in there earlier, having a delivery in the area, and Mr Meehan, who had always been a good friend, had suggested to Biddy that she might like to put her name down for a place with Mrs Freddy, at Accrington Court, just down the road from her present abode.

'Mrs Freddy's clean, a good cook, and a pleasant sort of person,' Mr Meehan had said, smiling at her. 'But her rooms are very popular, which is why she has a waiting list. Costs nothing to add your name, madam, and she charges three and six a week with evening meal.'

'I'll go at once and put my name down,' Biddy said. 'Thank you very much Mr Meehan, you are good to me. Can I have this one, please?'

Mr Meehan took the book and glanced at it, then flipped it open. '*Lorna Doone*,' he said. 'You've not read it, madam?'

'No, not this one,' Biddy assured him. Often she bought books she had read and enjoyed when her parents had been alive, but occasionally she took a chance and bought something she had never even seen before. She had been attracted to *Lorna Doone* both by the first few pages and by the illustration in the front, which was a brown and white photograph of the most beautiful river she had ever seen. She took the book from him and opened it at the photograph. 'Where's that, Mr Meehan? It's so beautiful!'

'It's Watersmeet, in Devonshire,' Mr Meehan said. 'The story takes place in Devonshire, on Dartmoor, if I recall. You'll enjoy it, madam.'

He took Biddy's money and they smiled at one another. He always called her madam, it was his little joke. 'Go round to Mrs Freddy's and say I sent you,' he advised as she turned towards the door. 'You deserve better than that Mrs Tebbit, and you would fit in very well at No. 3 Accrington Court.'

So Biddy had cycled round there and added her

name to what looked like a rather lengthy list.

'You're at Mrs Tebbit's?' Mrs Freddy had said, however. She shook her head sadly. 'Oh dear me! Well, even if I don't have a vacancy I'll see whether I can find you somewhere else. Those Tebbits!'

She left it at that but Biddy, cycling back to the shop, had felt a warm glow. She would escape from the Tebbits, either with or without Mrs Freddy, but it would be pleasant to feel she had an ally, someone else who wanted to help her.

But now, however, she had come down to earth. She would light her paraffin stove, make her French toast and a nice cup of tea, and then get into bed to keep warm and read her new book. The Tebbit household did not run to oil lamps upstairs, but Biddy had a supply of candles hidden away and one of them would last her until she grew too tired to read and wanted only to sleep.

She turned her bicycle into the entry down which she could reach the Tebbits' back yard. She kept her bicycle there, chained and with a strong padlock on the back wheel, but so far no one had ventured to interfere with it. As she secured the bicycle the snow, which had stopped for a while, started up again. Slow, lazy flakes at first, gradually growing thicker. Good weather to be out of, Biddy concluded, legging it for the back door. She burst into the kitchen to find the family assembled there, seemingly in accord for once. They were chattering and laughing, the fire blazed up and for once a reasonable smell of cooking came from the oven let into the wall beside the fire.

'Oh . . . sorry, I didn't realise you were in here,' Biddy said above the din. 'I'd have come through the front door if I'd known.'

'S'orlright, chuck,' Ray Tebbit said. He was a seaman, not home often, and Biddy always felt sorry for him because it seemed hard to come home from the sort of life she believed sailors lived, not to family comfort and good cheer but to the noisy quarrelling and frequent fights of the rest of the Tebbit clan.

Still, they all seemed happy enough tonight. There were chestnuts roasting on a coal shovel and the miserable Jane was toasting a crumpet, actually smiling as she shielded her face from the flames.

They must be celebrating Ray's return, Biddy thought, climbing quickly up the stairs. What a pity they aren't a pleasant crowd – how nice it would be to be part of a family again. Still, Ellen's Mam had asked her to spend Christmas Day with them, that was something to look forward to, and because of a general feeling of goodwill to all men at this time of year, her tips were building up once more. The lump in the pillow was quite uncomfortable some nights, when she turned over without care.

In her own room, Biddy tipped a good supply of paraffin into her stove and lit it. She left the door a little ajar, hoping that it would clear the fumes and make it unnecessary to open the window, then she took off her coat, hat, scarf and gloves and laid her groceries out on the edge of the bed. She was hanging her coat on the hook of the door when she remembered her tips; best put them in the lump at once, before she forgot them. She did not intend to leave them in her coat pocket all night, though really they would be pretty safe. No one ever came into her room when she was in residence.

She slid the money out of her pocket, counted it, then went over to the bed. She pulled her pillow out from under Dolly and her fingers found the neat slit in the seam. She pushed her hand in amongst the feathers, feeling for the lump. It wasn't there, but she always pushed it right down, well out of view and feel.

It took her all of five minutes to acknowledge the awful truth.

Her savings had disappeared.

The ship was iced up worse than Dai had ever known it and a heavy swell was running, so when the black frost began to rise from the water everyone had been too busy to notice it. You can't see black frost, but you can feel it; it is black frost which causes each breath you take to include tiny particles of ice, and ice in the lungs can kill a man.

But Dai kept his muffler round his mouth and nose, and he kept his great heavy gauntlets on, too. Because he – and every other man aboard who could be spared – was chopping ice. Desperately, with all their strength, they were chopping at the ice which had already all but immobilised the ship.

The trouble was, Dai knew, that a heavy sea which came inboard time after time, froze solid between each wave, so that the ship was becoming layered in ice which weighed her down in the water until her usual buoyant forward movement became little more than an uneasy wallow.

Clear the ice or die. Get her free of it or see her turn turtle ... it's the last thing you'll see as you gasp the iced air into your lungs for the last time.

They all knew the truth of it, all dreaded it. So they used picks and shovels and they battered and beat at the ice. Even the laziest man on board was galvanised into action. Greasy raised his pick and brought it down and diamonds flew across the deck, first small, then impossibly huge, koh-i-noors, every one.

'You're doin' fine, Grease,' Dai said through his muffler. 'We'll clear the whaleback in ten minutes – look at the masts!'

The masts were beautiful, slender candy sticks, blue-white and elegant. Dai felt he could have snapped one off and eaten it ... but the masts, too, must be cleared before any man aboard could go off watch.

'Aye. Like a woman, beautiful but deadly,' Greasy said thickly. 'Hey up, look 'oo's 'ere!'

It was the Skipper. He was of little use on the bridge; you cannot con a motionless vessel, so he had come to lend his strength to the ice-clearing party. Side by side with them, strength for strength, he worked all that long afternoon, until the *Bess* began to answer to the helm, to take on the seas at their own game, to respond.

'She'll live,' the Mate said at last. He stood back to let the crew go below first, then had to hack at his boot with his pick-axe because it had frozen to the deck in those few seconds. The crew began to shuffle down the companion-way, too tired to push and shove, to joke and blaspheme as they usually did, and the Mate followed them, talking as he came. 'She's a grand little ship, the *Bess*.'

'Obstinate little bitch, she wouldn't let the ice turtle her,' Colin said with affectionate pride. 'Eh, put the wind up us, didn't she though? Just like a bloody woman!'

'Gives you an appetite, mun, ice-clearing do,' Dai said with relish as they filed onto the mess deck. 'That's why the Skipper joined in, 'tweren't to give us a hand like, 'twas to get himself ready for Bandy's beef stew and dumplings.'

They all laughed. Bandy, the cook, was popular with everyone because he could cook in a raging arctic storm, his bread always rose and filled the small ship with its delicate, delicious smell and he made pancakes which a master chef would have envied – made them, what was more, with a heavy swell running and his stove moving up and down in rhythm whilst pans and pots flew through the air and thumped anyone standing in the galley.

'Never known the ice as bad as that,' Greasy remarked as he sat down at the table and plonked his plate of stew down in front of him. 'We've done a year on distant water, but we've never known ice that bad, have we, Taff?'

'Nor me,' Colin said. 'And this is my third year.'

There were murmurs of assent all round the room. 'Aye, it were pretty bad.' 'You don't often get it that thick on the masts.' 'It's always bad wi' a black frost, but that 'un beggars description.'

Dai nodded and attacked his stew. He ate it with relish, enjoying the new bread which accompanied it almost as much as the meal itself. Afterwards there was stewed apples and custard, after that coffee, hot and strong, in thick white cups.

'On watch, we are, in three hours,' he said to Greasy presently, as they sat back, replete. 'Let's get some shut-eye.'

They went to their bunks, took off their sea-boots and rolled into their blankets. Dai usually slept like a log the moment his head touched the pillow, but not tonight. Tonight his thoughts refused to let him sleep. They played round and round the scene out on the deck, with the old man giving the ice hell and every one of the crew working like devils, no one slacking, stopping for a rest, complaining. They had all known it was a race against time and they worked as a team until the sweat froze on them and their hands were covered in bleeding blisters.

He was never bored on the *Bess*, though he was often frightened, nearly always tired. But that had been a narrow escape, that icing up, he knew it by Colin's face, by the Mate's relief as he watched them go down the companionway, by the Skipper's mere presence on deck. I wish Mam were alive, she'd understand why I love it, why I'll keep coming back, he told himself wistfully. Da would have understood once, but not any more. All he can see, now, is Menna's white young body and the brassy yellow hair of her, all he can see is Davy Evans having his way with a woman young enough to be his daughter. He won't be interested in his son, not yet awhile.

But Bethan would have loved to hear about the *Bess*, would have understood. And suddenly, he wanted to talk to a woman, not a girl who would smile and kiss him and be willing or unwilling to go to bed with him but a woman, a motherly woman.

In the bunk beside his, Greasy sighed, then spoke. 'Taffy? I t'ink I'd like to go 'ome when we get back this time. Not to Victoria Street but 'ome. To me Mam. To Liverpool.'

There was a wealth of longing in his voice and Dai could have hugged him because it wasn't just he who had wanted a bit of mothering, Greasy did too.

'Yeah, mun,' Dai said, from under the blankets. 'My Mam said to go and see her friend in Liverpool, her name's Nellie Gallagher. If you go home, I'll come with you and find Mrs Gallagher. She may not even know my Mam's dead, yet. I should have visited, should have gone before. It was my Mam's last wish, you could say.'

'We'll both go,' Greasy said. His voice had deepened with exhaustion and the rapid approach of sleep. 'We'll both go, our Taff. Together.'

Biddy couldn't believe it at first. All that money, just gone, and she always so careful to push the small cloth bag deep into the feathers before she left for work each morning. She searched the bedding, the surrounding floor, she even looked in the pockets of every garment she possessed, just in case she had sleepwalked around the room and stowed her precious savings somewhere different.

But it was not a big room; the most diligent of searches could take her no longer than half an hour and at the end of the time Biddy descended the stairs, cold fury in her heart. She stalked into the kitchen and when the family went on squabbling and laughing she banged her hand hard on the half-open kitchen door.

It had the desired effect. Voices broke off in mid-sentence and every head in the room swung towards her.

When she saw she had everyone's attention, Biddy spoke, her voice hard. 'Where's my money?'

There was a short, uneasy silence. Mrs Tebbit was the first to break it. 'Gone, chuck . . . you'll owe again from tomorrer.'

'Not my rent,' Biddy said coldly. 'My savings. I kept my savings in a little white cloth bag inside my pillow. I went to it just now and my money had gone, bag and all. Someone from here must have taken it and I want it back, smartish, or I'll call the police.'

'None of my family would touch your money,' Mrs Tebbit said. Deep scarlet colour rose in her fat, lard-like cheeks. 'Ow dare you say such a thing, you baggage!'

'Who else would take it? Who else *could*?' Biddy asked. 'Strangers don't wander in off the streets and go up to my room and fiddle around in there. But someone does, I've known someone goes in and picks over my things when I'm at work, someone uses my paraffin, but this is going too far.' She stared at each one of them in turn, even giving the tatty, down-at-heel kids a long, chilly look. 'I'm going upstairs, now. If my money isn't handed back in the next ten minutes, I'm going down to the police station. I hope that's clear?'

No one answered. Eyes darted about, but no one spoke. Biddy threw them one last look and left the room. She went upstairs slowly, hoping against hope that someone would follow her upstairs, slip that familiar little cloth bag into her palm. But no one did.

In her room again, Dolly lay in an abandoned attitude on top of the ravaged pillowcase. A few feathers, dumb witnesses to Biddy's frantic search, floated lazily into the air as Biddy had opened the door, then settled slowly on floor and bed as the closing door cut off the draught once more.

Biddy waited for a good deal longer than ten minutes, but no one came clattering up the stairs, no one called her name, knocked, admitted the theft. Slowly, reluctantly, Biddy let the moments drift by, then she descended the stairs once more. At the foot she hesitated, then put her head round the kitchen door.

'I'm off for the police,' she said. 'Shan't be very long I don't suppose. Are you sure you wouldn't like to give me my savings back?'

She could tell by the looks on the faces that they knew who had robbed her, guessed that there had been harsh words exchanged, but they had obviously come to some sort of decision and it was clearly not to hand her money back.

'No one 'ere's got your filthy money,' Mrs Tebbit said at last, her tone as surly and aggressive as the expression on her face. 'Fancy you saltin' away all that money – or tellin' folk you 'ad, anyroad. Well, you're gonna get your comeuppance now, milady, an' no mistake, 'cos you've been pipped at the post. You say you'll tell the scuffers – well, tell away. Two can play at that game and we'll 'ave something to say an' all. What about the money missin' from me downstairs dresser, eh? Someone took it – oo's to say it weren't you, Miss 'Igh-an'-Mighty? Anyroad, our Jane went down to the cop-shop soon's you left, and reported it, said it were possible our lodger 'ad been sticky-fingerin' it. So chances is you'll be the one the scuffers wanna see!'

Biddy turned and left the room. She would go to the police, she would! As if they would believe a crowd of tatty, dirty Tebbits against Biddy O'Shaughnessy, who had never been wrong-sides of the law in her life! Though there was the flat . . . but that had been a long while ago and there had been no trouble. And there was poor Mr Bowker . . . he had been given a grand funeral and was buried in Ford cemetery, she and Ellen had taken flowers not all that long ago. Could any of this rebound on her? Of course it couldn't, she would go to the police and she just hoped they threw all the Tebbits into prison, or sold their miserable possessions to force them to pay her back!

But she found that instead of making her way to the police station she had climbed the stairs again so she went into her room, sat down on the bed, and began, very quietly, to weep. She could do nothing! The Tebbits had already made their complaint, what would any police-man think if she went along to the station now? They would think she was trying to cover up her own theft by reporting another . . . oh God, what should she do? She could not stay here and wait for the law to pounce though, she would have to leave.

'I'll change my name', Biddy thought frantically, chucking things into her trusty carpet bag. She tied her blanket round her pillow, stuffed Dolly into the bedroll, and headed for the door. She looked around the bare little room and gave a big sniff, then wiped her eyes with her fingers and went back to pick up the tin of paraffin. It was half full – should she leave it? But she did not want the Tebbits to get anything else of hers. Where would she take it, though? She had no money and no hope of any until the end of the week, and it was Christmas in ten days.

She would probably get tips next day and could buy chips and a tin of conny onny to see her though until pay-day. But what then? She had spent enough hours tramping the streets earlier in the year to know that good lodgings, even poor lodgings, were rare as hen's teeth in the city. Could she possibly go to the Bradleys and beg them to take her in, just until she found somewhere else? Mrs Bradley was ever so nice, a big, fat, friendly woman, tolerant of others, fond of all her sprawling brood. She had taken the erring Ellen back, surely she would let Biddy doss down on a floor somewhere for a couple of nights?

Biddy knew she would, and perhaps that was the trouble. Poor Mrs Bradley had worries of her own without Biddy adding to them. Ellen's baby, Robert, was much loved, but naturally his presence added to the Bradleys' difficulties, and if Biddy did beg the family to take her in then yet another person, in a house already bursting at the seams, might be the straw which broke the camel's back.

Until now, indeed, Biddy, as Ellen's best friend, had tried to pass on any bits and pieces which might make life easier for the new mother and her little son, but now . . . it's all I can do to keep body and soul together for meself, Biddy thought mournfully. I can't do a thing for Ellen or Bobby.

But it would only be for a few days, until I found somewhere else, Biddy reminded herself, closing her bedroom door slowly behind her and beginning to descend the stairs. I'll find somewhere else in a day or so, somewhere I can afford. Somewhere which doesn't want rent in advance . . . oh, I could kill that beastly Jane Tebbit, it took me years to save up that money and I might as well not have bothered, I would have done better to buy pretty clothes and nice shoes, or to give Ellen more of a hand, at least I'd have something to show for the money.

Half-way down the stairs, with her face set in hard,

defiant lines, Biddy saw the kitchen door below her open a crack. She continued to descend the stairs, ignoring the door. It would be a small Tebbit, spying on her so that he or she could turn and shrill 'She's gone!' to the others, so they would know themselves safe from her.

It was not a small Tebbit. It was Ray, the seaman son of whom Mrs Tebbit was so proud, looking very red-faced.

'Ang on a mo, Miss O'Shaughnessy, where's you off to?' he said. 'Don't you let them scare you off . . . I'm ashamed of me Mam, that I am. She knows very well we ain't lost no money, she's just trying to shield the person what took your savin's.'

'I'm going,' Biddy said with controlled violence. 'There's nothing for me here now, and nothing for a Tebbit to steal any more, so you might as well let me go without any fuss.'

'Ere, 'ang on queen, you've paid till the week's end, I'll see me Mam don't ask any rent off of you for a week or two. Where'll you go if you march out now, eh? What'll you do?'

'I've got friends,' Biddy said stiffly. 'Don't worry about me, I'll survive. I always have.' She jerked open the big old front door and almost tumbled onto the pavement. 'It's no use asking you to get my money back, Ray, because I daresay she's spent it by now, so if you'll just leave me alone to get on with my life . . . '

'Let me carry your bag,' Ray said, trying to tug it out of her grip. 'Then I can see with me own eyes that you're goin' to friends. 'Ow would I feel if they found you dead in a gutter tomorrer, eh? How'd me Mam feel?'

'Delighted, I should think,' Biddy said sourly, retaining her hold on the carpet bag. 'Just you let go of me, Ray Tebbit, or I'll scream for a policeman no matter what your Jane has told them. Go on, bog off!'

'I don't suppose Jane told 'em much,' Ray said, but

he stopped tugging at her bag. 'She's an awful little liar, our Jane. 'Ang on, le' me give you your tram fare, any-road.'

'I don't need a tram fare, I've got me delivery bicycle,' Biddy said, walking round the front of the house to the entry which led to the back yard. 'Unless some member of your family's swiped that as well, of course.'

'It's only Jane, the rest of us wouldn't,' Ray muttered uneasily. 'Look, 'ere's a bob, it's all I've got on me. Go on, take it, you never know when you may need it. What about your dinner tonight, eh?'

For the first time, Biddy remembered her plans for the evening; the two eggs, the ginger-beer bottle full of milk, the half loaf of bread. She had brought the food in her carpet bag because she was determined to leave the Tebbits nothing, but where could she cook it, what would she do with it? It was far too late to cast herself upon the Bradleys tonight, she would have to find somewhere to lay her head in the next couple of hours or she would be taken up as a vagrant and thrown either into gaol or the workhouse, she did not know which she dreaded more.

They had reached the back yard and Biddy unlocked her bicycle with trembling hands and then took the shilling Ray was offering.

'I shouldn't thank you, because your bloody family owe it me – but thanks,' she said rather unsteadily, putting the carpet bag into the carrier and beginning to push the bicycle out of the yard. 'You're all right, Ray. Good-bye.'

Ray might have followed her as he had threatened had she gone on foot, but on the bicycle she was far too fast for him. She leaned hard on the pedals and fairly tore up the Court and into the Scotland Road, and then she turned left and pedalled equally fast for the city centre, because though she still had no idea where she was going she felt she wanted to be on well-lit streets, with people about.

There were hotels, lodging houses, surely she could get a bed somewhere just for one night? But with a bob? And if she spent her bob on a bed then she wouldn't have any money to buy herself chips.

She cycled along the gaslit streets until she reached Ranelagh Place, then she turned into Ranelagh Street, her eyes seeking out Millicent's Modes. Was there somewhere here where she could doss down for the night? Some little nook or cranny where the scuffers wouldn't come poking around looking for drunks and tramps?

But apart from the shop doorway, which seemed suddenly extremely exposed, there was nowhere.

What about a station, though? Stations were busy places, she remembered trying to dispose of Mr Bowker in Wapping Goods station and being unable to do so for people, noise and traffic. So if she went up to Lime Street and pretended she was waiting for a train, then she might be able to snooze undisturbed and safe on a seat until morning. If I can just get through this night, she told herself, if I can survive until morning, then I can go to the shop, explain what's happened, see if Miss Whitney or Miss Harborough can tell me what to do or help me in some way. Come to that, I can go round to Ellen's once its daylight. Yes, that's what I'll do. All I want is somewhere to stay safe until day comes again.

The *Greenland Bess* was homeward bound with her fish-pounds heaving with cod, codling, sea bass and the smooth-bodied halibut. When the men were not hauling the trawl, shooting it, conning the ship, breaking ice, they were gutting the fish. Greasy, who seemed to take to the life of a fisherman with considerable verve, didn't like the gutting.

'A feller could lose a leg,' he remarked to Dai when a huge, eel-like fish, apparently dead as a dodo, suddenly came to life in the pound and attacked his sea-boot, ripping the strong rubber as if it were paper with its hundreds of exceedingly sharp teeth. 'No one ever told me a bleedin' fish would turn round an' try to gut *me*, for a change!'

'Happens all the time,' Dai said laconically, making a private vow to watch the big fish in future and to keep all his most precious parts well out of the reach of those needle-sharp teeth. 'Still, can't be too careful, mun. Don't turn your back on 'em.'

But that was all a thing of the past now; going-home time was clean-up time, the time you scrubbed every inch of deck, polished all the brasswork on the bridge, mopped down seating, tables, floors.

'I feel like a bleedin' 'ousewife,' Greasy grumbled as he and Dai scrubbed endlessly across the deck, removing the last traces of fish. 'I'm surprised the Skipper 'asn't give us a duster to tie round us 'air, like one o' them black mammies you see in Yankee fillums.'

'You would look good in blue and white check,' Dai nodded. 'I'm more for pink gingham, me. Come on, get scrubbing, mun, there's beer on the mess deck and Bandy's makin' chips.'

'Not fish, for Gawd's sake? Tell me we're not eatin' fish again?'

Dai laughed. Contrary to popular belief trawlermen going to distant waters do not live on fish, but they do eat an awful lot of it, especially towards the end of a voyage.

'No, not fish, honest. Corned-beef fritters.'

'Oh.' There was a short pause whilst Greasy stared into space and thought about his next meal, then he sighed and nodded his head. 'Corned-beef fritters, eh? Do I like 'em?'

'You love 'em,' Dai said solemnly. 'We all love 'em. But unless we get this deck clean as a new pin – cleaner – we won't be havin' 'em. We'll still be scrubbing.'

'Aye; that's what the Mate said, I seem to remember. Taff?'

'What's up now?' Dai said resignedly, attacking a new stretch of deck. 'Do you scrub as you talk, Greasy, or we'll still be cleaning this deck come midnight.'

'You meant it, didn't you? You will come 'ome wi' me after this trip, to Liverpool?'

'Why not? The Mate says we've two weeks this time, because of the damage to the trawl and the lifting gear, so we've plenty of time to get there an' back by the next trip. If we sign on, that is.'

'I'm signin' off after this trip,' Mal said, behind them. He was polishing the rail. 'Money's good, but by 'eck, the work's not. Reckon there's easier ways to earn a livin'.'

'Come up to Liverpool with us, sign on a coaster,' Dai suggested, very tongue in cheek. Trawlermen were a breed apart, they rarely went back to ordinary merchant shipping once the fishing had got them. 'Have yourself a rest, Mal bach.'

'Mebbe I will Taff, one day, but for now I'll save me wages and me bonus instead of spendin' it all in the pubs on Freeman Street. I may sign on again in a few weeks though. Not on a distant-water ship, but on a drifter, or somethin' trawlin' the North Sea. Somethin' a bit easier, not quite so . . . aw hell, you know.'

'That's done, then.' Dai and Greasy rose simultaneously. 'Let's go to the mess deck, see if the chips are cooked.'

As they passed Mal, still diligently polishing, another deck-hand overtook them and paused to speak.

'I heard Mal just now; says it every trip 'e does. Always signs off . . . then signs on again when we sail. It's in the bloomin' blood, this lark is. You can't just walk away.'

'Try me!' Greasy said. 'Once I'm 'ome in the 'Pool – jest try me!'

Biddy slept jerkily on a bench in Lime Street station and woke, stiff and aching. She went to work, did her best to do all that she should, and asked Miss Whitney and Miss Harborough if they could suggest anything. Miss Whitney rolled her eyes.

'Christmas only nine days away and you're wanting time off to search for a room?' she said coldly. 'It won't do, Bridget. Look in the *Echo*, ask your friends, but don't keep taking time off.'

Biddy did her best to get somewhere, but with Christmas rapidly approaching and with her penniless state, she could find no one willing to take her on without even a week's rent in advance.

On Biddy's second night of sleeping rough the really bad cold weather suddenly set in. She reached Lime Street station late, too late to secure a bench, so cycled off again, this time to the cathedral. She found a shelter for the workmen and crawled inside, but had a disturbed night, largely due to her own nightmares, which woke her at hourly intervals, convinced she was about to be discovered and charged with trespass by some very large, very unfriendly police constable.

On the third night she left work on time and went straight to the railway station, staking her claim to a good bench which was against a wall and therefore warmer than those in the middle of the forecourt. She had just fallen asleep, or so it seemed, when she was rudely awoken by a hand on her shoulder and a voice in her ear, both appearing more dreadful to her sleep-fuddled mind than they proved to be once she was properly awake. A very dirty old tramp was shouting at her, telling her that he always slept here and who did she think she was, stealing an old man's favourite kip? If she was catching a train, he told her querulously, she should use the waiting room, not his bench, and if she was not catching a train then she should leg it before he told the scuffers on her.

Biddy dared not leave her bicycle on the station; even with the chain on the back wheel and the padlock securing it, anyone could lift the machine onto a train and then tackle her security system at their leisure, so she did not take the old man's advice about the waiting room, nor did she try to argue with him over his right to the seat, though she did mutter something about possession being nine-tenths of the law. But he gaped uncomprehendingly and gave her a shove, so she and her bicycle left the station in the coldest and most depressing hour of the day, just before dawn, and she began to cycle slowly down Lime Street, wondering drearily whether she could continue to keep on the move until the shop opened, or whether she would presently fall asleep, bicycle or no bicycle, and be killed in a spectacular crash.

When she reached Ranelagh Street she turned into it and got off the machine. She began to push it along the pavement, without any clear objective in view, trying to wipe her nose on her sleeve as she did so, for the night was perishingly cold and she thought she was catching a chill. When she reached Millicent's Modes she turned into the doorway, and was pleasantly surprised at how warm it felt after the draughts on Lime Street Station and the cold of the streets.

This was not so bad after all! She glanced cautiously around but the road appeared to be empty, so she propped her bicycle across the entrance so that she was shut in by it, and with numb fingers chained the rear wheel and fastened the padlock. Then she undid her bedroll and hung one thin blanket over the bicycle. This was marvellous, her own little room! With even that slight shelter, things improved considerably, so she wrapped the remaining blanket round her shoulders, put her pillow in the corner where the shop window and the door met, and lay down.

Three nights earlier she would have found it impossible to sleep, on a frosty night, in a shop doorway wrapped only in a blanket, but after the worry and sleeplessness which had already been her lot, she could scarcely keep her eyes open. She felt safe here, far safer than on the station, and it was wonderfully private and, after the open streets, wonderfully warm. Biddy lay awake for about two minutes reminding herself that she must not be found here in the morning and then she simply fell asleep and knew no more.

She awoke, once again, to find someone shaking her and a voice complaining bitterly about something.

'You wicked, ungrateful . . . what do you mean by it, sleeping in the doorway of the very shop which employs you! Get up at once and be off and don't bother to come back! Yes, I'm giving you the sack, my lady, and richly you deserve it, too! Bridget O'Shaughnessy, will you wake up!'

Biddy opened dazed, sleep-filled eyes. Immediately she realised that her worst nightmares had come true. Miss Whitney and Miss Harborough stood over her, identical expressions of amazement on their well-bred faces, whilst she struggled to her feet, almost overcome with fear and humiliation.

'I'm – I'm truly sorry,' Biddy stammered, trying to roll up her bedding with fingers that were all thumbs. 'I c-couldn't find l-lodgings, everyone wanted a w-week's rent in advance . . . I did explain . . . '

There was quite an audience now; staff from other shops stared, their expressions amazed, as Miss Whitney and Miss Harborough heaped scorn on Biddy's head and explained to anyone – and everyone listening – that they had no idea the girl was sleeping rough, they paid her a good wage, she was frequently tipped . . . ah, the young these days, no sense of responsibility, no pride in themselves . . .

Biddy finished off her bedroll and took the padlock off the rear wheel of the bicycle. Miss Whitney could not mean to dismiss her just because she had had her money stolen, lost her possessions, was in dire straits! But it soon became apparent that Miss Whitney meant to do exactly that.

'Take yourself off, Bridget, and be thankful that I did not send for a policeman and give you over to him for trespass,' she said coldly, once the crowd had dispersed and the three of them and the bicycle had gone down the entry and in at the back entrance of the shop. 'I'm not saying you've not done a good job of the delivering, but we really cannot put up with this. The shame of it!'

'Where did you think I was sleeping, Miss Whitney?' Biddy asked tearfully, standing beside the bicycle and patting its saddle as though it were in truth her trusty steed. 'I told you a girl at my lodgings had stolen my savings and I'd been forced to leave, I told you I hadn't managed to find anywhere else . . . I even asked you for advice, asked if you could help! I had no choice but to sleep somewhere!'

'There are cheap places for young people to stay in the city, I know there are,' Miss Whitney said forbiddingly. 'But you did not intend to search in your own time, oh no! You preferred to trespass on both our good nature and our premises . . . it won't do, Bridget. You may leave at once . . . and do stop patting the bicycle in that absurd way!'

Biddy took her hand off the bicycle as if she had been stung. She stared at Miss Whitney for a long moment, then swung round to stare at Miss Harborough. That lady had the grace to look very embarrassed and uncomfortable.

'Miss Whitney . . . I understand how you feel, with Christmas coming up and everything, but although we rarely see Captain or Mrs Goring they do own Millicent's Modes and they might be highly displeased to find you had dismissed Miss O'Shaughnessy . . . deep though her fault has been there are mitigating circumstances . . . '

'Nonsense, Miss Harborough,' Miss Whitney said coldly. 'Take your things, Bridget, and please don't return here.'

'But Miss Whitney, who'll do the deliveries for you? And . . . and you owe me four days' wages,' Biddy said wildly. 'I am in desperate circumstances, you know that. If you really mean to turn me out, then I must have my wages for the past four days.'

For one truly dreadful moment she thought that Miss Whitney was just going to refuse to hand over a penny of the money owing, but the older woman hesitated, then shrugged sharply and moved out into the shop itself.

'Very well,' she said over her shoulder. 'I'll pay you the money owing, though in view of your behaviour I feel I should be justified . . . '

'It's her nephew,' Miss Harborough suddenly hissed. She was pink-faced and plainly agitated. 'Her nephew's been sacked from Lewises for prigging two pair o' gloves an' a silver gauze purse. He wants a job in time for Christmas. Oh Biddy, I do feel bad, she's been hoping to get rid of you for days, but she's no right . . . oh, my dear child . . . '

'Here you are,' Miss Whitney said. She gave Biddy a handful of small silver and copper. 'I think you'll find that's right. Goodbye, Bridget, and I hope that when you get employment again you give more . . . '

But Biddy, with her carpet bag weighing her down on the left side, the can of paraffin on her right and her bedroll under her arm, was trudging wearily across to the shop door, her head down and despair in her heart. What on earth was she to do? She could scarcely go to Mrs Bradley's place now, with no job to bring a little money in and no savings. If she went to the police station and explained her plight she would be kindly but firmly put in the workhouse . . . what on earth was she to do?

'Well I never did! Not a word of gratitude for my giving her money when I could just as well have said she was being sacked without a character and had no right to a penny-piece!'

That was Miss Whitney, her annoyance at Biddy walking away whilst she was in mid-telling-off clear. Biddy heard Miss Harborough murmur what might have been an expostulation, but she took no notice and did not so much as turn her head.

Things are bad, they could scarcely be worse, Biddy told herself as the cold air outside the shop made her nose start to run again and brought tears to her eyes. But at least, now she's sacked me, I don't have to listen to that sanctimonious old bitch going on and on. At least I can just walk away from her!

The *Greenland Bess* docked in Number One fish dock at noon. The previous night everyone aboard slept the sleep of the just, whilst bunks scarcely moved, beer bottles stayed where you stood them down and dreams were of shore-going, not of the monstrous dangers of the deep.

'We're ahead of the others,' the Mate said as they chugged gently up the Humber towards the dock. 'We'll get a good price.'

Seagulls had screamed out to welcome her in as she came up past Flamborough Head and Spurn Point. Now they held their positions on rail and mast and superstructure, swaying as the small ship swayed, heads turning, bright eyes questing for the fish that they could smell but could not, as yet, see.

Men looked different in their shore-going clothes; smaller, less aggressive and sure of themselves. Bright ties, suits with over-bold stripes, shoes with lift heels. The clothes themselves seemed ill-at-ease on the tanned toughness of the distant-water trawlermen. But Dai and Greasy joined the others to queue at the office to be paid off, with their bonuses all worked out plus their wages for the month's voyage.

'Signing on in a fortnight?' The clerk asked each man. 'All being well she'll sail then; she'll be in dry-dock ten, maybe twelve days.'

'Yeah, might as well,' Greasy replied. 'If we're back in time, of course. We're goin' 'ome to Liverpool for Christmas.'

It was only then that Dai realised their fortnight would include the holiday and felt a sharp stab of homesickness. Oh to be going back to Moelfre and to his home in the street which would up from the harbour to the top of the cliff! To see Bethan's loving smile, to boast of his adventures, to tell tall stories . . .

Still. Not much joy to be got out of home right now, not with Davy set against him and Sîan married and gone. Make the best of it, mun, he urged himself, signing the book. And see this Gallagher woman while you're about it. No harm. And it was Mam's last wish, after all.

They wasted no time but went straight to the railway station, which was close to the docks so that the fish spent as little time as possible in transit.

'We can't warn 'em we're comin', but that won't

marrer,' Greasy said confidently as he and Dai boarded the train and dived into an empty carriage. 'Me Mam'll 'ang the flags out whatever.'

'What about an uninvited guest, though?' Dai said rather uneasily. It seemed hard on Mrs O'Reilly to be descended upon by not one, but two. 'You're always saying the house is crammed with O'Reillys, how'll she cope with an Evans, and all?'

'We'll stop off at Great Homer Street an' buy some grub an' some bottled beer, mebbe some sweets for the littl'uns; nothin' fancy, mind. An' you've got your bedroll so she won't need more blankets,' Greasy pointed out blithely. 'She won't worry none; me Mam's norra worrier.'

'Right. And of course I'll go round to Mrs Gallagher's as soon as I can, and then I'll probably be staying there,' Dai agreed.

He did not, in fact, anticipate that an old friend of his mother's would ask him to sleep over, but he did not intend to embarrass the O'Reillys by his presence over Christmas. I'll get a bed in one of the Seamen's Missions, he told himself. Or even in a boarding house, heaven knows I could afford it. But I'll not spend more than two nights with Greasy's folk, it wouldn't be fair, no matter what Greasy may say.

It made him feel better to have made a decision and for the rest of the journey he slept. One thing about distant-water trawling, he told himself drowsily, waking once when the train clattered into a tiny station and heaved itself to a stop. One thing about it is that it stretches you fully, mind and body, so that you're grateful, at the end of a voyage, just for time to yourself to sleep and relax.

Cross-country travel is never easy, but they managed somehow to complete their journey only an hour or so after darkness had fallen. Dai tumbled out of the train, rubbing his eyes and coughing as the freezing, coal-scented air clutched at lungs which had been breathing the stuffy, smelly air of the overcrowded train for most of the day. But a trawler is all warmth and tobacco fumes below and the iced wine of an Arctic winter on deck, so he speedily recovered himself and stood, with his bed-roll under one arm and his bag at his feet, staring about him.

Because he was so tired and had slept so deeply it felt like the middle of the night to Dai, but glancing above his head, he saw from the face of the clock which hung above the concourse that it still lacked five minutes to seven o'clock. Good, they would be able to get to those shops Greasy had talked about, do their buying and still be back at Horatio Street before the O'Reillys settled down for the night. He turned to Greasy, who was standing there with a silly smirk on his face, just looking around him.

'Well, then? Do we walk, get a bus, or what?'

'Hey, less o' that, you iggerant bloody Taff,' Greasy said with great good humour. 'Ain't you never 'eard of Green Goddesses? Them's trams,' he added. 'Leckies. We'll get one 'ere what'll tek us straight where we wants to go. Eh, I can't wait to see me Mam again,' he added, then shot a conscience-stricken glance at his friend. 'Sorry, Taff, I forgot.'

'It's all right, it doesn't worry me,' Dai said gently. 'You've no cause to fret on my account.' He squared his shoulders and hefted his bedroll. 'Now where do we go to catch this "leckie" of yours?'

Chapter Seven

The two young men caught a tram which would take
them to Great Homer Street where they would do their
shopping. As the tram buzzed along through the gas-lit
streets, Greasy entertained Dai with stories of Paddy's
Market, where you could buy anything in the world you
wanted, probably for less than a bob. He also pointed out
local landmarks, including St George's Hall, which was
almost opposite Lime Street station, and the Free Library
and Museum, which looked like a palace to Dai. In fact
by the time the tram deposited them on Great Homer
Street, Dai was really looking forward to exploring the
city.

'It's a far cry from Holyhead,' he said ruefully, looking
out at the streets, still bustling with shoppers at eight
o'clock at night. 'I bet even London's no bigger or busier
than this.'

'I bet you're right, wack,' Greasy said contentedly,
steering his friend round a group of revellers outside a
pub and then accompanying him into a large provisions
shop, where it seemed to Dai's dazzled eyes that every
possible eatable was on sale. 'Now 'ave a look around,
then we'll decide what to buy.'

They were well-laden by the time they left the shop.
They had decided on a bag of oranges and another of
nuts, a slab of sultana cake and another of marble cake, a
big square of margarine and a slightly smaller one of
butter, a very large and smelly cartwheel of cheese and a
bag of mixed sweets, including the famous Everton mints.

'This'll keep 'em quiet for a week,' Greasy remarked, one cheek bulging with an Everton mint. 'It's 'ard for me Mam to manage, even wi' our Pete an' me both givin' her the allotment from our wages – no marrer 'ow she tries, the money don't stretch to feedin' eight kids, norrin winter, anyroad.'

'We didn't buy meat,' Dai said suddenly. 'Where's a butcher? I'll get a joint of some description, or a bird. Would they like a bird?'

'Best wait afore we buy a bird, in case Mam's got somethin', but you're right, they'll enjoy some meat. Now lemme think ... I gorrit ... sausages! There's a pork butcher on the corner up 'ere ...'

They were heading for the pork butcher when, ahead of them, a fight started on the pavement. At least, it sounded like a fight; sharp cries, a woman's shriek and then the thud and slap of flesh on flesh had Dai and Greasy, already heavily laden, in two minds whether to turn aside or go and take a look.

'We'd best get back,' Dai said. 'No point in us sticking our noses in; one look at a seaman's jersey and some people ...'

'We've gorra go that way, that's where the butcher is,' Greasy pointed out. 'Besides, wharrever it is'll be over by the time we get there.'

They pushed their way through the crowd thronging the pavement and discovered the most extraordinary scene. A big, burly man and a very much smaller person seemed to be disputing the ownership of a tattered carpet bag. The burly man was shouting that he was being robbed whilst the other said nothing, being too busy simply hanging on whilst the burly man hit out wildly and shook the bag – and the young person who held it – as a terrier shakes a rat.

Dai stepped forward. 'Stow that,' he said sharply,

grabbing the big man by the shoulder. 'No need to hit him, you're twice his size. Anyroad, it's easy to settle this particular argument. What's in the bag, mister?'

The man stopped slapping but he continued to try to tug the bag out of the other's hands. Dai glanced at his opponent and realised all in a moment that it wasn't a lad, as he had assumed, but a young girl. He caught a glimpse of tangled dark curls, large, furiously flashing blue eyes, and a mouth shut as tightly and as determinedly as a trap, before the burly man made another attempt to take the bag and, when the girl hung on, he swung his fist at her, catching her a glancing blow on the side of the head.

The girl winced, but hung on – actually came back to the attack. She kicked out, hard, and the man kicked right back so that she had to dodge, which she managed to do without once releasing her hold on the bag.

Dai, however, was having no more of this; other bystanders might think it amusing, but he did not intend to stand by whilst a very large man beat a very small girl.

'One more move from you and I'll flatten you, boyo,' he growled, grabbing the man's wrists in an iron grip. 'Where was you dragged up, eh? Hitting a lady!'

'Some lady – thievin' bitch, more like,' the burly one growled. His big, beefy hands were still clamped round the handles of the carpet bag. 'Mind your own business, you bloody nosy taff.'

All Dai's chivalrous instincts were aroused by this piece of nastiness. He gave a growl and transferred one hand to the burly one's nose whilst still retaining his hold on the other man's thick wrists. He tweaked it savagely so that the man shouted. The small girl, still hanging onto the carpet bag, gave a tiny, breathless giggle.

'Manners,' Dai said breathlessly. 'Now tell the lady you're sorry for using language before her.'

The man, mindful of Dai's grip on his nose, muttered something which could have been an apology and Greasy, who was standing guard over the shopping and personal possessions which Dai had dropped when he grabbed the man, leaned forward at this point and put his oar in.

'You wanna pick on someone your own size, matie! 'Sides, it's simple to solve the problem, as me bezzie said – what's in the bag, eh? You say first, 'ardclock, an' the lady says next.'

The big man began to bluster, but the two young seamen were determined and Dai's grip on his wrists was not to be denied. Dai had not spent a year hauling a trawl to stand any nonsense from a blubbery, cowardly sneak-thief, which, he had decided after one glance from the girl's blue eyes, was an accurate description of the burly one.

'Why should I say, eh? Wha' business is it of yourn?'

The girl, still clinging onto the bag, spoke out then. She had a clear, unaccented voice and she spoke with confidence, though her face was grimed with dirt and streaked with tears. 'I can tell you what's in it, since I packed it this morning! There's a change of underwear, a pillow, a blanket, six pennies and three ha'pence, a heel of bread, a bit of cheese, and a rag doll. That's all.'

'Them's ... them's me old woman's clothes ... me little daughter's stuff,' the man began, but as he did so he loosed his hold on the carpet bag for an instant.

It was sufficient. The small girl wrenched her property out of the man's hands, turned like lightning, and wiggled away through the crowd. Dai tried to follow her and tripped over his bedroll and Greasy thrust the shopping into his arms and told him, crisply, that he'd done his bit and now they'd best stop being unpaid scuffers and get into the butcher's before they closed.

'Yes, but we got to find that girl, mun,' Dai protested, pushing his way through the dispersing crowd. 'She's no guttersnipe, no sneak-thief – why did she run away from us? We were trying to help her!'

Greasy shook his head pityingly. 'She din't look like a thief, but she run away, so she may 'ave been,' he said sagely. 'She'll be awright, Taff – look at the way she 'ammered that feller's shins wit' 'er boots. Anyone what can kick like that can tek care o' theirselves.'

'But she only had a few pennies, I was going to give her enough for a hot meal . . . it's a cold night, she must be sleeping rough or she wouldn't carry a pillow and blanket round with her. Look, I feel responsible. Find her I must and will!'

'Taff, you don't know this area an' I do,' Greasy said positively. 'There's a million sidestreets, two million courts, there's the docks, the railway stations, the ware'ouses . . . she could be in any one of 'em. If she don't wanna be found, an' she don't, or she wouldn't ha' legged it, she won't be found. So we'll buy them sossies an' get back to 'Oratio Street; right?'

Dai heaved a sigh and looked desperately about him. There were faces all around, but none of them were crowned by tumbled black curls or owned a pair of big, scared blue eyes. 'Yeah, all right,' he agreed reluctantly. 'But 'ave a look round first thing in the morning I will though; might catch her in a doorway or something.'

'An' you might not,' Greasy pointed out. ' 'Ere's me Mam's favourite butcher's . . . shall we say two pounds o' best pork?'

Dai, following his friend into the sawdust-strewn shop, agreed that two pounds of best pork sausages sounded just about right, but he spoke absently; his mind was still fretting at his problem. He really must find that girl, it was his duty to find her.

All the way back to Horatio Street, all the time he was meeting the family, eating fried sausages with doorsteps of bread, laying out his bedroll on the back-bedroom floor, he thought about her. Quite a small girl, with a dark coat and a dirty face, stout boots and a great deal of determination. He did not know her name or her age or anything about her, save that she owned an old carpet bag with all her worldly possessions neatly packed away in it. He knew she would pack neatly; even in her present miserable circumstances she would be as neat as possible, he was sure of it.

When he was wrapped up in his blanket and preparing for sleep, the picture of her as she had looked up at him popped back into his mind. She was pretty, but he had seen prettier. She had courage, but girls who had grit and determination abounded. His Mam must have looked like that when she, too, had been just a girl. But in Wales, small, Celtic-looking girls with black hair and blue eyes abound. So what was it, then? Why did he have this conviction that she was special to him, that he must not lose her?

But though he fretted away at the problem for several moments it refused to be solved. Something in him had reached out to something in her, and from that moment on he had known he must find her again. Fate? Fellow-feeling? He had no idea.

But what did it matter, after all? I will find her, he told himself, settling down. I'll find her again if it takes me the rest of my life.

And on the thought, he slept.

Biddy, with her carpet bag firmly clutched to her bosom and her heart pumping like a traction engine in her chest, flew along the pavement, not having to push or shove since she was small and slim enough to get between the people fairly easily.

That awful, frightening old man! He had almost got her bag, the only thing left now between her and destitution! She wished she could have stayed to thank the seaman who had rescued her . . . she had heard him calling after her and had felt she was acting shabbily in running away from him as well as from the burly one, but she had little choice. She dared not risk losing anything more.

Her beautiful, hand-knitted woollen blanket had gone two nights previously, prigged whilst actually cuddled round her person. A young man with a wolfish face and a foreign accent had snatched it and gone . . . she had been happy to see him go, even with her blanket tucked under his arm. He had a really evil face, and he was flourishing a long, narrow-bladed knife which she was convinced he would have used without compunction had she tried to resist the theft.

The streets were a dangerous place indeed – now she knew the truth of the oft-repeated warning. She could have had her throat slit just for the possession of her blanket – that man just now had been prepared to beat her in front of a great many people and to lie boldly, just to get his hands on a bag containing he knew not what.

So Biddy, still clutching her bag, made her way rapidly along Great Homer Street and did not look back. She had found a safe place and she intended to go there and stay there until morning.

The 'safe place' was a shed in which a market trader kept his barrow, his awning and some of his unsold goods. Biddy had found the shed earlier in the day – found, too, the boards at the back which were loose and could be wriggled aside to let a small person slip in. She had spent the previous night here very cosily, bedding down on the gaily striped awning, and had only left the shed, in fact, to go and get herself some food.

Now, Biddy let herself into the shed, put the boards up again, and glanced contentedly around her. Some wrinkled apples would help out the bread and the cheese, and she had filled her ginger-beer bottle with water earlier, so she would have a drink as well. It was scarcely stealing, she told herself, biting into a small and wrinkled apple, to take market fades, especially such poor ones. And she had to live. Besides, the man who had stolen her blanket had not done so to fill his stomach but probably so that he could sell it. She, at least, stole from an urgent desire to keep body and soul together.

Kneeling on the awning, she opened her bag, got out her remaining blanket, her pillow and Dolly. She made up the bed, then sat back on her heels and fished bread and cheese out of the bag. The bottle full of water had been left under a fold in the awning – it was still there, she got it out and stood it handy – so now her evening meal was complete.

She ate quickly, for she was hungry, and as she ate she allowed her mind to go back to the incident on Great Homer Street earlier in the evening.

He had been awfully kind, that young seaman. Nice looking, too. She could see his face in her mind's eye clear as clear – the bunched up dark curls, the square-jawed, determined face, the dark and peaceful eyes. Yes, he was very nice looking, and she had hated running away from him – I felt more like running towards him, she remembered ruefully, more like just throwing myself into his arms and saying 'Look after me, because I'm so tired out with trying to look after myself!'

But you couldn't do things like that, of course, or only in your dreams. A young man would scarcely respect a girl who did that, the very first time they laid eyes on each other.

And yet . . . there had been something in those liquid dark eyes when they met her own, some message of familiarity and affection, as though they had known one another long ago and far away.

Bridget O'Shaughnessy, you are a sentimental little fool and you read too many of those stories in Peg's Paper, Biddy told herself. Love at first sight is just one of those silly, romantic stories which never happen in real life – I mean how could it? How could you just to look at a man and know he's the one for you? He could be married and a wife-beater, he could be an active white-slaver, he could be the sort of sailor who has a wife in every port! Forget him, she advised herself as she finished her food and began to pull her blanket about her. Forget him and start thinking how you will spend tomorrow. The young man is nothing to you and never will be, so put him right out of your head.

If it had been left to her sensible, practical mind, she would probably have obeyed and forgotten him, but her far from sensible and very susceptible heart had been touched, and refused to allow Biddy to forget that strong, calm face, the tanned hands which had rescued her, the logic which had proved who owned the carpet bag beyond doubt. He would always be special to her, it would be a long time before she stopped hoping to glimpse him again as she roamed the Liverpool Streets.

But only so I can thank him, of course, she told herself primly just before she fell asleep. I owe him my thanks, at least.

Oh, what a little liar, her heart remarked conversationally, when she was on the very edge of slumber. *You don't want to thank him and walk away, you want to be with him, get to know him . . . love him.*

And since Biddy's sensible mind had already fallen asleep, her heart continued to insert the seaman's sturdy figure and beautiful, dark-eyed face into her dreams all the night long.

It was strange, because when she woke next morning Biddy could not remember any of her dreams, though the face of her rescuer was indelibly printed on her mind, but something had definitely come over her. The sense of worthlessness, the conviction that she would never get a job, was a nuisance to friend and foe alike and might just as well be dead, had completely disappeared. Instead, she woke feeling positive, energetic and determined. She would stop being so foolish this very day! She would go to the Bradley house in Samson Court, off Paul Street, and explain that things had gone very wrong for her. She would ask permission to have a good wash, would borrow a clean skirt and jumper off Ellen, and would then go out, job-hunting. And, she told herself firmly, you will find a job and a good one too, because you're worthy of work. Everyone who has employed you in the past has been pleased with you, even horrible Miss Whitney had only sacked her because she slept in the shop doorway and Miss Whitney had a nephew who needed a job.

This sudden rush of self-confidence did not leave her either, when she crawled carefully out of the back of the shed, towing her bag behind her. It did not even falter when she remembered she had left her ginger-beer bottle behind . . . if she had done such a thing yesterday she would have burst into floods of tears and wished herself dead once more. What a difference that young man's championing of me has made, Biddy thought, raking her fingers through her hair and then setting off at a brisk trot. If she kept up a good pace she could be in Paul Street in no time.

Biddy arrived at the Bradley house just as the eldest son, Henry, was going off to work. He grinned at her, self-conscious in a jacket, with a tie round his neck. ' 'Ello, Biddy, you're around early! Wanna see our Ellie? She's still in bed, lazy trollop!'

'Hello, Henry,' Biddy said. 'Yes, I'd like to see Ellen. Can I go in?'

'Sure. Mam's gerrin' brekky for them as 'as time to eat it.'

He grinned again, then hurried out of the court and into Paul Street.

Biddy knocked gently on the door, then opened it. 'Cooee! It's me, Biddy,' she called. 'Can I come in, Mrs Bradley?'

Mrs Bradley's round and cheerful face appeared in the kitchen doorway. 'Oh, hello, Biddy,' she said at once. 'Don't 'over out on the doorstep, come right inside, queen. Our Ellie's been rare worried about you. She's in bed now though . . . want a spot o' brekky?'

'I wouldn't mind,' Biddy said, her mouth watering at the smell of tea and porridge which was wafting through into the front room. 'Mrs Bradley, I've come to ask a favour. Can I have a wash and borrow a skirt and jumper off Ellen? You see . . .'

The sad little story was soon told. Mrs Bradley, bustling round the kitchen with the porridge pot, tutted. 'You should ha' come 'ere at once, queen, we don't 'ave much, but what we do 'ave we share. 'Ere, get that down you.'

Hot tea tasted marvellous, the porridge better. Biddy tried to eat and drink slowly but somehow it was all

207

gone in no time and she was eyeing the loaf.

'There's margarine in the cupboard and a scrape o' jam,' Mrs Bradley said, cutting a hefty slice off the loaf. 'Go on, fill up. You're a growin' girl . . .' she laughed, '. . . like our Ellen,' she added. 'She's still fat, is our Ellen. You go up an' 'ave a word when you've ate.'

'I will,' Biddy said thickly through bread and marge. It had never tasted so good . . . and the tea was sheer heaven after so long on water. 'I'm going to ask her if I can borrow a skirt and jumper. I – I've not been able to wash my things and I didn't bring much away with me anyway. I left in such a rush.'

But before she could go upstairs, there was a heavy thumping and Ellen came down. She was, as her mother had said, still large, but she beamed with delight to see Biddy and came running across the room to give her a kiss. 'Oh, Bid, I've been so worried about you! I went into Millie's an' that sour-faced lemon wouldn't tell me where you was, only that you didn't work there no more.'

'She sacked me,' Biddy said briefly. 'I've been sleepin' rough.'

Ellen squeaked and put a hand to her mouth. 'Sleeping rough? Oh, Biddy, why didn't you come 'ere?'

'I don't know. I think I was a bit mad,' Biddy admitted. 'But I'm here now, Ellen. I'm going to borrow a skirt and jumper off you, if you don't mind, and have a wash, and then I'm going to apply for some jobs. I think I could ask Miss Harborough to give me a reference, because she was cross with Miss Whitney for sacking me, said it wasn't right.'

'Course you can borrow some clo'es; I can't wear any o' me nice stuff,' Ellen said regretfully. 'Want a squint at the *Echo*?'

'Oh, please! I've missed seeing the paper terribly,'

Biddy admitted. 'Not that there'll be anything for me, I don't suppose,' she added rather gloomily, 'with Christmas only a couple of days away they won't want shop staff.'

Ellen fetched the *Echo* and sat down opposite Biddy at the kitchen table. She handed the paper to her friend and took the bowl of porridge her mother was holding out. 'Ta, Mam. I know what you mean about shop work, but there's other jobs. . .'

Biddy's eye scanned the pages keenly, then she put the paper down, shaking her head. 'No shop work, or not the sort I could do, anyway. But I do wonder about one of the Register Offices? There's several of them about, that I do know.'

'One I can't forget is Bradley's, on Bold Street,' Ellen said with a giggle. 'Not that I ever tried there, because it's Domestic Servants, of course. But Mrs Aspinall's Registry, at No. 35 Bold Street, is well thought of, so I've heard. There wouldn't be any harm in trying there . . . but don't go until after Christmas, dear Biddy! Spend Christmas here!'

'I'd love to, but I can't risk missing out on a job,' Biddy told her. 'Someone may have been let down, or need a servant badly, I can't risk waiting and then finding everyone is suited. Look, I'll walk round there this morning, see what the situation is, then come back here tonight, if you're sure you don't mind.'

'Mind? We'll be real upset if you don't come back to us,' Ellen said vigorously. 'Wharra friends for, eh? I shan't forget what you did for me when I were in trouble.'

'You'll be in trouble right now, my lady, if you don't get your breakfas' ate and yourself and the baby down to the clinic,' Mrs Bradley said. 'Go on Biddy, you run upstairs an' 'ave a wash, then get into our Ellie's skirt an' jumper. An' don't go toting that bag off, call back later.

209

A job's easier to find if you're not cartin' your 'ome on your back, so to speak. There's a grey pleated skirt wi' a blue jumper . . . you'd look a treat in that. Ah, don't forget the jug o' water, I hotted you some special.'

Biddy went up the stairs and washed and changed, reappearing presently in the blue jumper and grey skirt. She had washed her hair and dried it, then tied it into a neat tail at the back of her head, using a length of Ellen's blue ribbon, secure in the knowledge that her friend would not mind. Now she stood anxiously at the foot of the stairs, watching her friend's expression. 'Do I look all right? Good enough to get a job?'

'Good enough to eat,' Ellen said exuberantly. 'Come on, we'll put each other on the leckie, an' we'll see you tonight. Don't be late, 'cos I made some curtains for Mrs Gregory last week an' tonight we're 'avin' mutton scouse to celebrate. You don' wanna miss that!'

'I'll be back,' Biddy said thankfully. 'Don't worry, Ellen, I'll be back.'

Bold Street was in a smart area of the city, but Biddy, thanks to her job as a delivery girl, knew most of it by heart. She had never actually visited any of the Employment Registers – there were three on Bold Street alone – but she always lingered when passing the Lyceum, the Liverpool Library, and Liberty's wonderful window displays.

Now, however, she ignored the lures of theatre, books and fabulous dresses and materials and went straight to the Employment Register run by Mrs Jane Aspinall. She lingered outside for a moment or two, adjusting her little hat – well, Ellen's little hat – and smoothing away a stray wisp of hair, but then she went inside.

It was a pleasant, bright little room with a long

counter, behind which sat two ladies. They looked up and smiled as Biddy entered, then looked down again. There were telephones before them, and large ledgers. It all looked very businesslike. Biddy wondered doubtfully whether she had been right to come.

Walking over to the counter she cleared her throat. The lady nearest her looked up again and smiled encouragingly. 'Yes, madam?'

It reminded Biddy sharply and poignantly of her friend Mr Meehan. Just as soon as she had a job she would go round and see him again and he would probably tell her that she had been silly not to come before. Why on earth had she panicked the way she had and kept away from all her friends? But the woman was looking at her enquiringly, so she gathered her wits and spoke.

'Good morning. I'm looking for a position in someone's house, as – as a domestic servant. I would like to live in, if that's possible.'

The woman was grey-haired with a pair of rather small but very shrewd brown eyes. 'Ah, yes. Parlour maid? Kitchen work? What previous experience have you, Miss...er...? My name is Mrs Edmonds, incidentally.'

'O'Shaughnessy; Bridget O'Shaughnessy. Experience? Well, I ran the home for my mother whilst she was ill,' Biddy said a little uncertainly. 'I've worked at a small sweetshop where the owner expected me to do the laundry, clean the house and cook the meals when she was otherwise occupied, but lately I've worked for a gown shop – Millicent's Modes. I'm sure they'll give me a reference, if you would like one.'

'Hmm. Let me see what's wanted at present. Cook general? Do you think you could do that sort of thing?'

Honesty forbade Biddy to agree completely. 'I'm not sure,' she said cautiously. 'If it was very simple cooking . . . but I can make confectionery, of course.'

'Wages?'

'Oh yes, I'd like to be paid,' Biddy said thoughtlessly, remembering Ma Kettle. The grey-haired lady gave her the sort of look idiots all over the world are probably used to receiving and Biddy, blushing, realised she had not given the expected reply. Trying to turn it into a joke, she added hastily, 'as much as possible, I suppose.'

A frosty look stole into the eyes of the woman behind the counter. 'Miss O'Shaughnessy, that is not the attitude you will be expected to display in domestic service, I suppose you realise that? We could not recommend anyone who . . .'

'I'm sorry, I wasn't really being impudent, it was because the lady I worked for at first didn't pay me any wages, just my keep,' Biddy said, her voice trembling a little. 'It – it wasn't a happy situation, so when you said "Wages?" I thought you meant . . .'

'Quite. A scandalous way to behave,' the grey-haired one said, appearing to relax a bit. 'However, perhaps you should discuss wages with your prospective employer rather than with myself. Now tell me, Miss O'Shaughnessy, why have you decided to apply for a job in domestic service? I don't hesitate to tell you that it is not as well paid as shop work and carries with it a certain . . . well, almost a stigma with some young people. They would prefer to work in a factory or shop, where at least their evenings and days off are entirely their own. In service, the mistress's wishes must always come first, even if it means you are working very much later than you had expected, or doing things which are not, strictly speaking, your job.'

Biddy took a deep breath. 'I was living with a family who were not honest,' she said. 'They stole my savings and when I gave them an hour to return my money or I would go to the sc . . . police . . . they went to the police at once and said that it was I who was the thief. So I left there; I had little choice. Now, I'm staying with friends in Paul Street, but it's a very overcrowded house already and I can't continue to live with them. So I thought . . . domestic service would mean I could live in, and I'd be paid a wage . . . it just seemed best.'

'Yes, by and large I agree with you. And why did you leave your last employer, Miss O'Shaughnessy?'

'Because a relative of Miss Whitney's came to the city and couldn't find work, and Miss Whitney decided to employ her relative in my place,' Biddy said promptly. 'But she was not dissatisfied with my work . . . I'm a hard and conscientious worker, Mrs Edmonds.'

The older woman stared at her very hard for a moment and then gave a little nod, as though she had read something she liked in Biddy's frank countenance. 'I shall give you a chance, Miss O'Shaughnessy. There's a lady who has a nice house just off the Boulevarde, in Ducie Street. Do you know it?'

'Yes, I know it,' Biddy said at once. 'It's close by Granby Street, isn't it?'

Mrs Edmonds looked surprised. 'Yes, that's right . . . you certainly do know the city, Miss O'Shaughnessy.'

Biddy smiled demurely. She did not intend to admit she'd been a delivery girl if she could avoid so doing. A shop assistant in a smart gown shop was much more acceptable to this sharp-eyed lady, she felt sure.

'Mrs Gallagher – that's the lady's name – needs a general servant, which usually means cooking, cleaning, answering the door etcetera. She has a woman in to do the rough scrubbing and so on. It's live-in, with all day Sunday and Thursday afternoons off, uniform provided, no other servant. Mrs Gallagher wants someone before Christmas, if possible, because her previous girl left some while ago and they haven't bothered to replace her since they've been away a lot. Oh, there are three in the family, Mr and Mrs Gallagher and a daughter of about fifteen, I believe.' She drew a pad of paper towards her. 'Would you like to go along for an interview? They are on the telephone, so I can ring her right now and we can arrange a suitable time.'

'Yes, that would be very nice,' Biddy said, hoping this was the expected response. Apparently it was, for Mrs Edmonds nodded and took the telephone receiver off its hook, though she kept her finger pressed down on the rest.

'Would you mind waiting over there, Miss O'Shaughnessy?' She indicated a chair set well back against the wall on the opposite side of the room.

Biddy went and sat in the chair. It was too far away for her to hear any of the ensuing conversation and in any case Mrs Edmonds deliberately pitched her voice low, but she could not help wondering what this Mrs Gallagher would be like – and Miss Gallagher, too. Miss Gallagher was only a year younger than herself, they might even become friends!

Presently Mrs Edmonds hung her receiver back on its hook and beckoned Biddy over. She folded the sheet of paper upon which she had been writing and slid it into an envelope which she then sealed and pushed across the counter. 'There you are, Miss O'Shaughnessy; a letter of introduction. Mrs Gallagher says if you catch the tram you can be with her quite soon, so she'll expect you when she sees you.' She paused delicately. 'I take it you have the tram fare, Miss O'Shaughnessy?'

Not for worlds would Biddy have admitted that her tram fare was also her dinner money. She nodded and smiled brightly, taking the envelope and slipping it into her coat pocket. 'Thank you, Mrs Edmonds. If – if I get the job do I come back?'

Mrs Edmonds shook her head. She was all smiles suddenly, as though simply seeing the last of Biddy was enough to cheer her up. 'No, Miss O'Shaughnessy. The rest of the business will be transacted entirely between Mrs Gallagher and myself. Good morning.'

It was a long walk out to Ducie Street, but Biddy was a good, fast walker when she set her mind to it. She was passed by two trams, but told herself that since Mrs Gallagher had said she would expect her when she saw her, she was unlikely to take against her just because she was perhaps a little later than she expected. Also, Biddy was quite shrewd enough to realise that someone who wanted a live-in servant by Christmas could probably not afford to be too fussy – everyone would prefer to spend the holiday at home or amongst friends rather than waiting on total strangers.

She reached Ducie Street at last and pulled the envelope out of her pocket. She glanced at the nearest house . . . not too far away, then. She walked on, found the right number and went up the short path to the door. For a moment she just stood there, suddenly sure she was making an awful mistake; she would be no good at this sort of thing, she had the wrong attitude. She had been nothing but a slave at Ma Kettle's, now she would find herself equally powerless, equally put-upon.

She very nearly turned and fled – but then she remembered the man who had stolen her blanket and the one who had tried to steal her carpet bag. She remembered the little house in Paul Street bulging with sixteen souls whilst poor Mrs Bradley scratted round to find everyone food and clothing.

She even remembered the baby Ellen had just had which would make life even harder for the Bradleys.

It would not be fair to run back to Samson Court and put upon her friends.

So she stood her ground and knocked, disciplining herself not to flee when she heard, from within the house, someone approaching the front door.

It was a pretty, slim woman with light brown hair and steady grey eyes. She had very pale skin and looked calm and self-assured – very different from me, Biddy thought; I'm a bundle of nerves. But when the woman smiled at her she smiled back, because it was a friendly and attractive smile.

'Good afternoon. Would you be Miss O'Shaughnessy? I'm Mrs Gallagher – do come in.'

Once in the hallway she held out her hand. 'How do you do? I'm afraid I'm not very good at this, Miss O'Shaughnessy, but if you'll come through to the kitchen perhaps you can watch whilst I prepare my husband's tea and we'll have a chat. It will give both of us some sort of idea . . .' her voice trailed away. 'This is the kitchen.'

The kitchen was nice and overlooked the back garden. It was modern by most standards, as modern as the house, with kitchen units all round the walls, bright linoleum on the floor, and a modern gas cooker as well as a blackened stove which probably heated the hot water as well as warming the kitchen itself.

'This is where most of the work's done, so I've tried to make it as up to date and pleasant as possible,' Mrs Gallagher said. 'As I'm sure Mrs Edmonds told you, there are only three of us, but we do entertain from time to time and we have quite a large dining-room.' She smiled at Biddy. 'Sit down, Miss O'Shaughnessy. Do you have a letter for me?'

Feeling her face go hot, Biddy guiltily produced the

envelope, looking a little the worse for wear, from her pocket. 'I'm sorry,' she said apologetically. 'This is the first time I've applied for a job in domestic service and I'm really rather nervous.' She had decided, on the spur of the moment, that she would much rather Mrs Gallagher knew the truth. That way, at least she was less likely to be disappointed if Biddy did not come up to expectations.

'Yes, so Mrs Edmonds says in the letter,' Mrs Gallagher said, having read the short note. 'I'll take you round the house, Miss O'Shaughnessy, show you the room you would have if you decided to take the position, and give you some idea of the work involved. I'm sure Mrs Edmonds told you that we have a woman in three times a week to do the rough work and a man who does the garden, cleans the boots and shoes and so on. But all the rest of the work will, I'm afraid, fall on your shoulders.'

'I don't mind hard work,' Biddy said. 'But I'm not sure my cooking is good enough . . . Mrs Edmonds said you needed a cook general . . .'

'I do most of the cooking myself,' Mrs Gallagher said gently. 'I enjoy cooking. But such things as peeling vegetables, preparing meat, making strawberry and raspberry preserve in the summer . . . things like that are easier with the work shared.'

'So long as I'm told what to do,' Biddy murmured. 'I don't want you to think I'm being difficult, but . . .'

'I think you're being sensible,' Mrs Gallagher assured her. 'Now just follow me and we'll do the rounds. . . . You can see the garden through the kitchen window, though there isn't much to see at this time of year, and only cabbages in the kitchen garden, which is right down the end, furthest away from the house.'

As she talked she was leading Biddy across a square

hall and she paused outside the first door she reached. 'The dining-room.'

It was a large room with an enormous table and a very grand mahogany sideboard. There were a dozen dining chairs upholstered in red leather, some pictures on the walls, a display of silver dishes on the sideboard and a large mirror behind them.

'You'd dust and clean generally in here, and help to serve food when we've guests,' Mrs Gallagher said, leading the way to the next room. 'Sitting-room.'

Another pleasant, large room, cluttered with chintz-covered chairs, occasional tables, several lamps, a wireless set and a quantity of strange objects plus a mass of coloured paper, whilst three young ladies, all aged about fourteen or fifteen, sprawled around a low central table on which was set out a large bowl of fruit, another of nuts, a jar of sticky paste and several pairs of scissors.

'My daughter, Elizabeth, the one with the plait, and a couple of her friends.' Mrs Gallagher raised her voice. 'Liz, you said making Christmas decorations, not eating all the nuts I've bought! Mind you clear up the shells.'

Liz of the long, light brown plait turned and grinned at Biddy. She was a pretty girl, lively and bright, wearing a deep pink woollen dress with a rather scruffy white apron over it.

'Sorry, Mam,' she said. 'We will clear up – and we *are* making Christmas decorations . . . see those beautiful chains and silver fir cones? . . . only it's hungry work, so we have raided the nuts rather, I'm afraid.'

'Well, never mind, there's still another couple of days before *the* day, so I suppose I can buy some more.' Mrs Gallagher withdrew, shutting the door gently behind her, and crossed the hall once more. She opened another door. 'My husband's study . . . not too large, and he's pretty tidy. He works for the newspaper, so he needs a telephone in here and we have another in the hall. Also we have one by our bed, because sometimes the newspaper needs him at night. He's a tidy type, my dear old Stuart, but he does hate things being moved, so since we don't want him having an apoplexy I always advise anyone cleaning in here to avoid so much as touching the papers all over the desk and if there is a pile of papers on the floor, just to leave them. He's very sweet tempered really, and extremely patient, but now and then he does *roar*, which frightens my charlady, Mrs Wrexham, dreadfully. At first she used to cower in the kitchen biting her nails and trembling, but she's grown accustomed now and takes no more notice than I do. Now that's all that need worry you down here; that room,' she gestured to her left, 'is a small downstairs cloakroom and the other door is just a glory hole for tennis racquets, boots, sleds and so on. Now we'll go upstairs and take a look at the bedrooms.'

There were five bedrooms on the first floor and two attic rooms. The bedrooms seemed the height of luxury to Biddy, especially Elizabeth's. It was all decorated in pink and white, with the prettiest curtains and a lovely, thick white rug, and Elizabeth had her own gas fire and a gas-ring, too, so that she could make herself a hot drink whilst she was up here studying.

'We want her to be comfortable and to consider study a pleasure,' Mrs Gallagher said simply. 'She's a clever girl, but she gets lonely, sometimes. And I must admit she makes a lot of work and does throw her things around rather, besides filling the house with young people and coming in for meals at odd hours . . . dashing upstairs and traipsing mud all through the place. However! This is our room, the dressing room's next door. I always do our rooms so you won't have to come in here unless I need a hand with something. The other rooms on this floor are just spare bedrooms, though they'll be in use this Christmas. I have a – a younger sister, Mrs Lilac Prescott she is now; she and her husband and their small children will be coming to stay over Christmas which is why I really am rather keen to get someone before then.' She looked ruefully over at Biddy, her eyes smiling though her mouth was serious. 'My sister is a dear girl and will do all she can to help, but her twins . . . well, they're really the naughtiest little boys you could imagine . . . does this put you off, Miss O'Shaughnessy?'

For the first time since she had entered the house, Biddy laughed. She liked Mrs Gallagher, she liked the sound of the sister, the awful twins, Liz and her friends thundering through the house scattering mud, Mr Gallagher *roaring* if his papers were touched. Even Mrs Wrexham the charlady, cowering in a corner and biting her nails because 'the master' was cross, sounded nice somehow. There was a cheerful informality about the Gallagher household which appealed to Biddy.

'No, Mrs Gallagher, it doesn't put me off, it makes me think I could be very happy here,' she said therefore. 'May I see the attic rooms, please?'

'Oh mercy, I always said honesty was the best policy,' Mrs Gallagher exclaimed. 'The rooms are both yours . . . I mean they go with the job, since you might yet turn me down! Follow me.'

They scampered up the attic stairs like a couple of kids, Biddy thought afterwards, and there were two small white doors, one to the left, one to the right, with a square landing in between. Intriguing doors, Biddy decided, staring at them. What was behind them?

'Bedroom,' Mrs Gallagher said, flinging open the left-hand door. 'Gas fire, in case it's cold, which it jolly well is right now. Single bed, plenty of blankets, a chair, a rug and of course wardrobe, chest of drawers . . . all the usual offices.'

'Very nice,' Biddy murmured. It was a delightful room, truly delightful, with every evidence of thoughtfulness and welcome.

'Yes, it is nice, isn't it? Liz said she wouldn't mind moving up here, so we guessed a girl could be happy, here. And the living-room.' She opened the right-hand door and gestured Biddy past her. 'What do you think?'

It was charming. The low window was curtained in warm red velvet and the rug was red with garlands of flowers. A small dining-table and two upright chairs stood in an alcove whilst in the main body of the room two easy chairs were set out before the little gas fire, a gas-ring just like the one in Elizabeth's room stood beside it and three pictures hung on the walls, all of them cheerful country scenes.

'It – it's perfect . . . absolutely perfect,' Biddy stammered. 'And this is all for your . . . your servant?'

'For you, if you would like to work for us,' Mrs Gallagher said gently. 'You see, Miss O'Shaughnessy, when I was your age I – I didn't have very much and I did work hard. To have a room like this would have been very precious to me, it would have made me very happy. So now I hope this room will make some young woman very happy too.'

'Oh, it will! And . . . and I can come and work for you, and have these two rooms?'

'Yes . . . but we haven't talked about money, yet,' Mrs Gallagher said, smiling and pink-cheeked. Biddy's rapture had obviously thrilled her. 'Would ten shillings a week suit you? It doesn't seem much, but it's all found, and it's what Mrs Edmonds recommended. If you can't manage . . .'

'On ten shilling a *week*, and not having to buy food? Oh, I'll manage just fine, Mrs Gallagher,' Biddy said, her tongue tripping over the words in her excitement. 'Can I start tomorrow? Can I move my things in then?'

'Tomorrow would suit me admirably, especially if you could manage quite early in the morning, since we're meeting the Prescotts off the London train at noon,' Mrs Gallagher said, her eyes sparkling. 'Oh, how wonderful to have help in the house again, with the evil twins on their way and Christmas almost upon us. You will not regret coming to work for us, Miss O'Shau . . . my dear, what is your first name?'

'Oh, I'm Bridget, but everyone calls me Biddy,' Biddy said joyfully. 'I'll be here by nine, Mrs Gallagher, if that will suit?'

'Admirably,' Mrs Gallagher said. She led the way down the attic stairs. 'I feel sure, Biddy, that you and I are going to get along famously!'

'I'd like working here even without the rooms,' Biddy said, following close. 'But with those rooms for my own – it'll be heaven, Mrs Gallagher!'

After Biddy O'Shaughnessy had left, positively bubbling with happiness, Nellie Gallagher sat in her kitchen, looking a little ruefully around her.

She liked Biddy, had liked her on sight, so that was good. She thought they would work well together, which was better. Because the last girl, Peggy Pound, had been a right little monkey. Idle, none too clean, an inventive liar . . . a bad influence all round who had made a deal of trouble before Nellie had managed to admit to herself that Peggy would have to leave.

The trouble was, Peggy was an orphan, as Nellie had been – still was, Nellie supposed ruefully now, sitting at her own kitchen table and pouring herself another cup of tea, since marriage and a daughter of her own did not endow her with parents. So because Peggy was an orphan, from the very same orphanage in which Nellie and her adopted sister, Lilac, had first met, Nellie had felt it incumbent upon her to try extra hard with Peggy.

But it had been trying wasted, because all Peggy ever thought about was having fun and doing as little work as possible. She had decided that carting water up two flights of stairs in order to wash her person was too much trouble, so she stopped washing. She seldom made the family a meal and when she did she burned more than she cooked. She had disliked Mrs Wrexham and told lies about her to Nellie, and she was jealous of Liz and frequently tried to get her into trouble with either parent, she was not fussy which.

The final straw had come when she started bringing young men in. Not even decent young men, Nellie thought indignantly now, pouring herself another cup of tea and leaving it to get cold whilst she remembered the many sins and wickednesses of Peggy Pound. She picked up the most dreadful young men on the streets, thieves, lay-abouts, the worst sort of scoundrels, and brought them back to Ducie Street, to the two attic rooms which Nellie had furnished so lovingly for some poor girl.

And I didn't even have the courage to sack her myself, Nellie remembered sorrowfully now. But darling Stuart, bless him, who had been an orphan in Liverpool, as well, darling Stuart had dealt with Peggy. Kindly but firmly, he had given her an ultimatum; stop bringing men into my house, stop thieving money from my wife's purse and my daughter's money-box, or out you will go. I mean it.

She couldn't stop, that was the trouble, and Stuart, even as he gave her the ultimatum, had known she couldn't stop. She was used to having a man in her bed and money in her purse; she could not just stop for the sake of a job she did not even value, let alone enjoy.

'She'll end up a sailors' whore on the waterfront,' Nellie had wept, lying next to Stuart in their big double bed the night after the ultimatum had been delivered. 'She'll die young, of some horrible disease. Oh Stu, my darling, what did we do wrong?'

'Nothing, sweetheart, nothing! She's a bad lot, we should never have taken her in; matron, if you remember, was very doubtful. Now go to sleep, and in a couple of days . . .'

And of course Peggy went, not even unwillingly. She had found a better way to make a living, she told Mrs Wrexham, whilst Elizabeth listened, wide-eyed. There were fellers around who just wanted to see a girl comfortable . . . all she had to do was crook her little finger . . .

'There's one other little thing she has to do,' Stuart said wickedly, when Nellie repeated the conversation that night. 'I bet she didn't put that into words, though.'

And ever since then, for months and months, Nellie had managed without a maid. Only it was beginning to get her down, because it was a big house and she had responsibilities. As a newspaper editor-in-chief, Stuart entertained quite often, and although Nellie rather enjoyed the cooking, she had to keep having temporary staff in to serve and wait on and help out generally.

'Employ someone else, only this time, go through one of the Employment Registers,' Stuart had insisted. 'Don't worry, my pet, they interview everyone they send to see you first; you won't get a long line of little Peggys knocking at the door.'

And the very first girl had been Biddy . . . Bridget O'Shaughnessy, who would do her best – Nellie just knew it – and was young enough to be a companion for Elizabeth yet old enough to be relied upon.

Oh Lor, Nellie said to herself now, sitting up straight and pushing the cold tea away. Oh Lor, I never asked her age! Oh goodness, and it'll be the first thing Stu asks me when he comes home tonight – he'll think I'm a real nitwit not to have asked!

Getting to her feet, she began to organise dinner. She and Elizabeth would have a makeshift luncheon when Elizabeth's friends had left, but tonight, with Stuart home, they would have a proper meal. Tonight they would have soup first, then pork chops and apple sauce, then apricot pudding. Stu was extremely fond of his Nell's apricot pudding. And she would be able to tell him that Biddy was starting next day, at nine o'clock, which would please him.

The day passed pleasantly, with Nellie doing the housework, reminding herself at frequent intervals that from the very next day she would have help and would not have to struggle on alone. At around five o'clock she began to prepare their meal, taking pleasure in it. The phone rang when she was opening the tinned apricots and she had to abandon the tin and run through into the hall, taking down the receiver with distinctly syrupy hands.

'Hello?'

It was Stuart. He was awfully sorry, but he would be late this evening; something had come up, something important. 'Have you cooked my dinner?' he asked anxiously. 'What was it?'

'Leek soup first, then pork chops, and apricot pudding to finish,' Nellie said, trying to sound cheerful and not resigned. 'But all I've done so far is start to make the apricot pudding.'

Stuart groaned. 'It's my favourite . . . tell you what,

make it and save me a piece. A big piece. Could you warm it up when I get in? I shan't be much after ten.'

'Of course I could,' Nellie said happily. 'Oh, Stu ... the Register sent a girl, like you said they would.'

'They did? Oh sweetheart, I'm so glad for you. What was she like?'

'Lovely. A dear little girl. Her name's Biddy O'Shaughnessy.'

He laughed. 'Crumbs, what a mouthful! When does she start?'

'Tomorrow, nine o'clock. But how d'you know she wanted the job? I only said the Register had sent her round.'

'She'd have been mad not to take the job if you liked her,' Stuart said simply. 'See you later, sweetheart; don't forget, a big piece of apricot pudding.'

They rang off and Nellie wandered back into the kitchen. Despite the news that Stuart would miss his meal she felt happy, because just to hear his voice, so full of understanding and affection, made her feel warm and comfortable, loved, precious.

It had been like that from the start, of course. Nellie began to make her pudding mixture, gazing out at the damp back garden without seeing it, remembering the first time she and Stuart had met.

She had been nursing wounded soldiers in France and Stuart had been convalescing from a splintered kneecap though, as a War Correspondent, he wasn't actually engaged in the fighting. She and a friend had been off duty, walking through the snowy countryside of Northern France, when he had heard her familiar Scouse accent and called out to her, offering, as one Liverpudlian to another, to take her tobogganing down the snowy slopes.

The toboggan had turned out to be a battered tin

hospital tray – it was a good deal more battered by the end of the afternoon – but despite this, Nellie had had the time of her life, and she had known from that moment that Stuart was the man for her. Of course it had not been that simple, nothing ever was, but after the war they had met up again and married, and since then Nellie's life had quite simply revolved round Stuart and their only child.

Reminiscing about those early years always filled her with wonder at her own immense good fortune. She had been a skinny little orphan with no particular skills, yet she had ended up married to the best man in the world, and had given birth to his beautiful daughter. Little Nellie McDowell, who had never expected much from life, was married to an important newspaper executive and happy as the day was long, though she would have been equally happy had Stuart been a tram driver or indeed a factory worker or a street sweeper. When two people are still deeply in love after – heavens, after getting on for two decades – then, Nellie knew, they were much blessed.

But gazing into space and counting her blessings would not get the meal cooked. She began to roll out her suety crust.

Nellie had finished the apricot pudding and was half-heartedly preparing vegetables and setting out two chops on the grill when the kitchen door burst open and Elizabeth came in. She smiled beguilingly at her mother and poured herself a glass of home-made lemonade, then sat down at the table with a thump. Her friends had gone to their own homes for luncheon, returned afterwards to take Elizabeth to the park for an impromptu game of three-a-side hockey, then they had accompanied her home again for tea and Nell's rich fruit-cake and butter shortbread.

'The girls have gone, Mam. They said to thank you very much for the tea. Can I help with dinner? When's me Da gettin' home?'

'Talk properly,' Nellie said reprovingly. 'Dad's going to be late, it was him on the phone just now. And you could get the soup out of the larder and put enough for two into a pan and put the pan on the stove if you like.'

'If it's just us, don't let's bother with soup,' Elizabeth said as her mother hoped she would. She drained her glass and burped, then patted her mouth with her hand. 'Pardon me! Are you mashing the spuds?'

'Are you creaming the potatoes?' Nellie corrected; it never ceased to amaze her that Elizabeth, who went to a private school and was getting a good education, still spoke, half the time, with a Liverpool accent. But then all the girls did, so she was only conforming, in the way children did. And she only talked like that when she was being a bit daft, and with either her close friends or family. On other occasions, nothing could have been purer than her small, clear voice.

'Well, are you? Mashing the . . . I mean creaming the potatoes,' Elizabeth said, laughing. She reached across and picked up the cabbage which Nell had got out ready. 'Can I cut the this up very finely, like you showed me, and do it with a little butter and an onion, in the French way?'

'If you like. Liz, did you like the girl I brought into the sitting-room this morning?'

'She looked nice,' Elizabeth acknowledged, beginning to slice the cabbage with great care. 'Is she going to take the job?'

'She is. I confirmed the arrangements with Mrs Edmonds of the Register an hour ago. I liked her so much. She'll be good for all of us.'

'Good for us? I don't see . . .'

The doorbell cut across her sentence. Nellie sighed and flapped a hand at Elizabeth, who had half risen to her feet, cabbage in one hand, knife in the other. 'You get on with that cabbage; I'll go to the door. I expect it's someone selling something.'

Dai had come up the road with some trepidation. Now that it had actually come to the point, he wondered whether he had been wise to come, or whether it was best to let sleeping dogs lie. His Mam, God bless her, was dead and gone. Her friend Mrs Gallagher had probably never been told that Bethan had died. Was it wise or sensible to open the wound, go round to the woman's house, talk about his Mam to someone who was, when all was said and done, a complete stranger?

He had spent quite a lot of the day fruitlessly searching for the girl with the blue eyes, though he had pretended to Greasy that he was buying Christmas presents. But he had had no luck. He had asked for her all over, describing her in some detail, but had met with no response. People had either not seen the blue-eyed girl or not noticed her. And when the day began to grow dusky it had occurred to him that he had best go round to this Ducie Street, if he intended to call on Nellie Gallagher, or go back to Greasy's place.

He liked the O'Reillys, they were a nice bunch, but he had promised himself that he would not impose on them over Christmas. And he only had a day and then it would *be* Christmas, so he should find Mrs Gallagher, introduce himself, and then book in at the Seamen's Mission, down on the waterfront. That way he would salve his conscience without hurting anyone's feelings, because the O'Reillys would think he was staying with his Mam's old friend, and his Mam's old friend would assume he was still with the O'Reillys.

It was quite a big house, though. Much grander than he had expected. Nice, he would grant you that, but grand.

He walked up and down the road a couple of times, looking curiously at the houses, and in particular the one which belonged to the Gallaghers. Nice front garden, brightly painted front door, clean, colourful curtains at the windows. . . . Damn it, he was going to knock; what was the point in coming all this way by tram only to turn tail and go back again without calling? Mam would be disgusted with him.

He walked up the short path and reached for the bell. He pressed his finger on the central button and rang it for several seconds. Then he stood back and waited.

He heard the quick, soft footsteps, the fingers fumbling with the door handle, then the door swung open. Golden light flooded out, temporarily blinding him, for he had been wandering the quiet, gaslit streets for the best part of an hour. He smiled in the direction of the person who had opened the door, however, and tugged off his seaman's cap. The maid who had answered the door – he caught a glimpse of a very large white apron and a small, delicate face with a dab of flour on the nose – gave a sort of strangled gasp as he did so. 'Davy? My God, it is you, isn't it? What in heaven's name are you doing here?'

'I . . . I wonder if I might see Mrs Gallagher,' Dai said, unable to make head or tail of the woman's words. She had obviously confused him with someone else – odd that it should have been his father's name that she had used, but then Davy was not an uncommon name.

'Oh, I can see now . . . I'm so sorry.' the woman's voice was soft. 'Just for a moment I thought you were someone else . . . can I help you? I am Mrs Gallagher.'

'I'm Dai Evans . . . Richart, I suppose I should say.

Mrs Gallagher, my Mam told me that if ever I was in Liverpool I should come to see you . . . my God!'

For Mrs Gallagher had given a sharp gasp, a small moan, and collapsed in a heap on her hall floor.

Dai didn't know what on earth to do. He went inside and bent over her and even as he did so her eyes flickered and opened, staring up into his face for a moment with cloudy puzzlement. Quickly, Dai put his arms around her and pulled her to a sitting position. He said, 'I'll fetch help – is there anyone else in the house?'

She gave a huge, shuddering sigh, then struggled to her feet. She gave him a watery smile.

'You're Bethan's boy,' she said slowly. 'My dear friend Bethan's boy. I had a note a while back . . .'

'My Mam died fifteen months ago,' Dai said wryly. 'I'm sorry not to have come to you before, Mrs Gallagher, but I'm at sea, distant-water trawling I've been this past year, and only now have I come to Liverpool.'

'I'm so glad you came . . . but my dear boy, you must come in . . . do you mind if we go into the kitchen? My daughter, Elizabeth, is in there . . . we're making dinner . . . you'll stay, of course.'

'But I don't think I should trouble you any more,' Dai said slowly. 'You aren't well.'

Nellie smiled and shook her head. 'I'm fine now; it was the shock, Dai. You are – you are so like your Mam, see, and I'd been thinking about her . . . your Mam wrote to me, she must have given the letter to a solicitor to be sent in the event of her death . . . I'm so sorry, Dai, Bethan was a marvellous woman. She had so much love and charity in her. She was – she was very kind to me, once.'

'She always said you were very kind to her,' Dai countered, smiling. He looked curiously at this little friend of his Mam's. She was quite a bit younger than

Bethan and she had gentler looks with the golden brown hair and the steady grey eyes. What foils they must have been to one another when they were friends as girls, he thought now, the one so fair and delicate, the other so dark haired, pink cheeked, sturdy! 'Look, let me come back another day, when you've got over the shock of meeting someone out of your past, so to speak. Better it would be, perhaps.'

But she was shaking her head at him reprovingly, taking him by the hand, drawing him into a pleasant kitchen, all firelight and the good smell of cooking, whilst a young girl, chopping cabbage at the big scrubbed wooden table, turned and smiled at him.

'Sit down, Dai, sit down,' Nellie said, beginning to bustle about. 'A cup of tea now, and some of my rich fruit-cake. Pass the tin over Elizabeth, there's a good girl. Oh, Dai, I'm forgetting my manners! Elizabeth, dear, this is Richart, usually called Dai, the son of – of my good friend Bethan Evans. Richart, this is my daughter, Elizabeth.'

The two young people eyed one another cautiously, then shook hands.

'Hello, Elizabeth; nice to meet you. Please call me Dai, when someone calls me Richart I always feel I'm either back at school or in disgrace.'

'Hello, Dai, it's nice to meet you, too. My Mam talks a lot about your Mam but I don't think she's mentioned you much.'

'No. Well, when they were friends, you and I, Elizabeth, had not even been thought of. Oh, tea . . . that's wonderful!' He took the cup from Nellie and turned back to the younger girl. 'I've been working on a trawler in the Arctic ocean, and I tell you, Liz, it's hot tea that keeps us going!'

Elizabeth, who had been eyeing him warily, laughed and seemed to relax. She was very like her mother but with her hair a shade deeper, an almost reddy gold, and her skin flushed with health. 'The Arctic ocean? Oh, Dai, will you tell us about it? Have you seen whales, polar bears, penguins?'

'I've seen 'em all,' Dai said, laughing back at her. 'Why, you should see the fish we catch! My mate, Greasy, had his boot torn off him by a dead conger eel once . . .'

'A *dead* conger eel? That's one of those tall stories they talk about – Dad calls them fishermen's tales, come to think of it! Now come on, the truth now!'

'No, honest! The eel had been in the fish pounds for the best part of a day . . .'

He ate with them, of course. Nellie took him up to the spare room and showed him how comfortable he could be over Christmas, though she understood that he must go back to his friends tonight and tell them that he would be moving in with the Gallaghers the following day.

'We're having a real family Christmas and there's no one in the world I'd sooner have to share it with us than – than Bethan's boy,' Nellie said, her eyes shining with affection. 'Stu knows how close Bethan and I were, it was sad that we never met after we married, but we wrote often. Friends can stay close that way – we could read between the lines, even, so that a cheerful letter that hid pain was quickly responded to in the right way.'

'Mam never showed no one the letters, but they were always by her side,' Dai acknowledged. 'Nellie . . . are you sure you don't mind my calling you that? Nellie, she said if I ever wanted mothering . . .'

Nellie patted his arm. Elizabeth had gone to bed and Stuart had not yet arrived home so the two of them were sitting, side by side, on the sofa in the living-room whilst, as Nellie put it, they got to know one another.

'You're a good lad, Dai,' she said softly. 'And it's my

belief that you – your Da has disappointed you some-how. Can you tell me about it?'

Dai found that he could tell her, found, even, that it eased him to tell her. 'They say, in the village, that Davy knew Menna even before my Mam passed on,' he said bitterly, as the story ended. 'Hate her I do, Nellie. A brassy, hard little bitch after what she can get, and my Da sniffing after what he can get . . . and my Mam . . .'

His voice broke and he stopped speaking. Nellie put her arms round his broad young shoulders and hugged him hard.

'Don't waste energy hating her, she's not worth it,' she said, surprisingly. 'You love your Da, but he's a weak man; he always was, from what Bethan told me. I do remember her saying he was – was always after the girls. Just love the side of him that loves you, and try to remember that he needs a woman to look after him. It's a shame that he couldn't pick on a decent girl, but Menna was around when he needed her. And don't let her stop you going home, Dai, bach. It's . . . it's your heritage, it's what your Mam wanted for you. . . . I remember her saying that you would inherit it all, the cows on the headland, the sheep in the meadow beyond, the fishing boat, the beautiful old house and garden. . . . And it isn't only that, Dai, it's all the rest – the beach, the hills . . . the Island of Anglesey, where you were born and raised. That's your heritage, too.'

'Aye, you're right,' Dai said. He was astonished at the depth of feeling he already had for this pale, slight woman who seemed to understand his feelings almost without speech. His Mam had been right, Nellie Gallagher was a friend worth having. 'I will go back, Nellie. But not right now; not yet. It's a small village and I can only live at my Da's house, and whilst she's there . . . I'm not strong enough to go back there.'

'Right. But don't leave it too long. And write to your Da, tell him that you're missing him and Moelfre. You'll have to come to terms with Menna one of these days or lose your Da, Dai, and you don't have to tell me you love him because I know you do, even if you aren't yet willing to admit it.' She sighed and got to her feet. 'Any relationship based on love is a good relationship, Dai. Davy was always very lovable, or – or so I understood from Bethan.'

Dai stood up as well. 'good you are for me, Nellie,' he said, smiling down at her. 'Better I do feel than I've felt for many a month. You're right, I may dislike Menna, but I do love my Da, and I'll be writing to him. And now you're sure I can come to you? I won't be in your way, won't spoil your family Christmas?'

'You'll make my Christmas,' Nellie assured him. 'And Stuart will be delighted to have another man about the place. Lilac's husband, Joey, is at sea most of the year so when he's home he spoils the twins disgracefully. Stuart will be glad to entertain someone who talks of something other than kindergartens, potty training and read-and-learn. Come back in time for lunch tomorrow, and bring your traps.'

'I will. I'm more thankful than I can say, Nellie, for your kindness,' Dai said sincerely. He had not felt so relieved about his father since his mother's death, but now Nellie had made him look at their relationship he realised that it was, as she said, based on a very deep love. He must not let that love dissipate just because his Da had taken a silly, fluffy little creature to comfort him for his dear Bethan's loss. Each to his own comfort, Dai reminded himself. Each to his own. 'And I'll post a card and a letter to my Da first thing in the morning, to reach him before Christmas,' he added as he stood on the doorstep. 'See you tomorrow, and thanks again!'

Chapter Eight

Nellie waved Dai off and then turned back indoors again. Stuart was later than he had hoped, but the large slice of apricot pudding was between two plates, waiting to be steam-heated through, and she had a jug of coffee keeping warm on the back of the stove.

She wondered how Stuart would take the news that he would be entertaining an extra guest for Christmas. She smiled to herself, pottering contentedly round her kitchen, setting out the breakfast for the morning. He would be pleased because she was pleased; he had heard her talking about her friend Bethan for years and had often suggested that the two of them should arrange to meet.

He knew nothing, of course, about Dai. Oh, he knew that Bethan had a son named Dai just as he knew Davy was Bethan's husband. What he did not know and need never know was that Davy had once been Nellie's lover – and that Dai was Nellie's own little son, the son she had born in Moelfre more than twenty-two years ago and left with Bethan, who had reared him as her own.

Unless he guessed, of course. Stuart and she were so close that keeping secrets from one another was next to impossible. She had often been aware, in the early days of their marriage, that Stuart, who knew she had born an illegitimate child, was deeply jealous of her first lover. No amount of telling him that she had never really loved the man who had fathered that child could entirely convince him.

But time had done the trick. With every year that passed, her quiet but deep devotion to him and to their daughter had soothed his jealousy, calmed his fears. She doubted that Stuart had given a thought, either to the illegitimate child he assumed she had had adopted (and in a sense, of course, he was right) or to her first lover, for a dozen years, so he was unlikely to start agonising over it now.

He was a nice young man was Dai. Frighteningly like Davy at first glance, the same clustering black curls, the dark blue eyes, the quirky, teasing smile. But when you looked closer you saw a steadiness, a seriousness even, which Davy had lacked. Dai was responsible, sensible, reliable, and he was only twenty-two years old, whereas Davy, who had been considerably older than that when he had fathered Dai, had always been a lightweight . . . and far too fond of women.

Nellie had never regretted losing Davy because by the time she had born Dai and left him with Bethan she had fallen totally out of love with the handsome young Welshman. Perhaps knowing what their love-affair could have done to Bethan had something to do with it, perhaps even his deceiving them both – for he had not told her he was married just as Bethan had never known he had a mistress – had taken that first fine gloss off their affair. But whatever the reason, by the time Dai was a year old she had recovered from her temporary madness and was growing up, mentally as well as physically.

Stuart had been her only true love. He was her strength, her rock. He was patient with her, explaining current affairs – the horrors of the Spanish civil war, the frightening way the Germans were behaving, as though they had forgotten the 'fourteen-'eighteen war – even the peculiarities of the British legal system and the difficulties faced by their new young King and Queen, became simple when Stuart explained them. Yet he managed never to make her feel foolish or ill-educated, sharing his knowledge easily, matter-of-factly.

And Elizabeth was her darling daughter and a companion second only to Stuart so far as Nellie was concerned. I'm a family person, she told herself now, a simple woman content with simple things. And though Davy and I made a baby together, it was just . . . just youth and silliness. There wasn't so much as a scrap of real love between us two, just friendship and a natural physical need for closeness, and a bit of flattery because I'd not had a boyfriend before him.

But it was so good to see Dai again! Last time he had been a bonny, dark-haired baby, crowing with delight when she had held him up to see the lambs playing in the field, gripping her hair with incredible baby-strength, smiling at her with that wide, totally trusting toothlessness which only the very young can show.

He's a man now, and a handsome one, yet he's still that baby, too, she told herself as she laid the table for breakfast and began to close the fire down for the night. It was almost midnight, and even if Stuart came in the next few minutes it was unlikely he would want to eat this late. I'm glad Dai's got in touch with me, and grateful for dear Bethan's generosity in putting us in touch. Sweet, selfless Bethan, giving Nellie back the son she had lost all claim to so long ago.

But there was little point in hanging around the kitchen; best make her way to bed now. Stuart would come in quietly, so as not to wake her. She made herself a cup of cocoa and had left the kitchen and was closing the door behind her when a key rattled in the front door lock. Nellie's heart bounded joyfully; Stuart! She ran across the hallway and pulled the door impatiently inwards so that Stuart, still trying to disengage his key from the lock, followed it and almost trod on her.

'Darling Stu, how late you are! I don't suppose you feel like apricot pudding, but I'll make you some cocoa, or hot milk with a tot of rum in it if you'd rather.'

Stuart's dark eyes were heavy with tiredness but his thin face creased into a grin at her words and he bent and kissed her, first teasingly on the nose, then seriously, on the mouth. Nellie put her arms round him and hugged, then exclaimed. 'You're soaking wet! Is it raining?'

'Raining? It's snowing, my love. We're in for a white Christmas! Ah, but it's good to be home. I've been trying to get a piece done for the paper tomorrow . . . did you listen to the six o'clock news?'

'On and off,' Nellie said. 'Come through into the kitchen, it's nice and warm in there still. Why do you ask if I listened to the news?'

'I wondered whether you'd heard; reports have been coming through saying that the Japs have attacked a British ship in the Yangtse River – HMS *Ladybird*. They killed a rating and injured several others. Apparently it was mistaken for a Chinese vessel, or that's what the Japs say, anyway.'

'They're as bad as the Huns,' Nellie said grimly. 'Horrible, cruel little men. I don't remember the *Ladybird*, but wasn't there something about an American ship?'

'Yes, that's right. The *Pansy*. She was sunk with the loss of several lives.'

'Oh Stu, where will it all end? I do hate it so. Why must nations fight?'

'It seems to be human nature,' Stuart said gloomily. 'It just seems worse at Christmas. But there's no point in discussing the news, it's bad enough to be working late all evening on such a dismal story, I just wondered if the BBC had reported it. Can I have hot milk, please?'

'Darling, of course. Here, give me that wet coat, I'll

hang it on the clothes rack whilst the milk heats, it'll be dry in time for you to wear it for work tomorrow.'

'Thanks, sweetheart,' Stuart said, watching affectionately as his wife measured milk into a pan. 'What would I do without you?'

'Go thirsty,' Nellie said, smiling at him. She put the pan on the heat, then walked across the kitchen and pulled the curtains a little apart. 'Oh Stu, look at that snow!'

Stuart followed her gaze; looking past her he could see the whirling flakes as they multiplied against the dark night sky. 'I said we'd have a white Christmas,' he said smugly. The milk began to hiss up the sides of the pan and he grabbed it off the heat just as Nellie abandoned the window and came across to him. 'What do you think of that, eh?'

'A white Christmas is a wonderful thing for us . . . but not so good for others,' Nellie said thoughtfully. She began to pour his milk into a blue-and-white mug.

'Oh, the Societies will be doing the rounds,' Stuart said quickly. He went over to the pantry and got down the big red cake tin with the picture of Queen Victoria on the lid. 'Any cake left?'

'Oh Stu, if you eat rich fruit-cake this late you'll get the most terrible indigestion and be up half the night! That's why I didn't offer you apricot pudding.'

'Cake won't hurt me; I'm starving, I had sandwiches for my dinner and a cup of weak coffee.' Stuart cut himself a large wedge and then sat on the edge of the table, watching as Nellie finished pouring the milk and then bustled over to the Welsh dresser and produced a bottle of rum from its depths. 'That isn't cooking rum, is it? I want the real McCoy!'

'It's the same sort you buy for the dining-room,' Nellie said. 'How big is a tot?'

'About tot-sized. Here, let me do it.'

Stuart poured the rum into the cup and Nellie made herself another cocoa with the small amount of milk remaining in the pan.

'That stuff smells horrid,' Nellie remarked as her husband, with the wedge of cake in one hand and the rum and hot milk in the other, walked with her across the kitchen. 'I wonder what it's like in cocoa?'

'You'd hate it, you always fuss when I breathe it on you in bed,' Stuart said. He sipped at the milk as Nell opened the kitchen door and ushered him through. 'Never mind, eh? Only one more day of producing a newspaper and then it's Christmas!'

Biddy arrived at the house in Ducie Street at nine o'clock on the dot next morning and Mrs Gallagher answered the door herself, just as she had the previous day. 'Good morning, Biddy; you are prompt,' she said. 'Is that all your luggage?'

'Yes,' Biddy said baldly. It was no use trying to explain how she came to possess almost nothing. 'Shall I leave it in the kitchen until later?'

Words could not have expressed her joy when Mrs Gallagher told her to take it up to her room, settle in, and then come down to the kitchen, where she, Mrs Gallagher, would be waiting.

'You'll find your uniforms hanging in the cupboard; I think they'll fit you, you're slimmer than Peggy but about the same height,' she said. 'Put one of them on and come down and I'll see if you need tucks or lettings-out.'

'Yes ma'am. And then what will I do?' Biddy asked.

'We'll start off by preparing luncheon together,' Mrs Gallagher said with her lovely smile. 'And then we'll go over the house, both of us, just dusting and so on. Mrs Wrexham and Mr Hedges come three times a week, so the place is pretty clean and tidy. Except for Elizabeth's bedroom, of course. And then later, we'll prepare the spare rooms.... Oh, I quite forgot, we have another guest, a young man, who will be arriving at about noon. We'd best do the small room out for him first, perhaps. Now off you go, Biddy.'

Biddy ran up the curving staircase and then up the narrower attic stairs, her heart almost bursting with pleasure and excitement. She had two whole rooms of her own now, and a place in this pleasant household, and she did not intend to spoil this wonderful opportunity. She would work extremely hard, get really good at the job, and stay here until she was too old to work any more.

She went into her bedroom, closed the door, and looked around her contentedly. In fact she kept looking round, to make sure she was not dreaming. Any roof over her head would have been welcome, but such a home as this was beyond her wildest dreams! And Mrs Gallagher was so understanding, so warm and friendly. And this room . . . she had never owned such a room in her life, nor expected to do so. She unpacked her carpet bag slowly, putting her pillow on top of the far nicer one on the bed, only her pillow was her friend, she could not imagine going to sleep without it. Then she laid her blanket on the chair, where it looked rather grand, and put Dolly on guard by the pillow.

Spare shoes in the cupboard, spare underwear in the chest of drawers . . . it looks pretty lonely now but once I get paid I'll begin to pick up some more clothes, Biddy told herself, turning regretfully towards the door. Oh . . . uniform!

She opened the cupboard and there were two grey gingham dresses, a black woollen dress, two big white aprons and one little, frilly one. She guessed that the pieces of shiny white linen were to wear on her head, but doubted that she could put it on correctly herself. Never mind, she would do her best and let Mrs Gallagher show her how to manage if she got it wrong.

The dress fitted more or less, and fitted better when she put the big white apron over it. I look really nice, she thought, standing on tiptoe to look at herself in the mirror on the chest of drawers. But all she could see was her head and shoulders, so she lifted the mirror off the top and gradually lowered it to get an over-all view, even if it was in small bits and pieces.

She looked all right. Smart, really. These clothes are the ones I'll be wearing most of the time, so my other things won't get worn out nearly as quickly as they used to do, she told herself. I'll be all right here, I just know it. Safe. And happy, too. It's the sort of house that welcomes you – I felt it soon as I came in the door.

She put the glass back on top of the chest of drawers again and tucked a stray curl behind her ear. Then she set off down the stairs.

The morning flew. Biddy found the work easy when it was done with Mrs Gallagher watchful at her side. At ten o'clock she met the charlady, Mrs Wrexham, who proved to be a wispy little woman of fifty or so with greying hair, a squint and a slight but definite moustache. Despite appearances, Mrs Wrexham had an enormous, booming voice and a laugh which echoed round the house, but she was quite timid and Biddy could well imagine her hiding in a corner if someone roared. She was much stronger than she looked, though, and seemed quite prepared to scrub acres of linoleum, brush acres of carpet, clean and lay a dozen fires and then tackle what she called 'small jobs', which meant cleaning windows and blacking grates and the stove.

At elevenses time Mr Hedges came in, removing his

boots on the doorstep and shuffling indoors in his socks. He was fiftyish, too, and not a talkative man, though he did have a few quiet words with Mrs Wrexham, and acknowledged Mrs Gallagher's introduction of Biddy with a smile and a mutter of, 'Ow d'you do, missus?'

'Now let's see how you can cook a meal for one young gentleman, one young lady – that's Elizabeth – yourself and me,' Mrs Gallagher said when Mr Hedges and Mrs Wrexham had both departed. 'Mr Gallagher doesn't come home for luncheon, you'll meet him this evening, at dinnertime. Or at least I hope you will – he sometimes works very late.'

The two women set about the task of making a light luncheon for four people.

'We'll do a thick vegetable soup, I think, since the baker will call in half an hour or so; I must remember to order some of those delicious milk rolls which go so well with soup,' Mrs Gallagher said. 'Can you prepare these vegetables, Biddy, whilst I make a rhubarb tart?'

Biddy was at the sink, peeling and chopping vegetables, when the front doorbell rang. She knew it was the front one because there was an object on the wall above the kitchen door which actually contained the bells, all clearly labelled, and the bell labelled 'front' was jangling.

'I'll go,' she said, her hands going up behind her to untie her apron, but Mrs Gallagher was before her.

'It's all right, Biddy, I'll go. It will be the young gentleman who's coming to stay with us for Christmas, Mr Evans. You go on with the vegetables.'

Biddy was rather disappointed not to have had the chance to answer the front door – she had her opening remark all ready, having been coached in it by Mrs Gallagher earlier. 'Good morning madam, (or sir, of course, if it was a feller) I'm afraid Mrs Gallagher is not here at present but if you will leave your name . . .'

Still, there would be other opportunities. The black dress, Mrs Gallagher had told her, was for evenings, when they had company and Biddy would be needed to serve the meal.

'But that is for business guests,' Mrs Gallagher had added hastily. 'At Christmas it's very much jollier. We'll all help, just wait and see.'

Now, Biddy could hear voices in the hallway, then footsteps. They mounted the stairs.

Mrs Gallagher is taking Mr Evans up to the blue room, Biddy thought, proud that she had got the hang of it all so quickly. The blue room was real smart, with a blue rug on the floor and blue cretonne curtains, and the dressing-table had marvellous mirrors which you could arrange, Mrs Gallagher told her, so that you could see the back of your own head. But the yellow room was even better with its Chinese wallpaper and the picture, over the mantel, of a willowy young lady with droopy hair and a very exciting red and black dress, apparently dancing all by herself in a wood.

Tomorrow, Mr and Mrs Prescott will have the yellow room and their twin sons will sleep in the little room off it, the one Mrs Gallagher said was a dressing room, Biddy reminded herself, working happily away at the sink. We'll be a houseful then all right!

Presently, the footsteps came downstairs again. Biddy had finished the vegetables and was hesitating by the big pan. When she and her mother had made soup they had chopped the vegetables just as Mrs Gallagher had told her, and then they had melted a little dripping in a big pan and added the vegetables, cooking them until they were bright and glowing, but still quite hard. Only then had they added the stock.

Mrs Gallagher came into the room, or rather she poked her head round the door. 'Biddy, I'm just taking Mr Evans to find Elizabeth – do you know how to make vegetable soup?'

'Yes, ma'am,' Biddy said after a slight hesitation. 'That is, if you make it like my Mam did; she sweated the veg in a spoonful of melted dripping first, then added her stock.'

'Yes, that's it. Not too much stock, since this is thick vegetable soup. Oh, and can you find me a bottle of rhubarb please, and strain it through a wire sieve?'

'Yes, ma'am,' Biddy said. 'I'll do that.'

She did not have the faintest idea where the bottled fruit was kept but she was an observant girl and thought she would soon run it to earth. First, furthermore, she must make the soup.

The soup was simmering when someone knocked on the back door. Biddy flew across and opened it and it was a boy of about her own age pushing a box-cart laden with bread of varying sorts, though mostly they were large, two-pound loaves, partly covered by a checked cloth. The boy whipped the cloth off in a very professional manner and the most glorious scent of bread rose to Biddy's nostrils.

'Mornin', chuck; she wan' any bread?' the boy said, jerking his head vaguely in the direction of the rest of the house. 'You're new.'

It was a statement but Biddy answered it as though it had been a question. 'Yes, that's right. I started this morning. Mrs Gallagher wants some milk rolls but she didn't mention how much bread.'

'She'll 'ave a large brown, a small white an' 'alf a dozen milk,' the boy said confidently, but Biddy knew delivery boys; they were all trying to make a living and this one wouldn't think twice about persuading her to give a large order just to have the money in his pocket.

'I'd best ask,' she said uncertainly. 'It's my first day, I don't want to get into trouble.'

The boy widened his eyes, which were very round and dark. 'I wouldn't tell you wrong . . . wha's your name, chuck?'

'Biddy O'Shaughnessy. What's yours?'

'Albert Brett.'

'Hello, Mr Brett. Have you worked for the baker long?'

'I work for Lunt's, I've been doin' their deliveries two years. Look, me name's Bert to you, Biddy, an' you'd best go an' ask Mrs Wozzit wharrit is she's after, seein' as Christmas is comin' an' I won't be callin' for a couple o' days. 'Sides, she'll want a word wi' me today, I reckon.'

'Right, I'll see if I can find her . . .' Biddy was beginning when the kitchen door opened and Mrs Gallagher came into the room.

'Ah, Albert's here already, I see,' she said cheerfully. 'I'll take a large brown and a small white, Bertie, and I'd better have eight milk rolls, I think.'

'I told 'er that was what you usually 'ad, missus,' Bertie said in an injured tone. 'But there, you can't trust folk these days an' that's a fact.' He handed the bread over and Mrs Gallagher paid him, then pressed a small envelope into his hand. 'Christmas box, Bertie,' she said, smiling. 'I hope you have a happy day.'

'Cor, thanks, missus,' Bertie said, giving Biddy a told-you-so look. 'See you when it's all over.'

He disappeared down the path, whistling jauntily.

'Now, how are we getting along?' Mrs Gallagher said, taking her purchases and putting them in a large enamelled box with the word 'Bread' painted on the lid. 'You've got the soup started, I see – well done. Now I'll show you where the bottled fruit is kept and you can see if your wrists are strong enough to break the seal on the Kilner jar. . . . I usually have to get Mr Gallagher to open bottles for me, but Mr Evans may feel equal to the task if you and I find ourselves unable to do it.' She walked over to the large, airy pantry and pointed. 'There, on the top shelf . . . I think rhubarb is quite near the front but you must use the steps to get it down.'

'Mrs Gallagher, may I watch you make the pastry so that I can do it next time?' Biddy said shyly presently, when the rhubarb had been fetched down off its shelf, opened, strained and stood ready.

'Certainly you may. And then you may thicken and sweeten the rhubarb juice for me – we sweeten it with sugar, of course, and thicken it with arrowroot, which gives it a lovely shine. I usually squeeze an orange into the juice to add that special touch of flavour, and some-times I grate the peel very finely and toast it under the grill and then scatter it on the tart. But Elizabeth doesn't like it much, it's Mr Gallagher who does, so we won't bother with that today.'

The two women worked on, chatting as they did so. Mrs Gallagher was so easy and approachable that Biddy soon found herself talking freely, telling her employer all about her parents, her sojourn with Ma Kettle and her time as a delivery girl, though she said nothing about her flight from the Tebbits or the reason she was dismissed from Millicent's. Already she loved her job and was desperate to keep it; she would do nothing which might make Mrs Gallagher think she had been mistaken in taking Biddy in.

When the meal was ready Biddy's was set out on the kitchen table and Mrs Gallagher and Elizabeth carried the rest through into the living-room on trays.

'It's not a real meal, it's just a snack,' Mrs Gallagher explained. 'But tonight we'll eat in the dining-room, because Mr and Mrs Prescott will have arrived – we'll be quite a party, so if you don't think you can cope just tell me, and Liz and myself will help you out.'

A snack! Biddy thought, spooning thick vegetable

soup into her mouth and following it with a bit of milk roll – so light and fluffy, so delicious. You couldn't call this a snack, a snack's a handful of potato crisps or an apple or a raw carrot. This is a wonderful meal, that's what it is.

There was a great deal of bustle and chatter when the Prescotts arrived. Biddy, helping them to take their traps upstairs, was very surprised to find that they were not rich or anything like that but quite ordinary people. Mrs Prescott – Mrs Gallagher called her 'My dearest Lilac', which Biddy thought a very unusual name – had glorious, red-gold hair and a pretty, lively face, but she wore an ordinary dark blue coat with a matching skirt which just brushed the tops of her smart little suede boots and she talked about the trials of housekeeping so that Biddy knew at once the Prescotts did not keep a maid. And Mr Prescott talked with a London accent and was a great joker, picked Mrs Gallagher up and kissed her on the nose, made a great fuss of his wife and the little boys, who were very alike but not, Biddy was relieved to see, identical, winked at Biddy when his wife began scolding the children for dragging at her coat and trying to examine the contents of her handbag and generally behaved, Biddy thought wistfully, just like her own father had, when he came home from sea.

'You must come into the living-room and meet my friend Bethan's son, from Anglesey,' Mrs Gallagher said at one point. 'Bethan died some time ago, and Dai came calling since he was in Liverpool, so we've invited him for the holiday – he's at sea, too, so he and Joey will have a lot in common.'

'You and your lame dogs,' Mrs Prescott said to Mrs Gallagher; but she said it so softly that Biddy thought no one else had overheard. 'I hope he's the only one.'

Biddy did not understand this, but anyway, Mr Prescott was speaking.

'The boys need some air,' he said. 'Wouldn't it be nice if Biddy here were to take the twins out for a walk? They will be good, won't you, boys? And it's no distance to Prince's Park.' He winked at Biddy again. 'She could buy them ice creams.'

Johnny and Fred Prescott leaped and bounced at the idea, clutching Biddy's hands and promising to be good.

'They slept in the train, the little demons,' Mrs Prescott said, 'So now they're bounding with energy. But are you sure, Biddy ? Only they do need to run off some of their energy.'

'I'd like it,' Biddy said shyly. 'I'd like to run in the park too – we could have a race, boys.'

'She'll be their idol from now on,' Mrs Prescott said, laughing, as Johnny and Fred squeaked that they would certainly race with her and beat her hollow, that boys were best, that ice creams were their favourite thing . . . 'I wish I had your energy, Biddy! But I'm afraid after a train journey with those demons, all I want is a nice cup of tea and a sit-down.'

'The kettle's on the hob, ma'am,' Biddy said, enjoying her new role. 'Shall I mash the tea before I go?'

But Mrs Gallagher, laughing, said that she and Lilac were not quite helpless and bade her get her coat down from her room and go off for her walk.

'The snow's not deep, but you should wear boots,' she instructed, then looked guilty. 'You haven't got boots, of course . . . I shall lend you an old pair of mine, our feet are about the same size. In fact, you may keep them, Biddy, if you find them comfortable. Go and fetch your coat and I'll get my wellingtons out.'

'Where did you find that pretty little creature?' Lilac asked Nellie, when introductions had been effected and Joey Prescott and Dai were talking about the sea and ships in front of the living-room fire, whilst the two adopted sisters sat on the comfortable velvet-covered *chaise-longue*, catching up on each other's news. 'You said you'd never have another maid, after Peggy.'

'She came through an Employment Register,' Nellie confessed. 'She was the very first girl they sent me and I liked her at once. I didn't even take up her references or anything like that. I do believe I've found a gem this time.'

'Or a very pretty lame dog,' Lilac said, dimpling at the older woman. 'No, don't get cross, Nell darling, I'm only teasing. When did she start work for you?'

'This morning. She made an excellent thick vegetable soup for our luncheon . . . Dai enjoyed it and so did Elizabeth . . . and she did several other jobs around the kitchen. She's neat, quick to learn, good with her hands. And a hard worker, to boot. I do hate it, our Lilac, when you pretend I do things for the wrong reasons. I needed help in the house, she applied for the job. . . . There's no question of her being a lame dog, truly.'

'No, of course not.' Lilac lowered her voice. 'But Dai . . . Nell, darling, who does he remind me of? He's most awfully like someone I used to know . . .'

'You never met Bethan, but he's rather like her.' Nellie looked into the fire, her cheeks flushing. 'Actually, he's a bit like Stuart was at that age . . . can you still remember?'

'Yes, that's it, of course. He's dark, he's got twinkly eyes and a curly mouth . . . yes, it'll be Stuart.' She pulled a face at her sister. 'Not a by-blow, I trust?'

'Lilac, you haven't changed at all, you're just as dreadful as ever! And do stop talking about someone who's in the same room . . . . Tell me about your horrid little boys, queen, and stop tryin' to shock me. I got them both clockwork train sets for Christmas, I do hope they like them.'

'Dai and my dear Joe are far too busy swopping tall stories to worry about us, Nell. And the twins will be absolutely delighted with everything they receive because . . . well, we have quite a struggle now that I'm not working. But clockwork train sets will give Joey and me as much pleasure as they will the twins, I'm sure.'

'Good. And I thought the twins could have a high tea with Biddy, in the kitchen, and then we can put them to bed whilst she gets on with the dinner. Elizabeth's gone to a party the other side of the park; she wanted to refuse when she heard you were arriving today but I insisted that she went. She'll eat with us, of course, but she'll enjoy helping with the twins. She doesn't say much, but she would have loved a brother or sister.'

'It just wasn't to be,' Lilac said, squeezing Nellie's hand. 'Let's have another cup of tea, shall we? I'm spittin' feathers.'

Nellie laughed. 'Whatever do they think of you down London way, you scouser, you?' she said. 'Spittin' feathers, indeed! I brung you up better'n that, our Lilac!'

Laughing together, the two women returned to the kitchen.

It had been a hectic first day for anyone to take on board and by the time she was to serve the dinner, Biddy was so tired she could have sat down on the floor and gone straight off to sleep.

The twins were dears, but little terrors, too. They had walked across the park and half-way Elizabeth, coming home from her party, had come bouncing up to them.

'Twins dear, it's your own Lizzie!' she said. 'Are you being good for Biddy, then?'

To Biddy she added, sotto voce, that the boys were spoilt rotten, but she said it indulgently. You couldn't say much else when they were only three years old and so lovable. Johnny was the bolder and naughtier of the two; it had been Fred who had put his little arms round Biddy's neck and asked to be carried home and then, with his mouth an inch from her ear, he had murmured, 'I love you, Biddy. Will you marry me when I's a big boy?'

'I will, Fred, if you're still of the same mind when you're big,' Biddy assured him. 'Now where's that ice cream gone?'

She was grateful for Elizabeth's company when they got home, though, and she realised where most of the ice cream had gone. Down the twins' little checked tweed coats, over their small hands, even up the sleeves of their red woollen jumpers.

'How did they get ice cream in their hair?' she asked Elizabeth, as the two of them tackled the sticky little boys with soap and flannel. 'No one gets ice cream in their *hair*!'

'We does,' Johnny said, as the flannel moved away from his mouth. 'We gets it all over; our Mam says so.'

And then there was the twins' high tea . . . boiled eggs with bread-and-butter soldier boys, warm milk in bunny mugs, a banana mashed up with brown sugar sprinkled over it. Their mother swathed them in voluminous bibs but even so the floor somehow managed to receive more than its fair share of their tea.

'We ought to have a dog,' Mrs Gallagher said, surveying the linoleum with despair. 'A dog would *enjoy* cleaning up after them.'

'I wanna dog,' Johnny said immediately. 'Do you wanna dog, our Fred?'

'Not our Fred, darling, just Fred,' Mrs Prescott put in. 'Oh dear, but I say it meself, I know I do!'

The men kept well out of the kitchen, but Biddy didn't mind. It was wonderful in here in the firelight, with the twins sitting up to the table banging with their spoons and slurping at their bunny mugs, whilst the women attended to their every want and Biddy ate a plateful of honey sandwiches, drank several cups of tea, and assured her employer that this would see her through until dinner was over.

'Bathtime now,' Mrs Prescott said briskly as the boys clambered off their chairs and began to tug at their bibs as though quite willing to behead themselves if only they could remove the hated sign of a meal sloppily eaten. 'You love a bath don't you, darlings?'

The darlings roared that they loved a bath and charged out of the kitchen, across the hall and up the stairs, making as much noise as a football team and, as Biddy discovered when she went upstairs herself that night, liberally smearing sugar, banana and egg yolk over everything they touched.

'Go and help, Liz,' Mrs Gallagher told her daughter indulgently. 'Biddy and I will cope down here won't we, Biddy?'

'I'm sure we shall, ma'am,' Biddy said. In the course of the afternoon she had made, under Mrs Gallagher's instructions, a pan of leek and potato soup, a wonderful concoction made with oranges, lemons, cream and sugar which Mrs Gallagher said was a citrus syllabub, and a savoury, which was liver, onions, bread and beef dripping all mashed and mixed together and then spread on little square biscuits.

'You'll put the biscuits on the sideboard, beside the drinks,' Mrs Gallagher had told her. 'Then I'll come and tip you the wink when to serve the soup. Liz will help. When you think we've had long enough to drink the soup you can bring the beef through – the roast potatoes, sprouts and so on will be in the tureens, keeping hot in the cupboard by the oven, so they must be taken out and brought through with the beef – the trolley's over there, just watch it on the edges of carpet. I'll see to the Yorkshire pudding . . . that isn't as easy as it looks. Oh . . . gravy . . .'

But at last all the instructions were given and understood and Mrs Gallagher had gone off to change.

'We don't bother, usually, but tonight, as it's our guests' first night with us, we shall,' she said. 'Poor Biddy, what a day you've had! Look, my dear, are you sure you can cope? I really should have got someone in to help you . . . but Elizabeth is awfully good, she'll be through like a shot if you need a hand.'

'I'll be all right; soup first, when you say,' Biddy said, white-faced but determined. Thank heaven for Mrs Gallagher, she thought. If she'd been some hardnosed old woman who gave orders and walked away I'd never have got through it. As it is, I've a fair chance.

She put the little biscuits out by the drinks tray, checked that the fire was made up, the table laid properly and the soft lamps round the room lit. Mrs Gallagher said the big central light was too bright and daunting for a family party. Then she went back to the kitchen.

The soup would be served from a huge china tureen, with a matching china ladle. Mrs Gallagher would serve the soup. It looked very good, just simmering on the stove, as Biddy hovered above it with a handful of chopped parsley. Add it at the last minute, Mrs Gallagher had said. And the vegetables in their tureens – silver ones this time – were in the oven along with the beef . . . the Yorkshire pudding had been made by Mrs Gallagher and put in the top of the wall oven, where it was cooking at a high heat, her mistress had said.

'Psst, Biddy! Soup!' Having nearly given her a heart attack, Elizabeth beamed at her. 'Want a hand?'

'No, I'm fine, thanks.' Biddy scooped the hot soup dishes out of the cupboard by the oven – heavens, they really were hot – and clattered them onto the trolley, then slid the tureen onto it as well. It was really heavy, she must be careful not to drop it!

She wheeled the trolley slowly across the kitchen, across the hall and through the dining-room door. There was a carpet in here, but she should not have to cross it; a gleaming parquet path led from the door to the head of the table, where she was bound. She kept her head down and her eyes lowered, intent on her task. Just get it there, that was all she had to do, then lift the tureen and put it down in front of Mrs Gallagher, hand the soup plates round, and she could go back to the kitchen.

She lifted the tureen and managed, just, to give it a safe landing right in front of her mistress. She gave a little sigh and stepped back, taking the soup plates off the trolley, and felt someone staring at her. She glanced uneasily down at herself. She was wearing the black dress, the little white pinny, the celluloid hair-tidy, only it was a cap whichever way you looked at it. Everything looked all right from up here; and the plates, though hot, were . . .

She looked across the table, straight into a pair of dark, intense eyes which were fixed on hers. Black, curly hair, a broad brow, a quirky, amused mouth . . . it was her rescuer, her hero!

She nearly dropped the plates. God knew, she thought afterwards, how she had managed to hold onto them, but she did. And not only that, she proceeded to hand them round as she had been taught, with a murmur of apology if someone had to move to accommodate her.

The seaman who had saved her was wearing the same clothes, probably, but he had a tie under his blue shirt collar. He was looking at her . . . well, it made her blush, the way he was looking. Someone would notice, say something . . . but everyone's attention was on Mrs Gallagher, ladling soup, telling everyone that Biddy had made it, that she was bidding fair to become a good little cook . . .

'Biddy.' The seaman said it under his breath, still watching her, making her name sound like a love-word, almost a caress. 'Biddy.'

'She's settling in very nicely, aren't you, love?'

With a start, Biddy realised that Mrs Gallagher was talking to her. 'Yes, ma'am,' she whispered. 'Very nicely.'

The seaman nodded, then glanced round the table and opened his mouth. He was about to speak, to tell everyone where he had seen her before and in what circumstances! Biddy shook her head at him, her eyes pleading for his understanding, his silence. If he said – if he told how he'd found her in the street, fighting over a carpet bag with an old tramp . . . If he told Mrs Gallagher how she had run away afterwards without a word of thanks . . . she would lose her lovely job, they would think her a street urchin, perhaps even a thief!

But he had read the message. He smiled, a slow, lazy, somehow very loving smile, and casually put a finger against his lips for a second, then held out his hand to take the bowl of soup Mrs Gallagher was offering.

'Thank you, Nellie,' he said. 'Good it looks, my favourite is leek and potato.'

He had such a lovely voice! She could not place his accent but his soft cadences warmed her heart. And he was not going to give her away, he would tell no one that he knew her! Relief made Biddy feel quite light-headed. Oh he was so kind! She did so love her job, she would do almost anything to keep it.

'Thank you, Biddy.' Everyone had been served and Mrs Gallagher was handing back the half-empty tureen.

'Thank you, ma'am,' Biddy said solemnly. She put the tureen back on the trolley and almost danced out of the room. Suddenly it struck her that he was the young man who was staying in the house over Christmas – Dai something-or-other, that was his name. She had longed to see him again but had not believed it to be possible. Seamen from all over the world come into port at Liverpool a couple of times a year, then perhaps they don't dock here again for years. And now she had not only set eyes on him but they were actually going to be living, over Christmas, under the same roof!

But she must not moon about thinking of her hero; there was too much to do. She gave them five minutes by the kitchen clock, then she began to unload the hot tureens from the oven onto the trolley. The beef was in a roasting tin; she transferred that, with the help of a couple of forks, onto its dish, rushed back to the gas cooker and picked up the pan with the gravy in it, tipped the contents into the shallow gravy boat, checked the trolley over . . . tiptoed out of the room to listen outside the dining-room door.

She was still hovering when the door opened; Elizabeth stood there, with a pile of soup plates in her hands.

'Serve up, Bid,' she hissed like a stage-conspirator. 'I want a glass of lemonade, they're all drinking wine and beer and stuff.'

'Oh . . . right!' Biddy scuttled back to the kitchen, seized the trolley, then slowed down as she had been told.

'Don't ever try to rush,' Mrs Gallagher had advised. 'If you take your time you won't trip or spill or have any other disasters of a similar nature. We shan't mind waiting, we've got so much to talk about.'

So Biddy pushed slowly and arrived safely. But this time she dared not glance across at her seaman; she kept her eyes down even whilst she was transferring the contents of her trolley to the table. She knew he was watching her, though. She could feel his eyes on her, it was almost like being stroked.

'Beef . . . potatoes, roast and boiled . . . sprouts, tinned peas . . . carrot sticks . . . that's lovely, Biddy. We can manage now.'

Biddy left the room, pushing the trolley ahead of her. Elizabeth, with a very large glass of lemonade in one hand, smiled and went to go past her as she entered the kitchen.

'All serene? Jolly good. I wonder if me Da will let me have the first slice of the beef? But they're all guests, and I'm family, so I'll have to take what I'm given . . . oh do have the soup, Biddy, it really is good.'

But Biddy was too keyed up to eat. She got the pudding dishes out of the dresser and put them on the trolley, fetched the wonderful citrus syllabub in its huge glass bowl and put that on the trolley too, and was about to bring the cream out of the vegetable scullery, where it had been put to keep cool, when like a flash of lightning she remembered.

The Yorkshire pudding! It was still in the little top oven, cooking away!

She threw open the oven door and snatched at the tin. It was far too hot for such treatment and tipped, spilling hot fat onto the floor before she managed to shove it back into the oven. She raced across the room for a cloth, rushed back and slid in the fat and landed on all fours, got up again, limping, and grabbed the cloth and went back, this time getting the pudding out successfully. She looked round for a dish, found a big brown pottery one, and turned the pudding out onto it, grabbed it and raced back across the kitchen. She burst into the dining-room, still limping, and held the pudding aloft.

'Oh, Mrs Gallagher, I forgot the Yorkshire! I gorrit out all right but I tipped some fat and slid in it, that's why I were a minute or two longer than I should've been. It's done to a turn, though . . . who's going to serve it?'

Everyone laughed. She had no idea why, but they did.

Even her seaman was smiling, his eyes sparkling with amusement.

Mr Gallagher stood up. He had dark hair with a touch of white at the temples, a thin, dark face and a long line which creased his right cheek when he smiled. 'Over here, Biddy,' he said. 'Nice to know you're not *too* perfect, chuck. But I can hear a genuine scouser under that nice little voice. How are you likin' your first dinner party, eh?'

'It's hard work, but it's exciting,' Biddy said. At that moment she loved them all. They had noticed her, had been hoping she would get on all right . . . oh, she was a lucky girl to work here, she really was!

Dai woke early and lay there, lazily smiling to himself. She was here, in this very house, his little blue-eyed girl! Her name was Biddy and she was Nellie's maidservant, she was new to the job but they were very pleased with her . . . she would stay here, he need never worry about losing touch with her again!

Not that they had exchanged so much as a word all evening. She had served the entire meal, including coffee and little chocolate biscuits – he had drunk three cups of coffee and eaten six biscuits, all absently, whilst watching the door, waiting for her to reappear.

Only she had not. In fact he, Stuart and Joey had remained in the dining-room, drinking port, whilst the women went and, he suspected, helped Biddy with the washing up. At any rate when they rejoined the ladies in the sitting-room presently, Stuart looked across at his wife, one eyebrow raised and she said at once, as though he had asked her a silent but perfectly understood question, 'I've sent her to bed, poor scrap. Didn't she do well? She's a lovely girl, Stu, she'll suit us admirably.'

'Clever girl to find her,' Stuart said, with such a wealth

of love and understanding in his voice that, unaccountably, Dai felt tears sting behind his eyes.

Oh, he could remember times when his Mam and Da had been like that; had spoken across a room without either of them opening their mouths! How could Davy have done it to her, slept with Menna whilst she was dying, in pain? How could he have brought Menna blatantly to live in the house, called her his housekeeper, when she was just a brassy little barmaid who was only at home behind a counter with the beer-pull in her hand?

But . . . was it really as bad as that? Rumour, in a small village, can be vicious. He did not know whether his father had gone courting Menna whilst Bethan was still alive, though he had suspected it. But surely all those long absences . . .

Give your Da a chance, Dai, love, his mother's gentle, amused voice said inside his head. *Give him a chance to explain for himself, to tell you where he went and why, when I lay dying. He won't lie to you about that, I promise you.*

But around him conversations buzzed; the young girl, Elizabeth, came and perched on the arm of his chair. He smiled lazily up at her. A pretty child, probably not much younger than Biddy, but life had dealt with them very differently, had conspired to keep Elizabeth young whilst Biddy had matured because she had no choice.

'Dai, tell me about your home. Tell me about when you were a little boy. Do you live in a city, like Liverpool? I've never been to the Isle of Anglesey you know.' ·

Joey was talking to Stuart and Nellie was listening. But Lilac, the girl whom Nellie called her adopted sister, was staring at the two of them. She looked both slightly puzzled and extremely thoughtful. Dai found that he was uneasy over her scrutiny and did not much want to talk about his childhood with those very large, violet-blue eyes fixed on his.

'Well you know that Anglesey's an island, luv, quite a small island off the coast of Wales. There's no city on the island. But isn't it time you went to bed? You've had a long day – we all have – and you'll want to be up early tomorrow, to see what Santa's brought.'

Nellie must have been listening despite looking as though she was concentrating entirely upon her husband and Joey. Without turning round she said, 'Yes, Dai's right, Liz darling. Go up now . . . and you might pop in on the twins, just make sure they're sleeping soundly.'

'If they weren't we'd all know,' Lilac said ruefully. 'They'd be shouting and yelling, or charging downstairs naked as the day they were born . . .'

'But they've got dear little sleeping suits on,' Elizabeth protested. 'I saw you put them on, Auntie Li!'

'And the first thing they do when they wake up is to take those dear little sleeping suits off,' Lilac assured her. 'Why we've produced two would-be nudists I've no idea, but we have.' She smiled wickedly at her husband. 'I suppose it's you, Joey. I suppose when you were a little boy you kept taking your clothes off and now your sons do it.'

'Me! When you were a child, my girl, you were the naughtiest, most self-willed . . .'

'Well, maybe, but I didn't take my clothes . . .'

'We've only your word for that, young Lilac!' Stuart said. 'When I think of the things Nellie told me about you . . . running away, leapin' about in Mersey-mud wi' your pals, nickin' fades from the market . . .'

'There!' Joey declared triumphantly. 'If there's bad blood in these lads we all know where it came from!'

Lilac jumped on Joey and a royal battle ensued, with Elizabeth taking now one side, now the other and Nellie and Stuart laughing and applauding. But again, Dai had got the feeling that, if Nell had not interrupted the conversation, someone might have said something . . .

You're being daft, he told himself now, lying on his back and looking across lazily at the window curtains. I wonder if it's snowing out there? I wonder if I'll get a chance of a word with Biddy at breakfast? I could offer to wash up . . . Nellie's awful kind, if I were to explain . . .

But Biddy didn't want him to explain, he'd known at once, and you could understand why. This was a happy household and Biddy did not want to put anyone off, to make her position here difficult. Well, nor do I want such a thing, Dai reminded himself hastily, because I like to know where she is. And this way I can get to know her properly, really get to know her. There are bound to be opportunities – there's her day off, for a start. She must have a day off, everyone does, and from what Nellie said at dinner last night she doesn't have parents to go home to. Only friends.

Yes, that's right, I'll see her on her day off. And I'll give a hand in the kitchen; it's the sort of house where people wander in and out of the kitchen. I'll offer to make a cup of tea, I'll peel the potatoes, I'll . . .

Bless me, it's Christmas Day! A present – that's it, I'll give her a present! He had explained to Nellie that he only had little things for everyone, and he knew that the Prescotts, for instance, had not known he was going to be here and so had not dreamed of buying anything. But he had a tiny bone carving of a dog for Elizabeth, a large cigar for Stuart, a small box of very good chocolates for Nellie . . . he racked his brain, trying to think what he might give Biddy, then remembered the chunk of amber.

It was a curiosity more than a present, really, except that it could probably be made into a piece of jewellery, he supposed. He had found it on a beach in Norfolk when the *Jenny Bowdler* had docked at a little place called Wells-next-the-Sea. He and Greasy had walked along the beach at low tide and he'd found it, just lying on the tide-line, gleaming with a red-gold gleam through the detritus the surf had left behind.

Thinking about it made him sit up and glance towards his ditty bag. It was within reach if he made a long arm . . .

He towed the ditty bag in and opened it, delving down the side of it until his fingers touched the hard, smooth sides of the amber. It was large, the size of a bantam's egg and would, he supposed vaguely, cut down into several pieces which could be worn. He brought it out and held it up to the light; you had to do that, otherwise it didn't look all that remarkable. He might never have bothered with it at all had he not been curious about its shape and, having dipped it in the sea, held it up against the pale wintry sun and realised it was translucent. A local gentleman exercising his spaniel on the beach and seeing Dai examining his find, had told him he was a lucky man.

'It's a very fine piece of Succinite, which is what mineralogists call the substance known as amber,' he had said impressively, having subjected the egg-like object to a long scrutiny through a pair of pince-nez spectacles which he produced from an inner pocket and perched on the end of his longish nose. 'Amber is the fossilised resin from the extinct pine forests which flourished millions of years ago along the Baltic coast. For many years the currents have deposited it on our northern shores, but few have been fortunate enough to find such a magnificent example. The Ancient Greeks and Romans used it as a cure for a great many disorders, rheumatism amongst others, and Roman women wore amulets made of amber as a protection against witchcraft.'

'Well I never,' Dai said, astonished at such an outpouring of information. 'But what use is it today? I don't suppose there's much belief in it as a charm, not these days!'

'Nowadays we prize it for its translucence and beautiful colour and make earrings, pendants and the like from it. This is a very fine example; you must have it polished and give it to the woman in your life.'

Dai had smiled and put the amber in his pocket, thanking the man politely, but the remark about the woman in his life had stung. He had no woman in his life any more, not since Bethan's death.

Now, though, Dai knew just what to do with his amber egg. He would give it to Biddy for a Christmas box, and tell her that, next Christmas, he would have it broken up and made into something pretty for her to wear. That would show her better than anything else could that he was serious. That this was not just a casual, here-today-gone-tomorrow friendship but a loving, lasting relationship. But right now he might just as well get up. He glanced at his watch, but it was still dark so he fumbled for matches, lit one, and read the time by its light.

Six o'clock, quite early still. But he was awake and he guessed that a maidservant would be expected to rise betimes, before anyone else. He would go downstairs now and put the kettle on – she would find a cup of tea waiting for her in the kitchen as well as Dai Evans! He could dress in two seconds flat; life on a trawler meant that no one ever undressed, though seaboots, jerseys and trousers were usually shed.

He dressed, dragged a comb through his curls and set off, in his socks so as not to disturb anyone, down the stairs. The house seemed wrapped in slumber still; Dai guessed that the twins, who would normally have been awake and investigating the stockings their parents had hung on the bedposts of their shared bed, were still suffering from the effects of their journey of the day before.

I'll riddle the fire through and put the kettle on, pull back the curtains, find the tea and the pot, Dai was planning as he opened the kitchen door with infinite softness and care. What a surprise young Biddy will get, to find me down before her!

Chapter Nine

The shrilling of the alarm clock gave Biddy the most dreadful fright, though she and Ellen had owned one in the flat and set it each night. But Biddy had been worn out by the time she got to bed and then, cuddling down and waiting for sleep to overcome her at once, as it usually did, she was sadly disappointed.

All she could do was think about him, the young man who had rescued her, Dai Evans! How he looked when he was serious, how he looked when he smiled. How he had not once taken his eyes off her all the while she had been in the dining-room last night. How he had been the subject of conversation, for a few brief moments, when Mrs Gallagher and her sister had returned to the kitchen to help Biddy to wash up and clear away.

That had been quite mysterious, now she came to think about it. Mrs Prescott had kept starting sentences and not finishing them, and Mrs Gallagher had spoken, not sharply, but with a kind of definite finality, which seemed to have been sufficient to make Mrs Prescott change the subject at least.

Mrs Gallagher had explained about the relationship between her and Mrs Prescott, though – how she had been a maid of all work at Culler's Orphan Asylum when a new-born baby had been left on the doorstep. The baby had been Lilac, which was Mrs Prescott's first name, and Mrs Gallagher had told Biddy that for years the two of them had clung together, leaving the orphanage together as well . . . how they were closer than sisters, sharing everything, even secrets.

It must be lovely to have a sister, Biddy thought wistfully, staring up at the dark ceiling above her head. And then, when she had given up on sleep and was lying there indulging in a beautiful fantasy in which Dai Evans came into the kitchen and said, deeply, 'It's you! I've searched the city for you, you lovely creature!', she fell annoyingly asleep and dreamed, not of Dai Evans's dark eyes, exciting smile and strong hands, but of Ma Kettle demanding that she return to Kettle's Confectionery at once.

'You're bound to me; your dear mother wished it,' Ma Kettle said, trying to persuade her to take a bath in a huge vat of cooling toffee for some obscure, dream-like reason. 'In you 'ops love, an' soon you'll be twice the woman you was! One lickle dip in this 'ere mixture an' you won't ever want to run away from me agin . . . poor but honest, that's us Kettles, from the best of us – that's me – to the worst, what'll be you when you wed our Kenny.'

'But I'm not going to wed your Kenny, I'm going to wed Dai Evans,' Biddy protested. 'And I've got a good job now, Ma, a job where they value me. I aren't leaving there for anyone!'

'Ho, an' 'oo might this wonderful employer be?' Ma Kettle sneered, struggling, now, to pour the vat of toffee over the recalcitrant Biddy. 'Per'aps she won't want you to stay when she sees you're jest a lickle toffee-girl!'

She tipped the vat, Biddy screamed . . . and woke.

The alarm was shrilling beside her ear, fairly hopping on the small bedside table, and the hands, when she lit her candle, pointed to six o'clock.

'Drat, I set it wrong,' Biddy muttered, standing the alarm back on the table again, for she had picked it up and peered, the better to make sure of the hour. 'Mrs

Gallagher said seven this morning, because they would all be late up. Still, no point in lying here, I might easily dream about Ma Kettle again. I'd rather get up and take my time preparing for the day ahead in the kitchen.'

She lit her candle, then got slowly out of bed, because it was Christmas Day, after all, and she had no need to hurry. Then she padded across the icy linoleum to her fire, turned on the gas, lit it, and went over to the window to draw the curtains back a tiny bit.

It was snowing! Lazily, the flakes floated down, each one big as a florin.

That's not the sort of snow which lies, Biddy told herself wisely. Not usually, anyway. It's the small, fast-falling flakes which build up. Still, it'll look like a picture-book out there by breakfast I reckon. I wonder if they'll go sledging? Wish I could, I used to love it so much.

But sledging was a pastime for the rich or for kids, she knew, not for maidservants, so she pulled the curtains back across again and went over to her gas ring. A panful of water boiled quite quickly so she had a hot wash, then dressed proudly in her new uniform. It was really pretty, especially now that Mrs Gallagher had taken the dress from her and put deeper darts around the waist and bust, so that it fitted well.

'It's hard-wearing stuff, unfortunately,' Mrs Gallagher had said as she pinned the new darts in place. 'I'm not keen on grey, but it doesn't need washing as often as prettier colours. In fact if you put it down for the laundry on a Friday morning and wear the other one the following week, you should do quite well.'

'The laundry?' Biddy had echoed. 'Don't I do your washing, Mrs Gallagher?'

'Bless you, no! You'll have quite enough to do without laundering, Biddy. Mind you, small things, underwear, stockings, things like that, are washed at home, but not big things, like sheets and dresses. Now, how does that feel?'

'Fine, thank you ma'am,' Biddy said. She would have said the same had a pin been driven an inch into her side, but it happened to be the truth. 'Shall I go and change so you can alter the other one?'

'No need, it's a simple job. I'll have both dresses done before you go to bed tonight and of course you'll wear your black to serve dinner.'

So here she was, putting on her pretty, pearl-grey dress and adjusting the big white apron over it. The cap was tricky, but she perched it on her head, clipped it in place with the white kirby grips her mistress had provided, and then turned and made her bed.

'I'll leave you in the warm today, Dolly,' she told her rag doll, sliding it under the covers until only its face showed. 'There, isn't that snug? Because it's snowing, and I'm going to turn the gas fire off before I go downstairs.'

She suited action to words, then doused the candle, went over and drew back the curtains, thought about opening a window to air the room but decided against it, and set off down the stairs, her slop-bucket swinging gently from one hand.

It was a modern house, which meant that the guests would use the bathroom and the upstairs toilet – no slop buckets for them, thank goodness. But she had to riddle the stove through and get it blazing, fetch more coke in so that it could be made up as soon as it caught hold, and then start on the other fires.

Bedrooms, again, had gas fires, which meant no work because when she asked Nellie if she should bring a tray of tea upstairs Nellie said at once that it wouldn't be necessary.

'Normally I would ask you to bring us a tray, but not over the holiday,' she said. 'And there's a gas-ring and a kettle in the Prescotts' room if they want a hot drink. As for Mr Evans, young men aren't used to being waited on, particularly seamen.'

Biddy thought of Luke, impatiently banging on his bedroom floor with the heel of a shoe if he thought she was late bringing his tea, and even of Kenny, who would put his head out into the hallway and holler, 'Bid? Have you dropped dead, our Biddy? Where's me cuppa?' No wonder it had killed poor old Ma Kettle, having to do all that herself after I left, she thought now, reaching the front hallway and crossing it, to push open the baize door which separated it from the kitchen regions. Glad this set-up is so different – oh, I'm so lucky!

She was still smiling at the thought of her own luck when she pushed the kitchen door open . . . then stopped in the doorway, staring.

The fire glowed through the bars, the gaslights hissed, illuminating the room which looked homely and warm, not at all quiet and deserted, as a kitchen should look to the first person down in the morning. The curtains were drawn back too and someone, who had been standing in front of the sink looking out at the lazily falling flakes, turned round and smiled at her.

'The compliments of the season to you, Biddy! Awake I was, so I thought you'd mebbe like a bit of company on Christmas Day.' Dai came across the kitchen and took the slop-bucket from her nerveless hand. 'Let me empty that now whilst you pour us both a cup of tea. It's made and mashed, all ready for you.'

'Oh . . . no, it's all right, I can manage quite . . .' Biddy began, pink-cheeked, trying to snatch the slop bucket from him, but he warded her off, laughing. 'Look, it's me job to . . .'

He ignored her, taking the bucket over to the sink and emptying it whilst Biddy continued to stammer helplessly. He was here, perhaps not uttering quite the words of her fantasy, but it was enough, suddenly, that they were in the same room. And alone, for a while anyway. A quick glance at the kitchen clock showed it still lacked five minutes to half past six. Yes, she was in good time.

But how did one behave when a young man you thought the world of appeared in your place of employment as the guest of your employer? As Dai turned away from the sink and stood the bucket on the draining board Biddy gave a little half-bob of a curtsy, looking down at her shoes as she did so. Immediately Dai crossed the room in a couple of strides and took both her hands in his.

'Biddy, this sounds daft, but I recognised you the moment I set eyes on you the other night. You – you were special to me, I could tell, my heart could tell. We're two of a kind, Biddy, and don't you go behaving with me as you would with other people – I don't think maids curtsy to anyone now, in any event – but you and I, we – we belong together.'

Biddy pulled half-heartedly at her hands but Dai just gripped them tighter, looking down into her face with eyes which blazed with sincerity.

'Isn't it all . . . oh, Mr Evans, you're here as a guest and I'm . . .'

'I'll leave,' Dai said promptly. 'I'll leave right now, I'll walk out through that back door and then knock and walk in again. Just Dai Evans I'll be, wanting to pay court to Bridget . . . what's your last name?'

'I'm Bridget O'Shaughnessy,' Biddy murmured tremulously. The feel of his hands on hers was doing very odd things to her stomach and there seemed to be a bird held captive in her rib-cage from the way her heart was fluttering 'You are daft, aren't you?'

She had not meant to say it and gasped at herself, but he just smiled more lovingly than ever and let go of her hands for a moment to tilt her chin with one strong, tanned hand.

'Course I'm daft, people in love do always act daft. Biddy, I never believed in love at first sight until I saw you struggling with that great bully in the market, and then I knew it was true because it had happened to me. Biddy? Do you like me a little bit, too?'

Ellen would have tossed her head and said it was all very well to talk about love . . . she would have given Dai sly glances through her lashes and flirted outrageously, her mouth saying 'No, no!' whilst all the rest of her said, 'Yes!' And men were good at conversations like that, they could make the sort of remark which had Ellen bubbling with laughter, saying, 'Oh, you are awful . . . what a tease you are, sir, I don't believe a word you say!' whilst the man pressed closer to her, tracing shapes with a forefinger in the palm of her hand, an arm brushing against her breast, the quick, double-meaning remarks tripping off his tongue whilst his eyes made bolder remarks still, just for her to see.

But Biddy was not Ellen, had never really understood the complex games of come and go, do and don't, which her friend had played with such consummate ease. She was just Biddy, who said what she thought, what she meant.

'I was the same,' she whispered now, staring fixedly at a point about half-way down Dai's broad chest. 'As soon as I saw you I felt that you were the – the person I'd waited for, only I never even knew I was waiting! Yesterday, when I walked into the dining room . . . oh, I was so happy, I could scarcely believe I wasn't dreaming!'

He nodded. 'Me, too. They'd talked about a new maid, Biddy, but you were the last person I expected to see. You came in with your head bent, and that cap-thing on your pretty curls, clutching the soup tureen as though it were your first-born . . . I knew it were you at once, though I couldn't see your face. Oh Biddy, a miracle it is that we've met up again! A bloody miracle!'

And Biddy, who disapproved of strong language, who would normally have winced at anyone describing a miracle in such terms, just nodded and looked up into his face once more. 'It is,' she said earnestly. 'It really is a bloody miracle – I prayed for it hard enough!'

And because she had raised her face at last and because he could read the worshipping expression in those big, blue eyes, Dai Evans bent his head and kissed her lips.

It should have been a light little kiss, a friendly kiss, but somehow it was not. Their lips clung, as though they had a will of their own and wished to remain close, and Biddy's body gradually relaxed until she was leaning against Dai's broad chest.

They might have remained there for ever, she thought afterwards, only they both heard a distant shout and then the patter of small feet, thumpety-thumping down the stairs.

'It's them little buggers,' Dai said, very reprehensively, Biddy thought. 'Come out wi' me after dinner . . . luncheon, I mean? I'll meet you outside the Baptist church on the corner . . . better that way, eh?'

'Much better. I'll come if I can, but . . . oh Dai, you'd better go!'

'Can't, they'll be here in two shakes. Look, gi's my cup an' I'll sit by the fire . . .'

He was innocently in position when the twins, closely followed by their father, burst into the room.

'Biddy, Biddy, look what farver Chrissmus give us!'

'Biddy, Biddy, what a go, eh? See our clockwork choo-choos!'

Peace, Biddy could see, was over for the day. The twins had been partially dressed but lacked shoes and socks and their fair curls stood on end as though they had wrenched themselves free half-way through a hair brushing.

'Come on aht of it,' their father said wrathfully, grabbing one twin by his left arm and the other by his right. 'Your mummy said dress first and she meant it. Leave Biddy alone, she's gettin' your breakfast and if you pester you won't get no grub. What about that for a threat, eh?'

But the twins were unimpressed.

'Biddy, there was choccy in our stockin's, an' a tangerine! Whistles too . . . see?' Johnny blew a long blast just to prove the truth of his words. 'Red for me, blue for Fred,' he added.

'An' we had a rag story book what you can't tear,' Fred shouted over his shoulder as he was towed out of the room. 'An' a b'loon in the top, red for me, blue for Johnny. An' . . . an' . . .'

Dai had slipped unobtrusively out of the room and was half-way up the stairs, his cup of tea in one hand. Biddy closed the kitchen door on them all and hurried back to get on with her work – to start her work, rather. But the kitchen clock only said twenty minutes to seven, so she was still early and could take her time.

Nevertheless, the breakfast today was to be a big one. Eggs, bacon, kidneys, sausages, bottled tomatoes, fried bread . . . and that was just what you might call the main course. The twins would have milky porridge and a poached egg each, the adults would have grapefruit first, then their main course and then lots of hot buttered toast and coffee.

It's a bloomin' wonder the rich can roll up the stairs to bed each night with all they eat, Biddy told herself, beginning to collect the ingredients for this mammoth meal which would last a poor person two days, if not a week. Kedgeree tomorrow, and I've no more idea how to make a kedgeree than fly to the moon. But Mrs Gallagher will show me; she says it's really easy. And this afternoon I'm going to meet Dai . . . oh, how ever shall I wait!

But in fact Biddy was so busy that the morning positively flew, and that was with all the women mucking in to get everything ready and on the table in time.

'We have our main hot meal at noon on Christmas Day, then a cold supper,' Mrs Gallagher explained. 'Then on Boxing Day we have cold meals all day, except for breakfast, which is kedgeree, and the evening dinner is usually served with a hot pudding of some sort. But Christmas dinner is always a bit daunting. Never mind, many hands make light work as they say.'

And with Elizabeth and Biddy doing the vegetables, Mrs Gallagher making bread sauce and stuffing and Mrs Prescott garlanding the half-cooked turkey with pork sausages and keeping an eye on the pudding, making the brandy sauce and laying the table, everything got done in the end, though there were several moments when Biddy was sure they would not eat until teatime.

And the Christmas dinner! Her own plate was brought through from the dining-room by Mrs Gallagher, piled high with good things. Great slices of creamy-white turkey breast, chestnut stuffing steaming on the side, golden-brown roast potatoes, red currant jelly, dark purple broccoli, pale green sprouts, emerald peas . . . and the gravy, golden-bubbled, over all.

'Don't worry about us, we'll take ages to get through this lot,' Mrs Gallagher said. 'Just eat it at your own pace. We'll come through when it's time to serve the pudding anyway, because we flame it in brandy, which the twins will love, and that takes practice.'

So Biddy took her time – and then could not eat half what was on her plate. She was terribly tempted to fetch a paper bag and put the dinner inside it and go out with it later, to find some poor tramp or half-starved child, but Mrs Gallagher, seeing her look guiltily at the food still piled on her plate, told her that it would not be wasted.

'It goes in the pig-bin, just outside the back door,' she explained. 'Then it's given to people who have a pig . . . Stuart doesn't believe in wasting food.' She smiled at Biddy. 'We've all been through bad times, just like you have,' she said softly. 'People don't forget.'

But Biddy, presently tucking into a very tiny slice of Christmas pudding, for she had assured Mrs Gallagher that she would burst if she was given a full helping, thought that her employer was wrong. People did forget, over and over. They fought their way up from poverty to bearable circumstances, from bearable circumstances to riches, and then their early experiences became transformed.

They began to believe they had fought their way up because they were, in some way, better and more worthy people than those who were still either struggling, or fixed at the bottom of the heap. They could no longer remember the ache of hunger, the pain of constant worry over where the next meal was to come from or the worse pain of seeing one you loved in miserable circumstances.

Now, the rich looked back and saw themselves as having been the deserving poor who had struggled out of the poverty pit by sheer hard work. Those who were still poor were condemned as idle and feckless, they drank too much, never saved money for a rainy day, frittered what they earned, when they earned anything at all, that was. Poverty had become, in their twisted minds, a punishment for failure – a deserved punishment what was more – and of course you didn't give to people like that, or pity them, or try to help. You despised them, pushed them away, preached at them . . . they were less human than your fat lap-dog, less regarded than the set of your jacket, the way your skirt hung at the back.

But the Gallaghers were not like that. They were caring people who knew all about poverty and remembered their own circumstances still. Mrs Gallagher belonged to the League of Welldoers and worked tirelessly to raise money for them, and Mr Gallagher was a Goodfellow – Biddy remembered how the Goodfellows had helped her Mam when she had first lost her job, and the wonderful food parcel which had been brought round after dark that first, terrible Christmas.

Biddy finished her Christmas pudding and jumped to her feet. Time to start the washing up, if she was to be ready to go out and meet Dai by the Baptist chapel this afternoon.

'I'll just make up the fire, ma'am, and then I'll go out for a bit of a blow, I'm thinking,' Biddy said, as the last dish was put away and the kitchen was as clean and tidy as though no one had worked in it for days. 'I'll fetch some more coke in from the shed.'

'Thank you, Biddy,' Mrs Gallagher said. 'The twins have been put down for a nap, though I think they're too excited to sleep for long, and the men are snoozing with their feet up in the study, so my sister and I will have a cosy chat in the living-room and tell each other what marvellous husbands we have and how lucky we are with our children.'

'You mean you'll have a moan about me Da eating too much and then snoring the afternoon away, and Auntie Lilac will have a moan about Uncle Joe having one too many at the dockyard pub when his ship comes in and reeling down the road shaking hands with lampposts,'

Elizabeth said, coming into the kitchen and heading for the scrap bag. 'Can I take some bits of bread and stuff out to the birds, Mam? I took some out earlier and it's all gone, they've scoffed the lot, poor little chaps. And I'll give them clean water at the same time because it keeps icing over and that isn't much fun for them.'

Biddy could dimly remember that when her father had been alive they had lived in a tiny house with a tiny garden, but she could not remember her mother feeding the birds. It was, however, a way of life with Elizabeth and Mrs Gallagher, who had told her that not only did they feed the birds three or four times a day, on three very fancy bird tables erected in different parts of the garden, but they had notebooks in which they noted down the species of birds which visited them, and they drew tiny pictures of each visitor to the tables with information concerning the length of their stay in the garden, what food they preferred, and whether they were what Mrs Gallagher called 'storm-tossed', which meant that they were not normally found in Britain, or simply a summer visitor.

'You want to feed the birds?' Mrs Gallagher looked at her little wristwatch. 'Yes, no reason why not. Try them with some warm water, it won't freeze so easily, and see if there's any dripping still soft in the larder. If so, pour it over the bread because it makes it more nourishing than bread alone. Then what will you do, dear? I'm afraid Christmas afternoon is usually rather flat.'

It had not occurred to Biddy before, but now she realised that despite her beautiful home, her friends and her wonderful family, Elizabeth was probably quite a lonely girl. She was encouraged to bring friends home, to go round to their houses when invited, to socialise in any way she chose, but her parents were very content with one another's company and there must be times when, with the best will in the world, Elizabeth felt a little bit left out.

'After feeding the birds? Oh, I dunno, mooch around I suppose.' Elizabeth glanced across at Biddy. 'What are you going to do, Bid? Can I do it with you?'

'Yes, of course,' Biddy said after only the very slightest hesitation. 'I'm, going out for some fresh air, we can go together.'

She could have done nothing else, but she felt a real stab of disappointment. She had worked so hard and was so looking forward to seeing Dai alone. . . . Elizabeth was a very nice girl, but . . .

But fate, for once, was on her side. She and Elizabeth had fed the birds together, laughing over the antics of a very cheeky robin, who actually flew to the bird-table whilst the two girls were still spreading out the feast and began pecking at the food. The snow was still falling, desultorily, but it was laying too, and Elizabeth had just remarked wistfully that she hoped it would be nice and deep by the time Christmas was over so that she and her friends might go sledging, snowballing and ice-skating, when Joey Prescott wandered out to them.

'Hello, girls,' he said. 'I've ate too much, my stomach's tight as a perishin' drum. Stuart and I thought we'd walk across to the lake in Prince's Park, see if the ice is holdin'. Fancy some exercise?'

'That would be lovely, wouldn't it, Biddy?' Elizabeth said at once. 'We were only going for a walk ourselves. . . . We'll go and put our coats and boots on – is Dai coming?'

'No, the lazy beggar won't. Well, he says he's goin' to pop over to his shipmate's place so he may not be back for tea, but he'll be in for supper. What about you, Biddy? Don't let Elizabeth answer for you, luv, or you'll never open your mouth again!'

Biddy laughed but seized the opportunity gratefully. 'I'd really like to go round to my friend Ellen and wish her a merry Christmas,' she admitted. 'Umm ... will it be all right if I don't come back for tea, though? She lives on Paul Street, a good walk from here. The trams won't be running on Christmas Day, will they?'

'No, not a chanst,' Joey said. 'I'll make it right with Nellie, though I'm sure she won't expect you back for tea; it'll only be a cuppa and a bit of cake, seein' as 'ow we guzzled fit to bust earlier.'

So Biddy hurried up to her room and put her trusty duffle-coat on over her uniform, though she did remove her white apron first. Then she donned Mrs Gallagher's wellingtons, tied Ellen's Christmas-present scarf round her head, put on the matching gloves and trundled down the stairs, feeling as hot and excited as though she were going to a party and not just walking down to the Baptist chapel on the corner.

Mrs Gallagher and her husband were in the hallway, both dressed up for going out. Mrs Gallagher was trying to make her husband wear the most enormous, stripy scarf and he was resisting fiercely. They swayed around the hall, laughing and knocking into the furniture, and never even noticed Biddy as she slipped out of the front door.

Out here it was a different world; a white world, with a keen little breeze blowing which ruffled the smooth surface of the snow and sent it up into the air in small, swirling eddies. But Biddy didn't mind what the weather did; she was off to meet Dai!

They met as arranged. Biddy came round the corner and there was Dai, hunched into a duffle-coat rather similar to hers, with his cap pulled well down over his brow and big boots on his feet. She could see almost nothing of him, yet already she would have known him anywhere, in any disguise. He did not hear her approach and was earnestly staring in the wrong direction through the whirling flakes when she touched his arm.

'Dai, I'm sorry I'm late.'

He turned and put his arms round her as naturally as though they had done it a thousand times before, instead of just the once. 'Biddy! You aren't late, it's me who's early. Where shall we go? I'd like to find a shelter of some sort so that we could sit down for a moment, but the place I've got in mind's a long walk, and I don't even know whether we'll be able to get in. Only Mrs Gallagher was talking about it at dinner, and . . .'

'Where?' Biddy asked. 'They're going to the lake in Prince's Park, so we'd better not go there.'

'No, I thought we'd walk across to Sefton Park. It's a long way but there's an aviary there, and a palm house. Mrs Gallagher said the palm house was often open . . . we could try both. There will surely be a seat in an alcove or something like that, wouldn't you think?'

'Oh, sure, to be,' Biddy murmured, falling into step beside him and feeling his arm slide round her waist with a delicious shiver. She did not care whether they found somewhere to sit down or not, so long as they were together. 'Which way will we go, though, to keep away from the lake?'

'We won't go into Prince's Park at all, we'll walk round it, along Croxteth Road and Lodge Lane. I bought a *Geographia of Liverpool* when I was searchin' for you, see, an' it's really good, gives lovely little maps of the whole city. Mind, I'm not the world's best map reader, but I've a fair bump of direction. Are you game to try and find this place?'

'Of course,' Biddy said. 'Even if I don't quite see . . . but I shall enjoy the walk.'

Her confidence was not exactly bolstered when Dai, having stared around him for a couple of minutes, announced, 'This way!' and led her boldly towards Prince's Gate West, then realised his mistake, muttered, 'Oh sugar!' beneath his breath and turned her round to face in the opposite direction.

'I do admire a man with a bump of direction,' Biddy said sweetly, smiling up at him. 'I'm sure you'll get us there, Dai, but going via the Mersey tunnel may take a while!'

'No sarcasm,' Dai growled, squeezing her waist. 'I'm on the right road now, feel it in my bones, I do. Quick march!'

They marched. The Croxteth Road was a long road, and on a snowy afternoon in December, a lonely road. But the two of them were soon so wrapped up in one another that they never noticed how far they had walked and in fact completely bypassed Lodge Lane, staying on the Croxteth Road until they reached the circus which heralded the Croxteth Gate. Here they walked between two wonderful mansions, only dimly seen through their surrounding trees despite the fact that the trees were leafless, and into the park at last.

'Not far now,' Dai said bracingly. 'Soon we can sit down and I can show you . . . well, what I want to show you.'

'How far's not far?' Biddy asked suspiciously. It was wonderful walking through the snow with Dai, but her feet were aching and she guessed that supper, albeit cold, would still tax her abilities to the utmost. Besides, they had not thought to bring an umbrella and since the snow had not held off for a moment the shoulders of her coat and the top of her scarf were already very wet indeed. 'About another five or six miles, would you say?'

Dai snorted and turned her to face him. He bent down,

for he was quite a lot taller than her, and rubbed her nose with his, Eskimo fashion. 'Poor little love, shall we give up and see if we can find a telephone booth? Then we could ring for a taxi and go home in comfort.'

'No, indeed,' Biddy said. She could no longer even feel her feet in the wellington boots, which was probably an advantage, since they must be freezing cold, she thought rather illogically. 'Come on . . . shall we run?'

They ran, slowing to a walk quite soon though, because even cutting straight across the snow-covered grass and between the trees, it was a good distance. As they went they glanced at the ornamental lake on which a number of ducks and seagulls were crossly huddled, tails to wind.

'The ice looks like it's holding,' Dai said with satisfaction. He squeezed her again. 'Got any skates, Biddy?'

'No. But I could put my stockings over my shoes,' Biddy suggested. 'I could slide great then, I bet.'

'I bet!' Dai turned her slightly and jerked his chin ahead of them. 'See that?'

It was not the aviary, not the palm house either, but it was what looked like a small workmen's hut beneath the trees. It also looked sturdy and firmly shut.

'That isn't the aviary,' Biddy objected. 'It's all shut up, we can't go in there.'

'Well, we'll take a look,' Dai decided. 'It's where they keep the deckchairs in the summer, I daresay. Come on.'

Since his arm was firmly looped around Biddy's waist she had little choice but to 'come on', so the two of them crossed the intervening snowy grass, leaving an arrow-straight path of double footprints, and went over to the hut.

Dai tried the door and to Biddy's astonishment, after a bit of creaking, it opened inwards, revealing a small, dusty but dry room in which, now that she looked about her, a caretaker or ticket-seller of some description must sit in summer, taking money or keeping an eye open through a small window whose shutters, however, were now firmly shut.

'This isn't bad,' Dai said. He pulled a canvas chair forward and Biddy collapsed into it, then he got one out and set it up for himself.

'Phew, that was a long walk,' he said, leaning back and closing his eyes for a moment. 'I wonder, was it worth it?'

Biddy giggled. 'See how you feel when we get back to Ducie Street,' she suggested. 'How does frostbite start?'

Dai's eyes shot open and he grinned provocatively across at her. 'I should know – it's one of the hazards of distant-water trawling. Tell you about it sometime I will, but right now . . . here, take it and tell me what you think, will you?'

He held a clenched fist out to her. Biddy could see by the way his fingers were curled that there was something quite large in his hand but she had no idea what it was. She wrinkled her nose doubtfully.

'I'm not touching something I can't see – for all I know it might be a toad or a lizard or – or a big, hairy spider.'

Dai shivered. 'It's not a spider; you wouldn't catch me grabbing up a spider, not even for the pleasure of having you jump into my arms,' he told her. 'It's nothing alive, honest.'

'Ugh! Not . . . not a *dead* spider?'

'Oh Biddy, how your mind do run on spiders,' Dai said impatiently. 'Can't you think of nothing else?'

'Well, no, because this strikes me as an awfully spidery sort of place,' Biddy admitted, glancing uneasily round. 'There are probably lots in here, under all the chairs, simply longing for a leg to run up . . . aaagh!'

She kicked out violently and Dai gave a shout of laughter.

'Mad you are, girl – tilting at windmills next you'll be! A large chunk of snow that was, melting and running down your knee and into your boot. And it's not a creature in my hand, I promise you that, it's something I'd like you to see. Be a brave girl, now.'

'It won't hurt or bite or make me jump?' Biddy said nervously. The little hut, which had seemed such a refuge when they were out in the snow, was shadowy and smelt of dust – and spiders. 'Do you promise, Dai?'

'See this wet, see this dry, cross my heart and hope to die,' Dai said, drawing a wetted finger across his throat. 'Don't you trust me, love?'

'Yes I do,' Biddy said. She held out her hand and gently took the object from his fingers as he released it. 'Oh, Dai, what is it? I can't see much in here, but it's warm and smooth . . . is it marble?'

'No, it's amber. It's what you females wear round your necks when it's made into beads, or on a chain when it's a pendant. It's quite a big bit, make all sorts with it you could. It's the most glorious colour, but you can't see it in this light, you need strong sunshine. Drat, never thought of that, I didn't, when I asked you to come out with me this afternoon.'

'It doesn't matter; it's still beautiful,' Biddy murmured. She tried to hand the amber back but Dai shook his head.

'No. It's for you, Biddy, a Christmas Box. And if you like it, I thought next Christmas I'd have it cut into beads, or a pendant and earrings for you.'

'A Christmas Box? For me? Oh, but Dai, it's much too beautiful! When would I wear amber, that's what proper ladies wear! Oh, isn't it a lovely thing, though? I just like the feel of it, all warm in my palm.'

'You'll wear it when you're a married lady, living in your own home with your man coming back to you from sea,' Dai said softly. 'You'll wear a blue dress with pleats, an amber necklace and a narrow velvet ribbon round your throat. You'll have your hair piled up on your head so you look like a little queen, only when I come home I'll put my hands into it and take out the pins and ribbons and it will tumble down over my hands, down to your shoulders, and it will hide your blushes when I kiss you.'

There was a long silence. In the dusk, Dai could see her small face, downturned, her eyes lowered, fixed on the amber egg in her lap. Then, just when he as thinking he must have been mad to talk to her like that, she got to her feet and came over to him. She put her hands on his shoulders and lowered her face until it was only inches from his.

'Dai, that was the loveliest thing anyone's ever said to me. I know I shouldn't, but I would love to keep the amber egg . . . at least until you find someone you'd rather give it to. We – we haven't known each other long, it was just that we met in such strange circumstances . . .'

'We've known one another long enough to share this seat,' Dai said. He pulled her down onto his knee and she did not resist. 'Biddy, you're very young – how old are you, by the way? - but I'm going on for twenty-three and I know my own mind. No one but you will there be for me. Not ever. Make up your mind to that.'

'I'm sixteen. I'll be seventeen next June,' Biddy murmured, her head resting comfortably in the hollow of his shoulder. 'And though I'm not as old as you, my mind is every bit as made up. I knew it as soon as I looked at you. Only we'll have to get to know one another better – I'm not earning very much, just ten shillings a week, but I can save, I'm an awful good saver.'

'I'm an awful good spender,' Dai said ruefully, against her hair. He had pulled off the wet scarf and cast it onto the spare chair as soon as she subsided onto his lap. 'But

I'll start to save from this moment on. We'll have a nice little home . . .'

'Two children, a boy and a girl . . .'

'A dog to take care of you whilst I'm at sea and a cow to give you milk . . .'

'A cow? In the city? Dai, I wouldn't know what to do to get the milk out!'

Dai laughed and kissed the side of her cold, snow-smelling face. 'No, you daft girl! We shan't live in the city, live on the Isle of Anglesey we will, near my people. Happy as the day is long you'll be, honest you will.'

'Oh! But they'll speak Welsh, and I only speak English.'

'And very nicely you speak it, too. Teach you Welsh in six months, I will – less, probably. And you'll pick up milking the cow easy as easy.'

'Oh, Dai, I'm a Catholic and I 'spect you're a Proddy.'

'Worse, I'm a Welsh Methodist; terrible old-fashioned and narrow-minded, to say nothing of bigoted, us Welsh Methodists. I go to chapel at home because my Mam did, but my religion don't weigh too heavy on me. I'm not a religious man, cariad.'

'Nor me, not when it comes to choosing a husband,' Biddy said drowsily. The cold outside and the warmth of Dai's arms were threatening to send her straight off to sleep. 'Besides, the Father at St Anthony's is a good man; I don't think he'd mind so long as we loved one another. And even if he does mind, if we aren't going to live in the 'Pool I don't suppose it matters much. Oh, Dai, am I dreaming? I keep thinking I should pinch myself. Are we really talking about marrying each other?'

'That's it. I wish I could say we'd marry tomorrow, cariad, but of course that's impossible. There's things we'll need to arrange first. But when summer comes we'll tie the knot, eh?'

'Oh yes please, Dai,' Biddy said fervently. 'Only we'd best not tell anyone else, not yet. Dear Mrs Gallagher is so pleased to have a maid she can trust, and I am very happy with her. I've never been so happy since I was a kid, nor known anyone kinder. I was desperate when she took me in, I couldn't hurt her in any way.'

'Aye, a good soul is Nellie Gallagher; you can stay with her for a while, anyway, because I've my way to make,' Dai told her. 'And sooner or later I'll have to go back to Moelfre and talk things through with my Da. We have quarrelled, cariad, but now I've a mind to go back, make things up. It'll be easier for me, knowing you're waiting in Liverpool.' He laid her back against his arm and bent over her, starting to kiss her soft but willing lips. 'Oh Biddy, I love you, I love you so much!'

'Mm . . . mm,' Biddy said, buzzing like a happy bee which finds itself deep in the scented heart of a rose. 'Mm . . . mmm.'

They reached home late, to find the women busy in the kitchen preparing the cold supper. Dai went round the front door and waited until his love was settled before he rang the bell. She came rapidly across the hall, he could hear her small feet clicking along, and opened the door to him. She smiled sweetly, wickedly, her eyes glowing with amusement.

'Oh, good evening, Mr Evans. Have you had a pleasant afternoon? If you'll just give me your coat and cap I'll take them through to the kitchen and put them on the airer; I can see you're very wet. Mr Gallagher and Mr Prescott and the children came in some time ago, so if you want to go up and have an early bath . . .'

There was no one else in the hall but the baize door was ajar and through it drifted the sounds of women talking and laughing in the kitchen. Dai grabbed Biddy and kissed her soundly, then put her back from him.

'Thank you, Biddy,' he said solemnly. 'I think I will have a bath . . . here's my coat and cap . . . and my scarf. What time is supper?'

'Supper's in half an hour, Mr Evans, but Mrs Gallagher said to tell you that if you fancy a snack before then there are biscuits and hot toddy in the study, where Mr Gallagher and Mr Prescott are sitting.'

'I'll bath first, Biddy,' Dai declared. He lowered his voice. 'What did you do with the amber egg?'

Biddy lowered her voice, too. 'It's in my pillow, amongst all the feathers, with my rag doll standing guard,' she whispered. 'I looked at it against the candle – oh Dai, I shouldn't let you give it to me, it must be immensely valuable! It's the most beautiful thing I've ever touched.'

'Then take care of it for me, cariad. And now go back to the kitchen; we don't want anyone becoming suspicious.'

On Boxing Night Dai lay in his bed and thought about Biddy, in her little attic room above him. They had known each other a little over two days, and yet he knew himself totally in love, thinking of no one else, dreaming of her, longing for her.

Christmas Day had been wonderful, even to the awful, cold walk to the park, the talk and cuddling in the cold little hut, with Biddy keeping an anxious eye out for invading spiders at first and so unable to give him her full attention – until he took her mind off spiders completely, that was, when she responded to his kisses and hugs in a most satisfying manner. And because they had found each other they had even enjoyed the walk home, both soaked to the skin, Biddy's teeth chattering like castanets, stopping now and then to hug, then running, then slowing to a walk .. laughing at each other, hugging again, almost enjoying the discomfort of damp clothes and icy extremities, because whatever they suffered they suffered together.

And afterwards they had all gathered in the big living-room and played charades and silly word games; Biddy as well. In charades, he, Elizabeth and Biddy had taken on the Gallaghers and the Prescotts and had beaten them in three games out of five. It had been great fun and, because of Biddy's presence, exciting.

Then came Boxing Day. The Gallaghers, armed with a quantity of envelopes and some very large cardboard boxes, had gone off in their motor car to deliver things. The Prescotts had taken the little boys off to visit friends. Which left Elizabeth, Biddy and Dai himself.

They got the sledge out of the loft above the garage and took it up to Everton Heights, found themselves a nice steep hill and spent most of the afternoon tipping it over, rescuing each other, laughing and pelting each other with snowballs.

They made a snowman, lent him Biddy's scarf, much to her indignation, then moved on . . . and had to come racing back over the snow to rescue the scarf before it was taken by a passer-by.

In the evening they had all piled into the motor car, Biddy as well, and Stuart drove them into Liverpool, to the Playhouse Theatre on Williamson Square, to see *The Story of Puss and his Amazing Boots*. Dai managed to get himself seated with Biddy on one side of him and Elizabeth on the other and though the two girls exclaimed and talked across him, he managed to hold Biddy's hand most of the evening and no one the wiser.

There were ices in the interval, and coffee or tall glasses of lemonade to drink. Dai would have liked a beer – Joey Prescott went out and got himself one – but he followed Stuart's lead and stuck to coffee. The pantomime was a good one, with two transformation scenes and a trapeze artist who might have seemed a little out of place in the Giant's palace to some people, but whose daring antics between the Giant's kitchen dresser and the hook on the back of his door seemed wonderful indeed to Biddy.

It was Biddy's first theatre trip and her wide-eyed wonder and tremulous enjoyment made the evening special for Dai. She sat with him on one side and the twins on the other and the three of them accepted everything which took place on stage as entirely natural. Together they marvelled over the magician who came on whilst the scenery was changed and drew rabbits from hats, miles of silk scarves from his own mouth, and sawed a beautiful lady in half, afterwards producing her all in one piece just to show you. Biddy bounced in her seat like a child of five, cheered Puss in Boots, booed the Giant, clapped the lady who came on and sang two beautiful songs and shouted 'Look behind you!' whenever cajoled by the cast to do so.

'Biddy made the performance special for all of us, especially the twins,' Stuart was heard to remark to Joey Prescott. 'She simply lost all her inhibitions and behaved like the child she is. And of course the twins – and even Elizabeth to an extent – followed her lead and enjoyed themselves twice as much as they would otherwise have done.'

Dai had managed to get one small kiss as they milled around outside the theatre, waiting for the car to pick them up. Just a little one, but all the sweeter for that. And now here he was, lying wakeful in his bed because tomorrow he would have to go round to the O'Reillys and talk to Greasy about the journey back to Grimsby. And on the floor above, his darling Biddy would be lying in her bed, no doubt soundly sleeping.

If I were to steal softly out of my room this minute, closing the door very gently behind me, if I were to climb the attic stairs very, very carefully, if I were to open her door, inch by inch, fraction by fraction, without so much as one tiny creak . . . I would see her, lying there in the cold moonlight, Dai told himself.

Her curls would be tumbled about her face and her long lashes would lie on her cheeks, and beneath the blankets the slim, strong body which he so loved to touch would be relaxed in sleep. And if I sat down on her bed and woke her with a kiss and then climbed into bed with her and cuddled down, put my arms round her . . . she would welcome me with a swiftly beating heart, a shy glance . . . but she would most definitely welcome me, Dai told himself.

But he would not do it, would not dream of it, just because she was such a sweet and trusting creature, his little Biddy O'Shaughnessy. She was too young for marriage, he should never have mentioned it to her, it was not fair because he was the only man she knew, the only man who had ever paid her the slightest attention. She should be allowed a year in which to get to know other men so that when she did make up her mind on marriage it would not be the leap in the dark which it would be if she made up her mind now.

However. She said she loved him and he loved her, so why shouldn't they plan to marry, plan happiness? Perhaps in six months he could mention the matter to Nellie as he would have mentioned it to his mother had she been alive – with a sort of shy pride, so that she would ask the right questions, become fond of Biddy, rejoice with him at his good fortune.

I'll do everything right, Dai vowed to himself, watching the moon mount the sky through a gap in his bedroom curtains. I'll mention it to Nellie, casual-like, before I go; I won't say anything's definite, I won't even say I've talked about it to Biddy, I'll just sort of hint that we're fond.

And on my next leave I'll have to go home to Moelfre and sort my Da out, he reminded himself. Got to do that I have, before I know what I've got to offer Biddy . . . not that she cares a fig, I'm sure. But I'll explain to her that it must be done, and I'll go home, talk to Davy. Who knows, maybe I'll take to Menna when I see her with an apron round her waist and a wooden spoon in her hand, maybe, if she's taking good care of my Da . . .

It would go against the grain to return to the island and not to see his darling, though. But it would be for everyone's good in the long run, he reminded himself sternly. Besides, what was one little shore-leave? Not much, compared to a lifetime's happiness. And on that thought he turned his head into his pillow and slept soundly till morning.

Dai was not the only person to lie awake in the Gallagher house that night. In her large double bed the lady of the house drank her cocoa, kissed her husband, settled down . . . and lay awake.

She had enjoyed Christmas even more than usual and that was because of Biddy. Such a good little girl, such a help . . . a treasure, no less. And Elizabeth was really fond of her, sang her praises, talked about her . . . but she talked about Dai, too.

Wouldn't it be lovely if I could tell Elizabeth that he's her brother, Nellie thought. She would be so thrilled, she's always longed for a brother or sister, that's why she's so good with the twins, so eager for Biddy's companionship. But it's impossible, I couldn't hurt my dear Stuart so.

And matters were complicated enough as it was. Lilac

had guessed. She had been a small girl of nine when Nellie had run away to Anglesey to have the baby, but even then she had been shrewd enough. Nellie had kept it from her for a good while but when she judged the moment was right she told Lilac about the baby she had been forced to leave behind.

She had never said where, or with whom, but Lilac had known Davy for a couple of years and father and son were so alike! Well, maybe not very alike now – Nellie had not seen Davy for more than twenty years – but the young man Davy had been then and the young man Dai now was were almost interchangeable. It was just the expression that was different; you only had to look at Dai to know he was a giver whereas Davy, with the best will in the world, had always been a taker.

Stuart had never met Davy, had no idea what the other man looked like, had never connected Nellie's friend Bethan with his wife's first lover. Unless someone said something – and it could not be Dai, who did not know his true parentage, and certainly would not be Nellie – Stuart need never know. He would take her fondness and friendship for the boy entirely at its face value and indeed, Nellie told herself, even had Dai not been her little boy grown to a man, she would have loved him for himself.

So Lilac was the only person who might inadvertently give her away, and Lilac never would. She loved and respected Stuart and she would never knowingly harm either of us, Nellie thought now, staring at the lighter patch at the end of her bed. So what are you lying here worrying over, for goodness sake? Just be thankful he's turned out so well, that he got in touch with you, that he's a son to be proud of, and forget that he ever lay in your arms and smiled up at you and tugged your hair. Love him as Bethan's dear son and you won't go far wrong.

She turned on her side and was soon on the edge of slumber, but even then a cautious little voice at the very back of her mind was warning her that there was something she had not thought of, had not allowed for, something that could still ruin everything. For a moment longer she lay there, trying to rationalise what must be a foolish, needless fear. But then sheer weariness overcame her and she slept at last.

Chapter Ten

Snow in August is nothing new; not in the Arctic, anyway. Dai battled his way across the deck, head tortoised deep into the collar of his coat, sou'wester pulled right down over his eyes so he could only see a small section of the deck beneath his feet.

Damned snow! They were seven days out of port and knew they were approaching the fishing grounds, but though they'd taken soundings earlier in the day they had not reached bottom yet. And when they did the Skipper would have to examine the mud or sand or whatever the lead brought up to see whether he thought they'd reached the feeding grounds, because you didn't shoot the trawl in weather like this in the wrong spot – no sir! Not only was it time-wasting, it could be worse. You could putter around searching and then find you only had coal enough for a couple of days' fishing before you had to run for home. Running out of coal in these seas was something no one dared contemplate – it was certain death.

Still, we've got a good Skipper, Dai reminded himself as he swung the lead and saw it plummet over the side and into the sea; at least he assumed it had gone into the sea since he couldn't actually see the water, what with the snow and the heaving of the swell. But he began to pay out the line, whilst beside him, Greasy moved his feet restlessly and kept shifting his weight along the rail as he narrowed his eyes against the whirling snow and tried to watch the line – when it slackened they would know they had reached bottom. Then the Skipper would want it held steady for long enough to bring up some mud, and with luck they might prepare to shoot the trawl.

Dai, also shuffling his feet, thought he felt a slight drag on the lead line; he stared downwards just as Greasy, beside him, lifted a gloved hand, one thumb erect. Dai nodded to show he understood and held on for a count of twenty, then began to bring the lead up once more. It broke surface, immediately becoming a great deal heavier, and the two men brought it inboard. Dai stared down at the sludge which had gathered round the lump of tallow wedged into the lead. It was blackish and full of tiny shell fragments, little specks of red and green which might be weed . . . he wondered if he would ever be sufficiently experienced to look at the mud, sniff it, stir it with a finger and announce that they would – or would not – shoot the trawl within the hour.

Lately, it had been suggested by the Mate that Dai might like to go for promotion. 'I started as a deckie, so did the Skipper,' he had said gruffly. 'You're young, intelligent . . . what about it, Taff?'

'I'll see what my young lady says,' Dai said warily, but he could not help feeling gratified. 'It 'ud mean moving across the country . . . but thanks, Harry.'

The Mate, a man of few words, grunted and moved away, and Dai had been thinking about it ever since, on and off. It was not everyone's game, distant-water trawling, but there was money to be made out here, by God there was! Whilst the British housewife went on buying cod, whilst the thousands of little fish-and-chip shops all over the country went on frying it, then there was profit to be made out here. If tastes ever changed, or if Arctic waters ever became overcrowded, then that was a different matter, but as things stood . . .

'Found bottom, sir.'

He had arrived on the bridge almost without noticing, and held out the lead. The Skipper took it, sniffed, touched, nodded.

'Aye; they'll be feedin' hereabouts. We'll be shootin' fairly soon so best get yourselves a meal.'

'Aye aye, sir.'

Dai ducked out of the bridge and folded his thigh boots down to calf height, then clattered below to tell anyone handy that they'd found bottom and would shoot shortly. Greasy was already sitting at the long table on the mess deck, eating what looked like a bacon sandwich. He waved it at Dai as he came in.

'Is 'e gonna shoot the trawl, Taff?' he said thickly, through a mouthful of bread and bacon. 'I thought it would be soon.'

'Yup. He'll send Harry round, get him to collect all hands. He wants us to eat first, then shoot. I'll give Bandy the word.'

The cook must have been listening because he leaned through his hatch, head and shoulders on the serving table. On their last voyage an unexpected surge had brought the hatch crashing down and Bandy had been trapped, swearing and blinding, until someone came below and released him, but it did not appear to have made him more careful.

'So we're shootin', eh? Not before time. There's steak an' kidney puddin' and two veg comin' up in ten, fifteen minutes.'

'Luverly grub,' Greasy said. 'Double helps for me, Bandy . . . an' for me young friend 'ere.'

'We'll need it when we haul,' Dai said, going over to the hatch and addressing the galley boy through it as Bandy withdrew to tend his stoves once more. 'Got a biscuit or something? Hungry I am.'

The galley boy was fourteen and a gannet; he ate everything that wasn't chained down but he could always conjure you up something between meals. Silently, he produced a bacon sandwich from somewhere and shoved it through the hatch. Dai thanked him and retreated to the mess table once more, where he sat shoulder to shoulder with Greasy and ate solidly until the sandwich was no more than a pleasant memory.

'I should be headin' for me kip now,' Greasy grumbled, eating the last of his own substantial snack. 'It's allus the bleedin' same, Taff, we allus shoots when you an' me's off watch.'

'I reckon every man aboard feels like that,' Dai said. 'Chuck us the pad, Grease; I'll write home, I think.'

'Oh, you an' your letters! Writin' to Biddy, are you? Or that other piece, on Anglesey?'

'My sister Sîan is not a "piece", she's a married lady. And yes, I'm writin' to Biddy. Just a few lines. I write a few lines most days, then when we get back to port I send off a big, fat letter. Besides, almost as good as seein' her, it is, to write.'

'But you said on your last leave you had a word with Stuart Gallagher an' he said she were too young an' you might 'old back a trifle,' Greasy said. 'If writin' every day's holdin' back a trifle then I'm the Pope!'

'He only meant not to get too serious with her,' Dai said. 'Oh shut up, Greasy, and let me write.'

He reached for the well-sharpened pencil and the pad of lined paper, brought Biddy up to date with what had happened on board the *Bess* in the last day or two and then sat back and sighed. Beside him, Greasy closed his eyes and, presently, began to snore.

Dai thought back to his last, longish shore leave, when he had managed to get back to Liverpool. Because they had had good catches and good trips from January to June he'd not gone back to Moelfre either – no time between sailings. But the money was mounting up nicely, and since the Mate had suggested he might get promotion he had borrowed books on navigation and seamanship and studied when he had time.

He telephoned Biddy though, whenever he was in port. He would ring through, let the phone bell sound three times, and ring off, then ring again immediately. That way Biddy would know it was him ringing and would run to the telephone. Sometimes the calls were more pain than pleasure, hearing her little voice so faint and far off, but at least they kept in touch that way.

Then he decided he would go up during a four-day shore leave and talk to Biddy once again about marrying, see how she felt about him staying in distant-water trawlers, but as an officer, eventually.

He got into Liverpool late one evening and knew he would have a bare forty-eight hours in the city before he had to leave again if he was not to miss his sailing. He went straight to the Gallagher house and was warmly welcomed by Nellie, Stuart and Elizabeth, Biddy hovering in the background, all smiles though her eyes sparkled with excitement and tears.

He ate with the family, talked about his recent voyages, explained that he had not been back since Christmas because catches had been excellent and the *Bess* had come through unscathed, so it was not necessary to put her into dry dock which always gave the crew a decent bit of time to themselves. But now he was here for a short spell . . . it was nice to see Liverpool in bright summer weather, to have the long evenings, to be able to admire the gardens and the parks, to tell the Gallaghers they had done wonders with their roses.

He insisted on helping with the washing up. Biddy washed, he and Elizabeth dried. Later that evening, he and the two girls went for a walk and talked a little about themselves. Biddy did not say much but Elizabeth prattled on – she was going to university, not many girls did but she would, her teachers thought she was clever enough and her Mam and Da saw no reason why not . . .

Dai told them about his hopes of promotion, the studying that he was doing when he had time both aboard the *Bess* and ashore. 'Not even been home to see my Da I haven't,' he said, addressing the words to Biddy, though he continued to look at Elizabeth. 'Came straight here as soon as I could.'

'Why don't you miss a voyage, just one? You said some of the fellows do,' Elizabeth asked him. 'Then you could see your Da and come here for longer; oh do, Dai, we could have such a good time!'

'I'm savin' up, I can't afford a voyage out,' Dai told her. 'We're well paid, but only so long as we stay with our ship.'

'What do you want to save for?' Elizabeth asked, with the disdain of one who has had everything she wants instantly provided all her life long. 'Is money so important to you, Dai?'

'Indeed it is, Lizzie. Savin' up to get married I am, one of these fine days,' Dai said, and saw his love blush delightfully, though Elizabeth just sniffed and said it seemed a pretty poor excuse to her.

That evening, very late, Dai and Biddy met in the kitchen. Dai had known she would come to him as he sat in the dying firelight, the *Manual of Seamanship Vol. I* open on his knee, his eyes fixed on the door.

She slid into the room, a small wraith in her white cotton nightgown with bare toes peeping out from under it. She went straight into his arms and they hugged with desperation, kissed hungrily, wrapped up in each other, each feeling the thunder of the other's heartbeat, each knowing the giddying joy of being together.

Presently, he sat down and pulled her onto his knee. She was so soft and pliant without all the fuss and botheration of her clothing, with only the thin cotton nightdress between them. Dai groaned and kissed her neck, then began to squeeze and fondle her, to smooth his hand over her breasts . . .

The kitchen door opening nearly caused both of them to die of shock. Biddy sprang off his lap and stood, trembling like an aspen, on the hearth. Dai stood up. 'Stuart! I'm doing some studying and . . .'

'It looked like it,' Stuart said with laughter behind his voice. He jerked his head at Biddy. 'Go off to bed, love, you've done nothing wrong either of you, but perhaps you've been a bit unwise. Don't worry, Biddy, I'll have a word with this young man and that's the last either of you will hear about it. I'm no tell-tale, it goes no further.'

Biddy went over to the doorway, then paused, staring at Stuart. 'Mr Gallagher, Mr Evans wasn't . . . wasn't taking advantage of me or anything like that. We – we are good f-friends, I came down to see if – if he needed anything, and . . . and . . .'

'I know, I was young myself, once. Off with you, Biddy, you'll catch your death standing around in that thin nightgown.'

Dai went over to the doorway and watched his love up the stairs, treading so softly that not a stair creaked, then he went back into the kitchen and closed the door. 'Stuart, I want to marry Biddy and I believe she wants to marry me. I've never done anything to her – with her – that either of us could be ashamed of, though we do kiss

303

and cuddle. If I'd had evil in mind I'd have gone to her room or persuaded her to mine . . . but we do have to talk sometimes, and it's very difficult to be with her without the whole household knowing about it.'

'And what's wrong with that? Us knowing, I mean?'

'Nellie said something to me the first time I stayed with you; she said she was glad she hadn't married the first man who took her around and paid her compliments, and she hoped both Biddy and Elizabeth would take their time, meet people, before they took the plunge into matrimony. Apparently she's known several girls who've married the first man who asked them and lived to regret it. She wasn't meaning me and Biddy, I knew that, but I could tell – thought I could tell – that she would say we ought to wait. Besides we can't afford to marry yet and Biddy's so happy here, she was terrified that if Nellie or you found out that we liked each other, she might be asked to go.'

'Never! But you know, Dai, Biddy really is rather young and very innocent. I doubt very much if anyone other than yourself has kissed her, certainly she doesn't go out with young men. I won't ask you to do anything foolish, like not seeing one another, clearly you are both very attached, but I do think that you should encourage Biddy to go dancing, meet other young men. And then, in a year's time . . .'

'I'd not dream of asking her to stay away from dances and fun, but she don't seem to want such things, not any more,' Dai said rather hopelessly. 'She used to go to the Acacia Dance Hall every Saturday night with her friend Ellen and meet young men and dance with them, but since she's come here she's lost interest, or so she says.'

'Oh! I didn't realise she used to go there.' Stuart, who had been standing with his back to the fire, sighed and sat down in one of the fireside chairs, motioning Dai to follow suit. 'Look, old man, I don't mean to interfere, but we're all only human. If you and Biddy keep meeting clandestinely, particularly when Biddy's only wearing a nightgown, what do you think is going to happen? I know you'll tell me you're a man of honour, but I know what would happen if I were in your shoes! And that would be very unfair on Biddy, very unfair indeed, with you out in the Arctic somewhere and her facing the music alone.'

'Oh!' Dai said. He had immediately seen the truth of Stuart's words because he knew that, had no one walked into the room, he would almost certainly have gone a good deal further than was right. But dammit, he loved her . . . if they married . . . . He put the point to Stuart who did not seem impressed.

'Yes, but you can't marry; not yet,' Stuart had pointed out briskly. 'You're still saving up, right? And Biddy is too. She'll want a wedding dress, a trousseau, all the usual things young girls want. She saves most of her wages and in a year she'll be in a comfortable position. So will you give her room to grow in that year? For Biddy's sake, Dai?'

What choice had he got, after that? And he knew it was true that if they kept meeting on the sly then sooner or later they would make love and Biddy could easily find herself pregnant. He had been with other girls, of course he had, but not young innocents like her. The sort of girl who roams the Grimsby docks knows how to take care of herself and is paid well for taking all the responsibility. Biddy was too good for him anyway, she certainly didn't deserve to be treated as if she was just another dockyard floozie.

'Right, Stuart,' Dai had said therefore, briskly but with a good grace. 'You have a point and I'll abide by it. No more cuddling in the kitchen after dark, just loving friends we will be. And in a year we'll marry and I'll steal her from you.'

Stuart had laughed and clapped him on the shoulder. 'It's a bargain! Your trouble, old man, was that you fooled us all. I never realised you and Biddy were more than acquaintances . . . . Do all the letters come from you, then?'

'Well, I hope so,' Dai said, grinning. 'Keep a postman occupied full-time we do, with the letters rushing across the country. I'll go to bed now . . . but it'll be good to know you're keeping an eye on her for me.'

Next day he gave Biddy a slightly watered-down version of their talk and Biddy had nodded thoughtfully.

'I'm not going dancing or anything like that, but I'll work hard and save up and in a year . . . in a year we'll talk about it again.'

That conversation, however, had taken place in the spring and now it was August and Dai's resolve was beginning to pall. Oh, not his resolve that he would never take advantage of Biddy, he was determined that they would not fall into that particular trap, but his resolve to wait a year before marriage. Better to marry than to burn, the Good Book said, and there were times when Dai burned for Biddy. Besides, it was over six months since they had met and fallen in love, he didn't see why they shouldn't at least get engaged. He was planning to spend his bonus this trip on a small ring, and if Biddy agreed they could at least name the day.

'All right you lot, grub up! Come on, get it in you whiles you got the chanst!' Bandy's round red face appeared through the hatch. 'Come on, the old man's swiggin' brandy an' stuffin' hisself wi' me beef an' kidney puddin'; you'd best look lively or he'll be bawlin' you all up on deck afore you've et!'

Elizabeth was growing up, and growing beautiful, what was more. She and Biddy often had their heads together over various matters, and Nellie had noticed that sometimes Elizabeth would accede to a suggestion which came from Biddy, whereas if she, Nellie, made that same suggestion, her daughter would unhesitatingly turn it down.

But Nellie knew it was all part of growing up so she just smiled and found a way of phrasing her suggestions so that they scarcely seemed to be suggestions at all, just ideas thrown out at random. That way, Elizabeth could believe herself totally independant of her parents, but Nellie could still keep her finger on the pulse of her daughter's activities.

Recently, Stuart had come home looking thoughtful, and had told Nellie, when they were alone, that he had been offered the chance to go up to Scotland and help to launch a new glossy magazine being started in Edinburgh.

'It's an opportunity, but I know how happy you are here, so I'll tell them I'm not interested,' he had said. 'No point in uprooting ourselves, though in a year or two it will be Elizabeth who will want to uproot, when she goes to university.'

'If she goes to university,' Nellie corrected, a slight frown marring her brow. 'You know our girl . . . she blows hot and cold, one minute she wants one thing, the next minute, another. Besides, things are so unsettled, Stu! The world situation, I mean. You believe there's going to be a war, don't you? There was the trouble over the poor Austrian Jews, then Hitler put the Austrian leaders into that Dachau place and no one tried to stop him . . . and the Air Force are running a huge recruitment campaign, you see the posters everywhere. I'm worried that war will come before poor Lizzie even leaves school, and if it does she won't want to go to university, she'll want to join one of the forces, I expect.'

'She's just at that stage in her development when the grass on the other side is always greener,' Stuart agreed. 'And you're right, sweetheart, I do think there'll be a war in the not-too-distant future. Even so, though, Lizzie may agree to further education, if that's still on the cards of course. She's a determined young lady, so she may easily stick to her guns over this.'

And then Dai turned up.

Nellie was alone in the house because Stuart had gone off to a meeting in Edinburgh – he might have decided not to take the job in Scotland but he was extremely interested in the magazine's birth-pangs – and Elizabeth and Biddy had gone into the city, to the Central Libraries on William Brown Street, where they would visit the Picton Reading Room and then go into the Lending Library where Elizabeth hoped to borrow books to help her with one of her subjects.

Biddy had gone along partly to borrow some books on her own account, though she also intended to visit her friend Ellen. Since it was her half-day it seemed a good opportunity to see Ellen since she would be in the city anyway, and could come home later, at her own pace.

'I'll go with Elizabeth to the library, then put her on the tram for home and catch another to Ellen's place,' she had said to Mrs Gallagher earlier in the day. 'We're going to have a snack at lunchtime – the Queensway Café, on London Road, is awfully good – and I'll have my tea with Ellen. I'll be home before the last tram, but I do love an afternoon with Ellen and little Bobby.'

So here was Nellie, standing in the kitchen making her Christmas cakes, although it was only September, and singing, rather appropriately, the song which came continually over the wireless these days, 'September in the Rain.' Some people might consider it too early to start Christmas cooking, but Nellie always made a great many rich fruit-cakes for her various charitable organisations and liked to do them in good time so that they could mature. So she was working away and singing lustily when someone knocked on the front door.

Nellie rinsed her hands hastily and ran across the kitchen and into the hall. The front door had a stained glass panel, all rich reds, glowing golds, jewel-like greens, and through it Nellie could see the outline of someone standing on the step. It looked like a young man, which meant one of Elizabeth's friends, Nellie thought rather despairingly, crossing the hallway at a trot. She remembered how shy she had been with young men when she was sixteen, but her daughter was completely at ease in any company and seemed to enjoy flirting with a number of rather nice young men. And she was so pretty, with that rich, golden-brown hair arranged at the moment in the popular Juliet pageboy, the clear blue eyes, the frank and easy manner which, Nellie privately thought, was the most attractive thing about her child. So undoubtedly it would be a young man wanting Lizzie, and Lizzie was far away and the onus of entertainment would be on Nellie, who wanted to continue to cook her Christmas cakes, sing her favourite songs and dream into the fire.

She opened the front door, however, with a rather guarded welcoming smile on her lips . . . which changed to delight when she saw who stood on the step.

'Dai! Oh my dear boy, how absolutely wonderful to see you! It's been such a long time . . . come in, come in!

I'm cooking in the kitchen since everyone else is out so you can come and watch me weighing tons of dried fruit, sugar, syrup, flour . . . and all the other good things which go into Christmas cakes.' She ushered him through into the kitchen, seized his ditty bag from him and slung it over the hook on the back of the door. 'Sit down, I'll make you a cup of tea . . . shan't be a moment.'

She filled the kettle, carried it over to the sink, took it back and put it on top of the stove. Then she turned to Dai. 'Well, your room's always ready for you, so that's no problem. How long can you stay, my dear boy?'

Dai smiled. He had taken off his navy jacket and now he sat there in his shirtsleeves looking calmly and contentedly about him, and when the kettle began to sing he told Nellie to get on with her cooking, he was a prince amongst tea-makers and would make her a cup in a trice.

'Well, I would like to get on,' Nellie admitted, cracking a dozen eggs into a jug, whisking them with a fork and then pouring them into her great yellow cooking bowl. 'And what brings you rushing over to see us, dear Dai, when I thought you wouldn't be back again until Christmas?'

Dai was making the tea, pouring water from the kettle onto the leaves he had just spooned into the big brown pot. Without looking round he said, in a slow, measured tone, 'Dear Nellie, I'm sure you must have guessed that I'm deeply in love with your girl. . . . I've brought her a ring and I'm going to ask her to be my wife. I know you'll say it's too soon, she's too young, but an uncertain world it is these days, with so many bad things happening. Felt I had to speak, see?'

Nellie dropped her spoon. A terrible, desolate unhappiness filled her and a deep sense of dread. This? She had dreaded that something bad would come of her behaviour with Dai's father all those years ago, but this went beyond her wildest nightmares! But she forced herself to think, to act calmly.

'Dai, my dear . . . she's too young! You both are, you've your lives before you . . . you mustn't jump into things, you must consider!'

Her adored daughter, her beautiful Elizabeth, she could not blame the boy for falling in love with her, she had noticed a certain fondness creeping into their relationship, but this!

'I know she's young, Nellie, and I'm prepared to wait, believe me. But I've saved up and bought this pretty little ring . . .' he was holding it out, smiling down at it, '. . . and I thought she could wear it on a chain round her neck if you feel she's too young for a formal engagement. It – it would give me such pleasure to know she wore my ring.'

A part of Nellie's mind acknowledged that Dai's logic was the sensible logic of a nice young man deeply in love, but another part could only scream a silent protest – she's too young, she's my baby, my little girl . . . and you were my baby once, my little boy – Dai, darling, you and Elizabeth are brother and sister!

But she could not say it. Instead, she took a deep breath and prepared to prevaricate. 'I see. I'm trying very hard to understand and sympathise, Dai, but it's been such a shock to me.'

'A shock?' He brought two cups of tea over to the table and sat down opposite her, pushing one of the cups across. 'I made sure Stuart would have told you – what a great gun he is, Nellie, to keep it to himself! The truth is, he caught us kissing one evening and guessed how it was with us and advised me to wait. Which I have done . . . only I long to give her a sign, I do . . . very dear to me she is.'

Stuart knew, and had not told her! But of course he

must have thought it was just puppy love and would be outgrown by both parties. And if it turned out to be true love, then why should Stuart object? Elizabeth was far too young, even Dai acknowledged that, but he did not mean to marry her for some time, he had made that clear. And if it had not been for the fact that they were brother and sister, Nellie realised, nothing would have given her greater pleasure than to welcome Dai officially into her family.

Oh, but she must stop it now, before it grew truly serious! She must put her foot down, tell him it was impossible – but she could not tell him why it was impossible, that was the rub!

'Dai darling, will you listen to me? Will you promise me not to take it any further until Christmas? Only till then . . . it's not much to ask. I'm sure you won't regret it. Stu thinks there'll be war . . . I'm in such a worry . . . if you'll just leave it lie for now . . .'

'We-ell . . . Nellie, is there someone else? Is that what you're trying to tell me? I'd rather have the truth, know where I stood.'

His face was pale, his dark eyes anxious. Nellie frowned across at him, biting the tip of her index finger. This would need careful handling; if he stayed and saw Elizabeth he would realise at once that she was still fancy free. Elizabeth was transparent, now that she thought about it she should have guessed – the way she looked at Dai, hung on his arm, begged him to take her to the park, skating in winter, playing tennis in summer. But Dai was still looking at her with that lost, vulnerable look . . . oh, how could she bear it? On the other hand if she lied to him, told him that Elizabeth had met someone else . . . but if it meant she would not have to break it to him that he and the girl he loved were brother and sister . . .

Nellie took a deep breath. 'Dai, there might be. She's

very young, but there's someone whom I begin to believe she really does like ... a little more than she realises herself as yet, perhaps. Just wait until Christmas, and then ... Dai! Wait! What on earth are you doing?'

But he had gone. He had snatched his coat from the peg, his ditty bag from the floor, and left. Without a word of goodbye, without a smile. She ran to the kitchen door; the garden was narrow but long, he could not have reached the end of it yet ...

The garden ended in a high wall in which was set a small green door. The door was still swinging, but although she ran down the garden and into the jigger at the back there was no sign of him. Dai Evans had completely disappeared.

Nellie returned to the kitchen and began listlessly pouring ingredients into the scale pan and from there to her yellow mixing bowl, but her heart was no longer in it and her song had died on her lips. She had hurt him so! But she had had no choice, she could not let him continue to love Elizabeth, to break all their hearts.

If only he had not gone so abruptly; if only he had waited until Stuart ... no, that would not have done, Stuart, in this instance at least, could not be relied upon to help her.

But the danger was over, at least for the time being. She had done a terrible thing, had hurt Dai to the heart. She acknowledged, now, that his affection for her daughter had been deeper and more profound than she could have possibly guessed. What else could I have done, though, she pondered, moving miserably round the kitchen, tossing ingredients into the bowl almost at random. How else could I have behaved? I had no choice, I had to drive him away, say something which would ensure that he never came back.

When she was putting the first cake into the oven, however, it occurred to her that she had not done it, not altogether. Dai would come back, any young man would. He would go now, bitterly hurt, and nurse his wounds for a bit, and then he would begin to think. He had not seen his love, nor heard from her own lips that she preferred another. He would be back, and next time he would not be so easily put off. Next time he would sit himself down at the kitchen table, smile at her coolly and a little grimly, and wait until he could see Elizabeth for himself. That tiny gold engagement ring with the little chip of a gemstone at its heart . . . her own heart ached at the thought of it. He really did love Elizabeth, he would have to see her if only once!

Nellie sat down with a thump at the kitchen table and put her head in her hands and prayed. There must be a way out, dear Lord, there must be some way of keeping them apart until they were older and had forgotten this first, early, attachment. He's a good young man, Dear Lord, and I love him, but their marriage would be an affront to Your church, it would be against nature! Please Mary, Holy Mother, look down on me in my fear and confusion and show me a way out, she prayed, squeezing her lids so tightly shut that whirling patterns formed in her head. Please, dear God, help me to help them!

And presently, as though the Holy Mother had pitied the little earthly mother so desperate not to hurt either of her children, Nellie saw the way.

When Stuart got back from his meeting very late that night he was met by a pale but determined wife who pounced on him the moment she heard his key in the door. 'Stuart, darling, I've been thinking. I want to go to Edinburgh; I think you should take the job they offered you. It's safer than Liverpool . . . but it's not just that, I think it would be best.'

She would say very little more, but was pale and distraught, making him a late-night snack, heating milk, adding a tot of rum so generous that he accused her, laughing, of trying to get him plastered.

'No indeed, you must have a clear head, but Stu, darling, you would like to take the job, wouldn't you?'

'Ye-es, but I'd quite made up my mind that it wasn't fair on you and Lizzie, I thought we'd agreed that . . .'

'Well, I've changed my mind. It would be very good for us, nothing could be better. We need a change, we've been here too long, I'm getting set in my ways. . . . Besides, we could see Lilac and the children quite as easily in Edinburgh as here and a change would be good for us. And dear Lizzie will talk with a Liverpool accent and I'd like to break her of the habit before she starts university, if she really means to start, that is. And . . . and if war does come, perhaps we would all be safer up in Edinburgh, further from bombs and dangers?'

'Have you asked Liz what she thinks? Darling, she won't want to go, all her friends are here, and I respect her feelings. But of course the job is rather important so your surprising offer is tempting, very tempting. It's not as if it's for ever, either, we needn't even sell this house, we could let it, because it would be a two-year spell in Edinburgh, that's all, just to set the thing up, get it running. . . . As for war, it'll come, but there's no point in worrying about it until it happens. Chamberlain's suing for peace; who knows? He may succeed in defusing the situation.'

'Then you'll do it? Take the job, move away? Oh Stu, darling, thank you so much! There is a reason why I think it will be best to go but I can't explain, not just yet. It's nothing awful, truly, but it's better that we go. When can we leave?'

Stuart looked down at her. She was pink-cheeked now, her eyes sparkling. Good thing I trust her, he thought wryly, giving her a hug. Because if I didn't I'd suspect that she was trying to get me out of the way and hiding some dark secret from me – a lover or something. But since I do trust her I guess it's some tiny little thing . . . probably one of the boys Elizabeth keeps turning up with has looked too long and lovingly at her darling, that would be enough to make her take fright. But it will probably come tumbling out presently, and prove to be some tiny, unimportant thing. Darling Nell!

Presently they went up to bed, but even in his arms she would only say, drowsily, that it was not important and that she was sure they would all be very happy living in Scotland.

'What about Lizzie's schooling, though?' Stuart said equally drowsily at one point.

'She'll find her level,' Nellie mumbled. 'It's for the best, truly, Stu. G'night, darling.'

Biddy was appalled by the news that the family were moving to Scotland, lock, stock and barrel, and within a month, too. She loved the family, trusted them totally, and was completely happy both in her work and her personal life. But going with them, tempting though it was, had to be out of the question, because of Dai.

'But we want you to come with us, of course, dear Biddy,' Mrs Gallagher said, smiling fondly at her. 'You'll be just as happy there as you are here, my dear, and you'll soon make new friends.'

'We shan't be gone long, either,' Elizabeth said threateningly. She had done her utmost to persuade her parents to change their minds, without one iota of success. Stuart merely said that the job was an important one and her mother knew best; Nellie tended to burst into tears, hug Elizabeth to her bosom and assure her that she would be grateful to her mother one of these days.

'I shan't be grateful at all,' Elizabeth had stormed when she saw there was no moving either parent. 'All my friends are here, how shall I *live* without Annie, Sheila and little Mimms? And there are others . . . what about Freddy Long? And Arthur? And nice, handsome Sullivan?'

'They'll all be here in a year or so, when we come back,' Nellie said soothingly. 'It will do you good, Elizabeth, not to have your own way for once in your life. Just settle down, there's a dear, and help me to pack. Your father has taken a beautiful fully-furnished house – it's a castle, really, out in the country with ponies and dogs and all sorts – but we'll need to take linen and all our clothes and personal possessions.'

A castle! Ponies, dogs and other animals! They had taken it for granted that Biddy would go too, but she spoke to Mr Gallagher quietly one day, as he was trying to pack in his study, and explained that though she would miss them horribly and be unhappy without them, she could not bring herself to leave Liverpool.

'I've felt like a member of the family, sir, but Mrs Gallagher doesn't know about Dai, and I don't think Lizzie knows, either,' she said shyly. 'It's only you that does know, Mr Gallagher. You see, Dai's coming back here at Christmas and – and we are to get engaged. I wouldn't like to go off to Scotland so that I wasn't here when he came home and I can't let him know because I had a letter only a day or so ago . . . he was just about to sail again. It might be four or five weeks before he docks.'

She did not tell Mr Gallagher, but the letter had been

rather a strange one, quite upsetting in fact. Dai said he understood that she needed to meet other people, he wanted her to do so, was all in favour of it. But then he went off at a tangent and said there was no one else in the world for him but if things had panned out differently for her then he could only wish her every happiness and do the decent thing.

The decent thing? What on earth did that mean, Biddy asked herself, reading the letter for the twentieth time. But even after all the re-reading she still could make nothing of it.

And after his fine remark about doing the decent thing the letter just rambled. There were bits in which he said he was ashamed of the way he had behaved towards Mrs Gallagher, another bit in which he complained that the journey back had been a hell on earth, with his mind going round and round what had been said – what *had* been said, Biddy wondered, thoroughly bemused – and that he had gone straight back on board the *Bess* to write to her before she sailed, despite what he now knew.

But I want to hear it from your own lips, the letter ended. *So I'm holding onto the ring until Christmas, when we shall meet again. All my love, darling, Dai.*

But fortunately Mr Gallagher did not want to see the letter; indeed, he seemed to understand perfectly why she felt she could not go to Edinburgh with them.

'We're letting the house to a gentleman from London and his family; he's the gentleman who will be doing my present job whilst I'm away,' Mr Gallagher explained. 'The family are called the Maitlands and they will be delighted to keep you on, Biddy. Same wages and conditions of service, of course. How would that suit you? I believe it will only be for a year at the most with the way the world situation is going, but if you and Dai intend to marry next spring, for instance, then you are quite right, your place is here, where you and Dai can be together.'

'I'll miss you all terribly, sir, but I shall have to stay,' Biddy said, feeling tears come to her eyes at the thought of losing the Gallagher family, who had been so good to her. 'But a year isn't so very long and I'll write often. Elizabeth will write to me, she's already promised.'

She did not add that Elizabeth had stormed at her and pleaded with her not to 'rat on us', as she elegantly put it, but to go up to Edinburgh as well, and Mrs Gallagher had wept and said that if Biddy should ever change her mind . . .

Biddy smiled and said again how she would miss everyone, but she was as firm, in her way, as Mrs Gallagher. She dreaded their going, knew she would miss them badly, but she could not let Dai down. She would not change her mind and go to Edinburgh, she would stay in Liverpool.

'I don't understand you. No, don't glare, Taffy, I ain't never knowed you sullen afore, but you're sullen now. Whass up, eh? You ain't been yourself not since you come back from the 'Pool afore this trip. C'mon, give!'

'There's nothing to tell, mun,' Dai said gruffly, trying not to look directly at Greasy's concerned face. 'I didn't see Biddy, I told you that – disappointed, I was.'

'Yeah, you told me, but I din't believe you,' Greasy said frankly. 'To go 'alf crost the country an' norra word or a look between you – well, that ain't like you, Taff. Any fool can see you're mad for that lickle judy.'

'Only a kid she is, that's the trouble,' Dai admitted. They were four days out of port and sitting on the mess deck eating ham sandwiches and playing cards whilst they waited for their watch. 'Everyone said so, Nellie, Stuart . . . everyone.'

'On'y a kid? C'mon, wack, where's your common sense? She's seventeen, ain't she? Me Mam 'ad two kids at that age . . . an' she were married, an' all. Your Biddy's a woman, norra kid, an' it's time they all come to terms wi' the fac's of life . . . Biddy, too. She oughter be glad there's a feller pantin' to get 'er. . . . You go 'ome, Chrismuss, an' grab 'er by the 'air an' do your caveman act! Drag 'er to your lair, Taff – she'll love it, they all does.'

Dai grinned, he couldn't help it. He'd felt downright suicidal when he had stormed out of the Gallagher house and all the way back to Grimsby the black dog of depression had sat on his shoulder. She didn't love him, he should have known she wouldn't, what woman would love a feller like him? Nellie was right, he should make himself scarce, keep out of her way, let her fall in love with some landlubber, not a seaman who would worry her sick by his absences and perhaps, one day, not come home at all.

He had signed on again and told himself that he must forget her -- but he could not! Biddy, Biddy! She had been the centre of his life and thoughts for almost a year, which was little enough time, but now he could not imagine continuing without her. Going home, not with her small hand tucked in his, but alone. Talking to his father, but not about what mattered, just about . . . the house, Menna, the boat. Seeing Sîan and her Gareth, congratulating her on the birth of her baby son, dandling the child on his knee, trying not to think that, had things been different, Biddy and he might . . .

But as the familiar work on board the trawler began to take up more and more of his time he became, insensibly, more optimistic. Nellie had said there was someone else, but not that Biddy was in love with the fellow. She had said that, given time, Biddy might be in love with him, but now that he thought about it, he knew his Biddy better. She was in love with him, she was probably just being polite to the other bloke. He would not give up, no matter that Nellie clearly thought he ought. I'll go back at Christmas, give her the ring, and tell here we're getting married at Easter, take it or leave it, he decided, and gave Greasy a real smile, a great big one, and felt a lot better.

'There, you see? Course she'll come runnin', soon's she sees you mean business. The pair of you'll be billin' an' cooin' in no time, once you mek 'er see reason. Wanna take an 'and o' cards? Gin rummy? No, I suppose you'll be wantin' to write one o' them great fat letters what tek you a whole trip to git down on paper.' Greasy sighed gustily. 'Oh well, on me own 'ead be it! I'd rather 'ave you cheerful an' writin' letters than downright bloody miserable an' playing gin. Chuck us the pack, Taff, an' I'll play a bit o' Patience.'

The new people moved in on the Saturday. The Maitlands were a couple in their early forties with four children, two boys and two girls. Mrs Maitland made up heavily and had a stiff, rather unnatural-looking permanent wave. She wore fashionable Russian boots, skirts which brushed her boot-tops, slashed sleeves and low necks in the modern imitation of Shakespearian fashion. Closer scrutiny showed her to be sharp-featured, but she seemed pleasant enough. Indeed the whole family would probably prove all right, though nowhere near as nice as the Gallaghers, but Biddy was determined to fit in and do a good job for them and worked like a young Trojan to get them settled.

On the Sunday, which should have been her day off,

she cooked them a roast luncheon, took the children to a rather smart Proddy church and then went on to Mass at the far humbler place of worship she herself favoured. Then she came back and served the luncheon, cleared and put away, got a very fancy afternoon tea (cucumber sandwiches, sponge cakes no bigger than your thumb and some stuff called Gentleman's Relish spread on tiny squares of hot toast) for the adults and something more substantial for the children, and then prepared a cold supper.

She went to bed that night and slept soundly, though she was disturbed by dreams in which the Maitlands decided to buy a dog-cart and also decided that they could not afford a pony so Biddy must pull it. She awoke from a furious confrontation with Mr Maitland over what sort of harness was best for her and whether she should be shod, to find the alarm bouncing on the bedside table and another day's work waiting.

Although the family was bigger and more demanding, Biddy would still have coped, and coped well, what was more. She stated calmly on Monday morning that she usually took Sundays off and would do so in future, and Mrs Maitland was very nice about it.

'Of course, dear. I'm so sorry, what with moving in on the Saturday we were in such a state I never thought . . . and you have Thursday afternoons off as a rule, don't you? Well, this week take all day Thursday, and we'll sort Sundays out on our own.'

Biddy said that this would be fine and continued to work hard for the Maitlands. Until Wednesday.

Wednesday was Mrs Maitland's bridge evening. She was, it transpired, a fanatical bridge player and as soon as she arrived in Liverpool she had made herself known to other players. On both Monday and Tuesday afternoons Mrs Maitland rang for a taxi and disappeared for several hours, and on Wednesday evening, dressed up to the nines and with her handbag full of change, she set off again.

'I make all my pin-money playing bridge,' she told Biddy chummily as she stood in the kitchen giving her last-minute instructions about the dinner she was to serve Mr Maitland and the hour at which the young Maitlands were to go to bed. 'I daresay I shall come home with some fairly substantial winnings tonight – we from the metropolis do have our standards and people from the provinces aren't perhaps *quite* as up to the minute as ourselves.'

'I thought you came from London,' Biddy said before she had thought, and saw Mrs Maitland give a knowing smirk. Biddy continued to make the apple pie she intended for Mr Maitland's dinner, but she found herself hoping, with quite uncharacteristic spite, that Mrs Maitland might be taken to the cleaners by the good bridge players of Liverpool, which would show her who was a provincial and who was not.

The evening proceeded smoothly after Mrs Maitland had left. The children, whose ages ranged from a snooty, self-satisfied ten year old to a delightful little moppet of three, had their high tea, played some quiet games and then went to bed. Biddy oversaw this, making a game of it, and thought, as she tucked the two youngest into bed, that they weren't bad kids and would be quite good company in time. The eldest, Master Samuel, could do with taking down a peg, but the others were nice enough and would improve once their new schools had knocked the conceit out of them and some sense in.

Back in the kitchen she served soup, roast pork and the apple pie with some rich yellow cream to Mr Maitland, who ate everything, scarcely exchanged a word with her, and then got up from the table, carrying the bottle of port, and shut himself in the study. How different from Mr Gallagher, Biddy thought wistfully, whizzing through the washing up whilst she listened to Mr Chamberlain, promising 'Peace in our Time', on the wireless. When the News was over she switched to a light music channel, beginning to tap her foot to the catchy rhythm of a jazz band. She wondered whether she ought to go through and offer Mr Maitland coffee, but decided against it for the time being. He seemed a very odd sort of man, but the rest of the family would probably be all right, once they settled in and grew accustomed.

Having only fed one man and herself there wasn't a lot of washing up, so Biddy got through it in no time. Having cleared up she went to the study to ask Mr Maitland if there was anything else he wanted, and when he had said no, he was quite all right thank you, she told him that she was off to bed but would leave the hall light burning for Mrs Maitland.

'Oh . . . yes, thank you, Biddy,' Mr Maitland said. 'She is usually very late; you need not wait up.'

Oh, aren't I relieved, Biddy said sarcastically to herself as she headed for the stairs. Because the last thing I intend to do is wait up for silly old biddies who go out gambling and don't come home till the early hours. I can just see Mrs Gallagher's face if I said I'd wait up for Mr Gallagher when he was out late putting the paper to bed. The idea!

She was in bed by ten and so she wrote a bit more of her current letter to Dai, telling him all the silly, funny things about the Maitlands and adding that she hardly knew how she would wait until Christmas, and then she blew out her candle, said her prayers, including rather a lot of fervent ones concerning the safety and well-being of Dai, his craft, and the Gallagher family, and pulled the blankets up over her shoulders. Dolly was heaved out from under the pillow, where she was unaccountably lurking, Biddy's hand delved into the feathers, found and extracted the amber egg, and she fell happily asleep.

She came abruptly awake for no reason that she knew, to find herself staring into the darkness, convinced that she was not alone. She could see nothing, scarcely even the lighter patch which was the curtained window, yet she was almost certain . . . yes! She could hear someone breathing!

Biddy sat up and reached for the candle and the matches. She fumbled the box open and as she did so someone bumped into her bedside table and muttered a curse. Immediately she felt much better and her heart, which had been hammering fit to bust, slowed to a more normal rate. It would be one of the Maitland children, of course, in a strange house and losing their way in the dark . . . or perhaps seeking her out for comfort and reassurance.

'Hold on,' she said, therefore. 'I'll just light the candle and . . .'

She struck a match and in its quick flare she saw Mr Maitland standing by the door looking at once owlish and extremely foolish. He was wearing a nightshirt, a striped affair in grey and white, and beneath it his hairy, knobbly legs looked horribly bare and pathetic.

'Mr Maitland, this is my room, you know,' Biddy said in what she hoped was a motherly tone. 'Have you got lost? Your rooms are on the floor below.'

He laughed, rather uneasily she thought. 'Ah . . . yes, my dear, very understandable; yes, no doubt I am lost and need to be d'rected to the place I sh-seek. Perhaps we should have a li'l chat about it, eh?'

And to Biddy's alarm he came across the room, sat on the edge of her bed, seized her by the shoulders and gave her first a little shake and then a squeeze.

Biddy stared at him, aghast. This plump, balding, middle-aged man with the hairy legs and the squashy pink lips couldn't possibly be under the impression that she liked him, could he? Just in case, she brought her knees up under the covers and began to try to position her feet so that a good kick would send him flying off the bed. He seemed unaware of this strategy, but leaned forward and tried to kiss her. He missed her face altogether but got her on the ear, the kiss making a moist explosion which nearly deafened her.

'Hey! Stop that!' Biddy said crossly. 'Gerroff me bed!'

'Ah, you'd rather I got *in* your bed I daresay,' the horrid old man said cheerfully, leering at her. 'Anything to 'blige a lady, my dear.'

He heaved at the blankets and despite Biddy's valiant efforts they slid down to her middle. 'Move over,' Mr Maitland ordered, his joviality slipping a little as Biddy made no effort to help him. He let go of her shoulders and stood up, in order to stick a hairy foot into her bed. 'Come on, don' hog the whole m-mattresh, my dear, or we'll never have our li'l bit of fun before my goo' lady comes back from her bridge; eh? Eh?'

'If you don't get out of me room this minute I'll scream the place down and Master Samuel will doubtless come tearin' up the stairs,' Biddy said desperately. She doubted that a ten-year-old child would be able to do much against this horrible person, but it was a good threat. 'And then I'll tell Mrs Maitland of you, sir.'

Mr Maitland took his foot out of the bed and tugged peevishly at the covers again and, because Biddy was not expecting it, they descended much further. He gave a crow of triumph and sat down on the bed, then tried to swing his legs in so that he could lie down. And then he turned with surprising swiftness for one so fat and unfit, and clasped Biddy to his paunch.

'Pretty li'l crittur,' he mumbled. He kissed her neck, his arms imprisoning her. 'Ooh, pretty li'l Biddy's going to have such a wonnerful time wi' her dear old mate Maitie in a moment! Oh, old Maitie givesh all the girls a wonderful time, you don't know how lucky you are . . . experienshed man of the world . . . no time for these jumped-up youngsters, you wanna nolder man . . .'

Biddy managed to heave one hand free. It happened to be the hand which grasped the amber egg. She said, 'Mr Maitland, I'm warning you, either you get out of my bed right this minute or . . .'

'Never! Neverneverneverever . . .' Mr Maitland declared, trying to get his pudgy hand inside Biddy's nightgown. 'Oh, you'll be coming down to fetch me up on a Wenn . . . Wess . . . Wednesday eve . . . evening, once you've met my famoush . . . famous . . .'

Biddy brought the amber egg down on Mr Maitland's head. It was an awkward angle but she did her best, though she did not hit hard enough, since he did not lose consciousness but merely shouted 'Ouch!' and then added, 'What wazzat?' before slowly slithering out of her bed and onto the floor.

'I do hope you're dead,' Biddy said, climbing out of bed and leaning over him. 'Are you dead, you old monster?'

'Dead, but not forgotten,' Mr Maitland said in a sepulchral voice. 'Jus' a teeny bit dead, thash all.'

'You're drunk,' Biddy said, with the air of one making a surprising discovery. 'You're a dirty old toss-pot and I'm not staying in this room another minute.'

This statement galvanised Mr Maitland into action, of a sort. He turned his head so that he could squint up at her and said heavily, 'Goin', sho shoon? But we haven't had our fun an' gamesh yet, little lady.'

'Oh yes we have,' Biddy said grimly, packing her belongings with great rapidity into her trusty carpet bag. 'And you owe me some wages, but I shan't be stopping to claim 'em. You can find yourself another maidservant just as soon as you like, Monster. I'm off!'

She was crossing the front hall when a key grated in the lock and Mrs Maitland came in, unbuttoning her astrakan coat as she came. She looked puzzled when she saw Biddy fully dressed and obviously about to leave.

'Biddy? What's wrong?'

'Everything,' Biddy said, not mincing matters. 'Your husband is lying on my bedroom floor; he's drunk. He's got some funny ideas, has Mr Maitland. I'll come back in a day or so to pick up my wages and the rest of my things, but I can't stay.'

'You're not leaving? Biddy, you can't leave, not just because my husband is a – a little the worse for wear! Look, you sleep in one of the spare rooms tonight and we'll sort things out in the morning.'

'No. I'm going. In fact, if you'll just give me some of my money now, I'll run after your taxi and go in that. The last tram must have left hours ago.'

Mrs Maitland looked shifty. 'I don't actually have any money. . . . I'm afraid I lost rather heavily, in fact I had to ask several ladies if they would accept my IOUs. Biddy, why are you laughing?'

'It's worth having to walk to hear you say that,' Biddy spluttered, opening the front door and stepping out into the balmy night air. 'Goodbye, Mrs Maitland,

I'm sorry things have turned out this way, but we in the provinces do have our standards.'

And with that Biddy walked rapidly away down the path, leaving her erstwhile employer staring after her.

Chapter Eleven

It was one thing to walk out of the house in the middle of the night, laughing like a drain and talking airily about taxi cabs, but it was quite another thing to find one. Biddy had enough money, since she had been saving up for some time, and though the bulk of her cash, at Mrs Gallagher's advice, had been lodged in the Liverpool Savings Bank on Smithdown Place, she still had several shillings wedged into her pillow. But there are times when money alone is not sufficient. In a quiet, suburban area of a large city there is little call for taxi cabs at one in the morning, so Biddy walked and walked and walked and began to realise that she might as well continue to walk; she would not find a cab until she reached the city centre, by which time she would have little need of one.

But she was very tired and not a little despondent by the time she arrived on Paul Street. She felt that the Bradley family would begin to believe that she was dogged by ill-fortune since she had already turned up on their doorstep, almost destitute, on a previous occasion.

The Gallaghers had been gone a week and she had worked for the Maitlands for only five days, that was the worst of it. What would Mrs Gallagher say when she found that Biddy had walked out after less than a week? For that matter, what would the Bradleys say when she confessed that she had not stuck with the Maitlands? Would they think she should have stayed, tried again? Or would they look back to her previous arrival on their doorstep and decide that she had no backbone and was always giving up?

Still. The last time she had cast herself on the Bradleys' mercy had been a year ago and since then she had done quite well for herself, and had given as much as she could afford to Ellen and the baby. And the Bradleys were such a jolly crowd that they would probably simply welcome her in and tell her to put her bed-roll down on the floor by Ellen's and not give a thought to her reason for coming.

Paul Street, when she reached it, was quiet and dark, save for a tabby cat which came out of a warehouse like a shot from a gun when it saw Biddy and curled itself fondly round her legs, purring like a sewing machine.

'Hello, puss – been shut out?' Biddy asked, bending to stroke it, though this meant temporarily standing her pile of possessions down on the pavement for a moment. 'Well, you can walk with me if you like, but I'm afraid that's no guarantee that either of us will have a roof over our heads tonight.'

Biddy turned into Samson Court, and the cat followed her. There was only one gaslight in the court and it was at the far end; it barely illuminated No. 7, where the Bradleys lived, but Biddy stumbled up the steps and raised a hand to knock . . . then hesitated.

It really was not fair to wake the entire household and it was a mild enough night. She would sleep on the doorstep, close up against the front door, then if by some unlucky chance a scuffer came by she would explain that she lived here but had been accidently locked out. Or if anyone tried any funny business she would screech and bang on the door.

Having made up her mind Biddy unfastened her carpet bag, withdrew her pillow, and placed it on the top step, resting it against the door. It looked really comfortable, she thought, and pulling out her blanket, carefully spread that out below the pillow. The cat, inquisitive as all cats are, climbed up the steps and examined both pillow and blanket carefully, and then, apparently deciding that Biddy had unpacked her possessions especially for its benefit, it gave a prolonged purr of approval and settled down on the pillow, curling into a neat ball.

'You cheeky devil,' Biddy said, but rather appreciatively than otherwise. 'Oh well, two's company, cat.'

She lay down on the blanket with her head on the pillow. The cat opened a yellow eye and stared at her, then closed it decisively. Now's the time for sleeping, it seemed to say. Don't watch me or I'll never drop off.

'Nor me,' Biddy muttered. 'G'night, cat.'

The cat did not again open an eye, though it continued to purr – or was it snoring? Biddy was still trying to work it out when she fell asleep.

Biddy woke when someone screamed right in her ear. She sat up groggily, her heart racing uncomfortably fast, and as soon as she did so she remembered where she was and why. She was on the Bradleys' doorstep because Mr Maitland had tried to get into her bed, and she had doubtless just given someone the fright of their life.

She looked up; Ellen, in a pink party-dress with her coat buttoned up wrong and no hat, was staring down at her. Biddy saw that her friend's face was greyish and unhealthy-looking, that her once-lovely blonde hair was lack-lustre and hung straight as string, and then, as sleep retreated, she realised that the front door was still firmly closed and it was still not morning. The sky was grey with dawn, but she doubted whether anyone in any of the houses was yet stirring themselves. It stood to reason, therefore, that Ellen had not just emerged from the house behind Biddy. She was returning to it after what, judging from her appearance, had been a rather wild night out.

'Good God, Biddy, you give me the most awful skeer! I th-thought you was a feller with a 'uman body an' a cat's 'ead! What in Gawd's name are you a-doin', lying on our doorstep?'

'I *was* minding my own business and sleeping soundly,' Biddy said in an aggrieved voice. 'Did you have to shriek like that, Ellen? And come to that, where have you been until this hour?'

Ellen looked a little self-conscious. She put a hand defensively to her mouth and Biddy realised that it looked sore and swollen.

'There were a dance . . . only when it ended I'd gorra friend, an' 'e asked me 'ome to 'is place . . .'

'Oh come on, Ellen pull the other one! What really happened?'

'Don't talk so loud,' hissed Ellen, looking agonised. 'You know what me Mam's like, she'd tell the Father soon as look at 'im, an' 'e'd start goin' on about mortal sin an' duty an' what'll become o' me an' I just can't abide lecturin'. Come inside, I've gorra key 'ere somewheres.'

Biddy rolled up her bedding, stuffed everything back into her carpet bag, and watched with some amusement as Ellen went through her clothing until she ran the key to earth. She had hidden it so well that it took her several moments, but she found it at last.

'Gorrit!' she hissed triumphantly. 'Now don't mek a sound, Biddy, or we'll both gerrit in the neck.'

Biddy followed her friend as silently as she could and they gained the tiny back bedroom where all the girls slept, without rousing anyone. In the bedroom five girls were all packed into one not very big bed, three in the bottom, two in the top, and Ellen's bedding lay against the wall with Bobby in a cardboard box beside her.

'E's too big for that bleedin' box,' Ellen hissed, pulling off her coat and pink dress and kicking off her shoes. 'I'm gonna gerra cot nex' week. I seen a lovely one in Paddy's Market, goin' cheap.' She pointed at a spare bit of floor. 'Kip down there, Bid. We'll talk in the mornin'.'

Biddy was as quiet as she could be, but even so Bobby began to mutter.

'I'm awfully sorry, I think I woke him,' Biddy was beginning, but Ellen shook her head tiredly and leaned out of bed to take the child in her arms.

'No, it ain't that. 'E likes to sleep wit' 'is mam, so's 'e can 'ave to suck when 'e fancies it. Come on then, Bobby, Mam's 'ere.'

She was wearing a soiled underslip and now she slipped one shoulder strap down and put the baby to her breast. Leaning against the pillow, her eyelids heavy with sleep, she smiled across at Biddy. 'Eh, 'oo'd be a mam, Bid? But 'e'll sleep like a top once he's et, then I can sleep an' all.'

And since Biddy was extremely tired herself and Bobby not all that hungry, in a remarkably short space of time everyone in the small back bedroom was fast asleep.

Explanations had to wait until morning, but then Ellen and Biddy went downstairs early and got tea for the rest of the Bradley clan, save for Eric and Tom, who worked in the docks and had left much earlier.

'Now then,' Ellen said when they had made and poured the tea. 'I'll take a cup up to me Mam in a mo, but I wanna know what you're doin' here when you should be in bed at Ducie Street.'

'I've run away,' Biddy said uneasily. 'I know you'll say that I didn't give it a fair try, but that horrible old man, Mr Maitland, tried to get into my bed. He were drunk as a lord, Ell, but I wasn't having any. I hit him over the head with me amber egg and legged it here as fast as I could. So I don't have a job right now. And what were you doing out at two in the morning, you bad girl?'

'I told you, I went to a dance an' met this feller, an' 'e axed me back to 'is place an' – an' we talked an' that, so I din't notice 'ow the time were goin' . . .'

'How much did he give you?' Biddy cut in.

'Two bob,' Ellen said promptly, then clapped a hand to her mouth. 'Oh Biddy, don't you go sayin' things like that, what sort of girl d'you think I am?'

'Daft and desperate,' Biddy said gently. 'Before I dropped off last night I couldn't help thinking about our flat on Shaw's Alley and how happy we were. Your Mam's awful kind, Ell, but this isn't a good place to bring young Bobby up, there's too many of you.'

Ellen looked at her for a moment and then burst into tears. She sat down on a broken chair and rested her elbows on the rickety table and simply howled. Tears channelled down her dirty face and Biddy, rather at a loss, patted her shoulder and murmured comfort and after a few moments Ellen dried her eyes, hiccuped, and turned to her friend.

'Biddy, I know it, but no one else does! I can't gerra job because Bobby's too young to leave an' me Mam's a lovely woman but – but she's got worries of 'er own, she can't add my lad to 'em. That cot we need – I've gorra find money for it from somewhere, 'cos I don't 'ave no money any more, all what I 'ad I spent when Bobby were new. So – so what's a girl to do? I wait till Bobby's asleep, then I put on one of me good dresses an' go down to the docks. I – I can earn a bit that way, an' workin' at night, like, means if Bobby did wake there'd be Minnie or Alice or Sal to see to 'im. But I know it's no use . . . I'm trapped, Biddy, the way I always said I'd never be!'

'There must be a way out, and I'll think of it,' Biddy vowed, taking Ellen's hands in hers and squeezing them gently. 'But until I do, don't go walking the docks again, there's a dear. I don't want to sound like your Mam, but . . . it really isn't right, is it, Ellie, love?'

Ellen grinned, a quick, bright grin, so that Biddy suddenly saw, behind the exhausted grey face and the dirty, stringy hair, the bright and perky little blonde whom Mr Bowker had loved.

'It ain't right, but it's a bit o' fun, Bid, a bit o' life! An' some of the fellers is good to me, in their way. Just stuck 'ere, day after day, that ain't life, Bid, it ain't even existin'. It's what makes young girls go after fellers for a few bob . . . or float away on Mersey-tide, when things go wrong.'

Her voice was light but Biddy could hear the desperation behind the words.

'Ellen, don't! Think of Bobby, think of what would happen to him if you weren't here to take care of him! And I'll find a way out, I swear it. Look, I've got savings and you and your family have done me many a good turn when I was desperate. I'll give you some money now, and when I've got a job I'll come back and we'll work something out for you. Only you'll have to get yourself cleaned up – wash your hair, have a good scrub down, – otherwise I don't suppose anyone will take you on.'

'I'll clean up . . . only when you walk the docks it puts 'em off if you're too clean an' fresh lookin',' Ellen said frankly. 'They like to know you're on the game just by lookin' at you, especially the younger ones.'

'No doubt,' Biddy said faintly. 'Look, take your Mam her cuppa. I'll be off soon, before I lose my courage. See you later, Ell – I'll leave my carpet bag and my bedroll here if you don't mind. I don't want everyone to think I was kicked out of my last place.'

'Right, Bid, I'll keep an eye on your traps. An' now I'll start in to get meself smartened up.'

Ellen went over to the sink and picked up the enamel

bucket which she had filled earlier from the communal yard tap. She tipped some water into a basin and began to wash her face. When it was clean she dunked her head under the water and rubbed vigorously with the bar of red soap, rinsed her hair in the water remaining in the bucket, then groped for a towel. Biddy put it into her outstretched hands.

'There you are, you've got your nice fresh complexion back,' she said as Biddy rubbed. 'When your hair's clean and dry you'll be pretty little Ellen again. See you tonight, Ell.'

It seemed only sensible to go back to the same Employment Register on Bold Street and Biddy had every intention of doing just that. But she had not stayed with Ellen to have breakfast because she guessed that there was very little food in the house, so having given her friend the last of her money she had set off to walk to the centre of the city.

And whilst she was still some way from Bold Street, hunger had suddenly made itself felt. My stomach's rumbling so loud that if I go and see Mrs Aspinall she won't be able to hear me above the din, she thought. I'd best get myself some breakfast first.

She went through her coat pockets and found four pennies which would buy her something to eat. I'm miles from the savings bank on Smithdown Place, so I can't get at my money yet, Biddy reminded herself, but I'd kill for a hot drink and a mouthful . . . where can I get a fill-up for fourpence? She did not regret giving the money to Ellen, but she rather wished she had thought to hang onto enough for a proper meal.

Still. Employment Registers did not open early, she knew that, so there would be no harm in walking up the Scotland Road to Paddy's Market. There was a busy café there which opened early to serve the porters from the market – Thorn's cannie house the local's called it, though over the door it said *Miss Elizabeth and Miss Agnes Thorn – Dining Rooms*. Their food was excellent, Biddy knew, and their prices reasonable.

It was not far from Kettle's Confectionery, either, but Biddy no longer worried that she might walk into Luke, Kenny or Jack. She was a part of their past, they might not even recognise her. And her guilt feelings over Ma Kettle's death had long since ceased to worry her.

So she did not turn right when she came out at the end of Paul Street, she turned left, anticipation making her mouth water, her fingers clutching the four pennies in her pocket. Along Bevington Bush she went, walking briskly in the pale September sunshine, for it was another nice day. She turned right when she reached Wellington Street, then left into the Scottie. Thorn's cannie house was not far and she could smell it even before she could see it; I'll have a big mug of hot tea and one of their roast beef sandwiches, Biddy decided. Or shall I have a bacon sandwich? Or I could have a bowl of that thick lentil and vegetable soup with a hunk of bread on the side.

She reached Paddy's Market and stood on the edge of the pavement, waiting to cross. It was still very early but there was already a good deal of traffic, mostly horse-drawn since they were mainly farmers and wholesalers delivering to the shops and markets. She heard someone shout her name as she reached the centre of the road but took no notice; there were a lot of Irish living and working on the Scottie and Bridget was a popular name amongst them, Biddy a popular shortened form. The shouter could have meant anyone . . .

She gained the further pavement and was able to see, through the doorway of Thorn's, that Miss Aggie was doling out a plateful of hot peas and bacon chops to a burly market porter. The scent of the food wafted out – it did smell wonderful, would that, perhaps, be even nicer than soup or sandwiches?

She was still wondering when a hand seized her arm. She looked down at it. A small, fat hand, with dirty nails. A strangely familiar hand. With a very odd feeling indeed curdling her stomach, Biddy looked up the arm, over the shoulder, and straight into the face not a foot from her own.

A large, round face, with shrewd little grey eyes and a rat-trap mouth. A blob of a nose and hair tugged up into a tight little bun on top. A small, determined chin resting on three more chins, all much fatter and softer than the first. A scruffy black dress, the collar grey rather than white. A shawl around the shoulders, and a big white apron slung low round ample hips.

It was, without a shadow of a doubt, Ma Kettle.

'Biddy, oh Biddy, I'm that pleased to 'ave found you!' Ma Kettle's small eyes brimmed with tears of sincerity – or something. Biddy was still too shocked to find her erstwhile employer apparently risen from the dead to query Ma Kettle's motives. 'Ow I reproached meself when you run off . . . you disappeared, chuck, disappeared off the face o' the earth. I t'ought you was dead, I t'ought dreadful things!'

Biddy could only stare for a moment, then she found her tongue. 'They told me *you* were dead – I saw the wreaths and Mrs Hackett, her next door, she said what a loss it was,' Biddy said at last. 'It wasn't long after I left . . . I *saw* the flowers, honest I did. Glory, Ma, I even saw the funeral and someone standing near me said you was well-liked.'

'And isn't that no more'n the trut', now?' Ma Kettle said complacently. 'Poor but honest, us Kettles . . . ask anyone. But that weren't me in the coffin, chuck. That were my poor sister, Mrs Olliphant. You remember her don't you?'

'Yes, though I never met her – but she didn't live with you, Mrs Kettle, she lived out Crosby way.'

'Oh aye. But she moved in to 'elp out when you went, chuck, an' not bein' used to city life, she stepped out from be'ind a tram and . . . well, that ain't a mistake you can make twice, if you understand me.'

'How – sad,' Biddy said. Ma Kettle sounded so matter of fact about the whole thing that it was difficult to sympathise. 'But the day I did leave you'd gone to Crosby for tea – that was to Mrs Olliphant's, I assume?'

For the first time, Ma Kettle looked a little uneasy. 'Oh, aye . . . that. Well, my poor widdered sister were findin' things difficult, so she'd sold up . . . I t'ought if she moved in wi' us, took an 'and on the counter or in the boilin' kitchen . . . Luke was gerrin' wed as you'll recall, so 'is room would 'ave been goin' beggin' . . .'

'And you made the arrangements the day before I went? Why did you do that, Mrs Kettle?'

'It were Kenny, mainly,' Mrs Kettle said. 'What say we 'ave a bite o' grub at the cannie 'ouse, queen? We can talk in there.'

'All right,' Biddy said readily. She thought it would be a rare treat to be bought a meal by Ma Kettle, who so hated parting with her cash! 'I'm awful hungry though; I've not eaten since teatime yesterday.'

Ma Kettle sighed but waddled beside her into Thorn's and nodded glumly as Biddy ordered thick soup, roast beef sandwiches and plum duff.

'A nice cuppa tea will do me . . . an' mebbe a wet nellie,' she told the woman who came for their order. 'Still, the young 'ave to be fed.'

'Good thing they's 'ungry, Ma Kettle, or you wouldn't

regret this day! And aren't I a lucky old woman to 'ave found you agin?'

'Iceberg on the port bow!'

The Bosun's stentorian voice was laced with panic. They had entered pack ice hours before, in the early evening, but now, at midnight, they had just hauled the trawl, a trawl loaded with more than sixty baskets of cod. Not until the trawl was safe inboard did they alter course and manoeuvre themselves into clear water once more.

And now every man on board who could be spared was down in the fishpounds, gutting, but the Skipper had ordered that the trawl be shot again immediately. They had found fish and could not afford to steam into safer waters, not whilst every haul brought such rich rewards. So the crew had seen the trawl crash down into the blackness of the ice-scummed sea and then returned to the gutting, talking of their next meal, of the sleep which their bodies needed, of a game of cards and a hot drink.

And now the iceberg. It was enormous, but because the visibility in an icefield is always reduced by the black frost which rises from the pack, icebergs round here were far more dangerous than one encountered in open water and good visibility, and though the ship had a searchlight on her bows it scarcely penetrated the black frost.

They could all see the 'berg now, catching a million colours from the ship's searchlight and multiplying them within its crystal castles. It came on slowly, almost gracefully, surrounded by the debris of collisions with other 'bergs.

'She's not fifty yards off our port bow . . . by God, she's a big 'un!'

As the Bosun's voice rang out the Skipper opened the bridge window and leaned out. 'This one's keeping her distance but there'll be others. I want two hands on watch . . . Taff, Greasy, you'll do. Don't budge from the bows until I give you the word and shout at once if you even think you've got a sighting. At once . . . right?'

'Right,' Dai and Greasy said in chorus, taking up their position in the bows of the ship. It was the only chance you had of an early sighting . . . but it was cold work out here, with the sea freezing in the scuppers when a wave came inboard before it had a chance to run out again.

'How does the ole man know there's others?' Greasy said, straining his eyes into the darkness ahead. 'As 'e gorra crystal ball in there or somethin'?'

The Mate was standing by the winch drum, staring ahead. He half-turned towards them as Greasy spoke.

'He can tell by the growlers round her, for one thing. She's met other 'bergs, smashed into 'em, moved on. And you get a feel for 'em, in the end. Good thing, or . . .'

He turned just as a huge wave came racing out of the darkness, straight at the ship. It crashed down on the deck, causing the whole ship to shudder, and bowled Greasy and Dai over, then smashed them against the whaleback. The Mate was still clinging onto the winch drum but now he was turning to make a funnel of his hands, warning the bridge.

'DEAD AHEAD! DEAD AHEAD! DEAD AHEAD!'

'It's another bleedin' iceberg,' Greasy said, staggering to his feet. 'That must 'ave been its bow wave.'

And just as Dai was preparing for the impact there was a tremendous explosion, so loud that he was temporarily deafened by it. He stared into the darkness and saw, as the ship veered and bucked, great chunks of ice which had obviously been hurled sky-high by the force of the explosion, hurtling down again into the ragged sea.

All around them was pandemonium. The Skipper

roared to the man at the wheel to starboard his helm, then shot open the bridge window.

'Where away? Taff, where away?'

Dai and Greasy, still half-deafened, got the message. They hurled themselves at the bows. If the wild and natural evasive action of the *Bess* had chanced to turn them in the wrong direction then the danger was still imminent, death still hovered out there in the black frost and the dark.

And then, suddenly, the blackness began to ease; above their heads the sky showed pale and the water came into view – clear water, the wave-crests restless still, but unencumbered by either pack ice or 'bergs.

'All clear ahead,' Dai shouted. 'All clear ahead! All clear ahead!'

He looked across at Greasy; his friend was grinning and Dai knew that an equally idiotic grin stretched his own lips.

'What 'appened?' Greasy asked, but Dai did not know, he could only turn to the Mate, drooping now by the winch drum.

'She exploded; icebergs do, sometimes. Something to do with the water and air temperature,' Harry said. 'Wonder what happened to the trawl? We're still towing . . . if it hasn't been crushed by the ice or had the cod-end torn to shreds.'

'When'll we know?' Dai asked. He was suddenly aware that he ached in every limb, that his mouth was dry and that he needed hot, sweet tea and a long sleep. But they would still be gutting down in the pounds and he – and everyone else – was still on watch.

The Mate consulted his watch. 'We'll haul in around three hours,' he said. 'Best go below now, Taff, in fours. Tell the hands, and say gutting will have to wait. Weary men can't haul.'

There was no argument. Dai went to the fish pounds to pass on the message; Greasy dashed onto the mess deck and grabbed a sandwich and a hot drink. He carried a slopping mug of tea for Dai too, and thrust it into his hand as the other man struggled out of his deck gear.

'Ere, get that down you,' he commanded. 'I could sleep for a week, but we'll be lucky to get two hours.'

'Aye,' Dai said, drinking the tea down straight off and getting wearily into his bunk. Harry and the Skipper would still be up there, working out a course which would take them clear of the pack ice but not of the feeding grounds. They would discuss what to do if the trawl was irreparably damaged, how long it would take to fit the spare – they always carried a spare – how many men could shoot the trawl once it had been hauled, how many might then go off watch.

Could he do it, if he was lucky enough to get promotion, become an officer? Could he be that dedicated, that selfless? But it had been a long and worrying night; before he had made up his mind, he was asleep.

It was strange being back in the Kettle household; strange and not too pleasant. Every time Biddy looked round the living-room she remembered how unhappy she had been here, but then she scolded herself. Everything was to be different now, Ma Kettle had promised and she would, Biddy was sure, keep her word. She had given Biddy Luke's room just for a start, no more talk of sharing, and had even gone out and bought a plant to put on the window-sill.

'Makes it more 'omely,' she had said proudly, centring the small and stringy aspidistra in the middle of the window-sill. 'Them's me summer curtings; I'll change 'em for me winter ones in a month or two. You'll like me winter ones; they're a nice warm brown.'

'These are fine,' Biddy had assured her. She did not like to say that it was possible she would not be here at winter-curtain time. 'The room will suit me very well, Mrs Kettle.'

But now, down in the boiling kitchen, she was preparing a big bowl of fudge whilst Ma Kettle sat in the shop and, she assumed, treated – and cheated – the customers as usual. Biddy had greased her tins, boiled her sugar, butter and conny onny and was about to test it for setting when the door opened softly and a skinny young girl entered. She had hair so red that you could have warmed your hands at it, a great many freckles, green eyes fringed with light lashes, and a beaming smile. She was wearing a garment which might have been brown or dark blue once, over which had been draped a very large and rather dirty apron which hid all of her person except for her cracked and patched boots.

'Ello, Miss. I'm Penny Ellis; I live wi' me aunt an' uncle in 'Ighsmith Court an' I'm fourteen come next March. I does me best to keep the 'ouse tidy an' I'm that glad you've come! Miz Kettle do get lonely . . . an' I likes to be 'ome in time for me supper.'

'I'm Bridget O'Shaughnessy, my friends call me Biddy, and I'm past seventeen,' Biddy said gravely. 'How do you do, Penny? I hope we shall be friends and I hope you'll get home in time for your supper now I'm here to help out.'

'Oh, you isn't to be axed to 'elp,' the child said anxiously, with a quick glance towards the shop, though it was unlikely that Ma Kettle could have heard a word they said. She was dealing, rather raucously, with a line of small children, mostly clutching ha'pennies or farthings. 'You're the best worker Miz Kettle ever 'ad, and she don't want you bein' driv into goin' off, she told me an' Gertie we'd gorra mind our manners wi' you.'

'Who's Gertie?' Biddy asked, dipping a spoon into her bubbling fudge and dripping it into the jamjar full of water standing by. 'I don't recall Mrs Kettle mentioning a Gertie.'

'Gertie's 'er gofor,' Penny explained. 'She's only eight but she comes in after school an' runs errands an' that. Gertie Parr, 'er name is. She's one o' them raggety kids.'

Biddy was about to remark, rather hotly, that Penny was no fashion-plate, when the door creaked open once more and a very tiny child burst in.

'Gorrany erran's, Miss?' the girl asked. She was thin as a pipe-cleaner, with fluffy hair that looked as though it had been cut with nail scissors and huge, round eyes which dominated her pale, thin little face.

'Not for me thanks, Gertie – you are Gertie? But you'd best ask Mrs Kettle,' Biddy said, feeling as though she had strayed into the workhouse, for the child Gertie was indeed raggety. She wore a very dirty man's shirt with a shawl tied round her waist and she was barefoot.

'Oh. Right.' Gertie padded purposefully across the kitchen and into the shop. They heard her shrill voice demanding, 'Gorrany erran's, Miz Keckle?' and then Penny jerked her head conspiratorially towards the shop.

'You thought I were bein' nasty when I said she were a raggety, but I weren't, were I, Biddy? An' she's a great gun, Gertie. Skeered o' nothin', not even o' Ma Kettle. She'll put 'er in 'er place right sharp, if the missus tries to bully 'er.'

'Well, that's good to hear,' Biddy said, taking her fudge off the stove and beginning to beat it with a big wooden spoon. 'Because I'm the same, and I hope you will be too Penny.'

'Jobs is scarce,' Penny said, sighing. 'I gets two bob a week – imagine that, Biddy, two bob! It keeps me uncle from thumpin' me, which is worth a bully or two.'

'Two bob,' Biddy said wonderingly. Leopards did not change their spots then, not underneath. Ma Kettle was still an old skinflint and would be until she died, but at least she was making an effort where Biddy was concerned.

'Aye, an' she on'y takes a few pence off if I'm slow, or eat too much, dinnertimes,' Penny said, plainly misunderstanding Biddy's wondering tone. 'So I don't wanna lose the job, like.'

'I'll tell you what, we'll stick up for each other,' Biddy said, visited by inspiration. That way, she could do her best to see that Penny got a fair deal without terrifying the poor kid. 'I reckon this is thick enough, don't you? Have a taste, tell me if it's smooth.'

Greatly daring, Penny peeled a small ball of fudge off the proffered spoon and sucked blissfully. 'It's jest right,' she declared as soon as it was swallowed. 'I'll get you the tins, Miss . . . I mean Biddy!'

When the sweetshop closed down for the day and Biddy and Ma Kettle had shared a meal of boiled ham, boiled onions and boiled potatoes – Penny was not an inventive cook – they sat one on either side of the living-room fire and talked for a bit.

'I'm axin' our Kenny round to tea, Sunday, when we're closed,' Ma Kettle said, eyeing Biddy anxiously. 'I ain't askin' you to tell no lies, Bid – poor but honest, that's us Kettles – but if you could 'splain to Kenny that you'd 'ave gone anyway, even if I 'adn't left you all that work, I'm 'opin' 'e'll see reason an' come back to us.'

'I'll explain, and I won't need to tell any lies, because I would have gone, anyway,' Biddy said. She could scarcely hurt everyone by telling Ma Kettle that Kenny's heavy-handed pounces would have driven her away regardless, but at least she could make it clear to Kenny that his mother was not entirely to blame. 'Does Kenny have a ladyfriend now? Or someone he likes more than he likes the others?'

'Our Kenny's been sweet on you ever since you walked t'rough that door,' Ma Kettle said impressively. 'Never looked at another girl, never mentioned one, neither. Why, if a lad casts aside 'is own Mam because 'e sez she ain't good to a gel . . . well, that tells you, Bid.'

'It was just because he didn't know many girls, I'm sure that was the reason,' Biddy said hastily. 'I do have a boyfriend, Mrs Kettle. He and I plan to wed next Easter at the latest.'

'Well, don't you go tellin' Kenny,' Ma Kettle said anxiously. 'We've 'ad one lorra bother, let's not 'ave another. Face Easter when we come to it, eh?'

'All right, but I do hate deceiving him,' Biddy said uneasily. 'Still, he'll have to come to terms with it sooner or later. And right now, Mrs Kettle, if it's all right by you, I'm going up to bed.'

'Certainly, certainly! Will I bring you tea in the mornin', dearie?' Ma Kettle asked, rubbing her plump palms anxiously against her skirt. 'Only young Penny don't get 'ere till eight.'

'I'll bring you a cup,' Biddy said magnanimously. A wage of eleven bob, she felt, entitled Ma Kettle to an early morning cuppa at the very least! 'Would half past seven suit you?'

'Alf past seven 'ud be prime,' Ma Kettle said, beaming so widely that her eyes all but disappeared behind the shelves of her cheeks.'Eh, you allus was a good girl, our Bid!'

The first thing Biddy did on gaining her room was to heave a huge sigh and sit down on the bed.

Why was life so complicated, she thought crossly? There she was, contented with her lot, just waiting for Dai to pop the question so that she might live happily ever after, and what happened? First, Stuart Gallagher got a job in Edinburgh, then 'Matey Maitland' tried it on with her so that she had no option but to leave his employ, and then having agreed to return to Kettle's Confectionery (upon certain terms, naturally) she had realised that Ma Kettle was hopeful not only that she would bring Kenny back to the Kettle fold, but that she might marry him into the bargain.

A nice little daughter-in-law who would make sweets, sell 'em, keep Ma Kettle comfortable in her old age . . . oh yes, that would be a complication all right!

But she had made it clear that Dai and she were to get married, and Ma Kettle – and Kenny – would just have to accept it.

Biddy sighed. There was no easy chair, no little gas fire in this room, but she had been really spoiled by the Gallaghers. Ma Kettle would suppose that Biddy would spend most of her time down in the living-room because that would be a natural, family-like thing to do and providing Ma Kettle with someone to talk to of an evening was what she was being paid for, amongst other things. So if she came up here once the cold weather started she would have to wrap her blanket round her and wear her winter socks over her cotton stockings. But right now she was warm enough, so she sat down on the bed and got out her pad and pencil. She was writing a nice, long letter to Dai and now she really did have something to tell him! There was Mr Maitland's strange behaviour for a start; she would have to tell Dai all about that, otherwise he would not understand why she had once again changed her address.

Then there was this odd business with Ma Kettle . . . oh, and she must tell him that the funeral had been that of Mrs Olliphant and not Ma Kettle at all, otherwise he would think she had run mad for she had told him all about her guilt over Ma Kettle's supposed demise and he had assured her that the old slave-driver had had it coming to her, that it had been nothing whatsoever to do with Biddy's defection.

And there were the little girls, Penny and Gertie. Where on earth did Ma Kettle find them? And how could she get away with paying Penny two bob a week – and docking her money when she was slow – to do all the housework and cooking and to start work at eight in the morning and finish twelve hours later?

Kids like that need someone to look after 'em, Biddy thought as she scribbled on and on, putting her darling Dai in the picture. There should be a society or something for 'em – a trade union, like. She wrote that down, then suggested that it might be something for Mrs Gallagher to look into, when she came back from Edinburgh.

'She's always so busy with her good works so I'm sure she'd take on keeping an eye on kids' she wrote. 'I wish they hadn't gone, but there's good in all things. Hopefully, Ma Kettle and Kenny will get back together again, and I'm here to do the best I can for young Penny. Gertie, it seems, can look after herself! She gets sixpence a week out of the Kettle for running errands, plus some toffees now and then, and thinks herself mortal lucky.'

She sat and sucked the end of her pencil for a bit, then said that she was about to go to bed where, with a bit of luck, she would dream about her dear Dai, but in any event she would not close her letter for another week or two seeing as how she knew he had only sailed quite recently so would not be back for a bit.

Then Biddy undressed, got into bed, and slept soundly till morning.

Nellie missed Biddy terribly, and so did Elizabeth.

'What's the good of a castle and dogs and cats if they

aren't yours and you've no one to share 'em with anyway?' Elizabeth said crossly when her mother told her to count her blessings. 'I don't like me new school all that much and I miss me pals and you keep sighing all the while and me Da's never home . . . I wish we were back in Liverpool!'

'Yes, well,' Nellie said guardedly. She was not particularly happy herself and sometimes, when Lizzie was grumbling at full throttle, it was really hard not to say, *If it hadn't been for you and your secret love affair, madam, we could all be in Liverpool still.*

But that would have been madness, of course. It had soon been borne in upon Nellie that the infatuation, love, call it what you will, between Elizabeth and Dai was completely one-sided. Elizabeth scarcely mentioned him, took it for granted that he would come up to Edinburgh to see them but was no more and no less enthusiastic over the visit than over Biddy's, which she was sure could not be long delayed, not when Biddy heard how unhappy she was.

Nellie had been shocked when Biddy had written to tell the Gallaghers of Mr Maitland's midnight visit to her room, though Stuart had laughed and said, 'The dirty old dog!' in a way which made Nellie suspect that her husband was not as surprised as he might have been.

'Stu, did you know Mr Maitland had . . . had *tendencies*?' she asked suspiciously after Stuart had had Biddy's letter read aloud to him. 'Because if so, it was wrong of you not to tell me. I would never have let Biddy stay with them had I suspected any such thing!'

'I didn't know he was going to cradle-snatch in his own home, but I did know he'd an eye for a pretty girl,' Stuart admitted. 'What a crass, insensitive fool the man must be, to get drunk and try it on with his wife's own maid!'

'But if she hadn't been his wife's maid, and if he'd carried on away from home, you'd have thought it acceptable behaviour?' Nellie said in a tone of sweet reasonableness. 'Is that what you're trying to say, Stu?'

'No, no indeed,' Stuart said hurriedly, seeing the trap his beloved was digging for him. 'What a swine you must think me, sweetheart.'

'You aren't a swine; just thoughtless,' Nellie said. 'Oh, Stu, I wish we'd never come, that I do! Poor little Biddy!'

'Judging by her letter, Biddy took very good care of herself,' Stuart said, chuckling. 'She hit him over the head and tipped him out of bed, then walked out on him. That isn't exactly the action of a milksop.'

'No, I suppose not. But I still feel we let Biddy down.'

'You don't like it here after all, do you?' Stuart said shrewdly. 'I didn't think you would, but you seemed so sure!'

'It's all right, it's just a bit strange, a bit different. And we've only been here a month, after all,' Nellie said with assumed brightness. 'I've written back to Biddy, telling her how sorry I am, and saying I hope she'll be happy with Ma Kettle this time round. And now I'm going shopping in the city with Elizabeth. She wants a new hockey stick.'

The *Bess* continued to steam on in appalling weather. They had hauled the trawl, or what was left of it, and chopped it free because it was no use to anyone in its torn and splintered state, and had replaced it with the spare, though that had taken time because of the conditions and the icing up on deck.

They were in uncharted waters now, in the darkness at the top of the world, and there was muttering from some of the old hands that not even the sort of catches they were taking would be worth the risk. But still they shot the trawl, hauled, filled the fish baskets, shot the trawl again. They had to pay for a new trawl now, on top of everything else, so they needed full fish pounds and the coal would have to be made to last.

Dai was at the wheel when they struck the iceberg, but it was no one's fault. The look-outs shouted their warning, but the *Bess* was steaming at speed, the collision could not be avoided. Dai kept the wheel hard over at the Skipper's instruction but it was as though the 'berg was pursuing them. The ship heeled over, came round ... and the 'berg followed, so that the *Bess* seemed to slide almost willingly into that icy embrace.

It was the hidden ice which caught them, not the great cliff of blue, amethyst and rose which towered above them. Dai saw that they had turned in time to miss the eighth of it which surged and curtsied above water and began a quiet prayer of thanksgiving. Then, looking down from his perch he saw, through the pale green of the water, the spires and turrets of the ice-palace, pointing up, like the pale fingers of sirens, beckoning the *Bess* to her doom.

She crunched home with a terrible crashing, squealing roar, then she backed off as the Skipper's frantic orders brought her full speed astern, but it was too late for the port bow, with the teeth of the ice already imbedded in it. The Bosun shouted that they were holed and swung himself below to assess the damage, and Dai kept his eyes ahead and obeyed instructions though his back ached with tension and his eyes stung where the sweat ran down.

Presently Harry came and took the wheel from Dai's hands. 'You done all right; now it'll be all hands to clear up the mess below,' he said calmly. 'First time you've struck, eh? Well, it won't be the last, and you'll still go for your certificates if you've the mind.' He clapped Dai's shoulder. 'We'll seal the damage with canvas, cement, anything that'll keep the sea out. The donkey-engine will pump out any water left. We've coal to get us home, full fish pounds, and the engine's still working. We've done well, Taff.'

Dai relinquished the wheel and rubbed his arms, walking off the bridge. As he went below, the Bosun was rounding up any crew not already working.

'Taff . . . icebreaking on deck. Mal, you're for the forward hold with the working party already down there. Bandy, you won't be needed here for a bit so you can clear ice with the rest. Where's the galley boy? Ah, make a big pot o' tea, lad, an' see all hands get a dram o' rum in each mug.'

It was so down-to-earth, so sensible! Dai went and got his foul weather gear, stopped off at the mess deck for his tea with rum, felt it coursing hot through him, and went up on deck.

Dai could see, now, that the *Bess* was heeling to port, partly from the strike and the resultant flooding, partly because of the weight of ice. He joined the other men, axes already beginning to bite. They could not afford to let her list too far or she'd turn turtle, leaks or no leaks.

Dai raised his axe shoulder-high and brought it down on the great mound of ice he knew to be the whale back. Beside him, the galley boy used a marlin spike to good effect, beyond him, Greasy worked like a maniac, ice chips diamonding the front of his smock.

A man's world. But probably every man on board, at the moment of impact, had thought of his woman. If I live through this, Biddy O'Shaughnessy, you're mine, Dai had told himself. I love you, I'll fight for you – and anyway, you're mine as I'm yours. No more shilly-shallying, no more trying to be fair. Biddy and me are two halves which together make up the whole. When – if – I get home I'm going to tell her so.

The thought comforted him through the trials and dangers of the rest of that long and dangerous voyage.

'Biddy! Eh, you look fine – well, well, well! Mam said a surprise, but I never thought it 'ud be our Biddy, back wi' the Kettles again!'

Kenny looked fine too, Biddy thought. He had grown up since she had seen him last, he was finer-drawn somehow, his face less complacent, less pudgy altogether.

Ma Kettle had brought Kenny through into the living-room and sat him down on the couch beside Biddy and gone out, ostensibly to see to the tea but really, Biddy realised, so that she and Kenny would have a chance to discuss the circumstances under which she had fled from the household. Well, she told herself, I shall do my best to see that Ma doesn't get all the blame; poor old soul, she's done her best, now, to put things right. And she does love Kenny so, he ought to come back.

'Hello, Kenny, it's nice to see you,' she said now, smiling up at him. He was wearing a dark suit and a blue necktie, and the spots which had marred his neck and jawline had disappeared, leaving his skin as smooth as anyone else's. Whilst he lived at home Ma Kettle had cut his hair once every six weeks or so but now Biddy supposed a barber must be doing it, and making a very much neater job of it too. Kenny had a nice-shaped head and his neck was clean and fluff free – a considerable improvement on the old Kenny. 'I expect you're awful busy, because I've been back wi' your Mam for over a month and not seen you earlier. How are the exams coming along?'

'Yes, I've kept pretty busy; and thanks to your 'elp I passed the first lot of exams last summer,' he said at once. 'I did awright – the boss was pleased wi' me. Though I shan't be takin' exams much longer if there's a war. Me sight's not up to much, but the Army will take me on, I reckon. And what about you, Biddy? How've you been? Where did you go when you . . . when you left? Did me Mam tell you what a tizz we was in – me specially? I worried about you, our Biddy, I really did.'

'That was kind, but I went and shared an old schoolfriend's flat, we stayed together for a long time,' Biddy explained. 'We'd always got on well, me and Ellen, and I worked in the city doing deliveries for a gown shop and lived with Ellen until she . . . well, until she decided to go home.'

'Oh ah. And then?'

'Oh, then I took a job in service. I liked it, they were such good people, so kind to me. But Mr Gallagher was moved to Edinburgh, just for a year or so to start up a new magazine, and I – I didn't like the new people so I moved out and I was staying with Ellen's Mam in Paul Street when I met Mrs Kettle again and she offered me my old job back. Only on – well, on better terms. And I took it.'

'Bet she begged, acos she's always said it weren't just her what made you run away from us. Is that true, Bid? Were there – other things?'

Biddy looked up at him. 'Yes, Kenny,' she said frankly. 'I wasn't old enough to know how to tell you I didn't want you as anything but a friend. I'm sorry, but it frightened me rather. I felt trapped.'

Echoes of Ellen, Biddy thought as the words left her mouth, but she knew they were true. Kenny had made her feel trapped, as though she had no right to spurn his advances whilst living under his mother's roof. But Kenny was nodding understandingly.

'Aye, I know what you mean. And I know because I did 'ave the feeling meself that you'd no right to refuse me. Awful young beggar, weren't I? But I know a bit better now, Bid. You won't catch me carryin' on like that again, I promise.'

'Then you will come back? You'll live with your Mam again? I think you should, Kenny, because I shan't be here for always and she does get so lonely. The young girl who does the housework whilst your Mam runs the shop is a nice little thing, but she lives out and she's a bit in awe of Mrs Kettle. It doesn't make chatting or having a laugh any too easy – well, it was the same for me last time I worked for your Mam.'

'My Mam's all right if you know how to handle her,' Kenny said knowingly. 'Yes, I'm movin' back, for the time bein', anyroad. There's nowhere like your own place an' all I've had since I left has been a room in someone else's house.'

'But it's done you good, Kenny,' Biddy said thoughtfully. 'You were a boy before, but now you're a man. And that doesn't happen when you're dependent on your Mam for everything you know, it happens when you take on responsibility for yourself.'

'Aye, I reckon you're right,' Kenny said. 'When you left here, Bid, you was a frightened little thing, you scarce said boo to a goose. But now you're a young woman with a mind of your own – I guess my Mam realised it, or she'd never have offered you a decent wage. It ain't that she doesn't want you real bad,' he added hastily, 'it's just her business sense. It steps in whenever she'd rather give a bit, act generous, and stops her smartish. Awful to be like that. Folk say she's mean, you know.'

'Well, she is a bit tight with her cash,' Biddy said mildly. 'Not to her boys, but to everyone else. She gives her little errand girl sixpence a week and the kid walks or runs miles to get the ingredients your Mam needs, to say nothing of shopping around Great Homer when she ought to be in bed.'

'That's business to Mam,' Kenny said a little too complacently, Biddy thought. 'But you'll keep her on the straight and narrer, see she treats folk fair, won't you, Bid? She means well, but . . .'

'I will whilst I'm here. But when I leave you'll have to do it yourself, Kenny,' Biddy told him. 'One day she'll not be able to manage the shop alone, either. Why don't you marry some nice young girl who would gladly help out for a decent wage? Then you could concentrate on moving up at work, knowing your Mam was well looked after.'

'When I marry it won't be to gerra minder for me Mam,' Kenny said a trifle reproachfully. 'Talkin' of marriage, Bid . . .'

'Yes, I am talking of it, with my young man,' Biddy said quickly. She simply could not allow Kenny to say something he would later regret, even if it did hurt a little right now. 'We're planning an Easter wedding.'

He nodded gloomily, looking down at his feet. 'Aye. I always knew it 'ud happen once you got clear of us. You're far too pretty, chuck, to be hangin' around waitin' for a feller like me. So; do I know the bloke?'

'I don't think so, in fact I'm sure you don't know him, because he isn't from Liverpool at all, he's from the Isle of Anglesey. He's a seaman, he was on a coaster but he's distant-water trawling right now.'

'Oh ah? Good money in it, is there?'

'Enough,' Biddy said briefly. 'Ah, here comes the teatrolley, I can hear it crashing along the hallway. Have you told your Mam yet that you'll be moving back in?'

Kenny grinned. He looked really nice when he grinned, Biddy thought. 'No, not yet. I'll surprise her when she comes in wi' the tea. And . . thanks Biddy.'

'Thanks? What for?'

'For comin' back after all the pain we must ha' caused

you. And for bein' so nice to me Mam. I'm fond of the old girl, in spite of everything.'

'Oddly enough, so am I,' Biddy said as the living-room door shuddered under the impact of a carelessly pushed trolley. 'Yes, against all the odds, I rather like your Mam!'

Chapter Twelve

It had been a beast of a voyage, they were all agreed on that. But somehow, with the ship's bows turned for home and their fish pounds groaning under the weight of fish, with everyone aboard secretly counting up the bonus he would have earned, and with just enough coal to get them right back into the mouth of the Humber, no one was inclined to quibble about the Skipper who had taken them into uncharted waters, rammed an iceberg – and got them out alive.

Dai worked like a Trojan because he felt that, by doing so, he was personally helping to get the ship back to Grimsby and that meant nearer to Biddy. The trip had taken much longer than usual, the Mate reckoned it would be seven full weeks before they docked, and he knew there would be worried faces at home whenever the ship's name was mentioned. But the *Bess*, which had borne up wonderfully under everything which had happened to her, was creaking home, unable to increase speed, eking out her coal, the donkey engine working day and night just to stop the forward hold from flooding, the radio useless, crushed into fragments by that collision with the 'berg.

The men, who had strained every nerve and sinew as the ship had made her way uncertainly through the dark, uncharted waters at the top of the world, could not rest even now. There was always work to be done. Ice had to be cleared every day, the gear kept oiled and in readiness, the leaks checked and plugged. Meals were a worry but

the men thanked their stars for Bandy, who would somehow stretch the four weeks' rations to seven so that they
didn't starve.

'Fish for breakfast, fish for dinner, fish for tea,' someone grumbled, but they all understood that it was sheer
necessity which sent Bandy down to the fish pounds for
provisions. The flour and margarine were holding out,
he reported, but they had eaten the last of the fresh
vegetables a week ago and nearly all the tins were gone.

'Thank your lucky stars it ain't raw fish,' Greasy said
quite sharply. 'Bandy's burnin' old socks in the galley to
save coal for the engine room.'

Harry laughed. 'So long as they ain't my old socks. . . .
Reckon I'll lose a toe this time, half my left foot's gone
black. Did you see that gannet?'

They had all seen it, frozen to the rail, dead as a dodo
before anyone realised that the black frost was rising
again.

'Unlucky, that,' Mal grumbled. 'Someone should've
noticed; as bad as having an albatross dead is a gannet.'

'It's only bad luck if you kill it, not if it dies,' the Mate
said patiently. 'All birds have to die in the fullness of
time.'

'Not on the rail, fruzz to it, its wings half out,' another
man said. 'Still, I reckon that's not goin' to bring bad
luck.'

'Except to the gannet,' Dai put in, and got a reluctant
laugh.

'That's it, Taff, you cut us down to size – what's a
Welshman think is unlucky, then?'

'A woman aboard? A seal swimmin' alongside? I
dunno that I believe in that sort o' bad luck, do you,
Grease? Mebbe we're more practical on the West side o'
the country than you Easteners.'

Greasy shook his head. 'Nah, I don't believe in that

sort o' bad luck. You makes your own, I reckon. Bad management, bad decisions, but I've norra lorra faith in a bird makin' the difference between good an' bad, life an' death.'

They were still arguing good-naturedly about the differences between luck, chance, and human failure, when the Bosun's head appeared round the mess-deck door. 'Ice-breakers wanted; this lot's comin' below for a fag an' a cuppa. Come on fellers, let's be havin' you!'

'A quarter of bull's-eyes? Certainly, madam. In two separate bags? Of course. And two ounces of peppermint fondant? Here we are, then.'

Biddy was working in the shop, enjoying the chance to meet customers and mingle with people instead of always slogging away by herself in the boiling kitchen. She had been allowed to take over in the shop for two reasons. One was that Ma wanted to do some Christmas shopping and the other was that Ma thought it would do Biddy good.

'You're lookin' that long-faced an' mis'rable, it's time you 'ad a change,' she had declared earlier in the day. 'Makin' yourself ill over some worthless young feller what don't know you're born . . . jest acos he's not writ for weeks . . . fellers are all the same, no doubt 'e's wettin' 'is whistle in some waterfront pub an' never givin little Biddy O'Shaughnessy a thought.'

'I rang the port authorities,' Biddy said, white-faced. 'They said the *Greenland Bess* was more than two weeks overdue. There's been no word from her for weeks, not even a radio message to another trawler. They can talk amongst themselves at sea the trawlers can, but they've not heard a word from her since she reached the fishing grounds three weeks or so back.'

'Likely the Lord'll look out for 'em,' Ma Kettle said

with all the comfortable blandness of one not personally concerned. 'Now gerrin there, queen, an' don't forget – no weighin' your thumbs!'

She gave Biddy a roguish wink, slung an extra shawl around the multitude of garments already disposed about her person, and rolled out of the doorway and into the busy street.

The customer, satisfied, left the shop and Biddy's mind turned in on itself once again. There was nothing she could do, that was the trouble. She made time during each day to ring for news of the *Bess* and always the voice answered, with compassion, that she was overdue by so many days and that there had been no word of her.

If we were married then at least I'd be able to go and watch for him; if we were married I could talk to other wives and girlfriends, Biddy thought, automatically turning to clean down a shelf and give the big glass bottles a rub whilst there was no one but herself in the shop. Oh if only Mrs Gallagher and Elizabeth were still in Liverpool, they would understand how desperately, horribly worried I am.

She could ring them! The thought, which crossed her mind just as a small, fat woman walked in with three even smaller and fatter children in tow, brought the first natural smile to Biddy's face for days. Mr Gallagher was in newspapers, he had to be on the telephone at home, she had the number in her room upstairs . . . she would ring as soon as Penny had a moment and could take over in here!

'Good morning, madam! Can I help you?'

The little, round woman looked gratified. She was a regular customer, more used to Ma Kettle's approach, which was to lean over the counter and clack the head of any child attempting to molest the trays of farthing dips.

'Mornin', chuck. Them's me grandchilder, they'd like

a penn'orth o' Kettle toffee an' I'll 'ave an ounce o' peppermints.'

'A penn'orth *each*,' the smallest child squeaked, hanging onto her grandmother's coat. 'Can I 'ave a sherbet dip?'

'If you're good for your Nan till your Mam comes 'ome,' the doting grandparent replied, smiling fondly down at the three children. She turned to Biddy. 'Gorrany kids, Missus? Eh, I wou'n't be wi'out 'em!'

Nellie was wending her way down Princes Street, trying to buy Christmas presents, but despite the enticing displays in the shops, she had not enjoyed the orgy of buying which she had indulged in over the last few days.

The truth was that Nellie was still, after more than two months, terribly homesick. She could not forget that the move to Edinburgh was all her doing, and she would have begged Stuart to let them go home had her conscience allowed her to do so. But she had leapt to conclusions about Lizzie and Dai, acted fast to prevent what she was sure would have been a catastrophe, and now she was stuck with the consequences.

So her Christmas presents this year would reflect the state of her conscience rather than her love, she thought, because she would buy Lizzie a wriggling, squiggling puppy from the pet shop, since it was her fault that her child was unhappy, and she would send Dai an expansive fisherman's guernsey she had seen for sale in a side-street, made of the thick, oily, island wool which would keep him warm as toast under his foul-weather smock. He was unhappy too, that stood to reason, but first love would pass, given time, and one day he would thank her for preventing him from declaring himself to the uncaring Lizzie.

Nellie had always fought against having a dog, feeling that one should spend any spare money on one's fellow human beings and not indulge an animal, but that was before she had lived in a cold, rambling Scottish country house and got to know the previous owner's dogs – Mattie, Angus, Willy and Bosh.

The dogs were looked after, fed, exercised and generally seen to by the gardener, old Jamie, but they soon realised that they had found a soft touch in the Gallaghers and insinuated themselves into the kitchen on every possible occasion.

'They're cold, they need to dry out and get comfy,' Elizabeth would plead, letting the four very large and shaggy retrievers into the kitchen, where they took up far more than their fair share of the hearth. 'Oh, they're the only things I'll miss about this place when we go home!'

Well, with a puppy of her own, at least she would not be able to reproach Nellie over having introduced her to the joys of dog-owning and then taking her away from dogs when Stuart's job came to an end . . . and it couldn't end soon enough for Nellie. As soon as she was certain Elizabeth did not share Dai's feelings she allowed her homesickness full rein and simply concentrated on longing for home. It was all very well to tell herself that Dai would thank her one day, but first, she knew, he would suffer dreadfully when he discovered that Lizzie really did not love him. His pain would hurt Nellie, but she could do nothing about it because discover he would; Elizabeth, sensible girl that she was, would never pretend an affection she did not feel.

And she had let Biddy down too, practically thrown her into the arms of that terrible old lecher, because she hadn't thought of a complication like that when she'd rushed into moving to Scotland the way she had. So to salve Nellie's conscience anew, Biddy would have one of those wonderful pleated skirts in the Black Watch tartan, and one of the very fine dark green wool jumpers to go with it. Unless I buy her a honey-coloured jumper, with a chocolate-coloured skirt, and forget the tartan, Nellie thought now, gazing into another window. Or there's always blue . . .

Fancy Biddy going back to Ma Kettle, though. Her first letter from Kettle's Confectionery had been so funny and sweet, the whole family had read it and laughed and agreed with Lizzie, who had announced that she was desperately homesick for Biddy, and couldn't they ask her up for Christmas, please?

'We'll ask,' Nellie had said doubtfully. 'But judging from what Biddy says, Ma Kettle will want her there for the holiday.'

'Oh, let the old horror want, for once,' Elizabeth said impatiently 'Bribe her, Mum – tell her Dai might come to Scotland for Christmas. She likes our Dai.'

Oh, wouldn't it be nice, Nellie thought now, staring into a window full of scarlet and green, wouldn't it be nice if Dai liked Biddy instead of my dear little daughter, and could be persuaded that it was Biddy he wanted to marry? All I want is their happiness, both of them – all three of them – she told anyone up above who happened to be listening. If only people fell in love sensibly, then there would be no such thing as the terrible ache that was unrequited love. She could scarcely forbid Elizabeth to ask Dai up for Christmas, but she did so hope something would come along to prevent his arrival – a more pressing invitation, anything!

But after a moment she shook herself and walked on. It was no use wishing, she would circumvent Elizabeth's invitation if she possibly could; she would even write to Dai privately and tell him the truth – that Liz was no longer interested in him in that sort of way. But it was no use meeting trouble half-way, she had watched the post carefully ever since arriving here and Dai was playing fair; he had not written to Elizabeth once. It will all work out, she decided, moving along to look in the next window. She always worried far too much and usually for no reason that anyone else could understand.

Nellie peered through the glass and tried to show an interest in a window full of snow-boots. She had not yet decided what to buy her dear Stuart; she had best look at a few more shops before turning her footsteps homewards once more.

Elizabeth was in the kitchen with the dogs when the telephone rang. She was tempted not to answer it because it was always for her father, but conscience was stronger than an urge to go on sitting before the fire, stroking Mattie's tangled fur and sipping at a cup of hot cocoa which the maid, Flora, had given her before going upstairs to tackle the bedrooms.

Flora hated the telephone, which she seemed to regard as an instrument of the devil, so Elizabeth got to her feet on the third ring, loped across the kitchen and into the hall. She sank down on the edge of the square hall table and snatched the receiver from its rest.

'Hello – Elizabeth Gallagher speaking.'

Faint and far off, she heard pennies clattering and someone pushed Button A. Someone was ringing from a call-box, then. Elizabeth brightened. It might even be a friend of hers for a change.

'Hello . . . you're through, caller.'

Another slight clatter, and then a voice spoke, faint but clear. Elizabeth's heart gave a great, happy bound. She would have known that voice anywhere!

'Biddy, it is you, isn't it? Oh, it's grand to hear your voice, absolutely grand! Are you comin' up for Christmas? Do, do come for Christmas. We'll have such fun . . . Dai might come too, if he's back home and has long enough between voyages. You'd like that, you two get on rather well, I've always thought. Biddy?'

The voice sounded fainter now, further off. But even so, Elizabeth could hear the desolation in it.

'Dai's ship is posted as missing, Liz. It's almost two weeks overdue. So he – he may not come home for Christmas at all.'

All Elizabeth's happiness drained away; Dai's ship was missing? This was terrible, a dreadful tragedy, surely Biddy must be mistaken? She said as much, her own voice small and frightened now, but Biddy's voice strengthened a little.

'No, I'm not mistaken, I ring the Port Authority every day and there's been no word for weeks,' she said. 'I – I don't know what to do, Liz. I'm very fond of Dai.'

'We all are,' Elizabeth muttered. 'Oh Biddy, I'll tell Mam an' Dad, see if they can think of anything. Ring me again tomorrow, whatever happens, won't you?'

'I'll try . . . no more time now, Liz, me money's running out . . .'

There was a very final sort of click and then the operator's voice came across the line saying that the caller had disconnected. Elizabeth hung her own receiver back and turned blindly away from the telephone. Tears had filled her eyes and now she let them run down her cheeks, made no effort to stop their flow.

Poor Dai, out in all that terrible cold! And poor Biddy, who was so fond of him – she must have been fonder than we ever realised, Elizabeth thought, to ring the Port Authority every day like that. But what can we do to help, what can anyone do? All we can do is wait, and pray, and comfort each other as best we can.

Nellie came into the house quickly, letting herself in through the front door and slinging her soaking coat at the hat-stand without even waiting to adjust it properly. She kicked off her short boots, massaged her icy toes with one hand for a moment, then pulled off the extra socks she had put on that morning; they were soggy, which meant she could do with some new boots. It was snowing outside and although she could have hailed a cab she had got the omnibus from the village and then walked, and now she wished she had had more sense.

I've probably caught my death, she was thinking as she went into the kitchen, positively wringing out her hair with one hand and watching a stream of water run out of it. I'm sure Scottish snow is colder than the Liverpool sort – certainly this house is colder than the one in Ducie Street, but it's scarcely worth doing anything about it, because we won't be here next winter, I'm sure of it.

Elizabeth was sitting by the fire, surrounded by dogs. She jumped to her feet as soon as her mother came into the room.

'Oh Mam . . . the most awful thing! You know Dai's ship, the *Greenland Bess*? It's two weeks overdue and posted as missing!'

Nellie stood stock still for a moment, feeling all the colour draining out of her face, leaving it cold as the snow which was falling outside. Then she sat down heavily on the nearest chair. One of the dogs, she could not tell which one, came and nuzzled her, pushing its wet nose into the palm of her hand, rubbing its head on her knees.

'Oh, dear God! Missing, you say?'

It was like some terrible nightmare, the sort where you ran in quicksand, unable to take a step, where the monster's hot breath is on your neck, his teeth a hair's breadth from your throat. Dai was missing, and she had been hoping, praying almost, that he would not be able to come up to Scotland and spend Christmas with them! She had brought this about herself, with her own selfishness, and now that her secret was safe she could see too clearly what a mean, pathetic little secret it was, how shallow and pitiful had been her attempts to keep the truth to herself.

'Mam, you look terrible! I'm sorry, I know you were fond of him, but we didn't know him all that well. . . . Mam, sit still, I'm going to telephone the office and get my father to come home.'

'Don't be silly, love.' The words should have come out strong and steady, but they emerged as a tiny whisper. 'I'll be all right, leave your Da out of this.'

'But – but Mam, I was going to ring Dad anyway, to ask him if there was anything we could do – anything the newspaper could do, really. Surely they could do something? Send out a – a rescue ship or something?'

Nellie suddenly ducked her head down into her lap. The room was starting to swim – she mustn't faint, she must be strong and sensible! If Stuart came home and saw her like this . . . no point in telling anyone that Dai was her son now, because . . . because . . .

A hand, warm, on the back of her neck. A face, young and soft, against hers. Elizabeth, as worried, now, over her mother as she had been worried just now over Dai.'Mam? It's all right, I'm sure he'll be all right, ships do get lost at sea, don't they, and then the crew turn up? I remember you telling me once . . .'

Her voice went on, telling a comforting story, but it had reminded Nellie. Davy had been posted as missing and mourned for dead during the war, but he had been safe. Picked up by an enemy ship, put into a prison camp . . . there was no war on now, but it could still happen, couldn't it? Men were sometimes saved at sea . . . she tried to put out of her head all that Dai had told them about fishing the Arctic, about the conditions which meant that a man overboard was dead before his body touched the water. No use to bring the bad things to mind, think positively, she urged herself. And pray, Nellie Gallagher, pray for your boy!

After Biddy had made her phone call she felt much better, as though having told Elizabeth meant, at least, that there were two of them going to be thinking and praying for Dai and the *Bess*.

She returned to the shop and sold sweets until Ma Kettle returned, a fat and chuckling Santa Claus, from her shopping trip.

'I done us proud,' Ma Kettle crowed, rooting through her brown paper bags with much mystery in the boiling kitchen. 'I've got more peppermint oil an' more almond essence, but the rest of the stuff's for upstairs. Wait on, chuck, I'll be t'rough there any moment, then you can put another boilin' o' toffee on. You've done well this mornin', but it's near enough to the 'oliday for sales to keep up an' it don't do to run out o' toffees.'

'All right,' Biddy said, but she was beginning to be aware, within herself, of a strange restlessness, a feeling that if she did not *do* something she would burst. What she was supposed to do she did not know, but there was something . . . should she go back to the Maitlands' house and see if there was a message? Should she ring the Port Authority again? But she had been round to Ducie Street earlier in the week and she had rung the Port Authority before getting in touch with Elizabeth.

She finished boiling the toffee mixture soon after noon and as soon as it was in its trays she found her hands going round to the back of her to untie her apron strings.

What's got into you, Biddy O'Shaughnessy, she scolded herself, with the apron in her hands instead of round her person. You've finished the toffee but there's no end still to do, you can't go yet!

Oh can't I, you try to stop me, a little inner voice replied defiantly. Just you tell old Kettle you're off and you'll be back as soon as you can and let her do some toffee-boiling for once. 'Twon't hurt her.

Biddy went upstairs and packed a few necessities into her carpet bag. Then she got her money out of her pillow and hurried downstairs again. She went through to the boiling kitchen and checked that everything was clean and as it should be, then she gave Penny a shout but before the younger girl had arrived she was going into the shop.

Biddy entered the shop quietly and closed the door behind her. Ma Kettle was weighing an ounce of aniseed balls for a waiting child and including quite a bit of thumb on the scales. Normally Biddy would have dug her in the back and Ma Kettle would have taken her hand away from the pan sharpish, but today Biddy didn't bother. She had her own affairs to attend to. 'I'm going out, Ma,' she said. 'I'll be back in an hour, but then I'll be off again maybe for a day or two. I'm off now, to fetch help.'

'Help? Back in a *day or two*? Biddy, I pays you good money . . .' Ma Kettle began, but Biddy swept round the end of the counter and headed for the shop door.

'You've already had most of this week free, because I won't charge you,' Biddy said recklessly over her shoulder. 'I've got to go, Ma, I really have. Penny's a good girl, she'll stand by you, and Kenny can give a hand in here Saturday afternoon, when he's not working. I won't be any longer than I have to be.'

'But you don't 'ave to go, no one 'asn't come after you,' Ma Kettle called plaintively after her retreating back. 'Think o' me, Biddy . . . think o' our livelihood . . . Christmas is our busiest time, if I got the toffees I can make a mint, Christmas, but without you to boil 'em . . .'

'Can't stop. You'll be all right Ma, honest you will. Would I leave you in the lurch at this time o' year? 'Course I wouldn't. But I can't stop now, I've got a goodish distance to walk.'

And Biddy was on her way, hurrying down the Scotland Road towards her destination.

She reached Paul Street and hurried along it, then turned into Samson Court. Despite the cold, half a dozen small children were playing out on the paving before the Bradley house.

''Ello, Biddy,' a small urchin squeaked cheerfully. 'Our Ellen's indoors. She's been cryin'.'

'She won't cry soon,' Biddy said recklessly, giving the door a bang and then opening it and entering the house. 'Ellen? Where are you?'

Ellen came down the stairs. Her eyes were pink-rimmed, but she smiled as soon as she set eyes on her friend. 'Oh Biddy, it's good to see you! I were that down . . . I went along to the market this mornin', bought Bobby a nice little coat 'cos it's gerrin' cold out, an' it's too bleedin' small, it catches 'im under the arms! Oh, I were fit to be tied!'

'Never mind that now,' Biddy said. 'Ellen, d'you remember in the flat, when you and I made sweets to sell, Christmas and Easter?'

''Course I do – we 'ad some fun in them days,' Ellen said wistfully, looking as though she was about to burst into tears again. 'Oh, poor Ted, if only . . .'

'Could you do it again?'

'Again? Do what again? If you mean live wi' a feller, there ain't no question . . .'

'Ellen, I could shake you!' Biddy said roundly. 'I'm in a tearing hurry . . . just listen to me! Could you make sweets still or have you forgotten how?'

'Course I could, even wi'out the recipes, what I've still got, anyroad,' Ellen said quite sharply. 'Small chance 'ere, though. No sugar, no butter, no . . .'

'And would you like a room of your own, decent wages, a kind o' uniform so's your own clothes didn't get mucky?'

'Would I! Bit it ain't no use, Bid . . . it's Bobby, I can't leave 'im 'ere wi' me Mam and no one wouldn't want me an' the kid 'cos 'e's too young to leave whiles I work.'

'I know all those things. Look, Ellen, sit down whilst I explain. The thing is that I've – I've got to go away for a day or so, perhaps longer. And Christmas is coming and old Ma Kettle is making masses o' sweets. She needs help, but I'm off, so I said I'd find someone. And Ell, dear, that someone can be you, if you'd like it and could cope.'

'Like it? Gawd, it 'ud be a real life-saver,' Ellen said fervently. 'But I couldn't boil toffee wi' Bobby on me 'ip, and I can't leave 'im . . .'

'You could leave him with Penny, the girl who does for Ma Kettle,' Biddy said slowly and clearly. 'Penny could keep an eye on him whilst you worked in the shop and the boiling kitchen. She's a good little girl, sensible and hard-working. And Bobby's no trouble, he'd be happy enough playing wi' bits and bobs whiles you were workin'. Right?'

'Yeah, absolutely right,' Ellen agreed. She was beginning to look hopeful. 'The trouble is, Biddy, that folk don't believe you can work wi' a baby around. There's always someone wi'out a kid who'll tek the job from under your nose. Believe me, I been for 'undreds o' jobs an' norra sniff 'ave I got.'

'No, but you can make sweets, which not many girls can, an' Ma Kettle's desperate. An' I'll vouch for your honesty, because I've never known you take what isn't yours, chuck, so the old girl won't have to worry about you prigging her toffees or her cash. So what about it? Will you come back wi' me now, leave a note for your Mam, an' give it a go?'

'Oh, Bid,' Ellen breathed. 'Oh, Bid, if it worked! If she liked me, wanted to keep me on! Oh, I'd work real 'ard, you know I would! Just to 'ave a place o' me own to lay me 'ead, just to 'ave Bobby looked after by someone who wasn't me, once in a while . . . oh, Bid!'

'I'll write the note, you sign it,' Biddy was beginning, when Mrs Bradley came into the kitchen backwards, towing a large sack of potatoes. She straightened up and grinned at the girls through the sweat running down her face.

'Gorrem cheap,' she said triumphantly. 'Spuds for a fortnight there, I reckon. 'Ello, Biddy, what's up wi' you, then?'

Breathlessly, Biddy explained about the job whilst Ellen flew upstairs to pack a few bits as she put it. And she was down almost before Biddy had finished her explanation, with a bulging bag and Bobby under one arm.

'Is it awright, Mam?' she said a trifle anxiously, standing her bag down for a moment. 'Only it ain't as if I get many chances.'

'You go an' grab it wi' both 'ands, flower,' Mrs Bradley said. 'You'd be best out o' here . . . too many of us.'

'Thanks Mam,' Ellen said. She picked up her bag and headed for the door. 'Come on, Bid, in case someone else gets there first – it 'ud be just my luck!'

It would not be true to say that Ma Kettle welcomed Ellen with open arms, because she viewed both girls with deep suspicion, but she was very taken with little Bobby.

''Oo's a fine feller, then?' she cooed, dangling a sugar mouse before his rounding eyes. 'Are you comin' to sit wi' Auntie Kettle for a moment then, whiles your Mam teks 'er bag upstairs?'

And seconds later Ma Kettle and Bobby were conversing in coos and gurgles and Ma was holding the child to the manner born, calling out to customers that she wouldn't be a mo, but she'd a young gennelman caller what was tekin' a deal of attention, right now.

'Be firm with her,' Biddy begged Ellen as they descended the stairs together. 'Remember if you walk out she'll be in a fair old pickle wi' Christmas so close and all. Oh, thanks, Ell, for coming over, and the best of luck.'

'But where are you off to?' Ellen said suddenly, realising that Biddy was actually about to leave. 'When'll you be back?'

'I'm – I'm going to Grimsby. I have to go and I dunno when I'll be back but it probably won't be more than four or five days. Thanks, Ell . . . bye, Mrs Kettle!'

'I only 'opes you're right about this young man's Mam,' an injured voice called through from the shop. 'She can start off by doin' me a boilin' o' the best Kettle toffee . . . . Don't you dare leave me for long, Biddy O'Shaughnessy, or . . . or . . .'

'Be good, both,' Biddy shouted out, then banged the door and fled along the icy pavement. Glancing back, she saw the first flakes of winter begin to meander down out of the grey and lowering sky. If it really began to snow that might make her journey a difficult one, but there was no point in worrying. Get to the port, Biddy, she ordered herself. Worry then if you must, but get there!

She was snug aboard the tram when the snow really started in earnest. I hope to God the trains don't get held up seriously by the snow, she prayed to herself, rubbing the steam off the window nearest her so she could look out. I need to get to Grimsby, I must get to Grimsby, I'll get there if I have to walk!

The pavements were wet so the snow was not yet lying, but the shoulders of passers-by were soon speckled with white and as the tram came to a halt on St George's Plain Biddy could barely see the big hotels which lined the other side of the road. This was not going to make her journey any easier, but she hopped down and hurried across the road, feeling ridiculously light-hearted. It was because she was doing something, not just waiting for whatever news was to come.

She reached Lime Street Station and glanced up at the clock; it was nearly three o'clock – what an hour to start a long, cross-country journey! But she went straight to the ticket office and put her problem to the expert, who was a rather tired-looking young clerk behind the little window. He was sipping a cup of tea, chewing a bun and reading what looked like a timetable, all at the same time; but he put everything down when Biddy tapped and shot up his little hatch.

'Sorry, queen, 'avin' me snap,' he said rather thickly. 'First quiet moment I've 'ad all day. Can I 'elp you?'

'I want to get to Grimsby, by tonight if possible,' Biddy said promptly. 'Can you work me out a route, please?'

Dai always moaned about the changes necessary on a cross-country route, but she was prepared for anything so long as she ended up in the port.

'You couldn't 'ave come to a better person,' the clerk said, picking up the big book he had been reading and flourishing it at her. 'New timetable, see? Just been familiarisin' meself with it, so to speak. Now Grimsby, you said, queen . . . hmm . . .'

Ten minutes later, with directions scribbled in the clerk's neat writing on a piece of L & NWR paper, Biddy set off again. She had half an hour before her train left, so she could go into Lime Street and buy herself a magazine and something to eat on the journey. The clerk was sure she would find herself waiting on various platforms and said she could probably nip out and buy herself something to eat then, but Biddy was taking no chances. Homelessness had taught her the importance of being prepared for anything, and she had no desire to spend a hungry, cold night on some lonely station in the middle of the country.

She found a café and bought sandwiches and some buns, then added a bottle of lemonade. It was rather heavy, but the horrors of thirst on a long journey could be imagined all too clearly. A nice new edition of *Woman* magazine came next, then Biddy returned to the station, brushing snow off her shoulders as she went.

She was in good time and easily secured a seat in the third-class section of the train.

'It ain't near enough to Christmas for the rush to 'ave started, and since folk don't travel much when it's wintry, wi' Christmas preparations to make, you won't find the trains overcrowded,' the clerk had explained as he sold Biddy her ticket. 'Good luck Miss, an' a pleasant journey.'

I don't think it will be all that pleasant, Biddy thought as she settled into a corner seat. It was already dusky outside but the train was not yet lit up and suddenly the adventure seemed more like a vain hope. Why am I going to Grimsby, when the ship isn't back and I'm a stranger there? Biddy asked herself helplessly as the train chugged out of Lime Street and into the whirling snow. I must be mad!

But in her heart she knew she was not mad at all. She had simply obeyed a feeling that Grimsby was the place to be and she intended to go on obeying that feeling until she felt the docks beneath her feet.

Presently she got her directions out and went over them again so that she would know when to get off the train and which connection she needed next. And having read it until the words were engraved on her memory she pushed the paper into her pocket, leaned her head back on the prickly upholstery, and allowed herself to doze.

'Thank you love, that was a kind thought. Now you go and – and do whatever you want and leave me quietly here. I need to think.'

Elizabeth smiled at her mother, then slipped out of the bedroom and closed the door gently behind her. On the opposite side of the galleried upper landing, Flora hovered. They had only been in Scotland a short while, Elizabeth reflected, but already Flora was extremely fond of her mistress and that fondness was reflected now in the worry on her small, bony face.

'Is she all right? No' ill, is she?'

Elizabeth shushed the maid with a finger to her lips and then walked round the gallery to where Flora stood.

'Hush, Flora, I gave her a couple of aspirin tablets and a hot drink; now I'm hoping she'll sleep. We – we had some sad news this morning.'

'Oh aye? Was it that telephone call?' Flora's small face reflected her distrust of the machine. 'I might ha' known it boded no good; that thing is an instrument o' the devil, have I no' telled ye so often and often?'

'Yes, you have,' Elizabeth admitted. 'But it wasn't the fault of the telephone, Flora. A friend called me to tell me that someone called Dai Evans, who is my Mam's friend's son, is lost at sea. Mam is fond of him, and I think since his own mother's death he looks on my Mam as her deputy. We – we were hoping he'd spend Christmas with us. It's been a sad blow.'

'Aye, aye,' Flora muttered. 'You'll get in touch with

your father, nae doubt, tell him your mother is unwell?'

'I was going to, but Mam doesn't want me to worry him; she says there's nothing anyone can do, not even my Da, but I thought perhaps the newspaper could help in some way.'

'Och no, men are lost at sea all the time,' Flora said. 'I'm frae a trawlin' family. Terrible sad it is, but all ye can do is pray, Miss Liz.'

'Yes. And now I'm going downstairs to make my mother a rather late luncheon. What do you recommend, Flora? I thought hot soup, because it's still snowing, and perhaps an egg on toast?'

'Aye, she's gae fond of an egg,' Flora said. 'I'll gi' you a hand, we've already got some fine leeks an' a ham bone in the larder an' Jamie will fetch in onions frae the shed if we need 'em.'

The two of them descended the stairs and presently began working companionably in the kitchen. Elizabeth, cleaning leeks, said that they might as well make sufficient soup for tonight since the snow, which had whirled ever since breakfast, showed no sign of letting up and it would be pleasant to have leek-and-ham soup at dinner.

By one o'clock the tray was laid, the meal ready. Flora went ahead to open doors, Elizabeth carried the tray with the soup steaming gently and the egg on toast under a silver cover.

They reached the bedroom and Flora threw open the door. Elizabeth sailed through with a big smile . . . then stopped suddenly. The soup, unwarned, slid across the tray, teetered frantically on the edge for a moment and then plummeted to the floor.

'Mam? Oh, she must have popped out for a minute to . . . hang on, what's that on the pillow? Oh Flora, I wish I'd not listened to her, I wish I'd telephoned my Da! There's an envelope addressed to my father and a tiny note for me, telling me not to worry, she's had to go out. Oh dear, I *knew* she was ill, I'll have to find her!'

'She won't be far, no' in this weather,' Flora said, having thought about it for a second. 'We'd best tell the men . . . we'll soon find someone who's seen her.'

And Jamie, the gardener, knew at once what had happened to his mistress.

'Went off on the bus into Edinburgh,' he said in his soft, elderly voice. 'Right as rain, she was, gave me a big smile an' said it was the Christmas shopping she was tackling today.'

'There, we're worrying for nae reason,' Flora said comfortingly. 'But telephone your father, Miss Liz, because of the letter.'

Elizabeth was on the phone almost before the maid had spoken, but she presently put it down again, disappointed. 'He's out on business, not expected back until five,' she said. 'Oh Flora, I am worried! Whatever ought I to do?'

Nellie boarded the first of her trains in mid-afternoon, and sat in a corner of the carriage wishing her feet would warm up and wondering whether she was doing the right thing. Not that she had had any choice. Once she had got over the initial shock of Elizabeth's news she had simply longed, with the whole of her heart, to be near Dai. I should have told him, she mourned, sitting icy in the carriage. I should have told him, quietly, that he was my boy. That way at least we could have exchanged letters, he could have confided in me. If only I'd not been so secretive . . .

But she had not wanted – still did not want – to hurt Stuart. The fact that she had run away to see whether there was anything she could do about the missing trawler should not worry or hurt him, she told herself, because he would simply think she was concerned for her friend's lad. But she could not sit at home and wait in idleness, this was the least she could do.

When the train stopped she got out and went into the small station buffet. She drank hot tea and ate a ham sandwich and wondered whether to telephone home from the booth just outside the station, but it would only lead to a lot of questions she did not feel capable of answering. So she climbed aboard the next train and settled herself for a long and very cold journey.

Dai was on deck when they first sighted the Spurn light, but the gulls were already aboard by then and circling overhead so everyone knew a landfall was imminent. The *Bess* was still proceeding cautiously, like an old lady with a gammy leg, low in the water and lopsided, too, but at least the coal would last out – just. And though the meals now consisted of fish with fish, followed by fish, with chunks of Bandy's soda bread the only relief, at least meals were still being provided – just. And no one was badly hurt; Dai himself nursed a sprained wrist from ice-breaking, Greasy had pulled a tendon in his leg and limped, the Mate was still in pain from the blackened toe. But there had been no loss of life though it had been a near-run thing.

They broke out the bonded rum in the Humber estu-ary and several of the men got drunk, but Dai was too excited to take more than a token sip. The *Bess* would be in dry dock for six weeks, possibly longer. The iceberg's toothmarks were deep and the damage done in the colli-sion would take a deal of work to put right. The little donkey engine toiled ceaselessly, pumping her out, and whenever you looked in the forward hold you had to wonder at the little ship's stubborn ability to remain afloat with so much water sloshing around below.

Next stop Liverpool, next stop Biddy, Dai kept repeating to himself. Oh, he'd stay in Grimsby long enough to collect his pay, to telephone the Gallaghers . . . oh no, he couldn't do that, Biddy wasn't with the Gallaghers any more but the Maitlands would still be on the telephone. Or he might get straight on a train; the surprise would be all the better when he turned up and swept her into his arms, told her no more silliness, they would get wed before he returned to sea and find themselves lodgings in Grimsby. He realised he had been mad to listen to Nellie because the only thing one should listen to regarding a loved one is your own heart. She can't love anyone else, she just can't, he told himself over and over, to still the niggling little doubt that sometimes came in the night and made him sweat with fear in case Nellie had been right. My Biddy's a girl in a thousand . . . wonder if there'll be a letter? If there isn't a letter . . .

The ship nosed slowly out of the fierceness of the North Sea, butting through the snow which was falling, heading up-river like an old hound who smells its home and its warm bed on the wind. Objects which had clattered ceaselessly to the wave's rhythm for six weeks fell silent and men looked around, puzzled by the stillness. You could play cards without having to grab the loose pack, you could stand a drink down and find it there when you turned to it once more, you could sleep without hanging grimly onto the side of your bunk, unable to relax because if you did you'd wake up half-way across the cabin.

You could smell the docks, despite having been amongst fish for six weeks. A strong, salty odour which was mixed with the smell of the land, an indefinable scent which Dai could not describe, but could only enjoy.

And as they made their slow way into the fish docks they saw other trawlers with men aboard who could understand what the marks on the bow meant, the reason for the lopsidedness, the constant discharge of water from the donkey engine. Men waved and shouted to them, asked questions, told them they'd been posted missing. . . . The crew called back, exchanged badinage, made light of Bess's wounds, her beast of a voyage.

'It'll all be the same in a hundred years; and we'll be having Christmas at home,' the Mate said as he stood beside Dai, watching the Skipper bring the Bess so neatly and quietly alongside that you never would have guessed all was not right with her. 'Hope you've been putting money away, lad. Six hungry weeks ahead, unless you sign on with another trawler, of course.'

'I'll go to Liverpool first, to see my girl, arrange our wedding,' Dai said matter-of-factly. It made it more real, somehow, putting it into words. 'Then . . . I'll go home, to Anglesey. Been meaning to go, meaning to talk to my Da these twelve months but never got round to it somehow. Now I'll go, sort things out. Take my girl so they can meet her.'

'Aye,' the Mate nodded thoughtfully. 'Never leave things till tomorrow, Taff, not if you're distant-water trawling. For too many there isn't a tomorrow. Riskiest business in the world bar none, ours. Not for everyone, not by a long chalk.'

'Not sure, after this little lot, if it's for me,' Dai admitted ruefully. He thought he would see the prow of the iceberg bearing down on their little ship in nightmares for the rest of his life. 'But I'll sign on again, just to see.'

The Mate grinned. 'That sounds like me, twenty year ago. Well, whichever way it goes, good luck, Taff. And see you in six weeks.'

The fenders were out, kissing the quayside, the gang-plank was lowered, the crew were lining up to leave.

There were shouts, rude jostlings, remarks about other people's wives and mothers which could only have been exchanged amongst men who knew each other very well indeed.

'Comin' to collect your wages, Taff?' Greasy said as they shuffled in line towards the shore. 'The fish'll fetch a good price, they say, 'cos we're one of the last boats in afore Christmas. Eh, look down there – someone's sweet'earts can't wait to see 'em!'

Down on the quayside two women stood, an older and a younger. They ignored the howling gale, the snow swirling past. They were both waving, but there was something in the way they stood which told Dai that tears were being held at bay, that the joyful smiles which he could just about make out through the snow were relief as much as pleasure. Of course, we were posted missing, he was telling himself, I hope Biddy didn't know, I hope she wasn't too worried . . . and all in a moment he recognised her.

Biddy! Soaked hair hanging in rats' tails down onto her shoulders, her coat almost black with wet, but the pink in her cheeks showing even through the snow, and the sparkle in those blue, blue eyes!

Dai had been at the back of the queue. Now he gave a hoarse, strangled shout and simply flew down the gangplank, knocking men twice his size and with double his seniority aside without a thought. He covered the snowwet, fish-slippery quay in half a dozen strides and she was in his arms, cuddling close, weeping, laughing, trying to talk whilst he tried to silence her with his mouth, kissing her eyelids, her cheeks, her ice-cold nose and then those tender, opening lips!

'I thought . . . I thought . . . you were posted missing. I'd – I'd been ringing every day . . .'

'There, there, sweetheart, and here I am, safe and

sound,' Dai crooned against her wet hair. 'Oh, Biddy, thought you'd met someone else, I did, then I told myself it just wasn't possible, but . . .'

It was her turn to croon now, her turn to comfort. 'Oh darling, as if I could ever think about anyone else, when I love you so very much! And we'll get married soon, won't we? Before you go back to sea again – as soon as we can arrange it?'

He stood back from her, the snowflakes floating between them kissing cheek and brow unnoticed. It could have been forty degrees below or baking hot for all they knew – or cared. The crew from the *Bess* streamed past them, ribald remarks were uttered, they were jostled and chuckled over, but neither one of them noticed.

'We'll get married in Moelfre, when we go back to see my people,' Dai said. 'I wish Mam could have known you, but . . . oh Biddy, I'm so happy!'

But Biddy had remembered her manners. She turned to the woman standing back, watching them with a gentle smile curving her lips. 'I'm so sorry . . . I quite forgot. Mrs Gallagher's come to welcome you home too, Dai. She – she's got something to tell you, my love.'

'Nellie!' Dai exclaimed. He turned and took both Nellie's cold little hands in his. 'Oh Nell, I'm sorry, I didn't see you standing there.'

'You two saw nothing but each other,' Nellie said, smiling up at him. 'Let's go and get a cup of tea and a bun; perhaps we should talk.'

'Sure,' Dai said. He put his arm round Biddy, holding her close, and then had to go on board the *Bess* again, to rescue his ditty bag, cast down at the moment of seeing Biddy. Returning to their side, he looked rather suspiciously at Nellie. 'Nellie, it was you who said . . .'

'I'll explain in a moment, dear,' Nellie said. 'Come along, we arrived here very late last night – we met on a station somewhere in the heart of Yorkshire and came the rest of the way together – and we've got a room on East Marsh Street, so when we came down to the docks we had to find somewhere to go and eat, dry out a bit. . . . There's a nice little place on Church Lane . . .'

'You arrived last night? But no one knew we were coming in, our transmitter was a casualty of the first iceberg. What made you decide to come to Grimsby?'

Nellie shrugged and beside him, Dai felt Biddy's shoulders rise and fall in an identical gesture.

'I don't know, Dai dear.' Nellie said quietly. 'I just felt I had to be here, and Biddy was the same. We've been on the dock since before dawn though, because the lighthouse saw you and reported that the *Bess* was heading for home. Now come along, we can talk in the cafe.'

The café was steamy, crowded, noisy. They managed to find a table in the window and all the while they were there the snow blew against the glass in little gusts as if to remind them that, outside, other men on other ships still risked their lives on the cruel and turbulent ocean.

They ordered a large pot of coffee, some hot buttered toast and a quantity of the small currant buns the proprietress was famed for, and started to eat and drink at once, at first almost without a word. But then Nellie put down her cup and spoke. 'Dai, when you came to me you told me you wanted to marry my girl . . . . Remember?'

'That's right. And you said . . .'

'Wait a moment, dear. Who did you mean when you say *my girl*?'

'Why, Biddy, of course. Whoever . . .'

'Ah, but when someone says *my girl* to me, I don't think of Biddy, I think of Elizabeth.'

Dai goggled; there was no other way of putting it. His eyes rounded and his mouth dropped open, but he could say nothing. Biddy could tell he was working it out, taking it in. Finally, he heaved a great sigh and grinned, a flash of amazingly white teeth in a face which had been weathered to a deep tan by wind and snow, never by the sun.

'Lizzie! You thought I was in love with little Lizzie! And she's got a boyfriend, eh?'

Biddy wondered whether Nellie would seize the offer of a get-out or tell the truth, but Nellie simply shook her head.

'No, not really, dear,' she said steadily. 'But there's something I've never told you – never told anyone but Biddy here, when we were stuck in that icy cold train, coming across country with infinite slowness. Dai, when I was very young I – I had a baby boy. I wasn't married, but the – the father of my baby was. He was a sailor on a coaster and his – his name was Davy Evans. When I found I was expecting his baby I went to Moelfre, and Bethan, your mother, befriended me. She was so good! But she had no child, she believed that her husband was dead, lost at sea, and there was I, about to give birth to Davy's baby, with no hope of giving the child a proper home, a real place in society. So when she said she would give you a home, and all the love at her command, I – I was glad to accept.'

Dai was staring at Nellie as though he doubted his hearing. Was this giving him pain, Biddy wondered compassionately? Did he hate the thought that his beloved Mam had not actually given birth to him, that he was the offspring of his father and his father's mistress?

'Nellie, what are you saying, woman? That I am not my mother's child? That I'm . . . I'm . . .'

'You're my son. Which is why, dear Dai, I panicked and lied desperately when I thought you were in love with Lizzie. She's – she's your sister, you see.'

Biddy had never taken her eyes off his face and now she saw the slow smile dawning in the dark eyes she loved so much, reaching his mouth so that suddenly he was smiling, then laughing. He leaned across the table and put his hands round Nellie's face, then kissed her forehead, suddenly sobering.

'When my Mam was dying she told me to turn to you if I wanted mothering,' he said slowly. 'Perhaps I should've known, guessed . . . but I didn't. Oh Nellie, fach, only one Mam there could ever be for me, and that one Bethan, but I can love you like a Mam, and I do.'

'That's more than I deserve,' Nellie said, tears trembling in her eyes, then spilling over. Dai leaned across and wiped them away with his fingers and Nellie laughed shakily. 'Oh Dai, what a sad mess I nearly made of your life, when all I wanted was to see you happy! And when I met our Bid in the station, with a face like a ghost and great, dark eyes; when she told me she was going to Grimsby . . . then I knew. It all came tumbling out, all the stupid things I'd done, and she said it didn't matter, because she was certain-sure that you weren't drowned, certain that we wouldn't both have been drawn to Grimsby without a purpose.'

Biddy smiled at Nellie and rubbed her face against Dai's sleeve.

'And when we reached the port they were talking about the *Bess* down on the docks, saying what a blessing it was that you'd not all been killed, talking about your catch, your Skipper . . . and we just hugged one another and grinned like loonies, didn't we, Mrs Gallagher?' Biddy said, smiling across at Nellie. 'So we're going to get married, eh, Dai? I'd best write a nice letter to Ma Kettle, telling her what's been happening, though I'll have to go back there, collect my things and so on, but I'd rather a letter reached her first, somehow. And you'll tell

Lizzie, Mrs Gallagher? She's been a good friend to me, I'd like her at my wedding, even if you and Mr Gallagher don't feel you could rightly turn up.'

'Of course I will, and you must call me Nellie since you're to be my daughter-in-law,' Nellie said gaily. 'In fact I'm going to tell Stu and Elizabeth the truth if you don't mind, Dai. There's a deal of harm done by lying, even if you lie for what you think are the right reasons.'

'Tell 'em all,' Dai said generously. 'But I won't spread it around at home, not in Moelfre. My Da doesn't know, I take it?'

Nellie smiled. 'No. Bethan would never have told him. My recollection of Davy is that one didn't tell him secrets.'

'Right. So that's settled. Now are you two lovely ladies coming down to the office with me, so's I can get paid off until the next trip? Or do you want to go back to your lodgings and try to dry out a bit? Because Biddy and me ought to catch the next train for Liverpool – we've a lot to do!'

'I'd best go straight home, I think,' Nellie said rather regretfully. 'You know we're living in Edinburgh now, Dai? I – I suppose you wouldn't both like to come back with me, just to get some of the explaining over? It wouldn't take long, then you could go to Moelfre for Christmas. Say you will, just for a few days! I'll pay your fares, of course.'

'I think perhaps we ought,' Biddy said slowly. 'Poor Nellie, you're going to have quite a lot of explaining to do, and if it would make it easier for you . . . I mean, you are Dai's Mam when all's said and done, and Mr Gallagher – Stuart, I mean – does deserve an explanation, all things considered. And I'd desperately like you Gallaghers at me wedding because I've no relatives of my own I can ask. Only it's up to Dai, really. What do you think, my love?'

'So long as no one starts brooding over what's long

past,' Dai said slowly. 'Yes, we'll come. Only he's a good feller is Stuart, not the sort to cast blame. I think you'll hear few reproaches, my little Mam.'

And he squeezed Nellie's hand and looked away as the tears ran down her cheeks.

They arrived in Edinburgh very late at night, and left the station to find themselves in the middle of a blinding snowstorm. The wind dashed snowflakes against the windows of their cab and caused the driver to slow to a crawl and to use some extremely Scottish words beneath his breath.

'I wonder if Lizzie's still up?' Biddy said as Nellie opened the big front door. 'She knows you're bringing us back, doesn't she, Mrs Ga ... I mean Nellie?'

'Yes; I rang her earlier though and said we would be late,' Nellie said, ushering them inside. Dai, who had stayed to pay the cab-driver, joined them in the hall, beginning to take off his coat, already damp across the shoulders even in the short dash from the car to the house. Nellie unbuttoned her own coat, then glanced up the stairs, beginning to smile. 'Ah, here she comes, tearing about, as usual! Lizzie darling, we're back! Take Biddy and Dai into the kitchen and make them a hot drink, will you? I just want a word with your father. He's in the study, I take it?'

Lizzie, bouncing down the stairs, kissed her mother and Biddy, then stood on tiptoe to kiss Dai's cheek before turning back to her mother. 'Oh Mam, I'm glad you're back, things have been a bit difficult here ... yes, me Da's in the study, go and have a word. I'll make a tray of tea for everyone and get out the biscuits.... I can make some sandwiches if you're really hungry, or I can heat up some soup.' She turned to examine Biddy and Dai as she led the way across the hall to the kitchen. 'You two look very

393

happy – but you can tell me what's been happening whilst Mam explains to me Da why she ran off like that. Come on.'

She bustled them into the kitchen and Biddy, looking over her shoulder, saw Nellie hesitate outside the study for a moment, as though she dreaded what was to come. Poor thing, Biddy thought, fancy having to tell Mr Gallagher what had happened all those years ago! Nellie was still wearing her damp and travel-stained coat, too. . . . Biddy would have advised her to take it off, but suddenly Nellie straightened her shoulders, tapped on the door and opened it, then went through and closed it softly behind her.

'Come on, Bid. You can give me a hand with the soup,' Lizzie said gaily, as they entered the kitchen. It was a large room with a flagstoned floor and a bright fire, before which three or four dogs lounged at their ease. Biddy entered the room rather carefully – she knew almost nothing about dogs – and looked around her whilst Lizzie went through a narrow doorway into what Biddy now saw was a very commodious pantry. 'It's leek and potato, made with cream – do you like that?'

Assuring Lizzie that she loved leek-and-potato soup, Biddy shot a quick and anxious glance at Dai, now standing beside her. 'Will she be all right? Nellie, I mean,' she hissed. 'Oh, poor Mrs Gallagher, Dai.'

'She'll be fine,' Dai whispered back. 'A grand feller, is Stuart. I've no worries there.'

'Oh, good,' Biddy said, turning back to the kitchen and trying not to imagine the scene in the study. Dai said it would be all right and he was older and wiser than she, he probably knew best.

But privately, Biddy had her doubts.

Nellie slipped inside the study and closed the door behind her. Stuart was sitting behind the desk, writing something on a pad of paper. He glanced up and stared expressionlessly across at her for a moment, then he bent his head over his work once more. He continued to write, finished his sentence, blotted the page, then put down his pen and leaned back in his chair. For the first time in their lives together, the glance that he sent her across the desk was cold and antagonistic.

'Ah, Nellie. So you did decide to come home.'

It was like a slap in the face, but though Nellie swallowed nervously she did not flinch. This was the reaction of a man who had been terribly worried and deeply hurt and she could scarcely blame him. She had not expected to be welcomed back with open arms – had she?

'Did you doubt it, Stuart?' she said, her voice trembling a little. 'I rang Lizzie and explained I'd gone to meet Dai's ship, I rang later and said I was bringing him and Biddy home here for a day or so. . . . Did you think I'd do that if I didn't mean to return?'

'Lizzie said you'd rung,' Stuart said heavily. He spoke without raising his eyes from the page before him. 'But your note gave no explanation for leaving the way you did. Lizzie told me you fainted when she gave you Biddy's message about Dai's ship being overdue. That doesn't seem a normal thing to do. Not for a friend's boy, anyway.'

'No. But . . . Dai's my boy, Stuart.'

That jerked his gaze up to meet hers, his eyes wide, darkening with shock, an expression of incredulity replacing the censure for a moment. '*Your* boy? Dai Evans is . . . I don't understand.'

'No. You couldn't possibly understand, but I'm here to explain, Stuart.' She took a step nearer the desk, trying to control the trembling which was racking her. 'Will you listen to me? It's – it's rather a long story and it starts rather a long time ago.'

'Will this *explanation* include the name of your lover, the name of the man who was so important to you that you insisted we move to Edinburgh? Will it include what you've been doing these past two days?' Nellie began to speak, feeling her face grow hot, but he overrode her, his voice rising to something perilously close to a shout. 'No, no, don't pretend indignation, I'm not a fool! There's always been something, something you wouldn't tell me, and I'm well aware that you had no message about Dai's ship, no telephone call to this house telling you he was safe. You went off somewhere else, then heard about Dai and used the information as an excuse for your sudden flight. . . . Nellie, I'm not a fool!'

Nellie put both hands to her hot cheeks and felt all her resolve, all her determination, draining away. How could she tell him, when he was so angry with her, so eager to believe her unfaithful, wicked? Yet if she did not tell him, did not make him listen, their relationship would founder, their marriage would become a mockery.

'Don't judge me, Stuart,' she said tremulously, trying not to glance at his hands, curled now into fists. She had never known him so angry and unyielding, not in all the years they had known each other. 'Not until you've heard the facts. As I said, it's a long story. May – may I sit down?'

He tightened his lips, scowling at her, but he nodded ungraciously. 'Very well . . . but pull the chair round to face me, if you please.'

She did as he asked, then sat down, facing him. It was impossible not to feel like a prisoner in the dock, on trial for her life, but she took a deep, calming breath, then began to speak, though she lowered her eyes as she did so, unable to meet the scorn in his glance. 'Years ago, before we married, I – I went with a man and fell for a child. I was very young and ignorant, Stuart, and very frightened, but my child's father had promised to marry me so when he did not come back for me, I decided to go to his village on the Isle of Anglesey and find out once and for all what had happened.

'I went to Davy's house – his name was Davy Evans – and found he was married to a dear girl called Bethan. She told me that Davy's ship had been sunk and Davy was drowned, and when I explained my state she asked me to stay with her, and to let her adopt my baby when he was born. She had no child, you see, nothing to remind her of Davy, and she said, truly, that the child would have a good life with her, and an inheritance. All I could give him would have been the shame of illegitimacy.

'So I agreed and in due course I gave birth to a son. I called him David, after his father. Everyone believed that Bethan was his Mam – we had kept my secret well – and when the baby was old enough I went back to Liverpool without him.

'Later, Davy went home. He hadn't been drowned, he'd been picked up by another vessel and taken to America I think it was, and when he got back to Anglesey he found he had a son. Stuart, we neither of us loved each other, it was just – just a mistake for us both. Davy settled down happily with Bethan and their boy and quite soon after that they had a girl, a sister for – for Dai, as they called him.'

As Nellie finished speaking Stuart looked across at her once more. His eyes were still cold. 'And when did your lover turn up again? Quite soon after Dai did – is that it? Freed by his wife's death, wanting you all over again? Finding you married to another man was clearly no bar to what *he* had in mind. And you couldn't resist the chance to see him again . . . you'll tell me that was all, I suppose? That you just wanted to see him, nothing more?'

'Who, Davy? Stuart, of course he didn't turn up, I've never seen him from that day to this and besides, Dai says his father has remarried.' Nellie smiled slightly. 'A girl young enough to be his daughter . . . typical of Davy, I imagine. But can't you see, Stu, that I couldn't tell you before? You knew I'd had a baby, I told you that, but I could scarcely tell you that my friend Bethan had passed the child off as her own, even to her husband! It wasn't my secret to share, was it?'

'None of that matters; I accept that you had an affair with this Davy Evans and that Dai's your child. But what matters to me is where you went these past two days? Why did you run away?' Stuart leaned across the desk now, his expression almost pleading, his eyes full of pain. 'If Davy Evans isn't your lover, who in heaven's name is?'

'It's you, Stuart, it's always been you,' Nellie said. Tears ran down her hot cheeks and dripped off the end of her chin. 'There's never been anyone else but you for me, Stuart, and you must know it! I went to Grimsby as soon as I got Biddy's message because I felt I must *do* something, be as near as possible to my boy. That's absolutely all there was to it. Stu, I'll swear it on the bible if that's the only way to convince you . . . but why should it be? We've never lied to each other, why should you think I'd lie now?'

'And coming to Edinburgh? When you'd quite made up your mind to stay in Liverpool?'

'That was stupid, but I thought Dai wanted to marry Lizzie and – and they're brother and sister, or half-brother and sister, anyway. He came round to the house in Ducie Street and asked me whether I would object to his asking "my girl" to marry him. And Stu, when anyone says "your girl" to me, I think of Lizzie at once, because she is my girl. I just never thought of Biddy.'

She was watching his face and saw, for the first time, a glint of what might have been amusement lighten his dark eyes. 'You thought Dai wanted to marry our girl? Nellie Gallagher, you want your head examinin'! And that was why you insisted that we leave the 'Pool? *That* was the reason you left your beloved home?'

'I know; I've been every sort of fool,' Nellie said ruefully. 'Do you remember me telling you I thought it would do Lizzie good to move up here? Well, that was why. I was terrified that she and Dai might want to marry . . . oh Stu, it was a nightmare, and I couldn't tell you, couldn't say why I was afraid. And of course quite soon I realised I'd made an awful mistake, that Lizzie and Dai were just friends, but I couldn't go back on it, could I? We were here, and you were settled into the job . . . so I had to make the best of it.'

'And . . . and you honestly set off in this dreadful weather, just to try to meet Dai? Just to see your boy? There wasn't anything else? Anyone else? You've not met Davy since you and he were lovers all those years ago?'

His eyes were soft, the expression in them anxious, but lovingly so, now. Nellie jumped up from her chair and ran round the desk. She cast herself into Stuart's arms and kissed him violently, then collapsed onto his lap with a blissful sigh.

'Oh Stuart, darling, if only you knew how much it hurt me to see you looking at me as if I was a stranger! I swear on – on Lizzie's life that I went to meet Dai and nobody else, and that I wouldn't want to see Davy if he turned up on our doorstep tomorrow. The last time I saw him, in fact, was when I was nursing in Liverpool. He was one of the injured to come onto my ward and I was so totally out of love with him that I applied for the job in France so that I wouldn't even have to set eyes on him again.

And then you and I met, so in a way you could say that not loving Davy brought us together.'

Stuart's arms went round her in a tight hug and he pressed his face against her tear-wet cheek. 'Oh Nell, sweetheart, if only *you* knew! I love you and trust you, only a fool would do otherwise, yet there has always been a little ache in the back of my mind because you'd never explained properly about the child you'd born, the man you'd . . . been with. It wasn't jealousy exactly, it was because I couldn't understand why you wouldn't be frank with me. And it hurt.'

'Well, now you know,' Nellie said contentedly. 'Do you mind about Dai, darling? Only he needed me and perhaps in a way I needed him. And now we've found each other, I'd hate to have to send him away.'

'He's a grand lad; I can't think of anyone I'd sooner have as a stepson,' Stuart said. 'But I'd rather that Davy fellow never knew.'

'Dai and I feel the same,' Nellie said fervently. 'Dai couldn't think of me as his mother – Bethan was all the mother he had or needed – but I hope we'll always be close. Oh Stu, no one ever had a nicer husband than you.'

'That's the truest word you ever spoke,' Stuart said. He tipped her off his lap and stood up, putting an arm around her shoulders and turning her towards the door. 'I bet all that talking's made you thirsty; let's go and find ourselves a drink. . . . God, woman, your coat's wet! Take it off and we'll put it over the airer in the kitchen. It'll be dry by morning.'

They went across the room and into the hall, where Nellie took off her coat and kicked off her short boots. Stuart found her slippers and put them on her icy feet and was about to open the kitchen door when Nellie caught his hand.

'Stu, the children are in there. I'd rather not face them tonight. Shall we go straight to bed?'

Stuart squeezed her shoulders, his expression very tender. 'Well, I still think you should have a hot drink after that long journey, but if you feel you can't face . . .'

The kitchen door opening cut his sentence off short. Lizzie stood framed in the doorway, a tray in her hands. She smiled at them. 'Ah, I was just about to bring your drinks through! Biddy and Dai have gone up – Biddy's in my room, Mam, and Dai's in the room over the porch – but I thought you'd like a hot drink and some sandwiches.'

'Good girl,' Stuart said, taking the tray from her. 'You're not such a bad kid after all, our Lizzie. Oh, hang your Mam's coat on the airer, would you? And we'll see you in the morning.'

Biddy and Dai stayed in Edinburgh, in the end, for the best part of a week.

Biddy said nothing to Lizzie as to what had passed between her parents that stormy night, but next day Stuart and Nellie seemed to be as loving as ever, and when Biddy, highly daring, asked 'Is it all right?' Nellie had nodded and smiled so blissfully that Biddy realised whatever had happened in the study the previous evening had probably strengthened the already strong relationship between the Gallaghers.

Dai, in the woodshed next morning chopping wood and hoping that poor little Nellie had not had a hard time, told Biddy that Stuart had simply come up to him and clapped him on the shoulder. Stuart's eyes, he said, were full of tears. 'My dear Dai, there's no one I'd rather have for a stepson,' he had said, his voice full of emotion. 'My poor darling Nell – the lengths she went to, and just so that I wouldn't be hurt when I'm not hurt in the slightest! I knew she was keeping something from me, you see, and

I imagined . . . dreadful things. Now I know the truth I'm just delighted that you felt you could turn to us, even before you knew of your relationship with my dearest Nell.'

'Give each other a hug, we did,' Dai told Biddy that evening, when they had gone out into the snow to give the dogs a walk before bedtime. 'Stuart's not the feller to hold a grudge, so pleased he was that Nell's secret wasn't a bad one he would have forgive her anything. Loves her deeply, does Stu.'

And Elizabeth was, quite simply, ecstatic. 'A brother! Well, all right, then, a half-brother,' she said to Biddy as the two of them worked side by side in the kitchen. 'And you as good as a sister to me, Biddy! It's what I've always wanted, a brother or sister of me own, and now I've got both of you.'

'I'll be a sister-in-law, not a proper sister,' Biddy reminded her, but Elizabeth just laughed and nudged her in the ribs.

'Who cares about that? You don't know what it's like, Biddy, having a Mam and a Da but no real uncles or aunts, let alone no cousins near enough to visit. I'm so pleased . . . and Mam says we will come to your wedding, even if it is just as friends. She says Davy will just have to get used to seeing her because she's going to enjoy Dai's company whenever she can, to make up for all the years she lost.'

But Biddy and Dai could not stay for Christmas, despite all the Gallaghers' urging.

'I've written to my Da, told him we'll go back there for the holiday,' Dai said. 'And Biddy's on pins in case Ma Kettle turns Ellen off. . . . Best get back.'

So just over a week after Biddy had left the shop to go to Grimsby, the two of them walked back into it again.

Ma Kettle was behind the counter and to Biddy's

pleasure, greeted her like an old friend and demanded to be introduced to the young feller she'd heard so much about.

'So you're gerrin' wed, eh?' Ma Kettle said, nodding wisely. 'That's a good girl you got yourself, young man. You tek care of our Biddy or you'll 'ave the Kettles to deal with.'

'And . . . and how's Ellen going on?' Biddy asked rather nervously, but she need not have worried.

Ma Kettle beamed. 'She's a good girl,' she said in a surprised but self-congratulatory tone. 'Eh, the lad's a bright 'un – puts me in mind o' Kenny when my lad were small. An' you teached that Ellen to boil a good, flavoursome batch o' toffee, I'll say that for the pair o' ye . . . and them fancy fudges, wi' nuts an' cherries in, they're goin' down well wi' Christmas comin' on. Oh ah, we shan't let young Ellen an' Bobby leave in an 'urry.'

'And how does she cope in the shop?' Biddy asked. 'Because she was in a very posh department store before Bobby was born.'

'She's a natural wi' our customers, young an' old, an' the little lad's a joy to the kids an' the grans,' Ma Kettle said simply. 'What's more, Kenny's right taken wi' the pair of 'em. Never did like 'elpin' in the shop, our Kenny, but I've noticed 'e don't mind doin' a turn be'ind the counter when young Ellen's 'ere. Course, I'm real sorry you've gorra leave, chuck,' she added hastily. 'But we'll manage.'

Ellen didn't have much chance of a private conversation, but she and Biddy exchanged a few words when Biddy nipped into the boiling kitchen for a minute, to find her friend, swathed in one of the huge white aprons, beating vanilla fudge.

'It's prime 'ere, Biddy, I'm ever so 'appy. Ma Kettle's ever so nice to Bobby an' that Kenny – I wish you'd brung 'im round to the flat years ago, our Biddy, 'stead of tellin' me about 'im all wrong. 'E's quite nice lookin' when you get to know 'im.'

'You're two very nice people, you and Kenny, and I hope everything goes on well for all of you,' Biddy said sincerely. 'Ma Kettle's not a bad old thing, you just have to know how to handle her – and it seems to me you're doing pretty well.'

Ellen dimpled at her. She was clean as a new pin, her hair was its old bouncy self and she was neatly clad in a grey cotton dress under the toffee-smeared apron. 'You aren't doin' too bad yourself! I like that Dai.'

'You don't know him! Did you see him just now, as I slipped through from the shop?'

'Aye. An' I listened at the door. He's right for you, Bid, I wish you every 'appiness. After all what you've done for me an' Bobby, you deserve it.'

'Yes, Dai is . . . is special. We're going away now to spend a few days with his people on Anglesey, but I'll be in touch when we get back.'

'Have a good time; they'll love you, never fear,' Ellen said generously. 'I'll explain to Kenny.'

'Kenny's grown up; he likes me, but that's all,' Biddy said serenely. 'Goodbye for now, dear Ellen. Give Bobby a hug for me when he wakes.'

The train was too slow at first and Biddy fidgeted and bit her nails in an agony of mixed boredom and apprehension. Then it seemed they were nearly there and the train seemed suddenly much too fast.

'It's all right, they'll love you,' Dai kept assuring her, but Biddy wasn't so sure.

'Why should they? They don't even know me, and anyway, your Da was cross with you when you last met,' Biddy said uneasily. 'They'll probably think I've caught you, that I'm just after a husband.'

He grinned at her, then leaned across and nuzzled the side of her face. 'Silly Biddy! Besides, you are just after a husband, be honest. Any man would do so long as he kept you out of Ma Kettle's ' .itchen.'

Biddy shook her head at him. 'Don't try and make me laugh, I'm too scared to laugh. Oh, oh, we've arrived! I wish I'd never come!'

'Arrived? We've miles to go yet. Come on, collect your traps and we'll get down and find ourselves a taxi.'

Biddy had stared in the train, but now, in the taxi, she got as close to Dai as she could and clutched his hand with feverish fingers. It was all so chilly and grey, so totally unpeopled! She was used to city streets, crowded housing, and people everywhere, this austere island with its grey stone cottages and slate-roofed houses frightened her.

'Are we nearly there?' she kept asking in a very small whisper. 'Is it far?'

They arrived. Down the hill they went and there was the sea on their right, a cold December sea but still more familiar to Biddy, reared by the Mersey, than was the gentle rolling Welsh countryside. The taxi was old and slow; it chugged over the grey stone bridge and Dai pointed out the foaming waterfall dashing down to the sea. They passed the beach, pale in the wintry twilight, and then turned left, away from the sea, the cottages and the pub, crowding close to the harbour, and began to climb a long hill.

'It's that house, the one with the ship's lantern outside the door,' Dai said. Biddy could tell from his tone that he was half-scared now, half so homesick for this place that even the memory of the quarrel between his father and himself could not make him hold back any longer. 'Put us down here . . . but don't go,' he told the taxi driver, 'we may need you presently to take us on.'

It was the first time he had acknowledged that he

might still have to back down, leave Moelfre and go to Sîan and her husband Gareth in the next village.

When it stopped they climbed a little stiffly out of the taxi and walked up the garden path. Dai waited in the porch a moment, then knocked on the door. There was a light in the room, softly burning, and someone came slowly across to the door and opened it.

A very young woman stood there, fair hair tied back from a pink-and-white country face, eyes fixed on them.

'Dai!' And then a gabble of Welsh which Biddy did not understand. It sounded threatening, but was probably nothing of the sort really, Biddy realised. Then the girl was ushering them in, calling something . . . and a man came in from the back, a large brown towel in his hand, his face still streaked with water. He must have been washing himself when they knocked, Biddy realised.

'Dai! Oh, Dai bach!'

The man was very like his son, so Biddy guessed that it was Davy and there seemed to be no ill-feeling here. The two embraced, then Dai turned and took her hand, pulling her forward.

'There's sorry I am to be so rude to you, cariad. Biddy, this is my Da, Davy Evans. And this is . . . is Menna, who is his wife now.'

'Aye married several months since,' Davy said. 'Wanted you to come to the wedding, we did. I wrote – did you not receive it, mun?'

'Not until long after the date – at sea we was, Da. But I'm here now.' Dai glanced across at Menna. 'Menna, Da, this is Bridget O'Shaughnessy; she and I . . .'

'Nice to meet you, Miss O'Shaughnessy,' Davy Evans said, giving Biddy a smile and offering a hand. Biddy shook his hand and smiled at Menna, then Davy turned back to his son. 'Dai, I wanted to see you at my wedding, but there was more beside. Menna's in the family way, truth to tell, and we was wantin' you home because Menna's Da isn't so well, see? A stroke he have had, very poorly he's been. So Mrs Owens wants us to take over the pub . . . only we could do no such thing whilst I had no one to take over here.'

'Take over?' Dai sounded dazed. 'What are you trying to say, Da?'

'If you'll come home, mun, an' take over here, look after the cows and sheep, go fishing, same's you used, then Menna and me can go back and run the pub in Amlwch. Good money there is in a pub, and easier, when a man's getting on in years, to stand behind a bar and smile and be mine host, rather than sweat in a boat and see to the sheep an' cows.'

'We'll have to think about it, Da,' Dai said. He sounded offhand, as though the thought of such a rural way of life was more amusing than practical. 'We're getting married, Biddy and me. We've not thought of coming back here, only to say hello to everyone, so you could meet Biddy and she could meet you.'

'It's a good old place,' Davy said. He smiled at Biddy and she saw he had a tooth missing in front which gave him a piratical air. 'Like living here you would, cariad . . . and fresh air and good food for the kiddies, when they come along. A good life and your man beside you, not off on a coaster eleven months out of the twelve.'

'I'm trawling now, Dad . . . distant water,' Dai said. 'I don't know, we'll have to talk it over, eh, Biddy? But we've not eaten since noon; do I go down to the Crown, book a room?'

'No indeed,' Menna said. She looked uncertainly from father to son. 'Spare rooms we do have, and a stew on the stove which can stretch like a piece of rubber for us all. I'll just peel a potato or two . . . a cup of tea, Biddy, while you wait for the meal?'

Biddy smiled at the other girl.

'I'll come and make it with you,' she volunteered. 'It'll give the men a chance to talk.'

Later, when they had eaten, Dai put his arm round Biddy and took her walking in the wintry night. There was no snow here – it rarely snowed on the island, Dai told her – but the stars overhead twinkled frostily and the wind off the sea lifted the hair from Biddy's head and tossed it behind her like blown spume.

'A quiet, rural life it is out here, Biddy, and I'm not so sure you'd take to it,' Dai shouted against the wind as they fought their way to the clifftop. 'There's folk in the village and sheep and cows in plenty – rabbits, too, and birds – but it's not what you're used to at all. If you'd rather, I can keep on with the trawling, or I can join another coaster . . . I don't want to make you unhappy.'

Biddy thought. She thought of the dreadful danger which he went into, jauntily, every time the *Bess* sailed. Could she stand it? The constant fear, the knowledge of his danger, the fact that a quarter of all those who sail the sea in search of the fish die of drowning? But he loved the excitement, the danger even, and the beauty of Arctic waters, she knew that.

If she asked him to do so he would join a coaster, which was far less dangerous, and she would see him between voyages. But his heart wasn't in a dirty little vessel nosing along inshore waters, he would lose all his pride in himself, all his gaiety and courage.

And what of me? she thought next. Biddy O'Shaughnessy, who has lived in the great city of Liverpool all her life and who loves it, understands it? What would I do out here, with the sea and the birds and cows which scare me and sheep about which I know nothing? There are people, but they speak a language I don't understand and live lives which are strange to me. Could I bear it?

But she knew she could, because she would have Dai beside her. He would go out in his fishing boat and she would worry, but he knew the waters, understood his small craft; she could come to terms with a worry like that. And he would be happy in a way she had probably never yet seen him, because he would be his own master in his own place, at last.

'Biddy?'

She leaned closer to him, so that she could feel the warmth of his body against her even through her coat. She kissed his chin, which needed a shave, and then her mouth found his lips. For a moment they simply kissed, then she drew back with a little sigh. 'Dai, wherever you are I shall be happiest. You're right that I don't know much and will be a burden to you, but if you please, let's live here, where you were born.'

He gave a shout of triumph and lifted her in his arms, squeezing her until she was breathless. Then he stood her down and took her hand. His delight and relief shone out of him – but he would have given it all up had she wished it, gone uncomplaining back to the trawling, or onto a coastal trader.

'Biddy, I do love you! Come on, let's run down the hill and tell my Da he's on – he and Menna can take over that old pub as soon as they like and we'll move in here. Oh, I've just thought of something!'

'What? Not something bad, I trust?'

'Well, cariad, it depends on your viewpoint. Only one spare bed we do have at Stryd Pen, and that's the big double in the back room. I'm afraid that they'll expect us to share it.'

Biddy squeezed his hand and started to run, tugging him behind her. 'So we'll get us a dear little baby, like

Ellen's Bobby,' she shouted, and the words were torn from her mouth by the wind of their going, but Dai heard every one. 'Come on, I'll race you!'

Hand in hand, they pelted down the hill and disappeared into the tall house in Stryd Pen. And presently the lamp was lit in the big back bedroom, and the soft golden light was like a beacon in the dark, leading weary mariners home.

KATIE FLYNN

The Girl from Seaforth Sands

arrow books

For Florence Walker, whose excellent memory of her father's work as a shrimp fisherman enabled me to write this book.

My most sincere thanks go to Heather and John Cross for introducing me to 'Auntie Flo', aged 102, whose delightful reminiscences gave me the idea for this book, and thanks, also, to the Liverpool Local History Library for finding me the ancient – but incredibly useful – book on Liverpool fishermen in the early years of the twentieth century.

Chapter One

1902

It was a cold day, although June was well advanced, and Amy Logan, cowering in the doorway of a shop on the corner of Berkeley Drive, wondered whether she had been wise to leave the house in such a hurry that she hadn't even put on a coat. She had peeped out of her shelter hoping that the rain would have begun to ease but it seemed to her, she thought sourly now, that it was pelting harder than ever.

Drawing back into the shelter of her doorway, Amy remembered that today should have been Coronation Day, but two days ago King Edward VII had been and gone and got appendicitis, whatever that might be, and the whole thing had had to be cancelled. Amy had supposed, vaguely, that it was an ailment only suffered by royal personages, but her mother had disillusioned her. 'Kings and princesses!' she had scoffed when Amy had aired her views. 'No, no, it's a thing anyone could have. Your stomach blows up and you get awful pain; your Uncle Reggie had his appendix out years ago when he was just a lad. Still and all, I reckon it's a nastier business when you're a man grown.'

Amy's mam was deeply interested in the royal family. She admired Queen Alexandra greatly and often said that she and the Queen had a good deal in common, though she had never deigned to explain exactly what she meant. Perhaps it was the fringe, Amy thought now, or the regal bearing, for Isobel

1

Logan always walked as though she had a poker up her back. At least, that was what Amy had heard her elder brother Edmund saying one day, his tone half laughing, half admiring. But in any event Amy had swallowed her disappointment over the loss of a day's holiday, because she had been told that as soon as King Edward recovered the date of the coronation would be fixed once more. And let's hope it won't be a day like today, Amy thought grimly, peering out at the downpour. It wouldn't help to have all those fine clothes and fancy hats dripping down royal necks. She grinned to herself. Suppose the colours ran? The Muspratt family who lived in Seaforth Hall would look really good with their faces streaked with purple or green. Amy, who saw members of the Muspratt family in church every Sunday, could just imagine their chagrin if their smart clothes were ruined, even in such a good cause as a coronation.

But right now, great cloud-reflecting puddles filled the road and when a vehicle came by the cart was preceded by a bow wave of water where, just opposite her doorway, two large puddles had joined to form a veritable lake.

Amy thought, a trifle wistfully, of the room she had left in such a hurry twenty minutes or so earlier. The kitchen had been warm and bright, and she and her sister Mary had been knitting and chatting happily enough when she had heard the rattle of a handcart over the rough cobbles which paved the jigger. Immediately Amy had known what this meant. Her father, Bill Logan, was a shrimp fisherman and the rattle of his handcart meant that he was bringing in his catch to be cleaned, shelled and prepared for potting. Potted shrimps were a great

2

favourite with the Liverpool housewives who shopped in the St John's fish market on Great Charlotte
Street, so shrimps potted today would be sold to the
stallholders, making the Logan family a fair sum.
The Logans had six children, although Edmund no
longer lived at home, and any money they could
earn was welcome.

But however much Liverpool people might enjoy
shrimps, both potted and plain, Amy absolutely
loathed them. When she had been small she had
simply disliked the smell and taste of the little pink
creatures, but as soon as she was seven or eight and
deemed old enough to help, she had had to join Gus,
Charlie, Mary, Albert and her mother round the big
kitchen table in their work of preparing the shrimps
both for market and for the potting. The shells of
shrimps are spiteful to small, soft fingers and Amy
very soon had the criss-cross, paper-thin cuts on her
hands – as had all the Logan children – caused by
the spiny carapaces of the little shrimps. There was
always a risk, furthermore, of being stabbed by a
spine of a yellow weaver fish, if one of them had
been netted accidentally. These small yellow fish had
poisonous spikes all over their bodies that could
cause agonising wounds, which would remain painful and swollen for many days despite the most
rigorous attention.

Amy very soon realised, what was more, that only
the swiftest possible withdrawal from the scene
would enable her to elude the job. A quick visit to
the privy in the yard might get you out of the way
for ten minutes, but then a brother or sister would be
sent to rout you out and return you to the kitchen to
do your share.

Amy, the youngest of the Logan family, had come

3

later to the shrimping than most, because her father spoilt his little girl and knew how she hated the work, but Isobel was adamant that all the children should do their share. 'Just because she's the youngest that does not mean she can shirk jobs she doesn't like,' she had said severely, staring at Bill over the top of her small half-glasses. 'She's young and quick with keen eyesight; that means she won't miss bits of weed and shell, and she'll be helping to earn her keep the same as the rest of us. Being the youngest isn't anything special. Why, if I were to have another littl'un, she wouldn't be the youngest any longer. You'd expect her to work then, I dare say?'

Bill had seen the justice of this – even Amy had realised it was fair enough – and had stopped trying to get her excused from the work, so now it was in Amy's own hands. If she heard the rattle of the handcart returning and could make herself scarce before Bill got into the yard, then she was safe so long as she stayed clear for two or three hours, for it took that long for the family to work through a batch of shrimps. Then, when she did return home, the chances were that her mother might not realise she had deliberately bunked off and Amy would be safe again – until the next time.

But right now, with the rain being blown almost horizontally across the front of her doorway, Amy was beginning to wonder whether she might have been better off picking shrimps. The kitchen would be warm and cosy, the family chatty and her father, if he had had a good catch, would be expansive and talkative, encouraging Amy's elder brothers Charlie and Augustus to talk about the fishing and their various adventures. There might be a cup of tea if

4

one worked fast and neatly, producing perfect shrimps with no stray legs still attached or tiny bits of transparent shell still in place.

On the other hand, though she had skipped out of the house before anyone else had heard the cart, mumbling an excuse about visiting the privy, Isobel was becoming suspicious of Amy's frequent absences when work was on hand and might easily extract a penalty if she guessed that her daughter was skiving off once more. Only a week previously Amy had returned to the house to find a quantity of shrimps still unshelled. 'Ah, Amy,' her mother had said with a narrow smile, 'just in time, chuck. You can finish off that lot while Mary helps me with the tea and the boys have a rest. I know you wouldn't want to see your brothers and sister do your share as well as their own.'

Amy had been mortified and had vowed to herself that next time she disappeared she would be sure to stay away until the hateful work was finished. She did not mind if she was given extra work about the house, so long as it was not preparing shrimps. Isobel could get her peeling spuds or mending nets or even cleaning creels, so long as she avoided the shrimps.

Having decided to stay out until the danger was over, however, did not mean that this miserable doorway was a good place to be. Amy peered out once more, trying to decide just what to do with her time. Her friend Ruth lived a couple of streets away and Ruth's mam would probably welcome Amy in, despite the fact that Ruth was the eldest of five children and their little house was always crowded. But Amy was barefoot – it was summer, after all – and the thought of splashing through perhaps a

5

quarter of a mile of chilly puddles and then having to retrace her steps a short while later did not really appeal. Besides, Ruth's mother would expect Amy to help amuse the little ones and to give Ruth a hand with whatever her friend was doing. It might not be as bad as preparing shrimps, but Amy was not overfond of helping to make a meal which she would not be eating, so going all the way to Ruth's was not a good idea.

If I had some money I'd go and buy a bun at the baker's on Rawson Road, Amy thought longingly. But Isobel did not give the children pennies for peeling the shrimps or doing other household chores. 'Earn money away from the house,' she was fond of telling her children. 'Don't take money out of it. Fisherfolk need every penny they can get.'

Having decided against a visit to Ruth's, Amy bent her mind to alternatives. It wasn't the weather for a stroll around Knowsley Road looking at the shops and there would be few games of ollies or skipping going on in such weather. Even her favourite place, Bowersdale Park, would not provide much amusement on such a day. It was a shame that Seafield Grove was, by and large, an elderly neighbourhood, so that there was little choice of companionship with children of her own age locally. The small terraced houses were largely inhabited by fishermen, most of whom had grown-up families. The two exceptions on Seafield Grove were the Logans and, at the far end of the street, the Keagans. Suzie Keagan had been widowed shortly after the birth of her son Paddy, and had moved in with her widowed mother-in-law and aunt. Isobel did not like the younger woman and disapproved of young Paddy who, despite being the same age as Albert,

6

was rarely in school and was clearly more than his mother could cope with. Bill, however, said that Paddy's heart was in the right place and felt that, in the circumstances, the boy had to take paid work whenever he could get it. He never made any comment when Isobel said that Suzie was a bad manager, making little effort to see that the money she earned got spent wisely, and Amy thought that this silence was a reluctant agreement. Left to herself, Isobel had once been heard to say that Suzie would seldom have cooked or cleaned, for she disliked housework, and this meant that their neighbour had all the makings of a slut. But Suzie's elderly mother-in-law and aunt kept the place reasonable, and though Paddy wore shabby, too-small clothing and did not seem to possess a pair of boots, at least he was fed most of the time and had, what was more, plenty of spirit, most of which he bent to mischief, Amy thought now.

So the two old ladies did the housework and cooked for the family, and Suzie worked, somewhat desultorily, at any job she could find, seldom keeping the same employment for very long. The money Paddy picked up through running messages and selling firewood and, Amy suspected, nicking from the stallholders on Scotland Road, was a very real help in keeping their little boat afloat. And Amy knew that her father did his best to keep the Keagans supplied with odds and ends of fish whenever his catch was good, despite what his wife thought of their neighbours.

Bill was prejudiced in favour of the Keagans because Abe Keagan, Suzie's dead husband, had been a fisherman like himself and had been lost at sea during a violent storm, which had sunk his boat and drowned every man aboard. Bill thought Suzie was more sinned against than sinning, Amy knew, but her father would never have dreamed of saying so in front of his wife. Bill had once told her that, until Abe's death, Suzie had been a good wife and mother, working hard to sell the fish her husband's family caught. If things had been different, if only Abe had not died, Suzie, Bill seemed to think, would have been every bit as sensible and reliable a housewife and mother as his own wife. Isobel was a good woman, but narrow-minded and strict. She had made up her mind to disapprove of the Keagans and that included Paddy. Nothing would change that, even though Albert and Paddy, both aged twelve and pupils at the same school, were bezzies and, during the school holidays, seldom apart.

Now, peering out into the rain, Amy saw a small figure sloshing through the puddles. It was a boy, coming up the street towards her, and even at this distance she recognised Paddy Keagan. Thinking about him had sort of conjured him up, she told herself crossly. Why on earth had she wasted a single thought on the Keagan family when they were far from her favourite people? In fact, she disliked Paddy intensely for several reasons. The most obvious one being that he disliked her and never lost an opportunity to tease, taunt, or even to bully her. He had divined that his family were disapproved of by the Logans, although clearly not by Albert, and because of this he was all too ready to find something wrong with her in his turn.

Another reason for disliking him was that he had a crush on Mary. Mary was lovely, Amy was very fond of her, but she thought that Paddy had a cheek to hang around their house hoping to catch sight of

8

the older girl. Not that Mary encouraged him – she thought him Albert's friend and no more than a kid anyway – but Amy still resented his liking Mary, particularly as it went hand in hand with disliking her. Of course, Mary was a blue-eyed blonde and very pretty, whereas Amy had red hair and greenish-hazel eyes and was not, she acknowledged ruefully, pretty at all. But her mam was always saying it was character that counted, not looks, so Paddy had no right to like Mary because she was pretty and dislike Amy because she wasn't.

However, Paddy was getting nearer by the minute and although Amy shrank into the back of her doorway she had little hope of eluding his eyes. Paddy would spot her, and would probably guess why she was there and what she was avoiding, and would make it his business to tell Mary and Albert, even if he would not dare to tale-clat to her mam. Accordingly, Amy turned her back on the roadway and shrank into the corner, knowing that Paddy was less likely to see her if the pallor of her face was hidden.

For a moment she thought she was safe but then, while she was still considering turning round to see where Paddy had gone, someone screamed 'Yah boo, Shrimpy!' right into her ear, at the same time gripping her shoulders and twisting her round to face him. 'Don't know why you were hidin' your face – I could tell it were you by the smell o' fish.' It was Paddy, of course, his grimy face split by a broad grin. Amy gave him a shove and then, when he continued to hold her skinny shoulders, turned her head sideways and, with some disgust, bit his filthy fingers as hard as she could.

Paddy let go of her as though she had been red

9

hot. 'You bleedin' little cat,' he said on a gasp. 'Oh, you wicked little slut, you've near on chewed me finger off! Oh, if you wasn't a girl I'd give you such a clack around the ear your head'd ring for a week. If you wasn't a girl I'd swing for you, so I would!'

'Well, me being a girl never stopped you from screeching in my ear and nigh on giving me a heart attack, let alone grabbing me hard enough to bruise,' Amy said crossly, rubbing her sore shoulders. 'What are you doing here anyway? It's perishin' wet and cold, and you've got no coat.'

'Huh! And you'll notice I aren't askin' what you's doin' out in the rain,' Paddy observed, giving her a malevolent glare. 'Your dad's barrowed in his catch and you're skivin' off as usual, leavin' the dirty work to someone like your Mary, who does more'n her share anyroad.'

'So what?' Amy said belligerently, stepping towards him, hands on hips, and then retreating hastily into the shelter of the doorway once more as the rain caught her. She might occasionally do bad things, she told herself now, but she was not a liar and did not intend to become one, even to spite Paddy. The way to hell began on the slippery slope of telling lies, Isobel often remarked, and since the Logan children knew their mother and father to be both truthful and honest, they tended to follow the parental example, even when it did not much suit them to do so. Of course, swearing around the house was inadvisable, to put it no stronger, so the young Logans watched their language within doors. But a child who did not occasionally use a bad word when in company with their friends would soon be picked out as different and Amy had no desire for such a doubtful honour. Therefore she said, 'Bugger off,

Keagan!' before setting off at a smart and splashy run in the direction of her home. Doing the shrimps might not be much fun, but when you compared it with being taunted and terrorised by Paddy Keagan, while at the same time getting soaked to the skin, it did not seem so terrible after all.

'What's the marrer, Shrimpy?' Paddy taunted, easily keeping pace beside her and making sure that everyone of his footfalls splashed her as well as himself. 'Changed your mind, eh? Goin' to do your share after all, tatty-'ead?'

'Mind your own bleedin' business,' Amy said breathlessly, then tightened her lips and put a spurt on. Small and skinny she might be – well, she was – but she knew from past experience that she could outrun most boys. Paddy's constant attacks had indeed proved this more than once, so now she speeded up and fairly flew along the wet road, swerving into the jigger several lengths ahead of him. She ran up the jigger, bounded through the backyard and was in the kitchen and across to the table very probably before Paddy had turned off the road. Breathlessly, with her heart still thumping from her run, she grinned at Mary, then slid on to the bench next to her sister and, without a word, began to attack the shrimps.

Paddy, foiled of his prey, slowed to a walk and sauntered passed the Logans' front door, casting a wistful glance at the house as he did so. He could never understand why he was not truly welcomed by Mrs Logan when he came calling. He acknowledged that she was a good woman and kind to him in her way, for during school time she quite often gave Albert a double carry-out. She must know that

Paddy's mam, who seemed to find it difficult to hold down a job for more than a few days together, was often hard pressed to find food for them all, let alone the time to prepare him butties. Yet though Mrs Logan might feed him without even being asked, she never encouraged him with so much as a friendly word or look and seldom allowed him to cross her threshold.

Therefore Paddy, aware of this, did not linger by the Logans' dwelling but continued to the tiny house on the end of the row where the Keagans lived. He went down the back jigger and in through the door, not remembering until he entered the room that he had been sent on a message and that Gran, stirring a large black pot over the fire, would be expecting him to return with a sack of the tiny potatoes, which the greengrocer on Elm Road sold off cheap at the end of each day's trading. But Paddy had no scruples about wrapping up the truth when necessary and said breezily, before his Gran could open her mouth, 'They ain't got enough yet to sell off; what's there is mainly earth and stones, to tell the truth. I's to go back in an hour or so. He reckons he'll have more stock in then.'

Gran gave a loud sniff and moved briskly across the kitchen, catching Paddy quite a painful blow around the ear with the long wooden spoon in her hand. 'You're a tarrible liar, Patrick James Keagan,' she said resignedly. 'Why, you ain't been gone long enough for the cat to lick her ear. You can't have reached the end of the road, you lazy little bugger. Comin' back, full of lies, 'spectin' me to believe some old tale . . .'

'Sorry, Gran,' Paddy said humbly. He might have known it didn't pay to try to pull the wool over

Gran's sharp old eyes. 'But it's mortal chilly out and wet as well; I've come back for me coat.'

'I t'ought as much,' Gran said, turning back to her cauldron. With her thin, greying hair made lank by the steam of her cooking, she looked more like a witch than a respectable householder. 'What was you really doin', young Paddy?'

Paddy took a deep breath; Gran was remarkably astute and probably had a fair idea of his 'goings on'. 'I were on me way to the shops when I spotted young Amy, hidin' in a doorway. I knew her dad had just brought in his catch – heard his barrow turnin' into the jigger as I passed it – so I guessed young Amy were bunking off, leavin' Mary to do all the work as usual. So ... so I kind of walked her home, saw her indoors. Well, you know what you've always said, Gran, it pays us to be nice to the Logans even if they ain't nice back. Then we's in the right and they's in the wrong, you said.'

Gran sniffed again. Despite the fact that she hardly ever left the house, she kept her ear to the ground and rarely missed a trick, Paddy knew. Still, the story was as near the truth as damn it. So now he took his ragged jacket off the back of the door and struggled into it. 'Sorry I forgot meself, Gran,' he said humbly, pulling open the back door. 'I'll get down to Evans's and be back with the spuds before you've missed me.'

'Who says I'll miss you?' Gran said pertly. 'Oh, you ain't a bad boy, Paddy. I've known worse.'

Out in the rain once more, Paddy hunched his shoulders and prepared for the dash round to Elm Road. He was grinning to himself as he jogged along. His gran was a good old girl so she was. She was seventy-six years old and had come to Liverpool

from Connemara as a bride over fifty years ago.
Michael Keagan and his family had been one of the
many Irish smallholders who had lost their livings
when the second potato famine had struck. Despite
the hardships the young couple had encountered in
Liverpool, they were both hard workers determined
to make a success of their new life. They had worked
their way up from doing any odd jobs they could
get, until Michael owned first a handcart and then a
stall, selling for a few pennies more, anything he
could buy cheap. Their business enterprise had
thrived until he was able to take a share in a
longshore fishing boat, while his wife sold their
catches to anyone eager to buy.

The time came when Michael and his brothers
were all working on the boat, which by now
belonged to the Keagan family. They had enjoyed
several successful years, often taking good hauls of
fish when other boats could not find. And then,
when Paddy was eighteen months old, disaster had
struck. A storm at sea had taken not only the lives
but also the livelihood from the Keagan family. In
one blow Paddy's mother, grandmother and great-
aunt had been widowed, and had moved from their
respective homes into the tiny end-of-terrace house
in Seafield Grove. With no catch of their own to sell
the women had taken what work they could get.
Great-Aunt Dolly, even then in her seventies, had
undertaken the household duties. Paddy could not
remember those early days but he gathered, from the
way Suzie talked, that they had been hard indeed.
She had worked for the odd day or so in the market
when Christmas came around and she cleaned for
anyone who would employ her, usually small
shopkeepers or one of the many pubs which

14

abounded in the area. Gran cleaned too and was famous for her scrubbing, but once Paddy was able to earn a little by his own efforts she was not sorry to take over the running of the house from Dolly who burned, Gran said, more potatoes and fish than ever she cooked. Aunt Dolly was childless and had never been much of a housewife.

As Paddy gained Elm Road the rain, which had seemed to fall unceasingly, began to ease. Paddy turned thankfully into the shop and dug a hand into his pocket for the pennies Gran had given him. Mr Evans, standing behind the counter in his stained brown overall and surreptitiously smoking a dog end, hastily pinched it out and shoved it behind his ear as he came forward across the empty shop. 'Afternoon, Paddy,' he said jovially, 'I dare say you'll be after spending a few bob, ain't that right?' He chuckled wheezily. 'Oh aye, did you back the winner of the Grand National, our Paddy? What'll it be, then? A couple o' dozen oranges and a nice pineapple? Or how's about some of them black grapes, eh?'

Paddy chuckled as well, although the joke was an old one. 'I wish,' he said. 'Two-penn'orth of small spuds please, Mr Evans.' He looked hopefully at the older man. 'Gorrany messages or little jobs for me today? The rain's easin' off and me gran's stewin' fish. I wouldn't mind bein' out o' doors for a bit.'

Mr Evans pulled a doubtful face. 'Well, I dunno as I've much in the way of messages,' he said slowly, 'unless you'd like to sort sacks o' spuds for a penny?'

Paddy sighed. Sorting spuds was tiring, dirty work but you could do a lot with a penny. There was the magic lantern show at the village hall, for instance. A boy could see the whole show, sitting on a wooden bench with his pals on Saturday mornings, and buy himself some sweets to suck during the performance, for a penny. But Paddy was not a bad boy and he knew what he would do with the money really. He would take it home to Gran, who needed a penny even more than he did. That way, the next time he earned himself some money he would probably be told to keep it, or at least the majority of it.

However, his gran wanted the small potatoes now and Mr Evans would not be too pleased if he went off without sorting his spuds. Paddy was still mulling over the point when a figure darkened the doorway and, turning, Paddy saw his friend Albert, cap on the side of his head, both hands shoved into the pockets of his grimy kecks. Rescue, Paddy thought thankfully. Albert was a bezzie worth having. When he had done his own messages, whatever they might be, he would be happy to deliver the bag of spuds to the Keagan household.

'Wotcher, Paddy,' Albert said cheerfully. 'How you doin', Mr Evans? Me mam sent me along for a couple a pounds o' carrots, a turnip – a nice big 'un – and some onions.' He smacked his lips. 'She's gorra neck o' lamb so she's makin' Irish stew – me favourite.' He turned to Paddy. 'What's you here for, Paddy? Don't say you's havin' Irish stew an' all?' He glanced down at the large bag of spuds by Paddy's feet. 'Blind Scouse?' he ventured.

'No, I think it's fish,' Paddy said rather gloomily. 'But I say, Bertie, could you run a message for me? I'd do the same for you if I wasn't so pressed for time. Gran needs the spuds, you see, but Mr Evans here could do wi' some spuds sorting, so . . .'

'That's all right by me,' Albert said breezily. Mr Evans had been weighing up Albert's purchases and putting them into the string bag which he had slung on to the counter. Now he totted up the prices on one of his brown paper bags and named a sum. Albert paid, picked up Paddy's spuds and his own string bag, bulging with vegetables. 'Will you come round to our place when you've done sorting spuds?' he asked hopefully. 'Me mam might give us a jam buttie, tell us to play out 'till supper's ready,' he ended.

'Sure I will,' Paddy said gratefully. He heaved one of the enormous sacks round into the back room behind the counter and began, methodically, to form the potatoes into three piles, large, medium and small. Albert was a good pal, he reflected. Two penn'orth of tiny spuds were heavy, but Albert hadn't hesitated. Odd, really, when you thought about it, how different the Logans were, one from another. Bill was a nice old bloke who would do anything for anybody, but Isobel was sharp as they came, while Mary was an angel – there was no other way to describe her – and Albert as good a bloke as ever breathed. And then there was the detestable Amy. She had ginger hair when the rest of the family were all blonde, and she was sharp and spiteful when the others – Mary, Albert and Bill at any rate – were all good-hearted and generous. Paddy knew full well that, had he asked Amy to carry spuds for him, or to do him any other favour for that matter, he would have received a dusty answer, probably laced with invective. Like mother like daughter, I suppose, he told himself, diligently sorting spuds with hands that were very soon as earthy as any potato. In a way, you could say us Keagans were

17

all different, too. Mam's easygoing and soft as marshmallow, while me gran is sharp as a needle, like what I am. Oh, well, Gran always says there's nowt so queer as folk. And with that philosophical thought, Paddy gave all his attention to sorting the spuds as quickly and neatly as he could.

Much later that evening Suzie came out of the canny house on Scotland Road, where she had worked for the past eight weeks, and looked, a trifle apprehensively, up at the sky overhead. It was full of scudding grey clouds but, although the road and pavements were still generously puddled, the rain seemed to have ceased, for the moment at any rate. Suzie only had a light shawl cast over her arm but she didn't bother to put it on, for it was warm despite the recent rain. Besides, she usually caught a tram home and on such an evening a shawl was not needed; the tram, though draughty, was a good deal warmer than the street. Added to which, the shawl was hiding something she would far rather her employer did not see in her possession. Mrs Hathaway, mean old cat, would not be best pleased to discover that her cleaning woman had managed to possess herself of a number of currant buns and the best part of a nice bit of ham. It wouldn't hurt her to give me some leftovers, the way she makes me slave, Suzie thought righteously, tucking the shawl securely round the purloined food. Anyhow, it ain't often us Keagans see meat; this'll be a rare treat for everyone, so it will.

There was a tram stop opposite the canny house where Suzie worked, so she crossed the road and joined the short queue of people waiting for the next vehicle. Other people might walk the five miles home, but Suzie did not believe in overexerting herself. The tram ride was only tuppence and she had some tips jangling in her apron pocket. The staff were supposed to share out their tips at the end of the day but Suzie, neither cooking nor serving but merely skivvying, rarely got tips. Instead, however, as she cleared tables and cleaned floors, walls and chairs, she whisked any pennies or halfpennies she might find into her apron pocket and outfaced anyone who suspected that she was feathering her nest instead of passing on the largesse to those who had earned it.

Mrs Hathaway was a marvellous cook, though, which was why Suzie had stayed in the job for so long, despite the pay being on the mingy side. She was employed to clean the room where the customers ate and the kitchen, of course; to do rough work such as scrubbing potatoes, cleaning vegetables and scouring pans, but when the main midday rush was over she sat down to a good meal with all the other employees. Work officially finished, for Suzie, at six in the evening, but she usually stayed later, despite not being paid to do so. There was the big dinner which Mrs Hathaway served to her workers when the place began to empty of regular customers, and there were what Suzie thought of as the 'leftovers'. Some people were given leftovers, but they were staff who had been with Mrs Hathaway a long time, not here-today-gone-tomorrow cleaners, who might well turn out to be no better than they should be. So Suzie nicked anything she could get away with, ate heartily at mealtimes and wondered how long she could stand such extremely hard work, for hard it most definitely was. Mrs Hathaway would not have kept her on for eight days, let alone eight weeks, if she had skimped her work.

However, all good things come to an end. Suzie had noticed, this very evening, that Jimmy, who did some of the cooking and a good deal of the waiting, had begun to look at her with a sort of wary closeness. She had no way of telling whether he had realised she took tips left for the serving staff, or whether he had counted the remaining currant buns that remained on the big dishes behind the counter, but she thought it possible that her job could finish abruptly. Hence the prigging of the bit of ham. It might be her last chance and, since it was summer and therefore not always easy to hide her 'leftovers', she might as well take what she could when the weather made a shawl a necessity and before Mrs Hathaway told her not to come in again.

The tram rumbled round the corner and came to a splashy halt, deluging the waiting people with water. Suzie sprang back and cursed with the rest, then climbed wearily aboard. She sat down on one of the hard wooden seats and reflected that it felt soft as goosefeathers to one who had been slaving for Mrs Hathaway all day. Still, she had a lot to be thankful for. The joint of ham and the currant buns would make more than one meal, and she reminded herself that a lot of widowed women in her position went home to a cold and empty house, and had to start lighting a fire and cooking a meal for their family. Suzie knew that Gran would have a warm room and a good meal ready to welcome her, that Great-Aunt Dolly would wash up and clear away after that meal, and that Paddy would have spent his day as usefully as he knew how. Yes, she told herself gazing out at the greying streaks, there were many worse off than herself.

The tram pulled up at another stop and several men climbed aboard. Suzie glanced incuriously towards them, then brightened. 'Mr Logan! Where've you been, then? I thought the Caradoc was your local?'

Bill sat down on the seat beside her and gave her a friendly smile. 'Who's to say I've been boozin'?' he asked cordially. 'I might've been to a Bible meeting for all you know.'

'You can't fool me, Mr Logan,' Suzie said, grinning. 'If you'd been to a Bible meeting you'd have had Mrs Logan with you. Besides, you wouldn't come into the city centre for no Bible meeting when there's St Thomas's church just around the corner. Anyroad, you aren't usually on this tram. Come to think, you don't catch trams much, do you?'

'Norra lot,' Bill agreed, shifting on the hard seat. 'No, I've not been to a Bible meeting nor yet to the boozer. Well, I did have a bevvy after seeing Arthur Stokes, but don't you go telling my wife. She doesn't understand a feller can like a drink without being wedded to the stuff.'

'Your wife's Temperance, isn't she?' Suzie enquired. 'Well, I ain't, but I might just as well be. There's no money for drink in our house. Not that I miss it,' she added. 'Never did take to it meself. And I'm hopin' young Paddy will steer clear as well. Me old father and me brother Tim could be violent when they'd had a skinful, and nothing breaks up a family quicker than a feller who abuses the drink and his own strength.'

'Aye, that's right enough,' Bill agreed. 'Your Paddy's a good lad, though. He and Albert are bezzies, and there's no one I'd rather me laddo went about with. Mrs Logan agrees with me, I know, even though she don't say much.'

Suzie, who had been staring straight ahead of her, turned to gaze at him, her eyebrows arching in surprise. 'Mrs Logan approves of our Paddy?' she asked incredulously. She put up a hand, stroking the rich, golden-brown hair back off her forehead and giving Bill the benefit of a teasing, provocative glance. She remembered Abe telling her once that it had been a teasing glance from her big blue eyes that had first caught his attention and his interest. 'I thought all Keagans were bad through and through in your wife's book,' she added.

Bill took off his cap and began to turn it round and round in his hands. There was a flush on his weather-beaten cheeks, but presently he looked up and grinned sheepishly at her. 'You mustn't mind Mrs Logan,' he said softly. 'It's just her way. Me wife's a good woman you know, Mrs Keagan, none better, even if her mind is a trifle set. Her old mam made all her children take the pledge when they were six or seven and taught them that pleasure of any sort was sinful. Mrs Logan knows better than that now, of course, but it's coloured the way she looks at life.' He sighed, giving Suzie a straight look out of his round, golden-brown eyes. 'Many's the time I've told her to be more tolerant and I know she does her best, but it's uphill work when you've had narrowness and self-righteousness preached at you since you was a kid.'

'Aye and I know she's been good to our Paddy often enough,' Suzie agreed, remembering the times her son had been fed by Isobel Logan. 'As for yourself, Mr Logan, you know how grateful we are for the fish. I won't deny if it wasn't for that we wouldn't always make ends meet. I does me best, but I find it hard to hold on to a good job even when I manage to get one. It's 'cos I mainly goes for cleaning or domestic work of some sort, where there's women in charge. Me old ma-in-law says I should tie back me hair and tek good care not to look too pretty, but ... well, I say self-respect's worth a bob or two.'

It was an invitation to Bill Logan to tell her that she was a good-looking woman, that other women would obviously be jealous of her, not want to employ her, but Bill did not respond in the way Suzie had hoped he would. Instead, he just nodded briefly as the tram drew to a shuddering halt and got to his feet. 'Don't you go worrying over such things,' he said. 'No point. As for the bits o' fish an' that, what's that to a feller in my trade?' He began to make his way down the tram, speaking to her over his shoulder as he did so. 'I'm gerrin' off here so's I can go to me aunt's house for half an hour, to see that she's all right and have a jangle. Goodnight, Mrs Keagan.'

Suzie smiled to herself as Bill Logan disembarked and the tram began to move once more. She guessed he would go to his aunt's house and chat and drink tea until not even the most suspicious would smell beer on his breath. Bill Logan was far too canny a man to make bullets for his wife to fire at him. Far too nice a man, Suzie's thoughts continued, for such a straight-backed, tight-mouthed wife. But he and Isobel must have been married for thirty years and a woman could change a good deal in that time; as, indeed, could a man. The girl that Bill Logan had fallen in love with could have been gay and amusing, but thirty years of bringing up kids and making every penny do the work of two could change anyone. Suzie knew it was changing her. There had been a time when her main aim in life had been to have fun and to get herself a decent man who would take her away from the miserable court off the Scotland Road where she had been born and brought up. Then she had met Abe and he had taken her back to the neat house in Seaforth and introduced her to his family, told her all about their boat, their trade. She had seen at once that marriage to Abe was bettering herself, especially when they had moved into a terraced house of their own and begun to furnish it nicely, to plan their future lives together.

They had wanted children and, although Suzie had been no fonder of housework then than she was now, at least she had found it bearable in a new little house, surrounded by nice things. She had cast off her family – had been glad to do so – and had entered wholeheartedly into the life of a small fishing community where the name Keagan was respected and where she herself had been totally accepted.

When Paddy had been born she had agreed with Abe that their boy should better himself, get an education, work at his books. In those days, selfish though she had been, she had not wanted Paddy to be forced into working as soon as he was able to hold down a job. She had dreamed of seeing her son the owner of a fishing vessel, as his father had been. But somehow the harsh reality of living in poverty in a big city had whittled away at her resolution until she found herself glad of every penny the boy could bring in and was no longer concerned when he sagged off school, so long as he was not caught.

Thinking it over now, she remembered also that she had been honest enough when Abe had been alive. Or was it just because there had been no need to prig joints of ham, to take tips left for others, to let her mam and her aunt do all the housework? She remembered life in the court, where she had had to fight for every mouthful of bread, every penny. Yes, in the old days, before she had met Abe, she had been as sly and on the make as anyone else.

The tram stopped once more and Suzie noticed that it was beginning to rain. Damn! She would have to put her shawl over her head and shoulders or folk would think it mighty odd. If only she had brought a shopping bag, but Mrs Hathaway would not let casual staff bring bags on to the premises. Too crafty, Suzie thought crossly. She was surprised that they let her bring the shawl – come to that, she wouldn't put it past old Ma Hathaway to insist that the staff removed their drawers before starting work, in case they stashed away food in them.

The tram lurched forward again just as a man came up the aisle, giving Suzie a grin as he passed her. Suzie cast down her eyes and pretended not to notice. She often thought about marrying again, for Abe had been dead now for more than ten years, but somehow she couldn't be bothered with all that courting business and she had no intention of taking a feller unless it was in marriage. Her ma-in-law was a tartar and wouldn't put up with any funny business, to say nothing of Aunt Dolly, who was in church five days a week and always telling her what happened to bad girls.

Still, marriage would be a way out of her difficulties; after all, it had been marriage that had got her out of the court and away from her dreadful family in the first place. Then death had robbed her of her pleasant life and had forced her to become a breadwinner once more. If she were to marry . . . but the trouble was she seemed to attract the wrong sort of man, or otherwise the right sort of men were married already. Take Bill Logan, for instance. He was twenty years or more older than she, but a reliable, strong sort of man and, she acknowledged to herself now, very attractive. If only he were not already wed. But he was and somehow the thought of marrying someone she did not know very well, only to discover that the new husband had feet of clay, was not one which appealed. Some day, Suzie told herself, Mr Right will come along and then I shan't have to work for bad-tempered old women who sack me because they're jealous of me looks. What's more, I shan't have to purrup with Gran and me Aunt Dolly bossing me around and telling me how I ought to behave. One day, one day . . .

The conductor rang the bell and people began to surge towards the rear of the vehicle. Suzie joined them and climbed down off the tram at the Seaforth Sands terminus, thankful that the rain had stopped once more, though the road and pavements were still puddled. She crossed the road and went under the Rimrose Bridge, just as a train passed overhead. The Caradoc Hotel looked most inviting on the corner opposite, but Suzie decided she must step out for home and pressed on down the Crosby Road. She passed the Royal Hotel, which at other times might have tempted her, and soon came abreast of the massive bulk of Seaforth Hall, set back from the road in enormous grounds. She crossed over the end of Shore Road and glanced to her left down to the beach. The sand was dark and the sea glimmered whitely as the waves crashed on the shore, but there was nothing else to be seen and soon she reached Seafield Grove on the right, lined on either side with terraced houses fronting directly on to the pavement.

She passed the Logan house with its brightly lit windows and wondered, enviously, what the family were doing. Waiting for the head of the household, no doubt, though perhaps the younger ones were already abed. She hoped that by now Paddy was sleeping soundly and told herself for the hundredth time that she really must begin to look for work that paid rather better than cleaning for Mrs Hathaway. Only she was so tired. Tired of trying to make ends meet, tired of the endless round of work and managing the money, tired of her boring existence, in fact.

Shocked at her own thoughts, she turned into the jigger, telling herself all over again that at least she was going home to a meal and a warm room. And no man. The thought popped into her head, shocking her by its forthrightness. She reminded herself how the thought of remarriage frightened her – had she not just been thinking so on the tram? She knew she was still an attractive woman but she knew also that she was lazy. The sheer effort of beginning a relationship with some young feller who might turn out to be more trouble than he was worth daunted her. It must be because I was so deeply in love with my dear old Abe she told herself, conveniently forgetting the way she had leapt at his proposal as an escape from the court. Once again she thought of Bill Logan, his friendly, open face, his generosity in often passing on some of his catch to the Keagan family. He was a handsome man, despite his fifty-three years. Any woman would be ...

But Bill Logan was, so to speak, spoken for and the other men she met tended to want a woman for almost anything but marriage. Suzie knew herself, despite appearances, to be less interested in the physical side of marriage than most women. In the ten years of her widowhood she had never been tempted to leave the straight and narrow for a bit on the side. She had had a difficult time giving birth to Paddy and had decided, quite coldly, that she would not have any more children. For the best part of a year she had kept Abe to his own side of the bed by pretending illness; then an old gypsy woman had sold her a little brown bottle, full of an evil-tasting draught . . .

The wretched stuff had worked, though it had made her almost as ill as she had pretended, she remembered now, slopping along the pavement. She had been told to take a tablespoonful of the stuff whenever her monthlies were due and since she had not fallen pregnant in the six months before Abe had died, she supposed it must have been the gypsy's concoction. But if she had had her way there would have been no need of medicine, for she could cheerfully have dispensed with having Abe all over her, especially when he'd had several pints of ale and was inclined to be rough with her. Odd how most women seemed to think that going to bed with a man was something special; Suzie simply considered it dangerous. Babies, after all, turned into children, into more mouths to feed. No, she did not think, somehow, that she would marry again. Of course, it would be different if she met someone really first-rate, someone who would support her, take care of her, keep the worry of Paddy and the old women off her mind. Someone like Bill . . .

But thinking like that never got anyone anywhere, Suzie told herself, as the back door opened under her hand. There was no point in coveting another woman's man, quite apart from its being a sin, particularly a man who's married to a plaster saint like Isobel Logan. She supposed, vaguely, that even if Isobel went and died on him, Bill Logan would look around for another prim, prissy-mouthed woman, who was prepared to work all hours and sell shrimps door to door without a word of complaint. And have ten kids, she reminded herself, wincing at the very thought. Oh, no, she did not mean to go through *that* again, she was better off a widow, much better off.

On this thought she emptied the contents of her hawl on to the kitchen table and grinned triumphantly across the room at Gran, who was dishing up stewed fish and potatoes into a cracked pottery plate. 'I'm home, Gran,' she said. 'Got some currant buns for Aunt Dolly to soak in a nice saucer of tea, so's she don't have to chew, and a nice joint o' ham for tomorrer's dinner. Mr Logan pop by wi' some plaice? Thought so. Honest to God, I'm wore out, but I'm still hungry as a horse after workin' like a slave all day.'

Gran sniffed. 'I suppose you'll say that hard-faced Hathaway woman give you the meat and them buns?' she said tauntingly. 'Well, so long as you don't expect me to believe you ...'

'Believe what you like.' Suzie cast the shawl in the rough direction of the hook on the back of the door and sat down at the table before the plate of food. 'I don't suppose it'll stop you eating them wherever they come from. That right?'

'Beggars can't be choosers,' her mother-in-law

admitted, coming over to the table with a mug of steaming hot tea and setting it down before her daughter-in-law. She picked up the joint of ham and looked at it critically. 'There's good eatin' on this, I'll say that for you. But how long will you last there, eh? A few currant buns is one thing, but a whole joint o' ham . . . well, they'll soon have your measure at that rate.'

'I'm sick of it anyway,' Suzie said, her mouth full of floury potato. Gran was a prime cook, she had to admit that. 'I were going to move on soon enough.'

'Oh aye? Before you're pushed, you mean? Oh, go on, don't bother to tell me no more lies. I'm tired, I want me bed. Wash up when you're done, gal.'

She left the room and Suzie continued to eat the fish and potatoes, and to sip at the scalding hot tea. Gran wasn't a bad old stick, a lot easier to get along with than Aunt Dolly with her religious mania and her spiteful tongue. Suzie finished her meal and stood up, the mug of tea in one hand. She would take it up to bed with her and drink it while she took off her outer clothing. She had no intention of doing the washing up and clearing away. Aunt Dolly, self-satisfied old fool, could do that. She might be eighty-two or three – Suzie was never quite sure of her aunt's precise age – but she wasn't helpless yet and she ate enough for two. She could do the washing up. Suzie doused the lamp and wandered across the kitchen and up the short flight of stairs to her room. Here, in her muddled and unmade bed, she settled down to sleep. Drowsily she considered Gran's words. Perhaps the joint of ham had been a little unwise. She would go back to the canny house next day, and if she was accused of thieving then, naturally, she would hotly and indignantly deny it.

Meanwhile, she could go along to the Caradoc Hotel, or the Royal, or even the International Marine and see if they had a vacancy for an evening barmaid, just in case she got the push. The Caradoc had advertised just such a position on a board outside the pub; she had seen it a couple of days earlier. She supposed she could stand working there for a few days, just until she found something better.

Soon Suzie slept, her conscience untroubled by thoughts of the day to come.

Bill Logan said goodnight to his aunt and set off on the walk home, glad that the rain had not restarted. He had had a good day and had concluded a nice little business deal with Arthur Stokes. He and Arthur had been at school together and though they had gone their separate ways – he to the fishing and Arthur into the retail grocery business – they had remained good friends. So when he and the other man had met up at the St John's fish market it had been natural for Arthur to suggest that he might come round one evening for a drink and have a chat. Bill had agreed, though he had guessed that there was more in Arthur's invitation than met the eye and so it proved. Arthur was keen to find a supplier of potted shrimps and had immediately suggested that he and Bill might work out a deal which would satisfy them both, and such indeed had been the case. The Stokeses were prepared to pay the Logans a very fair price since Arthur's shop, being well out of the centre of Liverpool, catered for customers who rarely got into the city and would be prepared to pay an extra penny or so for the convenience of buying potted shrimps from their own corner shop. Arthur, for his part, knew that the potted shrimps would bring the customers in, so was happy to cut his profit to a minimum for the sake of the extra business.

It had been a bonus, meeting Mrs Keagan on the tram, Bill thought now. She was a beautiful young woman, hard-working and good-hearted, if a little sloppy, and he often felt ashamed of the way Isobel regarded her. The girl had done nothing to deserve his wife's constant criticism – unless being younger and beautiful was a sin, which Bill sometimes thought Isobel must believe. His wife said that Suzie nicked stuff from her various employers, that she changed her jobs a good deal more regularly than she changed her underwear, that she put all the work of the house on the two old ladies, using her various jobs as an excuse for sluttishness. Yet when he thought about it, it did not seem likely that Isobel disliked Suzie merely because she was pretty, because such a view scarcely agreed with Isobel's feelings for Mary. Mary, her favourite daughter, was blonde and extremely pretty, very like Isobel had been when they had first married. Was that the reason for Isobel's partiality? Would this also account for the fact that his wife did not greatly care for plain little Amy and was as constantly critical of her small daughter, as, indeed, she was of Suzie Keagan? Bill reached the back door of his home and pushed it open, stepping thankfully into the warmth of his kitchen. It didn't do to start thinking too hard, he reminded himself. All parents have a favourite child – he was very fond of Amy – and there was nothing obvious to account for such feelings, it was simply the way one felt.

'Still raining?' Isobel asked, from her seat by the fire. 'Call itself summer? Well, I should think the poor King is downright grateful for his appendix blowing up the way it did, for this is no weather for a coronation. They would probably have had to swim up the Mall, getting all those lovely robes soaked. I've saved you some tea if you're still hungry, or did you eat with the Stokeses?'

Bill walked round the table and dropped a kiss on his wife's thick, greying hair. 'Aye, it's grand weather for ducks, not dukes,' he said, chuckling. 'Still an' all, the coronation's only postponed, not purroff for ever. Likely it'll be fine for the real thing when the King's better.'

Isobel ignored the caress but smiled up at him, shaking her head. 'Oh, you, Bill Logan! There's been a lot of disappointment over the King's illness, you know it as well as me. Now what about some food, or have you already eaten? It's Irish stew if you'd care for some. What did Mr Stokes want?'

'I did eat with the Stokeses,' Bill admitted, reaching into his jacket pocket for his pipe and then, with a sigh, putting it back once more. Isobel did not approve of tobacco any more than alcohol, and would grow tight-lipped and silent if he tried to smoke in the house. 'But that was a good while ago. I could just do with a plate of your Irish stew.'

'Right,' Isobel said, leaving her chair and crossing the room to the stove. With her back to him she added conversationally, 'You know our Amy lit out when the shrimps came in? Well, she came back after no more'n ten or fifteen minutes. I think maybe that young lady is learning at last that everyone's got to do their share in this world. She worked well, I'll say that for her. She helped with the potting as well.'

'Glad to hear it,' Bill said, going over and sitting down at the table. Isobel placed a brimming plateful of Irish stew before him and he picked up his spoon and began to eat. 'This is grand, queen,' he said appreciatively presently, reaching for a thick slice of home-baked bread and dipping it into the gravy. 'I'm a lucky feller, so I am.'

Isobel, seating herself opposite him, smiled. 'Aye, you're right,' she agreed. 'I'm a good cook, though I say it as shouldn't. And I'm not doing so badly myself, for there's many a worse husband in these parts.'

Chapter Two

As Bill had predicted, no sooner had the King
recovered from his operation than the date for the
coronation was fixed once more, this time for 9
August. Isobel read pieces out of the paper to the
children as they sat peeling shrimps, telling them all
about preparations for the celebration. There had
been the great feast the King had given thousands of
Londoners the previous month and, though his
bounty had not stretched as far as Liverpool,
everyone agreed it was a generous gesture. Then
there were the decorations. Wonderful arches which
spanned the widest of roads, monuments decorated
with artificial flowers and brilliant illuminations,
while enormous bouquets and garlands of real
flowers wreathed the major buildings. Amy, Mary
and Albert listened to these tales of wonder, and
envied Londoners and anyone else fortunate enough
to be going to the capital city for the great event. In
fact, the children all knew that there were people in
Seaforth who would go up to London, not perhaps
for the coronation but to see the decorations, which
would remain in place for several days after the
King and Queen were crowned. Seaforth was home
to several families who, while not as rich as the
Muspratts, were still very well-to-do. The Grimshaws, for instance, went to St Thomas's and were
very rich indeed. During the summer holidays and

usually at Christmas, too, they had their grand-children to stay. Philip was fourteen and Laura twelve; the children knew that much since Isobel sometimes sold fish at the big house on Crosby Road, but they scarcely saw the Grimshaws during the services, for the Grimshaws had a closed-in pew with high wooden walls, which hid the occupants from ordinary worshippers. Laura was not allowed much freedom, not nearly as much as Amy, but Philip, being a boy and also older, frequently made his way down to the shore to fish. A couple of times he had begged an illicit ride in the shrimp boat, and both Bill Logan and Amy's brothers said he was a decent young chap and not a bad fisherman either.

However, Amy was not particularly interested right now in the Grimshaws or, indeed, in the coronation itself. She considered it thoughtless, if not downright selfish, of the King to rearrange his coronation so that it was during the school holidays instead of in term-time, but no one was perfect. Isobel was a keen royalist, knowing every detail about the royal family and she was a great admirer of Queen Alexandra, so when the papers reported the great event Isobel would be in her element. Indeed, she would be too busy reading all about it to worry overmuch what her daughters were up to. But Coronation Day having dawned at last, Amy and Mary had obtained permission to take their midday meal down to the sands and to spend their time on the beach, digging for cockles if they felt inclined but otherwise having a lazy day. So now she and Mary skirted Seaforth Hall and made their way past the Grimshaws' big house, heading for the particular spot where they had decided to spend their holiday. 'For it is a holiday,' Mary told her sister as they left the house, their carry-out in the string bag that swung from Mary's hand. 'It isn't often our mam let's us off for a whole day, let alone gives us a picnic.'

'It's not often the King and Queen get crowned,' Amy pointed out, skipping along beside her sister. 'Oh, but isn't it a lovely day, our Mary? I wonder what Albert's doing – something he shouldn't ought to, I reckon.'

'He's not a bad lad,' Mary objected. 'Not like Paddy Keagan. He leads our Albert into more mischief than a cartload of organ-grinders' monkeys. But there's no real harm in him, our Dad says. And he offered to carry my basket last time I did the messages for our mam.'

'I think there's harm in that Paddy. And anyway, Albert needn't do as he says,' Amy pointed out righteously. 'Mammy would say he could choose the good road or the bad, same as the rest of us. I say, Mary,' she added as a thought struck her, 'why don't we call Albert Bertie, same as Paddy does? Come to that, Mam always uses full names, even for Augustus. Everyone else calls him Gus.'

'Mam doesn't like nicknames,' Mary said as they reached the sand and began to walk along it, scuffing their bare feet in the warm, golden grains. 'She'd call Dad William, if she could, only he told her when they were first married that he wouldn't stand for it. That's why we girls have short names which you can't muck about with. You can't shorten Amy or Mary, can you, chuck?'

'No-o-o,' Amy admitted after some thought. 'But why choose Augustus or Albert? They are names which everyone shortens, wouldn't you say?'

'Dad chose 'em,' Mary said briefly. She plonked

herself down in the sand and pushed the straw hat she was wearing to the back of her head. 'Phew, isn't it hot, though? And it can't be more than ten o'clock, if that. Shall we start on our drink? Just a sip or two each, mind.'

'That's fine by me.' Amy rooted for the bottle in the string bag. 'Oh, Mam put in a bottle of water and one of ginger beer. Shall we start on the water and save the ginger beer till later?'

'Yes, that'll be best,' Mary agreed, taking the bottle of water from Amy's hand, uncorking it and lifting it to her lips. She took several thirsty gulps, then replaced the cork and handed the bottle back to her sister. 'Do you want a drink, Amy?'

Amy took a mouthful, but she was not particularly thirsty, and quickly replaced the cork and carried both bottles down to the edge of the waves. Here she dug a hole with her hands as a dog might and, when the water had crept halfway up the sides, she put both bottles in it, knowing that the sea would keep the drink cool. Then she kilted up her skirt and waded into the water. Mary, after a moment's hesitation, followed suit and for some time the two children simply revelled in the water, splashing backwards and forwards and trying to spot shells, seaweed and tiny crabs, which they could see through the waves but could not pick up without getting soaked.

After half an hour of this rather frustrating game, Amy went ashore and took off her white cotton apron, her long grey skirt and the two petticoats beneath it. Then she rolled up the legs of her frilled drawers and took off her blue blouse. While Mary was still gaping at her, wide-eyed with horror, she marched back into the water until it was up to her chest, gasping at the cold but thoroughly enjoying the sense of freedom that her near-nudity gave her.

'Amy!' Mary squeaked. 'Whatever are you doing? Mam would half kill you if she saw you now! You should know better, indeed you should. Mam would say no decently brought-up girl would kilt her skirts up, let alone take them right off. Remember we're on a public beach, our Amy, and though it's early still, folk are going to start coming on to the sands any minute now. Why, anyone might come along and see you and think you a nasty, common sort of kid. Come out of that at once, do you hear me?'

'No, I shan't,' Amy said defiantly, splashing with her arms and pretending to swim. Indeed, when each of the little waves came inshore it lifted her up and carried her with it, making her feel as though she really was swimming. 'I don't see why you're making such a fuss, anyhow, because no one's here yet. Besides, ever such smart ladies and gentlemen go swimming these days, you know they do! Don't you remember the pictures in that old copy of the *Sketch*, which Mam brought home from the Grimshaw place? I'm sure what they were wearing wasn't nearly as respectable as my drawers and chemmy.'

'The folk who go swimming have proper costumes and ... oh, Amy, someone *is* coming, honest to God they are! Now will you come out and stop shaming? I do declare, if I were to tell our mam ...'

'But you won't,' Amy pointed out. Mary might disapprove, but she wouldn't go tale-clatting to Mam, not she. Nevertheless, she glanced along the beach and saw that someone really was approaching. Two – no, three – figures, one of which held what she took to be a fishing rod in one hand and a basket of some sort in the other. 'Oh, damn,' Amy muttered. But she knew her sister was right. Seaforth Sands was a popular venue with half Liverpool when the weather was fine and today was to be a holiday for a good many people, though schoolkids, already on holiday, were missing out. Accordingly she began to wade out of the sea, though her tilted chin and defiant glare would tell her sister, she hoped, that she was coming because she wanted to do so and not because she was afraid of the consequences.

Indeed, the little wavelets were no more than lapping at her ankles when she took another glance along the beach and realised, with considerable dismay, that she recognised at least one of the small advancing group. The detestable Paddy Keagan, hair on end, ragged jersey tied round his waist, kicking a round pebble before him and singing what was probably a very rude sea shanty, was approaching, thankfully at a saunter. And it stands to reason, Amy told herself, hastily splashing ashore, that if Paddy's here, Albert's with him and that could mean . . . oh, all sorts of trouble.

The far worse trouble, that of being soaked with salt water and without so much as a handkerchief with which to dry herself, did not occur to poor Amy until she was approaching their bag of food. Then, glancing down at herself, she saw how far from glamorous one looked in a sodden chemise with drawers which had managed to trap, in their one plain frill, a quantity of grey-looking sand. 'Oh, God love me, I'm in a pickle this time,' she muttered under her breath. 'Oh, oh, they're getting awfully close, so they are, and that pig of a Paddy is starting to grin like ... like an ape!' She seized her skirt and pulled it on all anyhow, then began to struggle into her blouse, which was too small for her anyway. Her long hair was dripping down her back, soaking her all over again, and Mary was expostulating, telling her that she couldn't possibly put dry clothes over soaking underwear and wasn't she the stupidest, naughtiest kid ever to disobey her elders, now.

But Amy was past caring what Mary might say. What worries me is what that bleedin' Paddy would put about if he sees me in my drawers, Amy told herself, continuing to struggle into her – by now – damp clothing. Oh, he would jeer at her, he would scoff, he would ...

A great guffaw of laughter interrupted her thoughts. Paddy stood not six yards distant, grimy hands on hips, his belongings cast down, a grin from ear to ear splitting his horrible, dirt-smeared face. 'Ooh, look at ole sainted Shrimpy, Mammy's good little darlin', a-wearin' of frilly kecks an' soaked right through to her miserable speckled skin,' he shouted. 'And she's been a-swimmin' in her bare skin just like us fellers does, only she can't swim for toffee-nuts, bein' a stupid, brainless *girl*, acourse.'

The three boys were grinning but the eldest of them, who must be Philip Grimshaw, Amy supposed, suddenly stopped smiling and said, 'Oh, come on, Paddy, there's no need to be rude, is there?'

'I's always rude to her,' Paddy said airily. 'She's a tale-clat an' a nuisance; she thinks she's someone special. She's rude to me so I's rude to her.'

'Fellers shouldn't be rude to girls,' the boy, Philip, pointed out. Not self-righteously, Amy thought, but rather as a matter of course. 'And you can't blame her for taking a swim on such a grand day. I wouldn't mind a swim myself.'

Amy, having struggled at last into her clothing, turned to face the boys. She glanced rather shyly up at Philip, thinking him handsome and much older than he looked, for she knew from Albert that he could not be more than fourteen or fifteen. He was a good deal taller than either of his companions, however, with crisp, taffy-brown hair and matching eyes, a firm chin and a mouth with a good deal of humour in its swift, curling smile. Accordingly, she gave him a quick grin, to show she appreciated his championship, then faced up to her old enemy. 'I can swim then, Paddy Keagan, I taught myself just this minute, so I did! And I may be freckled, but I'm not clarted up with dirt like you are.'

'Swim! All you did was flap like a stranded plaice an' come in on a wave – I saw you wi' me own eyes. Aw, you're a great ole fool, Amy Logan, to think you can swim the first time you try.'

If it had not been for Mary's restraining hand, Amy would have hurled herself back in the water, clothes and all, just to prove to Paddy Keagan that she could indeed swim, but Mary hung grimly on to her and Amy realised that this was a good thing, since she knew, in her heart, that Paddy was right. She could not really swim at all; it was the sea which had been kind and lifted her up just for a moment. Had she been out of her depth, however, she suspected that she would have gone straight down into Davy Jones's locker no matter how she might flail around.

'Paddy, do leave off,' Mary said, as she clung to Amy's arm. 'As for you, our Amy, just you ignore him. He's out to annoy you, that's all, and don't you rise like a fish to a fly? I told you it was very wrong to go right into the water and now you know for why. Oh, and look up the beach, girl! There's a heap of folk walking along the sand, so maybe our Albert and Paddy and their pal just about saved you from making a real cake of yourself.' She turned to the boys. 'Do you have a carry-out?' she enquired. 'If so, why don't we all sit down and have it right now, and forget our differences? It's a special holiday, after all, our mam won't expect us back until this evening.'

'I've gorra bit of food,' Paddy said gruffly. He could never argue with Mary, Amy knew that very well. 'And some water in a bottle. You've gorra stack of stuff, though, haven't you, Albert?'

'Same's the girls, I guess,' Albert said. 'Phil?'

'In the basket,' Philip told him. 'The housekeeper packed it so I don't know what it is, but she said it'd stop me from starving until dinner time. Oh, and there's a bottle of raspberry syrup. We can all share.'

'Right,' Albert said. 'And no more snipin' at the girls, Paddy, 'cos it makes for awkwardness. I'm goin' to set up me fishin' line first, though. We can watch it as we eat, the girls too. Good thing we came right up this end o' the beach, the other end's thick wi' folk already.'

It was true. Amy, glancing along the way they had come, could see family parties, groups of young people and children already industriously digging in the wet sand at the edge of the waves. What was more, she knew from experience that as the day went on, even the less popular part of the beach where the marram grass grew and the shoreline tended to be muddy at low tide would grow crowded with people. Therefore it behoved them to get as much pleasure from the day's holiday as they could while a large area of sand around them remained empty of people. Amy had never gone fishing with her brother, because Albert almost always went with Paddy. The older boys, most of whom fished for a living, preferred to take a rod into Wales or the Wirral for a day's sport. As for the fishing boat, she had never asked her father to take her shrimping and thought she probably never would. Even had she done so, she doubted that Bill would want her on board. She imagined he would think it unlucky to take a woman out fishing and was devoutly glad of it.

However, fishing with Albert and the others might be quite fun, so she watched with interest as the boys set up their lines. Her brother and Paddy had short hazel wands, which they stuck in the sand after they had thrown out lines baited with what looked like grubs of some sort. Philip, however, had a proper rod with a line and a float and bait, which looked more professional somehow. He cast expertly, too, sending his baited line a good deal further out to sea than either Albert or Paddy had managed, but then he, too, stuck his smart, cork-handled rod in the sand, and strolled back to where Mary and Amy were watching.

'There, that didn't take long, did it?' he asked, sitting down on the sand beside Mary and reaching across for the basket he had been carrying. 'It's early still, but I could do with a snack.' The basket lid was cunningly closed with two loops and a wooden peg. He unfastened it and threw back the lid, revealing several compartments filled with interesting-looking packages as well as an oddly shaped bottle full of a dark-red liquid, neatly corked. Amy was fascinated to see that the lid of the basket held cutlery, a couple of enamel mugs and plates.

'There's all sorts in here.' Philip fished out two of the packages and began to unwrap them. 'My grandmother's cook is an awkward old blighter, but she has a soft spot for me. Besides, if she packs me a decent picnic, she knows she'll be rid of me all day, which makes her life easier, I suppose.' He held out the package towards the two girls. Amy, looking at the chunks of cheese, slices of thick bread and cuts of ham, found that her mouth was watering already. If this was the cook's idea of a carry-out, what sort of meals did Philip normally enjoy?

'Cor!' Amy breathed reverently. 'Your cook must've thought your sister was going to share your carry-out, eh? No one could think one feller needed this lot.'

Philip laughed. 'My sister's gone to the city centre to visit our great-aunt,' he said. 'She and Grandma will get a grand luncheon at Great-Aunt Betty's. Laura loves iced puddings so Great-Aunt's cook always makes one for her.'

The Logan family had ham at Christmas, but iced puddings? She'd never even heard of such a thing, let alone tasted one. They had cheese from time to time, but it was still very much a treat. And fancy having plates and mugs on the beach, where such things were virtually unknown. It must be wonderful to have so much money and so many possessions that one could risk the loss of cutlery or even plates and mugs. The Logans guarded such things with jealous care. Isobel would never have dreamed of letting so much as a teaspoon leave her neat kitchen.

But if the rich had many possessions, the poor could have good times too. Amy remembered one of her brothers telling her once how Dad had taken the older ones on an expedition to New Brighton. They had dug cockles, boiled them in an old Glaxo tin over the driftwood fire they had built and eaten them as the sun began to sink. Gus had never forgotten the trip, and now Amy felt dimly that though it was wonderful to have loads of money and a picnic basket full of delicious food, there were compensations in being poor. She did not think that even the most succulent ham could ever be as delicious as food you had won from the sea, cooked over your own fire and eaten in the sunset's glow. She remembered some of Isobel's favourite sayings, that money was the root of all evil and that riches gave only the delusion of pleasure, and for the first time she thought she saw some meaning behind her mother's words. For all the Grimshaws' money, they would not know the intense pleasure that Amy and her family – and the Keagans come to that – got from the small excitements in their lives. Ham at Christmas, cheese when the money stretched to it, a trip on the ferry, a ride on the overhead railway and cooking your own supper on a sunset beach. To the Logans and the Keagans such things were the very stuff of pleasure, something to be treasured all the more because of their rarity and remembered in the years ahead.

'What'll you have, young Amy? Cheese or ham? Only better take a bit of bread first, so you can make a sort of sandwich.'

'Thanks,' Amy breathed, delighted by such generosity. 'Can I have a bit of both? Just a little bit you know.'

'Amy!' Mary was scandalised. 'It's greedy to have

both. Besides, this is Philip's dinner. We shouldn't . . .'

'Oh, let her have both, there's plenty for us all I should think,' Philip said airily. He watched while first Amy and then Mary selected their food, folding the bread over the meat and cheese, and then did likewise, while Albert and Paddy, as a matter of course, helped themselves. The five children sat on the sand, munching in companionable silence, until Amy happened to notice that one of the hazel wands was being tugged almost out of the sand by some movement in the sea. She grabbed Mary's arm. 'Look, Mary! Does that mean someone's caught a fish?'

'Bejaysus, that's my stick – rod, I mean – so it is,' Paddy exclaimed, jumping to his feet. The other two boys promptly followed suit and very soon Albert and Paddy were up to their knees in the waves, both attempting to catch hold of the slippery line and draw it in by hand, for only Philip had a proper reel. Amy went as far as the edge of the waves and watched the struggle, which ended with Paddy and Albert drawing the fish so close to the shore that Paddy fell upon it and presently staggered from the waves, bearing in his arms a sizeable codling. 'Will you look at that!' he wheezed, as he reached Amy's side. 'Isn't he a fine aargh . . .'

The fish, wriggling and flapping wildly, had momentarily escaped from Paddy's grasp, but the three children – for Amy did not intend to be left totally out of the chase – fell upon it in the creaming waves and Paddy dispatched it, chiefly by falling upon it and driving it into the sand. Scrambling to his feet, he grinned triumphantly at his fellow fishers. 'Gorrim! And he's dead as a Dodo,' he said, holding up the limp and sandy grey body. 'Shall us cook him for our dinners?'

'Oh, we've got our dinners,' Albert said. 'We have fish often. Paddy, you take him home for your mam.'

Amy was relieved when Paddy, having considered the size of his fish, nodded agreement. 'All right. Me mam'll be glad of it,' he said. He began to slosh the fish to and fro in the water until, Amy thought, you could almost have believed it alive again. 'Do you reckon there's enough on this 'ere for me gran to have some as well? Still, you never know, if I rebait me hook I might get another. They's bitin' well today, wouldn't you say?'

'That one certainly did,' Albert said appreciatively. He looked up to where his own rod stuck up out of the sand. 'Tell you what, Paddy, if I gets a bite you can have that 'an all. But we'd better get your hook rebaited and into the water, to give your fish's pals a chance to join 'im.'

'Right you are.' Paddy shoved his fingers into the fish's mouth and withdrew the hook, examining it with a grunt of satisfaction. Clearly its sojourn in the fish's gut had done it no harm, Amy concluded.

The three children emerged from the water and made their way to where Albert's rod stood in the sand. Amy watched with interest as Paddy rooted around in an old tobacco tin and produced a wriggling grub, which he impaled upon his hook. He ran down to the edge of the sea and cast his line as far as he could, before returning to stick his hazel wand into the sand once more. Then, for the first time it seemed, he looked long and hard at Amy. 'Oh, Gawd,' he said in an awestruck voice. 'What'll your mam say to this, 'eh? She'll think I baited me hook wi' *you* instead of one of me grubs. 'Cept you'd better not tell her it were my fault, 'cos I never asked you to go jumpin' in the sea and interferin' wi' me day's sport.' Still staring at Amy, he began to giggle. 'I wish you could see yourself, girl, you're enough to make a cat die laughin'.'

Amy, recalled to reality by these rude remarks, glanced down at herself. She was soaked and sandy from halfway down her blouse to the hem of her draggled skirt and knew that, in the excitement of the chase, she had somehow managed to get her hair wet and sandy too. Despite herself, she began to grin. Paddy might be a horrible boy who teased and tormented her, but at least he was honest. It had not been his fault and she did look a sight, she acknowledged the fact. It would be bad enough when she went up the beach to rejoin Mary – she could not imagine what her mother would have said had she been present. However, Isobel was safe at home, no doubt eagerly awaiting news of the coronation. The hour of reckoning, therefore, might be decently delayed until evening. By then, with a bit of luck, she would have dried off and have been able to brush away the sand and to appear at least moderately respectable. She glanced up the beach towards where her sister sat and decided that Mary must have seen what had happened, so hopefully would not chide her for the state she was in.

Albert, beside her, gave her skirt a tweak. 'Take it off, queen,' he suggested. 'If we swish it in the water like Paddy did his fish it'll get rid of a deal of sand. Better do it now, afore any more folk come walkin' past.'

Amy, with a sigh, agreed. She began to struggle out of her skirt and presently she and Albert

49

swished it through the water and then squeezed it as dry as they could before Amy replaced it upon her person. 'It won't make much difference,' she said with a sigh, 'because when I sit down to have my dinner the sand'll stick like glue. Still, no one can say we didn't try.'

When the younger ones went roaring into the sea, Mary and Philip walked back up the beach to where they had left their possessions. As Mary had anticipated, the beach was already filling up and, with so many people about, she did not think it safe to leave things unattended. So she sat down by her string bag and Philip, after only the slightest of hesitations, sat down beside her.

'I wonder what they've hooked?' he said idly after a moment, looking back towards the sea where the three younger ones seemed to be having a private fight of their own against some monster of the deep. 'Surely it shouldn't take three of them to tackle one little plaice?'

'It might not be a plaice,' Mary objected, wincing as Albert fell to his knees and was immediately up again, though clearly drenched. 'I should think it's a shark, or a whale, judging by the commotion. Oh, Lord save us, Amy's forgot to kilt up her skirt; she'll get soaked to the skin all over again! Honest to God, that girl should've been a lad, she just doesn't know how to behave and that's the truth.'

Philip glanced at her; Mary saw that he had golden-brown eyes with very thick, fair lashes and a dusting of freckles across his rather aquiline nose. 'Your sister's a spunky kid. There aren't many girls who'd jump into the water like that just to save a pal's fish.'

'Well, I wouldn't, for one,' Mary admitted. 'I like paddling all right and I might like swimming, if I had a swimming costume, but I wouldn't go jumping in with all my clothes on.'

Philip turned and looked at her again, his mouth quirking into an engaging grin. He nodded slowly, still smiling at her. 'No, I guess you wouldn't plunge fully clothed into the briny,' he agreed. 'But if you'll excuse me saying so, Miss Mary, you're a young lady, not a kid. And you've had responsibilities as the elder, which young Amy won't ever have. I'm older than Laura and when we're together I'm responsible for her, so I behave in a more serious fashion, I suppose. Do you feel freer when Amy's not with you? I'm sure I do when Mother takes Laura off my hands.'

'I don't know about that,' Mary said, having thought the matter over. 'It's just that . . . that Amy doesn't think before she acts. She's not a bad girl, just a thoughtless one. And Dad encourages her. He thinks she's a spunky kid, too, but Mam doesn't agree. She'd like Amy to be a real little girl; she says Amy's neither one thing nor the other. And she's a real worry to me, acting the way she does. I never know what she'll do next and that's the truth of it.' She had been facing Philip, but now she turned to glance once more at the sea and gave a shriek. 'Oh, my Gawd, she'll be drowned for sure. Oh, oh, oh!' She jumped to her feet and would have run down the beach, but Philip seized her arm and pulled her into a sitting position once more.

'She's up again and I think they've got the fish,' he said, as Mary settled herself by his side. 'It's a codling, by the looks, and a decent sized one at that. See? Paddy's got it in his arms, just as though it were

51

a baby. Oh! It jumped clear back into the sea. Well, will you look at that.'

For several moments the two young people sat and watched, fascinated, as the three children collapsed on the edge of the sea in a whirl of foam, and flailing arms and legs. But fortunately for Mary's nerves, the battle was a short one and presently Albert, Paddy and Amy came dripping up on to the beach and clustered round Paddy's fishing gear. 'They're rebaiting the hook,' Philip said wisely. 'They'll try for another one now, after such a good start. I say, d'you fancy an apple?'

At six o' clock, tired but happy, the Logans and Paddy trailed home. Paddy carried, slung over one shoulder, a string of three decent-sized codling and was in a boastful and triumphant mood. He had caught two of the three fish himself, despite his inferior fishing tackle, and could hardly wait to show off his catch. Amy guessed that he did not intend to tell anyone that Philip had caught the largest fish but would take credit for all three. Though she would have liked to sneer, she thoroughly understood how Paddy felt; in the circumstances she knew she would have done the same herself.

They had parted from Philip some time earlier. He had taken his own catch of two fine plaice back with him, though he had tried to persuade either the Logans or Paddy to take them as a gift. Albert had pointed out that the Logans had all the fish they needed and Paddy, who was a realist, had also refused the offer – three codling was praiseworthy, but add two large plaice to his bag and even the fondest relative might show some incredulity. So

Philip had taken his catch home, along with an empty picnic, for the goodies which cook had packed so carefully had been eaten long since.

Mary remembered the meal with awe and pleasure. It was the first time she and Amy had met Philip, and now, making their way home, she turned to her sister. 'Well, Amy? Enjoy yourself?' she asked.

'Oh, I did.' Amy sighed. 'That Philip's all right, wouldn't you say, Mary? He handed out his grub like a right one and wasn't it grand grub, too? I'm sure none of us have eaten like that, except at Christmas. Why, he thought no more of cold ham than if it'd been bread!'

'Oh, Amy, you don't judge a fella by his carry-out,' Mary said reproachfully. 'He liked you, though. He said you were a spunky kid.'

Amy giggled. 'I'm a wet one,' she observed. 'But I'm drying out nicely.'

Mary gave a little smile and then, rather adroitly she thought, changed the subject but inside her head she went on thinking about Philip. She thought he liked her – for they had talked easily and pleasantly while they waited for the young ones to return for their dinner – though he had not called her a spunky kid. He had called her a young lady and Mary, just beginning to be conscious of her pretty looks, thought this a far more valuable compliment. Secretly she thought him easily the nicest boy she had ever met. He had talked gravely, too, in a way which was somehow so friendly and pleasant that she was sure he liked her more than he could possibly have liked Amy, who was still a child, after all.

Glancing ahead of her at Paddy's lopsided figure, weighed down by his string of fish, Mary reflected that to have Philip's friendship would be a good deal more welcome than the obvious admiration which Paddy often showed. The younger boy was always hanging around their house, bringing Mary small, unwanted gifts. She knew he constantly praised her to Albert, while equally constantly running Amy down, for there was no doubt that Paddy Keagan truly disliked her small sister. Unfortunately this dislike seemed totally irrational and, though Mary had attempted to reason with him once or twice, Paddy persisted in being horrid to Amy whenever an opportunity occurred. Philip, Mary reminded herself now, had teased and laughed at Amy that very afternoon, but it had been the teasing of one friend to another with none of the malice Paddy showed towards the younger girl.

All the while Mary's thoughts had been busy, Amy had been chattering blithely away, but now she turned to her older sister and asked curiously, 'What did you really think of Philip? What did you talk about when we were catching fish?'

'I thought he was nice,' Mary said cautiously. She did not intend to tell her small sister that she thought Philip quite as handsome as any of the stars she saw at the Rotunda, acting their parts on the wide stage. 'He's a good friend for Albert and Paddy. I've seen him in church, of course, but we've never talked before. And it was ever so interesting, Amy. They live in an even bigger house in Manchester than the Seaforth one. The Grimshaws have heaps of money. Philip goes to boarding school – a really expensive one – and they have maids and servants and ponies of their own. They've got relatives in London who have them to stay whenever the Grimshaws want to visit the capital. Why, Philip told me that his grandparents are taking them up to London to see the coronation decorations. They're going tomorrow on the train and staying for two nights with his Uncle Richard and Aunt Mabel. His mam and dad go off to foreign parts most summers – aren't they lucky, Amy? I'd give a lot to see all those arches and lights and stuff, wouldn't you? And I'd love to go to foreign parts. He said something about Paris.'

'Oh aye,' Amy said indifferently. Happily skipping down the jigger beside Mary, it was clear that the younger girl had forgotten the state of her clothing and the row that would probably follow her appearance in the kitchen. She had had a lovely day, Mary thought indulgently, and hurried to catch up with her sister so that they both entered the kitchen together. Isobel would be brimming with talk of the celebrations and, with a bit of luck, the girls could get up to their room and change into clean clothes before their mother noticed Amy's dishevelment. If they hurried across to the stairs . . .

The ruse worked, Isobel merely turning from the range to tell them to hurry for the meal was almost ready. Mary, getting out clean calico aprons and fresh gingham skirts for them both, reminded herself that dreaming about a friendship with Philip really wasn't practical. Apart from the fact that he only came to Seaforth during the summer holidays, their different circumstances would, in any case, keep them apart. So she put him firmly out of her mind, changed into her clean clothes and went downstairs to help serve the meal.

Philip entered the big house by a side door. In the small cloakroom he kicked off his boots and took off his jacket before taking his fish through to the kitchens. Cook was standing by the sink, supervising one of the kitchen maids who was scrubbing potatoes with zest and throwing the cleaned ones into a large enamel saucepan which stood on the draining board.

'Well, you *have* had a good day, Master Philip,' Mrs Darwin said, staring admiringly at the large plaice. 'Pity you're off t' London tomorrow or I could have fried them for you and Miss Laura to have for your dinners. You can't have 'em tonight 'cause I'm roastin' a couple of nice capons, since your gran's asked the Frobishers to dinner.'

The maid, standing at the sink, turned and looked from Philip to the fish and back again. 'You could have 'em for a fish course, Mrs D,' she suggested. 'Cut 'em into strips and curled round the way you do, wi' a bit o' lemon on the top and a nice white sauce. That always goes down well.'

'No, I'm doing raspberry sorbet,' Mrs Darwin told her. 'Never mind, Edie, gal, we'll have 'em for staff supper with some fried potatoes. That'll make a nice change.' She eyed Philip closely, suddenly seeming to notice his dishevelled state. 'You'd best get upstairs, Master Philip,' she said, holding out her hand for the fish. 'Dinner's in an hour and your gran will want you to look neat and smart with the Frobishers here. I know their kids is grown, but I remember in the old days, when they were your age, and they were always smart as paint.'

Philip sighed but handed over the plaice and turned back towards the kitchen door. He was never allowed to forget the Frobisher twins. They were three years older than himself and were always held up by his grandma as a shining example of how young gentlemen should both look and behave.

Philip thought them a couple of boring milksops but it would never have done to say so – not to his grandparents at any rate. So he left the kitchen and thundered across the hall and up the long flight of stairs to his room where he washed and changed briskly, throwing his sandy clothing into the linen basket outside his door as he made his way to his sister's room. He was about to knock on the door when it opened to reveal Laura in her new evening frock. 'Philip, you're back,' she said in a relieved voice. 'No one told us, but the Frobishers are coming to dine and you know what a state Grandma gets in if we're late or untidy.' She eyed him critically. 'Oh, you've already changed – you look very smart – so that's all right. We'd best go down to the drawing room, though, Grandma will want you to do the pretty, especially since those wretched boys will be coming with their parents.'

Together the two children began to descend the stairs. 'We had iced pudding for luncheon,' Laura told him, 'and Aunt Betty gave me the prettiest hat for London. What did you do? Get any fish?'

'A couple. Well, more than that, actually. I met up with two of the boys and their sisters that we've seen around and we went fishing together. We had a good time, but I gave the little one – his name's Paddy – most of my fish, his need being greater than ours, as they say.'

Laura sighed. 'Sometimes I wish I were just an ordinary kid, like the ones you've been off with today. They might never get to see the decorations in London, but they wouldn't have to put up with the Frobisher boys being held up as an example the way we do. What were their names – the girls, I mean – were they nice?'

'They were all right,' Philip said indifferently. 'Mary's the older of the two – she's a bit prim and goody-goody, but I dare say she can't help that. Amy, the little one, was a real little devil. She went into the water with all her clothes on and got soaked. But did she mind? Not her. Plain as a boot, though,' he ended regretfully.

'Fancy going into the water in your clothes.' Laura was wide-eyed. 'I bet I'd like that Amy from what you say, better than I like the Frobishers, anyway.'

'You can guess why they've asked the Frobishers,' Philip said as they neared the end of the flight. 'It's because Mr Frobisher is something important in newspapers and will have all the latest news on the coronation.' A thought occurred to him. 'Dear God, you don't suppose they're going up to London tomorrow as well? The Frobisher twins, I mean. That really would be too bad.'

'I'm surprised they didn't go up for the coronation itself, seeing how important they are, or think they are,' Laura said with a giggle. 'Desmond thinks he's the cat's whiskers and Darcy is even more pleased with himself. Oh, I do hope they're not coming to London with us. It would ruin everything.'

Philip thought about Amy in her salt-stained, sandy clothes and about Mary, beautiful as a rose, both thinking themselves lucky indeed to be given cold meat and some fruit. He knew vaguely that the 'ordinary kids' of whom his sister had spoken were not really enviable. Their lives might seem free from the restrictions which bound him and his sister, but they were trammelled by their own parents' conventions, just as he and Laura were. And for the Logans and Keagans, treats such as the trip to London on the morrow were out of the question. What was more, when he and Laura grew up, their lives would continue to be cushioned by their parents' wealth, whereas the Logans and Keagans would have to fight hard just to keep food on the table and clothes on their backs.

But it was no good saying any of this to Laura, who mixed very little with the local children. Indeed, though Philip knew of the hardships suffered by the poor in theory, in practice he was as ignorant as his sister. He had never been into one of the tiny houses in Seafield Grove, never visited the fish market in Great Charlotte Street nor been with his friends when they were earning a few coppers by running messages, chopping up boxes for firewood, or selling bags of shrimps from door to door. He could not really imagine these pastimes and though he knew most of the kids went barefoot in summer it had not previously occurred to him that this was not from choice.

The front-door bell pealing, as they were crossing the hall, made Laura give Philip a dig in the back. 'That'll be them, arriving,' she hissed. 'Get a move on, Philip, so we can greet them with Grandma and Grandpa in the drawing room.'

'Damn,' Philip muttered, but nevertheless obeyed his sister's injunction. He wondered wistfully what Paddy and Albert would be doing now, but then he caught a whiff from the kitchens of roast capon and Cook's home-made stuffing. Despite Mrs Darwin's generous lunch he realised he was starving hungry and was already looking forward to the meal ahead. Perhaps having money and a position in life weren't so bad after all, he concluded, as he and Laura entered the drawing room.

Paddy and his fish were welcomed home by Gran who told him briefly that his mam was off searching for another job. When Paddy asked why she had left the canny house, Gran mumbled something about other members of the staff being agin her but she looked away from him as she spoke and Paddy, well used to putting two and two together where his mother was concerned, thought ruefully that it probably had something to do with the leg of mutton which Gran was even now slicing on to three tin plates. 'Makes a nice change from fish,' she remarked, as she saw her grandson looking at the meat. 'Though fish like them you caught, what was swimmin' in the briny an hour ago, are a rare treat an' all,' she ended hastily.

Paddy carried his catch over to the sink and began to clean and gut them. 'Shall you eat the fish now, Gran, and save the mutton for tomorrow?' he asked tactfully. 'Fish is best served fresh.'

'No, its all right, I'll wrap the fish in cabbage leaves and stick them on the cold slab; they'll keep fine there until tomorrer,' Gran said, continuing to slice mutton on to the plates. 'The spuds is almost cooked and there's a grand big cabbage steaming on the back of the fire, so the King ain't the only one to be havin' a coronation feast.' She jerked her thumb at the door. 'Go and tell your Aunt Dolly we's about to eat. She's rare fond of a bit of mutton, though she'll have to cut it up terrible small to get it down, her not likin' the new teeth they made for her up at the Brougham clinic. They cost her a pretty penny an' all.'

'What about me mam?' Paddy asked, turning back as he reached the door. 'Aren't we waitin' for her?'

Gran, now draining the potatoes over the low

stone sink, shook her head. 'You know what your mam is,' she said resignedly. 'She'll be goin' up and down the Scotty, poppin' into all the pubs, tryin' to get a bit of work. If she don't get an offer she'll be that down, she'll mebbe take a drink or two to cheer her up, and if she does get a job she'll take another drink or two to celebrate. I doubt she'll be home before closing time.'

Paddy, who knew very well how his mother would behave when either depressed or elated, nodded and went through to give a bang on Aunt Dolly's door. 'Grub up, Aunty Dot,' he shouted cheerfully. 'Me mam's brought in a leg o' mutton.' There was an answering squeak from within the room and presently Aunt Dolly emerged and made a beeline for her place at table. She was a tiny, mouselike woman, bent into a 'C' by rheumatism, so that Paddy often thought that the heavy crucifix which hung on the rosary round her neck might easily trip her up. But despite her disabilities she liked her food. She watched keenly as Gran served potatoes and cabbage, then glanced round the room. 'Where's the gal?' she demanded. 'Ain't she home yet?'

'No, not yet, Aunty Dolly,' Paddy said, since his gran was still serving the food. 'She's after a new job, Gran says.'

Aunt Dolly gave a sniff and delved into the pocket of her shabby black skirt, producing a gleaming set of dentures, which she scrunched into her mouth before beginning to tackle the meal. 'She'll turn up again, like a bad penny,' she mumbled through a mouthful of potato. 'She's no better than she should be, your mam.'

'Mam's all right,' Paddy said defensively, beginning to eat his own food. The mutton was delicious. 'She has to earn for all of us, Aunt Dolly, or we'd likely starve.'

'Aye, but she thieved this 'ere mutton an' well you know it,' Aunt Dolly said. 'She were never taught right from wrong. She was spoilt rotten as a kid.'

Gran, beginning to eat her own meal, shot her older sister an accusing look. 'If you're so high and mighty, Dolly Pringle, you'd best not eat the mutton,' she said. 'Otherwise the sin's on you as much as on our Suzie.'

It was the right thing to say. Dolly gave her sister a malevolent glare, but she continued to eat the mutton, and presently Paddy told the old ladies about his day on the beach with the other kids and about Philip's wonderful lunch basket. This turned the talk away from morality and mutton into safer channels, and by the time the meal was finished all three were in good charity with one another, and Aunt Dolly washed the dishes and sang hymns as she did so, always a sign that she was happy with life.

Suzie had still not returned from her job search by the time Paddy went to bed but this did not worry her son in the slightest. If Mam had got bar work she would not return anyway until after closing time for she would be required to clean down, wash glasses and make all respectable for the next day. But, Paddy thought drowsily to himself as he curled up under his ragged blanket, Mam being out late was a good sign; it meant she had almost certainly got work of some description. Money therefore would continue to enter the Keagan house for a while longer at least.

On this happy thought, Paddy slept.

Chapter Three

Amy was standing in front of the sink, scrubbing potatoes, when the back door burst open and Albert, lugging a heavy shopping basket, entered the room. He went over to the table and piled the contents of the basket upon it, giving vent to a relieved whistle as he put his burden down. 'Phew! Them's heavy,' he said, as Amy turned away from the sink to grin at him. 'Me arms is as long as a gorilla's. How come the older I am the heavier the shopping gets? Do you think it's 'cos we eats more as we get older, queen?'

'Well, you bleedin' well eat more, I can vouch for that,' Amy said. 'I never knew how hard our Mary worked till she left school and went into service.' Mary had gone to what their mother had described as 'a good family', who lived in Manchester but had had connections with Seaforth and so had advertised for members of staff locally. 'Now that I'm doing what she used to do I'm fair wore out, honest to God I am. You don't know you're born, our Albert. You want to give our mam a hand with the fish stall, or go from door to door with bags of shrimps, before you moan about a few messages.'

'That's women's work,' Albert pointed out, throwing himself on to one of the hard kitchen chairs and reaching into a bag from which he produced a large purple plum. He saw Amy looking at him and hastily bit into the fruit. 'It's all right, Mr Evans give it me, seeing as I bought up half the bleedin' shop,' he said, holding out the remains of the fruit to his sister. 'Halves is fair, though, wouldn't you say?'

'Thanks, Albert.' Amy bit gratefully into the sweet flesh. He wasn't a bad boy, she concluded. It wasn't his fault that Mammy worked her so hard and seemed to expect more of her than she ever had of Mary. The truth was, Amy knew, that Isobel had grown used to Amy's habit of doing a bunk whenever the opportunity occurred, almost always when work was in the offing. Consequently she worked Amy twice as hard, in the certain knowledge that Amy would do her best to get out of at least half the tasks she was set. What Isobel did not appear to realise was that, with Mary gone, there was no one else to do the work. If Amy only delivered half the shrimps she was given to sell, then only half the money would arrive home when evening came and since Mary was no longer able to finish off the selling for her sister, Amy's slackness would be immediately discovered – and punished.

Albert, on the other hand, was still treated as someone who would one day have to earn his own living at that toughest of all trades, inshore fishing. Therefore, as with her other sons, Isobel seemed to think that his childhood should be relatively untrammelled except, of course, when he went to sea with his father to help with the fishing, which he did from time to time.

Amy finished the plum and threw the stone into the rubbish pail under the sink. Then she went over to the table and began to unpack the shopping, since Albert, with his feet up on another chair, was reading an elderly copy of the *Echo*, which had been wrapped round a couple of fine cabbages, and seemed to have no intention of finishing the work.

'Do you know what we were doing a year ago today?' she asked, carrying some of the groceries over to the pantry. It wasn't a proper pantry, it was a cupboard which was floored and shelved with slabs of slate, and because the outer wall had a northern aspect it was the easiest part of the kitchen to keep cold. 'Or can't you remember that far back, puddin' head?'

'A year ago today?' Albert said vaguely, not looking up from the paper. 'How the devil should I know? Trust a bleedin' girl to ask a bleedin' silly question like that!'

'It's not a stupid question at all,' Amy protested indignantly. She carried the last of the shopping into the pantry and slammed the door shut, turning back to Albert. 'I called you puddin' head but I should think even a puddin' has more brains than you,' she went on derisively. 'What's the date, you stupid clunch?'

'Dunno. This is an old newspaper.' Albert grinned at his own wit. 'I think it's yesterday's, or tomorrer's, I ain't sure which.'

Amy heaved a deep, dramatic sigh and returned to the sink. 'It's the ninth of bloody August,' she said over her shoulder. 'Doesn't that mean anything to you, puddin' head?'

By way of answer, a plum stone whizzed passed her ear and disappeared through the open kitchen window. 'I knew all the time, eejit,' Albert said breezily – and untruthfully, Amy guessed. 'It were the coronation, o' course, and we went fishin' on the shore wi' Philip and Paddy. You and Mary come along too, as I remember. Eh, we had a grand day! Us fellers got a grosh of fish.' He laughed raucously.

'And you gals got soaked to the skin and sent to bed early, as I recall.'

'It was a lovely day.' Amy ignored the slur on her good name. She distinctly remembered hurrying up the stairs and changing her clothing before her mother had had a chance to comment upon the state of her. Supper, she recalled, had been liver and onions, followed by marmalade pudding; a feast which had been eaten in the King's and Queen's honour. But it was no good reminding Albert of that; he'd likely say she'd made it up. 'Do you remember, Albert, how the sun shone and there wasn't a cloud in the sky? The King had a grand day for his crowning, Mam said, and the pictures were prime. I know the King's children aren't kids any more, but they all looked pretty happy. Well, it must be a bit of all right to have a king and queen for your mam and dad, wouldn't you say?'

'Not bad,' Albert said. He leaned back in his chair so that it stood on its hind legs, like a rearing horse, then lifted up his feet so that the chair crashed to the ground once more. 'What's for supper, eh?'

'Belly on legs,' Amy muttered. 'We're having white fish, boiled spuds – I've just finished scrubbing them, I'll put them over the fire presently – and some of those carrots you got from Mr Evans. Mam's upstairs; when she's ready I'll go up and change.' She looked down at her fish-stained apron and the skirt, draggly from pushing the handcart through the dust of the warm August day. 'I don't envy Mary being in service, doing someone else's housework and so on all day, but it must be grand not to smell of fish. Coming home, a feller shouted out as he passed me, "Two penn'orth o' cod, miss – and go easy on the bluebottles." I could have died it was so

67

humiliating. Why, even when I'm working on the market stall and could afford a tramride home I usually walk, on account of the pong. It's awful when folk move away from you on the tram, or young women give up their seats just to get away from the smell.'

'I don't see why it bothers you.' Albert returned to his perusal of the paper. 'After all, it ain't as though you can smell it yourself ... and when you wash it goes.'

'Ye-es, but I hate people shouting at me in the street. I don't know how our Mary stood it, honest to God I don't.'

'She never helped Mam wi' the gutting,' Albert said briefly. 'She just sold the stuff. But I'm sure I remember her saying there was a sink at the fish market and she sluiced herself down there before she came home. And didn't she keep a fresh apron there, too? I suppose that's how she got rid of the pong.'

'Did she? Well, I'll ask Mam if I can do the same, then.' Amy brightened. She had put the cleaned potatoes into a large pot and now staggered with it over to the fire. As she passed Albert she kicked him neatly on the ankle. 'Cor, this bloody thing weighs a ton; if you were a real gentleman, Albert Logan, you'd offer to lug it across for me. Fellers are meant to help ladies with the heavy work.'

'If you were a lady I might,' Albert said, prudently removing himself out of Amy's range, however. 'Where *is* Mam anyroad? She's usually in here by now, getting the supper ready.'

'Oh, she's having a bit of a lie-down,' Amy informed him. 'I dare say it's the heat, but she's ever so tired. And we didn't do as well as we might have,

what with Dad bringing back a record catch yesterday. We sold all the shrimps, mind; the ones left
over from the door-to-door went like hot cakes on
the stall. But we had some plaice left over and a few
haddock as well, and you know Mam. She won't put
them on ice for tomorrow; she says our reputation is
for fresh fish and she won't jeop ... jeopa ... oh,
well, she won't put it at risk by using ice.'

'She's right,' Albert said authoritatively. He might
not work on the stall nor sell shrimps door to door,
but he did go out in the fishing boat, *Mersey Maid*,
and knew how important it was to bring the catch in
and sell it as soon as possible. 'Well, since I've done
the messages, I might as well take the scraps round
to the Keagans and then go and see if Dad wants any
cleaning up done. How long to supper, our Amy?'

'Say half an hour.' Amy had glanced up at the big
clock over the mantel. 'I'm going to take a cuppa up
to our mam. It's not often she has a lie-down and I
thought she looked downright peaked by the time
we'd walked home. She could have caught the tram,'
she added, 'but it was that hot she said she'd rather
walk.'

'Half an hour it is, then,' Albert said, crossing the
kitchen and throwing open the back door. 'And
don't you be late, because us fellers'll be rare hungry
by then.'

Amy snorted. She was busy filling one of the
enamel mugs with tea and, after a moment's
thought, added a spoonful of sugar. Isobel only took
sugar in her tea when she was feeling what she
usually described as 'a bit cagged, like', but Amy
knew she was not the only person to notice her
mother's unusual pallor that day. Mrs O'Brien, who
was a regular customer, and Mrs Kelly, who usually

visited the market late in order to buy as cheaply as possible for her large family, had both remarked that Mrs Logan looked poorly and ought to rest more, now she'd a daughter earning and another helping out.

Rather to Amy's surprise, her mother had seemed more embarrassed than pleased by the attention and interest in her health. She had said gruffly that she was just tired, that it took some getting used to having Mary gone, that the heat got her down. And on the walk home, when Amy had tried to ask her mother what was the matter, she had been quite short. 'I said, didn't I?' she had asked crossly, putting a hand up to her head as though it ached, then changing the action to push back the fringe of grey-blonde hair which curled crisply across her forehead. 'I'm just pulled by the heat, nothing more.'

But now, when Amy entered her bedroom with the mug of tea and a cut off the fruit cake which she kept in a tin in the pantry, Isobel looked up and actually smiled at the sight of the tea and the round tin plate with the slice of cake on it. 'Well, isn't this nice?' She hauled herself upright so that she was propped against her pillows. 'My daughter's looking after me – aren't I the lucky one? I thought Mary was the best of daughters, but you're running her close, young Amy. Before I know it you'll be as useful as our Mary was.'

The somewhat sideways compliment made Amy blush with pleasure, however, for it was a sign that she and her mother were getting on better. Before Mary started work, Amy had received plenty of slaps and very few kisses from her strict and strait-laced mother, but now it appeared that there was a softening and this thrilled Amy. Everyone wants to be liked, she told herself, putting the cake down on her mother's knees and holding out the mug of tea. If Mam is going to try to like me the way she likes Mary, then I'll work my fingers to the bone for her, so I will. It's just when she criticises and finds fault no matter how hard I try that I get to think I can't do right, so I'll stop making the effort. She handed her mother the mug of tea and perched on the side of the bed. 'I'm glad you think I'm a bit useful, Mam,' she said earnestly as her mother took the first sip from the mug. 'I do try – but I'm not naturally good, neither can I cook and clean like our Mary.'

'I'll teach you,' her mother promised. She blew on the tea, then looked out of the small window, avoiding her daughter's eye. Amy saw that Isobel was in her nightgown and felt the first stab of genuine fear. She must be really ill; she had said she was going to lie down for a few minutes while the meal cooked, not that she intended to go to bed. No one in the Logan family went to bed during the day unless they were very ill indeed; even the kids tended to be rousted out after the first flush of some childish ailment – measles, chickenpox, a septic sore throat – had run its course. 'Umm . . . Amy, I've got something to tell you.'

Amy's heart gave a lurch. Mam was going to tell her that she was really bad, perhaps dying. Mothers did die. Aggie French's mam had died last year and now the family was ruled by an old and irritable grandmother, who spent most of her time telling the children that it wasn't fair or right that she should be bringing up a young family at her time of life. Aggie was Amy's age but the rest of the French kids were all younger; Aggie said she couldn't wait to get a job and leave home, so her gran wouldn't be able to nag and whine at her so much.

However, it wouldn't do to let her mother know what she was thinking. 'Oh . . . I've got the supper on the go, Mam,' she said, gabbling a little. 'I've done the spuds, and I've gutted the fish and it's all ready to go in the pan. And Albert's done the messages, he's brought back some good, long carrots and . . .'

'I don't know whether you've noticed owt, Amy.' Isobel's voice rose resolutely above her daughter's. 'I should have told you some time back – Mary knows – but somehow I couldn't bring myself . . . a woman my age . . . I hate to think what young folk like that Suzie Keagan will say . . . and you and me's not known each other all that well, queen, for all you're my youngest child. But I said to your father that it wasn't fair . . . I'll be asking more of you even than I did of Mary, especially when I get near my time.' She looked at Amy with the air of one who has told all and now expects a reaction.

Amy stared straight back. What on earth did her mother mean? Mary knew? And her dad must know too, but he had been more than usually cheerful lately, not at all like a man who has received bad tidings, who has a sick woman on his hands. But her mother was sipping tea again, even taking a nibble of cake, looking at her with a little half-smile. It was no use, she would have to say she didn't understand or the most awful complications would result. 'What d'you mean, Mam? Are . . . are you ill? Is that why you've put your nightdress on in the daytime?'

'Oh. Well, I'm not ill, but I'm old for . . . women of my age don't . . . I mean, you're my youngest child and you're all of eleven years old . . .'

'You aren't old, Mam,' Amy said quickly. 'My dad's older than you and so's heaps of the women in the St John's fish market. What d'you *mean*?'

Isobel stopped glancing out of the window, down at her hands, around at the whitewashed walls, in fact, at everything but Amy. She then looked squarely into Amy's eyes. 'Oh, chuck, I'm expecting a . . . a baby,' she said and, to Amy's astonishment, tears came into her mother's eyes. 'I've not told the boys yet, nor my friends, but as I said, I told Mary and . . . and I thought you ought to know. As I get – well – get bigger, I shan't be able to bend so easily, nor I won't be as quick with the gutting and filleting, so you'll be doing all sorts and if you don't know, don't understand . . .'

'Oh, Mam, I'm that relieved, I thought you must be dying when you looked so pale and chucked up your breakfast the other morning,' Amy said. 'And what's wrong with having another baby, anyway? I'd be right glad to have a little brother or sister, even if it does mean a bit more work. I've often envied Ruth, having all those young 'uns about the place. When will it come, Mam? Will it be soon? When will you stop working?'

Isobel laughed. She looked relieved, Amy thought, as if she had been dreading telling her daughter of the expected arrival, though why she should feel like that Amy had no idea. A baby is a delightful thing, Amy told herself, taking the empty mug from her mother's grasp and watching as Isobel finished off the last crumbs of cake.

'I bet Dad's pleased as pleased can be,' she said and was rewarded by the look of delight that crossed her mother's face. 'Do you want a girl, Mam? You wouldn't want another boy, surely?'

'It doesn't matter whether it's a boy or a girl, so long as it's healthy,' Isobel told her. 'Your dad's going to tell the boys, now I've broken the news to yourself. But if you like, queen, you can tell Albert, seeing as how he'll be wondering what we've been talking about up here. Maybe he'll wonder what I'm doing in bed, too,' she added.

Amy, halfway to the door, stopped for a moment to smile back at her mother. 'You know what today is, don't you, Mam? The King and Queen were crowned a year ago today. So if it's a boy you could call it Edward, and if it's a girl . . .'

'. . . Alexandra.' Isobel returned the smile. 'What a mouthful for a little girl, though, queen. Maybe I'd best stick to the ordinary names and leave the long ones for royalty. D'you know, I'm feeling more rested already? If you give me a shout when the food is on the table I think I'll join you downstairs. I won't start interfering with what you've done, but I might give you a hand with the washing up. And we'll plan the meals for tomorrow between us, shall we?'

Amy, agreeing, went downstairs with a full heart. She felt that an understanding was growing between herself and her mother, perhaps for the first time in her life. She had always thought it would be a grand thing to be friends with your mam, as Mary had been and indeed still was, and now it looked as though she, too, was beginning to share in their friendship. Suddenly the hard work at the fish market and the slog of door-to-door selling no longer seemed such a weary way to spend her spare time. Summer holidays from school might never be the same again, but to be friends with her mam would make losing the freedom of the streets and shore almost worthwhile. Besides, it was the first real sign that she was growing up, becoming a woman. What was more, mam had said she would need a deal of help when the baby came and this might well mean she would keep Amy by her until the child was four or five. She would be unable to cope with all the housework, the preparing and selling of the shrimps, and with a young child without help from someone. Why should it not be Amy? Amy, who had always loathed the idea of going into service, found she was delighted at the thought of being a real help to her mother. She had no idea whether she would be paid a wage for such work, but found this scarcely seemed to matter. Mam will do right by me, she told herself, descending the narrow stairs. And though three months earlier she would have doubted this statement, she now realised it was true. Isobel was as fond of the new, grown-up Amy as she was of Mary.

Amy entered the kitchen feeling that her cup of happiness was full and beamed across at Albert, who was struggling to pull the heavy pan of potatoes to the side of the fire. He looked up as she entered the room and cursed as hot water splashed out of the pan, narrowly missing his feet. 'Where the hell have you been?' he enquired caustically. 'These bloody spuds have boiled over twice already and I've near broke me arms heavin' them off the fire. What was you doin', for God's sake? You've been gone *hours*, Amy Logan!'

Amy went over to the fire and pushed Albert to one side so that she might move the pan without scalding either of them. 'I've been talking to Mam,' she said importantly. 'She's been telling me we're going to have a new baby, what about that, eh?'

Albert stared at her, round-eyed. 'A *baby*?' he said, his very tone incredulous. 'She can't be havin' a baby, queen, women her age is grannies, not mams. Why, our Edmund's twenty-one.' Edmund was working the trawlers now and sailing from Fleetwood, and what was more, was courting a local girl whom Isobel had disliked on sight. Consequently they saw very little of him, though Bill, Amy thought, visited his elder son from time to time.

'It doesn't matter how old you are, if you're a woman,' Amy said knowingly. 'Anyhow, our mam isn't old and she *is* having a baby, she told me so this minute, so that's one in the eye for you, Albert Logan.'

'Well, I think that's disgustin',' Albert said morosely, slouching across the kitchen and throwing himself into his chair once more. He picked up the paper and flung it down again with a groan. 'What'll I tell me pals? Damn it, I'm thirteen goin' on fourteen – I'll be in work soon. The fellers will laugh their heads off, I'm tellin' you.'

'Well, none of my friends will laugh,' Amy said stoutly. 'Women don't laugh about babies, they like them. And don't you go telling our mam that you aren't thrilled, because she'll be mortally upset if you do. She . . . she said something about being too old herself, so the last thing she'll want is to hear you talking such rubbish. Now, shift yourself, Albert, and give me a hand for once. Mam's coming down when the grub's on the table and I know Dad would say we've all got to show her a cheerful face. So start grinning and stop scowling or I'll give you a clack. And when I dish up I'll make sure you get the smallest plateful, so there!'

Albert got to his feet and went over to the dresser.

He pulled open the drawer which contained their meagre supply of cutlery and selected a handful, then reached up for the enamel plates. 'Right you are, I hear you' – to lay the table – 'but it'll mean a deal of work for you and me, chuck. Babies always does. Still an' all, it's better than if Mam had been really ill. I were beginnin' to wonder, to tell you the truth.'

Amy, sliding the floured fillets into the frying pan, nodded her head in violent agreement. 'Aye, you're right there,' she admitted. 'I was really worried, Albert, and that's the truth.' The fat in the pan started to spit as it heated up and she flinched away from the flying droplets. 'Gawd, these perishin' dabs are fighting back! I never knew fish could be so fierce.'

'You oughter try catchin' them, heavin' the net up when it's loaded with slippery, snappin' critters from the deep,' Albert said with relish. 'That's man's work if you like, gal. Fancy moanin' about fryin' a few fillets.'

'Then you do it, if you're so clever,' Amy said briskly. She tilted her head as her ears caught the sound of the back gate clicking open. 'Hey up, here comes Dad and the boys. We'd best get a move on, Albert, or we won't have the food on the table by the time they've washed up.'

Amy woke and lay for a moment staring into the dark and wondering what had roused her. She glanced towards the window but could tell that it was not yet morning by the grey glimmer of light showing round the curtains. In fact, from the heavy feeling of her head and limbs it was probably no more than one or two o'clock. She had been lying on her side, but now she rolled on to her back and listened. Nothing. No one talking or moving in the house, no traffic passing by in the street below. Yet something must have woken her. The scratch of a mouse as it emerged from beneath the skirting board? A sparrow's sleepy chirrup as a cat passed by? Sometimes she was woken when the weather was rough by the sound of waves crashing on the shore, but it was a calm, still night in mid-February. Nothing, in short, should've brought her so annoyingly wide awake, so she had best curl down under the blanket again and try to recapture some sleep.

She obeyed her own instructions and closed her eyes firmly, curling her left hand under the pillow while her right held on to several strands of hair. This was how she always slept, but tonight the familiar magic did not work and she remained awake.

She had just decided that she had better begin to count sheep when she heard the mewing. It wasn't loud or particularly close, she thought, but somewhere out in the cold dark, a cat was in trouble. The Logan family had never owned a cat, or indeed any other pet; Mam and Dad said they had their work cut out to feed the family without stretching their meagre resources to cover animals as well. But Amy knew that stray cats did hang around the premises and that Bill sometimes fed them odd scraps of leftover fish. If one of those stray cats had got shut into the wash-house there would be all sorts of trouble. For a start, it might devour and generally mess up a quantity of the fish that would be sent to the fish market the following day, or – horror of horrors – it might fall into the copper, which her father usually kept full of water, and drown itself.

On that thought Amy jumped out of bed. One of the stray cats she had seen in the yard was little more than a kitten; she doubted that it would survive long if it did fall into the copper, which was slippery from the shrimps cooked in it and probably very attractive to feline appetites. She slung her shawl round her shoulders but did not bother with her boots. It took ages to lace them in daylight, heaven knew, so what it would be like in the dark she could not bear to contemplate. Instead, she padded across the room, out on to the tiny landing and began to descend the stairs.

Halfway down the flight, however, the mewing sound came again and this time she was sure it had come from behind her. Immediately, before she had time to think, she had whipped round, run up the stairs again and hurled herself at her parents' door. The baby! The baby must have come, although she had heard no sound of a nurse arriving. She no longer believed in the fairy tale of the stork, flapping in through the window and leaving the baby on the fortunate mother's bed, because Ruth had long ago disabused her of this fanciful notion. But she still had very little idea of how a baby actually arrived and thought, in her innocence, that its journey from the parental tummy into the light of day was a quick and simple matter. She knew the nurse would come but had very little idea why this was necessary and assumed, vaguely, that it was another of the adult mysteries into which her parents were so reluctant to admit her.

She shot the door open, bounded into the room and stopped short, both hands flying to her mouth.

Her mother lay on the bed, scarlet-faced and sweating profusely, with her legs drawn up and the covers pushed down to her waist. The nurse, a local woman by the name of Mrs Scott, was sitting in a chair by the bed. She had obviously been chatting to her patient but stopped suddenly at Amy's abrupt arrival.

'Oh! Oh, I'm sorry,' Amy stammered, feeling the hot blood rush to her cheeks. 'I . . . I thought I heard a baby cry. I thought it'd come already and I wanted to help.' She glanced nervously from face to face. 'Where's my dad? Is there anything I can do?'

At the sound of her voice Isobel had heaved the covers up over her stomach and breasts, and now she gave what Amy imagined was meant to be a reassuring smile. 'It's all right, queen,' she said huskily. 'The baby won't be here for a while yet, but as soon as it arrives, nurse here will let you know. As for your dad, he's downstairs making Mrs Scott and me a cup of tea. If you'd like to go down and give him a hand, I'm sure he'd be grateful. Unless you think you might be able to go back to sleep?'

'I'll go and give Dad a hand.' Amy, ignored the last question as not worthy of comment. How could she possibly sleep when such momentous events were taking place? Albert, Gus and Charlie, of course, would be sleeping straight through all the excitement, but that was fellers for you. No soul, Amy thought disgustedly, assuring her mother that she would bring her and Mrs Scott a cup of tea as soon as it had brewed.

Isobel was beginning to thank her when there was a movement beneath the sheet and her face became contorted with pain. She bent forward and grasped her own knees with both hands, and Amy left the room, hastily closing the door behind her. She realised that the mewing noise she had heard must have been small cries of pain and found she had no desire whatever to see her mother suffer. Instead, she decided to go down to the kitchen and do whatever her father bade her, so that the time would pass quickly until the baby's birth.

The baby was born almost forty-eight hours later, after what the nurse described as a really difficult labour, and was a tiny but perfect girl, with lint-white hair and big, dreamy blue eyes. Amy saw her for the first time before breakfast, only a few hours after her birth, and was delighted with her, though she thought her mother looked drained and exhausted, and quite twenty years older than she really was. Despite her hopes, the baby had not been called Alexandra but was to rejoice in the name of Jane. And she isn't a plain Jane, Amy thought to herself, timidly stroking the baby's cheek. Still, it's Mam's choice when you come down to it. Liverpool folk always add a bit to a short little name and chop off a bit from a long one, so if she had been named Alexandra she would have ended up being called Allie, which isn't all that special.

Mary had come home as soon as their father had got a message to her telling her that Isobel was in labour. She had been a tower of strength both to Amy and to their mother, and seemed to know by instinct what best to do for the baby. Like Amy, she was disappointed by the plain name Isobel had chosen and had managed to persuade her mother to give the child a second name. She and Amy put their heads together and it was finally agreed that their new little sister would be christened Jane Rebecca when the time was ripe.

To Amy's disappointment, Mary was only able to stay for two days, helping to look after her mother and the baby, but at the end of that time she had to return to the family who employed her. They lived at too great a distance from Seaforth to allow Mary to spend her day off with them, so having her home for two whole days was a real treat. The two girls gossiped endlessly during the day while they were working, for Amy was being kept off school while her mother was still in childbed, and at night, lying close together in the bed they had shared for so many years, Mary told Amy all about life as a housemaid. She had done her best to explain how she felt. 'I thought I'd hate being in service and so I did at first,' she told her sister. 'But it's a bit like school – ordered, sensible, so you know just what you should be doing all the time. You brush and polish, wait on the family, lay tables, clear away. You don't have to cook your own meals, answer doors, clean fish, or sell shrimps, because your tasks are laid down and once they're done you're free. It's wonderful to have time to yourself, your own little room, and friends who work beside you. And best of all, no smell of fish, no icy hands and feet, no . . . no responsibility for anything but your own work and your own pleasure. So I wouldn't want to leave Manchester to come back to . . . to *this*.' Her gesture encompassed the little house, the family – their entire life Amy thought, rather dismayed. Mary had indeed changed, grown away from them.

It did not sound much fun to Amy, but Mary clearly enjoyed the life. She had made a great many friends, both among the staff at the Cottlestones' house and the neighbours, and was much in demand as a dancing partner when she and her friends had an evening off. She seemed to be doing well in her work, too. She was a good seamstress, clever with her needle, and actually enjoyed polishing the silver until it shone like a mirror, and dusting in every nook and cranny until the rooms she had been set to look after were spotless. She did not seem to miss the small house in Seafield Grove, nor to hanker after the beach and the park where the girls had spent what little time off they had had. Mary was expected to serve the family wholeheartedly, to attend church with them on a Sunday and to obey the wishes of the upper servants who could, and did, order her about. She told Amy that when she wrote a letter home she couldn't even take it down the road to the nearest postbox without getting permission from one of the upper servants to leave the estate house. This would have irked Amy terribly, but the placid and sweet-tempered Mary actually seemed to prefer what she termed 'an ordered existence' to the rather more haphazard life of the family in Seafield Grove.

'But you're enjoying helping with the baby and with our mam,' Amy pointed out, as she and Mary prepared for bed one night, 'and you seem to like cooking and cleaning up after the boys well enough. How will you feel, Mary, when you have to go back to being bossed around all the time? Won't you miss being able to walk down to the shore when you want to? And visiting your pals now and then?'

'It's grand being home all right,' Mary agreed, 'but how often have I had a moment to myself after I got back, eh, queen? And although I've met a pal or two when I've been doing the messages, I've never had time to stop for a jangle. In fact, there's not a lot of time for anything, the way we live. At the Cottlestone house things are more ordered, more tidy, like. When you're free you really are free. No one asks you to run messages or clean fish or bake a pie. But at home there's only us to do everything. Can you understand that?'

'Ye-es, I know what you mean,' Amy said grudgingly, after some thought, 'but I'd still rather have my life than yours, Mary. It's because I'm untidy by nature and you're the opposite. What about marrying, though? You'd like to do that one day, wouldn't you?'

'I might,' Mary said guardedly. 'And then again I might not; I do have a particular friend, but folk don't get married when they are barely fifteen, chuck. I wouldn't want to be a housemaid for the rest of my life, but marriage changes everything. What about you, Amy? I know you're still in school, though it's a bit off and on, isn't it? Mam was saying what a help you'd been to her, and that must mean you're missing school every now and then I suppose. And of course, if you're missing school you'll miss playing out as well. So your freedom isn't what it was, wouldn't you say?'

'Yes, I've been missing school on a Friday,' Amy acknowledged. 'But the rest of the week Mam manages pretty well. I help after school, of course, and I do miss seeing my pals in the long summer evenings, but I'm getting on ever so much better with our mam, Mary. Now you aren't here, she relies on me, you see, and I like that. I never thought I would, but I do. Dad says it's all part of growing up and I dare say he's right. And Mam says once she's up and about she'll be able to do a good deal more. She'll take the baby with her when she goes door-to-door selling.'

Mary pulled a face. 'Well, it might work out,' she said thoughtfully. 'But it'll come hard on you, Amy. Mam's never expected the boys to do anything she thinks of as woman's work and there's a deal of that in this house, with potting the shrimps and all. It'd be fairer on you if Mam were to pay a woman to come in and give a hand three or four times a week. After all, if you go on sagging off school there'll be trouble.'

Amy sighed. 'I dare say you're right.' She climbed into bed. 'I might as well blow the candle out; we can talk just as well in the dark.' She suited action to words and cuddled down. It was so nice to feel Mary's familiar warmth beside her in the bed. It was odd, she thought, how she had not really missed Mary until she returned home; only now did she recognise the gap that the loss of her sister's company had left in her life. Mary was due to return to the Cottlestones next morning and Amy knew she would miss her terribly. But at least I'll know she's truly happy being a housemaid and living away from home, she told herself drowsily, as sleep began to claim her. We would neither of us want the other's life, as we're very different people. It's a good thing that Mary is the older, though. Imagine how awful it would've been if I'd ended up in service and Mary had had to stay at home. On this horrid thought she fell asleep.

Two days after Mary and Amy had kissed each other goodbye under the clock on Lime Street Station Isobel woke, feeling hot and feverish, and aching in every limb. Bill roused Amy and told her to give an eye to the baby and to fetch her mother a cup of tea. He was off to have a word with Mrs Scott. The old woman still came in twice each day and would continue to do so until Jane Rebecca was three weeks old, but she had told Bill to call her at once if either his wife or the baby ailed. 'Your missus ain't exactly a chicken,' she had said bluntly. 'Better to be safe than sorry.'

Amy got out of bed, dragged her jumper over her nightdress and padded down the stairs to the kitchen. The room was empty, apart from the baby in her cradle – Bill must have brought her down before he had woken his daughter. A glance at the back door showed Albert's cap and coat were missing, so Amy guessed that her brother had been sent to fetch Mrs Scott, while Bill himself had gone back upstairs to Isobel. Amy shivered a little, for the kitchen was chilly, but she knew it would soon warm up once she had stirred up the fire, which had sunk to a bed of ashes with only a red glow in its centre to show that it had not done the dirty on her and gone out.

Amy got the poker, stirred up the fire, riddled the ashes and then put fresh fuel on to the embers. In a moment it was blazing and quite hot enough for Amy to pull the kettle over the flame. While she waited for it to boil she got the loaf from the bread bin and cut a couple of thick slices. It was nowhere near breakfast time, but she found she was hungry and guessed that Albert, when he returned from his errand, would be hungry, too. She would toast the bread in front of the fire while waiting for the kettle, then she and her brother could have a snack as soon as he came back with the midwife.

The toast was made and the tea poured when the

back door opened to admit Mrs Scott, with Albert close on her heels. 'Mornin', young 'un,' Mrs Scott said breezily. 'My, that toast smells good. I'm that clemmed I swear I could eat a horse.'

Silently Amy handed her a round of buttered toast and watched, enviously, as the older woman devoured it in three enormous bites. Then, without being asked, she handed one of the mugs of tea over, but Mrs Scott, though she gazed at it wistfully, shook her neat grey head. 'Not now, chuck,' she said, heading for the stairs. 'Just you bring up an extry cup when you bring your mam's. I wouldn't let a patient wait above stairs whiles I drank tea in the kitchen.'

'She's norra bad old stick,' Albert remarked, taking the remaining slice of toast and beginning to eat. 'Some of them old women what call themselves nurses drink gin and leave your mam to gerron with it, the fellers at school say. Was that your bit of toast, gal? If so, I'll make you another while you take up the tea.'

But in fact, Amy did not get a chance to take the tea to the bedroom. Halfway up the stairs, carefully balancing two mugs of well-sugared tea, she met Mrs Scott thundering down. 'Thanks, chuck, I'll take that,' Mrs Scott said briskly. 'But I want you to go straight downstairs and tell young Albert to fetch Doctor Payne. Tell Albert to say Mrs Scott says as it's urgent and he's to come right away, if he pleases.'

Amy, thoroughly frightened, pushed the mugs of tea into the nurse's hands and fled down the stairs again, entering the kitchen with the message already on her lips. Albert was sitting in front of the fire with a round of bread on a stick held out to the flames, but to do him credit, he wasted no more time than

Amy had. 'Take this,' he said brusquely, thrusting the stick into her hands and grabbing his coat and cap. He jammed the cap down over his unbrushed hair and headed for the back door, saying over his shoulder, 'Where's me dad? What's happenin' up there?'

'I dunno,' Amy said with equal brevity. 'I only got halfway up when I met old Ma Scott coming down. Oh, Albert, do hurry! I think our mam must be awfully bad.'

The rest of that day and all the next were a nightmare, which Amy knew she would remember for the rest of her life. She longed for Mary's comforting presence, but knew better than to suggest her sister might be fetched; things were too desperately bad for that. It would've been a comfort to her had Bill been able to explain what was happening, but on the only occasion when he left Isobel's side for a moment to come downstairs and take a drink of tea he looked so grey and ill that Amy hadn't the heart to cross-question him. 'It's milk fever, only some specially bad sort,' he said in answer to Amy's one timid question. 'She's mortal bad, chuck.' He got to his feet and headed across the kitchen. 'Nurse will be down in a minute,' he added over his shoulder. 'She'll tell you what to do about the baby.'

Mrs Scott did indeed tell Amy what to do about the baby, though it was not welcome advice. 'Is there anyone hereabouts nursin' their own young 'un?' she enquired, busily making a brew of some description in a small pan on the stove. She tutted. 'Why am I asking you when I know better than anyone who's had a baby recently? You tek young Jane Rebecca along to Mrs O'Hara, on Holly Grove, an' ask her to give it suck for you.'

Amy looked doubtful. 'But we hardly know Mrs O'Hara,' she objected. 'Couldn't we make her up a milk feed with conny-onny and water? Lots of women can't feed their own babies, Mam told me. Why, she couldn't feed my big brother, Charlie, when he was born, on account of getting influenza and being right pulled down by it. She said he throve on conny-onny, honest to God, Mrs Scott.'

'We-ell,' Mrs Scott said doubtfully. 'I dare say you're right, chuck. I were thinking your mam might be feedin' her again in a day or two and forgettin' it weren't likely, not with puerperal fever. We'll try the conny-onny, then, see how she takes to it.'

So Amy mixed condensed milk and water in a little jug, warmed it through and then offered the baby a tiny spoonful when next she awoke. Since the baby made no objection to the mixture Mrs Scott advised Amy to find a feeding bottle and teat, and see whether she would accept it. Amy knew where there was an old bottle – she had used it for her doll Betsy – but the rubber teat proved to be perished beyond recall, so Amy wrapped the baby in her shawl, got Albert to tie the shawl securely round her person and set off for the shops. She bought two rubber teats, returned home, and boiled them and the bottle on the stove, meanwhile nursing an increasingly indignant child to her breast, and at last, she was able to offer the baby the milk she was badly in need of. Despite the fact that Jane Rebecca had never before drunk from a bottle, let alone tasted conny-onny, she drank quite half the contents of the bottle, burped immensely and fell deeply asleep.

All this had taken some time, what with changing the baby's napkin and bringing up her wind, but at last she was restored to her cradle and Amy started to worry about her mother once more. The doctor popped in three or four times, looking worried. Mrs Scott appeared and disappeared from the kitchen, and occasionally a neighbour popped in to ask how Mrs Logan did, for Isobel was a popular figure in the neighbourhood. Nevertheless the day dragged, with Amy feeling she was the only person in the house who was completely ignorant of what was happening in the bedroom upstairs. When teatime arrived the doctor came down and bade Amy boil up his instruments, tipping a number of wicked-looking objects into the small pan she offered him. When the water had boiled for five minutes Mrs Scott came down, drained it from the pan and carried it upstairs, telling Amy as she did so in a falsely jovial voice that things were beginning to look up at last. 'Doctor Payne knows what he's doing,' she assured the anxious young people sitting around the kitchen awaiting some news, for by now the older boys had returned from their fishing trip. 'Doctor Payne is going to let out some of the badness, so soon your mam will be right as rain, you just see.'

She disappeared up the staircase and the terrible waiting started once more. Amy could imagine only too well what must be happening in the bedroom upstairs; she had been appalled by the sharpness and number of Dr Payne's instruments, and despite her best endeavours ghastly pictures of those knives and probes entering flesh would keep popping into her mind.

But for a long time nothing whatsoever happened. No one came down and, although Gus tiptoed to the bottom of the stairs and stood, head cocked, listening, when he returned he could only report a soft murmur of voices coming from the bedroom and no sign of either doctor or nurse. In fact, Amy had begun to cut them some sandwiches and the kettle was on for yet more tea when Bill Logan came heavily down the stairs and into the kitchen. He stood in the middle of the room, staring straight in front of him and not appearing to notice any of them until Charlie, as the eldest present, went over and pushed his father gently into a chair.

Charlie was very like his father, tall and broad with soft, dark hair flopping over his forehead and a gentle, patient expression, but now anxiety was creasing his brow into a frown and his voice, when he spoke, was sharper than usual. 'Well, Dad? What's happening to me mam? ... Is she ... is she ...?'

Bill Logan put his elbows on the table and his chin in his hands; for a moment he said nothing, then raised a haggard face and his eyes, full of pain, met those of his son. 'She's gone,' he said huskily, his voice breaking. 'They did all they could, it weren't no one's fault. Doctor Payne told me it were pretty well hopeless right from the start; her temperature went sky high and he couldn't get it down, nohow.'

Albert broke the silence that followed. 'Are you sayin' our mam's *dead*?' he asked. He got to his feet and, leaning across the table, actually seized his father's hands and shook them. 'Is that what you're telling us, Dad? That she's dead?'

For a moment Bill didn't speak. Amy, staring at his bent head, was horrified to see tears trickling down his face. Then he gave a gulp, nodded his head and said, 'That's right, son. I can't believe it meself and that's the truth, but she's gone. Presently, you can go up and see her, I suppose that's best, but . . .'

As his words died away Amy jumped to her feet. 'It isn't true, it can't be true!' she shouted into the sudden silence. 'It's that doctor's fault, he hurt her with those shiny tool things and now . . . and now . . .' She bolted for the back door as a babble of sound broke out behind her and was halfway across the yard when Gus caught up with her. He put his arms round her and gave her a hard hug, then walked her slowly back into the kitchen, one arm still across her shoulders. 'We've got to face it, queen,' he said gently. 'Mam's gone, and because she ain't here no more we'll need to hang together and take care of one another, because that's what she would want. No one can run away from sorrow because it runs faster than any of us can. As for casting blame, that's norra very Christian attitude, is it? Our mam made us go to church because she believed in it, not because it was the thing to do. And don't forget the baby. You'll have to take special care of her now, queen. Be brave, Amy, and help us fellers to help Dad, because Mam would've wanted that, too.'

Mary came home, but she was a very different girl from the one who had shared Amy's bed after Jane Rebecca's birth. She was wide-eyed and white-faced with shock and misery, as they all were, but after the first few days were over it occurred to Amy that her sister was also rebellious. To be sure, she did whatever work was demanded of her, but never willingly or with good grace. February was a bad time for the fishing, but because of a sudden spell of mild weather catches were not as bad as they might have been, so there was fish to sell both in the Great Charlotte Street market and from the handcart. Amy understood her sister's reluctance to start selling fish again, but she saw no reason why Mary should baulk over looking after the baby or cooking the meals.

Fortunately, Mary's reluctance was not as obvious to the rest of the family as it was to Amy. In front of her father and brothers she managed to put on a good face over whatever tasks were to be done, but Amy could read the signs of her sister's reluctance in Mary's tight lips and impatient, jerky movements.

It did not make things easier that Mary refused to tell Amy why she no longer seemed to want to help her family. When questioned, she would only say that she missed her job in Manchester and the friends that she had made there. She also made it plain that she had returned for Mam's funeral and had remained because it was her duty to do so, but she would be off again just as soon as Bill felt he could manage without her. 'I've been earning good money, regular money, and we can't afford to lose my wages,' she told Amy. 'Servants aren't hard to find, so if the Cottlestones replace me I may never get another job as good, let alone one where I'm valued and happy. I'm telling you, Amy, I can't wait to get out of here and back to a place where I'm appreciated.'

'But you're appreciated here,' Amy wailed, thinking how impossible life would be without her sister's help, even if that help was reluctantly given. 'I'm sure the folk in Manchester couldn't need you as much as we do, queen. Why, how could I possibly manage without you? There's baby Becky, and the fish, and the housework, to say nothing of getting the washing done, potting the shrimps . . .' The family had now agreed to call the baby Becky, because Janie was so easily confused with Amy and they were sure Isobel would have agreed.

'I know what you mean,' Mary said with a sigh. The two girls were lying in bed and talking in whispers since baby Becky was asleep in her cradle beside the bed. 'But I've got my own way to make, chuck. I'm going to tell Dad he ought to get a woman in to give you a hand. Even with the pair of us, the work's more than we can manage and it's winter now, with small catches. In the summer, when the nets are full and Dad brings in tons of shrimps to be potted, we'd simply never manage, not if we worked all day and all night, too. I never realised how much Mam did until she died, but now I *know* it's too much for a couple of girls.'

'Ye-es, but Dad doesn't have that sort of money, does he?' Amy asked. Mary opened her mouth to reply, beginning to say that her father would have to find the money somehow, when baby Becky, who had been stirring uneasily for some moments, began to scream and that was the end of that particular attempt, Amy thought, to get Mary to admit she was needed at home.

Because of the spell of mild, unseasonable weather, housekeeping became temporarily easier. Nappies hung on the washing line in the morning were brought in dry and fluffy from the gentle breeze before darkness fell and even the sad business of arranging for Isobel's funeral was conducted beneath blue skies. However, after about ten days the weather reverted to more normal winter conditions of cold and even of snow, though this last rarely laid so close to the sea. But it did mean very much smaller catches. In a way this was a relief. The girls had their work cut out to cope with the baby and what fish there was. Potting shrimps would have been impossible. Bill, who had always been an understanding and sympathetic father, had changed on losing his wife. He grew taciturn, unable to discuss the problems which beset him, because he had always relied on Isobel to arrange the shore side of the fishing. It speedily became apparent that he knew little of the preparation and potting of shrimps, save that they had to be shelled first and, truth to tell, he knew remarkably little about sales. Isobel had had her regular contacts at the fish market and Amy had realised some time earlier that her mother had different arrangements with almost every customer.

The trouble was that Amy did not know what these arrangements were and, when questioned, neither did Mary. Bill, when appealed to, merely said that it was now the girls' job to do such deals, which left his daughters in an unenviable position. To overcharge a valued customer or to undercharge one who would boast of it could do their business irreparable harm so, since Mary seemed to prefer staying at home and keeping house to dealing with the fish, Amy decided to cast herself on the mercy of Mrs O'Leary, but first she must sell the good catch of shrimps, which Bill had brought triumphantly home earlier that day.

He had gone out again, but had not taken Albert with him, so Albert had gone down to the shore to fetch driftwood and, while Amy was pulling on her only decent pair of boots, he came in with his arms full of salt-stained wood. 'I'll chop that presently,' he was beginning, when Mary, at the sink, turned round and spoke sharply.

'You can do that later, Albert,' she said. 'Someone's got to sell the bleedin' shrimps and it isn't going to be me. I've put all that behind me, I have. Besides, there's a deal to do in the house, yet. I had a word with Dad earlier this morning, trying to make him see that Amy and me can't cope alone with the fish, the house and the baby, but it wasn't any manner of use. I told him he'd have to pay a grown woman to come in and give us a hand, but he just said he couldn't afford the wage and when I tried to persuade him he got downright nasty. He said he wouldn't replace our mam with some idle slut from the workhouse – as if I'd suggest such a thing! Anyway, so far as I can see, Dad's idea of us all pulling together simply means that Amy and myself do all the work. Certainly Dad never lifts a finger in the house and he's getting far too fond of visiting his pals of an evening . . . if he does visit them, that is. It's my belief he goes round to the Caradoc and drowns his sorrows, as they say.'

There was a shocked silence, then Amy spoke: 'But Dad's Temperance, Mary. He doesn't take strong drink.'

Mary turned from the sink, shaking her head sorrowfully. 'No, queen. Mam was Temperance and brought us up to think the same, but it's my belief that Dad never was. Fishing's a cruel, hard job, and Dad and the older lads deserve a pint and a bit of company at the end of a day's work. I don't *blame* Dad for taking a drink now and then, but he's got to be made to accept help. Otherwise, I'm telling you, we'll all be in the workhouse in six months' time.' She turned to point an accusing finger at Albert.

'And you will help sell the shrimps, me laddo, even if it goes against the grain.'

'What's wrong wi' Amy sellin' the perishin' shrimps?' Albert asked sulkily, turning to hold his hands out to the blaze, for it was a cold day with an icy wind blowing. 'I've bin' on that bleedin' shrimp boat since before dawn and I'm so cold it's a wonder me fingers don't snap off like icicles. Let Amy go, she's better at sellin' shrimps than any feller. Gals always is.'

Amy, who knew her chances of escaping the task were small, sighed deeply and went towards the scullery where the sack of shrimps awaited her. 'All right, all right, only you might come along as well, Albert, because I'm thinking of going to see Mrs O'Leary when I've sold the shrimps. Someone's got to have a word about the stall and prices and so on, and it might as well be me.'

'In that case Albert can push the handcart and you can carry the baby, Amy,' Mary said, brightening. 'I want to give this house a good clean through, get the messages up to date and clean down the wash-house and fish scullery – God knows it could do with it, it hasn't been done since well before me mam died. Also I want to see if I can hear of a respectable woman who can do with a few hours' work. You'd best take a bottle for the littl 'un and some carry-out for yourselves. I made scones and a meat-and-potato pie yesterday. You can have them. Now, don't start carrying on, Amy,' she added, as Amy began to protest. 'Baby Becky's a good little soul, I've heard you say so often and often. Why, folk come over to coo at the baby and end up buying shrimps, so you'll be sold out afore you know it. Now hurry up and leave, do, so I can get on.'

So it was, with Albert pushing the cart and with baby Becky in her arms, that Amy finally left the house. She was well wrapped up in a thick though ragged shawl and the baby was well muffled too. Even so, the cold wind cut like a knife and as the three of them turned into Crosby Road they gasped as it hit them, snatching the breath from their mouths. Amy instinctively curled closer round the child and Albert grabbed at the sack of shrimps.

'It's hellish cold on the boat, but at least I ain't pushin' a bleedin' great barrer over slippery cobbles,' Albert shrieked above the wind. 'Must we do the big houses today? It's them long drives and often, when you reaches the house, some snooty bitch of a maidservant says, "Not today, thanks," and slams the door on your snout. Let's try some of the streets off Knowsley Road in Bootle, shall us?'

'Good idea,' Amy shrieked back. Like Albert, she did not enjoy either the long walk up gravelled drives or the snubs that could result if an unfriendly servant came to the kitchen door. People in the poetry streets, as her mother had called them, were friendly and sympathetic towards young shrimp sellers and if they had the money would always buy. Shrimps were a treat to such people, not a garnish to already luxurious meals. In fact, the main reason that Isobel insisted on the children trying the larger houses was because such families ate more fish. Since they had no fish to sell today, common sense as well as the bitter cold dictated that they follow Albert's suggestion.

Accordingly the children, battling their way along Crosby Road with the wind off the sea hurling itself at them, dived into the temporary shelter afforded by the Rimrose Bridge and turned into Knowsley

Road. It was a real relief to enter Byron Street, out of the worst of the wind, and knock on the first door. A tall, plump woman, swathed in an enormous calico apron, smiled down at them from the doorway. 'Well, if it ain't the shrimp seller!' she said, her hand going to her apron pocket, 'and on such a wild day, too. About all I've got in the house is bread and marge, but shrimps goes well with everything, so I'll have a pint, if you please.'

Amy picked up the tin measure and filled it generously; Mam had always said it didn't do to skimp. If you were generous, your customers bought time and time again; if you were mean they would turn you from the door next time you called. 'Sixpence, please, missus,' she said, tipping the shrimps into a brown paper bag, and letting Albert screw it closed and hand it over, since she had the baby in one arm. The customer, noticing the child, leaned over and chirruped, but baby Becky never stirred. Sheltered from the wind and in her sister's familiar embrace, she was as snug as in her own cot.

'Ain't she a good little soul?' the woman said wonderingly. 'And pretty as a picture, too.' She looked searchingly at Amy. 'She don't favour you much. Your sister, is she? I suppose your mam's busy today?'

'Mam died a month back,' Amy stated briefly. It was a question she was growing used to hearing and it no longer brought tears to her eyes, though she still missed Isobel dreadfully. 'But we're a big family. My sister Mary's doing a spring clean, that's why me and Albert took baby Becky on the shrimp round.'

'Ah, that explains it.' The woman nodded. She produced a sixpence, which she handed to Albert and, after a second's hesitation, a round brown halfpenny, which she pressed into Amy's hand. 'For the littl'un,' she mumbled, and was back in the house with the door closed before Amy could thank her.

'Well, isn't that just lovely?' Amy asked as they approached the next door. 'Mary said Baby would sell shrimps for us and it looks like she was right. Come on, Albert, let's try our luck again.'

Three hours later, with the last shrimp sold and their pockets bulging with pennies, they made their way towards the nearest tram stop. By now both children were exhausted, so each took a handle of the cart and dragged it behind them with Albert taking the baby from his sister, since he was the stronger of the two. 'Are you sure you want to go to the fish market today, our Amy?' he asked as they reached the stop. 'It's gerrin' late, an' you must be tired out – I know I am. Besides, the littl'un will want feedin' again pretty soon I dare say.'

Amy, though she was sure she was every bit as tired as Albert, shook her head. She intended to see the older woman and get things sorted out today, otherwise they would go on fumbling through life, never knowing whether they might have been selling too cheap and buying too dear. 'It's all right, I'll have a nice sit-down on the tram and I've still got a bottle for Becky in my skirt pocket.' Amy let go of the barrow and took the baby from Albert's none too reluctant grasp. 'I know the barrow's heavy for you to push alone, but it won't matter how much you jostle and jounce now it's empty. Tell Mary I'll try to be back in time for tea.'

Albert snorted. 'I ain't goin' straight home,' he

said self-righteously. 'Our dad's goin' to be seeing to the boat for a while yet. So I'll go an' give him a hand.'

It was Amy's turn to snort. 'In this weather our dad'll be round at old Ben Carpenter's havin' a glass of his wife's home-made wine an' a nice bit of fruit cake,' she said, just as a tram drew up alongside.

'Yeah, well . . .' Albert gave a guilty grin. 'I'd sooner be wi' the Carpenters than have Mary buzzin' round me lugs, tryin' to make me scrub floors or chop wood, or even make the perishin' beds. Our Mary's good at dele-whachamacallit, but she's not so keen on workin' herself, I've noticed.'

'Delegating,' Amy said as she swung herself on to the platform and headed for an empty seat. She turned briefly to wave to Albert, but her brother was already heading back towards Trevor Street and the Carpenters'.

Amy leaned back in her seat and settled the baby more comfortably in her lap. By a piece of good fortune the tram was a number 24, which would take her all the way to her destination, for Mrs O'Leary had her stall in St John's fish market in Great Charlotte Street. Mrs O'Leary was a fat and friendly body who bought a good deal of fish, particularly shellfish, from the Logans. She was in her late sixties and because she no longer felt able to work every day in the market she had lent the use of her stall, on Mondays, to Isobel. If there was sufficient fish, Isobel would thus be able to sell at least some of their catch direct to the customers, while paying Mrs O'Leary a small sum for the privilege. Because of this sharing, convenient to both, the two women had become good friends and Isobel had impressed on Amy the importance of always leaving the stall immaculate for the real owner's return the following day.

So if there's one who'll advise me, it'll be Mrs O'Leary, Amy told herself. It might have been easier to talk to Mrs O'Leary, she reflected, had she been alone, but she was not sorry to have baby Becky with her, for the baby was company even though she could not talk and, what was more, holding her little body beneath the shawl meant they helped to keep each other warm. The wind was still bitterly cold and though the baby seemed light, Amy knew from experience that she would grow steadily heavier with each passing hour.

Amy saw several people she knew and greeted them politely, but as the tram rumbled along the Stanley Road getting ever nearer to her destination she began to feel the weight of responsibility descending on her narrow shoulders in a very unpleasant way. If Mary couldn't bring herself to do it, then Dad should have, she thought miserably. It was no good looking for help from either of her older brothers. Because the fishing was so poor at this time of year, Charlie had taken work in the brewery maltings in the Midlands and would not be returning until early May, so he could be discounted as far as help went. Gus and Albert, of course, worked with Bill on the boat and could not be spared. Even so, Amy felt increasingly put upon, especially when it crossed her mind that she was going into the city centre in the most blatant manner on a day when she should have been in school. Sagging off school was a popular pastime among the young lads, but because of Isobel's rigid principles, Amy had never feared the attendance officer before. Now, however, she knew that it would go hard with her if she were caught. The family might need her – did need her – but the authorities would not see it this way and the fact that she had been forced to go on this errand in order to keep her family solvent would not make a jot of difference.

The tram arrived at Lime Street and Amy and her burden got down without incident. She made her way round the corner into Roe Street, past the Royal Court, glancing curiously at the billboards outside the theatre as she did so. How lovely it would be to attend a performance at the theatre, she thought wistfully. Her mam had taken her and Mary to a pantomime once and she had never forgotten it. But she could not linger today to examine the photographs of the actresses nor the details of the present drama and turned into Great Charlotte Street, heading for St John's fish market.

Mrs O'Leary was sitting behind her stall but the moment she saw Amy she got to her feet and surged into the aisle between the stalls, enveloping girl and baby in a loving but odorous embrace. Gently disengaging herself, Amy remembered her mother saying that Mrs O'Leary was one of the many old shawlies in Liverpool who seldom washed the bits that didn't show. 'When they get old they get cold,' she had told her small daughter. 'Oh, they buy new clothes all right, but they just put them on over the old ones. That's why so many of 'em look fat as fivepence when they're really skinny as a sprat. So when Mrs O'Leary gives you a hug, just you take a big breath first, like someone divin' into deep water, and give her your best smile. She's a good woman, better to us than most; I wouldn't hurt her feelings for the world, nor let you girls do so.'

'Well, well, well, if it ain't little Miss Amy and the

babby,' the old woman said wheezily. 'Come round be'ind the stall, queen, and you shall have some tea from me bottle and a nice piece o' cake. There's allus a lull around now so I gorra moment to meself.'

Amy accompanied Mrs O'Leary to the back of the stall, where she perched on an empty fish box reflecting unhappily that she would pong as badly as her hostess if she stayed here long. She accepted a tin mug of cold tea, though she declined the proffered cake, producing a scone which had been left over from the carry-out she and Albert had shared earlier and biting into it. 'Me dad said I'd better bring a mouthful since I'm not likely to get home until late,' she explained thickly. 'Mrs O'Leary, we're in terrible trouble at home and I remembered my mam telling me before she died that if I ever needed advice to come to you. She said you were a good friend to us Logans and would be sure to put me on the right path, like. My dad's a grand fellow, so he is, but he's that moithered without Mam and that puzzled what to do that I can't put any more on him right now.'

Amy looked appealingly up at the old woman, feeling guilty because she knew very well that Mrs O'Leary would assume Isobel's words had been spoken just before she died; a sort of last request, if you like. Whereas, in fact, Amy had gleaned the information about her mother's old friend from chance remarks Mam had let drop over the last couple of years. Isobel had been too busy fighting for her life to give a thought to last requests, Amy knew, and felt tears rise spontaneously to her eyes.

'There, there, queen,' Mrs O'Leary said, clearly much moved. 'Don't you go starting to bawl, because your mam was right. What I can do I will, though that may be little enough, the Lord knows. So you're in a pickle at home, eh? Well, I suppose that's scarcely surprising for a better organised, more businesslike woman than your mam I've yet to meet, and folk like that take everythin' into their own hands and never consider how the people they take care of would manage without them. I'll be bound your da doesn't know how to boil an egg or wash a babby's napkin, let alone change one. But now I think back, don't you have an elder sister what's in service? Don't tell me your da hasn't sent for her? So why ain't it her askin' for me help? She'll be the fair-haired, pretty one.'

'Yes, that's Mary,' Amy agreed. 'And she's come home all right, but the fact is, Mrs O'Leary, she doesn't understand much about the fish and shrimps and that. She said she'd rather look after the house and leave the business side to me.'

Mrs O'Leary pulled a doubtful face. 'You'se awful young and small,' she said thoughtfully. 'They'll scarce see you acrost the top of the stall. Or wasn't you thinkin' about takin' your mam's day? Only I doubt you'll mek the same money sellin' wholesale as you do direct. An' if your da lets his fish go to the wholesale next door, you'll soon be scrattin' round for rent money since it ain't likely that a couple o' kids will strike the bargains your mam used to make.'

'Oh, but we want the stall, if you please, Mrs O'Leary,' Amy said eagerly. 'I'm still in school and there isn't much I can do about that, but Mary will run the stall, except at holiday times, and then I can stand on a fish box – or two, if that means folk'll take me more seriously.' She had not discussed the matter with Mary but assumed the older girl would take on the work for the sake of the family, though she knew her sister hated the thought of selling fish. 'But Mam never told us what rent she paid you, nor the prices she asked from the other stallholders for the shrimps and the crabs and that.' She lowered her voice. 'I know Mam had arrangements with folk over fish prices, but I don't know what they were, and I'm afraid of making a mess of it so folk get angry and won't buy any more.'

Mrs O'Leary smiled down at her and pulled a scruffy piece of paper and a stub of pencil from a pocket in her voluminous skirt. 'You're a sharp one,' she said approvingly. 'I'll write it all down, as much as I know that is, an' you and your sister – an' your da too, o'course – can mull over it this evening. See what's best to do. Of course, at this time o' year, with fish bein' difficult to get 'cos catches is small, us'll all pay more for what you bring in. Your da will know all about wholesale prices and seasonal variations, I'm sure of that, it's just your mam's side of the business that she kept close to her chest.'

Amy was beginning to thank her profusely when baby Becky, obviously noticing that the pleasant rocking motion of tram and walk had ceased, began to grizzle. The old woman, with a delighted chuckle, held out two fat, cushiony arms, and Amy placed the baby in them and then handed over the bottle of milk. 'Do you want to give her this, Mrs O'Leary?' she asked. 'It's time she had a feed, I guess.'

'It's cold,' Mrs O'Leary objected, folding fat fingers round the banana-shaped bottle. 'Tek it to Dorothy's Dining Rooms down the road an' ask them to warm it up for you.' She chuckled, gazing down at baby Becky's small face. 'I'll keep the littl'un quiet while you're gone. Babbies like me so don't you worry that we shan't get along.'

Since the baby had stopped crying as soon as she was handed over, Amy concluded that either Mrs O'Leary was right or the child was too stunned by the older woman's odour to utter a peep. Accordingly, she set off for the dining rooms and was soon back and watching with satisfaction as Mrs O'Leary crooned and cuddled, and the milk sank in the bottle.

When the baby was fed and changed, Amy tucked her back into the shawl once more, got Mrs O'Leary to retie the knot so that she was held securely against her and set off for the tram stop. She had all the information she would need scribbled down on the scrap of paper and felt a good deal happier. Mrs O'Leary had suggested she should tell Bill Logan to pop into the market the next time he was in the area. 'For what you young'uns need is a growed woman to keep an eye on the babby an' do the actual potting of the shrimps,' she said impressively. 'I don't deny you and young Mary is goin' to do your best but you should be in school, queen, and when times is good and catches is large, the two of you will have your work cut out to pot the shrimps, let alone sell 'em. What's more, pottin's an art an' I'll be bound your mam never let either of you tek a hand in it. That right?'

'That's right,' Amy had been forced to agree. 'But Dad reckons we'll kind of pick it up, once we start. He said he'd get a recipe . . . or at least I think that's what he said. But Mary's been in service; I'm sure she must have an idea of how to pot shrimps.'

'And by the same token, if your sister would rather keep house than sell fish, why have you got the littl'un?' Mrs O'Leary had said suddenly. 'You'd think a gal of her age – what is she, fourteen? Fifteen? – would love a-lookin' after her little sister.'

Amy had been struck by the obvious common sense of this remark. Now that she thought about it, it seemed downright strange that Mary had chosen to burden her with the baby who would have been happier, and better off, in the cradle which the two girls lugged downstairs each morning and up again at night. What was more, Mary did seem to enjoy looking after Becky, often telling Amy how to do small jobs, such as bathing the baby in a comfortable manner, for Mary could still remember how her mother had treated Amy herself when she had been small.

But Mrs O'Leary had looked at her questioningly so Amy said inadequately, 'I don't know, I'm sure, except I suppose she'll be able to get on better without having to see to baby here. Thanks again, Mrs O'Leary.'

But right now, standing at the tram stop with the bitter wind cutting through her second-best skirt and whipping strands of hair out from under the shawl, she thought rather bitterly that Mrs O'Leary's question had been a good one. Whatever had possessed Mary to insist that she take the baby on such a freezing cold day? To be sure, Becky was sleeping contentedly enough, warm in the shelter of the shawl, but Amy could see that her little nose was like a cherry where the wind had caught it and knew that such intense cold was not good for babies. She decided that she would have a talk with Mary when she arrived home and would make it plain that she, Amy, was not a servant who would do all the work and take all the responsibility, while Mary flicked a duster around their small house.

Standing there in the cold, she grew more and more indignant with her sister, until her cheeks burned with righteous anger. She rehearsed the pithy speech she would make when she got indoors, and planned to tell her father that such behaviour was unfair and should be punished.

By the time she got off the tram at the Seaforth Sands terminus, she found she was quite looking forward to getting home. The kitchen would be warm, there would probably be a cup of tea waiting, she had got the information they needed and her courage was high. She would make Mary see that; as Gus had said the day her Mam had died, the Logan family must pull together.

She began to walk briskly in the direction of Seafield Grove, and the baby awoke and started to grizzle. 'Never mind, baby,' Amy said breathlessly. 'Soon have you home in the warm and then won't we tell our Mary some home truths!'

She reached the jigger, trotted down it and entered their yard. The men were not yet back from the fishing for there were no seaboots lined up in the wooden porch against the back door and no cart full of fish awaiting gutting. She opened it stepped into the kitchen and paused. It felt chilly, almost unlived in, and though the fire was alight it burned sullenly beneath a layer of white ash. Amy began to undo the knot of her shawl and put the baby down in the cradle, realising as she did so that she was very tired indeed.

'Mary!' she shouted sharply. 'Mary, where in heaven's name have you got to? The fire's damn near out, and me and baby is fruzz wi' cold. Surely

I've done enough today without having to remake the fire while you lie around in bed?'

But even as she spoke some instinct told her that she was wasting her breath. The house was empty. Mary might have gone to do the messages or simply round to see a neighbour but she was definitely not at home. With a most uncomfortable feeling in the pit of her stomach, Amy ran up the stairs and flung open the door of the bedroom that she and Mary shared. One glance was enough to tell her that her sister had gone. None of her clothing or personal possessions remained in the small room. A second glance revealed a pencilled note pinned to Mary's pillow. With a sinking heart, Amy unpinned the note and read it as she made her way downstairs.

Amy, don't be cross, [the note began], *I just can't live like this and our dad won't fetch anyone in to help while I'm at home. Dear Amy, I know you will think I'm being hard on you, but it's for the best. Don't let our dad try and fetch me back for I'll only run away again. This is so important to me and not just for now but for my future. I'm really sorry, but one day, you'll understand.*

Your loving Mary.

Amy put the note down and slumped into a chair. This changed everything. For a start, there was no way she herself could run Mrs O'Leary's fish stall while school was in session. Nor could she look after the baby or pot the shrimps, let alone sell from door to door without her sister's help.

But a little hard thought brought a ray of sunshine to lighten what had seemed at first a real catastrophe. Mary had shown no enthusiasm at all for staying at home, let alone coping with the multitude of tasks her mother had daily tackled. She and Mary had longed for Bill to employ a grown-up woman, someone who knew all about rearing children, and coping with the task of potting shrimps and selling fish.

However, sitting here worrying would not get the fire going again, nor sort out what the family were to have for their suppers when they came in. Amy got off her chair, went and riddled the fire, and walked into the pantry. It was odd, really, she mused as she took potatoes from the sack and dumped them in the sink, how at first Mary's defection had struck cold and chill. Now, having thought about it only a little, she realised that Mary was right. Two girls might stumble along somehow, but sooner or later they would need outside help. Whereas if Dad was forced to get a woman in . . .

Please, God, let it be someone kind, who can cook as well as my mam and who'll love baby Becky, she prayed, as she began to scrub. Someone cuddly, like that nice widder-woman from Belgrave Road, who made those lovely apple pies for the harvest festival supper last year. Or there was a kind soul on Clarendon Road who had been known to give kiddies sweets when they sang carols outside her door come Christmas. Just so long as Dad doesn't go giving us over to some slut like Suzie Keagan, who doesn't bother to do her own work, let alone anyone else's. Only Dad would have more sense, surely? He must know as well as she did that Suzie never did anything if she could get someone else to do it for her. He must know that she liked a little drink as well; that she wasn't above pinching the odd copper or two from an employer's till and that the fellers said she gambled on the horses and the dogs whenever she could afford it, and sometimes when she couldn't.

Thinking of these drawbacks to Suzie's character eased her mind; Bill would never allow such a woman into his home and among his children.

Satisfied on that score, she continued to scrub potatoes. Surely, with Mary gone, her dad would have no option but to employ some woman? So if Mary's flight forced his hand, it would be for the best . . .

Chapter Four

It was a bright September day, with a soft breeze bringing the sense of the countryside into the small end house on Seafield Grove. Suzie was hanging out the washing, knowing that in the kitchen behind her Gran would be making the breakfast porridge for the three of them. Paddy had gone off long before Suzie had got up; Gran always roused early and got his breakfast, although Paddy tried to assure her that he would do very well on a slice of bread and jam, and a sup of cold tea. He was now lowest of the low, working for the dairy on Dryden Street, off Great Homer Street. He started at five in the morning and he mucked out the cows, saw to their clean bedding, their feed and their general health, and was responsible for rolling the milk churns out of the cowshed and into the dairy itself. The work was poorly paid, but Suzie thought her son quite enjoyed it. It was better than being cooped up in a shop or a factory and the staff were kind to him, giving him odds and ends of food that were not quite up to the dairy's usual standard.

Suzie herself had been working for the Logan family ever since early March, when Mary had run off back to Manchester. She rather enjoyed being able to come and go as she pleased in someone else's house, for the Logans were mostly absent while she did her work. She also enjoyed running Mrs O'Leary's fish stall on Mondays each week, because it brought her into contact with other people, both customers and stallholders, and enabled her to salt away the odd bob or two, as well as taking home for the Keagans' tea any unsold fish still fresh enough to eat.

During the school holidays, of course, Amy looked after the baby and did a good deal of the housework, which was a bonus since Suzie very much disliked scrubbing floors, polishing furniture and preparing enormous meals for the family. But in term-time she was forced to do quite a lot of these things, and disliked the dullness and repetitiveness of the work.

Not that she worked very hard. She didn't mind looking after Becky who was nearly seven months old now. At first the baby had been colicky and difficult, quick to cry and slow to smile but gradually, as the weeks passed, Suzie got her into a routine and now she was easier. Housework itself, which meant cooking, cleaning and washing, was divided pretty equally between Amy, Gran and Suzie herself. Suzie had pretended to be shocked when she discovered that Bill boiled the shrimps in the Logans' copper, but it had been a good reason to take their washing back to her own house, where Gran dealt swiftly and capably with it. 'I don't know about you, queen,' her mother-in-law was fond of remarking, 'you oughter be a colonel in the army or an admiral in the navy, 'cos you're so bleedin' good at gettin' other people to do your work.' She had shaken her head sadly, only half joking. 'Us Keagans've always bin workers and your Abe was just another such, but you've got a lazy streak as wide as the tramlines runnin' down the Scottie.

You'll never do owt you can wriggle out of – ain't that so?'

Sometimes Suzie admitted that it was and sometimes she simply shrugged and laughed, but in her heart she knew that her mother-in-law was right. Without the two old ladies to give a hand, her home would soon have degenerated into a slum and without the money which she was now bringing in she would have been in deep financial trouble months ago.

The truth was, she reflected, pinning baby Becky's nappies on the line, that she had to watch her Ps and Qs in front of Bill. He did not approve of women gambling, or drinking, though he thought there was no harm in himself going out of an evening and having a bevvy or two with his pals, or with his two elder sons. The idea that she might either go drinking or gambling had not, she was sure, ever entered his head. And because it was clear that he both liked and trusted her, Suzie was determined that such ideas should remain a mystery to him. She had always liked Bill Logan but now, being around him so much, she liked him even better. He was a generous, amusing, even affectionate man for, though the loss of his wife had grieved him deeply, he was gradually coming to terms with it. She pinned the last nappy to the line and returned to the kitchen, reminding her mother briskly that she would be gone from the house now until about four that afternoon, when Amy returned from school and could safely be left in charge of both house and child.

Old Mrs Keagan gave a derisive sniff but made no other comment. However, she went to a large pile of linen standing on the draining board and shovelled it into an oilskin bag, remarking as she handed it to her daughter-in-law, 'Don't forget all them shirts *you* so neatly ironed nor all them nappies *you* boiled till they was white as snow, queen. It wouldn't do to let anyone else take the credit for *your* work, would it, eh? And if young Amy were to come round a-fetchin' of it, she might see more than you'd like, Mrs Clever Keagan.'

'Oh, young Amy's gorra head on her shoulders and a mean streak even wider than the tramlines on the Scottie,' Suzie said with a chuckle. 'I doubt she believes I do me own washin' and ironin', let alone theirs. But she don't go tale-clattin' to her dad, I'll say that for her. And though I don't like the kid, she won't try an' put a spoke in me wheel so long as the work gets done. Now that we've got the pottin' of the shrimps sorted out, she's content to sell 'em for as much as she can get. And I never get a sniff of that money,' she finished, with only the slightest trace of bitterness. She glanced around the kitchen. 'Paddy go off all right this mornin'?'

'Aye,' Gran said briefly. She held out the bulging bag of clean linen. 'Here you are. You'd best gerroff now, queen, 'cos young Amy can't go to school till you're there to look after the babby. Unless Albert's staying behind today?'

Suzie snorted, taking the bag of clean linen, and turned towards the door. 'Bill wouldn't let Albert stay behind on a day like this, Gran. A fine September is a grand month for the shrimps and now that Charlie's livin' away, Bill needs Albert as well as Gus. Mind, if it looks as though I'm goin' to be held up, young Amy will bring the babby down to meet me. Not that she minds bein' late in school 'cos she's a clever kid, top of her class. She's got big ideas, has Miss Amy, and her dad encourages her. Still, there you are. Men's often fools over their daughters I'm told.'

'I wouldn't know,' Gran said, as Suzie opened the door, 'havin' only had sons meself. And how come Mr Logan is suddenly Bill, eh?'

Suzie, halfway out of the door, chuckled. 'That's just between ourselves,' she said. 'Don't worry, there's a load of perks attached to this job an' I'm not goin' to risk muckin' things up by gettin' too familiar. I'll call him Mr Logan . . .' she smiled wryly at the older woman '. . . until he asks me to use his Christian name,' she finished and shut the door gently behind her.

Walking up Seafield Grove with the heavy bag of clean linen, Suzie saw Amy poised on the pavement outside her own home. As soon as the girl noticed the woman approaching she jerked her thumb at the open door behind her. 'She's asleep,' she called softly. 'Awright if I go now?'

'Aye, you bugger off,' Suzie bawled cheerfully. She would not have said such a thing had Bill been at home, but it amused her to try to shock Amy when there were no other members of the family within earshot. Not that Amy ever acted shocked, but Suzie had a shrewd suspicion that the girl was aware how Isobel would have disliked such language. 'Got your carry-out, chuck?' The question was rhetorical, since Amy always saw that the family had food of some sort for their midday meal; Bill liked his bread cut fresh in the morning and not prepared the night before. Suzie baked the bread, or rather Mr Marsh, the local baker, did the actual cooking, while Gran or even Aunt Dolly usually made and proved the round cottage loaves. Suzie could cook and at first had taken some pride in making bread for the Logans, but Bill had complained that the loaves were heavy and lay on his stomach like lead. He had suggested that Suzie should buy bread, but since Isobel had not done so, Suzie pretended that the loaves were heavy because she was trying to use Isobel's recipe and had commandeered Gran for the task. Bill, totally unaware of this, had been heard to tell friends and relatives about Suzie's delicious bread, and although Amy might purse her lips and give an exasperated sigh, she had not mentioned the facts of the case. Suzie concluded that either Amy was ignorant of the ruse or she had some other motive for keeping her own counsel. Whichever it was, it suited Suzie's book to be thought a first-rate cook, for she had a plan of her own, which she had confided to neither the Keagans nor the Logans.

Softlee, softlee, catchee monkey, Suzie thought to herself, as she moved around the Logans' house, which was twice the size of her own and infinitely more pleasant. If I play me cards right I'll be so indis ... indis ... Oh, I'll be so useful to 'em that when I say I's got to leave they'll do anything, just about, to get me to stay. Oh aye, Bill Logan has gorra rely on me so much that he won't know how to go on wi'out me. Once I gorrim to that stage, it'll be plain sailin' for Suzie Keagan, 'cos nothin' will be too good for me. Thank Gawd, our gran knew how to pot shrimps, though, or there wouldn't be the money for any extra perks lerralone the ones I get already.

She dumped the basket of linen on the kitchen table and went over to the cradle. The baby was sleeping, as Amy had said, but Suzie knew that it would not be long before the child awoke and

118

demanded attention. In the meantime there were the breakfast dishes to wash up, the porridge saucepan to scour and a number of small jobs to be done, before she dressed the baby and took her up the road to do the messages. Amy could be persuaded, or even commanded, to do a great deal, but she stuck her heels in over such things as the porridge pan. She told Suzie frankly that she was too busy on school mornings to heat water for the dishes. 'I do more than my share,' she had said bluntly, right at the beginning, when Suzie had first started working for the Logans. 'But I'm not a skivvy to keep your hands out of water, Mrs Keagan, when my dad thinks you do the lot. And if you don't wash up and keep baby Becky nice when I'm at school, I'll tell my Dad, honest to God I will. I'll do what I can, but I won't be pushed around and nor will Albert, not if I can prevent it.'

But that had been back in March, when Albert was still in school. Now, with Albert working on the fishing boat alongside his father and his brother Gus, there was no question of Suzie having two helpers. When it came to peeling the shrimps, of course, she had both Gus and Albert to help, and often managed to rope Paddy in as well, but for the ordinary everyday running of the house she had to make do with Amy.

It often crossed Suzie's mind to wonder why Amy, who she knew had never liked her, did so much of the housework without ever complaining to her father. There must be something behind it. Perhaps she's writing lists of what I do and what she does and one of these days, when I need to have her on my side, she'll split on me to her dad and it'll be all up wi' me, Suzie thought. But she had always lived for the moment and knew that whatever the challenge, she would face up to it when it came. She was aware that the longer she worked for Bill the less likely he would be to believe ill of her. So if young Amy was storing up grievances she would probably find, when the time came to reveal all, that she had left it too late. By then, even if he believed her, Bill Logan would not be able to envisage life without Suzie.

Smiling with satisfaction, Suzie hauled the big kettle over the fire and began to pile the dirty dishes in the low stone sink.

Amy, meanwhile, making her way to school, was also thinking about Suzie and the future. Not that she called her Suzie, of course; Bill would have been outraged at such familiarity. He always addressed her as Mrs Keagan and expected the children to do likewise. But Amy, though she did as she was bidden, always thought of Suzie by her first name and usually with contempt. She told herself that she was well aware of the game Suzie was playing but was not prepared to put a spoke in her wheel, since she knew, probably even better than her father did, how dependent they were on the older woman. Without Suzie they would not have old Gran Keagan's help, just for a start. Nor would Paddy allow himself to be roped in for the shrimp shelling and even Paddy's Great-Aunt Dolly had her uses to the Logan family, though Amy was not supposed to know this.

So, for the time being at least, as Suzie had guessed, Amy made a mental note of each and every one of Suzie's peccadilloes and having a phenomenal memory – which stood her in good stead at school – knew she would be able to recite the ever lengthening list, should it become necessary. This gave her some comfort when she was up to her eyes in work and saw Suzie idly slopping around the kitchen with a cup of tea in one hand and a cigarette in the other. Bill did not approve of women smoking, but so far he had never caught her at it. Amy thought the smell of the Woodbines, the cigarettes which Suzie favoured, was disgusting and always knew when the older woman had been having a crafty puff, but Bill was a pipe man, so she assumed that his nose was so used to the smell of the strong shag he smoked that other smells tended to pass him by. When Amy had first started noticing how Suzie behaved she had faced Bill with some of her less pleasant tricks and had been astonished at Bill's reaction.

He had grabbed her by both shoulders, given her a good shaking and slapped her face so hard that his fingermarks had lingered for a whole day. 'You wicked, clat-bearin' little liar,' he had shouted, his eyes glittering with fury. 'We couldn't manage wi'out Mrs Keagan and well you know it! She's been a grand friend to this family, none better, and I'll thank you never to let another spiteful word pass your lips when you're speaking of someone who's saved our family from bein' split up. If it hadn't been for her, likely you an' baby Becky would've been sent to the Culler children's home by now. How d'you think I'd ha' looked after two little girls on me own, once your mam was gone, eh?'

Amy, who had been her father's favourite for so long, had been appalled by his violence towards her and shocked that he could call her a liar. As for his blindness over Suzie's faults, she could only marvel at it, but for the time being, at least, she held her tongue.

'Hey, Amy! Ain't you a-goin' to say hello to your pals, then? I hollered to you twice as you were comin' up the road and you never so much as looked up.' Ruth, with a younger sister on either hand, came panting up beside Amy and immediately all thoughts of Suzie and the Keagan family went out of Amy's head.

'Sorry, Ruth,' Amy said contritely. She took hold of the other hand of the smallest Durrant and the four of them began to walk along the pavement in the direction of the school, 'Have you got a carry-out or is it a ha'penny for a milk roll today?'

'Slice of bread and jam, but the jam's spread awful thin,' Ruth said, patting the pocket of her faded tweed jacket. It had once belonged to a man and had probably been bought second- or even fifth-hand from Paddy's Market, but Mrs Durrant was good with her needle and had cut it down to make her daughter a coat for school. 'I say, you know that Paddy Keagan, the one whose mam works for you?'

'Course I know him, worse luck,' Amy said scornfully. 'Wish I didn't know him, nor his mam neither, but I do. Why? What's he done *this* time?'

'He's been an' gone an' got hisself caught nickin' sweets from Miz O'Mara's confectionery on Whitefield Road,' Ruth said. 'He's gorra good job, too. Me mam says he don't need to nick sweets when there's two of 'em in work and they's ever so generous in the dairy. He gets milk, butter, cheese – oh, all sorts – give him to take home at the end of each week. So why nick?'

'I dunno,' Amy said doubtfully. She did not like Paddy any better for being thrust into his company

122

when shelling shrimps, but she did acknowledge, albeit grudgingly, that he did his share without more than the usual grumbling. Furthermore, she did not envy him having a mother like Suzie, who always put herself first. 'I think he probably has to make his own carry-out and I expect his mam takes most of his money, if not all. Besides, who said he nicked the stuff? That Mrs O'Mara is a right spiteful old gal. If he so much as touched a liquorice stick, or a sherbet dab, she'd want to be paid for 'em. Did she call the scuffers?'

'No-o-o,' Ruth admitted, having thought the matter over. 'I don't know as how she'd caught him, come to think. But she told Mrs McGregor and she told my Aunt Ethel, and Aunt Ethel told me mam that young Keagan had been nickin' when the shop was busy, so I thought . . .'

'Well, of all the nerve!' Amy gasped, truly shocked that her friend could repeat such unfounded gossip as if it were fact. 'I'm not saying anything against your Aunt Ethel, but I wouldn't trust mad ole Ma McGregor as far as I could throw her, which isn't far since she's the size of an elephant. Don't you go saying that to anyone else, Ruthie, or you'll get in real trouble, so you will. Paddy's horrible, I can't stand the sight of him, but fair's fair. I mean, when we were kids, most of us nicked the odd fade off the market – what's one rotten apple to a stallholder, after all – or a handful of aniseed balls, if they were parked low on the counter. Human nature, isn't it, when your mam and dad can't afford to give you the odd ha'penny?'

'Yes, I suppose so,' Ruth admitted. 'I won't say nothin' to nobody else then, Amy. It was just . . . well, now he's got a job . . . it seemed worse somehow than a schoolkid takin' the odd sweetie. Still an' all, mad Ma McGregor is a nasty piece of work and she do hate Mrs Keagan. She reckons Mrs Keagan took her job at the pub last year and she says as how she might've fallen for the shrimp pottin', if Mrs Keagan hadn't shoved her nose in.'

'Huh!' Amy said succinctly. She did not like having Mrs Keagan around the house, but the thought of mad Ma McGregor shuffling around their kitchen, smelling like a midden and poking her long nose into everything, made her realise that things could have been worse. And she felt quite proud of having scotched the nasty story about Paddy before it had really got going. She might not like him – in fact she absolutely hated him – but she had defended him almost as though he had been a Logan.

She had looked into the shippon when doing messages for Suzie along Great Homer Street and had thought Paddy was lucky in his work. She liked horses and a dairy had a great many horses for pulling the milk carts, and she also liked cows, with their big soft eyes and, at certain times of year, their wobbly-legged calves trotting at heel. She thought it must be an amusing place to work and when she went into the dairy to buy a dewy slab of butter or a triangular cut from one of the big cheeses she quite envied the young girls in their neat white coats, who sliced the butter, weighed and wrapped it in an instant. She was only twelve, of course, but she was sure that her time remaining in school would pass like a flash and she wanted to choose a job for herself, rather than take anything that was offered. She was bright, top of her class in almost everything and her teacher, Miss Musgrove, had told her mother the previous autumn, 'Young Amy has great potential and might easily go on to higher education, if you so wished.'

Amy was well aware, however, that further education was unlikely to be an option now. While her mother was alive and Mary at home, they would have managed somehow, but as things stood at present Amy's help, and eventually her wage, were essential to the Logan family. So instead of letting her mind dwell on a future as a teacher, secretary, or bank employee, she thought about shops, the dairy or possibly even a waitress in a dining room. But she would have preferred a job that kept her out of doors; she had had enough of being cooped up in the house to last her a lifetime she had decided.

But right now, she was just a schoolgirl, making her way to school with her pals. Work – or, rather, paid work – was something for the future.

Paddy, sitting in the hayloft with his pal Tommy Chee, was eating his snap in the twenty minutes allowed by the dairy. He and Tommy often took their carry-out up there, to keep out of the way of the milk cart drivers. Tommy was Chinese and though he had been born and bred in Liverpool, some of the men made crude jokes about his father cooking rats, lizards and other disgusting things for the family meals, and pretended that Tommy could only speak pidgin English. They also thought it amusing to set the two boys tasks which prevented them from having a sit-down while they ate their carry-out. They had tried various tricks on Paddy when he first came to work there, sending him off to the hardware shop to buy three-penn'orth of square holes, or a couple of yards of scotch mist, but Paddy would have none of it. 'You must think I were born yesterday,' he had said scornfully. 'If you mess wi' me you'll find yourself deliverin' watered milk, or that old dobbin you drive will cast a shoe just when you're in a hurry to get back to the bleedin' dairy. So it's your choice, me dear old mates. Leave me alone or live to regret to it, right?'

They had not liked it, of course, and one or two of the younger men had tried to take him on at his own game, but Paddy was too streetwise to be taken in for long and very soon the jokers were regretting their actions, as he had said they would.

Tommy Chee, however, had led a far more sheltered existence. He was the youngest of seven brothers, sons of the owner of a Chinese laundry on the Smithdown Road. Because he was the youngest there was no job for him in the laundry and besides, he had been keen to work at the dairy, longing for some independence from his close-knit, almost smothering family. The Chinese were known to be hard-working, clean and tidy, and Tommy must have known that he stood a good chance of getting the job be wanted; at any rate he told Paddy he wanted to work in the dairy because he thought it quite possible that he might rise to a managerial position in a few years. Mrs Briggs, who owned the business, had no children and was already in her late sixties. Clearly, there would be an opening there for a bright lad and Tommy was very bright indeed.

However, he had not reckoned with having to start on the very lowest rung of the ladder, actually in the shippon. He was not fond of animals and hated the work of mucking out morning and night, though he had grown accustomed to the chores of feeding, changing bedding and other such tasks.

Neither had he reckoned with the drivers' coarse sense of humour and, until Paddy had come to work there, had spent a good deal of his time running fruitless errands and being mocked and derided by men who should have known better. He had tried to take all such teasing in good part, but Paddy's championship had come just in time to stop him throwing in the sponge, sick and tired of the constant barracking. So when Paddy made it clear that he would not allow his pal to be bullied he was only too delighted to have found such a friend and, although he was the older by more than a year, he hero-worshipped Paddy and would have done anything in his power for the younger boy.

So when, sitting in the hayloft, Paddy remarked that later on he would be forced into helping to shell shrimps for the Logan family instead of having his evening to himself, Tommy volunteered at once to give a hand. 'I've shelled shrimps at home, for me mam and dad,' he assured his friend. 'I'm quick at things like that – we all are, all us boys – so mebbe wi' the two of us we could get through it in half the time. Then we could walk on the beach, or see if we can find someone playin' pitch and toss.'

Like most of his race, Tommy was a gambler, though not an obsessive one. He would put money on a horse, or on the dogs, and he would bet on which of two snails would crawl up a wall first, but he never went too far. He never gambled with money he could not afford to lose for a start and in Paddy's book that meant merely that he liked a flutter, not that he was a true gambler. Unlike me mam, Paddy thought now, remembering the times that his mother had left the house with money in her pocket intending to buy food and had come home penniless, without so much as a slice of bread to show for her shopping trip. Still, she had improved no end since she had taken the job with the Logans.

But right now they were talking about peeling shrimps, not pitch and toss. Paddy was thankful that he himself was not a gambler, was not even interested in such things, so pitch and toss was not his favourite way of spending an evening. He took a big bite of food and considered Tommy's offer. It was a good one. Picking over the shrimps would be a good deal more fun with a pal beside you, someone to grin at and have a laugh with. 'That 'ud be grand, though you'll have to put up with horrible Amy, the youngest Logan gal,' Paddy said through a mouthful of bread and jam. 'She's a mean one if you like. Always on at me, criticisin', findin' fault, sayin' I've left the legs on half the perishin' shrimps when I done no such thing. Nasty little red-haired beast; I dunno how me mam puts up wi' the gal, honest to God I don't. Now her sister Mary was different . . . oh, different as shrimps and sparrers. Pretty as a picture, wi' lovely golden hair and the bluest eyes . . . I were sweet on her, truth to tell.'

'Will she be there?' Tommy asked hopefully. 'She sounds more fun than her sister, that I will grant you.'

'No, Mary went into service in Manchester, as a parlour maid or some such thing, and she hardly ever comes home no more. Don't know as I blame her, though it seems a rum thing not to visit your parents save once in a twelve-month. But goin' back to the shrimps, Tommy, many hands make light work, so no doubt we'll finish miles quicker wi' you as well as me a-pickin'. In fact, we should have some time to ourselves when the shrimps is done, so what about a bit of night fishin' afore you goes home?'

Tommy took a swig of milk from the tin mug at his side and considered. He was a good-looking boy, with the soot-black, straight hair of his race, brilliant black eyes and skin that was a smooth, very pale golden-brown. Despite his name and parentage, Paddy thought he looked only slightly oriental and of course, as soon as he opened his mouth one forgot his antecedents entirely, for his voice, expression and mannerisms were pure Liverpool. Right now, he was clearly tempted by the thought of a night's fishing on the beach, for the weather was still very good for September and, judging by the clear blue sky, the night was likely to be fine and moonlit. What was more, September was an excellent month for fishing and the Chees, Paddy knew, were extremely fond of fresh fish.

'Well?' Paddy said, when Tommy went on staring into space and chewing thoughtfully. 'Are you game for a bit o' night fishin'? It 'ud be a rare old lark, Tommy boy, and it seems ages since I had a lark. The trouble is, once you leave school there ain't much time for larkin' about. So what do you say?'

Tommy swallowed the last of his bread and jam, folded up the piece of greaseproof paper in which his food had been wrapped and pushed it into his pocket. Then he dusted his hands together and smiled apologetically at his friend. 'I'll come and shell shrimps wi' you, but I can't come night fishin',' he said. 'Me mam's a born worrier, bless her, and me dad's almost as bad. They won't fret if I'm home by nine, even though it'll be dark, but they'd have the scuffers out searchin' for a missin' lad if I were much later. If there was some way of lettin' them know . . .'

But there was not and both boys knew it. If the drivers had been friendlier or more reliable, they could have sent a message by Joe Coutts who lived in Thornycroft Road and had to pass the Chee laundry on his way home. Old Joe wasn't a bad sort and very likely would have popped a letter or a note through the letter box in the front door, if Tommy had asked him to do so, but you never knew. Joe was rather simple and if he had been persuaded by one of the other drivers that it would be more amusing to chuck the letter into the nearest bin, then Tommy would be in real trouble at home and neither boy wanted that.

'Oh, well, it was a thought,' Paddy said, getting to his feet and heading for the ladder which led down into the stables below. 'But you'll still come and shell shrimps? Me mam will give you tea, a'course, and it'll be a good one.' He grinned sideways at his friend. 'Only the best for me pal, I'll tell me mam. A nice slice o' fried rat, garnished wi' beetles . . .'

Tommy tried to grab him; Paddy dodged and flew for the ladder. Swearing and scuffling, the two boys made their way back to the offices where they would be told what their next job was to be.

Mary was having an afternoon off and spending it with her friend Josie in the park. They meant to have their tea out and then to visit the theatre, which was showing a tragedy, *La Dame aux Camélias*, that both girls were keen to see. In their opinion there was nothing like a good cry to set one up for a happy day out. But now, having bought and eaten a cream-ice each, they were killing time and enjoying both their leisure and the lovely sunshine, until such time as they were hungry enough to make their way to the

Kardomah Café for the high tea they had planned before the visit to the theatre.

Mary was lying on her stomach, searching for four-leaf clovers and watching an ant busily making its way through what must seem to it to be a great forest of grass blades. It was an idyllic afternoon and she was almost asleep, when Josie spoke: 'Mary, why don't you go home when you get a bit of time off? You've worked for the Cottlestones for an age, but you only seem to go home for a day or so, no longer. Don't your mam and dad ask why not? Oh, I know some girls have rotten homes and bad parents, and naturally they ain't keen to go back; you don't often talk about your dad and your mam and even your brothers and sister ... but you seem fond enough of 'em. It's only natural to wanna spend all your time with your young man.'

'I've got a stepmother,' Mary said briefly. She liked Josie but had made it a rule never to discuss her home life, except in the vaguest of terms. Even admitting to a stepmother was a concession and she was vaguely surprised that she had told Josie about her brothers and sister. Then she remembered the letters, and supposed that Josie had noticed how frequently Amy wrote and had guessed the sisters were fond of one another. Whatever her faults, Amy was a pretty good correspondent. She was still at school, of course, but Mary guessed that Suzie worked her sister pretty hard whenever she wasn't actually in class, yet Amy still found time to write to her at least once a week and now and then, perhaps every other month, Bill also dropped her a line in his large, ill-educated scrawl. Mary supposed, now, that Josie must have taken a good peek at the envelopes – she always destroyed the contents, once read – and put two and two together and rather neatly made four.

'Oh? I didn't know you had a stepmother, but wouldn't it be nice to see that sister of yourn? And ain't there a baby, too? You like babies; think what you're missin' by never goin' home.'

'My dad's a fisherman and the house always smells of fish,' Mary said without thinking. 'It makes me sick, that smell. And ... and when I'm home they'll expect me to clean the bleedin' fish and gut them, and shell the shrimps and dress crabs ... Anyway, I will go home next time they give me a week or so off. Probably.'

'Well, I don't understand you,' grumbled Josie. She was a pretty girl, with a neat figure, and long, dark hair, which waved luxuriantly away from a high, white forehead. She and Mary, one so dark, the other so fair, were perfect foils for one another and were well aware of it. Young men, they knew, were fascinated by such opposites, not that this mattered much to either of them. Josie had a 'steady', a well set-up young fellow who was gentleman's gentleman, or valet, to a rich industrialist. He and Josie were saving hard and meant to marry in a year or two so, as far as Mary was concerned, Josie was the ideal friend. They were able to go out and enjoy meeting young men without ever wanting to form relationships with them.

Mary had met a young bank clerk when she had first gone to work in Manchester. His name was Roderick Campbell and, like Mary, he was a stranger in the city, having arrived there only a few weeks before they met. He was from Scotland and was working for Scott and Burrows Bank, whose main headquarters were in Glasgow. However, the branch in Spring Gardens was a big one, with plenty of opportunity for advancement if you were a young man with ambition, which Roderick certainly was.

Mary often suspected that the reason Roderick was not willing to talk much about their relationship was due to that very ambition. He thought it beneath him to be going steady with a housemaid, and Mary knew that had she not been both extremely pretty and very smart, she would not have held him for long. So instead of going home for her holidays, she usually took on some part-time paid employment, to help to keep her in the smart clothes and shoes which Roderick admired. Mary did not think that Roderick liked smart clothes for themselves, he liked the impression they made upon other people. Folk meeting him when he was out with Mary would never have guessed that she was a humble housemaid. They would have taken her, she thought proudly, for a sales assistant in one of the smart shops on King Street, or perhaps even for a fellow worker in Roderick's bank, since they were a go-ahead firm who employed some female clerks.

On two evenings a week Roderick went to night school to study for examinations which would enable him to apply for a better-paid position in the banking world. He was already doing better than most young men of his age, but often told Mary that his career was only beginning; once he had the exams he needed he would forge ahead, right to the top, if such a thing were possible.

Perhaps Mary was infected by Roderick's ambition, but it was certainly true that she very soon realised she would have to keep pace with her young man if she wanted to marry him one day and be a credit to him. So Mary, in her turn, began to go to evening classes a couple of times a week. She enjoyed domestic service, but would not have hesitated to leave and get a job in a shop or an office, where her good appearance and quick intelligence would have been more appreciated than they were in the Cottlestone household. However, the Cottlestone lifestyle would have been way beyond the means of a shop girl or office worker, no matter how ambitious. Mary enjoyed having good food provided, which she did not have to cook, having her own little room in the attic, with a soft bed and a wardrobe full of uniforms, which were laundered for her along with the rest of the Cottlestones' linen. She loved the beautiful furniture, carpets and curtains by which she was surrounded, and did not fancy changing all this luxury for a shared bed-sitting room, in some sleazy back street, which would have been her lot had she not taken to domestic service.

So Mary studied English Literature, because she had always loved reading, and the French language, since she had a hazy idea that French might be useful to her, should she ever become a lady's maid, or seek employment in an office.

Fond though she was of Roderick, Mary had few illusions about him. He would have been astonished had he known how few. And because she was ambitious and also down-to-earth, she had never told Roderick that she was a fisherman's daughter. She had not told him either that she knew Philip Grimshaw, because that would have meant revealing her humble origins.

When she had first come to Manchester, Mary had been walking in the square garden enjoying the spring sunshine, when a voice had hailed her.

Turning to the sound of her name, she had seen a tall young man, in a brightly striped blazer and cricketing flannels peering at her through the railings. Hesitantly, for she knew no one in Manchester apart from the other servants in the Cottlestone house, she had walked towards the young man and had been astonished to recognise Philip Grimshaw. Indeed, at first she could scarcely believe her eyes, for the last time she had seen him must have been quite two years before on the Seaforth beach. She remembered *that* Philip clearly enough, with his hair rumpled by the breeze and his trouser legs rolled above the knee, but this Philip was a young gentleman, though his smile was as friendly and unassuming as it had been on the day of the King's coronation. In fact, so unaffected was he, so friendly and natural, that Mary had no hesitation in returning his greeting. 'Well, if it isn't Philip Grimshaw,' she said, not trying to hide her astonishment. 'Whatever are you doing here, Philip?'

'I live here,' Philip answered, grinning. 'What about you though, Mary? You really *are* a long way from home.'

'Not really; I live here as well now,' Mary had told him and proceeded to explain all about her job with the Cottlestones. Some young men, on finding that she was a housemaid in the home of a neighbouring family, might have dropped the acquaintance forthwith, but Philip clearly never considered such a thing. In fact, he went out of his way to be kind to Mary, always greeting her in a friendly fashion when their paths crossed, and something in his glance made Mary suspect that he admired as well as liked her. Had things been different . . .

So in the back of Mary's mind, whenever she

thought about her future, there was the tiny almost unacknowledged hope that one day, if she and Roderick did not marry, she might get to know Philip a little better.

But this was only dreaming and Mary had never mentioned to anyone that she knew Philip Grimshaw. What was more, although Philip was perfectly polite when they met, this was seldom and, in her heart of hearts, Mary knew that she was nothing to him and never would be.

'I'm gettin' a trifle peckish,' Josie remarked suddenly, bringing Mary abruptly back to earth and out of her pleasant daydream. 'Whatever were you thinkin' about, Mary? You looked all daft and soppy for a moment.'

'Oh, just fellers and that,' Mary said vaguely. She sat up and began to brush bits of grass off her clean pink blouse. 'I could do with a snack myself, now you mention it; let's go.'

Amy was not having a good day, which was strange because the weather was lovely and Evie O'Brien had a wonderful new skipping rope, with real painted wooden handles. Of course, it could not improve one's skipping and was really no better than an orange box rope, but there was something about the sensation of the rounded wooden handles nestling in their palms which made the girls feel as efficient as any circus performer.

Evie let everyone have a go and, because it was such a lovely day and the autumn term had only just begun, Miss Musgrove allowed the girls to stay in the playground for an extra half-hour, which was a great treat. Yet even as they played, jumped rope and sang the innumerable skipping songs, which every girl knew as well as she knew her own name, Amy felt uneasy.

The day had not started well, of course. Mrs Keagan had been late arriving to take care of baby Becky, so Amy had had to run all the way to school and had arrived just as Miss Musgrove was calling the register. Amy had slid breathlessly into her seat beside Ruth, who had hissed, 'Where *was* you? I waited for ages but you never come, so I had to run meself, an' only got in 'alf a minute before you. The Muzzle won't 'arf give it to us!'

It was unfortunate that 'The Muzzle' should have looked up just as Amy was, in her turn, telling Ruth why she herself had been late. The teacher said sharply, 'What was that, Amy Logan? Kindly give the class the benefit of your explanation as to your late arrival.'

Amy, with a hot face, had mumbled that she was very sorry, but the babyminder had been late arriving. 'Baby is only seven months, so I can't very well leave her alone in the house,' she explained. 'But I ran all the way, miss, honest to God I did.'

Miss Musgrove gave Amy a hard look over the top of her little gold-framed glasses. 'Please don't take the name of the Lord in vain,' she said briskly. 'And why didn't you take the baby round to the childminder, miss? Wouldn't that have solved the problem?'

It would have, of course, but Amy knew from bitter experience what happened if the baby went to the Keagans' place. Granny Keagan promptly took over the care of the child, Suzie Keagan took herself off on any excuse and, when Amy got home, the house would be precisely as she had left it, with the breakfast things still on the table, the fire very likely dead, and no preparations for supper even begun. Naturally, however, she could not say any of this to Miss Musgrove. Instead she mumbled that in future ... and hoped that Miss Musgrove, who was in reality a very understanding person, would let it go at that.

'We was lucky not to get order marks,' Ruth remarked later that morning, as they sat companionably on the low brick wall which divided the coke tip from the playground. 'Old Muzzle must ha' bin in a good mood on account o' the sunshine. It were lucky she didn't pick on me as well, since she'd say waitin' for a pal was no excuse for lateness.'

'It was the whispering which got her goat,' Amy said wisely, 'rather than us nearly being late. After all, *nearly* doing a thing isn't wrong, it's not doing it at all which they get you for. I mean, if I were to nearly tip you into the coke pile, you wouldn't have a mark on you, whereas if I gave you a good shove ...'

The two girls wrestled half-heartedly on the wall, then they linked arms in perfect amity and began to walk round the perimeter of the playground, chatting as they went. Amy had confided her vague discontent with the day and, even as she spoke, had suddenly known the cause. She stopped short, grabbing Ruth's arm so hard that Ruth gave a squeak of dismay, which Amy ignored. 'It's the shrimps!' she said triumphantly. 'It's fine weather, Dad and the fellers were out at the crack o' dawn, so the chances are they'll be home around three, with sacks of bleedin' shrimps. Oh, Gawd, Ruthie, and we'll spend the whole evening shelling the little buggers.'

Ruth, whose main knowledge of shrimps came

from picking over a handful and eating them between two rounds of bread, giggled. 'I dunno why you hates peelin' shrimps so much,' she observed. 'You was sayin' only the other day that Suzie never pinches any of the money you get for potted shrimps. You said that no one checks what you gets for loose shrimps what you sells from door to door, so you an' Bertie can keep back a penny or two for the things your dad won't shell out for.' She giggled again. 'Did you hear that, Amy, shell out! That were a joke.'

'Oh, aye,' Amy said gloomily. 'Very funny I'm sure, particularly if it isn't you who gets to shell the bloody things. Oh, Ruthie, I do hate it. Still, if I play my cards right I'll mebbe get out of it this once. After all, I work like a perishin' dog to keep things right. Why should I shell shrimps and all?'

Ruthie, still giggling, remarked that shelling shrimps was a regular tongue twister. 'Like sister Susie shelling shrimps for sailors,' she said. 'Though why sailors should want selled shrimps ... oh, shelled. Oh, hang it, you knows what I mean.'

This made Amy laugh and presently the bell rang and they had to go back to class, but although Amy joined with the rest of the girls in tackling the long division sums which the teacher chalked on the blackboard, her mind continued to plot how she would avoid picking the shrimps.

When school was over she and Ruthie set off briskly for home. Amy went breezily into the kitchen, where the baby was grizzling on the hearthrug and Mrs Keagan was desultorily scraping carrots, and asked if there were any messages. Suzie looked up. 'Change the baby before you does anything else,' she said at once. 'I been meaning to do it, but somehow something else always crops up. I went round to Elm Road and got some scrag end for a stew, and then I remembered your Dad said he'd likely be bringin' fish home. Still an' all, you can get mighty tired of fish when you've had a good season, and I know your dad and the boys are mortal fond of a scrag end stew.'

Amy went straight to the rag rug on the floor where the baby was struggling to sit up. At the sight of Amy she beamed broadly, showing two tiny pearly teeth, and held up her arms. Amy whisked the child off the rug, wrinkling her nose as the smell of stale urine, and worse, assailed her nostrils. There was a pile of clean nappies on the dresser and she snatched one up as she passed, then took the baby with her into the little low scullery and laid her on the shrimping table, where the shrimps were dealt with once they had been boiled. She whipped the sodden nappy off and dropped it into the wooden bucket half full of salty water kept for the purpose. Then she poured clean water into an enamel bowl, seized a worn scrap of towelling and got to work.

Ten minutes later a clean and happy baby was set down once more on the rag rug, this time with a piece of oven-dried bread in one hand. 'That seems to have shut her up,' Suzie said without turning round. 'She's bin squalling this past hour or more; enough to drive you crazy.'

'She doesn't cry when she's clean,' Amy pointed out. 'You didn't oughter leave her dirty, Mrs Keagan, she gets awfully sore and that makes her bad-tempered. I can't see why you don't change her regularly for your own sake, if not hers. She's a good kid, but you can't expect her to be happy when she's in pain.'

Suzie sniffed. 'I got all the work of this house to do,' she said. 'I did oughter have help wi' the littl'un. It's all right when it's school holidays and you can give a hand, but what'll I do when she's walkin' an' gettin' into everythin'? I'll have to speak to your dad.'

Amy, who was even now considering speaking to her dad about the state the baby was getting into, sighed. Bill was proud of his little daughter and fond of her too, but knew nothing about the care of young babies. He would not understand that clean nappies, several times a day, were necessary for the baby's comfort. I'll have to find a way of blackmailing Suzie into doing right by the kid, Amy decided. Even as the thought crossed her mind, however, she knew she was being unfair. Suzie had many faults, but neglecting the baby was not one of them. Amy knew this to be true, but nevertheless she felt angry with the older woman. Lately Suzie had left the midday nappy change for Amy to deal with, which meant that Becky's nappy area was usually in a bad state by the time Amy got back from school. She glanced at the clock above the mantel. Any minute now the men would return home, trundling the handcart laden with sacks of shrimps. If she was to escape, she would have to find an excuse to do so pretty quickly; she glanced at the baby and made up her mind.

She picked up Becky, settled her comfortably on her hip and made for the back door. 'The poor little beggar's got running sores on her little bum,' she said as she left the house. 'I'm takin' her up to the pharmacy to see what Mr Keir can give me for her.' She did not linger to give Suzie the opportunity of saddling her with other messages, but walked briskly down Seafield Grove and turned left into Crosby Road. When she reached the corner of Elm Drive she turned into it, already aware that she had been foolish to rush out in such a hurry. Becky was getting heavier and was far easier to carry in the loop of a shawl – better still, if she had thought of it, was the ancient wooden cart which the boys used when collecting driftwood. However, that was what happened when you let your temper get the better of you and had she lingered for even a moment, Suzie would undoubtedly have added to her errands.

The pharmacist had a neat shop front on Elm Road, the window decorated by two enormous glass flagons, one filled with a brilliant red liquid and the other with green. Many a time, when her mother had been alive, Amy and Albert had played around outside the shop, while Isobel went in. If you got the right distance from the window and then slowly walked towards it, you could see strange reflections of yourself, either bright red or bright green, looming and leering in the glass. When she had been very small, Amy had thought the liquid in the flagons had some sort of magic which made a small girl appear to be hugely fat, scrawnily thin, or strangely mishapen, but Isobel had briskly disabused her of this idea. 'It's only coloured water in those jars,' she had informed her children. 'Water and glass, when they get together, act like one of those mirrors at the fair, the sort that make you die laughing at your reflection.'

Despite knowing that there was nothing wonderful in the green and red jars, Amy lingered by the window a moment, moving her head from side to side and grinning as her small nose grew as long as a duck's bill one minute and shrank to a button the next. She tried to interest the baby in the reflections, but Becky merely gurgled and went on clutching at a hank of Amy's hair, wound securely and rather painfully round her small and chubby fist.

Inside the shop Mrs Keir was sitting behind the counter, knitting something in soft pink wool. She looked up and smiled when Amy entered and got to her feet. 'What can I do for you, young Amy? Baby not well?'

Presently Amy left the shop once more, with a fat tube of cream for the baby's sores and a rather dusty liquorice stick for herself. She liked Mrs Keir, but reflected that for some reason, liquorice bought – or given – at the pharmacy, always tasted a bit like medicine, whereas liquorice bought at the sweetshop on the other side of the road was unmistakably a treat.

She did her best to linger on the way home, but Becky was too heavy for her to hang around for long. She wondered whether to go round to Ruth's, but the impulse to get out of the house – and away from the task of shelling shrimps – was leaving her. What was the point, after all? If she went back now she would make a pot of tea and spread some bread with margarine and jam, and she could be comfortably fed before the task began.

She was just turning off Crosby Road when she saw, ahead of her, a couple of lads. She recognised Paddy, even from the back, and groaned inwardly; despite the fact that his mother worked for them he was still as rude and nasty to her as ever. Indeed, he had more opportunity now, since his mother made him come in and help shell shrimps or gut fish when the catch was good. Amy was glad that he seemed to dislike the task as much as she did, and also glad that her father had resisted Suzie's blatant attempts to get him to take Paddy aboard the *Mersey Maid* as another hand. 'One boy is all I can cope with for now,' Bill had said gruffly, when Suzie's suggestions that he should employ her son became perilously close to demands. 'There ain't the room for more than the three of us and that's the truth, Mrs Keagan. But if Gus ever decides to move on ...'

The matter had rested there, but Amy guessed that Paddy himself would have preferred life aboard the boat to the dairy on Dryden Street and was meanly glad that he had been rejected. He might get nicer if he had to muck out cows and cart heavy milk churns for a few years, she thought. And then there were deliveries. He might get called in to work on the milk carts and in winter, when they went off in the dark and cold of early morning, he wouldn't be too keen on that.

She reached the jigger at the back of the house and turned into it. Moments later, she opened the back door and went into the kitchen. The small scullery was to her left, and already she could hear the boys scuffling themselves round the table. Gus helped with the shelling, despite being almost a man, so did Albert and herself, of course, and even Suzie occasionally lent a hand, but Bill held aloof. He was the skipper of the boat, after all, and did most of the gutting and cleaning of the fish, and besides, there was really only room round the table for six at the most. So Amy skipped into the kitchen and sat the baby down on the rug, surrounded by cushions; then she went over and took a slice from the plateful of bread and jam, which Suzie – miracle of miracles – must have prepared when she realised that Amy would not be back in time to do so. Only then did she go into the scullery.

Gus, Albert and Paddy were already seated at the table, with a great glistening pile of shrimps in front of them, but seated beside Paddy was a stranger. He was tall and thin with dark hair cut in a fringe across his forehead and liquid black eyes which, when he glanced at Amy, sparkled with amusement. He was shelling shrimps with amazing speed, scarcely seeming to need to glance down at his work, for his thin, strong fingers continued to pick the shrimps, even while he was looking up at Amy. A second glance at the stranger confirmed that he was not English, though Amy could not have said with any accuracy from which country he had come. His skin was a very pale golden brown and, though his eyes were almond-shaped, they were not slitted, like those of many Chinese, nor was his skin dark enough to lead her to believe him of Indian blood.

However, it was none of her business where the boy came from. She slid along the bench and settled opposite him, beside Gus, who was working away stolidly, head bent, shoulders rigid with effort, for the tiny, finicky movement necessary for peeling shrimps was harder for Gus's big, clumsy fingers than for the smaller ones of the younger members of the family.

Amy picked up a shrimp and began to peel, kicking Albert under the table as she did so. 'Who's your pal?' she enquired, low-voiced.

Paddy looked up and grinned maliciously. 'He ain't Albert's pal, he's mine,' he said. 'Tommy, that there's 'orrible Amy, what I've telled you about. This is Tommy Chee, me bezzie at the dairy.'

To Amy's amazement Tommy promptly held out

145

a thin hand, smiling at her as though, she thought, he was in the Queen's bleedin' drawing room instead of the shrimp scullery. However, they shook hands and grinned at each other, before Amy turned back to Paddy. 'If I'm 'orrible Amy, then that there's perishin' Paddy,' she said composedly, continuing to peel shrimps. 'Why are you helping us, Tommy? You're awful good at it, I could see that at a glance, but it isn't a job as many people want. If I could get out of it, I'd never peel another perishin' shrimp all my life long.'

'Oh, I don't mind it,' Tommy said easily. 'Many hands make light work, they say. Besides, Paddy an' me's going to take a walk up the Scottie, get ourselves a paper of chips, when the shrimps is done.'

'Right.' Amy told herself she was not particularly interested in Paddy's friend or in what they intended to do that evening. What mattered to her was getting the shrimps peeled, so that she could have a good wash and get to bed early for once. Suzie went home when they had had supper, which meant that a good many other chores, such as washing up and damping down the fire for the night, would fall to Amy's lot. Bill sometimes took pity on her and told her to run off to bed, saying he would finish her chores for her, and Albert did his share by drying the dishes and bringing in water for the morning. But even so, Amy usually got to bed late and worn out. But this evening it was clear that the shrimps would be finished betimes. Amy had been doing them for years now, and had never seen anyone work with the speed and efficiency which Tommy brought to the task. She began to copy him, modelling her movements on his and, in an amazingly short space of time the shrimps were finished, the empty shells disposed of and the little pink curls of shrimp flesh placed in the big black cauldron, ready for potting.

'I'll have me supper when I get back,' Gus said, eagerly jumping to his feet. He was courting a girl who lived in Rawson Road and knew that Peggy's mother would be glad to feed him if he and Peggy meant to go out for the evening. Gus turned and grinned at the younger ones. 'Thanks, kids. See you later, Dad.'

Supper tonight was the scrag end stew, with mounds of potatoes and carrots. This was followed by apple pie and Amy stared covertly at Tommy, as they sat down to eat. On hearing his name, she had guessed he was of Chinese origin and wondered whether he ate ordinary food, as well as the rats and small dogs, to say nothing of cats, which rumour and hearsay had attributed to them. It was soon obvious that Tommy was well used to ordinary British food, however. He tucked in with the rest and congratulated Mrs Keagan on the apple pie, which made Amy smirk; she knew Granny's pastry when she tasted it.

Bill walked over to the fire and stood with his back to it, warming himself. 'If young Paddy's off out with his pal, I'd better walk Mrs Keagan home when she's finished with the washing up,' he said. with studied casualness, which did not fool Amy for one moment. 'You'll keep an ear open for the littl'un, won't you, Amy?'

Amy nodded, but raised her brows at this, pulling a face. Her father never walked Suzie home – why should he? She only lived at the end of the road, no more than thirty yards further along the pavement, so she assumed that Bill had something to say to Suzie, which he did not want the rest of the family to hear. She devoutly hoped that he intended to give old Suzie a good telling off, for surely by now Bill would have realised that Suzie shirked her work and gave poor value for money? She wondered if she might sneak quietly out and hide in the back jigger to hear what Bill wanted to say, but Albert put the lid on any such plan by suggesting that he and she might accompany Tommy and Paddy up the Scottie and have a paper of chips on their own account.

'Dad won't be two minutes, takin' the old girl home,' Albert said, lowering his voice to a whisper. 'And baby Becky's asleep, so she won't bother. What do you say, Amy?'

Amy's hopes of an early night promptly disappeared. A walk in the dark up to the shops, a bag of chips and some light-hearted banter was just what she needed. But suppose her father decided to pop into the Keagans' house, or took longer than usual for some reason? She guessed that Albert would want to leave at once and she could not risk baby Becky waking to find herself alone in the house. 'Oh, but we can't leave the baby . . .' she began, only to be interrupted by Bill, emerging from the fish scullery.

'That's all right, chuck,' he said heartily, 'I dare say Mrs Keagan can see herself safe home if I go into the road and watch till she reaches her door. You go off and enjoy yourselves.' He delved into his pocket, producing some coins which he held out to them. 'Here, buy yourselves a bottle of ginger beer to drink wi' your chips.'

Amy took the coins, thanking her father profusely, and presently the four of them made their way along the road, all thinking gleefully of the bright lights

148

ahead and the fun they could have, since they had finished early for once.

It was getting on for ten o'clock when Albert and Amy made their way back along Seafield Grove. Paddy had decided to walk part of the way home with Tommy but though Albert said he would very much like to accompany them, he felt the walk would be too much for Amy's shorter legs.

'If you think them linen poles is short,' Paddy growled, 'then you's is madder than old Ma McGregor. The gal looks as though she's on stilts. Still an' all, gals ain't got no stamina, I grant you that. Why not let her go home, whiles you come wi' us? No one ain't goin' to interfere wi' a beanpole like young Amy here.'

Amy bristled and gave as good as she got. 'I dunno how you dare say things about my legs, which you've hardly seen, when your ugly face is on view all the time and enough to turn the milk sour,' she said briskly. 'Can't you find nothing else to do than to be rude to your betters? I'm a lady, but if I weren't I'd thump you on your bloody snout.'

'Oh, very ladylike,' Paddy sneered.

But Tommy, though he was grinning, tugged at his friend's sleeve. 'You've gorra give her best, old son,' he said. 'Ta-ra Albert, Amy. Been nice meetin' you. See you again some time.'

'I hope you do see us again, 'cos you're the quickest shrimp picker I ever did meet,' Amy called over her shoulder, as she and her brother headed for home. The chips were all eaten, but there was quite half a bottle of ginger beer left and they shared the drink, turn and turn about, until Albert drained the last drop as they entered the jigger.

'It's been a grand evening, Albert,' Amy said gratefully, as they made their way across the cobbled yard. 'Thanks ever so much for taking me along.'

'That's all right.' Albert opened the back door and ushered her inside. 'It were good of Dad to keep an eye on the baby for you an' all.' He glanced round the empty kitchen. 'Think he's gone to bed?'

'Not likely, it isn't even ten yet,' Amy said, glancing at the clock above the mantel. 'Mebbe he's nipped out back for a jimmy riddle. No, he can't have done that, the lamp's still on the hook by the door.'

'I dare say Becky woke,' Albert observed, glancing towards the stairs. 'I'll pull the kettle over the fire, then we can all have a drink before we goes to bed.' He chuckled. 'It'll be a change for our dad not to have a pint to send him to sleep, but he's never been one for havin' drink in the house, so it'll have to be tea.'

Amy stared round-eyed at her brother. 'Do you mean that he goes out to the pub every night?' she enquired incredulously. 'Mary told me he wasn't Temperance and hadn't signed the pledge, but she said he wasn't a drinking man either.'

'Nor he is,' Albert said stoutly. 'But he's only human, Amy. Fishing's a hard job and he likes a bit o' company, apart from us kids, I mean, so he goes down to the pub and meets his pals and has a pint or two. What's wrong with that?'

'I dunno.' Amy's, illusions of her father's character were crumbling round her ears. 'Does he get drunk, Albert? Only I'm never up when he gets back, or not often anyway.'

'One beer don't make a feller drunk,' Albert told her. 'It's the company he goes to the pub for, not the

150

drink. There ain't a better man livin' than our dad, queen, even Mam never grudged him the odd drink now and then just to relax, like. Now she's gone and he's got all the responsibility and that, it's a wonder he don't take more than a glass. Ah, hear that? I said he were probably givin' an eye to baby.'

Sure enough, Amy heard the sound of feet crossing the bedroom and beginning to descend the stairs, and presently her father, looking very self-conscious, entered the room. He looked across at them, and it struck Amy that there was a flush on his cheeks and a glittering brightness in his eyes, but before she had done more than notice the fact, someone else came down the stairs. It was Mrs Keagan, pink-faced and bright-eyed, with her hair, which was usually pulled back from her face, tumbling about her shoulders and her blouse done up on the wrong buttons.

Amy, never renowned for her tact, said blankly, 'Wharron earth ...? I thought you said you were seeing Mrs Keagan home when we left for our chips, Dad.'

'Oh aye.' Bill turned to stare at the woman beside him. 'But we ... that's to say ...'

'The baby woke,' Suzie said brightly. 'Anyhow, your dad's got something to say to you.' Her glance, Amy saw, was defiant and even as she looked, Suzie reached down and took Bill's hand in a possessive grasp. 'Go on, Bill,' she urged, 'tell 'em'.

Bill took a deep, steadying breath. 'I've asked Mrs Keagan to be me wife,' he said bluntly, 'and she's accepted. We'll be wed before Christmas and all one big, happy family. And now, since the two of youse is home, I'll just walk Mrs Keagan – I mean Suzie –

back to her place, so's we can break the news to Paddy, Gran and Aunt Dolly.'

Neither Albert nor Amy said a word. They simply stared unbelievingly, as Bill got cap and coat off the back of the door and helped Suzie to throw her shawl round her shoulders. Then the two of them left, with only a valedictory wave from Bill, and a gloating and glittering smile from Suzie.

'Well, I'm buggered!' Albert said slowly, as the sound of his father's footsteps faded. 'Who'd have thought it, our Amy? What'll happen, d'you suppose? They can't all move in here, that's for sure. Well, I suppose Paddy could share with us boys, but there's nowhere for Gran and Aunt Dolly. Your room's a squeeze for you and Becky ain't it, and Mary, when she's home? I suppose they'll keep both houses on, even though it's double the rent.'

'He can't do it! Living in the same house with *her* and having Paddy here all the time, would be hell on earth,' Amy stated vehemently. 'Do married people always live in the same house? Couldn't they be married and still stay the way they are right now?'

Albert sighed at her ignorance but shook his head decisively. 'Course not. Married folk don't just live in the same house, they sleep in the same bed. Remember what it says in the Bible about the pro . . . procreation of children? You've gorra sleep in the same bed to do the procreatin' bit,' he ended.

On the other side of the kitchen the kettle began to hop and sizzle. Amy crossed the room automatically and made a pot of tea, set out three mugs and went to the milk jug in the scullery. When she had made three cups of tea, she carried one over to the sofa and, sitting down, began gingerly to sip. Albert followed suit and for a long while the kitchen was silent as the two youngsters were lost in thought. Then Amy got to her feet, picked up the third cup of tea and tipped it into the slop bucket. When she spoke at last it was with little or none of the shock and bitterness she had shown earlier. 'Dad won't be wanting that,' she said heavily. 'This is going to change everything and not for the better, either. Oh, Albert, why couldn't things have stayed the same?'

Chapter Five
JANUARY 1908

Amy came out of the small house in Seafield Grove and gasped as the wind blew large cold flakes of snow against her warm face. She wrapped her scarf more tightly round her neck, then turned and headed along Crosby Road towards the tram terminus where she would presently catch the tram into the city centre. She was seldom unhappy to leave her home now, not since Bill's marriage, about three years previously, had given her a stepmother. It would not be fair to say that Suzie disliked Amy – but she certainly made use of her. Indeed, starting work had been, in a way, a relief.

Baby Becky had to rely on either Suzie herself or old Granny Keagan for her upbringing, because Amy was now out of the house from eight in the morning until seven in the evening. By that time, of course, Becky was safely tucked up in bed and, though Suzie left as much of the housework as she could for Amy to tackle, she had long ago realised that she must treat the younger girl reasonably, or Amy, who had a very strong will of her own, would manage to ignore any tasks set her.

But right now, hurrying towards the Rimrose Bridge with her head bent against the blizzard, Amy almost regretted leaving her home. The kitchen had been warm and cosy, the fire burning up brightly and Bill sitting before it, with a round of bread on a toasting fork held out to the flames. In weather such

as this there was no point in even going down to the
beach, let alone taking the boat out, so Bill would
occupy himself with domestic tasks which needed
doing and would then mend nets in the comfort of
the kitchen.

Amy was almost at the tram stop, could actually
see a tram about to depart, when a voice hailed her,
shrieking above the wind: 'Hey, Amy! It *is* you, ain't
it? My word, I've not clapped eyes on you for ages.
How're you doin', queen?'

'Ruth!' Amy squeaked. She had not seen her old
friend since Ruth had gone into service with a family
in Southport. Somehow, when Ruth had been home
Amy had always been at work, but she had heard
rumours that her pal was sick of service and wanted
a job where she could live at home. She had thought
it would be grand to have Ruth back once more and
now it looked as though the rumours had been true,
for here she was, muffled in coat and scarf, heading
for the tram terminus, as she was herself.

Trams, however, wait for no man. 'I've got to get
on this tram, Ruthie,' Amy said breathlessly, raising
her voice above the sound of the wind. 'It's a
number 24 so it takes me all the way to Lime Street.
Where are you going?'

'A number 24 will do me fine,' Ruth said, as the
two of them scrambled aboard the waiting tram.

The conductor, blowing on his hands in their
fingerless mittens, grinned at them. 'Hon you gets,
young ladies,' he called cheerfully. 'Me driver's
raring to go because, what with the slippery roads
and the bleedin' snow blowin' in his face, we's
almost bound to be late and the inspectors fair haunt
this route in bad weather, hopin' to catch us out.'
Another shrouded and bent figure, in the all-

enveloping shawl and draggly skirts of a street trader, came slogging towards the tram. She was struggling with a huge basket covered by a checked cloth and the conductor shouted to his driver, 'Wait onna moment, George, ole pal. This 'ere passenger needs a hand by the looks. Once the lady's aboard, you can go fast as you like.'

Amy smiled at the old woman as she was heaved on to the step and collapsed into the nearest seat. She recognised her as one of the women who sold flowers outside Lime Street Station, but could not imagine there would be much sale for such wares, even if she had managed to acquire flowers in this dreadful weather. Probably she was now selling oranges, apples and the like.

However, it was Ruthie's presence on the tram which interested her right now. She waited until they were seated and the tram had jerked into noisy motion, then turned to her old friend, who was removing her dark-blue headscarf and brushing snow off her shoulders. 'Ruthie! So you *are* home! Well, that's a piece of luck for me, I tell you straight. What with working at the fish market and doing all my stepmother's housework, keeping an eye on the kid and trying to see the boys don't go short, I've not made a friend of my own age since you left. It'll be grand to have you home again. But what are you doing on the workers' special? Don't say you've got a job already!'

Ruthie replaced her headscarf, tying it firmly under her chin, and smiled at Amy. She had not changed much in the years since she and Amy had been to school together, though her pale-brown hair was coiled into a low bun on the back of her neck and Amy suspected that a dusting of powder covered her friend's small, straight nose. 'Yes, I'm home for good. Two years of service is enough for anyone – not that they wasn't good to me in their way, but it weren't our way, Amy. It was all right while I had a young feller interested in marriage, but when he took up with the second parlour maid – oh, I dunno, I just wanted to come home and do a job of work which finished at a proper time, so's I wasn't always on call, like. And I have got another job, though it may only be temporary. But what's been happenin' to you, Amy? And the rest of the family, of course? Have you gorra feller?'

'Not so's you'd notice,' Amy said ruefully. 'As for the family, the boys and my dad are fine, and Becky's fine, and Mary seems to like service more than home life; at least she never comes back for more than a couple of days and even then she's raring to go back to Manchester just as soon as she can. She's got a feller, I believe, though she doesn't talk about him. As for me, I used to go to the dances at the Daulby Hall, but it wasn't much fun without a pal. Of course, I've been out with fellers from time to time – remember that Tommy Chee, Ruthie, the boy Paddy was friendly with? Him and me went to the theatre once or twice and last summer we went over the water a couple of times, but to tell you the truth, my dad didn't approve. It was stupid because we're just good pals, there's nothing in it really. Still he's a deal nicer than most of the fellers Paddy hangs out with. But I'm sorry about your feller, queen. Were you much upset?'

Ruth snorted. 'Upset? Over a two-timing bugger who thought if he played his cards right he could have the pair of us? No, chuck, I weren't upset so much as furious. In fact, now I've got over the shock

157

I pity Flo Williams – that's the gal's name – because it won't be long before he's seein' someone else on the sly. That's men all over for you. But you can put it down to experience I suppose.'

'It's experience I'm short of,' Amy said ruefully, glancing enviously at her friend's smooth prettiness. She could well imagine the sort of effect Ruth's cherubic countenance had had among the young men of Southport. 'Still, with you to go around with me, Ruthie, perhaps I'll begin to have some fun as well as working every hour God sends. Where did you say you had a job?'

'You know Dorothy's Dining Rooms on the corner of Rose and Elliot Streets? Well, I'm workin' in the kitchens there and doin' some waitin' on because they's several people away with influenza. This'll be me first day. Mrs Owen said I was to start this morning and work for at least three weeks, mebbe longer. She said it depends on me work and on whether everyone who's off ill comes back.'

'Well, I'm blowed!' Amy exclaimed, turning to beam at her friend. 'Those dining rooms are ever so popular, chuck. They're always crowded with folk from the offices, fellers poppin' in from the station when they want a quick bite before their train and, of course, with actors from the theatre – as well as one or two from the market, when they've a few pence to spare. Oh, Ruthie, it will be grand to have you so close! We'll be able to catch the same tram to and from work, and tell each other how our day has gone – so long as you don't mind the smell of fish,' she ended, sighing regretfully.

'You don't smell of fish,' Ruth said mildly. 'You never did, Amy, even when you were running the fish stall in the school holidays. But you always thought you did, I seem to recall,' she added with a reminiscent smile.

The tram, which despite the conductor's fears had done the journey in good time, swung into the terminus by the station and the girls, lifting their scarves to cover their mouths, climbed reluctantly down into the teeth of the blizzard. Amy looked across at St George's Plateau, where the snow was already lying in a thick white blanket, criss-crossed with footmarks. She was amused to see the lions wearing neat white snow caps and smiled to herself as she accompanied her friend into Elliot Street and saw her into the dining rooms, before heading towards Great Charlotte Street and St John's fish market. Normally she would have walked the other way down Roe Street because this would enable her to have a good nose at the theatre as she passed it, but in weather such as this the quickest way was best. The familiar smell surged out to meet her as she approached the enormous green-painted wooden doors. There were clouds of steam coming from the direction of Mrs O'Leary's stall, so Amy knew her employer had arrived before her, despite the fact that she herself was at least ten minutes earlier than usual. She went over to the stall to hang her shopping bag on a hook beneath the counter and greet Mrs O'Leary cheerfully. 'Morning, Mrs O! Isn't it a cold, horrible day? It's enough to freeze the wotsits off a brass monkey, as my dad says.'

'Mornin', queen,' Mrs O'Leary answered. She was cleaning down her concrete stand, red in the face from the effort. Amy promptly took the long brush, the big bar of red soap and the bucket of boiling water from her employer's hands. 'You sit yourself down, Mrs O,' she said gently. 'It's my job to clean down and yours to sort out a float for the till. It won't take me but a minute to get this done and then I'll be off to Harry Roper's for the ice. Though if you ask me, we might as well get it free in weather like this by scraping it off the pavements.'

Mrs O'Leary chuckled wheezily and sank thankfully into the creaking old basket chair in which she now spent most of her working day. 'You're a good gal, Amy.' She mopped her brow with a large checked handkerchief. 'I dunno how I ever managed wi'out you and that's God's truth. As for ice, I dunno as we're goin' to need much wi' that bleedin' blizzard a-blowin',' she added ruefully.

Amy smiled. 'Yes, it's the sort of weather to keep customers at home,' she agreed. 'What's more, the boats won't be going out while it's so bad, you can be sure of that. My dad and the boys will be mending nets, knocking up new fish crates, checking ropes and sails and doing anything else ashore that comes to mind, but they won't venture out in a blizzard, not for all the fish in the sea.'

'And the shrimps all lie low while the weather's bad,' Mrs O'Leary remarked. 'But it's a grand time selling potted shrimps, smoked and salt fish, so it is. And praise be to heaven, we don't need ice for such as them. Still an' all, we're not out of fresh fish stocks yet nor likely to be, so when you've finished scrubbin' down the floor, you'd best get off to Harry's for the ice.'

Amy sluiced the last few inches of hot and now filthy water into the channel which ran along the front of the stalls and hurried the little river along faster with her broom. Then she turned back to her employer. 'Right, I'll do that. I say Mrs O, what a piece of luck I had this morning! I was getting on the tram out at Seaforth when someone called my name. It was my best pal, Ruthie Durrant, who was in school with me. She's been in service away from home but she's back now and working in Dorothy's Dining Rooms. What about that, eh? It'll be grand to have a pal to chat with on the tram going home after work. I'm that pleased, even the weather doesn't get me down.'

Mrs O'Leary surged to her feet and took broom and bucket from Amy, to stand them against the back of the stall. 'I'm real glad, queen,' she said sincerely, 'there's no one your age workin' in the fish market, or no one 'cept young lads what's too ignorant to pass the time of day, it bein' mortal hard to get young 'uns to work here on account o' the smell and the cold. Why, if you've gorra pal you might even rent a room in the neighbourhood here, so's you could do wi'out the journey to and from.'

Oddly enough, this thought had not occurred to Amy, though she had been longing to leave home ever since her father had remarried. Suzie took advantage of her, she knew that and thought that if she were not around the older woman would have no alternative but to do her own work or be shown up before Bill and the boys. What was more, it would get her away from Paddy, whose dislike became more difficult to deal with every day. He had bitterly resented her friendship with his pal Tommy and at one point had actually accused her of deliberately stealing his bezzie away from him. 'It's norreven as though Tommy could possibly be interested in a scrawny little red-headed beast what smells o' shrimps, like you,' he had shouted at her when he had first spotted the two of them sitting on the grass in the Bowersdale Park one day the previous summer. 'You're not even the same colour – it's all wrong – you want to leave Tommy Chee alone!'

'We aren't thinking of getting wed, you know,' Amy had said, giggling, 'We're just pals, same as you and Tommy are.'

'There you are, then!' Paddy had yelled, red as a turkeycock with frustrated anger. 'Tommy's *my* bleedin' pal, not yours! He's me workmate and me bezzie, and I won't have you horning in and spoiling things, so just you back off, Shrimpy Logan.'

Amy had not wanted a fight so she had said nothing more, but if she had bitterly resented Bill's interference in her friendship with Tommy, how much more bitterly had she resented Paddy's attempts to force her hand and make her give up seeing his pal. She would not have changed her behaviour one iota because of Paddy's words, but her father's strictures were a different matter. Therefore, since she had no intention of forming any relationship other than friendship with Tommy Chee, she had gradually stopped seeing him altogether, though it had cost her some pangs to make excuses every time he issued a casual invitation.

Consequently Amy had begun to feel herself friendless indeed. Her school friends had scattered, many of them working away, and those who were still at home had made other friends among their new workmates. So Amy, working hard at the fish market all day, preparing and selling shrimps in the long summer evenings and working for her step-mother in the house whenever she was free to do so, was scarcely conscious of the social life she was missing and had begun to feel like a caged rat on a wheel, with escape impossible.

Now, Mrs O'Leary's suggestion danced enticingly before Amy's inner eye, presenting a delightful picture of independence, not only from Suzie Keagan but from the abominable Paddy Keagan as well. If only Ruthie would agree they could have a lovely time, just the two of them, managing for themselves. So Amy set off to fetch the ice, with an empty bucket swinging from either hand and with her mind full of exciting plans. She was forced to reflect, however, that the money she was at present paid would scarcely cover half the rent of even the tiniest room, let alone feed and clothe her. But there were other jobs; in winter her working day ended early and she supposed she could get a job from, say, six to ten, working behind a bar in one of the many public houses which surrounded St John's Market or even waiting, or skivvying for the cook in a popular dining room. Alternatively she and Ruthie could approach a third girl to share a room with them. This would make the rent cheaper and, what with odds and ends of fish which Mrs O'Leary would doubtless give her and whatever the other two could provide, surely it would be possible for three of them to find somewhere they could afford?

'Mornin', Amy,' Harry Roper said cheerfully, as Amy clanked her buckets on to his cold stone floor. 'Wharra day, queen! Have any difficulty reachin' the market today? You come in from Seaforth way, don't you? I dare say it'll be possible to get into the city for a while, but what with this blizzard and the folk all wantin' to go home at the same time, you'd best ask Mrs O'Leary to let you leave work after dinner while the trams is still runnin'. It's a helluva walk out to Seaforth from here.'

'Don't I know it,' Amy agreed gloomily, as Harry began to chop at a block of ice and drop the pieces into her buckets. 'Mrs O'Leary was asking why didn't I think about moving into the city, sharing a room with a pal, so I didn't have the journey in winter. But I dare say it would cost more than me and a pal or two could afford. Rooms are pricey round here, so I've heard.'

Harry filled the second bucket and pushed both across the floor towards her, then straightened, his hand in the small of his back. 'If it were just a room you were after, I dunno as it'd break you to take a bit of a room in one of the courts, or somewhere like that.'

'The courts?' Amy said doubtfully. Ever since she had been small she had been warned by Isobel about the courts and those who inhabited them. 'Dens of iniquity, that's what they are, those courts,' she had told her small daughter, as the two of them hawked shrimps round the city streets. 'They live there, all crowded in like animals, ten to a room, they say, and if there's money missing or some old woman hit over the head for the sake of the few pennies in her purse, then it's to the courts that the scuffers go first. So we'll not hawk our shrimps round the courts, queen. We'll take 'em to honest folks.'

Bill, who was less prejudiced than his wife, informed Amy privately that the folk who lived in the courts were not all bad. 'Some of 'em's just poor, luv,' he told her when she repeated Isobel's remarks. 'You get real respectable folk livin' in the courts, folk who'd take as much care of their little houses as your mam does of ours. Proper little palaces, some

164

of 'em. But your mam went sellin' shrimps round the courts on the Scottie when we was first married. She were expectin' and she got a mouthful of abuse and a stinkin' old boot hurled at her head by a drunken docker. Your mam ain't never forgot it and you could say it coloured her feelings about the courts. So don't condemn folk out of hand just because of where they live.'

However, it seemed that Suzie had shared Isobel's bad opinion of the courts, though possibly for a different reason. 'I get more customers for the shrimps in the pubs than in them courts,' she had told Amy, when Amy had suggested trying the narrow, crowded little alleyways. 'Besides, landlords reckon shrimps give you a thirst, so we're always welcome in the pubs.'

'There's nowt wrong wi' the courts, queen,' Harry said gently now, walking with her to the doorway. 'I only suggested it because I know a little place at the back of Skelhorne Street, off Hilbre Street, where's there a widow woman by the name of Mrs Beckham, ever so respectable, who lives at number 8 Kingfisher Court and who might let a room to a couple of nice young girls what wouldn't mess up her home.'

Amy, who had been about to cross Rose Street, stopped on the edge of the pavement. 'I'm sure a place like that would suit me and Ruth just fine,' she called over her shoulder. 'Thanks ever so much for suggesting it, Mr Roper. Me and Ruth will have a talk and I'll come back to you. Thanks again.'

The rest of the day went with amazing speed. Despite the fearful weather – for the blizzard continued to blow for most of the day – there were sufficient customers to keep Amy busy gutting and filleting fish. Because of it, however, Mrs O'Leary closed the stall at four in the afternoon and advised Amy to go home while the trams continued to run. 'If they're still runnin', that is,' she added darkly, buttoning her long black cloak up to the neck and winding her black scarf round her face to the eyes, so that her voice emerged muffled. 'If the trams have stopped there's always the overhead railway, so be a sensible girl and make for it, if the trams ain't runnin. You don't want to be benighted here, do you? See you tomorrer.'

'Thanks, Mrs O'Leary,' Amy said but she did not commit herself to going home at once, since she intended to wait for Ruth, so that they might discuss the exciting proposal of renting a room between them. She went through to the sinks at the back and washed as thoroughly as she always did, rinsed her apron and hung it over a hook, took off the clumsy wooden clogs she wore for work and donned her outer clothing. Having muffled herself up, she went briskly out of the fish market into the bitter wind and headed for Dorothy's Dining Rooms. She had money in her pocket for a cup of tea and a bun, and decided that if she did not see Ruth she would send a message to the kitchens by one of the waitresses. If Ruth could tell her at what time she would finish work she could stay in the dining rooms, spinning out one cup of tea, or possibly two, until her friend was free to join her.

When she reached the dining rooms they were already crowded, with people staring anxiously out at the snow and ordering tea and crumpets or something more substantial. The bustle and busyness were a revelation to Amy, who did not frequent such places as a rule, and she realised that it would not be possible to do as she had planned and wait in a corner until Ruth was free. Instead she decided to approach the woman sitting in the little glass-fronted box at one end of the room, taking the bills and the money, and handing out change with a smile and a pleasant word to her customers.

This must be Mrs Owen, who owned the establishment, Amy supposed, so she approached her with a certain amount of caution, not wanting to get Ruth into trouble on her first day in the job. But Mrs Owen no sooner heard her say that she was Ruth's friend than, with a harassed glance at the crowded room, she said, 'Why, if you're going to wait for Miss Durrant then you might as well be useful! We're rushed off our feet, as you can see, and there's piles and piles of dishes and cutlery waiting to be washed up, so if you nip through into the kitchens and borrow a clean apron you might give Ruth a hand with 'em.'

'Well, yes . . . of course, if I can be . . .' Amy began uncertainly, to be briskly interrupted: 'Good girl. Off wi' you, then!'

In a daze, Amy followed the woman's pointing finger and pushed her way through a baize door, nearly knocking over a perspiring waitress as she did so. She tried to apologise but the woman merely said, 'Gerrout of me way, young 'un. Two beef dinners for table 6!' and continued across the dining room as though Amy did not exist.

In the kitchen Amy saw Ruth up to her elbows in hot suds, frantically working her way through a large pile of dinner plates, cups, saucers and glasses. She also saw, on a hook above the long wooden draining boards, a number of white aprons. Hesitantly, she took one down, hung up her heavy coat and put on the apron. Then she approached the sink. 'Ruthie? Your boss told me to come through and give you a hand, so you'd be free sooner and we could go home. The snow's still falling, so Mrs O'Leary let me go early, but it seems your boss thinks trade's too good to turn down. Shall I wash or wipe?'

Ruth turned and grinned at her, then unhooked a red and white striped cloth from a line of them under the sink and handed it to her friend. 'Wipe,' she said briefly. 'Someone just told me this is the teatime rush and we'll go home soon's it's over. Mrs Owen – she's the boss – isn't a bad sort, but she lives in the city so she don't have to rely on trams an' such to get her home. Start on the plates, will you? It's mainly the smaller ones coming through now; they're not half so mucky as plates what've had dinners on 'em.'

So Amy, used to hard work, settled down to wipe up the mound of crockery and, because the water was very hot indeed and Ruth a thorough and conscientious worker, it was not too bad a job. The dried plates soon began to pile perilously high on the big kitchen table behind the sink, while the piles of unwashed crockery dwindled at last.

At first, Amy had simply worked as hard as she could, but gradually, as the pile of clean plates grew, along with another of cups, saucers and side plates, she began to realise that she was enjoying herself. It was warm in the kitchen and the workers seemed to be a happy crowd. They called out, chaffed one another and even teased Ruth, though she was a newcomer and this was her first day's work. It was hard not to draw comparisons between this sort of work and that of the fish market. The older people in the market were friendly with one another and were quite kind to Amy, but everyone was selling for themselves just as fast as they could and the camaraderie, which was so evident in the Dorothy kitchen, was simply not present in St John's fish market.

Despite Mrs Owen's fears that they might have to close early, business continued to be brisk. It was soon obvious to Amy, peeping into the dining room, that a good many of the customers had come in for a bite to eat because their trams or buses were either not running or running so late that they would miss their evening meal. 'It's good business for Mrs Owen, that's for sure,' she whispered to Ruth as she thumped a pile of plates on to the draining board. 'But what's it going to mean for us, queen? If our tram isn't runnin we'll have to get the overhead railway and I don't know the times of the trains, do you?'

'No, I don't,' Ruth admitted.

'Well,' said Amy, 'I usually catch a tram. Still, if we're late our folks'll guess it's the weather what's held us up. How long will we be here, do you suppose? Only Mr Roper, who sells ice to the fish market, told me about a good sort of woman called Mrs Beckham who lets rooms cheap.' She went on to tell Ruth all about Mrs O'Leary's suggestion and Harry Roper's information, and Ruth listened, bright-eyed.

'If only we could rent the place,' she said longingly when Amy finished her tale. 'I won't deny I'm happier at home than I were in service, but I miss havin' me own space, if you know what I mean. And I shall miss not being able to relax when the day's work is done, because Mam will expect me to set to and help wi' the younger ones. You can't blame her, but if I weren't livin' at home . . .'

'Shall we go round to this court, off Skelhorne Street, when we finish here, then?' Amy asked eagerly. 'I'm game if you are, Ruthie. After all, we're going to be late whatever we do, so we might as well get some good out of it.'

This somewhat garbled reasoning seemed eminently sensible to Ruth, so the two girls continued to work hard until seven o'clock, when Mrs Owen came into the kitchens to tell them that they had done very well and might go home now. 'I'll see you tomorrow morning,' she said to Ruth and then turned to Amy: 'Thank you very much, young 'un. If you ever need a job you can come to me for a reference.' She held out a hand and dropped several coins into Amy's palm. 'You've earned every penny, my dear,' she added as Amy stared blankly at her. 'You didn't think I'd expect you to work for me wi'out so much as a penny piece in payment, did you?'

'I . . . I didn't really think, Mrs Owen,' Amy stammered. 'It was so nice and warm in the kitchen and I was helping Ruthie to get finished sooner . . . but thanks ever so much. Why, I reckon we could go home in a taxi cab if we wanted!'

Mrs Owen laughed, but shook her head. 'Gerron a tram, chuck,' she advised, turning to take down her heavy coat from its peg and beginning to struggle into it. 'There's bound to be a tram goin' your way.'

Presently the two girls, well muffled against the storm, stood on the edge of the pavement waiting to cross. Despite the lateness of the hour the street was still busy and, as they waited, a tram swept past, sending a bow wave of filthy slush towards them.

Amy jumped back with an exclamation of disgust, grabbing Ruth's arm to pull her out of danger as well and, as she did so, saw a white and malignant face leering at her from the tram window. It was Paddy, plainly delighted to see her soaked and probably imagining that she had missed the last tram into the bargain, which might well get her into trouble at home.

'Still, he'll tell Mr Logan you're goin' to be late,' Ruth observed when Amy told her who had been pulling faces at them from the tram. 'So you needn't be afraid they'll worry or owt like that.'

The roadway being temporarily clear, the two girls hurried across straight into Skelhorne Street. It was wide and well lit, but when she glanced to her right, for the bulk of Lime Street Station lay to the left, Amy saw that the streets leading off were very much narrower and far darker. 'Let me see, Mr Roper said the court was off Hilbre Street. He said number 8 Kingfisher. Can you see it, Ruthie?'

'Dunno, but this here's Hilbre Street,' Ruth said, turning briskly to her right. 'Better try the first entry we come to.'

The courts off Hilbre Street proved to be as dark and confusing as Amy had imagined. At first the two girls wandered up and down the central pavement between the tiny terraced houses, hoping to meet someone who could tell them where Mrs Beckham lived. Because of the inclement weather, however, doors were firmly closed and finally they were forced to begin to leave the courts and search for a friendly shopkeeper who might have the information they required.

The first small general store they reached was run by a weary, grey-haired old woman in a draggly purple skirt, with a grey shawl closely wrapped round her meagre frame. She did not know Mrs Beckham but suggested they try the fried fish shop a short distance away. 'They know everyone, the Dempseys, and if they don't the customers will,' she assured them, going to the doorway to point them in the right direction. 'Folk in the courts all know one another, even if they'd slit each other's throats for a farden,' she added with a toothless grin.

This was not encouraging but the two girls took her advice. 'We're only *looking*,' Amy pointed out as they made their way through the fast-falling flakes. 'We can say we've got to talk it over with our folks and if we don't like it, we just won't go back ever again.'

Ruth agreed that this seemed sensible and when they reached the fried fish shop the atmosphere was so friendly – and the smell of frying fish and potatoes so tempting – that it was easy to forget the old woman's embittered words. What was more, at the mere mention of the name Beckham the man behind the counter paused in his task of heaping a generous scoop of golden chipped potatoes into a square of newspaper to say cheerfully, 'Oh, yes. I know her well, queen. She lives at number 8 Kingfisher Court, though I dare say you won't be able to see the street names at this time o' night. It's the second entry along.' He finished serving the customer before them and raised grizzled eyebrows. 'Want two penn'orth o' chips to keep out the cold, girls? I dare say you can share a paper between you.'

Feeling that the information was worth at least tuppence, Amy and Ruth handed over a penny each and leant on the end of the counter, eating their chips and watching Mr Dempsey's deft movements, enjoying their impromptu meals. Then they set off once more, tracking down their destination without more ado.

'Though this place hasn't seen a kingfisher for a hundred years, if then,' Amy grumbled, as the two girls followed Mr Dempsey's instructions. 'Blackbird would be a deal more appropriate, wouldn't you say?'

'You may be right, but kingfisher is more cheerful,' Ruth said, as they turned into the dark and grimy court, lit by one flickering gaslight. 'Lordie, ain't it dark, though? I can't see a number on a single bleedin' door.'

Once they had established that this was where Mrs Beckham lived by the simple expedient of knocking loudly on the nearest door until their knock was answered, it was the work of a moment to walk another four doors along and knock there.

Mrs Beckham, though she had not expected visitors in such appalling weather, asked them inside and, clucking over their wet coats and shoes, sat them down in her kitchen before a cheerful fire. 'I've just put the kettle on for a nice cup o' tea and I was going to toast meself a couple o' rounds o' bread, 'cos it's no weather to be chasing down to the Dempseys for fried fish,' she observed, settling herself in a creaking basketwork chair. 'I dare say someone telled you I have a room to rent?'

Amy explained about Mr Roper. She had already decided that she liked the older woman – who, despite being in her late sixties, seemed both lively and humorous – and thought that she and Ruth could be happy in this cheerful little house.

Mrs Beckham immediately got to her feet and gestured to them to follow her. 'I'm not sayin' as it's a palace,' she said over her shoulder, as the three of them mounted the narrow stairway. 'But it's newly decorated every spring and nicely furnished, though I do say it as shouldn't'. She flung open one of the brown-painted doors on the small upper landing and stood back, so that the two girls could look into the room by the light of the lamp she held.

It was not a large room, and the beds were narrow and pushed back against the wall to give more space, but the walls were freshly whitewashed, the linoleum shone with polishing and the curtains, already drawn to shut out the night, were brightly patterned and cheerful. Amy saw two comfortable fireside chairs, a primus stove and a washstand with an enamelled jug and basin upon it. Both beds had matching pink and white counterpanes and the small fireplace had a narrow mantelpiece above it, on which were a couple of china figures, one a flower seller with a basket of blossoms at her feet, the other a shepherd boy with two lambs.

'I asks ten shillin' a week and you've use of me kitchen, since there ain't much you can cook on a primus and the fireplace is turrble small,' Mrs Beckham said. Amy was grateful that the information was unsolicited, since she would have felt shy about asking the rent of the room. She nodded and smiled, and Mrs Beckham added that she provided neither towels nor bed linen, but was happy to allow the girls to wash such items either in her kitchen or the communal wash-house in the court. 'I've gorra line what stretches from my place to Mrs Haddock's,' she explained. 'These houses is back to back, you see, so there's no jigger nor no yard, worse luck. But there's two taps at the far end of the court and two lavvies, o' course.' She turned to leave the room, ushering the girls before her and closing the door. Then she went ahead of them down the stairs, lighting the way with the lamp.

In the kitchen once more, she removed their steaming coats from the wooden kitchen chair on which she had placed them and handed them to her guests. 'You'll want to talk this over between yourselves,' she said briskly, ushering them through the doorway by which they had entered. 'But I'd be obliged if you'd give me an answer in a couple o' days. Me rooms is popular; I've got two nurses sharin' the attic room already, but I don't deny I could do with a couple more lodgers. We're conveniently situated here,' she went on, 'only a step away from St John's Market, so food's cheap and it's not far to go for your grub. Dearie me, I never asked your names, but plenty of time for that if you decide to take me room.' She flung open the front door, gave them a bright smile and exclaimed that it was a devilish cold night, so she'd not linger in the doorway. Almost before the words were out of her mouth, the door slammed briskly shut, leaving Amy and Ruth with only the slight illumination of the solitary gas lamp to guide their footsteps back to the road.

'Wasn't it a dear little room, though?' Amy said wistfully, as they trudged across the snow-covered paving. 'But five bob a week each – we wouldn't have enough money to buy food with, let alone clothes and that.'

'I might,' Ruth said thoughtfully. 'I get tips when I'm waitin' on the customers and the other girls say they mount up. But of course, the job ain't permanent, I might be out of work in a couple o' weeks. You ... you really don't think we could afford it if we got ourselves a second job, like? I'd be willin' to try ... and we'd save our tram fares.'

But delightful though the thought of being independent was, both girls knew that taking the room as things stood was impossible, so it was rather sadly that they turned their steps towards the main road.

'Tell you what, though, I'm ever so glad we saw the room,' Ruth said, as they paused in the court entrance. 'I never knew what I wanted before. Now I do. I want to live in a little house like that, with a dear little room two pals can share.'

Amy, agreeing, felt exactly the same. At least it was a goal, something to aim for. Escape from Suzie's despotic rule would have been good, but to share a room like that with her best friend would have been even better. So it was in reasonably high spirits, despite their disappointment over the rent, that the two set off on their journey back to Seaforth.

The girls had gone on their court hunt for Mrs Beckham at seven o'clock, but it was past nine before they had finally left Mrs Beckham's little house and as soon as they re-entered the roadway Amy realised that, far from easing, the storm raged harder than ever. She stopped short as they left the comparative shelter of the narrow little road and gazed at Ruth in blank dismay. 'We'll never get a tram in this,' she said, pulling down her muffling scarf so that Ruth could hear her words. 'Shall we make our way to the Pier Head and catch the overhead railway? 'Cos I don't fancy trying to walk in this weather.'

'Ye-es, only I ain't too sure which way we should be headin',' Ruth said, glancing at the confusion of whirling flakes which had already effectively hidden such aids as street names. 'Is it far, Amy?'

'Shouldn't think so,' Amy answered cheerfully. She did not intend to admit that, what with the confusion of searching the courts and the way the snow changed the aspect of the little streets, she had no more idea than Ruth in which direction the Pier Head lay. But surely when they reached the more frequented streets there would be somebody from whom they could get directions? So she pulled her scarf over her mouth once more, linked arms with her friend and set off in what she devoutly hoped was the right direction. She told herself that, no matter how ferocious the weather, the docker's umbrella would continue to function, but a nagging doubt reminded her that she did not know the time of the last train, so they had better not linger. But of course Ruthie, who had been away from Liverpool for so long and had never worked here before, would not think of such a thing. Therefore it's up to me, Amy told herself stoutly, head bent against the gale, to think for both of us. So it was with the resolution to keep Ruthie cheerful and unworried that she set off into the storm.

Bill grew anxious as the evening progressed, and Amy did not put in an appearance, and suggested to his wife that it might be as well if he walked up to the terminus to see whether the trams were still running. 'Amy's terrible late,' he said bluntly. 'It ain't like her, Suzie. I can't see Mrs O'Leary keepin' her till after dark on a night like this, but I suppose somethin' must have come up to detain her. If she catches the tram it's a fair walk against the wind, she'll do better with my arm to hang on to.'

'You spoil that kid, Bill,' Suzie grumbled. She was sitting in front of the fire, roasting chestnuts and whenever a nut blackened she would hook it out with the end of the toasting fork, shed the husk and, as soon as it was cool enough, would crunch the delicacy down. 'What's a bit of a walk through the snow when you're her age? It's a lark, that's wharrit is, but you'll go off and leave me alone wi' young Becky, just so's your precious Amy gets give an arm.'

Bill, halfway across the kitchen to fetch his coat, stopped and glanced uneasily across at his wife. He did not understand her attitude. She often accused him of favouring Amy, yet the girl worked hard, both in her job for Mrs O'Leary and at home. On the other hand, Suzie was very good with the baby. As he sighed and scratched his head over the problem of his daughter's lateness, he wondered, not for the first time, why on earth would his wife resent the kid? Making up his mind, he went over to the door and took his coat off the hook. No matter what Suzie thought, or why, he knew his duty and that meant a walk in the snow on such a night. 'There's a worse storm ragin' out there than there's been for many a year,' he said, slipping into the coat. 'She's mebbe young and healthy, as you say, but Amy's a skinny little thing; this wind could blow her down like a ninepin if she weren't careful, so I'll just walk up the road and . . .'

He was reaching for his cap and scarf when the back door opened abruptly, cutting him off in mid-sentence. Paddy entered the kitchen, looking like a snowman, with a package in his hands which he slammed down on to the table, before beginning to divest himself of his snow-laden garments. 'It's bleedin' terrible out there,' he said breathlessly, stamping his feet and rubbing his hands to try to get the feeling back into them. 'Where's you goin', Uncle Bill? I wouldn't send a dog out on a night like this, honest to God I wouldn't.'

'Amy's not in,' Bill told him briefly, reaching for his muffler. 'Did you catch the last tram, Paddy, or are they still runnin' like normal?'

'I've been back in Seaforth an hour or more.' Paddy pointed to the package on the table. 'Them's chipped potatoes. I come home wi' Donny Fisher and we had to queue at the fried fish shop. I dunno about the trams, but I saw Amy crossin' Lime Street.' His tone grew sharp with malice. 'She were clutchin' some fella's arm – I reckon it were Tommy Chee – and makin' for the backstreets, so no wonder she's late.'

Bill stopped in the act of pulling on his thick wool gloves and stared unbelievingly at Paddy. 'You saw her with Tommy Chee?' he asked incredulously. 'That can't be right. I telled her months back that she weren't to see no more of that young feller. She wouldn't go agin me.'

'I'm only tellin' you what I saw,' Paddy said rather belligerently. 'Theys was all muffled up but she don't know any fellas 'cept for my pal Tommy, what she's been and gone and stole off of me. Still, I suppose if you want to walk up to the terminus, there's no harm in it.'

'Yes, there is,' Suzie said aggressively, rising to her feet. 'I'm tellin' you, Bill Logan, if you go out after that spoilt brat and mek yourself ill, I shan't be nursin' you, 'cos you'll have asked for it, that's what you'll have done. Look at Paddy there, more like a pillar of ice than a human bein' and he's not half

179

your age. Just you tek them things off and give over bein' so foolish and I'll mek you a nice hot cuppa. By the time you've got it down you, likely the gal will be back – and the young feller with her if he's got any sense.'

'I told her not to have nothin' to do wi' Tommy Chee,' Bill said, going towards the back door and opening it into the teeth of the gale. 'I'll not have me daughter larkin' around in this sort o' weather with anyone, let alone a chap as I've forbid her to see.' And before Suzie could say another word, he was out through the door and battling his way towards the tram terminus.

It was gone midnight before two thoroughly exhausted girls reached Seaforth once more. For the overhead railway had not been able to battle all the way out to Seaforth, so they had been forced to walk from Alexandra Station. As Amy dropped Ruth off at her door, however, she remarked that the storm seemed to be lessening at last and, weary though they were, the girls agreed to meet next morning on the tram that would take them both in to work – if they were running by the following day. But the salt wind from the sea usually saw off snow and ice quite quickly, so there was a good chance that by next morning things would be at least nearly normal.

Amy let herself into the kitchen as quietly as she could, guessing that the rest of the family would be in bed. Sure enough, the kitchen was empty. When she had hung her soaking outer garments over the clothes horse to dry before the fire, put on some more fuel so that it would not go and die on her and made herself a hot drink to take up to bed, she heard a sound from the stairs. She thought that perhaps Albert might have worried over her lateness but to her astonishment it was Suzie who came out of her bedroom on to the little top landing, a scruffy shawl round her shoulders and her hair in curl papers. 'Where've you been, you wicked gal?' she hissed, as Amy began ascending the stairs. 'Oh, you deserve a good thrashing for keepin' your dad out so late in this terrible weather. What's more, I've not slept a wink for worryin' over the pair of youse. I telled Bill you was old enough to manage for yourself and come in when you felt like it, but would he listen? No, off he goes into that fearful weather to wait at the tram terminus till you turned up, no doubt. Is he still below? You should ha' sent him up first, 'stead of scurrying for your own bed, like the spoilt little madam you are . . .'

'Tram terminus?' Amy exclaimed, quite bewildered by this flood of invective. 'But I didn't come by tram, I came by the docker's umbrella. The last tram was hours and hours ago, so Ruthie and me went along to the Pier Head and caught the train. Only it stopped at Alexandra and couldn't go any further, so we had to walk.'

'You didn't . . . Oh, my God! But you must have walked past the terminus. Didn't you see no sign of your dad? I'm tellin' you, he set off to walk there hours since and he's still not back.'

'There wasn't a sign of anyone waiting,' Amy said doubtfully. 'There was one tram standing in the middle of the road, all covered in snow, but no sign of my dad. He must've gone into a house nearby for shelter – Mr Benbow lives near there, on Peel Road, doesn't he? Do you suppose he's popped in there and got benighted?'

'No, of course he hasn't – wouldn't dream of doin' such a thing and worryin' the life out o' me. Oh, Gawd, wharrever's happened to my Bill, then?' Suzie spun round and hurled the door of the boys' room so wide that it crashed against the wall. Amy could hear her hollering at them, and guessed she was shouting at Gus and shaking Albert and Paddy, who slept like the dead once they had gone off. 'Oh, my Gawd, oh, my Gawd,' Suzie wailed. 'Gerrup fellers, we're in real trouble. Here's that blamed Amy come home by the docker's umbrella and she says she never saw my Bill when she passed the tram terminus. So gerrup the lot of you, you've gorra go and search for him.'

Amy took a hasty swig of her hot drink and then went towards the clothes horse where her coat still steamed. She began to struggle into it again, as sounds of stirring came from upstairs. She was still searching for a dry headscarf to replace her wet one when the boys came clattering into the kitchen, Gus in the lead. All three of them were pale-faced. Gus stared at her as though he were still dreaming. 'Amy? Is it true what Suzie just said? Is me dad out in this awful weather?'

'He must be, since she says he's not come in,' Amy said briefly. She went over to the dresser and rummaged through the cupboards for another pair of woollen gloves to replace her wet ones, then pulled them on. 'Is Suzie coming to search, too? Or is it just us three?'

'Four,' Albert said gruffly. 'Unless you'd rather stay in, our Amy? Only you're already awful wet – I reckon our dad would rather you didn't go searchin' for him in this weather and at this hour.'

'I'm coming,' Amy stated, but did not explain that

she had not expected Paddy to join them. He was not a Logan, after all, though had she been forced to give her honest opinion she would have had to admit that she thought the boy was very attached to her dad. Despite the fact that there had been no work for him on the shrimp boat, Bill took Paddy with him as a replacement for Gus or Albert when they had a day off, and said that Paddy was useful and had all the right ideas. 'But three's plenty for a boat the size of the *Mersey Maid*,' he was wont to say half apologetically. 'If Gus ever wants to go his own way, same as our Ed and Charlie have done, then I'd tek Paddy aboard like a shot. But until that day it's the just three of us.'

So now, the boys wrapped up, all four of them set out, Amy walking with Gus. They reached the tram terminus in good time and, having seen nobody waiting, were about to turn back when Albert gave a shout. 'What's that ... in that doorway? It may be some old tramp ...'

The four of them ran, slipping and sliding through the thick layer of snow, to where a figure lay slumped, half in a shop doorway, but more across the pavement. The reason he had been difficult to see was that he, too, was thickly covered with snow, but as soon as Gus rolled him over, Amy gave a cry. 'It's our dad!' she gasped and began to try to lift him, with the boys doing the same. 'Oh, whatever's come to him, Gus?'

Gus was a quiet young man, not given to much shows of emotion, but when Amy looked into his face, as they gradually lifted Bill up into a sitting position, she saw tears shining in his eyes. 'Reckon he had some sort o' attack,' he said. 'Or mebbe slipped and hit his head. There's a bump over his right eye . . . see?'

Amy looked, but could make out little in the dim light. 'But . . . but he's alive, isn't he, Gus?' she quavered. 'He wouldn't die from a fall, would he? Suzie says it's my fault because I was late coming home, but how could I possibly know our dad would come looking for me and have a fall? Oh, Gus, I do love our dad, I can't bear to think of him hurt bad!'

As though he had heard, Bill gave a deep, rather frightening groan, then said in a husky whisper, 'I'm awright, thanks. If you'll help me to me feet, gentlemen all, I'll be mekin' me way home for me wife will be worried that I'm so late. I must ha' fell as I got down from me fishin' boat . . . the snow's that confusin' . . .'

'We aren't gentlemen, Dad, it's me, Amy, and the boys,' Amy said, her voice breaking. 'Don't you know us?'

Bill looked vaguely up at her, then his eyes slid away and his head sagged. He was plainly barely conscious; had probably not heard what she had said.

'Don't worry him, Amy love, he's not hisself,' Gus said authoritatively. 'Albert, you're a sturdy feller, you take hold of him round the waist and we'll make him a chair atwixt us. Paddy, you take him under the knees and see he don't slide forward. Amy, you run home and get the brandy out of the little end cupboard in the fish scullery. Oh, and warm a blanket, and pull the kettle over the flame.'

Anxious to do everything she had been told, Amy fairly flew back to the house, burst into the kitchen and told Suzie, in a gabble, that they had found Bill, that he had been lying in the snow and was, she feared, ill. 'He seemed not to know us, but Gus said I was to warm a blanket and bring out the little bottle of brandy in the end cupboard.'

Suzie immediately bridled, as though Amy had somehow insulted her. 'No, that you won't.' Her tone was vicious. 'Anything that's to be done for my Bill I'll do meself, I thank you. You've done harm enough already.'

'I've done nothing wrong,' Amy said, defensively, heading for the stairs. There were blankets on her bed which she could bring down for her father. 'I didn't *know* he was going to wait up for me, did I?'

She disappeared into her room, grabbed a couple of blankets and came hurrying down the stairs once more. Suzie came over, took the blankets and spread them over a chair before the fire, then said spitefully, 'Get out of me sight. It's your fault that we're in this terrible fix, your fault . . .'

The opening of the door stopped her dead in her tracks. Gus and Albert came in, Bill's moribund form between them, with Paddy holding the door wide, then closing it quickly behind them to keep the weather out. Without another word they began to get Bill out of his wet clothes and into the warmed blankets, while Suzie made a drink from the boiling water in the kettle.

'We need a doctor,' Gus said, after they had settled Bill as comfortably as they could upon the sofa. 'Albert . . .'

Albert was out of the door on the words and Amy followed him, anxious now only to get away from Suzie's sharp tongue. Once her father was better she would explain to him why she had been late. Dad would understand, she was sure.

The matter, which had seemed grave enough in all conscience when the young people had brought Bill home, turned out, upon the doctor's arrival, to be even more serious. 'He's concussed, following a nasty bang on the head, and freezing cold from exposure,' he said briefly, having examined Bill. 'He'll be best in hospital.' He had looked rather hard at Suzie. 'Might he have taken a drink or two?' he asked. 'If he was somewhat uncertain of his footing...'

Suzie was silent, looking a little self-conscious, but Gus said at once, 'My father only has the occasional pint, Doctor Payne. He couldn't have had a drink tonight anyway, 'cos he went out far too late.'

'Then perhaps he slipped on the icy pavement,' the doctor said quickly. 'I don't think he should be moved, not immediately at any rate. I'll come in first thing tomorrow – only it is today already, of course – to see how he's going on. In the meantime keep him warm and quiet. There's nothing broken, only a nasty bruise on his head.'

Amy looked in on her father early next morning before the rest of the family were up and found the kitchen quite warm, despite the fact that the fire had burned very low. Of Suzie there was no sign, but while she was making up the fire with fresh logs brought in from the backyard, she came in from the scullery. She had a shawl wrapped round her shoulders and must, Amy supposed, have been out to the lavatory, for she was holding up her night-gown so that the hem would not get wet and wore on her feet the short rubber boots which she kept by the back door. She gave Amy a baleful glance, then went and sat in the old armchair, which she had drawn up close to the sofa.

Amy finished mending the fire and pulled the kettle over the flame. It was already hot and soon boiled, so she made a pot of tea and poured out two cups, carrying one across to her stepmother. 'Has he woke at all yet?' she asked, eyeing her father's pale face anxiously. The livid bruise had swollen the right-hand side of his brow, giving him a lopsided, angry appearance. 'He doesn't look too bright, poor Dad.'

Suzie appeared to give this question some thought before replying, briefly, 'He ain't stirred all night. I've not moved from his side save to go out to the lavvy just now.' She took the proffered cup of tea without a word of thanks and sipped it noisily.

'The doctor said he'd be round early; I wonder if I ought to wait until he's been?' Amy said. It worried her to see Bill lying there so pale and still.

But Suzie shook her head.

'You gerroff to work. Your dad ain't going to be fishing for a bit, so we'll need every penny the rest of you can earn.'

Amy finished her tea and began to struggle into her coat. She went over to the sofa and kissed her father lightly on the forehead. 'See you tonight, Dad,' she said in a low voice. 'Wish I could stay, but I wouldn't be welcome – I reckon you know that. The boys will be up soon, though, and they'll see to anything Suzie wants done.'

For a moment Amy thought she saw Bill's eyelids flicker, but he continued to lie absolutely still and she concluded that it was wishful thinking. He was still far away, in a land of his own, where none of them could follow him. So she wrapped herself as warmly as she could and left the house, closing the door behind her.

The previous day's storm had given way to a brisk, salt-laden breeze and a clear sky. The snow still lay piled up beside the road, but Amy guessed that it would probably not linger long. She did not know whether the trams would be running, but thought it would be better to walk in to work, rather than return to the house to face Suzie's anger and resentment. She did not know why her stepmother was blaming her so cruelly and unreasonably for what was most certainly not her fault, but she already knew that Suzie's bouts of ill temper were best avoided.

She reached Ruth's house just as her friend emerged from the jigger and hurried eagerly to meet her. 'Oh, Ruthie, we're in awful trouble at home, just wait until I tell you ...'

Chapter Six

The day of the storm, which was to remain vivid in the minds of the Logan children for many years, was almost equally bad for others. When Amy arrived at the fish market the stall was not manned. Mrs O'Leary, it transpired, had gone to the home of her married daughter but had insisted on setting out for her own house as soon as tea was over, on the grounds that if she did not leave soon she would miss the last tram. She had caught it all right, but had also caught, along with it, a severe chill through hanging around in the snow and wind. She was now in bed and would be for some time. The man on the next stall informed Amy, with a certain amount of relish, that he had had a visit from Mrs O'Leary's sister Bridget, who ran the flat they shared nearby. She had told him that Mrs O'Leary was in bed, with a fire lit in her room, a hot toddy by her bedside, with Bridget waiting on her hand and foot and telling her at frequent intervals that she had been a fool to rush round to young Maria's place in such weather instead of coming straight home.

'I wonder what I ought to do?' Amy mused, more to herself than to Mr Mosscrop, but he answered her anyway, being a man fond of both the sound of his own voice and the airing of his own opinions.

'Do? Why, gal, there's no point in you hangin' around here, for no craft will set out in weather such as this, so there'll be no fresh fish bein' brung in.

Why, your da is a fisherman. I doubt he's took the boat out today, has he?'

'He's ill,' Amy said briefly. Mr Mosscrop could be pleasant enough, but being the stall next to Mrs O'Leary, he was also their chief competition. Amy knew very well that if there was any business going Mr Mosscrop would do his very best to see that it came to him and not to herself. If that meant encouraging her to go home and leave the stall unattended, he would not think twice about it. Accordingly she said, 'I'll hang on, thanks all the same, Mr M. We've still got a bit of fish left in the icebox and you never know. Customers do turn up when you least expect 'em.'

Mr Mosscrop, his advice clearly flouted, grunted and turned away, and Amy began to scrub down and then set out the stall. As she worked she thought once more of her father, then of the possibility of her moving out of the house in Seafield Grove. She had always been a favourite with Bill and she adored him, but since Suzie – and Paddy, of course – had entered their lives, things had not been so simple. She knew that Suzie was jealous of the affection between herself and her father; knew that Paddy, in his own way, was equally jealous of the friendship between herself and Albert and probably, for all she knew, of the good feeling which existed between Gus and herself. But she did not see why Suzie should resent so bitterly a relationship which was no threat to herself, that of father and daughter.

But whether she understood it or not, Suzie's antagonism had, of late, made life in the little house in Seafield Grove very difficult. Paddy never missed an opportunity to let Bill see his daughter in a bad light and Suzie not only criticised everything she did, but grumbled to Bill that his daughter thought more of her job in the fish market than she did of the 'little tasks' she was asked to perform at home. And though she took five of the seven shillings and sixpence which Amy earned each week, she was always saying it was not enough to feed such a greedy great girl, though admitting sourly that the fish Amy brought home from the stall at the end of each day's work was a bit of a help towards her keep.

Yet Amy knew it was not simply the fact that she was not happy at home which made her want to move out. Ruthie was very happy at home, but she felt she wanted a bit more independence. They might tell each other it was because they needed to be nearer their work that made the move attractive, but Amy knew this was not so. They were growing up, growing away from the family background, the brothers and sisters sharing beds; for the bed which she and Mary had shared was now occupied by herself and baby Becky. 'Little birds want to leave the nest and spread their wings,' a particularly annoying teacher had been wont to say to the class, when talking about what jobs they would wish to do. At least, Amy had thought her a particularly annoying woman, but she had merely been putting into words what all the class should have been thinking – that growing up meant getting away, leaving home, finding a place of one's own.

Despite early fears that she was wasting her time by setting out the stall, Amy soon realised that she had done the right thing, which was comforting. Mr Mosscrop and herself did good business, for folk who had not shopped the day before because of the inclement weather were doing so now in earnest. By four o'clock, when dusk was falling fast, Amy was able to clean down and change out of her fishy apron and her stained wooden clogs, knowing that there was a nice little sum of money in the black japanned box to take round to Mrs O'Leary, now that work was finished for the day.

Mrs O'Leary lived with her sister Bridget in a two-bedroomed flat over a millinery shop on Mount Pleasant. Amy had visited the place before and had thought it very snug, and this evening, with a bright fire burning in the bedroom grate and Miss Bridget Flynn toasting slices of bread before it, it seemed an idyllic place to live, particularly when compared with her own home.

The young girl who had let Amy into the flat and accompanied her to Mrs O'Leary's bedroom said, 'Here's someone to see you Miz O'Leary,' ushering Amy into the room and closing the door behind her.

Bridget turned away from the fire and smiled at Amy, while slipping a slice of toast off her fork and beginning to butter it. When it was done she held it out to Amy with the words, 'You'll be fair clemmed, workin' all day in the fish market wi'out me sister's help. Eat this whiles I pour me sister a cuppa. Then you can tell her how it's gone today.'

Amy crunched the toast and watched, as Bridget set about pouring the tea and waking her sister, who had clearly fallen into an uneasy slumber. Presently, with Mrs O'Leary supping the tea, Amy was able to ask Bridget in a quiet voice how her employer was going on. The younger sister was a skinny, self-reliant woman in her fifties. Amy knew she worked as a supervisor at a big clothing factory and was much valued by her employers, for Mrs O'Leary was proud as well as fond of her sister and frequently

192

talked about Bridget's 'career', a word she would never have used about her own work. Amy guessed that the little girl who had let her in was the maid the sisters employed to keep house while they were at work, so there would be no necessity for Miss Flynn to be away from the factory while her sister was ill.

'She's got a bad chill, there's no denyin' it,' Bridget told her. 'And it's gone on her chest, like her chills nearly always does. But I've known her a good deal worse than this and we've caught it early, so mebbe, in a week or ten days, she'll be back in the fish market.' She eyed Amy keenly. 'Can you manage till then, chuck? I know you're only young, but me sister sets great store by you, so she does. There'll be a few bob extra in your hand at the end of that time, 'cos I know it ain't everyone who'd stand by Mrs O'Leary the way you will. I s'pose there's no chance of your dad or one of your brothers givin' a hand? You won't need help while the weather stays severe, but if we have a mild day or two, when the fleet can get out, then folk'll fancy fresh fish again and you'll mebbe need some help.'

Mrs O'Leary, who had been sipping her tea, suddenly seemed to realise that Amy was in the room. 'It's good of you to come, queen,' she said huskily. Amy could hear the breath wheezing in her chest as she spoke. 'Done much today?'

Amy went over to the bed and opened the japanned box. 'Look, we've done quite well,' she said proudly. 'And we're clear out of fresh fish to sell. But it's been a fair day today, so maybe the fleet will have sailed and there'll be more to sell tomorrow.'

'You're a good gal,' Mrs O'Leary wheezed. 'Has

your dad sailed today? If so, I'll warrant he'll bring his catch straight to us.'

'My dad's ill with concussion,' Amy said dolefully. 'But maybe Gus and Albert will have taken the boat out. I'll find out when I get home.'

'Your dad's ill!' Mrs O'Leary exclaimed, real sympathy in her thickened voice. 'You shouldn't ha' bothered to bring the money round, queen, when you must be anxious to gerroff home and see how he's a doin'. Tomorrer, I'll send young Alfie – he's me grandson – to collect the money, so's you don't have to trail round here. Off you go then, Amy, and give your dad me best wishes for a quick recovery.'

'Thanks, Mrs O'Leary.' Amy headed for the door. 'But I reckon I'd rather come round myself, if it's all the same to you. It wouldn't be fair to put all that on a little lad. Good night, both.'

Freed from the responsibility of her employer's money, Amy fairly flew along the pavement towards the tram terminus at Lime Street. Her luck was in and the tram waiting was a number 23, which would take her all the way to Seaforth Sands.

During the journey on the tram her thoughts had been divided between a half-apprehensive fear of the responsibility of looking after the fish stall while Mrs O'Leary was ill and pride that her employer was willing to trust her. Once she was on Seafield Grove, however, worry over her father simply took over, and it was with quickened step and fast-beating heart that she hurried down the jigger, across the yard and in at the back door.

Suzie was standing by the fire, staring down into the flames. Her face was bloated and blotched by the heat, Amy thought, but on hearing the door open Suzie swung round and Amy realised that the older woman's face was wet with tears. Her heart jumped into her mouth. 'Is ... is Dad ...?' she faltered, staring at Suzie. 'Oh, Suzie, is me dad worse?'

'They've took him to the hospital.' Suzie's voice was thick with tears. 'He were real bad, delirious, the doctor said. I stayed with him until it were time for the boys to come in; then they said I should come home and they would spell me for a bit while I got meself some food. He were still unconscious and he sounded mortal bad.'

'Which hospital?' Amy asked baldly. She had unbuttoned her coat and now she buttoned it up again. 'Which ward, come to that?'

'They've took him to the Stanley,' Suzie said dolefully. She sniffed, dabbing at her face with a filthy rag of a handkerchief, then she seemed to remember that she disliked Amy and looked up, her mouth twisting spitefully. 'But don't you go there worriting the nurses, Amy Logan, for I won't have my Bill made any worse than you've made him already.'

Amy, who had been pulling on her gloves and turning towards the back door, stared at Suzie. 'What on earth do you mean?' she asked, genuine puzzlement in her voice. 'It wasn't my fault that I worked late and came home by the docker's umbrella instead of the tram, though you keep saying it was. There's no sense in casting blame anyroad. It doesn't do anyone any good, it might even make my dad worse if he knew what you were saying.'

'Knew what I were sayin'?' Suzie tipped back her head and laughed without amusement. 'Why, your dad knows all about it. He were that distressed when my Paddy told what he knew that nothing would do but for him to go out into the storm to make sure you didn't get into no more trouble. Bad enough that you ignored my Bill's wishes and did what he 'spressly told you not to do ...'

'Suzie, I haven't got the foggiest idea what you're talking about,' Amy said helplessly, but she was beginning to be very angry. 'I never did what my dad told me not to do, though he wasn't one for laying down the law, not in general, he wasn't. So just what did your Paddy tell him about me? Because I'd take money it wasn't true, whatever it was.'

Suzie ruffled up indignantly, her cheeks reddening at the implied insult. 'Why, Paddy telled your father that he saw you junketing around the Liverpool streets wi' that chinky feller what my Bill telled you never to see no more,' she said triumphantly. 'He were on the tram, but he said you weren't even tryin' to catch it, the two of you went giggling off into one of the side streets – up to no good I'll swear, what with you comin' home after midnight, brazen-faced as any streetwalker. Oh, yes, me lady, your father knew what you were up to and ...'

'If your son told my dad that I were with anyone but my pal Ruthie, then he's a worse liar than all the rest of your bloody family put together,' Amy screamed, crossing the room in a couple of bounds and ending up almost nose to nose with Suzie. 'I told you I was with Ruthie and I'm not in the habit of telling lies, unlike some! As for Tommy Chee, I stopped seeing him when my dad told me to, though I thought it were a pack of nonsense, and if Paddy told him different then it's him who's responsible for my dad being in hospital 'stead of home with the rest of us. So what've you got to say to that?'

Suzie had stepped back a pace but now she said, 'Paddy had no reason to lie. He just told my Bill what he saw and . . .'

'You make me sick,' Amy spat, turning to the door. 'I'm going to see my dad and you may be sure I'll tell him that your precious son filled his head with a pack of lies. And don't you try to stop me,' she added, as Suzie grabbed at her sleeve, 'because you've done enough harm, you and your precious Paddy!'

Amy arrived at the hospital just as Albert and Paddy came down the stairs and crossed the foyer towards her. Albert put an arm round her shoulders and gave her a squeeze. 'Dad's still unconscious, Amy, but there's a bit of colour in his cheeks and the nurses seem a little more hopeful. He was awful grey when we first arrived and he's breathing kind of funny, but he doesn't seem so bad, somehow, as he did at first. Gus has gone to the telegraph office to let Edmund, Charlie and Mary know what has happened,' Albert said gently, and Amy saw that both boys were pale and anxious-looking.

She had known for some time that Paddy was very fond of her father; thought of him as though he were a much-loved uncle, but she found she could not even look at him after one quick, initial glance. He had told lies about her to her father and she had been unable to repudiate them. She thought desperately that Bill's recovery might be held back by what Paddy had said. She had never liked Paddy, but now she hated and despised him, and would do so, she told herself, for the rest of her days. 'Do you mean Dad's still very ill, Albert?' she asked and her voice only had a tiny shake in it. 'But Suzie said they'd sent her home to get a meal and a change of clothing – I thought he must have improved, must be holding his own.'

'The doctor thought the same and likely he's right; but he's with Dad now. They told us to come down and get a breath of air while he's examined,' Albert replied. 'Seems they're worried about the possibility of pneumonia, what with him lying out in the snow for so long.' Albert's voice broke and he hugged her shoulders convulsively.

'Pneumonia!' Amy thought of her father, his loving ways, his gentleness. People died from pneumonia, she knew. As soon as she possibly could she must tell Dad that Paddy had mistaken Ruth for Tommy, which would clear up the whole horrible misunderstanding. If only Albert was wrong and it wasn't pneumonia. It would break her heart if Bill were to die, particularly thinking ill of her. She felt tears rise to her eyes and closed them, praying with all her might that her father would recover, would not leave them, as her mother had done. Amy felt another hand on her arm and realised that both boys were steering her across the foyer towards the stairs; the wards, she knew, were all on the first floor. She opened tear-drowned eyes and saw Paddy's face, only inches from hers. She glared at him and tried to drag her arm away, but he held on.

'I told him, Amy,' Paddy said in a constricted voice. 'I told Uncle Bill I'd been mistook, that it weren't Tommy you was with. I ... I'm sure he heard ... I'm real sorry, Amy, I never meant ...'

'Get your bleedin' hands off me, Paddy Keagan,' Amy said and now her voice was rock steady and cold as ice, and even the tears seemed to have dried on her cheeks. 'You're a liar and a troublemaker and I don't want anything to do with you, now or never. Bugger off! It's my dad lying ill in this place, mine and Gus's and Albert's, not yours. Go back to your mammy – she believed your lies and tried to make things worse ... why, she did her best to stop me coming to the hospital.'

Albert jerked his head at Paddy. 'She's right, Paddy ... oh, I know you love Dad near on as much as we do, but for now ...'

'I'll wait here, then,' Paddy said in a low voice. 'Amy, I swear to God I didn't mean no harm ...'

'Shut up!' Amy said, but still coldly, not with the heat that the phrase implied. 'Go back to Seafield Grove, to your gran's house mind, not ours. Because I never want to set eyes on you again.'

To her secret surprise, Paddy turned and went down the stairs with dragging steps.

The two Logans made their way towards the ward where Bill lay. Albert turned to his sister. 'You were a bit hard on him, queen,' he said gently. 'I know you think he were tryin' to make mischief – likely he was – but you could have accepted that he were sorry. He did try to tell our dad that he'd been wrong, it hadn't been Tommy Chee you were with, but ... to tell you the truth, I don't think Dad believed what Paddy had told him in the first place, honest to God I don't. I think he wanted to go out to meet you, and Paddy saying what he did was a good excuse for ignorin' Suzie and getting out of the house anyway.'

There was a commotion up the corridor, and a group of people came through the swing doors on the left and walked towards them. 'It's the doc,'

Albert whispered, drawing Amy to a halt. 'We'll have a word.'

The doctor was a tall, elderly man, with tiny gold spectacles perched on a long, thin nose. He was almost bald and he looked weary and preoccupied, but when his eyes fell on the two youngsters he smiled kindly and patted Albert's shoulder. 'You'll be young Logan, William Logan's boy, and this must be your sister,' he said in a thin, educated voice. 'Well, I'm afraid your father does have a touch of pneumonia, but he's a strong man with plenty of staying power and I see no reason why he shouldn't pull round – with good nursing, that is.' He glanced at the two young women who flanked him, one on each side. The ward sister and a staff nurse, Amy guessed. 'These ladies will see to that, you may be sure. I've had a word with your father . . .'

'Oh, sir, is he conscious?' the words broke from Amy and Albert simultaneously. 'I thought my brother said he hadn't come round,' Amy added.

'Yes, he's conscious, and presently we hope he'll take a mouthful or two of nourishing broth,' the doctor told her. 'You may go and see him to calm your fears, but you may only stay two minutes. He's still very weak and needs all the rest we can give him.'

'Won't we be allowed to sit with him?' Albert asked with a strange mixture of timidity and belligerence. 'Me stepmother and me big brother was spelling each other by the bed, and we were going to take over until one of them comes back.'

The doctor smiled at them very kindly, but shook his head. 'No need, now, to keep a constant watch on him,' he said. 'He'll rest a deal easier without eyes on him for, as I've said, it's sleep and nourishing food which will restore his strength. You tell the rest of your family they may come in for ten minutes only tomorrow morning and then we'll see.'

'I don't like the sound of that,' Albert muttered, as the doctor strode away from them. 'What if Dad needs something? I'd sooner one of us is by, even if it's Suzie.'

But the staff nurse, who had stayed with them, smiled and shook her head. 'No, lad, your dad's on a general ward now he's come round and norrin the end cubicle by hisself. The nursing staff will keep an eye on him, of course, but the other patients will fetch someone if your father needs anything. Why, if we had relatives at every bedside twenty-four hours a day, we wouldn't be able to get inside the ward, let alone nurse the patients.'

As she spoke she had guided them into a long ward with at least twenty beds, in the nearest of which Amy immediately recognised her father. He was propped up in the narrow iron bedstead, with a number of pillows and another nurse was bending over him, helping him to drink out of an object which looked like a small white teapot. Bill took a long swallow; Amy could see his throat convulsing, then he shook his head and the nurse stood the teapot down on his bedside locker. 'Well done, Mr Logan,' she said softly, 'you'll feel all the better for that I'm sure. And now you've got visitors, so I'll leave you for a while.'

Albert slid a wooden bench out from under the bed and pulled it close, so that Amy could take her father's hand in hers. 'Oh, Dad, you're looking much better,' she said eagerly. 'We've been so worried – especially me. I felt it was my fault that you'd had to go out in the snow because if you'd not gone to meet me, none of this would have happened.' She gestured vaguely towards the bed.

Bill looked puzzled. He put a hand up to his head and winced as his fingers encountered the enormous lump on his brow. 'I slipped on the ice when I were comin' to meet you off your tram,' he said in a small voice, totally unlike his usual firm tones. 'Only you never come. Where was you, queen?'

Amy hesitated. She did not really want to tell her father what she and Ruth had been doing, but she reflected that lies and evasions never did anyone any good in the long run. 'Do you remember my pal, Ruthie?' she enquired. 'Well, she's come back to Seaforth to live. She's got a job quite near the market so, after work, her and me went looking for a room to share, so's we'd be nearer our work, like. We found a place ...'

Bill had been listening, with his eyes fixed on her face, but suddenly his hand shot out and gripped hers. 'Amy, you mustn't leave home, queen,' he said urgently. 'Suzie's a good wife to me, but she's not a manager like your mam was. I know she hasn't always treated you like she should, but I'll change all that if only you'll promise me you won't leave us in the lurch.'

Amy was touched by the entreaty in her father's blue eyes and worried by the trembling grip of his hot, damp hand. 'It's all right, Dad,' she said soothingly, 'we couldn't afford the room we saw, but if you truly want me at home then we shan't go looking for anything else. Honest to God we won't.'

Bill's fingers slipped from hers and he heaved a satisfied sigh. 'You're a good girl, queen,' he said huskily. 'I dunno what we'd do wi'out you and that's the truth. Promise me ...'

The staff nurse who had brought them up to the ward appeared by the bedside and tapped Amy on the shoulder. 'Your two minutes is up, dear,' she said briskly. 'You run along home now and come back to see your dad again tomorrow. By then he'll be much more the thing – and don't forget to tell Mrs Logan that Mr Logan is on the general ward now and she can come in for just ten minutes tomorrow morning, no longer.' She turned to Bill. 'Nurse tells me you had a couple of sips of beef tea for her, so how about having another couple of sips for me?'

All the way home on the tram, Amy sat beside Albert in thoughtful silence, murmuring replies to his remarks, but never making any contribution of her own to the conversation. She had promised her father that she would go home, would not leave either the family or Suzie in the lurch, but she was beginning to realise that if life in the Logan household were to be bearable she would have to have a serious talk with Suzie. What was more, she would have to sort things out with Paddy, because no matter how you looked at it, if she kept her threat and never spoke to Paddy again it would make for a very uncomfortable atmosphere.

The tram was an old and noisy one, however, and very soon Albert fell silent, defeated as much by the effort of shouting to Amy above the rattle and roar of the vehicle as by Amy's long silences. But when they reached the Rimrose Bridge and climbed stiffly down, Albert asked her outright what she intended to do. 'I didn't know you were so unhappy, queen,' he said gently, giving her shoulders a brotherly squeeze. 'But I heared you tell Dad you'd been after a room share wi' young Ruthie Durrant and, now I think about it, it can't have been much fun for you livin' in the same house as Paddy. I dunno what's the matter wi' him,' he added broodingly. 'When you was kids he were always rude and nasty to you, but I thought that was on account o' Mary – him havin' a crush on her, I mean. I thought he were nasty to you to ... to kind of contrast with how he danced attendance on our Mary. I thought it'd stop once Mary left, but it didn't, did it? He's still gorrit in for you, though he don't call you "Shrimpy" so much, nor shout at you in the street.'

'Well, I don't like him much,' Amy admitted honestly. 'Looking back, I can't for the life of me remember how it started, or who started it for that matter. It should be different now we're older, but somehow Paddy always seems to want to get me into trouble and once he moved in ...'

'Yes, I know, it's just gone from bad to worse,' Albert cut in. 'But it'll be different now, Amy. He's rare ashamed of what he telled our dad and if you play your cards right he'll be your pal from now on, I'm thinkin'. All you've gorra do is accept his apology. Then you can start afresh, like.'

'But I said I'd never speak to him again and I meant it,' Amy pointed out. 'He told a deliberate lie to put me in Dad's bad books and look what has happened as a result, Albert. Our dad's ever so ill. He could easily die and it was all Paddy's fault.'

'No it weren't, queen,' Albert said reprovingly. 'You've gorra take some of the blame, you know. You went gaddin' off to look at rooms and missed the last tram, off your own bat, in a bleedin' blizzard, you know you did. Why, our dad would've gone chasin' off after you, Paddy or no Paddy, once it got to ten o'clock in that weather an' no sign of you. Be fair, our Amy.'

Since this uncomfortable thought had already crossed Amy's mind, she felt her cheeks grow hot and nodded grudgingly. 'Yes, you've got a point, Albert. It's no use trying to blame Paddy for everything – what is it Dad says? It takes two to make a quarrel. But Albert, you should have heard the way Suzie lit into me. She called me every bad name she could lay her tongue to, screaming like a fishwife and saying it was all my fault her Bill was took bad.' She snorted derisively. '*Her Bill*, indeed! He's our dad, isn't he, and he's been our dad a lot longer than he's been *her Bill*!'

'Yes, I know what you mean,' Albert admitted. 'When they was first wed I thought Suzie had hooked him like you hook a big sea bass, and hauled him aboard her boat an' all, but since then I've watched 'em a fair bit an' that Suzie's rare fond of our dad, queen. He's older than her and he don't take her about much, but she fair worships the ground he walks on. The reason she's nasty to you is jealousy, pure an' simple. You're our dad's favourite and always have been, so she resents it o' course. Now, be honest, our Amy. Ain't that the truth?'

'Ye–es, but there's nothing pure or simple about jealousy,' Amy pointed out. 'I can't help being Dad's favourite – if I am, that is. Why, I'm a kid and Suzie's a woman grown. She ought to know better than pick on me the way she does. I often want to tell her to do her own work when I come in from the market to find cleaning and housework waiting to be done, but I never do. Sometimes she's not too bad, but Paddy sets her agin me whenever he can. He's tried tale-clatting to Dad, too, in the past, but he knows his mam wants to believe bad of me, so he does better telling his tales to her. So what'll I do, Albert? I can't move out now I've promised Dad I'll stay, but things are bound to be awkward.'

They had walked down Crosby Road, so busy discussing their problem that Amy had scarcely glanced at the big houses which lay between them and the sea. Turning into Seafield Grove, she tugged at Albert's arm, drawing him to a halt. 'What'll I do?' she asked plaintively. 'I know I promised Dad and I'll stick to my word but it isn't going to be much of a life for any of us if Suzie goes on picking on me, and Paddy and I don't speak.'

Albert laughed. 'Talk to them,' he advised. 'Tell Suzie you're doing your best and don't need the constant nagging she hands out. Tell Paddy you'll be civil if he will. If that don't do the trick you'll have to talk to Dad again – when he's well, I mean. But Paddy's awright really, you know. He's been a good pal to me in the past and maybe, once things are sorted out, he'll be a good pal to you as well.'

Amy sniffed, but began to walk towards their home once more. 'I'll do it for Dad's sake,' she said decisively. 'Oh, Gawd, I think I'd rather face a man-eating tiger than that Suzie when she's got a cob on and she isn't going to be happy when we tell her she can't see Dad except for ten minutes tomorrow morning. Still an' all, I'm doing this for Dad. Come on, Albert.' And with head held high and bumping heart, she headed for home, with Albert close on her heels.

Amy hurried along Crosby Road, taking deep

breaths of the mild spring air. She was excited because Dad was coming out of hospital today after almost two months of illness, for he had indeed contracted pneumonia and, despite good nursing, there had been times when even the doctor had doubted Bill's ability to pull through.

But Bill had fought the disease and conquered it. Some four weeks ago the medical staff had known they were going to win the fight, and Sister had told Amy that Bill's lungs were clear and it was just a matter of building up his strength. Since then, Amy had been able to chart his improvement on her daily visits, and she and Suzie had watched with delight as Bill began to fret against his imprisonment. He wanted to be out and about for, though he trusted Gus, Charlie and Albert so far as it went, he could not believe that the lads could possibly bring in catches such as he habitually did when spring arrived.

What was more, although Charlie had been willing to help in the boat while Bill was in hospital, he was eager to return to the maltings, where he had not only a good job but a young lady, whom he missed badly. 'They're keepin' me job for me and Lottie's not the sort of girl to let a feller down,' he had told Amy. 'But I'm doing well down there, queen, and though I know Dad's happy with Suzie, I can't say I care for her much meself. I'll stay whiles I'm needed, but as soon as Dad's well enough to work again I'll be off.'

However, it had not been necessary for Charlie to remain, once Dad had turned the corner. Bill's old friend Ben Carpenter, who had been a fisherman in his time but was now mostly retired, had agreed to help the boys work the boat and Charlie had gone back to the Midlands, knowing he had not let his family down.

Walking briskly towards the tram terminus, Amy reflected that she had done a great deal of growing up over the past couple of months. It had started, she supposed, the night after Bill had been taken into hospital when she and Suzie had finally got down to brass tacks and talked plainly, because they had realised that night that they shared a common fear – that Bill might be taken from them.

'I love me dad better than anyone else in the whole world,' Amy had said earnestly, staring at Suzie's pale and woebegone face across the table which had separated them. 'The way the two of us are behaving, Suzie, isn't likely to help his recovery, because he loves us both, you know, though in different ways. I'm willing to stay here and do everything I can to help you bring up baby Becky and to look after the boys, but I can't do it if you're set agin me. I told Dad this evening that I meant to move out, take a place of my own, even if it took my last penny, but he begged me to stay. I dare say you'd rather I went, but it'd put Dad in a rare worry to know you were trying to manage alone, so if we can come to some agreement . . .'

'We must agree,' Suzie had said, looking Amy squarely in the eye. 'I don't deny I've been hard on you, queen, but I knew right from the start that you didn't want me takin' Isobel's place. You didn't want Bill marryin' anyone, least of all meself. I knew you were watchin' me and thinkin' your dad could have done a deal better, an' it made me mean towards you. Then Paddy weren't no help, were he? I reckon he knew how you felt about me – I am his mam, after all – so he made things hard for you, same as I did. And he lied about Tommy Chee, didn't he. Well, he told me himself not an hour since that he couldn't tell who the feller was, he were so muffled up. He said it were Tommy because he thought Bill would lose his rag wi' you and leave you to gerron with it. But it had the opposite effect. An' now Bill's in hospital and ... and we've gorra pull together, queen, for his sake and for our own. Paddy's gone to sleep at Gran's tonight, 'cos he said you'd not stay if he were in the house ...'

'It's true I said I'd never speak to him again, but that was in the heat of the moment,' Amy had said quickly. 'Mind you, it'll be for the best if he stays with Gran for a bit, seeing as how Gus telegraphed Edmund, Charlie and Mary to come home. There won't be room to swing a cat once they arrive, so Paddy will be best at Gran's.'

That night, Amy thought now, heading for Ruthie's house, had been the beginning of a completely different relationship between her and her stepmother. It was as though Amy's eyes had been opened to the very real love which Suzie had for Bill. She had never looked past Suzie's shiftless and lazy ways to the depth of affection that she showed in every action she performed for Bill. Suzie had made her way to the hospital two or three times a day with small comforts for her sick husband. She had bought the *Echo* each evening and stumblingly read him news of local events, though reading had never come easily to her. Little Becky had not been allowed on the ward, but Suzie knew how Bill adored his little daughter and had recounted all Becky's exploits with as much interest and affection as though the child had been her own. What was more, on several occasions she had taken Becky to the hospital and lifted her up to the window nearest to Bill's bed, so that he could see for himself how well and happy the child was. It had meant a lot to Bill, Amy knew, but it had been just one more task for Suzie, who suddenly found herself with more work than she had ever had to cope with in her life before.

For within a couple of weeks of Bill's being taken ill, Gran, too, had fallen sick. She had contracted influenza and had been very ill indeed for three weeks, with the doctor calling daily and Aunt Dolly almost out of her mind with worry. The older woman had nursed her sister devotedly and had done her best to bring her back to health, but though she was now pottering around and doing her own housework once more, Amy acknowledged that Gran would never again be able to carry Suzie, as she had in the past.

So, though at the time she had felt some pangs of conscience over her insistence that Paddy should live with his grandmother, Amy soon realised that it was a blessing in disguise. She might dislike Paddy – well, she did – but she had always known that he was neither workshy nor lazy. When Gran had taken to her bed, all the messages, cleaning and a good deal of the cooking had fallen to Paddy's lot, for Aunt Dolly was too old and frail to do much besides nurse her sister. Paddy had risen to the occasion and, though he had come round to the Logan house for advice from time to time, he had never asked them for help in his own predicament. Though she could not like him, Amy was forced, reluctantly, to admire the way he had coped. He was a young man, after all, not used to housework or cooking, let alone taking care of two old ladies, but somehow he had managed to keep the household going, though he must have been heartily glad when Gran had been able to leave her sick bed once more, albeit falteringly.

Ahead of her the front door of the Durrants' house opened and Ruthie shot out on to the pavement. She was carrying a round of toast, folded over, and spoke rather thickly between bites. 'Awright, chuck? It's your big day today, in't it? Did they say it was still all right for your dad to come out today, eh? I bet you're excited, ain't you? But how will you stop him tryin' to help wi' the fishin', now the weather is so fine?'

Amy laughed and tucked her arm through her friend's. 'Dad's not a fool, chuck,' she said, answering the last question first. 'He knows as well as the rest of us do that tomorrow or the day after the weather will probably break and turn windy and rough. He's been in hospital so long that he won't risk putting himself back by taking foolish chances with his health. As for being excited, of course I am, same as the rest of the family. Edmund wrote and said he'd come home and see Dad again, once he's settled in, and Mary's going to do the same. As for Charlie, he's been home most weekends, as you know, so he'll probably leave it a bit before he visits. But the rest of us are so excited ... Little Becky's made him a picture to hang on his wall and Suzie's been cooking all the stuff he likes best since yesterday morning. Gus and Albert have clubbed together to buy him a new muffler and even Paddy came round with a bag of bull's-eyes for him to suck while he's mending nets. The doctor reckons he must take it easy until the weather's truly warm.'

As they had been speaking, the two girls were hurrying towards the terminus and now they climbed aboard a tram and took their seats just behind the driver. 'My mum's bakin' some currant buns for your dad's tea,' Ruth said presently, as the tram began to rattle along Knowsley Road. 'And I've bought him a bag of seed potatoes for his allotment. It ain't much, I know, but I talked to Albert when he were bringing the catch ashore last week, and he told me he and Paddy had dug over your dad's allotment as a bit of a surprise, like, so I thought mebbe they would put the seed potatoes in for him as well.'

'That was kind. Dad'll be just thrilled,' Amy said appreciatively. Bill had put his name down for an allotment five years previously, but had not managed to get one until the last year, and it was his pride and joy. Despite the hardness of a fisherman's life, he had told Amy that he found digging, planting, weeding and above all, harvesting his crops thoroughly relaxing and enjoyable. In summer he went there every night, making his way along Sandy Road until he reached the bridge over the railway, from where it was only a step. And Bill swore that the combination of soot from the engines and salt from the sea improved the soil and was partly responsible for the excellence of his crops. Once he had got well enough to worry, he had fretted over his beloved allotment and, though the family assured him that lying fallow until the spring came could do it nothing but good, he was unconvinced. Amy guessed that Albert and Paddy had dug the allotment chiefly so that Bill would have no excuse to do so himself before he was fit for the work, and was grateful, though she was sure it had been Albert's idea, rather than Paddy's.

'I bet it'll be like a party tonight when your da

comes home,' Ruth said enviously. 'I'll bring me seed potatoes and me mam's buns, but I won't stay. Mr Logan will want his home and his family to hisself after so long away.'

'It won't hurt to pop in for a moment.' Amy smiled at her friend. 'I wouldn't be surprised if Dad went to bed pretty early tonight. It's an exciting day for him, but though he's much stronger, he won't be his own self for a while yet. The doctor said not to work until the summer, but I can't see my dad sitting there idle. He'll be mending nets and doing the accounts before many days have passed, if I know him.'

'Well, I'll pop in for a moment,' Ruth conceded when the tram came to a halt beside a long queue of would-be passengers. As they began to scramble aboard, she turned to her friend. 'I haven't liked to ask, chuck, but does your dad know Paddy is living with Gran? Has anyone told him?'

Amy heaved a sigh. Despite the fact that there was now an uneasy truce between Paddy and herself, she had insisted that he continued to live with the two old ladies rather than in the Logan house. She had told Suzie that Paddy was needed more by Gran and Aunt Dolly than he was by themselves. It eased the congestion in the boys' room, especially when Charlie came home to see his dad, and it also gave Paddy freedom to have his friends in and to come and go as he pleased, for Gran and Aunt Dolly did not attempt to restrain him.

However, she had a nasty feeling that Bill would not approve of this arrangement, so satisfactory to herself but so galling both for Paddy and his mother. She wondered how long it would be before Bill realised that his stepson was no longer living under his roof and thought apprehensively that it could not be many days before he twigged. Paddy had most of his meals with the two old ladies but occasionally, when he had been helping with the boat, he had his tea with the Logans. Bill was sure to notice his absence at mealtimes, particularly at weekends, and would doubtless comment on it.

Suzie and Amy had been getting on very well ever since they had come to terms with one another and Amy was able to see Suzie's point of view better than she had ever done before. Despite her step-mother's casual-seeming attitude towards her only child, she was very fond of Paddy and, though her life was busier than ever with Bill in hospital, she made a point of seeing him at least once every day. She agreed with Amy that the old ladies needed Paddy, particularly since Gran's illness, but Amy knew Suzie missed her son and imagined that, at times, she must feel quite beleaguered by Logans, especially with Bill not there to protect her. But she had never even suggested that Paddy should come back to live with her, so Amy supposed they would all have to wait and see how Bill reacted to the change.

The tram jerked to a stop, the conductor bawled down the length of the vehicle, 'Lime Street Station! We doesn't go no further, ladies and gents all,' and Amy and Ruth joined the exodus. Ruth was still working at Dorothy's and was very happy there, so Amy usually walked her as far as the kitchen entrance, then continued round the corner into Great Charlotte Street and along to the fish market. Mrs O'Leary and Amy reached the stall simultaneously and smiled at each other as they automatically began their morning preparations.

'Mornin', chuck,' Mrs O'Leary said breezily, struggling out of her thick winter coat and changing her button boots for wooden clogs. 'So, today's the great day, eh? I reckon your stepma is all of a twitter with her man comin' home after so long. And I dare say you and your brothers is pretty excited.'

'That's right, Mrs O,' Amy agreed, hanging up her coat and shedding her boots. 'Gus and Albert will be along later, because they had a right good catch yesterday and they'll be wanting to set sail as soon as they can today, since the weather's clement at the moment. Gus said they ran into a regular shoal of whiting yesterday afternoon, though they were a bit small. And when he pulled up the crab pots he got at least a dozen decent-sized ones, and crabs always go well.'

'Crabs!' Mrs O'Leary exclaimed, her face lightening. 'Now crabs is something that we can always sell and seein' as they're alive, alive-oh it wouldn't matter if they did hang about for a day or so, 'cos no one could say they wasn't fresh. What time do you think the lads will be along?'

Amy was about to reply when a rumbling made her look up. Gus and Albert, pushing a handcart between them, came skidding across the slippery cobbles and stopped, panting and grinning, alongside the stall. 'Your fish delivery, ma'am,' Gus said, bowing mockingly in Amy's direction. 'All fresh as a daisy, especially them perishin' crabs. I got a nice tweak from the big 'un in the right-hand corner, 'cos he started trying to make his way out. You'll want me to leave the basket, I 'spect?'

'Yes,' Amy said, coming round the stall to help the boys to unload the catch, while Mrs O'Leary briskly weighed the fish and wrote down price per pound in the shabby little ledger she kept for the purpose. None of the Logan family ever haggled with Mrs O'Leary over the price, because it had long ago been agreed between herself and Isobel that she would pay according to scarcity value, demand and quality, and they knew that Mrs O'Leary would never cheat them.

Mr Mosscrop, on the stall next door, was a different proposition, though. When he cast envious eyes at the heavy basket of clacking and furious crabs, and asked if he might buy some to boil and dress, Gus promptly named a price which made Mr Mosscrop stagger back in pretended horror. 'I bet you didn't pay that for 'em, Mrs O,' he grumbled, eyeing his neighbour. 'Still an' all, I dare say I'll get a bit extry for dressin' them and no one else seems to be bringing crabs in today, so I'd best pay up wi' a good grace.'

Accordingly Mrs O'Leary, who was a fair woman, picked out the two largest crabs and handed them to her neighbour. The boys, pocketing the sheet of prices and the money she gave them, reminded Amy to bring something good back for tea since it was Dad's first day home and rattled off, pushing the cart before them.

'Suzie's already got a steak and kidney pud ready to put on to boil when the time's right,' Amy shrieked after them. 'And Gran's made a nice apple pie for afters, so don't you be late, fellers.' She turned to Mrs O'Leary as the boys disappeared. 'If Dad's being in hospital has done one good thing it has made me and Suzie get on much better; you could say we were friends even. She's worked like a right one these past weeks and never a cross word between us. Dad'll be right pleased when he realises we're pals.'

Mrs O'Leary, who had set about cleaning some of the whiting for display on the front of the stall, looked up quickly. 'Aye, it's true you've been much easier wi' one another whiles your Dad was out of the way,' she said slowly, 'but human nature is human nature, queen, and jealousy is one of them emotions you can't just stifle – or not for long, any road. I don't want to seem to look on the black side, but it wouldn't surprise me if your stepma don't revert to her old ways once your dad comes home.'

'Oh, I don't see why she should do that,' Amy said. Surely the good understanding which had grown up between herself and Suzie could not simply disappear just because Bill was home? 'I'll keep on being friendly and helping her as much as I can without giving her dirty looks, so Dad will be able to love the pair of us and not have to choose.' She turned back to the stall and picked up the two big wooden buckets which stood behind it. 'Shall I go for the ice, now, Mrs O? Looks like we'll need it with all those lovely whiting to sell.'

It seemed strange to Bill to leave the white, echoing cleanliness of the Stanley Hospital and to breathe the cold March air into lungs that were used to the mixed smells of disinfectant, carbolic soap and boiled cabbage, which seemed to make up the air in his ward. What was even stranger was the chill which touched his cheeks and hands, and the sudden realisation that his legs were no longer to be relied upon. Instinctively he clutched at Suzie's arm and felt the reassuring strength of it, even as Charlie, on his other side, grasped him firmly by the elbow.

'Feelin' kind o' shaky, Dad?' Charlie asked gently. 'Never you mind, I dare say anyone would feel the same if they have been flat on their backs for gerrin' on two months. But don't worry, we ain't goin' to ask you to walk all the way to Seaforth, there's a cab waitin' in the road, so you'll travel home like the King of England.'

Suzie, on Bill's other side, gave his hand a comforting squeeze. 'Tek it slow,' she advised, helping him across the pavement. 'The cab's no more than three yards away and Charlie and me's strong, so lean on us.'

'I'm awright,' Bill said a trifle breathlessly, as he climbed the creaking steps into the cab. He lowered himself gingerly on to the warm leather seat, while Suzie settled herself beside him and Charlie jumped aboard, carrying a small carpet bag which contained Bill's few possessions. 'My, but don't it take it out of you? I've always been a chap as could tackle any physical work and I thought I were doin' well in hospital, but right now I feel as weak as any kitten.'

'Never mind, Dad.' Charlie gave him a reassuring grin. 'They tell me when a woman has a babby she feels uncommon shaky when she first leaves her bed. Just you pretend you're a nursin' mother and . . .'

'Stop your clack, you wicked young devil,' Bill said, giving a reluctant grin. 'I don't need to pretend nothin'; it's not many fellers as recover from con . . . concussion *and* the nastiest attack of pneumonia the doctor said he's seen for a long while. Anyroad, once I'm in me own home and had a good night's sleep in me own bed, I'll be beatin' you at your own game, young Charlie. Why, I'll be fishin' in a week or so!'

Suzie and Charlie exchanged quick, guilty glances

and Bill, settling back against the seat with a sigh of relief, grinned to himself. He knew well enough that it would be impossible for him to stroll down to the beach, let alone go out in the boat, for many weeks to come, but it would do no harm to pretend to be fitter than he really was. He had no intention of risking his future health by being foolish, for though he knew the boys had done well – or well enough – in his absence, he also knew that neither Charlie nor Gus had yet gained that special knowledge of the waters they fished, which it had taken him almost fifty years to acquire. Besides, Charlie's heart was in the Midlands. The boy enjoyed the work and the independence and, of course, the company of his young lady and would, Bill knew, be reluctant to exchange his new life for the terrible harshness of fishing. Charlie worked under a roof during the severest months of the winter, whereas a fisherman would be out in all weathers, risking his life for his catch, which sometimes rewarded him well and at other times seemed scarcely worth the effort.

Edmund, working on distant water trawlers, had an even worse and harder existence, but trawlermen did at least get amply rewarded for their work – they were not known as 'three-day millionaires' for nothing. Bill sometimes thought that if something should happen to him, Gus might follow Edmund up to Fleetwood; perhaps the two boys might end up sharing a trawler between them, for fishing off the Great Burbo Bank was becoming harder, as fish stocks shrank and more boats came in to search for what fish there were. Now that he came to think of it, if Gus did go, Albert, Paddy and himself could manage the *Mersey Maid* and still make a living. Paddy was not experienced, but he was a hard worker and was already a useful member of the crew when one or other of the boys was unable to work; he would do very well once he had built up some experience.

The cab lurched as the horse left the smooth surface of Crosby Road South and entered Seafield Grove. It jolted on for a short way, then the driver's face appeared in the trapdoor. He was grinning encouragingly. 'We's arrived, lady and gents,' he said, then withdrew and descended. He opened the door, seized Bill's bag, stood it on the pavement and offered Suzie his hand. 'Out wit' you, queen,' he said breezily. 'You go ahead and open the front door, so's I can give your man me arm.'

And presently Bill, with a sigh of contentment, found himself sitting in his own chair, beside his own fire, with the kettle hopping on the range and Suzie bustling around making the tea. Despite himself Bill felt a slow smile spread across his face. They had been kind in hospital, the food hadn't been bad, the other patients were friendly and the staff nursed the inmates devotedly. But it was not home. Bill, looking around him, felt confident that his true cure had begun.

Paddy came along Crosby Road and turned into Seafield Grove, then hesitated. It was Bill's first day home and he knew he ought to go into the Logans' house to have his tea and say hello to his stepfather. The nicer side of his nature wanted to do just that, for he was extremely fond of the older man and thought of him as the father he had never known. Bill had been kind to him from the very beginning – not just when he became his stepfather – but ever since he and Albert had become bezzies. Paddy often told himself that he no longer hated Amy, who had stood by his mother when she had needed help most. However, old habits die hard. Try though he might, Paddy could not forget the stuck-up, know-all Amy, who had so often made him look a fool by twisting his words, so that a sneer meant to make her look small ended up by making him appear spiteful and ignorant.

So now, standing undecidedly on the pavement, he reminded himself that if he went in for his tea, Bill would not realise that he had been forbidden the house by Amy Cleverclogs Logan. It was not that he wanted to get Amy into trouble, exactly. It was not even that he wanted to live under the Logan roof once more. He rather enjoyed staying with Gran and being the man of the house, though he missed Albert's constant companionship. It was more that he felt he had been cheated of his rights as a stepson. Amy, when all was said and done, was only a girl with no right to boss him around. Dammit, she was two years younger than him and, though he admitted he had been in the wrong when he told Bill Amy had deliberately flouted his wishes, that had been two months ago. He had apologised, hadn't he? Surely by now the unpleasantness should have been forgotten? He could not imagine Bill bearing a grudge and thought that if he played his cards right he might yet see Amy humbled and himself brought back into favour.

So if he went into tea now, Bill would think everything was normal and would not discover that his stepson only came into the Logan kitchen on sufferance. On the other hand if Bill was still in the kitchen when tea was over and Paddy about to depart, surely he would ask where the boy was bound?

While Paddy hesitated, a hand smote him between the shoulder blades and a voice bellowed cheerfully, 'Hey up, Paddy! Wharrer you doin' standin' in the middle of the road, gaping like a cod? Ain't you comin' in for tea? It's Dad's first night home and your mam's made a steak an' kidney pud.'

'Albert! You damn near knocked me teeth down me bleedin' throat,' Paddy said aggrievedly. 'Well, I dunno. It's your sister; she . . . she may rather I went back to Gran's.'

'Well that's something new, you worrying what our Amy thinks,' Albert observed, linking his arm with Paddy's. 'Amy never says a word when you come in for tea, you know she don't.'

'Ye-es, but today's kind o' special,' Paddy pointed out, but he allowed himself to be pulled down the jigger and into the Logans' small backyard. Presently he found himself in the warm kitchen, with his mother about to dish up a large steak and kidney pudding and Amy bustling about, setting the table and making a big pot of tea. Baby Becky, who was scarcely four, had had her tea and been put to bed earlier, and Bill was sitting in his usual chair, looking tired but happy, and Paddy forgot his doubts and the desire to see Amy in trouble, melting away under the warmth of Bill's greeting. He handed over the bag of bull's-eyes and Bill stuck one in his cheek at once, promising the rest of the family that they might have one later, once tea was finished, but adding that most of the bull's-eyes would follow the one at present in his mouth, for they were easily his favourite sweets.

Paddy was still grinning over the success of his small gift when Gus came in from the backyard, carrying more driftwood for the fire and Charlie followed close on his heels with a net slung over one arm. They both greeted Paddy pleasantly and very soon the family were settled at the table, with the best meal they had had for weeks before them, though Bill remained in his fireside chair with a tin tray on his lap. And somehow, Paddy did not quite know how, he realised that clever Amy had managed to slip into the conversation the fact that he, Paddy, was no longer living squashed up in the boys' room above stairs, but was staying down the road with Gran and Aunt Dolly.

'Since Gran's been ill, Paddy's been the man of the house, doing all their messages and keeping an eye on the old ladies,' she observed, smiling with saccharine sweetness into Paddy's enraged face. She had done it again, he thought bitterly. If he told Bill now that Amy had slung him out of the house on the night Bill had been taken into hospital it would merely make him look bad. What was more, everyone round the table, and possibly even Bill himself, would realise that he was trying to get Amy into trouble. All his old animosity against Amy flared for a moment, then died into sulky mutterings. It was no use; he would have to accept what Amy had said with a good grace and see how things panned out.

'If you've finished your tea, Paddy, you might take a tray round to Gran and Aunt Dolly. I promised them their tea tonight, seein' as it was somethin' special,' his mother said when Paddy's plate was empty. 'And your gran's got an apple pie cookin' in her oven, so you can bring that back with you. If she hasn't cut it, you can take off a couple of slices for them and bring the rest back here.'

Paddy got to his feet but Amy was before him. 'No need for that,' she said sweetly. 'Paddy can take the pudding helpings round – they'd be a bit heavy for me – but I'll go with him and bring back the apple pie. He can eat his piece with Gran and Aunt Dolly so there won't be any need for him to go out in the cold again.'

Paddy opened his mouth to protest but Bill said, rather wearily from his place by the fire, 'I don't think I'll be having apple pie, thanks, queen. I dunno how it is but I feel as if I've run a mile today. I'll be makin' me way up to me bed and maybe, Amy love, you'd fetch me up a cup o' tea next time you put the kettle on.'

So Paddy took the tray with the two helpings of steak and kidney pudding and floury boiled potatoes, without demur and set off, with Amy tagging at his heels. He put the food down on Gran's kitchen table and the two old ladies settled themselves eagerly before it. Then he went to the oven, drew out the apple pie and plonked it rather crossly on the draining board. He got out three battered tin plates, while Amy poured cups of tea for the old ladies, then addressed her in a hissing whisper: 'Well you've done it again, young Amy. You've seen me off on Uncle Bill's first night home without anyone but me seein' what you're up to. But just you wait. One of these days I'll be workin' on the boat wi' the other fellows, and you'll still be selling shrimps door to door and slaving for old Ma O'Leary in St John's fish market. And when I've a share in the boat . . .'

But Amy was not staying to listen. She gave him her sweetest smile, snatched up the apple pie, called her farewells over her shoulder and disappeared through the kitchen doorway.

Paddy, sitting down to his own share of the apple pie, wondered why he bothered to try to needle Amy. He always got the worst of it in the end. And what did it matter, when all was said and done? They were no longer a couple of kids, vying for Albert's or Bill's affection; they were young people in work with their own lives to lead. He determined, not for the first time, that he would stop irritating Amy. After all, she was Mary's sister and Mary was an angel.

Pouring custard over his apple pie, he decided the best thing to do would be to ignore the girl completely. After all, he longed to join the crew of the fishing boat, hoping in his heart of hearts that one day he and Albert would own it between them, with a young lad as the third member of the crew. Once that happened he would have the position in life that he wanted and the hateful Amy, though ugly as a can of worms, would doubtless find some poor sucker to marry her and would go away from the little house in Seafield Grove.

Smiling to himself, Paddy ate the last of his apple pie and collected the empty dishes. 'You goin' to wash up, Gran?' he enquired cheerfully. 'If so, I'll give you a hand with the wiping before I fetches in water for the morning. Then I'll make up the fire and be off to bed, for I've an early start tomorrer.'

It was a brilliantly sunny day in July, and Amy had got off the tram at the St Martin's Market stop (usually known as Paddy's Market). She needed a lightweight jacket for the warmer weather, which she should be able to pick up in the market and, since she ran the stall on a Monday and business was usually slack after the weekend, she had decided not to open until eleven o'clock that day. What was more, because there was no fishing done on a Sunday she sold mainly salt fish, smoked fish and potted shrimps, which meant that takings were usually down. Now that Mrs O'Leary had given her a second day on the stall, most of her money was made on a Thursday, so opening late on Monday was acceptable both to Amy and her customers. Accordingly, she decided to walk the rest of the way, enjoying the sunshine. She also wanted time to think and the walk would enable her to do so without interruption.

Once again, after a gap of several months, she was seriously considering moving out of the little house in Seafield Grove. For within a month of Bill coming home, Amy knew that Mrs O'Leary had been right. Gradually, over the course of those weeks, Suzie's attitude had begun subtly to change. At first she only found fault with Amy's work or attitude when Bill was out of the way, but because Amy did not fight back and simply accepted the criticism with what good grace she could muster, Suzie began to return to her old ways.

Bill was back on the fishing boat, but he was far from his old self; after so long in hospital it would have been strange indeed had he not found an ordinary job exhausting, let alone the extraordinarily taxing job of catching fish. Amy worried about him and knew Gus and Albert did as well, but she hesitated to mention the matter to Bill himself. His pride in his ability both to find and to catch the fish was understandable and Amy thought that to take this pride from him – to insinuate that he was no

226

longer capable of such work – would be cruel indeed. However, she wished fervently that there were some tactful way he could be persuaded to find himself an easier job.

Apart from the fishing, Bill seemed to be coping admirably with the rest of his life. His allotment was flourishing – although any heavy digging was still being done by either Albert or Paddy – with new potatoes, peas, tender young carrots and even a row of onions, as well as the thick hedge of pinks and sweet-williams, which Bill grew for the house. Because of the allotment and because of Bill's deep knowledge of the fish they searched for, the Logan family were doing well and pulling back from the lean days of the winter in excellent style. Amy knew they would miss her dreadfully if she were to leave, but she did not know for how long she could continue to put up with the atmosphere in their small house.

Baby Becky was now at a dame school and although this would seem to lessen Suzie's responsibilities, it soon became apparent that taking Becky to school each morning and fetching her in the afternoon was an excellent reason, or perhaps excuse would be a more appropriate word, for Suzie to leave a good many tasks to be done by her stepdaughter. This usually consisted of large piles of ironing, for although Suzie sold shrimps from door to door when the catch was good, taking little Becky with her during the school holidays, she no longer did any other work inside the home. Instead, she had managed to find herself a job laundering the linen from one of the big houses along the front. She used Gran's copper to boil the whites because the shrimps were boiled in the Logan copper, but the ironing, great mounds of it, were piled up in the kitchen waiting for Amy's attention. Amy had to concede that the flat irons were always stood ready for her in the hearth, the nearest one to the fire being the first employed, but this did not help much when she came home tired from a day in the fish market to find the back-breaking work of pressing the dry linen awaiting her.

Suzie left her other jobs, of course. She had never been able to make good bread and had relied on Gran to do so for her. But since her illness Gran had not baked her own bread, let alone Suzie's. So on a Sunday, before church, Amy would get up early and go down to the kitchen to begin the task of making bread. She would leave the loaves to prove beside the fire while she went to church with the rest of the family and then, upon her return, would pop them into the small bake oven beside the fire. Amy quite enjoyed making bread – she certainly enjoyed the result – but she resented being no longer able to call her Sundays her own. Bill was strict about the family going to church, Amy thought more in memory of his dead wife than from any profound conviction, but he had always been happy for his children to make themselves scarce once the service was over. Even on Sunday the main meal of the day was eaten in the evening, which should have given her several hours in which to meet her friends, walk along the beach and visit the Bowersdale Park. But because Suzie could not be relied upon to check the loaves and stand them to cool on the kitchen table when they were done, Amy was denied even this freedom.

At first she had not realised why Suzie either took the bread out too soon or left it in until the crust was black as coal, but it was soon borne in upon her that this was yet another skirmish in the war which she had declared on her stepdaughter. She told Bill that Amy couldn't even make bread without spoiling it, said the loaves were heavy when they were merely undercooked, complained that Amy had weighed the ingredients wrongly when the crust was burnt to a crisp. So Amy decided she must stay with the bread until she had it safely out of the oven, and since the family was a large one and she was baking bread for Gran's household as well as her own, the task usually lasted her until early evening.

Now, with a sigh, Amy turned into Paddy's Market and immediately forgot her troubles in searching the many and various stalls for the garment of her choice. Ruth had recently bought a nice one in a dark-grey gabardine and Amy wanted something similar. After some good-natured haggling, she managed to buy a brown linen jacket, which seemed ideal. Having completed her purchase, she slipped the jacket across her shoulders, for it was easier to carry it thus on such a warm day, and set out once more for the fish market. She was passing the free library when she remembered glancing at the clock over the jeweller's on Byron Street and realised that it had shown only half past ten; she had another half-hour before she needed to go to work. Accordingly she headed for St John's Gardens, wishing she had had the foresight to purchase a bag of buns. She had passed a confectioner's window displaying mouth-watering cakes and could easily have spared a copper or two. It would have been nice to sit on the benches beneath the cherry trees and have a little picnic; a sit-down would be infinitely preferable to arriving at work half an hour early.

Crossing William Brown Street, she headed for the gardens and was on the further pavement when she heard a considerable commotion coming from her left. She glanced towards St George's Hall and realised, with a shock of surprise, that the plateau before it, the long rows of steps and even the roadway itself were crowded with figures, most of whom were shouting, gesticulating or singing what sounded, at this distance, like ribald songs. For a moment she simply stood where she was, staring, and then decided to take a closer look. The pavement upon which she stood was relatively empty but as soon as she got nearer the hall and the stone lions which guarded its frontage, she realised that this must be a political meeting of some description. The police were out in force, apparently trying to control the crowd, who were taking absolutely no notice of the long arms of the law. The people surged to and fro, and roared applause whenever the small figure perched at the very top of the long line of steps stopped speaking for an instant.

Amy had watched for several moments before she realised that, with one or two exceptions, the crowd consisted entirely of women. Old ones, young ones, fat ones, thin ones; women shabbily dressed in calico aprons and clogs, women in smart town clothing, country women in gingham gowns and stout boots, and young women in straw hats, leg-o'-mutton blouses and straight, pale-coloured skirts.

Quite near Amy, a man began to shout abuse at the speaker and immediately the women nearest him turned on him, telling him to shut up in no uncertain terms. 'Shut your bleedin' face, you hairy little nothing,' a hugely fat woman, wearing a straw hat richly furbished with curled ostrich plumes, screamed at him, her face inches from his own. 'If you don't shurrup I'll ... I'll flatten you and believe me, if I were to roll on you, you wouldn't be eatin' no dinner, nor shoutin' at your betters for a week or more.'

The man began to reply, his words clearly couched in offensive terms, when two policemen approached. Amy thought hopefully that this would end the fracas but, to her astonishment, the policemen walked straight by the offending man and grabbed the fat woman by both arms. 'You just keep your evil mouth shut, you great boiled puddin',' the larger of the two policemen said. 'Gawd, you bleedin' suffragettes make more work and more trouble than a couple of hundred protesters – the male sort, that is. Now, are you goin' to shut up or shall we take you in charge?'

Amy stepped forward, full of indignation; this was prejudice the like of which she had never encountered before. The poor were always discriminated against, she knew that, but in her experience the scuffers were more inclined to stand up for the poor and indigent than to persecute them and had always seemed well-disposed towards women. Before she could interfere, however, a tall, stately woman in her mid-fifties, carrying a small parasol and wearing an extremely smart walking dress, had acted. With one swift poke of her parasol, the first policeman's helmet was sent spinning into the crowd and, turning as if to apologise, a neatly judged blow from her elbow had the second policeman releasing his prisoner to straighten his helmet and tenderly caress one tingling scarlet ear.

'So sorry, officer,' the woman said in a cultured, self-confident accent. 'These little ... accidents ...

happen when too many people are squeezed into too small a place, don't you know?'

The first policeman was chasing after his helmet and paid no heed to her words, but the second one growled ungraciously, 'Ho, I dare say, but a decent woman wouldn't be seen dead among all these trouble-makin' bitches, I'm telling you.'

Amy, open-mouthed, watched this drama, trembling for the fate of the tall woman but then the crowd surged forward again and the policeman, muttering beneath his breath, lost sight of both combatants and went grudgingly off to find his companion, still rubbing his inflamed ear.

The woman standing at the top of the hall steps had a megaphone and, as she spoke, whole phrases suddenly began to make sense in Amy's mind. She was talking about women's rights and Amy remembered that the policeman had called them suffragettes. Instantly she knew what this was all about – getting women the right to vote for members of parliament, a right which had been denied them for so long. But listening as hard as she could, Amy realised that the speaker was addressing other issues, issues which affected her far more than the parliamentary vote. The woman was talking about the right to work, to earn a decent wage, to be regarded equally with men in the workplace, ideas so revolutionary that Amy gasped and began to wriggle through the crowd in order to get closer to the speaker.

She had got within perhaps ten feet of the bottom step when someone addressed her. It was a girl of about her own age, dressed in a striped toilinette blouse and a dark-blue skirt, her small waist clipped into a neat black leather belt with a silver clasp. Her light-brown hair was piled on top of her head and held in place by a silver and tortoiseshell comb, and she held a straw hat, with a chequered ribbon round the crown, in one hand. She looked neat, smart and collected, but the smile she gave Amy was warm and natural, and when she spoke her voice was low-pitched and pleasant, with no trace of a local accent. 'Hello! Is this your first suffragette meeting? I was quite frightened initially, because the police seem so aggressive. It's almost as if they hate us, wouldn't you say? Mrs Blenkinsop is such a wonderful speaker, though, that I've stopped minding about the crowds and the police. In fact, I'm really enjoying myself.'

Amy smiled at the other girl. 'I wouldn't say it was my first meeting, because I'm not here really at all,' she explained. 'I was on my way to work, only I'm half an hour too early, so I thought I'd sit down in the gardens for a bit, seeing as how it's a lovely day, but then I heard the rumpus and I came over to take a look. I saw the scuffer grab hold of ever such a nice lady, who'd done nothing wrong, and I was moving forward to tell him what I thought, when another lady knocked him for six and sent him running after his helmet. Then I heard what Mrs . . . Mrs Blenkinsop was saying and it caught my fancy. Only it's hard to hear, because the women keep shouting and cheering, and the fellers at the back keep hollering to drown out her voice.'

'She's talking a great deal of sense,' the other girl said. 'We could try and get a bit nearer, though. Put your arm round my waist and I'll put mine round yours and we'll shove our way through somehow. She's been talking about education for women, saying that ordinary girls, girls like us, ought to have equal opportunities with young men, so we could take degrees and go to college like they do. My employer would be mad as fire if he knew where I was, but it's my day off and I told everyone I was going shopping in Blackler's to choose a nice new hat for my cousin Lucy's wedding. I bet half the girls here had to tell untruths to someone, just to get away for a few hours. It isn't right that we should have to descend to such expedients, but . . . Oh, look, there's a gap! Let's see if we can squeeze through. If we could reach one of those pillars . . .'

But at this point it was as though all hell had broken loose. A phalanx of policemen had forced their way through the crowd, mounted the stone steps and completely surrounded the speaker. One moment the crowd was quiet and orderly, the next a policeman had seized her megaphone, another twisted her arms behind her back and, while the crowd was still gaping, unable to believe what was happening, they found more policemen were among them, swinging their truncheons, cursing and kicking, and doing their best to break up the meeting.

Amy and her new friend had been forced apart by the sudden pressure of women tumbling down the steps to avoid the police, but now the other girl grabbed Amy's hand and together they began to fight their way out of the mêlée. It was not easy. Men who had no connection with the police force had joined enthusiastically in the rout, hitting and punching indiscriminately at the women and, it must be confessed, frequently being hit back. Amy saw sturdy shawlies dealing mortal blows with their shopping bags, smart women using their parasols to good effect and even girls like her and her new friend, kicking and punching with all the strength they could muster. Indeed, Amy herself punched a whooping boy on the nose when he tried to grab her friend's hat from her hand and was delighted to see she had drawn blood. Though by the time they had escaped from the crowd and were sitting innocently in the Lyons Café in Lime Street nearby, she found she was trembling with a mixture of fright and excitement, and saw in the window glass that she had managed to get considerably rumpled by her recent activities. Her hair, which had been pulled back from her face in a severe bun, straggled in witch locks round her shoulders. Her neat white blouse was torn and had two buttons missing, and though she had been unaware of it at the time, she now realised that her feet had been trampled and kicked in the scrum and were extremely sore.

But it had been an adventure and one she would not have missed for the world. She accepted the cup of tea which the waitress handed to her and turned to her new friend. 'Phew! I feel as if I've been run over by a tram, but it's the most exciting thing that's ever happened to me. Oh, my name's Amy Logan, by the way, and I work in St John's fish market. Who are you?'

'I'm Ella Morton,' the girl said, taking a sip from her own cup of tea. 'I work in the Bon Marché on Church Street. And I share a room with another girl who works in Bunney's on the corner of Whitechapel. Where do you live, Amy? In the city?'

'No, I live out at Seaforth with my dad, my brothers and my little sister Becky. Oh, and with my stepmother. But to tell you the truth, Ella, I've been thinking for a long while that it was time I moved out – came into the city to be nearer my work. I've got a pal called Ruthie and last winter we began looking for a room to rent, but the prices were more than we could afford on the sort of money we earn. Then my dad was taken ill and spent nigh on eight weeks in hospital, and I realised I couldn't walk out on them, not with my dad so poorly. Only now that he's better I'm beginning to think about a room share again.'

And presently, with Ella's gentle encouragement, she found herself telling her new friend everything, beginning with Isobel's death and Mary's defection, and continuing to the present day with Suzie's jealous attacks and the amount of work through which she, Amy, was supposed to wade unaided.

Ella had listened with interest and sympathy to Amy's story, and her friendly attitude allowed Amy to utter the thoughts which she had been unwilling, at first, to voice. 'Excuse me asking, but is your room very pricey? Only I guess you earn a deal more than I can, seeing as how the Bon Marché is a posh shop and you speak nicely and look so smart.'

'I don't know what you earn, but I don't get paid anything like they would pay a young man in the gents' department,' Ella said. 'The rent of the room does seem to swallow up a good deal of my wages and, of course, one must dress respectably if one is selling clothing to women with a great deal of money. They're fussy, you see, which is why the managerial staff tend to pick girls with unaccented voices and a good appearance. But Amy, you must have been in work a year or so, since you look to be about my own age. I don't imagine selling fish is either much fun or well paid, so why not try for something different? There are jobs for women to be had in big offices and banks. In fact, I am attending evening classes at the YWCA in order to better myself. Have you ever thought of doing that? It is one of the things Mrs Blenkinsop believes in and she is an example to us all.'

Amy felt quite dazed, as though one moment she had been trudging along in her own dull old world and the next had been dragged, without her own volition, into somewhere quite different. She looked carefully at her companion, noting the smooth young face with its big brown eyes and merry mouth and then, at a second glance, seeing there was sadness in the eyes and the wariness of experience behind what she was sure was usually a sunny and trusting gaze. 'How is it that you don't have any trace of an accent though, Ella?' she asked. 'And why aren't you living at home? If you're my age – and you look about sixteen, same as me . . .'

'Oh, it's a common story,' Ella said with a tiny sigh. 'I was born and brought up in my parents' home in Southport. We were what you might call well to do . . .'

'That means rich,' Amy said, grinning, 'you can't pull the wool over my eyes, old Ella!' She half thought that this was a test; if her new friend secretly regarded herself as superior to Amy then she would dislike the familiarity of the remark.

But Ella grinned back at her, clearly not at all offended. 'Oh, well, I didn't mean to boast or anything like that, I just wanted to tell you the truth. Now, are you going to let me get on with it, or are you going to keep putting your spoke in?'

'I'm going to have to teach you to speak Scouse,' Amy said, smiling more broadly. 'We say "Gerron with it" in these parts, so you do just that. Gerron with it and I won't put any spoke in any wheel; in fact, I'll hold my clack till you reach the end.'

'Gosh, she's giving me a carte blanche,' Ella said in an exaggeratedly posh voice. Then, returning to her normal tones, she added, 'Right then, Amy, I'd better tell you from the start.'

The story, as Amy heard it, was both a dramatic and a sad one, for Ella Morton had had the privileged life of an only child of rich and loving parents until a year previously. Mr Morton had decided to take his wife on a tour of Europe, visiting places of which they had both heard but had never seen. His business partner was prepared to take full responsibility for the firm in his friend's absence and had urged the Mortons to go ahead with the trip. The tour was to have taken them three to four months, but Ella was away at a boarding school in the south of England for most of this time and, when she came home, there would be a house full of servants who had loved her since she had been small and would, she knew, take great care of her. Ella herself had had no qualms over her parents' extended absence, but had quite looked forward to having friends to stay.

Mr Morton had been in partnership with a Mr Fortescue in the running of a large finance company. Since the relationship was purely a business one, Ella had scarcely known her father's partner, but what she had known of him she disliked. Her father had often remarked ruefully, 'Jim can be a bit too sharp at times; one of these days he'll cut himself and I hope to God I'll be able to staunch the blood before he ruins both of us.' Since this had been said half laughingly, however, Ella had been totally unprepared for what followed. One day her father's chief clerk had come to the house with a worried expression on his usually cheerful face. 'Oh, miss, I've got to get in touch with your father. Can you give me his direction? I shall have to send a telegram – it is of the utmost importance that I contact him without delay.'

Ella had been unable to help him since her parents had merely told her the extent of their tour and not precisely where they would be situated at any one time. She had received letters and postcards, but usually these were headed with the name of the town in which they were staying and gave little or no indication of where they would be next.

However, Mr Jones, the chief clerk, was a man of considerable persistence and as soon as he realised that Ella was unable to help him he set about finding his employer via the telegraph office, even consulting such persons as the mayors of small towns who might be able to help trace the Mortons.

'Sometimes I ask myself if it might not have been better had he not managed to find them,' Ella said ruefully, now. 'For he did find them, you know. They were in a tiny principality in the Pyrenees called Andorra, famous for its wild scenic beauty, I believe. Mr Jones's telegraph message had reached them there and the news that Mr Fortescue had absconded and the business was ruined brought my parents chasing home. Much alarmed, my father hired a coach and they set off for Toulouse, where they could have caught a train for Paris and then on to Calais.'

She gazed ahead of her, as though she were seeing pictures of the past. 'If they hadn't been in such a hurry they might not have had the accident which killed them.' She turned her large eyes on

Amy and a tear slid slowly down one cheek. 'I sometimes fancy that the driver of their conveyance must have been the worse for drink because he managed to overturn the vehicle, God knows how, on a narrow mountain track, high above a steep ravine. Mr Jones told me later that death would have been instantaneous, for they must have fallen a good three hundred feet, ending up half submerged in one of the raging torrents which abound in those parts. The driver was killed as well, however, so no one will ever know the truth of it.'

Amy could only stare at her companion as her own eyes filled with tears. 'Oh, Ella, what a terrible thing to happen,' she said, her voice trembling. 'You poor creature – how did you bear it?'

'I bore it very badly at first,' Ella admitted. 'I raged against Mr Fortescue and railed against the fate which had taken my parents from me. When they said there was no money, that the house would have to be sold to satisfy the company's creditors, I was so sad that I barely took it in – scarcely realised what it would do to me. I told myself that they were welcome to have every penny of the money, to take the house, my pony, everything I owned, if only it could all have been a mistake. All I wanted was my parents back. But it wasn't a mistake. They had gone and the house, our possessions, every penny that we had in the bank had gone too. Mr Jones thought I should appeal to my papa's relatives, but I did not intend to do that. They had not approved of his marrying my mother and had never attempted to get in touch with us, not even a letter of condolence when the tragedy was reported in the newspapers. So I left my boarding school for, at seventeen, I felt I had been educated enough and in any event there was no possibility of paying the fees once my parents were dead. Mr Jones managed to get me a position in a small shop on the Scotland Road, owned by a relative of his. I was grateful, of course, but she was a slave-driving old creature, who let me sleep on a mattress under the counter in her shop, underpaid me dreadfully and used me pretty much like a slave. Still, it kept the wolf from the door until I managed to get a better place and moved out to share a room with Minnie Miniver – her real name's Ethel Miniver, but everybody calls her Minnie and she's a good laugh.'

At the end of the story there was a long silence while Amy gazed, awestruck, at her new friend. It astonished her that a girl who had clearly been raised in cotton, as the expression goes, should have been able to earn her own living, dress herself well and become independent in the way that Ella had. In fact, it made Amy feel ashamed. She had her father, brothers and even Mary, to say nothing of Mrs O'Leary, all of whom would have supported her had she got herself into some sort of financial trouble. But Ella had had no one and had been strong enough to turn inwards and to use resources which she had probably been unaware she possessed.

She said as much to Ella, who leaned across the table and clasped her hand. 'We women are stronger than we realise ourselves,' she observed. 'You aren't happy at home, Amy, but if something terrible happened, if your father and stepmother were no longer able to support you, I'm certain you would do just as I did. Why, I thought from the moment I saw you that you looked the sort of girl I could be friends with and I'm a pretty good judge of character, let me tell you. If you want to take Mrs

Blenkinsop's advice and better yourself, then come along to the YWCA with me this evening when you finish work and see what's on offer. Don't ever sit down under the weight of your troubles; push them aside and start changing things, as Mrs Blenkinsop advises. For a start, you can spend a night sleeping in a blanket on the floor of our room, so you don't have to go all the way back to Seaforth after classes. Well? What about it? Are you game?'

'I certainly am,' Amy said, her voice still revealing her astonished surprise. 'When do they hold these classes, queen? Can I start at once? Only I'll have to go home first and tell my dad I'll be staying away for – what? A couple of times a week?'

'That's right, only it's Mondays, Wednesdays and Fridays,' Ella told her. 'We won't charge you to sleep on our floor so long as the landlady doesn't find out, but I do think you might provide us with a bit of supper on those evenings, just bread and marge and some jam, perhaps, or half a pound of broken biscuits and a pint of milk.'

'How about a nice piece of smoked haddock, or a pair of kippers?' Amy suggested, giggling. 'I dare say your landlady might not like the pong, mind.'

'Kippers!' Ella said longingly. 'It seems a lifetime ago that I had kippers for breakfast and, if you fit in and can afford it, perhaps we might manage to turn our two bedder into a three bedder, particularly once your family can manage without you. Why, we might even rent a larger room between the three of us.'

'Or the four of us, if Ruthie came in,' Amy said eagerly. 'Oh, Ella, you don't know what this means to me. You're a sport and the nicest girl I've ever met. What's more, you've made me see that even a working girl like me can better herself. You're a pal, so you are!'

Chapter Seven
JUNE 1911

The train was crowded. Amy and the others had known it would be, which was why they had arrived at Lime Street Station early. The four of them – Amy herself, Ella, Ruth and Minnie – had thought long and hard before deciding to take their week's holiday from work and spend it in London, attending a big suffragette rally in the Albert Hall, then staying on to see the coronation of King George V five days later. Unfortunately others had also decided to arrive early in order to get seats on the train, so though the four girls had done their best to stick together, they had speedily realised it was to be every woman for herself. Amy and Ella had managed to get into the same compartment, but were separated at each end of it and could scarcely exchange more than smiles.

However, a train journey of such length was a delightful novelty for Amy. She had been lucky enough to get a corner seat, and now she settled down to gaze out of the window and reflect how her life had changed since she had met her friend.

It had all begun with the evening classes, of course. Miss Maple, who taught shorthand, typewriting and bookkeeping, was startled and impressed by the speed with which Amy assimilated knowledge. After barely two terms in her class she had suggested that Amy might like to try for a position as an office junior, which had just become vacant in the Adelphi Hotel. She pointed out that Amy would have to continue with her classes in the evening for some considerable while, but that working in an office all day, instead of in the fish market, would greatly increase her chances of passing the necessary examinations.

If it had not been for Ella, Amy reflected now, she might never even have applied for the post, but Ella had taken her in hand as soon as Amy had explained about the job.

'I don't want to hurt your feelings, Amy, but the very first thing an interviewer will notice is your clothing and general appearance,' Ella had said. 'You really should do something about your hair and complexion, you know. I realise it's difficult for you with a large family crammed into a little house, but you've got really pretty hair. If it were washed regularly and well cut to get rid of split ends, then it would do a great deal for your appearance. And though your complexion is good, just a touch of pencil on those fair eyebrows would give your face more ... more character. I hope you don't think I'm being critical, love, but jobs for women are scarce and if you really want to get one ...'

'I know you're right.' Amy had sighed, looking despairingly at her reflection in the small mirror which stood on the dressing table in the girls' room. 'The truth is, Ella, that when my mother was alive she used to wash my hair every week, regular as clockwork, and we had a bath every week, too. But now I'm working on the fish stall, it doesn't seem to matter what I look like, and Suzie's so mean with hot water that I'm lucky to get a bath once a month. As for clothes ...'

'I'll lend you something suitable,' Ella said

eagerly. She looked critically at her friend. 'Yes, I've got a lavender blouse with a high neck and long, full sleeves and a navy skirt with a frilled hem which will suit you very well and impress the interviewer, whoever he or she may be. Tell you what, Amy, you come and stay with us the night before the interview and we'll send you off the next morning, neat as a pin and smart as paint, and if you don't get the job I'll eat my new chapeau.'

Amy had been delighted to fall in with this suggestion and, despite Suzie's grumbles, had insisted on a lengthy hot bath in the scullery the previous day. Back in the girls' room, Ella had scrubbed Amy's hair until the water ran clear, while Amy cleaned her nails with an orange stick. When Amy's abundant auburn locks were dry, Ella piled the red-gold tresses on top of Amy's head, holding them in place with three curved tortoiseshell combs. Only then did Amy don the clothes which Ella had set out and presently, looking at her reflection in the mirror, she had seen a young woman she scarcely recognised as the Amy Logan who served each day behind Mrs O'Leary's fish stall. The blouse clung tightly to her slender figure, the well-tailored skirt emphasised her tiny waist and the face which smiled back at her was pink and white from vigorous washing, the large, hazel-green eyes bright with excitement. 'Oh, Ella,' Amy had breathed rapturously, 'I never knew I could look like this – why, you could take me for a real lady.'

'You *are* a real lady, goose,' Ella said, laughing, 'and once you're away from that wretched fish market and working in an office or a shop or something similar you'll know I'm right. Of course I hope you'll get the job at the Adelphi, but there's bound to be stiff competition, so we mustn't despair if you don't get offered the very first position you apply for. And having seen how nice you can look, dear Amy, I'm sure you'll want to keep it up. Now, it's time you were off. Good luck!'

Amy had duly gone for the interview, along with a great many other young ladies of her own age, and had been waiting to hear whether she had got the job when Mrs O'Leary had her fall. Sluicing down cobbles when they finished work one evening, she had stepped back on to her empty bucket and had fallen heavily. She had made light of the accident at first, though it was clear she was in great pain, but the next day her sister had come to the fish stall to tell Amy that Mrs O'Leary's leg was broken. Two days after that Mrs O'Leary had asked Bill and Amy to call on her and had told father and daughter that the doctor who had set her leg had said that she would be unable to walk on it for three months. 'For as you know, I'm past seventy and I've an uncommon heavy frame,' she said frankly. 'What's more, I don't fancy employing someone to help Amy out just for three months, so it seemed to me and Bridget that the best thing would be for me to retire and sell the business.

'As you know, I rent the stall from the council,' she told them, sitting in a fireside chair, with her injured leg resting on a stool drawn up before her. 'But I've a good little business and the money I'll get for it will give me a bit of a nest egg for the years to come, though me and me sister have always put a bit by, like.' She looked from Bill to Amy and back. 'But your girl's worked hard for me, Mr Logan, with never a moan or complaint, and you've let me have the pick o' your catch even when you might have sold it better elsewhere, so I's offering you first refusal, like.'

She named a sum and Amy waited for Bill to consult her or to say that they could not afford it, but instead he leaned forward in his chair, rested his elbows on his knees and said earnestly, 'To tell you the truth, Mrs O'Leary, I've known ever since me illness the winter before last that I'd have to give up the fishing, lerrit go to a younger man. Gus is capable and finds the fish, and Albert's near on as good. I reckon if they takes on young Paddy Keagan the three of them will do just about as well as we did when I were aboard. But I've no mind to retire yet, so I've been looking about me for a nice little business. And what could be better than the stall? It'd keep it in the family, like, and now young Becky's in school I'd mebbe get me wife to give a hand.' He turned to Amy, sitting on a stool at his feet, and patted her shoulder. 'If you wanted to run the stall wi' me, queen, that'd be just grand, so don't think I'm trying to ease you out. But ever since you started them evening classes at the YWCA last September I've knowed you had your eye on an office job of some sort.' He turned back to the older woman. 'So the answer's yes, Mrs O'Leary. I'll buy the business with the greatest of pleasure and take over as soon as it's all signed and sealed.'

Amy had gone to her evening classes that night with a light heart. Although she had longed for the opportunity to work in an office and use her newly acquired skills, she had felt that by so doing she would be letting both Mrs O'Leary and the family down. But her father's buying of the fish stall changed things completely and her heart swelled with love for Bill, who had understood her yearning

248

to be something other than a fish seller, and was now happy for her both to move out of her home and to take up different employment.

For Bill had made it plain, as the two of them had made their way to the tram stop, that living in a room share in the city with friends of her own age was the natural thing to do. He told her that with himself on the fish stall, the boys running the boat and Suzie selling the shrimps, they should be able to manage very nicely without Amy's money coming in. Secretly Amy doubted that Suzie would agree with him, but she cared nothing for that. At first she would have her work cut out to feed and clothe herself, and pay her share of the rent, for office juniors got very little more than she had earned on the fish stall. She did not, however, intend to remain an office junior for ever. She had been overawed by the appointments of the great hotel, though the offices, when she reached them, were far from plush. She was to work in a small room with five other girls, sitting at plain deal desks with their typewriting machines before them.

'We have a policy of promoting from within,' the office manager told her. 'So the successful candidate might rise to giddy heights if she stays with us, Miss Logan.' And with this in mind, Amy had been glad to take the job when it was offered. Ella and Minnie immediately said she must move in with them and Amy did so, quite content with a mattress on the floor and with a diet which consisted largely of porridge, bread and margarine, and the oddments of fish which her father saved her from the stall, though while on duty the staff were given their meals at the hotel.

She had been a little in awe of Minnie at first; the

other girl was five years older than she and worked as chief assistant in Bunney's china department, earning a good deal more than either of the others. She and her widowed mother had originally lived in the lower half of a house in Huskisson Street, opposite St Bride's church, but after Mrs Miniver's death, Minnie had retained the largest room for her own use. Some months later, however, loneliness had impelled her to put a notice in a newsagent's window, asking for a room sharer, and Ella had applied.

The two girls had got on famously, but had found the rent of such a large room in such a pleasant neighbourhood difficult to find; hence Ella's invitation to Amy and subsequently Amy's own suggestion that they should ask Ruth to join them.

It had been, Amy thought now, gazing out at the flat fields of Cheshire as they passed the window, a good move for everyone. She visited the house in Seafield Grove at least once a month, sometimes oftener, and though Suzie had been strange and stiff with her at first she had managed to hide her animosity under a pretence, at least, of friendliness. Bill and the boys were always glad to see her, though Paddy was apt to mutter some excuse and leave the house as she entered it. He was living with the Logans once more, since Aunt Dolly had died soon after Amy had moved into the city and, though Gran had always behaved as if Aunt Dolly was nothing but a burden, she had not survived her sister by many weeks. So the house had been let to someone else and Paddy had moved back into the boys' room.

The train, which had been puffing along slower and slower, drew to a halt. Amy peered out and saw that they had reached Crewe. Every seat in the carriage had been taken and a great many men were standing in the corridor outside. There was a great deal of bustle and movement as people began to rise from their seats and push their way out on to the platform, while others reached up to the luggage racks for their possessions, heedless of those still seated. In the ensuing scramble Ella managed to get a place beside Amy and the two of them smiled at each other as the train began to fill up again. 'That's a bit of luck,' Ella observed, settling herself into her new seat. 'I wonder how many people on this train are bound for Hyde Park, like us? Did you notice there are a great many women aboard? I saw one woman on the platform with a purple, green and white riband under her jacket, but I couldn't read what it said. I'll be bound she was one of us, though.'

'I expect lots of them are heading for the rally,' Amy agreed. She and the other girls had their sashes beneath their jackets and did not intend to reveal them until they reached the rallying point in Hyde Park, where they were to march on the Albert Hall to hear the speakers. Amy was secretly fairly indifferent to getting the vote, which she thought was of little or no importance, but she understood Mrs Pankhurst's point that in order to get equal opportunities with men, women must first have a say in who ran the country and how they did it. She had supported the suffragette movement ever since that first memorable rally before St George's Hall, but neither she nor the other girls were active members.

'We're too young and too poor to be able to risk a term of imprisonment and bad marks against us,' Ella had said long ago, when the matter came up for discussion. 'We aren't going to chain ourselves to railings or throw ourselves under steam locomotives, but we'll do what we can to show our support for the movement.' So when the girls heard of the rally in London, and realised that it was to take place just five days before the coronation of King George and Queen Mary, they had decided, recklessly, to blow their week's holiday and the money they had saved up on a week in the capital. They had managed to get lodgings quite near Euston Station, where they would cheerfully sleep two to a bed, and planned to attend the rally, to see the sights of London and, on the day before the coronation, to take up good positions somewhere along the route. They had brought with them umbrellas, a warm coat and a blanket each, and intended to spend the night on the pavement rather than miss the wonderful spectacle of the royal procession.

'I think we ought to go straight to our lodgings and leave our suitcases,' Ella said, as the train began to pick up speed once more. 'Euston Station is a huge place so we'll have our work cut out to find the other two. The train is so crowded we can't possibly search for them until we reach London. Is Ruth wearing her poppy hat? That should be easy to spot.'

Amy chuckled. 'Yes, I think she is, and Minnie's got that carpet bag with the red fringe. Anyway, they'll be looking for us too, remember.'

'True,' Ella said. 'I suppose the thing to do is just to stand still. Then when everyone else is gone we'll be able to spot each other easily. Oh, Amy, I haven't enjoyed myself so much for years. Dear old London, I'm longing to see it again.'

'What a glorious day!' Amy lay on her back on the

cool green grass, gazing up into the blue sky above her. 'And isn't this the most beautiful place you ever saw, Ella? Aren't I glad we decided to have a day off from sightseeing before the coronation tomorrow. Mind you, when you suggested Hampton Court, I remembered old Cardinal Wolsey and Henry VIII and all that history stuff, and thought that we were in for another boring old museum. But this is prime!'

Ella, lying beside her on the grass, smiled and rolled on to her tummy. Propping herself on her elbows, she reached for the bag of buns they had bought earlier, selected one and proffered it to Minnie and Ruth sitting beside her. 'Yes, I know what you mean,' she admitted, taking a large bite out of the bun in her hand, 'but to tell the truth, Hampton Court is one of the few places around London I've never visited before myself. So coming here was a bit of a gamble.'

'Well, it was a gamble that paid off,' Minnie observed, chosing a bun covered in virulent pink icing. 'The rose garden is really beautiful, the scent of those big, dark-red ones made me feel as drunk as the bees. And the palace is most impressive, from the outside, that is. Our tickets allow us to go inside, only it's such a glorious day ... but I suppose we ought, don't you think?'

'I think we oughter have another go at the maze,' Ruth observed, taking a bite out of her own bun. 'We very nearly got to the centre last time, you know, and I'd rather do that than go inside a palace, no matter how impressive.'

'It's too hot,' Amy moaned. She picked up her straw hat which she had laid down beside her on the grass and fanned her face vigorously with it. 'Only fancy if the weather is like this tomorrow! But at least we shan't spend the night huddled under our umbrellas. That wouldn't have been much fun, would it?'

'Oh, I don't know,' Ella remarked, finishing her bun and rolling on to her back once more. 'It seems to me we have fun whatever we do, us four. Don't you agree, girls?'

It was true, Amy thought, remembering life in their large but crowded room in Huskisson Street. Having spent the first years of her life in a male-dominated household where women were expected to do all the jobs, save for such things as the bringing in of fuel and water, she appreciated more than the others how good it was to share household and domestic chores. Everyone did their own washing and ironing – sometimes the lines of washing criss-crossing the yard seemed to belong solely to the girls in the large front room – and took turns at practically everything else. Shopping and cooking were arranged on a rota basis, but it was a free and easy rota. If you were down to cook the Sunday roast and wanted to go out with a young man, or visit a relative on that particular day, you simply swapped with someone who was not so engaged. If doing the messages meant a visit to the dairy and another of your room-mates was going in that direction, then a simple request would be enough.

'If we're going to try and solve the puzzle of the maze again, then we really should be moving,' Minnie observed, standing up and beginning to dust crumbs off her long grey skirt. With varying degrees of reluctance the others joined her and, passing a bench where trippers had been picnicking, Amy spotted a copy of the *Evening Standard* and pounced on it.

'A free paper! And it's last night's, too,' she announced. She began to flick idly through the pages as they made their way towards the maze and presently, her eyes caught by the word Liverpool, she stopped short, a hand flying to her mouth. 'Hang on a minute, girls. You'll never guess what it says here! There's been trouble at the docks, a strike or some such thing, because they wanted a ten bob a month rise and the bosses turned it down. Good lord, aren't we the lucky ones? There's bound to be more fuss and we're out of it. It says here that there's been unrest in the streets, whatever that may mean.'

'Ooh, perhaps they'll stop the trams running, then I shan't have to go and tell me family all about the coronation,' Ruth said, grinning at Amy. 'Mind you, I'd walk to Seaforth sooner than miss telling Mam and the kids all about London and the King and Queen and everything. What's more, there's the souvenirs. The kids will be that eager to get their hands on what I've bought them, they'd probably walk into the city centre theirselves.'

'Good thing they aren't striking in London, that's what I say,' Ella remarked, as they stopped outside the maze. 'Still, as you say, it will all be over by the time we get back. Now, shall we tackle the maze separately or in pairs?'

It was still fine that evening when the girls made camp on the pavement along the procession route. They were by no means the only people so disposing themselves and, by the time they began to eat their sandwiches and drink tea from the bottles with which they had provided themselves, they were already on friendly terms with the people camping on either side of them. Both parties were Londoners, large family groups with what seemed, at first, like a dozen children apiece, all of whom raced up and down the road carrying news and gossip from one group to another, and being rewarded with sweets and fruit.

'This'll be the fourth night this century as I've spent on the pavement,' the mother of the family on their left informed Amy. 'Fust there were Queen Victoria's funeral, then King Eddie's crowning, then poor old Eddie's funeral and now young George's coronation.'

Amy would not have described King George as young, but she was intrigued to learn that her new friend – Mrs Potter – was such a connoisseur of royal events. As the night drew on, she encouraged Mrs Potter to talk about her previous experience of royal processions and was very moved to hear how, at King Edward's funeral, his charger was led behind the coffin with King Edward's riding boots reversed in the stirrups, and all the girls wept over the fate of the King's little dog, Caesar, who followed the coffin, searching constantly for his master.

'He were only a little mongrel,' Mrs Potter informed them, 'but on his collar it said "Caesar: I belong to the King". Oh aye, there's no doubt Teddy adored that dog; Caesar went with him everywhere – he'll be lost wi'out Teddy, poor little chap.'

It was after midnight before the excited, chattering crowd began to settle. Amy wrapped herself in her blanket and, using her bag as a pillow, managed to snatch a few hours' sleep. She guessed that the other girls had done the same, but woke slowly and grudgingly as a grey dawn crept across the sky, with a nasty taste in her mouth and her elbows and hips as stiff as boards. She sat, knuckling her eyes and looking around her. Presently someone further up the line lit a primus stove and boiled a kettle of hot water. She served her companions first, then came along the pavement edge, offering hot water to anyone who, as she put it, was 'dyin' to wet their whistle'. The girls eagerly proffered their enamel mugs and made themselves milkless tea, which greatly refreshed them and, as Ella put it, 'woke them up with a vengeance'.

Behind the pavement on which the girls had camped lay a park and on the previous evening they had noticed a drinking fountain on a small circle of gravel. Accordingly they went to it in pairs and had as good a wash as was possible in a public place. They combed their hair, pinned on their hats, shook out their jackets and brushed down their skirts, then made their way back to their camping site where they ate bread and margarine and apples for an early breakfast.

They recognised several of the women camping on the opposite pavement as members of the suffragette movement whom they had seen in the Albert Hall, and exchanged waves and smiles, but it really did look as though they were the only Liverpudlians, in this part of the crowd at any rate.

As soon as it was light enough, various entertainers began to stroll along the sides of the road. There were men with mouth organs, concertinas and penny whistles; there were tumblers who performed amazing acts, climbing upon each other's shoulders to form a huge pyramid, tightrope walkers who brought their stand and rope with them and danced as merrily along it, six feet above the roadway, as though they were performing on a stage. They got a great reception from the waiting crowds and were doing quite well when the police began to clear the roadway – obviously something was about to happen.

'We've got an excellent place here. We shan't miss much,' Ella remarked to Amy, as the first of the carriages containing the dignitaries began to arrive. The upper ten thousand, as Amy remembered Isobel calling them, would take their places in Westminster Abbey long before the royals arrived and Amy wondered what would happen should one of them wish to use the privy. There were public lavatories in the park and the girls had made use of them in the early hours, realising how crowded they would become later. But a lord or a lady, dressed in heavy ermine-trimmed robes of state, would be in no position to make a dash for the outside world, no matter how urgent his or her need.

By the time the young princes had driven past Amy felt quite hoarse from cheering, but when the King and Queen arrived, in an open carriage drawn by six cream-coloured ponies, she managed yet another cheer and waved her little Union Jack with as much enthusiasm as, five days earlier, she had waved her 'Votes for Women' banner.

'Oh, ain't I glad we came,' Ruthie said rapturously when the last of the colourful companies of soldiers had marched past. 'I won't ever forget today, our Amy. Are we goin' to wait until they come out? Only if we're goin' to catch our train ...'

'I think we ought to be getting back to our lodgings,' Amy said regretfully. 'Judging by the newspaper report, we may find Liverpool in a bit of a state when we reach Lime Street, even though the strike will probably be over by now. What's more, I could do with a proper wash and a good meal. What do you say, Ella, Minnie?'

The girls all agreed that they had best begin to think about their journey home and turned, rather regretfully, back towards the environs of Euston Station.

The station was crowded, as they had guessed it would be, but not, Amy thought, as crowded as it would probably become later in the day, when the procession had returned to Buckingham Palace, shouted and cheered every foot of the way. She and her friends settled down with their baggage on one of the green wooden seats provided by the railway company, but as soon as their train came in they made a dash for it, hoping this time to be able to sit together.

They found a carriage in which two young men were piling their cases on to the luggage rack and settled themselves in a row. The young men finished with their luggage and one of them turned courteously towards them and offered to help them heave their belongings on to the string rack above their heads. For a moment Amy stared at the young man, wondering where she had previously seen him. But before she could say a word he suddenly beamed at her and, seizing her hand, shook it vigorously. 'It's Amy Logan, by all that's wonderful! Well, I'm darned, I've not seen you since you were a scrubby little kid with your skirts hiked up to your knees, helping to haul a fish ashore on Seaforth Sands. Don't you remember me? I'm sure you've changed a great deal more than I have.'

'Philip!' Amy said, considerably astonished. She thought he had changed greatly, despite his words.

He was wearing a boater tilted at a rakish angle, which he raised momentarily to reveal his light-brown hair, and he had a moustache which, in Amy's view, completely changed his appearance, making him look years older.

'Yes, it's me,' Philip agreed, grinning. 'My goodness, Amy, how you've grown! You're quite the young lady – but what in heaven's name are you doing in London? Don't say you've left home?'

'Yes, I have left home,' Amy admitted, 'but I don't live in London, we just came up for ... for the coronation, me and my pals here.' She indicated her friends with a wave of her hand. 'Come to that, what are you doing in London yourself, Philip? Or do fellers watch coronations as well as girls? And what are you doing on this train? You live in Manchester, near where my sister Mary used to work; she said so in her letters. Oh, I suppose you're getting off at Crewe and catching another train, is that it?'

Philip laughed. 'You aren't the only one who can leave home,' he observed, sitting down opposite Amy and leaning forward. 'I've been living and working in Liverpool for almost a year now. My father's firm has its head office in Manchester, I know, but two years ago we decided to expand and started up a branch in Liverpool. You could say I was in charge of it.' He suddenly struck his forehead, looking abashed. 'But whatever am I thinking of? Amy, this is Mr Maynard, one of my colleagues and a very good friend. Dick, this is Amy Logan, the sister of my pal Albert. Not that I've seen either of them for years. After my grandfather died the family sold the house in Seaforth, which meant Laura and I didn't visit there any more. A pity, because I loved the place, but life's like that.'

'I should have introduced you to my friends,' Amy said, conscience-stricken. 'This is Miss Morton, sitting next to me, Miss Miniver on her other side and Miss Durrant in the corner. Girls, this is Mr Philip Grimshaw and Mr Maynard.'

The girls murmured polite greetings just as the train jerked violently, causing Ella, who was sitting on the edge of her seat, to fall forward, landing almost in Philip's lap. This broke the ice in a way which nothing else could have done and presently the six of them were chattering away as if they had known one another all their lives. Amy took advantage of the situation and leaned forward to tap Philip on the knee. 'Philip, do you see much of our Mary? She's done well for herself and risen in the world. She used to work for a family who lived near your parents so I dare say you saw her now and again, but she's working in a departmental store on Deansgate now. She's in ladies' hats and doing ever so well, only she hardly ever comes home and we've never met her young man.'

'I do remember seeing Mary two or three years back,' Philip said slowly, after giving the matter some thought. 'Yes, now you mention it I did see her with a young man more recently. Well, not young exactly. In his mid-twenties I would say, but then she may have had several young men since then.'

'No, I think she's been going steady with Roderick ever since she moved to Manchester,' Amy said. 'He's in a bank and doing most awfully well, Mary says. She often mentions him in her letters but, reading between the lines, I don't think they mean to marry until they're in a really good financial position.'

'Marry? But she can't be more than twenty-two or

three?' Philip asked. 'They'll want to be able to afford a decent place of their own and also be able to do without Mary's wages before they wed. At least,' he added hastily, 'I imagine they will, because once they're married and the little ones come along ...'

Amy giggled. It seemed strange to think of Mary marrying some unknown young man, let alone having children. Without fully understanding why, she realised that Mary had never talked about a home and children, only about marriage. Her sister was ambitious and the young man with whom she was going steady had his whole mind fixed on advancement. Perhaps, she thought now, they would never marry but would continue to keep company for years, until each attained the height of their ambition.

But Philip was talking now, telling her about the service flat which he shared with Mr Maynard and asking her about Albert, her parents and, of course, the Keagans and Paddy. Taking a deep breath, Amy told him rapidly all that had happened since that day on the beach. The birth of baby Becky, her mother's death, Bill's remarriage and her own move into the city. She said as little as possible about Suzie's attitude to herself and nothing about her job in the fish market, but she did tell Philip of her father's illness. She also told him that Bill now had a stall in St John's Market selling his own fish and was, consequently, better off than he had been since her mother's death. 'My stepmother's not a worker like my mam was,' she said. 'But she really loves my dad and she's good to the boys and little Becky, and since I'm not living there any more it's the most I can hope for.'

'What about Paddy?' Philip asked after a moment.

'I seem to remember you and he weren't exactly pally when we were kids.'

Amy laughed. 'We were sworn enemies from the first time he called me "Liverpool Shrimpy" and said I smelled of fish,' she admitted frankly. 'It was really difficult living under the same roof, once Bill and Suzie married, because he didn't like me any better for sharing our home and of course I simply hated him. But now he's working the boat with Gus and Albert, and when I go home he usually slopes off so I don't have much to do with him at all. A good job, I reckon.'

'I don't think he disliked you for yourself,' Philip told her, after a thoughtful pause. 'He was that fond of Albert that he was jealous of you. And he had a terrific crush on Mary, you know. He thought you were against him there and might set Mary against him too. I remember him going on about it one afternoon when the three of us went digging for cockles. Albert kept telling him he was talking nonsense and afterwards your brother told me privately that Paddy might as well forget all about Mary, because she would be after better game as soon as she was able. Anyway, don't tell me Paddy still dislikes you? You're a young woman and he's a young man now, not a couple of kids. Feelings change as you get older, the person you disliked may be quite different now that . . .'

At this point they were interrupted. 'If you two have stopped swapping family histories, how about a bite to eat?' Minnie said plaintively. 'We've got ham sandwiches wi' mustard, cheese-and-tomato rolls and a bag of sticky buns. They'll go round six easy, if you'd like to share 'em with us.' The young men agreed eagerly and Philip said that when the train stopped at the next station he would get out and buy six paper cups of tea from one of the platform vendors. Very soon a pleasant picnic was taking place and the conversation had become general.

Ella, always a lively and vivacious talker, told the two young men all about their room in Huskisson Street and made everyone laugh with a description of getting up in the early hours of a winter's morning, while it was still dark, and becoming horribly entangled with a pair of wet stockings which someone had strung on a line across the room. 'I thought it was either a web spun by the biggest and most horrible spider in the world, or a desperate robber, trying to tie me up,' she admitted. 'I shrieked so loudly that poor Minnie nearly had a heart attack. When I managed to find the candle and light it, she was sitting up in bed clutching a boot in one hand and the front of her nightgown in the other, with eyes as big as saucers and her mouth open to shout for help.'

'Why a boot, queen?' Ruth asked, giggling. The incident had happened, it appeared, before either she or Amy had come to live in Huskisson Street. 'Was you thinkin' of gettin' dressed and runnin' out on your pal?'

'No, indeed,' Minnie said with dignity. 'I thought it was a burglar, too, so I was going to brain him with me boot.'

'You make sharing a room sound great fun – much more fun than living in a hostel as a lot of girls do,' Philip said presently, his voice almost wistful. 'Dick and myself have a good time, of course, but we're sober citizens compared with the four of you. We go to the theatre, eat out most nights in the dining room below the flats, go dancing sometimes ... do you ever go dancing?'

'Course we do, when we can afford it and there's a decent dance on,' Amy said at once. 'But even with four of us sharing, money's a bit tight. Why, we saved up for a whole year so that we could go to London for the ... the coronation.'

'Tell the truth and shame the devil, Amy,' Ella said, smirking. 'We went to the suffragette rally first, fellows. We don't chain ourselves to railings or throw ourselves under steam trains or racehorses, but we do support the movement. We think we should have as much of a chance to earn a decent living as any young man. Don't you agree?'

'I do, up to a point,' Philip said cautiously. 'But I'm not sure I approve of the suffragette movement. It ... it's unwomanly, don't you think? Surely there must be a better, *gentler* way of making your point and getting your own way? I mean, fighting the police, going to prison, chaining yourselves to railings ...'

'The *gentle* way, as you put it, has been proving itself useless since the dawn of time, Mr Grimshaw,' Ella pointed out. 'No one wanted to have to use violence, or go to prison, or be force-fed in order to get what should be ours by right. Nor, for that matter, do any women I know want to give men carte blanche to bully and ill-treat the weaker sex as we are called, because that is how a good many members of the police force behave. Nothing gives them greater pleasure than to be allowed – nay, encouraged – to attack and beat distinguished and intelligent women who are merely asking that they be taken seriously. Such women, the average police-man knows, are intellectually and morally their infinite superiors. So they are taking a sort of revenge on every suffragette whom they ill-treat and arrest.'

'Gosh!' Amy said, very much struck by this speech. 'Well, Philip, I hope that's given you something to think about. And there's no need to be *ashamed* to support the suffragettes, you know, for a great many gentlemen do. Even members of parliament,' she added.

Philip, who had been bending forward and listening to Ella with great attention, leaned back in his seat and expelled his breath in a long whistle. 'Phew! Well, thank you, Miss – er – Morton for the lecture, which I'm sure I richly deserved. I can't say you've changed my opinion, exactly, but you've certainly made me think.' He turned to his friend. 'You haven't said much, Dick. Are you a secret supporter of the suffragette movement? If so, you've kept it very quiet until now.'

Dick looked uncomfortable. Amy had often observed that among gentlemen who had not yet taken a stand, discomfort seemed to be their chief emotion. But finding himself the object of everyone's attention he cleared his throat and spoke: 'I don't know what I felt before, Miss Morton, but like my friend here, you've certainly given me something to think about. I must admit I've seen the police behaving in a very brutal and uncouth fashion during demonstrations ... but then, what choice have they? I suppose they have to use rioters roughly, whether they be male or female.'

Amy was about to reply wrathfully that violence against women who were for the most part incapable of using equal force, could never be right or fair when Minnie, ever the peacemaker, spoke up.

'Let's not argue,' she said placatingly. 'After all, there's been a seamen's strike in Liverpool while we were away, and I don't suppose anyone of us girls intends to go on to the streets and join the dockers' protest, even if we believe their cause to be just. So why should we expect these gentlemen to interest themselves in our cause? Let's change the subject, girls, and ask Mr Grimshaw and Mr Maynard to tell us a bit about their work.'

From then on conversation became general. The six of them discussed plays they had seen, actors and actresses they admired and the new kinema-color shows which had appeared for the first time at the Argyle Theatre in Birkenhead.

'Have you seen Vesta Tilley at the Empire? We went a week ago and we all thought she was superb – she looked more like a man than some men do,' Ella said.

'Do you go often to the theatre?' Philip asked eagerly. 'We might meet you there some time and perhaps go for a meal afterwards. Then we could tell each other what we thought of the show while we ate. Why, if four young women and two gentlemen seems wrong, we could get a couple of the fellows from the office to come along – just to make up the numbers you know,' he added hastily.

Amy was about to agree enthusiastically that this would be a great idea when Ella spoke. 'It might be fun, but you know we're all in work and fully employed until seven or eight in the evening,' she pointed out. 'Apart from this, our holiday, we don't get much time we can call our own. Mind you, we can go to the last house on a Saturday, because then we can lie in on Sunday, but other than that . . .'

'We do get half-days,' Amy put in. She sighed.

'But they aren't usually the same, unfortunately. Working at the Adelphi as I do, I often work shifts, which cuts down my social life, you might say. Ella and Minnie aren't too badly off because Bunney's and the Bon Marché close at a reasonable hour, but poor Ruth works in Dorothy's Dining Rooms and she can be kept really late some nights.'

'Dorothy's Dining Rooms!' Philip exclaimed, his eyes brightening, 'I *thought* I'd seen you somewhere before, I just couldn't think where. Dick and I often pop along to Dorothy's for a quick snack when we are working late and sometimes we take business clients along there for luncheon. It's very handy for Lime Street Station and most of them come and go between Manchester and Liverpool on the train.'

Ruth, who must have felt a little out of it, Amy considered, was delighted to find herself recognised and, after staring very hard at Dick and Philip for several moments, said she believed she remembered them as well. 'You're the young gentlemen who came in last week with a huge feller, old-fashioned looking, with a shiny top hat and a dickie bow,' she said triumphantly. 'He weren't with you,' she added hastily. 'I think he was in the Music Hall Show at the Royal Court Theatre. He's a magician or something, and ever so kind and jolly to us girls. He tips well and all,' she finished reflectively.

Philip's brow cleared and he grinned delightedly. 'What a memory you've got,' he marvelled. 'Yes, I remember now, old Marvo, the magician – he was in front of us last Tuesday and bagged the window table we'd got our eye on so we went and sat with young Stebbings and Mr Alcock.' He turned back to Ruth. 'Well, fancy you remembering that! Every time

I come into Dorothy's Dining Rooms in future I shall demand to be served by Miss ... Miss ...

'I'm Miss Durrant,' Ruth said, smiling shyly. 'Well, isn't that a coincidence? Are you sure you haven't met Miss Morton when you've been shopping in the Bon Marché? Or Miss Miniver when you go after sports equipment in Bunney's?'

The two young men laughed, but shook their heads. 'We don't frequent the department stores much,' Philip said, 'but now we know where to find you, perhaps we'll do so.' He turned to Ella. 'Why, you might even give me a discount, Miss Morton.'

With much similar chatter and a great deal of laughter, the journey passed in a flash and soon they found themselves on Lime Street Station once more. The young gentlemen offered to help pile their bags into a taxi cab but the girls refused, having every intention of getting a tram back to Huskisson Street. They walked along to Renshaw Street and very soon they were scrambling on to a number 15 and heading for home, tired but happy after their holiday in London and delighted to think that they had made two new friends.

A week later the girls were sitting round the open window of their room, eating supper from plates on their knees, for the day had been oppressively warm and they felt they would sleep better for some fresh air. Amy finished her brawn sandwich and set the plate on the floor, then picked up a letter from Mary, which had been delivered earlier in the day, and slit the envelope open. 'I wrote to Mary the day after we got home from the coronation, but I didn't expect a reply for a couple of weeks,' she observed, pulling out the thin lined sheets of paper. 'But here she is,

269

writing to me a matter of days later. I wonder what's up? Perhaps she's coming home. Well, if she is, I'll have to see her weekends or evenings, because I've used all my holiday and I don't intend to take unpaid leave just because Mary's coming home.'

Ella finished her sandwich and put her own plate on top of Amy's, then shook her head sadly. 'What a one you are for leaping to conclusions,' she remarked. 'Poor Mary probably only wants to tell you what she did on the King's Coronation Day. Why don't you read it instead of making nasty remarks?'

Amy giggled. 'All right, all right, I'm just going to, no need to bully me,' she said and smoothed out the first sheet. She read the letter right through once, turned back to the beginning and read it again. Then she raised round eyes to her friends' faces. 'Mary *is* coming home,' she said in a dazed voice. 'I must be psychic, Ella, because she hardly ever comes home and I didn't really believe she meant to do so this time either. That's right at the end of the letter, mind. She begins by telling me that she and Roderick had the day off for the coronation and went out into the countryside on their bicycles with a picnic. Then she goes on about the street party which she and Roderick attended in the evening and the fun they had, and how people danced on the cobbles, and someone turned her ankle, and she and another girl took her to hospital . . . and after that she just sort of mentions that she's coming home and says she's looking forward to seeing me.'

'I wonder what's bringing her back all of a rush like that?' Ella mused. She stood up and began to collect the girls' used plates. 'I suppose she's going to stay with your parents, Amy? I mean, there isn't room for a visitor here, no matter how tiny. Well, I suppose she could share your bed . . .'

'No, she couldn't,' Amy said firmly, going over to put the kettle on the gas ring. 'My dad would be terribly upset if Mary came to us instead of to Seaforth and besides, Mary's got a bit . . . a bit high and mighty you could say, these past years. One of the reasons she doesn't come home often is because she's ashamed of being a fisherman's daughter and living in crowded conditions. No, if she's coming home – and from her letter it looks as though she's planning to stay a week – then it's for some definite reason. If I didn't know about her bank clerk I'd wonder . . .'

'You'd wonder what?' Ella asked after a moment when Amy said no more, but Amy only shook her head. This did not mean, however, that she had not had what amounted to a revelation. She had written to Mary and had not omitted to tell her how they had met Philip and his friend on the train and what a jolly journey they had. Was it possible that Mary's early fancy for Philip was actually causing her to come back to Liverpool? Now that she thought about it seriously, she realised that it was highly unlikely Mary would have known that Philip no longer lived in Manchester until she had received Amy's letter. But the more Amy thought about it, the less she believed it possible. She did not know much about Mary's young man but surely her sister would be well aware that a bird in the hand was worth two in the bush? To come flying back to Liverpool just because Philip, whom she hardly knew, had returned to that city seemed an act of madness and Mary had always been level-headed, with an eye to the main chance.

I'm letting my imagination run away with me, Amy decided, taking the kettle off the gas ring and pouring hot water into the basin which they used for washing up. But having allowed the thought to take possession of her mind, she knew she would have to go to Seaforth that very Sunday and find out just why her sister had decided to come home.

Amy had planned to catch the early tram on Sunday, so that she might arrive in Seaforth in time to go to church with the rest of her family, but she had reckoned without the number of people who would want to travel from the city centre to Seaforth Sands on a fine Sunday in June. Three trams sailed past her, crammed to the eyebrows, with at least fifty people perilously strap-hanging, before she was able to climb aboard the fourth. So it was well past noon before she eventually got off the tram at the Rimrose Bridge.

It had been several weeks since she had last visited her family and she had not told them that she intended to do so today, so she was delighted, as she turned into Crosby Road, to find a small figure hurrying towards her along the pavement. It was Becky, pigtails flying, one ribbon already missing, but with a broad beam on her small face. 'Amy!' Becky squeaked, hurling herself into her older sister's arms. 'I come down the road 'cos our mam said our Mary were goin' to be on the next tram and there's you!' She gazed anxiously up into Amy's face. '*Was* Mary on your tram, our Amy? She writ to our dad sayin' she were gettin' a train today, 'cos her young man were takin' her to the pictures, Sat'day, only Sunday trains ain't good, our dad says. She weren't on your tram, were she, Amy?'

'No, she wasn't. And she may not be on a tram for some time, queen, because it's a lovely day and everyone wants to get to the seaside, so the queues for the trams are miles long – I had difficulty myself in getting aboard.'

'What'll I do then, our Amy?' the small girl enquired. Amy smiled down at her sister; she was a pretty thing, with her blonde hair cut into a fringe across her forehead and the rest plaited into two fat little pigtails. She had a rosy, cherubic face and large, light-blue eyes, and Amy had to admit that Suzie dressed the child beautifully now that she had the money to do so, and always saw to it that she was spotlessly clean. Today Becky wore a blue and white gingham smock dress, covered by a frilled white pinafore with white cotton stockings and neat brown shoes. Amy remembered how she and the others, including Paddy, had always gone barefoot in the summer, and thought there were advantages in being the spoilt youngest of the family, when the older children had all grown up. But she did not grudge Becky her boots or pretty clothes and was just glad, for the child's sake, that both Bill and Suzie clearly adored the little girl.

'Amy!' Becky shook the hand she was clasping impatiently. 'Shall I wait for the next tram or can we go home? I didn't really want to come up to meet Mary all that much 'cos I don't know her very well, not nearly as well as I know you. Besides, she's stayin' for a week this time an' I dare say you've only popped in to have tea with us. So shall us go home, Amy? The boys are home, of course, though Gus usually goes out of a Sunday. Oh, Amy, did you know Gus has fallen out wi' Peggy Higgins? And they've been goin' steady for three years – longer!'

'Well I never,' Amy said, as the two of them, hand in hand, began to walk up Crosby Road. 'Mind you, people do fall out from time to time, you know; it's probably what they call a lover's tiff and in a few days they'll be going steady again.'

'They won't, though,' Becky said positively, swinging vigorously on Amy's hand. 'Peggy's gorra little sister what's only two years older than me and she says Peggy don't care for Gus no more; she's gorra feller who ships aboard the *Devanha* what goes regular to India and the Far East. Elly, that's Peggy's sister, says he brung back a china tea set for Peg wi' little cups like eggshells, all painted wi' pagodas and such. She says Gus never give Peggy nowt but the odd bag o' shrimps.'

'Well!' Amy said, considerably shocked to hear her small sister passing on such gossip. 'I tell you what though, queen, if all Peggy thinks about are what presents a feller can hand out, Gus is better off without her. Although it seems a shame he wasted all those years courting her.'

'Oh, Gus don't mind,' Becky said cheerfully. 'He says women just hold a feller back and he's goin' to take a berth aboard a trawler like our Edmund done and make his fortune that way. Then Peg will be sorry, he says.'

'I dare say she'll be sorry long before that,' Amy said, as they turned into Seafield Grove. 'You know the strike everyone's been talking about, queen? Well, it means there's a great many sailors hanging about the city, bored with having nothing to do. Probably Peggy's new young man is one of them and when the strike's over and his ship sails he won't give Peg another thought. And serve her right,' she ended, as the pair of them crossed the

274

yard and entered the Logan kitchen. She could not help reflecting, however, as she glanced round the room, that things had changed greatly in the years since she had lived at home. The kitchen had been freshly painted and the worn and shabby furniture she remembered had been replaced by a new upholstered sofa and two easy chairs. The old stoneware sink, with its slippery wooden draining boards, had gone and there was a modern sink unit where it had once stood. Instead of the rickety sideboard, which Isobel had told her had been left in the house by the previous tenants, a smart mahogany one now leaned against the wall. Also, bright damask curtains hung at the windows and, when Becky sat down, it was on a sateen-covered pouffe instead of the three-legged wooden stool which had usually accommodated the youngest Logan child.

The changes had come gradually, of course, and Amy had long realised that the ownership of the fish stall had done wonders for the family's economy. As Bill said, they had cut out the middle man completely, selling virtually from the boat to the public so that the fish was always the freshest available and customers' recommendations meant that there was scarcely any waste.

What was more, now that they only paid the rent on this one house, Bill had taken on an extra allotment and he, Gus and Albert – and probably Paddy, too, for all she knew – grew vegetables there, for when Suzie took her shrimps from door to door, she had begun to sell fresh vegetables, and found they were as popular as the fish and sold every bit as well.

With a little more money available, things had

become easier all round. Suzie no longer took in washing and the family ate shop-baked bread, though Suzie's cooking had improved considerably. Gran had left an old exercise book in which she had noted down her favourite recipes and Suzie, carefully conning it, began to present her family with cakes, pies and puddings, and was delighted with their enthusiastic response.

Now Bill, who had been sitting reading an old copy of the *Echo*, puffing away at his pipe, turned at Amy's entrance and stood up. 'Well, blow me down!' he exclaimed, crossing the room towards her and taking both her hands in his. 'Here was I expectin' one daughter and who should turn up but t'other! I'm delighted to see you, queen, but where's you sprung from, eh? We were expectin' Mary. She wrote and said she were comin' home today so Suzie sent our Becky down to the tram to meet her. Though I'm powerful glad to see you, Mary or no Mary,' he ended, giving her a kiss and a hug.

'There's a deal of fuss going on in the city because of this here strike,' Amy said, carefully unpinning her hat and hanging it on the back of the kitchen door, 'and on a fine day, everyone wants to get away from trouble and down to the beach. So the trams were chock-a-block. Still, I got here in the end. The truth is, Dad, that Mary wrote to me as well and I thought, since I was off today, I'd pop over and see her – and the rest of you, of course – so we could have a good old jangle. But it looks as though, if I want to see Mary, I'll have to make some other arrangement.'

Bill had returned to his newspaper, but now he looked up. 'Suzie, Gus and Albert have gone up to the allotment. They won't be long but Suzie fancied cookin' a mess of peas for our supper, so they've gone to pick any that's ripe. You know we sell 'em now. We do well with 'em in summer and in winter the root vegetables go down a treat, so one way and another we ain't doin' bad.'

'I know and I think it's grand,' Amy said, taking the chair opposite her father's. 'The kitchen looks lovely, too, Dad. Isn't Mary going to have a surprise when she gets here? It must be months since she was last home.'

Becky, having come in with Amy, asked brightly, 'Can I go to the 'lotment, Dad? I can help carry the veggies home.'

'Yes, but don't you go eatin' all the peas afore we've had a chance to shell them,' Bill said, grinning. As the back door slammed behind Becky, he turned to his older daughter. 'Did our Becky tell you about Gus?'

'Yes, she couldn't wait to tell me,' Amy said, smiling. 'It's a pity, but these things do happen.'

Bill was beginning to reply when the back door opened and the rest of the family surged into the room, with Becky dancing ahead. Suzie came over and kissed her stepdaughter with a warmth that Amy appreciated, since when she had lived at home such warmth had been notable only by its absence. Albert came over and punched her in the shoulder, the way brothers do, and Gus ruffled her hair, saying jovially, 'Where's you sprung from, our Amy? We were expectin' Mary, but not yourself. Have you heard about . . .'

'If you mean that you and Peggy have split up, you can't enter Seaforth without someone giving the news,' Amy laughed up at her big brother. 'I'm not going to offer you my condolences, though, because the general opinion seems to be you're well out of it. Met anyone else yet?'

Gus snorted. 'No, nor I don't want to,' he said gruffly. 'I wasted the best years of me life on Peggy Higgins; now I'm goin' to have me some fun before I'm too old to appreciate it. Wharr I want is a fast woman – do you know any, young Amy?'

Amy spluttered and rose to her feet to give Gus a slap, but he had carried the heavy basket of vegetables through into the scullery, so she sat down again. Albert, who held a string bag full of pea pods, came over to her, tipped a quantity into her lap and stood a heavy saucepan down by her side. 'Shell 'em for our tea, there's a good little sister,' he said, going over to the door to kick off his muddy boots. Over his shoulder he went on, 'No one said as how you were comin' home today, Amy, you could've let us know. That young Durrant girl comes home most Sundays, don't she?'

'I don't really know,' Amy said, surprised, 'just lately I've been doing a lot of shift work, so I haven't had many Sundays off myself. Still, I couldn't have told Ruthie I was coming home because I only made up my mind yesterday, when the boss said he wouldn't be needing me in today. Hotels aren't like shops and such, we have to have a full staff in seven days a week.'

'Well, it doesn't matter; you're here now,' Albert said lazily, sitting down beside her and beginning to ping peas into the saucepan. He followed Amy's example and dropped the empty pods in a neat pile by the fast-emptying string bag. 'Wharrabout young Peggy Higgins, then, did Gus tell you . . .'

'Everyone's telled her,' roared Gus from the scullery. 'Honest to God, there's no need of a town crier in Seaforth; every perishin' person knows your business almost before you know it yourself.'

'Well, it's the most excitin' thing to happen in Seaforth for half a century,' Albert said, grinning. 'I wonder when our Mary will arrive, though? Paddy said he were goin' to come home via the Rimrose Bridge to see if he could meet her, so mebbe the two of them will turn up in time to eat supper, if not help prepare it.'

Amy was making a joking reply when the back door burst open and a tall, broad-shouldered young man entered the room, closely followed by a girl, dressed in the height of fashion and wearing a hat so large and flower-bedecked that it was all she could do to get it through the doorway. Amy stared hard at the young man, scarcely able to believe that this was Paddy, but when Becky jumped up from her pouffe, squeaking 'Ooh, ooh, our Mary, ain't you grand!' she was almost betrayed into a gasp of astonishment.

Apart from the hat, which completely hid Mary's abundant curls, her sister was wearing a plum-coloured silk two-piece suit, with a lace jabot at the neck and a nipped-in waist. The skirt was full and brushed the ground. It must, Amy thought, have been uncomfortable for such a hot day, but her sister did look very smart and she supposed that her appearance mattered more to Mary than her comfort.

There was a concerted shout from the assembled family and, while Paddy crossed the kitchen quietly carrying Mary's bags, Amy managed another covert glance at him. She had not seen him for several months, since if she came on a Sunday and he was pre-warned, he always absented himself from the house and on a weekday, of course, he was out with her brothers in the fishing boat. Now, reluctantly almost, she saw that Paddy had grown into a sturdy and self-reliant young man. He was not handsome but he had a pleasantly tanned face and his dark hair curled attractively across a broad forehead.

He saw her looking at him and shot her a quick glance, accompanied by a smile which revealed even white teeth. 'Hello, Shrimpy,' he said as he passed her chair, his eyes twinkling wickedly, and Amy, who had intended to be coolly friendly, found that at the mere mention of the old nickname her hackles had risen and her brows had drawn into a frown. She would have liked to ignore the remark – and Paddy – altogether, but remembering how she had promised herself not to be nasty, said coldly, 'Hello, Paddy.'

She expected him to pass on, but instead he lingered. 'You've changed, queen,' he said, sounding almost surprised, as though he had expected her to remain a child for ever. 'You were such an ugly, gingery kid, but now you're quite a looker! Gerrin' away from this household – and me, of course – seems to ha' done you a power of good.'

'How nice of you to say so,' Amy said sarcastically. 'I wish I could say the same of you, but honesty forbids it. Though you're a lot larger, naturally.'

He grinned, a flash of white teeth in his tanned face. To Amy's fury he looked amused rather than outraged. 'Well, now, isn't that just typical? I never knew you to say a nice word if you could think of a nasty one. And despite your looks, you're still not half as nice as your sister Mary.'

Amy opened her mouth to say that she knew very

well Mary was beautiful and she was not, but he had continued on his way past her and was mounting the stairs. When he came down again, having left Mary's bags in her room she assumed, he went over to where Albert and Gus were sorting out vegetables and fell into conversation, leaving the two girls and Becky to chat among themselves. And presently, when Amy stood up to carry the peas and their pods into the scullery, she saw Paddy disappearing, without a word of farewell, through the back doorway.

Paddy had been genuinely impressed by the change in Amy. As he walked along, heading for the beach, he marvelled at how the ugly duckling of a few years back had changed into a beautiful swan. Not that she resembled a swan in the slightest. With her flaming red hair, and eyes green as sea water, she was far more exotic than any swan. What was more, though she had changed so much, she still had the sharp tongue and quick wits which he had once hated but now rather admired.

Pity they had never got on, because in different circumstances he would have liked to take her out, enjoy her company, instead of feeling bound to remain her enemy.

But there you were; she disliked him, so no chance there of a reconciliation. Shrugging philosophically, Paddy continued to walk and whistle, and to try to forget Miss Amy Logan and her fascinating but prickly personality.

Amy saw no more of Paddy until supper was actually on the table, though the rest of the family remained at home, making much of herself and

Mary. When she asked Albert, on the quiet, where Paddy had gone, he gave her a hard stare and said, 'He'll have gone to the allotment. Why do you want to know, queen? Paddy always clears out when you're around, you know that.'

'Yes, but he's that keen on Mary, I should have thought he'd have stayed indoors,' Amy said rather feebly. She told herself she did not care whether Paddy stayed or went, but she did wonder if his old feelings for Mary had survived their years apart. She could not say this to Albert, however, and allowed the subject to drop.

The tête-à-tête which she had wanted with Mary did not occur until late in the evening, when supper had been eaten. Becky had been put to bed and the family had spent a pleasant hour exchanging news. Bill told them all about life in the Great Charlotte Street fish market, Albert prattled on about the fishing, as did Gus, and Suzie spoke in a sprightly and affectionate manner of Becky's progress at school and of the pleasure she herself took in home-making, now that there was a little more money available.

But Mary, rather to Amy's disappointment, did not do much talking at all. On previous occasions when the two girls had met, Mary's tongue had run on wheels; the other girls in her department, her neighbours in Young Street, friends of both sexes whom she had made in Manchester and the grand entertainments available in that city, had come pouring out. But now, although she answered questions readily enough, she was strangely reticent about her own life. She commented, rather sourly, upon the bedlam that had been caused on all forms of public transport during the recent unrest and how bad it been for sales in her department. Amy, who had thought the strikes had been confined to Liverpool alone, was surprised, but did not say so. It would not do to antagonise Mary by making light of the troubles in Manchester compared with those of Liverpool, so she decided to hold her tongue. Under cover of the general conversation, Amy looked long and hard at her sister and realised, with a pang of mixed astonishment and dismay, that Mary was looking almost haggard. Her cheeks, which had always been round and pink, were hollow and the white skin in which she had taken such pride looked weary and almost sallow beneath the layer of fine powder that disguised it. Amy thought her sister had lost weight and she had certainly lost the air of confidence which Amy remembered.

Rather to Amy's surprise, Paddy had not put in an appearance until the family were halfway through their meal, but then he had come in and taken the place beside Mary. He had spoken little, simply eating his food as rapidly as good manners permitted and gulping down three cups of strong tea. Then he had scraped back his chair, muttered to Mary that he would see her later, raised a hand to the rest of the company and left the house. Albert, noticing Amy's surprised glance after his friend, told her that Paddy meant to fetch up the nets which needed mending, so that they might work on them before the light failed, but since Paddy did not reappear, Amy guessed that this was just an excuse. No matter what anyone might say, Paddy could not bear to be in the same room with her. Not that it mattered; she was happier with his absence than his presence and with the rest of her family around her he was quickly forgotten.

Presently Amy glanced at the clock over the mantel and realised that, unless she wanted to miss the last tram, she had best begin to say her goodbyes. She stood up. 'Bless me, look at the time,' she said gaily. 'I've got to be going just in case the tram's on time, though with this bleedin' strike there's no saying what will happen. Thanks for a grand supper, Suzie – my day off's Wednesday this week, so maybe I'll come over again . . .' She turned to Mary. 'Unless you'd rather come into the city, queen? We could have a day out together and I could introduce you to the girls I live with.'

'I'd enjoy that,' Mary said quietly, 'it seems an age since I walked down Church Street and visited the big shops. Yes, a day out together would be fun.'

Amy walked to the back door and, reaching her hat down, pinned it on, then turned to find Mary standing beside her and donning her own magnificent headpiece. 'I'll walk down to the Rimrose Bridge with you, our Amy,' Mary said with almost studied casualness. 'It's a warm night and I could do with a breath of fresh air.'

Amy waited for Albert or Gus to offer to accompany them, which would have spoilt everything, for she guessed that Mary wanted to talk, but neither of her brothers moved from their places around the table. Albert was carving a piece of driftwood into a little horse, which he intended to give to Becky, and Gus was deep in his father's cast-off newspaper. Hastily, before either boy looked up, Amy called her goodbyes and the two girls slipped out into the cool of the night.

Until they reached Crosby Road they walked in silence, apart from Amy murmuring that it was good to smell the salt breeze again, but once they turned the corner Mary began to speak: 'Amy, I've got to tell someone and I'd rather it were you than anyone else. You know Roderick, my feller?'

'You've mentioned him once or twice in your letters,' Amy said cautiously, 'but you never *said* much about him, if you understand what I mean. I don't know if he's tall or short, dark or fair, fat or thin. In fact, to be honest, Mary, I don't even know if he was the sort of feller I'd like above half. Tell me about him.'

Mary sighed and stared ahead for a moment without speaking and, when she did, it was in a low tone, almost as though she were speaking to herself. 'There's no point in talking about Roderick,' she said, 'because he isn't my feller any more. Just about the time your letter came, telling me about your trip to London, I found he was two-timing me with a young piece who worked in Buss and Sons, the ironmongers on Deansgate, just next door to William Wright's, where I worked. So that's five years of my life down the drain, queen.'

'Oh, Mary,' Amy gasped, 'I'm so sorry, but you must think of it same as Gus thinks about losing Peggy. He says better to find out now than later and I'm sure he's right. How could anyone do that to you, Mary? He must be a real swine.'

'He was ambitious,' Mary admitted. 'But so was I, come to that. He was doing well in his bank, looking to be head clerk one of these days and I've moved up from just being a counter hand to being second-in-command of hats and gloves. We've been putting money away and in a couple of years we'd have had enough to buy a decent little house in the suburbs ...'

'Buy?' Amy squeaked, quite stunned by this

remark. People in their situation simply did not buy property, it was far too expensive. Everyone she knew rented their own homes, so why should Mary and this Roderick have been different? But perhaps renting property was not so easy in Manchester; her experience of such matters only encompassed Liverpool and its environs.

'Yes, we meant to buy,' Mary confirmed. 'Roderick said that owning property was an investment for the future and he was keen on the future, was Roderick. What was more, he always liked me to look nice and dress well, because appearances are so important. He said he was proud of me – but then he goes gadding off with some horrible little tart what's no more than sixteen. I ask you, Amy, what would you do?'

'I'd do what you've done,' Amy said immediately. 'I'd come home for a bit of a holiday and maybe look around me for a job in Liverpool, where I wouldn't have to see horrible Roderick or his tart. Is that what you mean to do, Mary?'

'Well, I'm definitely thinking about it,' Mary told her. 'Fancy you guessing, Amy! The truth is, I've applied for a job as senior sales lady in Blackler's department store and if I get it ... Why, I've even sorted out accommodation. A friend of mine from Manchester moved to Liverpool six months back and she's offered to let me share her rooms – she's a bit out of the city but on a good tram route, so I shall be able to get in to work easily enough. If I take the job, that is. It's a big move, but I'd be nearer home and nearer my family ... Do you think I'd be doing the right thing, though? I mean, I've been in Manchester a long time now and I know the city a good deal better than I do Liverpool.'

The two girls had reached the tram stop but the driver was not in his seat, so Amy leaned against the vehicle for a final word before climbing aboard. 'I don't know whether I'm the right person to give you advice, since I've spent all my life in Liverpool and never so much as seen Manchester,' she said after a moment's thought. 'But I've heard Blackler's are a good firm to work for, and if you really don't think there's any chance of you and Roderick getting back together . . . well, it seems sensible to come home and . . . and sort of start a new life. You are sure you won't want to . . . to start things up again with Roderick? I don't know much about young men, you know, because I've never had one and neither have any of my friends, not the ones I room with, I mean. We're all fancy free, you might say.'

There was a short, somehow startled silence, then Mary gripped her arm and spoke. 'But what about Philip?' she asked. 'You told me in your letter you had met up with Philip and were going to see him again. Don't tell me you're not interested in him, because I shan't believe you. He liked you when we were just kids. He told me so and to tell the truth, Amy, I think he liked me as well. Whenever we met in the square or down Deansgate he was always most polite, raising his hat and giving me the friendliest smile.'

Amy stared at her; so her first wild guess had been right; Mary had come back to Liverpool in the hope of getting to know Philip once more. However, she knew better than to let Mary realise she had guessed and was on the point of saying that her sister should not read too much into smiles exchanged in the street, when the driver and conductor abandoned the cigarettes they had been smoking and climbed aboard the tram. 'Come along, ladies both,' the conductor shouted jovially. 'No time to lose, we'll have folks all along the route cursing us if we don't gerra move on, 'cos this is the last tram tonight.'

Hastily Amy scrambled aboard. She turned in the doorway and called back to Mary, 'See you on Wednesday. Come to Huskisson Street around ten o'clock – don't be late – and we'll talk then.'

Within a month of the visit to Seafield Grove, Mary had accepted the job in Blackler's and settled in to her friend's rooms in a small house in Mather Avenue, out Allerton way. It was a suburb of the city which Amy did not know at all, but she had called for Mary after work one evening and gone home with her, and had been pleasantly surprised, almost envious, at the two airy rooms the girls shared, with the use of a kitchen and – wonder of wonders! – a real bathroom. It was not cheap and Mary had to get up early in order to catch the number 8 tram which would carry her in to the city centre, but she and Faith, her friend, were clearly very satisfied with their little home. In fact, Amy thought as she sat on the last tram back into the city centre later that night, Mary had really fallen on her feet and seemed happier – and better tempered – than she had been for a very long time.

All those ambitions to be something she wasn't hadn't done much to make her happy, Amy told herself, as the tram rattled and creaked onward. Nor did trying to live up to that Roderick feller. But being a person in her own right, earning her own living, meeting up with her relatives now and then . . . well, it had turned Mary back into the gentle, thoughtful young person who had adored her mother and loved her little sister, and Amy was happy that it was so.

Presently the tram stopped in Renshaw Street and Amy stepped down, thankfully climbing on to a number 15 almost immediately, which would take her the rest of her way home. She turned into Huskisson Street, thinking that it was nice to have a sister close enough to visit for an evening and hoping that Mary, too, would come visiting in the not too distant future.

Chapter Eight

It was a burning hot day in August, and Amy and Ella were walking in to work, not because they felt they needed the exercise but because, due to the railwaymen's strike, which was now established, and the consequent riots that had been rocking the city, the trams were running a restricted service. The tram drivers had gallantly refused to go on strike too, but because of the ugly mood of the rioters they had insisted upon some form of protection. Every tram now carried an armed soldier on board, but despite the fact that the troops came from the barracks in Seaforth, the girls felt uneasy in their presence. Many strange soldiers had been drafted in to help control the crowds and Amy felt that such men might fire first and regret it later, unlike the men who usually manned the Seaforth barracks. So rather than face the few trams that were running, the girls had decided they would walk in to work that morning.

'I never knew a strike of railway workers could lead to such complete chaos,' Ella grumbled as the heat rose off the paving stones, making their feet feel like live coals. 'There's hardly any food in the shops and someone told me that last night the crowds pelted the police with fruit, which seemed a great shame. I could just do with a nice basket of raspberries right now and I wouldn't throw them at anyone; I'd eat the lot. When you think of all the fuss the authorities made over the suffragette rallies – and now look at this crew! There are scarcely any public service vehicles running, most of those who want to work have to walk into the city, the rioters have been giving the police as good as they get, looting shops, chucking bricks, and you can walk a mile and not find a loaf of bread or a pound of sausages for sale.'

'Yes, I know what you mean. But better not say it too loud,' Amy advised, tucking her arm into Ella's. The two girls had always been good friends, but since Ella had got a job in the offices of the Adelphi Hotel and worked side by side with Amy, they had become almost inseparable. Not that they were doing the same work; Ella's good education had won her an unusual sort of job, for as well as taking shorthand notes and typing them up on her machine, she was called for regularly when French or German guests arrived and had difficulty in making themselves understood, whereupon she would interpret for the management.

'There's a lot of folk about,' Amy said rather uneasily, as they continued to make their way towards the hotel along crowded pavements. 'Oh, look, that window's been smashed, and there's fellers all in among the display ... they're helping themselves ... oh, Ella, look out!'

A group of men were charging along the pavement towards them, all dressed in working clothes, and behind them, in hot pursuit, came a number of policemen, batons in hand, clearly intent upon catching the miscreants, if miscreants they were. Amy and Ella ducked into the nearest shop doorway, their light shoes crunching on broken glass, but even the doorway was no refuge for long, for behind the policemen came an excited crowd of men, many of whom brandished various objects with which they clearly intended to do violence. The shop doorway they had chosen – or rather had been forced to choose – belonged to an ironmonger and, as soon as he realised this, a large, disreputable-looking man from the crowd swung the brick he was carrying at the window. It shattered and long, wicked-looking shards of glass showered everywhere, some of them descending like daggers into the flooring where they stayed upright, quivering every time anyone moved.

Clinging together with their hands up to their faces to save them from flying splinters, the two girls crouched against the shop door. Amy put up a hand and tried the brass doorknob, but the door remained obstinately closed; clearly the owner had been too wary to open his premises while the unrest continued. Without taking her hands from her face, Amy thought she could tell very well what was happening by the sights and shouts alone. Booted feet trampled on broken glass, heavy objects fell with a thud and men's voices exclaimed as they picked over the contents of the window. Amy guessed that for the most part they were looking for weapons rather than simply looting, for beyond the policemen she had seen the flash of military uniforms and the light reflecting off gun barrels. So they had called the army in. But during the many weeks that the strike had been in force she had begun to understand the desperation which drove the strikers. If need be, she thought now, they would fight the army as well as the police, using any weapon that came to hand.

As the footsteps began to leave the ironmonger's window once more, she risked a peek from between her hands and saw men armed with garden spades, forks, rakes and weighty-looking carpentry tools, brandishing them as they abandoned the premises. To Amy's amusement, one of the strikers had protected himself by placing a coal scuttle on his head and another followed suit with a large white chamber pot, which fitted snugly round his outstanding ears. She could not help reflecting, however, that one good blow from a policeman's baton would shatter the chamber pot, probably causing the wearer more trouble than it had saved him. She also noticed that most of the men streaming past looked as though they had not had a square meal for a week and her heart bled for them when she saw the stout, well-fed policemen who followed close on their heels.

Beside her, Ella dropped her hands from her face and gave vent to a long, whistling sigh. 'Cripes!' she said inelegantly. 'What have we got ourselves into this time? This isn't just a protest meeting, nor a gathering of strikers, this is a full-blown riot. Should we go home, do you think, or will it be safe to press on to the Adelphi?'

Amy, picking pieces of glass out of her cotton skirt, looked at the crowd pressing close against the doorway as they passed. 'I don't think we're going to have much choice,' she said doubtfully. 'I think the moment we poke our noses out on to the pavement we'll simply get carried along with the crowd. It isn't that they won't let us go in the opposite direction, it's a bit like throwing yourself into the Mersey when the tide's coming in. You don't get any choice and nor does the river; it'll carry you inland, willy-nilly, until the tide starts to ebb again.'

'Oh, very poetic,' Ella said, shaking her own skirt free of splinters. 'Well, we can't stand here for ever, we'll have to make a move sooner or later, so how about now?' And without giving herself time to think, she grabbed Amy's hand and the two of them plunged into the maelstrom of people who they could now see filled the roadway as well as the pavement.

'Put your arm round my waist, Ella!' Amy screamed at the top of her voice. The one thing suffragette rallies had taught her was to hold on physically to anyone from whom you did not wish to be parted. 'The first chance either of us gets, we'll turn aside, pulling the other one with her.' She turned to a burly, cloth-capped man in the coat and gaiters of a carter, who was being borne alongside her. 'Where's the crowd heading?' she shouted. 'And when did the troops arrive?'

The carter shrugged massive shoulders, or at least Amy guessed that he had, for it was difficult to see small movements when being urged forward by people behind. 'I don't know as we're goin' anywhere,' he bawled back. 'I guess we're running away from the scuffers and the soldiers. There ain't much unarmed chaps like us can do against a bleedin' brigade wi' fixed bayonets and loaded rifles.' He glanced curiously down at them from his great height. 'Whot's a couple of young ladies like yerselves doin' in this 'ere scrum, anyway?' he enquired. 'This is no place for the likes of you. Come to that, I ain't seen a female all mornin', 'cept for you two.'

'We were on our way to work at the Adelphi Hotel when we got caught up and carried along with the crowd,' Amy shouted back. 'Where are we, do you know? I can't see anything, save for people all crushed together and moving like a river.'

'Dunno,' the man roared back. He opened his mouth to say something else but in the strange way which happens in a crowd he suddenly dropped behind them, while Amy and Ella, quite without their own volition, surged forward. The last Amy saw of her friend the carter was his hand reaching for his cloth cap as it was knocked from his head by an advertisement sign.

Half an hour later, still trapped by the many people around them, Amy at last managed to recognise their whereabouts. Towering to the right of her were the well-known cream-coloured stones of the free library, where she and Ella spent a good deal of time searching for the books they needed. And on the other side of William Brown Street, as she well knew, were the shaded lawns and pleasant pathways of St John's Gardens. If they could only push their way through the crowd and reach that haven, surely they would be safe?

She shrieked the information into Ella's ear and the two of them began, for the first time, actively to attempt to push their way through the crowd, though they both realised that this was a dangerous move, for one stumble would mean you could be thrown to the ground and trampled to death beneath heedless feet, the owners of which were not even aware of your presence.

Nevertheless, Ella must have thought it was worth a try for she nodded, indicating that she understood and the two girls began to try to make their way through the close-packed crowd.

They had actually succeeded, though not in time

to enter the gardens, for the forward movement of the crowd had not stopped, so it was close against the St George's Plateau that they finally got more or less free. Amy was just drawing in her first unhampered breath of relief, when she saw, on her left, a number of men in military uniform. They appeared to be kneeling and pointing something across the heads of the crowd, but before she had taken in what was happening there was a shout of command and a ragged volley of shots rang out. Amy gave a violent start and turned to her friend, as Ella, with a face as white as a sheet, dropped like a stone to the ground.

Philip and Dick Maynard had decided the previous day not to open their offices since, with the riots becoming worse with every hour that passed, there would be little or no business transacted in the city. But it was a hot and sunny day, not at all the sort of weather to remain within doors, so Philip had suggested that the two of them might make their way down to the Pier Head to see whether the ferries were running. There were no trams or buses, of course, but surely there would be someone willing to take passengers across the great width of the Mersey? If not, Philip thought they might hire a fishing boat, so at least they could gain the further shore and spend a few hours away from the city, which had become more like a battlefield than a busy commercial centre.

They had scarcely begun the walk to the Pier Head, however, when the crowd had come roaring along the roadway and simply engulfed them. They were both strong and determined young men, but wasted a good deal of time in searching for one another since, lacking the experience of suffragette rallies, they had not held on to one another when they plunged into the crowd.

Philip was a tall young man but even so he had difficulty in spotting his friend in the sea of heads that surrounded him. There was a good deal of noise as members of the crowd shouted to one another, whistled and cat-called, and adjured their neighbours to 'Get your bleedin' elbow out of my mouth', or, 'Doncher know whose perishin' feet you're stampin' on, sonny?' But even so, Philip raised his voice in a shout: 'Dick? Dick? Give us a wave, old fellow.'

To his relief, Philip heard a voice answering him almost immediately and saw a hand raised. Dick was no more than twelve feet away and by dint of shoving and pushing against the tide, he managed at last to reach him.

'Link arms,' Philip commanded as soon as they were together once more. 'Where are we, do you know? We could be treading on acres of grass in some park for all I can tell. Hang on a mo', though – that's St George's Hall – you can't mistake that.'

As Philip spoke, Dick pointed to the line of figures above and ahead of them on the St George's Hall steps. 'Soldiers, with rifles at the ready,' he said. 'We'd better get out of this in case there's real trouble.' Almost before the words were out of his mouth, firing broke out and at the same moment Philip heard a scream and saw a slim, girlish figure, topped by a cluster of red-gold curls, fall from his sight. He knew her instantly and immediately began to fight his way towards her. 'Did you see,' he gasped, dragging Dick with him through the crowd, which was now fighting as desperately to get back as they had tried before to go forward. 'It was Amy

Logan, the girl we met on the train on the day of the coronation. She's been hit. I saw her fall. Come on!'

The two young men had been only yards away from where the girls stood and in a remarkably short space of time, for they were the only ones going towards the hall, they reached Amy's side. She was kneeling on the ground, trying to lift her companion in her arms, but the other girl's head flopped back, her face a deathly white, save for a scarlet furrow, sluggishly bleeding, across her left temple.

'Amy! Good God, we thought you'd been hit – who's your friend?' Philip said breathlessly. 'How come she's ... My God, it's the little suffragette, the one who lectured me on women's rights – Miss Morton, isn't it? Let me take her from you and carry her out of this. The soldiers fired over the heads of the crowd but I suppose a bullet must have ricocheted and hit her. Here, Amy, have you got something to staunch the blood? I'll make my handkerchief into a pad and hold it over the wound if you can find something to secure it.'

Amy, without a second's hesitation, bent down and ripped the frill off her petticoat, offering it mutely to Philip who took it and bound it swiftly round the padded handkerchief he had placed over Ella's wound, which was already soaked with blood. He hoisted the girl into his arms and Dick helped Amy to her feet. Then the three of them, with Philip carrying the unconscious girl, began to make their way across the road towards the North Western Hotel.

'Is ... is she dead?' Amy asked fearfully as they entered the imposing portals. 'I didn't think she was because she stirred and moaned just before you arrived, but now she looks so white and lies so still . . .'

'I don't think she's dead, because bleeding stops when the heart does and she's still losing blood,' Dick commented, giving Amy's hand a reassuring squeeze. 'I'd say the bullet ploughed along her skull, causing a very nasty wound, which needs attention urgently, but there's bound to be a doctor, or a nurse perhaps, who can be summoned by the clerk on reception.' He glanced around the empty foyer. 'Why is it so dark in here? The place is usually ablaze with lights and full of people.'

Philip looked too. 'For the same reason that the trams aren't running – no electricity,' he said briefly, then pointed to a sofa against a wall. 'I'll lay her on that couch, Dick. You go and get help, and make it snappy.'

While Philip and Amy made Ella as comfortable as they could on the shiny, gold, satin-covered chaise longue, making a pad of Philip's jacket beneath her head in the hope of not staining the sofa with Ella's blood, Dick went over to the desk and could be heard shouting for attention. Meanwhile Philip sent Amy scurrying to fetch a bowl and some water, so that they might bathe Ella's face and wrists, for even in the cooler darkness of the hotel it was still very hot.

Amy flew across the foyer, her experience of hotels telling her not to waste time searching for someone in authority but to go straight through the green baize doors which would lead, she guessed, to the kitchen quarters. She ran along the dark corridor, heedless of the clatter her shoes made on the tiles, and burst through some swing doors and into the first of a series of kitchens. Startled faces turned towards her, but she ignored them all, making for the big stone sinks she could see ranged along the wall in the next room. A man in a tall chef's hat and the white jacket and checked trousers of his calling stood up as she ran past and tried to grab her, but Amy was too quick for him. 'There's a girl been shot,' she said over her shoulder, grabbing a large white pudding basin from the sideboard and whipping down a pudding cloth from where it hung on the overhead rack. She turned the cold tap full on, half filled the basin, then turned back to retrace her steps, going very much more slowly so that she would not lose the water she was carrying.

'Did you say someone's been shot, chuck?' a fat woman in a frilled cap and apron asked incredulously. 'Well, if that's so, it's a doctor you'll be needin' – and some antiseptic – I've got a bottle of Listerine in me room; where's the young woman at?'

'She's in the foyer, on one of the sofas, with two of my friends taking care of her,' Amy said briefly, not pausing in her steady onward progress. 'If you could bring the Listerine along there . . .'

She reached the foyer without further incident, the housekeeper close on her heels, to find the little tableau very much as she had left it, save that Dick now stood by the sofa as well as Philip. Both men were wearing the distraught yet helpless look worn by young males the world over when a woman they regard highly is sick or in trouble.

Philip swung round at Amy's approach and said briefly: 'There's a doctor coming. Dick rang and explained. He said ten minutes and five have passed already.'

'Let me through, young gents,' the housekeeper said, briskly pushing both men to one side and dropping to her knees by the patient. 'We'll loosen her clothing – it's what you do when they faint, as I well know, for if there's one thing housemaids excel at it's faintin' fits.' With careful fingers she undid the tiny buttons, slippery with blood, at the high neck of Ella's blouse, then at the cuffs and finally, at the waist of her skirt. Amy took the Listerine from her and tipped some of it into her basin. Then she began to stroke her friend's brow, cheeks and neck with the water and antiseptic mixture.

She was wondering whether to move the handkerchief in order to clean the wound, when Philip's hand shot out and caught her wrist. 'Don't!' he said urgently and Amy could feel his strong fingers trembling. 'She's unconscious at present and feeling no pain, but if you put antiseptic on to raw flesh . . .'

Amy shuddered at the thought and was about to assure him that she would do no such thing, when the street doors opened and a short, sandy-haired man in a frock coat and high collar came briskly across the foyer towards them. 'I'm Doctor McKay, is this my patient?' he asked in a strong Scottish accent. 'Someone said she'd been shot.'

He sounded so incredulous that Amy's hands moved instinctively to show him the wound, but once again Philip stopped her. 'Yes, doctor, it was probably only a ricochet but she's been shot, nevertheless,' he said quietly. 'I don't think the bullet entered her body, I think it has merely ploughed a furrow along the side of her skull, but as you can see, she's bleeding heavily. Ought she not to be in hospital?'

'Ah, a flesh wound,' the doctor mused. He had been carrying a small black bag, which he now stood down and opened. He brought out a pair of scissors with which he snipped through the strip of petticoat holding the handkerchief in place. He stared for a moment at the mess of blood and hair which had formed beneath the impromptu dressing and then, to Amy's horror, began with practised ease to snip away her friend's long, blood-drenched tresses. When the wound was revealed, Amy had to turn away for a moment, a hand flying to her mouth. The wound must have been at least six inches long, and narrow, and the bullet – if it had been a bullet – had carried away the top inch of Ella's ear. Amy imagined that most of the blood had probably come from the shattered ear, for the head wound, though still bleeding, did not seem as bad as she had feared from the amount of the blood that had soaked through the dressings.

The doctor, however, continued to clip busily until a good half of Ella's beautiful hair lay on the floor. 'This will need cleaning and probably stitching,' he said at last, 'now I can see it properly without all that damned hair in the way. I would have liked to get her to a hospital, but we'd never do it, not with the crowds, the police, the troops and no possibility of finding a vehicle which could carry her.' He turned to the housekeeper. 'Prepare a room on the ground floor, Mrs Ellis. I'll want a great deal of hot water, bandages and someone with a steady hand to assist me. Normally I'd send for my nurse, but if this young lady is to recover quickly we must act at once.' He turned to look consideringly at Amy. 'How about you? It seems you don't faint at the sight of blood.'

'I'd help you willingly,' Philip said, before Amy could reply. 'I have had some experience, since I joined a first-aid class in my last year at school.'

The doctor gave a snort, which he tried to turn into a cough, but shook his head. 'Thank you, but I'd prefer the young lady, since I shall have to examine my patient to make sure there are no other wounds; a ricocheting bullet can cause more than one, you know.'

So Philip and Dick carried Ella, with great care and gentleness, through to the room which Mrs Ellis had prepared and laid her tenderly on the bed. She had still not recovered consciousness, which Dr McKay seemed to think a good thing, but as he left the room, Philip turned to take one more look at her. The still whiteness of her face went to his heart. She must get better, she must, he told himself, as he and his friend crossed the foyer and began to clear away the blood-draggled hair and all other signs that the wounded girl had lain there. Philip then took advantage of the gentlemen's cloakroom to wash off the blood that had soaked into his jacket and had even penetrated as far as his white shirt. Then they sat on the shiny little sofa and waited, Philip suddenly conscious of a dreadful sense of foreboding. Dammit, I liked the girl from the first, he told himself, staring towards the door of the room they had just left. She's brave and outspoken and ... and a real little darling; I can't bear the thought of her suffering, let alone ...

But even to himself he could not admit that Ella might die of her wounds, so he sat and waited, with Dick beside him, and said a silent prayer for the girl lying so pale and still beneath the doctor's hands.

Ever afterwards, Amy could not remember the time she spent assisting Dr McKay without giving a strong shudder. It was not too bad while Ella remained unconscious, but when she suddenly came to herself and uttered a long, whimpering scream, it was all Amy could do not to run out of the room, running and running until she no longer had to hear, or even think about, her friend's agony.

The doctor, who had been inserting stitches in the wound, merely stopped work long enough to say gruffly to Amy, 'You'll find a small bottle of chloroform in the side pocket of my bag and a soft pad of gauze close beside it. The chloroform bottle has a dripper fixed in the neck; allow two or three drops, no more, to fall on the pad, then hold it firmly over Miss Morton's nose and mouth.' He looked up at Amy over the small pince-nez glasses, which he had perched on his nose as soon as he began the operation, and gave her a penetrating but friendly glance. 'You've done your friend proud so far, lassie; don't go letting her down now. Keep a steady hand and a brave heart and Miss Morton will be unconscious again in moments.'

With fumbling hands Amy got the necessary items out of the doctor's bag, dripped the chloroform – which smelled perfectly beastly – on to the muslin pad and shrinkingly held it to her friend's face. Ella had been breathing jerkily and uttering moans and little cries, her eyes opening and rolling desperately from side to side, even though the doctor had momentarily paused in his work, but within seconds of the pad being applied her breathing slowed and deepened, and the half-moons of her dark lashes sank on to her cheeks. With a sigh of pure relief Amy continued to assist Dr McKay until at last he stood back, laid down his needle and reached out a hand to grip Amy's shoulder reassuringly. 'You've done well, Miss Logan, and greatly assisted both myself and your poor friend,' he said gruffly. 'I'm no' in the habit of complimenting the young women who assist me, but they are trained nurses, which I take it you are not?'

'No indeed,' Amy said faintly. 'I've often wondered if I might like to be a nurse, but today has changed my mind. I work in the offices of the Adelphi Hotel as a shorthand writer and receptionist, so perhaps I'd better stick to what I know.'

The doctor, busily cleaning his instruments in a kettle full of boiling water, laughed shortly and once again gave her a penetrating glance. 'It's a very different thing assisting at an operation with none of the facilities of a hospital theatre,' he observed. 'And what's more, you know the patient – she is, I gather, a close friend of yours. Even I, Miss Logan, would hesitate to perform an operation without benefit of proper anaesthesia upon a loved one, so accept my congratulations.'

Amy glanced towards the bed, where her friend now lay peacefully upon her back, her head and neck swathed in bandages and her eyes closed. 'Thank you, Doctor McKay,' she said humbly. 'But what must I do now? I don't suppose the hotel will allow her to remain here until she is fit to be moved and God alone knows how long this strike will last. Liverpool people are not easily cowed; sometimes it is worse to try to outface them when they feel themselves to be in the right. Unless the government is prepared to give *something*, the strike could still be going strong at Christmas.'

The doctor, packing away his instruments and clearing up the debris from the operation, tutted and shook his head gently. 'The hotel will keep Miss Morton until I can find a conveyance to carry her to

305

a hospital,' he said firmly. 'As soon as I am able I shall send a nurse round to look after your friend.'

'But the cost ...' Amy breathed. 'We none of us have much money, doctor, although there are four of us sharing our room. I don't know how we shall ever repay you, let alone the hotel and a nurse ...!'

'Don't try to meet trouble halfway,' the doctor said briefly. 'This wound was caused by a stray bullet, presumably fired by a member of the army. They may well be responsible for the cost of putting right what they did.'

With that he left the room, and Amy was sitting by her friend's bed and wondering what was to become of them, when there was a tap on the door and Philip's head appeared round it. 'The doctor says she's come through it pretty well,' Philip whispered, tiptoeing in. 'He said you were worrying about the cost – don't. I'll see to everything, not that I think we'll end up with a huge bill. Now stop fretting and as soon as the nurse arrives I'll take you home. The crowd outside seems to have dispersed, so I'll get you there easily enough.'

'I can't leave Ella, not with the best nurse in the world,' Amy whispered back. 'I'll stay. But Philip, could you go round to Huskisson Street and tell the others what's happened?'

'I'll go right away.' But Philip lingered, looking down at Ella's pale face and mangled cropped head. 'Poor little devil, I'd give anything ... but the doctor seemed to think she'd be all right in a day or so. Is there anything else you want, though, Amy? I don't like to think of you sitting here alone without so much as a book to read or a drink. I could nip out and bring something back at once, before I make for Huskisson Street. How about if I fetch you in a newspaper and some ... some biscuits, or peppermint humbugs? Come to that, you may need proper food later on. And how about a book to read while you wait for Miss Morton to wake up? And toiletries? A change of clothing?'

Amy laughed softly, but shook her head. 'Thanks, Philip, but Mrs Ellis said the hotel would feed us, and I'd rather you went straight to Huskisson Street and didn't waste time fetching me stuff I can do without. But when you do come back it would be nice if you could bring in some beef tea, if such a thing is available, because the doctor said Ella would want fortifying drinks at first rather than food. Oh, and some lemon barley water, if you would be so good.'

'I'll bring whatever I can find,' Philip promised. He grinned ruefully across the bed at Amy. 'I'll be as quick as I can, I promise, but because of the looting it may not be easy to find everything you want. Still, I'll do my best. Goodbye for now.'

When he had gone, closing the door softly behind him, Amy leaned back in her seat with a tiny sigh. He was a nice chap, was Philip, she had always known it but now she knew he was a good friend in a crisis as well. After all, he scarcely knew Ella but was prepared to stand by her for his old friend Amy's sake. Presently, worn out by the rigours and excitements of the day, she snoozed in her chair, though she never allowed herself to fall asleep completely. She was too anxious about Ella to risk missing her friend's slightest move.

Amy could not have slept for more than ten minutes when the doctor himself came in, telling her that he had arranged for Ella to have a bed in the Royal

Infirmary nearby. 'I met Mr Grimshaw in the foyer,' he told Amy. 'He had managed to get hold of a hansom cab, so I told him to keep hold of it . . .' he smiled grimly at his own joke '. . . so that my patient might ride to the Infirmary in relative comfort. If you will wrap her in a blanket I will fetch Mr Grimshaw. He has volunteered to carry the wee lass out to the cab and since he tells me it was he who brought her in after the shooting, I'm sure he is quite capable of doing so.'

When Amy, Philip and Ella arrived at the hospital they were shown directly to a long ward and as soon as the stretcher bearers had gently rolled the still unconscious Ella on to a high white bed, Amy and Philip were told to wait in the corridor, while the patient was examined by a hospital doctor.

'Doctor McKay told us the history of the case when he booked Miss Morton in,' a middle-aged sister, in a navy blue dress with white celluloid collar and cuffs, told them. 'But even so Mr Rivers, the consultant, will want to make his own examination. A blow to the head can seem straightforward but it can also lead to complications.'

Left to themselves, Philip and Amy sat down on the long benches provided and looked anxiously at one another.

'Complications? Could that mean damage to her skull? Or can a blow on the head affect the brain?' Amy asked in a worried undertone.

'I'm sure if there had been any question of brain damage, Doctor McKay would not have let her travel between the hotel and the hospital in a hansom cab,' Philip said reassuringly. He took Amy's hand between both of his own and looked earnestly into her round, worried eyes. 'Your friend is young and strong, and has had a blow on the head, which she might have got during a game of hockey. She was seen very quickly by an excellent doctor, but naturally, the surgeon in charge of this ward wishes to reassure himself as well as his staff that the damage is only superficial. So stop *worrying*, you little goose. In five or ten minutes we'll know what Mr Rivers thinks and you can be easy.'

'It's only that Ella's my best friend, Philip,' Amy said apologetically. 'We understand one another as though we were sisters – better than sisters, because I never have understood Mary. Although we are so different, Ella and I could scarcely have been closer. Ella is an only child and her parents were wealthy . . .'

Sitting there in the corridor, waiting to be allowed back on the ward, Amy related to Philip Ella's sad story, emphasising how brave she had been in the face of such appalling adversity. 'She had had so much, yet at the age of seventeen she found herself with nothing,' she told him. 'For the first time in her life she was forced to earn her own living, working in a miserable little clothing shop on the Scotland Road and sleeping at night on a mattress behind the counter. A lot of girls would have forgotten their ambitions, gone on struggling just to keep alive, but Ella has the courage of a lion, honest she has, Philip. She worked hard to learn what sort of staff the big departmental stores wanted and very quickly got her herself a job in one of them, and answered an advertisement for a room share. She was only a junior assistant, filling the shelves when stocks ran low, running up and down from the basement to the top floor, carrying heavy boxes of goods. But she soon rose to be a counter hand, then a sales assistant and now, as you know, she works with me at the Adelphi. Only she's more important than I am, because she translates French and German for the management and is already indispensable, although she has been with them less than six months.'

At this point the doors to the ward in which Ella lay opened, and the surgeon and his team came out. They walked up the corridor towards Amy and Philip, who both rose to their feet. Mr Rivers was a tall, skinny man, probably no more than forty years old, with a calm and confident manner, which instantly put both young people at their ease. 'Your friend has an admirable constitution and an extremely strong skull,' he informed them, smiling genially as he did so. 'She has not yet regained consciousness – I fancy she may have a touch of concussion – but I am sure she will come to herself over the course of the next few hours. I would strongly advise you both to go home now, leaving Miss Morton in the capable hands of the nursing staff. You may return this afternoon with such small necessities as the patient needs – her own nightgown perhaps – and by then your friend will have regained consciousness.'

Amy's relief was so great that she found she could only stare at the surgeon while her eyes filled with tears, but Philip said at once, 'Thank you, sir, I know you have relieved both our minds and we will feel happier as a result.' He turned to Amy as the surgeon and his team moved off down the corridor. 'Well? Has that satisfied you? I think we ought to take Mr Rivers's advice and go home now, and come back this afternoon.'

Paddy, Albert and Gus brought the boat up into the

estuary alongside Seaforth Sands and lowered the brick-coloured sail, each one performing his task without a word spoken, so familiar were they with this daily routine. They had sailed at dawn, realising that the heat would become oppressive as the day progressed, and had filled their dragnet before the shrimps had sought shelter in deeper waters. Thus they were now heading for home after only a few hours' fishing. This meant that the shrimps could be boiled and piled on the handcart in plenty of time to be sold straight to the public that same day. And fresh shrimps, especially at this time of year, always commanded top prices.

As soon as they were in shallow water Paddy and Albert jumped out and began to pull the boat ashore. In winter, when they performed this task, they would have been clad in great fishermen's thigh waders but now, because of the heat, they were barefoot, with trousers rolled up as high as they would go and Paddy, splashing in first, thought the cool water against his hot and sunburned legs was a delightful experience.

Like most of the lads in Seaforth he could swim like a fish, though the older men still insisted that it was bad luck for a fisherman to be able to swim. 'Askin' for trouble, thass worrit is,' the old salts, sitting outside the Caradoc would tell each other. 'A fisherman's place is atop the water not innit. My da always told me that fishes were the only ones what needed to swim and since I'm still here to tell the tale, I reckon he were right.'

But right now, with Gus joining them to pull the boat up the beach, Paddy thought longingly that a quick swim would be just what the doctor ordered. He was so hot and carrying the shrimps back to

Seafield Grove would be hot work as well, to say nothing of boiling them in the crowded little wash-house and then shovelling them, still hot, into the large, loose-weave sacks.

Of course, in the usual way his mam would take over at this point, setting off with the handcart to sell the shrimps round the houses and pubs, but because they had such a large quantity of shrimps he, Gus and Albert would probably take the remainder of the catch into St John's fish market for Bill to sell on his stall. They had bought a second handcart a while back and though Bill had often talked of investing in a donkey to bring the fish from Seaforth to the city centre more rapidly, nothing so far had come of it.

Normally the two younger boys would have pushed the handcart into the market by themselves, but because of the strike, and the looting and rioting that had followed, they felt a good deal safer with Gus along to help, in the event of trouble. By and large, the rioters did not interfere with the poor, but attacked the city centre shops and stores, though on one occasion a group of rowdy, undisciplined youths had overturned the handcart, thinking it a great joke to see Albert and Paddy scrabbling on the cobbles to retrieve what shrimps they could.

The boat being satisfactorily beached, Albert and Paddy checked the sails, sheets and oars, and then began to fasten the necks of the sacks. Gus, meanwhile, had strode up the beach and was returning, dragging the handcart behind him. He did not come too far, because the sand was soft and the cart, when laden, could easily get bogged down, so presently he abandoned it and came and joined them. Each of them hefted a sack on to his back and began the hard slog up the beach. Paddy, with sweat trickling down his brow and stinging his eyes, looked sideways at Gus. 'Any chance of a swim, Gus?' he asked plaintively. 'I'm as hot as fire and we'll be red as lobsters afore we're much older, what wi' boiling the shrimps and carting them to St John's Market. And it won't take nobbut a few minutes, just to set ourselves up, like, wi' a dip in the briny.'

'Tell you what,' Gus said, as they reached the handcart and began to unload their sacks on to it, 'I'll take a couple of sacks along to the house, so that Suzie can get on wi' cooking them, and you two can have your dip. I won't bother with the handcart, you can bring that when you've had your swim.'

Paddy and Albert agreed with this suggestion and very soon, clad only in their working trousers, they were washing the sweat and the heat away in the cool waves. When they reached the house in Seafield Grove half an hour later Paddy announced breezily, as they hefted the remaining sacks of shrimps into the wash-house, that he felt a different feller. 'If you want to go down to the shore now, Gus, and have your dip while we boil the remaining shrimps, I'm sure Albert and me are willin',' he said.

Gus, however, shook his head and said that he meant to go indoors and have a strip-down wash and put on clean kecks and shirt. 'For when we've delivered the shrimps to Dad I've a mind to stroll round to the Crown and have a beer or two,' he said with assumed casualness. 'That is, if you think the two of you will be able to get the handcart back to Seaforth wi'out the aid of me bulgin' muscles?' he added with a grin.

Paddy and Albert exchanged meaningful looks, but said nothing. They were both well aware that Gus had taken a fancy to the little blonde barmaid who worked at the Crown public house, and was plucking up his courage to ask her out. Rather to Paddy's surprise, the girl was not unlike Peggy Higgins to look at, but there was no accounting for tastes. If I'd been dumped by a blonde, the way Peggy dumped our Gus, then I reckon I'd go for a brunette next time around, Paddy told himself, as they began to empty the sacks of uncooked shrimps into the boiling, salty water. But there you are, everyone's different and no doubt Gus will take out several girls before he starts getting serious again.

Aloud Paddy said, in answer to Gus's question; 'Oh aye, we'll get the handcart home all right, don't you worry about us, old feller. But seeing as we're early today, I think I'll go round to the dairy and have a word wi' me old pals. It's ages since Tommy and I met – we might make an evening of it.'

'Well, if we're going to make an evening of it, then we'd best all change our kecks and shirts,' Albert said hopefully. 'What's on at the Palais de Luxe in Lime Street, Paddy? I wouldn't mind seeing a film ... Mind you, there's dances and all sorts in the city centre. Anyway, we can decide what we want to do later. We'll leave the handcart wi' our dad and get him to pay a kid a few coppers to wheel it back to Seaforth.'

Accordingly, as soon as the shrimps were boiled, Paddy and Albert hurried into the kitchen. Suzie was sitting by the open window darning a pair of Bill's socks, and Becky and her small friend Etty were playing at shop with a number of empty packets arrayed on top of a wooden box, which served both as counter and stall room. Paddy tugged one of Becky's blonde pigtails as he passed and she turned to smile up at him. 'Hello, Paddy! Me an'

Etty's playin' shop,' she said unnecessarily. 'Amy told me, the last time she was home, that she an' Mary played shop when they were small. So Mammy's been savin' empty packets and jars, an' now I'm the shop lady and Etty's me customer.'

'That's grand, queen,' Paddy said absently, but the mention of Amy's name made him remember when he and she had been forced to share a roof. How they had argued and even fought one another when there was no one about to keep them apart! He had called her nastier and nastier names but somehow she had always got back at him. Life was much quieter now she had moved out but, he reflected ruefully, it was much duller too. She had been – was – a sparky little thing, with plenty to say for herself, always full of tales of her work or her friends' doings. Looking back, he knew that both he and his mother had been jealous of Bill's affection for his younger daughter, so it was better for all of them to live separately, as they did now.

He skirted the chair in which Amy had sat and exchanged tart remarks with him the last time she had come home, and found himself remembering every detail of her appearance on that day. The small, pointy chinned face, with its large, greenish eyes, the pink lips which could fold so tightly in disapproval and the long auburn hair, piled on top of her small head and held in place by tortoiseshell combs. He had called her a looker, not intending to compliment her, but simply speaking the truth. And what had she done? Snubbed him as usual. So she was best forgotten, he decided, mounting the stairs at a run. Heaven knew, their paths did not cross often and when she came home he usually kept well clear. Last time they had met he had hoped to bury the hatchet, but Amy's attitude clearly made this impossible, so he would think of her no more.

Having washed, slicked down their hair with brilliantine and donned clean shirts, kecks and shoes, the boys thundered down the stairs again and it was not long before the sacks of cooked shrimps were piled on the handcart and being pushed along Crosby Road by three neatly attired young gentlemen, eager for a bit of fun.

Neither Gus nor the younger boys had been into the city centre for several days and they were shocked to find the streets buzzing with policemen and with obvious signs, such as smashed shop windows and litter everywhere, that a crowd had recently rioted there. Now, however, apart from the obvious police presence, the streets were almost empty and the boys and their catch proceeded without interference right up to Bill's stall in the fish market. There were few customers and even fewer stallholders, but Bill thanked them for the shrimps and sent Kenny, the little lad who helped him when he was busy, round to Roper's for more ice.

'We had a rare do here this morning,' Bill told his sons as they unloaded the shrimps. 'The strikers came in a body to hear some feller address them from St George's Plateau. It seems things got out of hand, though, and there was no end of damage done. They called the troops in, I've heard, and someone was shot. We heard the burst of gunfire from here, but Jack Gibson, who were doin' a delivery along Lime Street, said the troops fired over the heads of the crowd. Bullets go astray, though,' he added wisely, 'and sometimes it ain't only the troops what get themselves armed – there's fellers here what fought in the Boer War an' never handed in their weapons, so I've heard.'

'It's quiet enough out there now,' Gus observed. 'The place is crawling wi' scuffers, mind, so I suppose it would be. I were goin' round to the Crown for a beer, but will they be open? I noticed several shops closed as we came along.'

Bill shrugged. 'Who knows? I reckon the pubs closed at the height of the trouble but they may well be open again by now. Publicans have got a living to make, same as the rest of us. No harm in going along there to check, anyroad.'

So presently, having arranged with Kenny to push the handcart home in exchange for a threepenny joe, the boys split up. Gus made determinedly, for the Crown; Albert went off towards Lime Street Station and Paddy headed for his old workplace.

Paddy walked into the dairy and grinned across the counter at Tommy who was serving a customer with milk, dipping a ladle into a tall churn and filling the woman's enamel jug. He greeted his friend cheerfully, but continued to serve the small queue of waiting women until the last one had paid for her order and left. Only then did he turn to Paddy. 'Hello, stranger,' he said affably. 'On the run from the scuffers, are you? Or haven't you heard about the riots yet?'

'On the run from the scuffers yourself,' Paddy said indignantly. 'We were a mile off shore draggin' for shrimps when the trouble broke out. We had a jolly good haul, too, which is why we've come into the city early, so's Uncle Bill could start sellin' before all the housewives go home. Where were you, anyroad? In here, I s'pose, like a good little lad, sellin' jugs of milk and pats of butter to nice old women who wouldn't know a riot from a ... a ... prayer meeting.'

'Yes, you're right as it happens, ' Tommy admitted. He sighed regretfully. 'I missed all the fun and games by a whisker, though. Joe Coutts broke his arm last winter and from time to time he has a check-up at the infirmary. He was supposed to go today and I were goin' to do his round, but he went to his doctor at the surgery last night and the old feller signed him off, so he come in as usual this morning and did his own round.' He grinned at Paddy. 'Never mind, eh. Better luck next time. Why've you come a visitin', anyroad?'

Paddy explained his errand and Tommy agreed it would be just grand to have an evening out together. He was beginning to expand on this theme when a group of housewives entered the shop. Tommy promptly waved Paddy away, saying in a hissing whisper, 'See you outside the Palais de Luxe at six,' before turning to his customers with a courteous enquiry as to their wants.

Having made his arrangements with Tommy, Paddy decided to go to the shippon and stables, and see who was working there. The shippon was empty but he found Joe Coutts in the stable, whistling tunelessly between his teeth as he cleaned down his horse, a large chestnut gelding called Conker. He grinned at Paddy. 'Well, so you've come a visitin', young Paddy. I tek it you wasn't a part of that there riot this mornin'? I did wonder, seeing as how you're a fisherman now and fishermen is seamen?'

'Oh, no, they ain't,' Paddy retorted, 'and besides, it isn't the seamen strikin' now, you oaf, it's railway workers. What about you, Joe?'

'Oh, I were in the thick of it, I were. I were knocked off me milk cart and bowled head over heels into the gutter right outside Lime Street Station. The station were barricaded and folk were screaming and shoutin' . . . oh aye, it were a nasty moment. I could see clear across to St George's Hall – that's how I come to see everything. I seed the troops, watched 'em fire over the 'eads of the crowds . . . I even see the girl go down.'

'What girl?' Paddy asked lazily. He knew Joe was simple, but he also knew the man was honest. 'Was a girl knocked over, then?'

'Aye, she were shot an' what's more, I knew 'er,' Joe said triumphantly. 'Come to think of it, you'll know her an' all, Paddy. It were young Amy Logan, what used to work in the fish market. I allus buy my fish there on a Friday to take home to the wife, though it's young Amy's dad what runs the stall now. Oh aye, it were young Amy all right – I see the troops fire and she went down like a ton o' bricks, an' were took up for dead.'

Paddy stared. For one awful moment he actually thought he might faint, as a terrible coldness swept over his entire body in spite of the heat of the afternoon. Then anger stiffened his spine and he felt a wave of scarlet heat invade his face. He grabbed Joe by both shoulders and shook him vigorously. 'What the devil do you mean, you silly old fool,' he shouted right into the man's startled face. 'Are you tryin' to say me stepsister's dead? I don't believe it. I were in the fish market no more than an hour ago and Uncle Bill said nothin' about it.'

Joe tugged himself free from Paddy's vicious grip and flapped a hand in the younger man's face. 'Don't gerrin such a takin', la',' he said soothingly. 'I

319

said took up for dead, which is what folk were sayin', but later I heard she'd been took to the Infirmary, so maybe she's just badly injured. There was a deal of blood,' he went on ghoulishly. 'When the crowd had cleared, me an' old Conker 'ere went over to take a look and the paving stones were scarlet where she'd lain.'

But he was talking to empty air. Paddy had whipped round and rushed out of the yard with one thought only uppermost in his mind. Amy was injured and from what Joe had said she might be at death's door. She had snubbed him and cold-shouldered him, and tried to make trouble for him, but he realised now that he regarded her as a part of the family. He had known on that day when both sisters had returned to Seaforth that he no longer idolised Mary. The older girl had become hard-faced and selfish, with little resemblance to the sweet, mild-mannered young woman he had believed himself to love. Amy, with her sharp tongue and sharper wit, was far more his sort of girl – and now she was sick unto death and he might never get the chance to tell her how sorry he was for the way he had treated her in the past.

It was a long way from Dryden Street to the Infirmary. Reaching Scotland Road, he was about to continue running along the pavement when it occurred to him that he might catch a number 3 tram, which would drop him on London Road, well over half his way to his destination. However, he had no idea when the next tram would come along. In his urge to hurry he cursed the strike, which had made life in the city centre so difficult.

By the time he reached the Infirmary he was so out of breath that he realised he would be unable to ask sensible questions regarding Amy's whereabouts, and stopped for a moment to lean against a pillar and get his breath back. After a few moments he walked towards the glass doors which lead into the hospital foyer and saw, reflected therein, a wild figure. His hair, which had been neatly slicked back, was standing up like a gorse bush with the wind of his going and his sweat-streaked face bore the marks of many smuts. His tie was askew and his unbuttoned jacket rucked up on one side. Hastily he flattened his hair with both hands, tugged his tie straight, buttoned his jacket and rubbed his face as clean as he could get it on his pocket handkerchief. Only then did he go into the hospital foyer and move towards the clerk behind the reception desk.

He was about to ask in which ward Amy lay when two things occurred to him. The first was that it had been his duty to go immediately to Bill and tell him what Joe had said. The second that he might be denied admittance here, simply because he was not a relative in the strictest sense of the word, but that last, he decided, could soon be remedied. He would announce himself as her brother and, even if she were conscious, he doubted she would be well enough to refute the claim.

The foyer was crowded and for a moment Paddy hesitated, unsure of which way to go; then, amid the bustling throng he spotted a porter in uniform and made a beeline for him, hailing him as soon as he reached him. 'Excuse me, mate, I'm lookin' for me sister. A pal told me she'd got herself mixed up wi' some riot or other and been shot. Can you tell me . . .?'

The porter swung round and pointed towards one of the long corridors leading off the foyer. 'She's just been taken to Nightingale Ward,' he said in a strong Irish brogue. 'Sure an' isn't it a terrible thing, a pretty young critter like that. Third bed from the end, you'll find her.'

Almost before the words were out of his mouth, Paddy was running across the foyer, muttering beneath his breath, 'Nightingale Ward, Nightingale Ward, third bed along.' He found that his knees were actually shaking and deemed it sensible to stop for a moment outside Nightingale Ward to get his breath and collect his wits. It was probably as well that he did so, since a middle-aged nurse in a stiffly starched uniform swept out of Nightingale Ward, giving him a suspicious glance as she passed him. Hastily Paddy composed himself and walked past the ward doors with the air of one who knows exactly where he is going and is in no hurry to get there. As soon as the nurse disappeared, however, he turned back and entered the ward, his eyes going straight to the third bed from the end.

A figure lay in the high white bed, bandaged and still – so still that for a moment his heart missed a beat – but almost as he began to approach the bed the figure turned her head slightly on the pillow, to smile up at someone standing beside her and he realised that this was not Amy. For a moment he stopped, frozen in his tracks, staring unbelievingly at the two figures beside the bed. The girl who was holding the patient's hand and smiling down at her was Amy, looking neither injured nor unhappy. In fact, in her green cotton dress and straw hat, with her abundant hair curling around her face, she looked as composed and at ease as though nothing unusual had happened. And beside her, in a grey flannel suit with a straw boater in one hand and the other resting lightly on her shoulder, was Philip Grimshaw – it was unmistakably he, though Paddy had not set eyes on him for years.

Bewilderment kept Paddy rooted to the spot for several seconds – several seconds too long – before he began instinctively to turn away. In that moment Philip recognised him. He turned Amy so that she, too, was looking down the ward, and came towards Paddy, a pleasant smile on his handsome face. 'Paddy!' he exclaimed. 'What on earth are you doing here? Of all the odd coincidences ... or are you visiting Miss Morton too? I didn't imagine you knew her, but being part of the family now ... I suppose ...'

Feeling trapped, Paddy searched his mind desperately for a good reason to be standing on the ward and came up with the truth, though as soon as the words were out he cursed himself for having said them. 'I were told it were Amy,' he blurted out. 'A feller I used to know when I worked in Dryden Street told me he saw Bill's girl shot by the troops on St George's Plain. I ... I thought I'd better make sure it were true before fetching Bill over.'

He could not resist a quick glance at Amy's face and saw the big, green-grey eyes widen for a second before she said thoughtfully, 'Yes, I can understand how such a mistake could come about. When Ella fell – Miss Morton that is – I dropped to my knees to try to help her. Well, there was so much blood ... for an awful moment I thought – I thought ...'

Philip put his arm around Amy's slender shoulders and gave her a little shake. 'Stop it now,' he said warningly. 'Miss Morton is going to be just fine. I know she's got a head wound, a good deal of bruising and a suspected fractured rib, but the nurses say she'll be out by the end of the week, all being well.'

'Philip and I brought her in here this morning and we've just taken in an overnight bag for her,' Amy explained. 'But I can't help wondering whether I did the right thing . . .'

'The doctor said you acted with good sense and promptitude,' Philip interrupted. 'And since we don't want you going into a decline, stop wondering what else you could have done and start thinking about what you're going to eat when we nip over to Lyons Corner House for a sustaining meal.' He and Amy turned back towards Ella, clearly intent on bidding farewell to their friend, but the girl in the bed was sound asleep. 'Best not to wake her,' he whispered, 'we'll be in again later, anyway.' He turned to Paddy, the familiar quirky grin lighting up his face. 'Paddy, old pal, would you like to join us? Amy's had nothing to eat since breakfast – nor have I for that matter and there's no point in either of us starving ourselves.'

Paddy found himself staring at the arm which still circled Amy's shoulders. His sudden realisation that Amy meant something to him, despite their history of childhood squabbles, made him resent Philip's familiarity. For two pins, he told himself savagely, he would have asked Philip to stop mauling the girl, yet for all he knew, Philip might be Amy's latest beau – probably was, since she had clearly called on him in her hour of need. Not that she would have called on me, he reflected bitterly, not if I'd been the last feller on earth. Why, I might as well face it, no matter how I feel about her – and that's something I haven't really worked out yet – she hates my perishin' guts.

'Well, Paddy Keagan, are you coming with us or not, because we haven't got all day and I'm starving hungry.' It was Amy, her tone tart as ever.

Paddy pulled himself together with an effort. 'No, thanks,' he muttered. 'Two's company, they say, and three's a crowd. Besides, me mam wouldn't want me to spoil my appetite for supper.'

'Oh, come on, Paddy,' Philip said, his tone almost wheedling. 'It's been years since we met; I want to hear all the local gossip. Why, I've no idea what you're doing now – nor where you're living – and we were good pals once, when we were kids.'

'Oh, let him go, if that's what he wants,' Amy said, slipping her hand into the crook of Philip's elbow. 'Any gossip you want, I can tell you . . .' The two of them moved down the ward towards the swing doors at the end and Paddy followed, deliberately hanging back so that the others might get well ahead. Bloody Amy, he thought furiously, she had a real knack of ruining everything. Well, if Philip wanted a girl with a tongue like an adder then he was welcome to her. And with that thought Paddy slipped out of a side entrance, hoping, but not expecting, that the other two would feel concerned and come back into the hospital, only to find him disappeared.

That evening, after she and Philip had revisited the hospital and seen Ella sitting up in bed and chattering, quite like her usual self, Amy returned to Huskisson Street in a very much happier frame of mind. She explained what had happened to the other girls, trying to play down the drama so that they were not too worried, and managed to convince them that though Ella had had a horrible experience, the medical staff were sure she would recover completely, given time. After this, totally exhausted by the day's events, she took herself off to bed.

Cuddling down beneath the blankets, she expected to fall asleep immediately, but instead found herself wondering, for the first time since they had left him, just exactly what had brought Paddy to the hospital in such haste. Recalling the moment when Philip had drawn her attention to the tall, dark-haired figure, standing stock still in the centre of the ward, she also remembered how white his face had been until it suddenly flooded with scarlet and how his dark eyes had burned as his glance fell on her. He had been shocked to find her uninjured, she was sure of that, but she could not recall any look of pleasure when he had realised she was unhurt.

The old Amy would have assumed Paddy was disappointed to find her whole, but Amy knew that this was nonsense. Paddy might not like her – did not like her – but she did not really suppose for one moment that he actually wished her harm. After all, she did not like him, but she would have been truly distressed had he been injured when working on the boat. Indeed, when she thought of the sort of conditions the fishermen faced whenever they went to sea in bad weather a chill of dread crept over her. He could easily be knocked overboard by a wildly swinging boom and tossed ashore by the great, white-tipped waves which accompanied such conditions. And there were a thousand and one smaller, less fatal accidents, which were almost everyday occurrences among the fishing fleet.

Now that she had begun on this train of thought, she had hard work to dismiss it from her mind but she knew she must do so, reminding herself that her beloved brothers, Albert and Gus, were also fishermen and faced the same horrendous dangers daily. She was just thinking that the old animosity between herself and Paddy must be beginning to fade, just drifting into sleep, when she distinctly heard his voice, taunting and shrill, the boy Paddy, screaming after her as he had so often done, 'Shrimpy, Shrimpy! Who stinks of bleedin' fish, then? Keep to windward of her, fellers, else the pong will knock you out.'

Instantly Amy found herself sitting bolt upright in bed, all her gentle thoughts of Paddy forgotten. He had been a horrible little boy and was probably now a horrible young man. The fact that she did not see much of him must therefore be considered a huge advantage and she would most certainly not worry about his possible fate aboard the fishing boat, nor continue to exercise her mind with fruitless wonderings concerning his hospital visit.

Resolutely she turned her face into the pillow and presently slept. But even the best of resolutions cannot always be kept and, as she dreamed, she smiled. And the Paddy who accompanied her into dreamland was not the irritating little boy but an extraordinarily attractive young man.

At the time that Paddy was leaving the hospital, Albert was taking his place at a small corner table in Dorothy's Dining Rooms. When the waitress approached him he grinned up at her, and ordered a pot of tea and some buttered toast and then, with seeming casualness, he asked her if Ruth Durrant was on the premises.

The girl looked at him closely, then smiled. 'I seen

you before,' she said almost accusingly, 'you come in a week ago, dincher? Did Ruthie serve you then? She must ha' made an impression for you to come back so soon!'

Albert felt rather offended but did not intend to show it. The girl made him sound like one of those – what did they call them? – Yes, stage-door johnnies who hung around outside theatres trying to scrape acquaintance with a member of the chorus. He felt like telling her that he and Ruth were old friends, but instead said loftily, 'Ruth's a neighbour of mine; we both live out at Seaforth. Is she around? I'd like a word.'

The girl grinned but vouchsafed no answer, merely moving to another table to take a customer's order and presently went through the swing doors into the kitchen. Albert hoped that his message would reach Ruth and that she would not think he had a nerve to come visiting her workplace. But nothing ventured, nothing gained, his dad had often remarked and this was definitely a case in point. He had known Ruth since their early schooldays; known her better than he knew most girls, because of her friendship with his sister. He liked Ruth very much but had somehow lacked the courage to ask her out. Now, with an afternoon and evening free, he intended to do it. If she agreed to go with him he meant to take her to the Rotunda on the Scottie, since it was on their way home and would not, he thought, be likely to attract either Gus or Paddy, who would go for a theatre in the city centre.

'Hello, Albert. Lily said you was asking for me.' Ruth stood by the table, looking interrogatively down at him. She was a small, pale girl with light-brown hair and honey-coloured eyes and, though she was not pretty, there was a good deal of appeal in her neat, quick movements and ready smile. She smiled at Albert now and began to arrange a teapot, cup and saucer and milk jug on the table before him. 'Your buttered toast won't be a minute – the kitchen hand is makin' it now.'

Albert took a deep breath. 'What time do you finish, Ruthie? Only we gorroff early today on account of the strike an' that. I thought you might like to see the show at the Rotunda; we might have a bite to eat an' all.'

Ruth smiled down at him with an unaccustomed twinkle in her sparkling eyes. 'I can't leave work till after eight o'clock and the last house starts at half past seven,' she said demurely, 'but it's a lovely evening; a walk down to the Pier Head and along the waterfront might be nice, and there's bound to be somewhere open where we could get tea and a buttie, despite the strike.'

Albert beamed at her. 'It's a date,' he said exultantly. 'I'll be outside the kitchen door waitin' for you at eight o'clock on the dot.'

Ella was in hospital for a week and during that time, though she had a number of visitors, no one was as regular in their attendance as Philip Grimshaw. At first he came whenever Amy did and the two of them sat, one on either side of Ella's bed. They told Ella what they had been doing, chaffed one another over small incidents which had happened on their way to the hospital and generally behaved in a manner which, at first, led Ella to suppose that they were more than friends. This surprised her, since

Amy had seldom mentioned Philip after that meeting in the train and then usually only in connection with her sister Mary.

I suppose it was my accident which drew them together, Ella told herself – until, that was, Philip began to visit her on his own. He popped in at odd times of the day, charming the nursing staff, deferring to the doctors and usually bringing small gifts for Ella herself. Ella, pondering his attentiveness, did not for one moment imagine that he was courting her; his manner was in no way loverlike. What was more, she knew herself to look a positive scarecrow with her hair shaved away on the right-hand side of her head and, because she was not allowed to get the wound wet, the rest of her locks greasy and dishevelled. Furthermore, for the first few days of her stay in hospital she had been pale and listless, reluctant to move in the bed because of her fractured rib and hating the sight of her face, disfigured as it was by an enormous purple and yellow bruise. No one, she thought ruefully, could enjoy looking at a visage so battered. However, she could not believe that he was trying to ingratiate himself with her friend either – how could it be so?

Amy never even knew about the visits beforehand and, when Ella told her, took them for granted. 'He's ever so nice, Ella,' she said earnestly. 'A really kind young man who is always thinking of others and putting himself second. Why, you've even converted him to approving the suffragette movement! He told me the other evening, when he was walking me home, that he has the greatest respect for the way women are trying to claim their rights and wishes them every success.'

So when the doctor told Ella that she was well

enough to leave hospital, she was in two minds over it. Naturally, a part of her was delighted that she was escaping from hospital food and hospital routine – while another part of her thought wistfully that she would really miss Philip's company. She had begun to realise that the two of them had much in common. They had both received an excellent education and had read many of the same books. They had both visited France and Italy and, though Philip had studied mathematics and the sciences, he could also speak passable French and knew the rudiments of German. Ella loved her room-mates and appreciated their good points, but acknowledged ruefully that they had not had the opportunities which she and Philip had enjoyed and were therefore unable to share her feelings on certain issues.

However, when she told Philip that she would be leaving hospital later that day his face brightened. 'I'll fetch a hansom cab to the door and see you back to Huskisson Street,' he said at once. 'And having found you, Miss Morton, I don't intend to lose you again. Nor your friends,' he added hastily. 'Has the doctor told you when you may return to work? Until you do so, I'm sure outings to the seaside or the country would do you a great deal of good. And if this is so, I'll happily take you anywhere you want to go.' After this formal speech he cocked his head on one side and gave her a grin of such pure delight that Ella burst out laughing. It was grand to have a friend like Philip, she told herself exultantly – and even grander to know that he intended to stay her friend, whether in hospital or out of it.

Fortunately it was a simple matter to get a message

to Amy that Ella would be leaving hospital that afternoon, forestalling Amy's daily visit, which usually took place as soon as she had finished work for the day. Ella wrote a note and Philip delivered it to the front desk at the Adelphi. When the cab arrived, all Ella had to do was to get into it and be driven back to Huskisson Street in comfort. Philip took the seat opposite her, asking every few minutes if the cabby should be told to slow down, whether she found the breeze from the open window too cool and, almost in the same breath, enquiring as to how she was enjoying being outside once more after so long in the ward.

They reached Huskisson Street and Philip carried Ella's bag for her, standing it down in the front hall. The front door was seldom locked, but the door to the girls' room always was, since there was usually a new tenant somewhere in the building who might, or might not, prove to be dishonest. Ella fumbled her key into the lock, suddenly realising with considerable dismay that there would be no one at home at this hour. She could scarcely turn Philip away without asking him inside, yet she knew that her parents would have been horrified to learn that she was entertaining a young man alone.

The problem, however, was solved by Philip. He went ahead of her into the room, holding the door open for her and standing her bag down on a small table just inside the door. Then he gave her his sweetest smile and turned towards the front door once more. 'This has been a big day,' he said over his shoulder. 'The change from an institutionalised way of life to your ordinary, everyday one is always tiring, especially when you've been as ill as you have. I'm going back to the office now, and I think

you should lie down on your bed and have a sleep.
When you wake up, you might make yourself a cup
of tea and sit in the window until your friends get
back from their work. Honestly, Miss – oh, this is
ridiculous since I feel we've known one another for
ever – may I call you Ella?'

'Yes, of course, if I can call you Philip,' Ella said
gaily. She could feel the heat rising to her cheeks and
pressed the palms of her hands against them. 'I'm
sure you're right, because although I've done nothing except sit in a very comfortable cab, I feel
absolutely exhausted. So I'll take your advice and
have a rest on my bed, but before I do so Mr Gr – I
mean Philip – I'd like to thank you very much
indeed for bringing me home in such luxury. You've
been most awfully kind.'

'It was a pleasure,' Philip said briefly, turning in
the doorway to smile at her. Ella saw that, in his
turn, Philip's colour had brightened. 'I wonder if
you will feel fit for a short outing tomorrow? If so, I
could take the afternoon off from work easily
enough.'

'That would be very nice,' Ella said demurely.
'Shall you call for me here or shall we meet at some
mutually convenient spot? Perhaps that would be
better. I should be able to get into the city centre
quite easily.'

Philip, however, did not think much of that idea.
'No such thing; I shall call for you here at two
o'clock,' he said firmly. 'Mind you're ready for me!'
And with a valedictory wave he was gone, leaving
Ella to close and lock her door, to take off her long
cotton skirt and the crisp white blouse, which Amy
had brought to the hospital the previous day, and to
lie down on her bed. She did not immediately go to

sleep, however, but stared at the ceiling and thought, with pleasure, about Philip. He was all that Amy had claimed him to be and more, and she, Ella, was becoming remarkably fond of him. And, she told herself as her lids began to droop, I do believe he is becoming fond of me.

Chapter Nine

It was October before Ella finally returned to work and by the time she did so she and Philip were going steady in earnest. He had taken her on so many pleasant expeditions, both to the country and to the seaside, that returning to work had been hard indeed, but since she either met Philip for a hasty lunch soon after noon, or in the evening, she was able to pass her working days pleasantly enough.

After the first few weeks Philip had suggested that Amy might like to join them. He was feeling a trifle guilty at leaving his flatmate, Dick Maynard, alone most evenings, so a foursome with Ella's friend seemed the ideal solution.

Ella enjoyed the outings and knew that Amy did too, though she did not think that Amy thought of Dick as anything but a friend. He was a pleasant, intelligent person but Amy, it seemed, did not wish to get involved with any young man; or so it appeared to Ella. Ella found it impossible to guess why her friend seemed almost indifferent to Dick; it was not that Amy was secretive, merely that long experience of the treatment she had received from her stepmother had made her keep her own counsel, so though she clearly enjoyed both the outings and Dick's company, by the time Christmas was drawing near Ella was still no wiser as to the extent of her friend's feelings. What was more, Amy had heard with equanimity that Dick was to return to his home for two weeks over Christmas and was planning her own holiday with obvious enjoyment, clearly unaffected by Dick's proposed absence.

Since her parents' death, Ella had rather dreaded Christmas. It was such a family time and even the sight of carol singers in the street or a bedecked tree would bring tears to her eyes as she thought, with loving nostalgia, of Christmases past.

Once she was sharing the room with the other girls, of course, things became easier. The room was Minnie's home and had been ever since Mrs Miniver's death, and the two girls had made as merry as circumstances allowed, even endeavouring to cook a small chicken over the open fire, which caused much hilarity, as well as a strong smell of burning when the skin of the bird became enveloped in flames. With Amy's and Ruth's arrival, the run-up to Christmas was no longer something to be dreaded, but on the day itself, when the two younger girls returned to their families, Ella knew that she and Minnie both had to work hard not to let themselves fall into gloom. Amy would have liked to take Ella home with her, and Minnie too, but because of the size of the Logan family – and the size of their tiny house – this was clearly impossible. Ruthie, too, lived in a small, overcrowded house, so could do little entertaining.

It seemed, however, that this year was to be different again. Philip had actually asked Ella if she would like to accompany him back to his parents' home in Manchester to share their family Christmas. For the first time in their relationship Ella was in a quandary. It was such a commitment and, although she was extremely fond of Philip, she did not yet feel sure enough of her own feelings – or his – to want to put them to the test. Inevitably, if she went home with him everyone, probably including Philip, would assume that marriage was a likely event in the not too distant future. Although Ella was an enthusiastic suffragette, she believed that a happy marriage was the best thing which could happen to a woman. She also believed in the old saying 'Marry in haste, repent at leisure' and thought fearfully that if Philip were to see her under his parents' roof he might realise that she was not, after all, the sort of girl they would wish him to marry. She chided herself for this fear, for was this not 1911? If it was generally accepted that many young women had, of necessity, to earn a living in order to keep themselves, then it followed that the Grimshaws must know such young women existed, might even admire them. It was common knowledge that, in order to get a decent position in any walk of life, a woman had to be ten times more intelligent and determined as any man. Philip himself acknowledged it, but would his parents? He had a sister, Laura, of whom he was very fond; suppose Laura did not take to her?

Ella tried, rather timidly, to put these questions to Amy, who simply stared at her round-eyed. 'You think *you* are going to feel uncomfortable among the Grimshaws?' she asked incredulously. 'You think they'll look down on you? Well, if they do so, all I can say is they aren't worth knowing. Besides, don't you think that Philip probably takes after one or other of his parents? If that's so, then they'll be lovely people who will accept you for what you are, a brave and resourceful woman, making her own way in the world.'

'But I don't want to be thought of as a brave and

resourceful woman,' Ella wailed, running her hands through her short, curly hair, for she had had to cut the left side to match the right as soon as her hair had reached a respectable length. 'I want to be thought of as pretty, eligible and ... and charming.'

Amy laughed at this honest declaration. 'Votes for women, indeed,' she scoffed. 'You're just like the rest of us women, queen. In our heart of hearts we all want to be cherished and protected, and thought of as helpless little darlings. Well, Ella, just you go ahead and visit Philip's folks, because you're pretty as a picture and smart as paint, and worth a whole flock of empty-headed society beauties.'

'Do you know, I believe I will?' Ella said slowly. She looked around their room, which was already decorated with brightly coloured paper chains, a miniature Christmas tree and sprigs of holly tacked on to the picture rail. 'You and Ruthie will go home, of course – but what about Minnie? I can't and won't leave her here to celebrate Christmas alone.'

'Why, she must come home with me, of course,' Amy said at once, without appearing to give the matter so much as a moment's thought. 'We'll go to Seafield Grove for Christmas Day and Boxing Day, but come home to Huskisson Street at night. Then there won't be any question of who's to sleep where – though come to think of it, Mary probably won't be coming home for Christmas, so Minnie and I could share with Becky just for one or two nights. I meant to tell you, I went into Blackler's yesterday in my dinner hour and had a chat with Mary. She's thinking of staying with a pal over the holiday and not coming back to Seaforth. She took a leaf out of our book, you know, when she came back to Liverpool, and began to go about more with friends from the store. So unless she comes over for the New Year, we shan't be seeing her in Seaforth for a while. And you'll never believe it, Ella, but she's actually found a feller, someone she really seems to like for himself. I don't say she's serious, probably he's just a friend, but nevertheless, she does like him and he's only a tram driver and plain as a plum pudding, apparently. And you know our Mary, she's always put looks, money and position high on her list of requirements, so the fact that she's looked twice at a tram driver, and an ugly one at that, must mean she's head over heels.'

Both girls laughed at the thought of Mary actually falling in love with anyone, let alone with a young man whom she would plainly think her social inferior. So having decided what to do with Minnie, they continued with their plans for Christmas.

Mary had enjoyed her meeting with Amy, for the two girls did not see each other very often. She had told Amy briefly that she had met someone called Haydn Lloyd, who had made a great impression on her. She had not, however, gone into any more detail because, even to herself, the friendship had seemed a strange one. At least, it would have seemed a strange one to the old Mary, the Mary who had gone steady with Roderick Campbell for five years, during which time she had grown more and more similar to Mr Campbell and less and less like the girl who had set out to conquer Manchester with such high hopes.

At the time, Mary had scarcely been aware that she was changing, hardening. She had not realised, until Roderick had left her, that she had been slowly but surely becoming like him, embracing his attitudes, ambitions and values, and allowing her own to become almost completely submerged.

At first, when he had taken up with his little tart, as Mary had called her, she had felt bitter shame and rage for her lost years, along with the feeling that she could not hold a man, not even one as thoroughly unworthy as Roderick had proved to be. But gradually, as the weeks passed, she had begun to feel a lightness of spirit and a burgeoning of hope. It was this, at last, which gradually made her realise how bad Roderick had been for her and how infinitely better off she was without him.

She had gone back to Seaforth, however, when her bitter shame and rage over Roderick's defection had been at its height. Then she had agreed to meet up with Amy for a day out, and that day had determined her on the move back to the city of her birth. For they had met Ella, Minnie and Ruth after work and had walked back to Huskisson Street together, staring into shop windows, covertly eyeing the young men they passed and light-heartedly announcing their preference for dark men, fair ones, tall ones or cheeky ones. Then they had purchased fried fish and chipped potatoes for their supper and had eaten their meal out of newspaper wrappings, and had spent the jolliest evening imaginable in the girls' big room, chatting, laughing and exchanging frank comments about life in general and married life in particular, until Mary had truly envied Amy her room share and had begun to see that young men were really not as important as she had once thought.

She had remembered afterwards how she had

arrived in Seaforth in a white heat of rage, determined to find Philip Grimshaw so that she might somehow become his young lady, which would have shown Roderick that Mary was not to be trifled with. She knew that Roderick had been jealous of Philip, whose superior looks and intelligence had made him popular with young men and girls alike, so to flourish Philip in Roderick's face would have been a triumph indeed. She had speedily realised the futility of this plan when Amy had explained how brief their meeting had been and had added that they had not seen Philip since, nor did they expect to do so. But by then it no longer mattered. Mary had realised the fun which could be had with a group of girlfriends and had returned to Manchester no longer interested in spiting Roderick but determining, instead, to make a new life for herself in Liverpool which would not, in the early stages at any rate, include the capturing of a young man.

Deciding on this course, she had taken the job at Blackler's and accepted Faith's offer of the room share. Bearing in mind the enjoyable evening she had spent with Amy and her room-mates, once she had settled in, she had invited three girls, from the departmental store in which they all worked, back to her room one evening for a light supper and a cosy chat. This had proved so successful that later the four of them had gone off to the Empire Theatre on Lime Street to see Cecilia Loftus and Albert Whelan. This had led naturally to the suggestion that they should go dancing together at the dance academy on Renshaw Street and it was here that Mary had met Haydn Lloyd for the first time. He had asked her to dance with him within half an hour of her arrival at the hall and Mary, who was seldom without a partner, had slid gracefully into his arms and had barely noticed him as a person, save for the realisation that he was no more than an inch taller than she. Very soon she realised that he was a marvellous dancer, with a degree of expertise considerably superior to Roderick's. He was an interesting companion, too, talking in a lively fashion and, what was even nicer, his hands did not continually stray, so she was able to enjoy his company without worrying that he would presently begin to take advantage of having his arm about her, the way so many men did. In fact, she found dancing with him such a pleasure that for the rest of the evening he became her chosen partner, even taking her out during the interval and buying her a small sherry at the nearest public house.

Haydn Lloyd was as Welsh as he sounded and Mary had always rather looked down on the Welsh, considering them country bumpkins not worthy of the attention of a sophisticated city girl like herself. And now, here she was, the beautiful Miss Logan of Blackler's, who had had so many offers in her time, actually contemplating spending her Christmas holiday somewhere in the wilds of Wales with a man who was neither wealthy nor influential – a man, furthermore, who was a widower with two small children.

He had told her about his kids at their very first meeting, had admitted that he missed them most dreadfully and that they lived in Mold, in the county of Flintshire, with his mother. When he had worked down the coal mine at Llay, they had lived in a miner's cottage quite near the pit. However, his wife had died shortly after the birth of his second child and he had moved his family to Mold to live with his mother. There, he had taken work on the land but had speedily found that he could not keep his family on the wages of an unskilled farmworker. Having worked in the open air for a few months, he had no desire to return to the pit. So, with his mother taking care of the children, he had left North Wales to try his luck in the great city of Liverpool. He had speedily found work driving the trams and had hoped, at first, to bring his family to the city so that they could all be together. However, he soon realised he could not cope both with the children and with his job on the trams, and his mother, though a most amenable woman, had utterly refused to leave her neat little terraced house at her time of life. She hated cities, besides which, lodgings in Liverpool were not cheap. Accordingly, Haydn continued with his job, sending money home and retaining only enough to keep himself.

Any sensible girl would have drawn back immediately at this point, because it was as plain as the nose on his face – and that *was* plain! – that Mr Lloyd was looking for a wife to take the place of the one he had lost and Mary, like all girls of her age, wanted romance, a good life and, eventually, children of her own; she did not want to be made use of as a mam for a fellow's motherless kids. Yet despite knowing all this, Mary had not drawn back. She had liked Haydn for his ready grin, his strength of character and for the sheer *goodness* of him, which was a delight after Roderick's self-seeking, humourless attitude to life.

And now Mary was sitting in her comfortable little armchair in her rooms on Mather Avenue, wondering whether she had gone slightly but definitely mad. It was one thing to like a fellow, to want to continue seeing him, but she was actually contemplating going away for Christmas with a man she had met a bare two weeks before, and not a rich or an influential man either, but a tram driver in his forties, with a thick thatch of greying dark hair, a pair of sparkling black eyes and a rather large nose.

She was still telling herself that she must be mad to consider Haydn Lloyd's proposal, when a small voice spoke in her head. *What's wrong with a tram driver – or a miner, come to that?* the little voice said. *Who are you when you're at home? Why, you're nothing but the daughter of a humble fisherman, like the girl in the fairy story, the one they told you in infant school! Oh, I know you may tell yourself that you're a senior sales lady, doing well for yourself, but what does that matter, after all? Even if you rise to be head buyer in Gowns, you'll still be nothing but a fisherman's daughter, when all's said and done.*

The little voice was right, Mary knew it, and not only did she know it, she also acknowledged it as no more than the truth. She had never taken Roderick home because she knew he would despise her background, her father and brothers, even the smell of fish that hung around the house in which she had been born and bred. But Haydn was a different person altogether. He would *like* her father and feel completely at home with her brothers. He would probably consider the little house in Seafield Grove a palace compared with the pit cottage in which he had grown up. She could imagine him helping the boys to heave the boat ashore, gathering up arms full of dripping net, carting boxes laden with flapping fish up the beach and on to the roadway. In short, Mary thought joyfully, Hadyn would be one of them; he would not think for one moment that a tram driver was either superior or inferior to a fisherman. That was not his way. He would simply think them likeable folk and would settle down to become a part of the family.

Mary jumped to her feet. She ran across the small room, dragging her coat off the hook of the back of the door and casting a light shawl over her hair. She knew where Haydn lived, though she had not previously visited him there, but she would do so now. She would tell him joyfully that she would love to go home with him at Christmas and that she very much hoped he would come home with her for the New Year. In other words, Mary told herself, as she descended the stairs and went out into the cold night air, I am about to burn my boats for the very first time in my life and I don't feel worried, or guilty, or anything like that. I feel . . . I feel as though I'm at the very start of a real adventure.

It was a very cold day. Paddy, who had just boiled a supply of shrimps in the wash-house, crossed the courtyard, opened the back door and entered the kitchen, the basket of steaming shrimps in his arms. 'It's norra good day for the fishin',' he observed, going through into the scullery to dump his burden. 'It's bleedin' cold out an' all, Mam, so if you like I'll sell these few shrimps house-to-house, while you gerron with the cookin'.'

Suzie was baking in the kitchen, humming a tune beneath her breath as she worked. She glanced up as her son passed her, nodding thankfully at his suggestion. 'That'd be grand, Paddy,' she said, pushing a wisp of hair off her damp forehead. 'You'll soon get rid of them. It's not many people will bring shrimps in on a day like this.'

345

Paddy continued on his way to the scullery, glancing down at Becky as he passed her. She was fiddling around with a small grey ball of pastry of her very own, imitating her stepmother, using the miniature rolling pin which Gus had made for her, flattening the pastry into a large, round circle. Then she rolled it into a ball again, wondering aloud why it was such a funny colour, whereas Mam's pastry was a nice, cool, creamy shade.

'You've worked your bit rather hard, our Becky,' Suzie told her, but she good-naturedly broke a ball off the pastry she was rolling out to fit a pie dish, and handed it to her stepdaughter. 'Don't keep rollin' it back into a ball again. If you flatten it quite lightly, just the one time, I'll give you a dab o' mincemeat and you can mek yourself a mince pie.'

Paddy, listening from the scullery, smiled to himself. His mam had really taken to Becky, loved her like her own and would go to any lengths to see the child well-clothed, well-fed and happy. Indeed, looking back to his own childhood, Paddy had to conclude that his mam had mellowed with the years. In those far-off days she had been impatient, quick with a kiss, true, but also with a slap. It had been Gran who had played games with him, taught him his letters, made arithmetic interesting as she set him to counting a bag full of dried peas, using them both as playthings and as a means to teach him simple addition, subtraction and multiplication. Gran had been a marvellous cook, he still remembered the puddings and pies she had made when circumstances permitted, but there had never been enough spare pastry over, he supposed, for her to let him play with it. Instead, he and Albert had made sand pies from the wet and muddy sand which was reachable only at low tide. They carted it up the beach in a leaky wooden bucket, crouching down amid the dunes and decorating the pies with bits of broken shell, pebbles and stems of marram grass.

Paddy sighed; thinking about his childhood always brought Amy to mind and the truth was that Amy had been on his mind for some weeks, ever since he had thought her injured in the riots. He could never forget the awful sinking feeling and the rush of cold dread which had invaded him at that time. Because of his feelings he had made a couple of honest attempts to get on a better footing with her, but these had failed pretty dismally, he thought now. She was polite, she smiled coolly at him, she had even allowed him on one occasion to carry her heavy basket back from the Rimrose Bridge to Seafield Grove. But throughout the course of the walk home she had scarcely spoken, replying in monosyllables to anything that Paddy said and making it clear as crystal that even if his antagonism had disappeared, hers had not.

After that walk, Paddy had vowed that he would stop thinking about her, but the truth was she had become an obsession with him. When she visited the house in Seafield Grove he found himself covertly watching her. He had never thought her pretty, not even passable, but now he discovered that there was a charm in her small vivacious face and tilted smile, which was missing in many prettier young women. He had watched her as she went about the kitchen noticing, without wishing to do so, the neat economy of her movements. She could heft a great basket of fish and carry it across the room without so much as growing breathless, yet she did not appear to be strong. She was slim and slightly built and, although she dressed plainly, there was something elegant, Paddy thought, in the way she wore her simple clothes. Why couldn't she like him? Or if not like, at least not actively dislike, for he knew that at present his own warmer feelings had absolutely no chance of being returned. She might no longer hate him but she certainly never thought of him as anything but a young man who had once been an unpleasant part of her childhood.

Paddy had finished cleaning himself up, so he picked up the basket of shrimps and headed to the back door once more. 'Shan't be long, our mam,' he said cheerfully. 'I'll take this lot to Bootle – any messages?'

Suzie looked up from her baking. 'You might fetch me back another couple of pounds of sultanas and some apples; I'll need to make some more mince-meat since it seems we're entertaining extra over Christmas,' she said.

Paddy pricked up his ears. 'Extra?' he said interrogatively. He glanced across at his mother, still working placidly away at her pastry. 'Oh, I suppose you mean Charlie and his young lady?'

'Oh, them. No, I weren't thinkin' about them,' Suzie said almost absently. She picked up a slice of apple and ate it. 'It's that Amy – she's bringin' a friend home for Christmas and Boxing Day. Not that I mind, particular,' she added, flushing a little under Paddy's hard stare. 'I mean, I know it's her home when all's said and done, but it's not a big house, and with all you fellers, and Becky . . .' Her voice trailed off.

'A friend?' Paddy asked rather blankly. 'Oh, yes, I did know . . .' He turned once more for the door. So I were right, he told himself savagely, as he crossed the little yard. She and that Philip were more than just friends – I should ha' knowed it. I dare say she's been meetin' him every day and gettin' friendlier and friendlier ... well, it's no skin off *my* nose, 'cos she's never pretended to like me even a little bit. Her having Philip courtin' her won't make any difference to *me*.

But as he trudged round the wintry streets, knocking on doors and selling his shrimps, he was aware of a deep sense of disappointment, almost of loss. Despite all the facts, he had hoped that over Christmas a better understanding might happen between himself and Amy. Now it was clear that even if it did, it would not help his cause.

His cause? Now what exactly do you mean by that, Paddy Keagan? he asked himself, as he knocked on yet another door. You aren't tryin' to tell me that you thought you'd ever get anywhere with Amy Logan? I thought you just wanted to be friends, nothin' more?

But in his heart of hearts he was beginning to realise that, if he lost Amy to Philip, or indeed any other, he would be a very unhappy young man.

Ella and Philip travelled to Manchester by an early train, then took a taxi to Philip's home. Manchester seemed to have had quite a heavy snowfall during the night, for though the sun shone now, it shone on a city gleaming and glittering with snow. The streets, however, were churned-up and filthy, and Ella noticed that most of the women shoppers were lifting their skirts to avoid the slush, even on the pavements. Ella had realised, as the train drew nearer the city, that she was extremely nervous, which seemed odd considering how she had looked forward to this visit. She was very fond of Philip, knew that he was fond of her, even accepted that his intentions were honourable. He had talked of marriage, though she had never let him think that marriage was her ultimate aim. She was a working woman, earning a respectable salary, who had a career she enjoyed. The fact that she would have thrown it up willingly to marry Philip was something that she kept to herself, almost ashamed of how her high principles and desire to be a woman of independent means had crumbled beneath the warmth of his affection and his obvious and increasing desire to shelter her from the harsh realities of life.

In the cab, threading its way through the busy pre-Christmas streets, Philip took her hand in a comforting grasp. 'Nervous?' he asked, giving it a little shake. 'Well, if you aren't, I am. I've got butterflies the size of elephants lashing around in my stomach. It isn't that I'm worried my parents won't like you – they'll love you as I do – it's just ... oh, I don't know, it's just that they're bound to think we're a bit young ...'

'Just because I'm staying with your parents for Christmas doesn't mean we're anything but good friends,' Ella said rather feebly. She knew as well as Philip did that a young man did not ask a young woman to stay with his parents unless he had serious intentions. Of course, a whole week spent in one another's company might cause either party to change their minds, but she knew for her own part that this was unlikely to happen. The trouble was that Philip was not yet twenty-four and a good many parents would consider him young to be thinking seriously of marriage. On the other hand he was living away from home, managing a busy office and coping with the usual requirements of daily living. His life would be very much easier if he shared it with a wife, or so Ella thought now, as the cab drew up before a tall, red-brick house, with a flight of whitened stone steps leading to an impressive front door, upon which hung a wreath of Christmas greenery. The steps, which must have been covered with snow, were now in full sunshine but, like the pavement below, were puddled with melted snow and would have to be ascended with caution. The last thing Ella wanted to do was to make a fool of herself by slipping in the icy water and ending up on hands and knees in front of the door.

Philip gave her hand another reassuring squeeze, climbed from the cab and helped her down on to the pavement. The cab driver picked up their bags, carried them up the steps and heaved at the bell pull, and almost immediately the front door was opened by an imposing figure who beamed a welcome. 'Master Philip! It's good to see you after so long. Miss Laura's out shopping but your mama is in the drawing room.'

'Thanks, Richards,' Philip said. 'This way, Ella!'

Twenty minutes later Ella sat before the dressing table in the large and airy bedroom to which her hostess had led her, unpinning her hat, glad to be rid of its weight and beginning to brush out her crumpled locks. To her great relief she had found Mrs Grimshaw a delightful person, who looked far too young to be Philip's mama. When she entered the drawing room, which was bright with evergreens and Christmas decorations, Mrs Grimshaw had welcomed Ella with warmth and gaiety, apologising for her daughter's absence but explaining that Laura was buying Christmas gifts and would be home in good time for luncheon. 'We've planned all sorts of entertainment for you, my dear,' she said in her pleasant voice. 'We've booked seats at the theatre and there will be a great many private parties to which we have all been invited. Laura wanted to take you shopping today, but I think it would be better, personally, if you spent this afternoon settling in and this evening, when Mr Grimshaw returns home, perhaps we might introduce you to some members of the family who live nearby. Nothing formal, just Philip's grandmother and some cousins who will come in for a glass of wine before dinner.'

So now, as Ella combed out her short curls, she found herself wondering what she should wear that night. Her evening dresses, she knew, were several years out of date, but the material was good and, where it was possible, she had made changes so that she would not look frumpish or old-fashioned. She was looking forward to meeting Laura because Philip was clearly very fond of his younger sister. She sounded great fun, but in any event Ella was determined to like her for Philip's sake.

Having tidied her hair and changed her cotton voile blouse for an uncreased one, Ella was debating whether to go straight downstairs again to find her hostess when there was a tap at the door, which opened to reveal a maid in a blue print dress and white apron. 'Madam sent me to ask if I may unpack for you and iron out any creases in your clothes, Miss Morton,' the girl said in a small, shy voice, with a strong Mancunian accent. 'Is there anything else I can do for you – I dare say your shoes might need cleaning?'

Ella looked down at her neat black shoes adorned with a small velvet bow. They were new, having been bought only days earlier at Thierry's in Bold Street. They were also still both clean and dry since she had only taken a few steps between the cab and the front door on arrival in Manchester, and in Liverpool there had been no sign of snow. 'No, these are fine, thank you,' she said, hoping she was striking just the right note between mistress and maid.

She turned her foot to glance at the heel and the girl said admiringly, 'Them's the new Cuban heels, ain't they, miss? Oh, I do think they're smart!'

'Well, thank you,' Ella said, touched by the friendliness in the girl's tone. 'Oh, I never asked you your name.'

'I'm Myrtle, Miss Morton,' the girl said, 'and Mrs Grimshaw has told me to wait on you, so if there's anything you want, all you've got to do is pull that there bell and I'll come running.'

'Very well, Myrtle, I shan't forget,' Ella said bravely. 'And now if you wouldn't mind coming with me to the head of the stairs and pointing out the drawing room – if that's where I shall find Mrs Grimshaw – then I'll leave you to get on with your work.'

Myrtle, who could not have been many years younger than Ella herself, obligingly came halfway down the stairs with her, saying that Mrs Grimshaw would be in the morning room, where she had ordered coffee to be served. 'Young Mr Grimshaw is in there as well,' she said breathlessly, as she turned to retrace her steps. 'I've only worked for the family for eight weeks, so I've not met him before. Oh, miss, isn't he ...?' She clapped a hand to her mouth, a pink flush invading her face, but her eyes sparkled at Ella over her spread fingers.

Ella smiled, but had no opportunity to comment one way or the other since the door of the morning room flew open, revealing Philip, who glanced up at her, smiling. 'Ah, Ella, you're just in time for coffee and bourbon biscuits,' he said, crossing the hall to meet her as she descended the last stairs. 'And Laura will be joining us in a few minutes; she's run upstairs to change out of her street clothes.' He held out both hands and took Ella's in a warm grasp, and immediately the worry, which must have shown on Ella's face at the thought of meeting his beloved sister, faded from her mind. 'You're going to love one another, like two sisters,' he whispered as they entered the room together.

When Myrtle had helped her to get ready for bed that night and left her, at last, in her brightly lit room, with the fire blazing and a drink of hot milk on her bedside table, Ella was able to reflect on all that had passed. It had been a wonderful day, from the moment that Philip had picked her up in Huskisson Street to the present, sitting warm and comfortable in her beautiful bedroom and anticipating with real excitement the days still to come.

She had, as she had hoped, loved Laura almost as soon as she met her, partly because she was so very like Philip, with the same taffy-brown hair and matching eyes, although in Laura's case the hair had been elaborately curled and was tied back from her face with ribbon. She was about Ella's own height and had a good deal of self-confidence, although she

354

was not at all assertive. What was more, she was clearly determined to like Ella and had speedily dispensed with the title 'Miss Morton', and had begged Ella not to keep calling her Miss Grimshaw, either. 'For we are going to be great friends,' she had said gaily, slipping her arm round Ella's waist, as the two of them went to their rooms after luncheon to get ready for a shopping expedition.

After some earlier discussion, Laura had persuaded Ella that their shopping, if it was to be successful, had best be done that day. 'For tomorrow is Christmas Eve,' she had said, 'and the shops will be crowded with people searching for last-minute gifts. If we go immediately after luncheon, we should be home for tea. That will give you plenty of time to prepare for the family party this evening.' As they continued up the stairs, Laura turned to Ella once more and gave her a teasing glance, from her large, long-lashed eyes. 'And though I know we shall be friends, from what Philip tells me, I may yet be able to call you sister.' She smiled at Ella's astonished expression and gave the other girl a little shake. 'Silly! You must be as aware as I, that Philip would scarcely bring you home and introduce you to his family unless he was ... was serious about you. I do hope you are serious about him as well,' she added naively, 'because he's the nicest young man I know, even though I *am* prejudiced, he being my brother.'

'I like your brother very much,' Ella said rather stiffly, 'but this visit is by way of being a ... a sort of test. I'm working very hard to become an independent woman, someone who can look after herself and earn sufficient money to be comfortable, no matter

355

what may happen to me. I haven't seriously considered marriage . . .' She met Laura's quizzical eye and felt her cheeks grow hot. 'Well, I suppose everyone considers marriage but . . . but we aren't engaged or anything of that nature.'

They had reached Ella's bedroom door by this time. She opened it and would have gone into the room but Laura detained her, a hand on her arm. 'Philip told me that this was a sort of test as well,' she admitted. 'Oh, but Ella, I do so want it to be a success!' And with that she flitted down the corridor and disappeared into her own room.

Despite the slight feeling of embarrassment which Laura's assumption had caused her, Ella had still enjoyed the shopping expedition immensely. She had asked Laura which of her evening dresses she should wear that night and Laura had unhesitatingly picked out Ella's favourite, a lavender silk gown with a low-cut neck, a dark-purple velvet sash round the high waist and tiny, embroidered, laced sleeves. With this gown, Ella had intended to wear her white lace elbow-length gloves, but Laura had shaken her head.

'Lavender kid gloves,' she had said decisively. 'And I know where just such a pair may be purchased for a reasonable price. Bradshaw and Blackmore's are having a pre-Christmas sale. We can catch a tram and be there in ten minutes, and while we're there I'd like to look at some of the oriental trousers that the magazines have been raving about. Not that I would dream of wearing them,' she added. 'Particularly not this evening, since Grandma Grimshaw would probably have a heart attack if I wore anything so daring.'

The shopping expedition had gone off well. Ella

had purchased not only the gloves, but a pair of elegant high-heeled shoes, decorated with beading and embroidery, in a lovely shade of deep violet, which contrasted beautifully with the lavender gown. Laura, having examined with close interest the outrageous harem trousers and turbans on display, bought a boa made of white swansdown which would, she assured her new friend, go with everything she possessed. The two girls returned home and spent a great deal of time dressing for the evening. Although Mrs Grimshaw had said it was scarcely a party, Ella thought that she had been afraid of frightening her young guest; according to Laura it was to be a dinner party and the cousins would all be dressed in their best.

'And Emmeline Griffith is bound to come, since her parents live next door and are great friends of papa's,' Laura remarked.

She glanced sideways at Ella, clearly wondering whether to continue with what she had been about to say. Ella, who had bound a lavender chiffon scarf around her curls, and was rather doubtfully regarding the effect in her dressing-table mirror, raised her brows. 'Emmeline Griffith?'

'She ... she likes Philip,' Laura blurted, then looked conscience-stricken. 'He doesn't like her,' she added hastily. 'Oh, he thinks she's frightfully smart and terribly amusing, but he doesn't like her, not one bit.'

Now, taking a sip of her hot milk, Ella reflected that Miss Griffith most certainly *did* like Philip and had spared no pains to show him that she was available. She had also shown that as far as she was concerned Ella was a provincial nobody who had somehow managed to enter the Grimshaws'

357

charmed circle by a method she herself would never have needed to employ.

The dinner had gone well; Ella had been seated between Philip on her left and a young man called Davidson on her right, and had managed to conduct a reasonable conversation with both of them, despite Miss Griffith's constant calls on their attention, for she was seated on the opposite side of the table and had made eyes at Philip throughout the meal.

The part of the evening which had filled Ella with lively dismay in advance, however, proved to be far less of an ordeal than she had anticipated. Old Mrs Grimshaw was a tall, straight-backed octogenarian, with white hair piled up on her head in the Queen Alexandra style. She had glittering blue eyes, which Ella found focused upon herself disconcertingly often, and a clear, commanding voice that she used to good effect. After dinner Philip took Ella to the sofa upon which his grandmother was seated and, rather basely Ella felt, sat her down beside the old lady and went off to get them both a cup of coffee.

Mrs Grimshaw promptly began to reminisce about her own girlhood, which had been spent in Southport. 'For I was a Seymour before I married Mr Grimshaw,' she explained. 'We lived in a very fine house on Lord Street and had a great many friends among the neighbouring families and Southport was a whirl of gaiety in Victorian times. Not that we were allowed the licence you young people enjoy today,' she added, fixing Ella with her glittering eyes. 'Balls were private affairs, unless one went to a subscription ball, of course – they were a little more informal. Yet though we could not go out without a chaperone, we still managed to enjoy ourselves. And naturally we met the right people, not the wrong ones,' she finished, which Ella felt to be a remark directed at her.

'My own grandmother was born and bred in Southport, and married a Southport gentleman,' Ella said quietly. 'I imagine she must have had the same restrictions that you speak of, though she died when I was only two, so I never really knew her.'

'Oh, so you're a Southport gel,' Mrs Grimshaw said at once, her interest clearly aroused. 'What was the name again?'

'My mother was Henrietta Morton, but ...'

'Mortons? Never heard of them,' the old lady said decisively. 'Can't have moved in my circle.'

'No, that was my mother's married name,' Ella said, patiently. 'She married my father, Oswald Morton, when she was only nineteen. But before her marriage she was a Hillerman.'

The old lady, who had been eyeing the young people talking in a small group by the long dining table, abruptly turned towards Ella, seeming to lose interest in the conversation going on ahead of her. 'Not Rebecca Hillerman?' she said incredulously. 'She was my greatest friend. Why, even after we both married we remained on the very best of terms – I was godmother to her eldest daughter, Matilda.' She stared hard at Ella, the bright blue eyes unblinking. 'Now that I look at you closely, I declare I can see a resemblance to your dear grandmother. She had just those big, dark eyes and always with such a quizzical gleam when something amused her. Yes, there is a *marked* resemblance – and your grandmother was a great beauty in her time.'

The incident had set the seal on the evening and not only on the evening, Ella thought now, finishing her hot milk and climbing between the sheets, but on her whole visit. From the moment that old Mrs Grimshaw had begun to tell people how she and Ella's grandmother had been great friends, Ella felt herself accepted not only by the Grimshaws themselves, but by their numerous friends and relations. The fact that Ella was now a working girl, sharing a room with three others, no longer mattered; she was a Hillerman, the child of important and wealthy people, and in future would be accepted as such without question.

I'm not a snob, Ella told herself as she settled down to sleep. Everyone wants to be accepted for themselves, but I can't deny it's very comfortable to feel that my birth does mean something. Amy says she's proud of being a fisherman's daughter and so she should be, which means I can be proud of my connections, too.

There had only been one dissident voice when her connections in Southport had been discussed and unfortunately, perhaps, Ella had overheard it. Indeed, thinking back, she found herself torn between a desire to giggle and another to slap Emmeline Griffith's face.

Ella had been sitting with a group of Philip's cousins, half listening to their animated conversation, when her own name caught her ears. Without turning her head she promptly switched her attention to the young woman who had spoken, realising immediately that the soft, affected tones, belonged to Miss Griffith.

'Ella Morton?' the voice drawled, with an edge of dislike to it which was unmistakable, 'and the old lady recognised her you say? I think it likelier that she recognised the dress.'

For a moment Ella's cheeks had burned with

mortification, but then the funny side brought a smile to her lips. It was true that her dress had been remodelled from an old one belonging to her mother, but glancing towards Miss Griffith's rear view she reflected that anyone with a bottom which could be compared unfavourably with that of a carthorse was bound to make catty remarks about someone as slim as herself. What was more the bottom in question, being upholstered in red velvet, drew attention to its size; black would have been more sensible, Ella found herself thinking. Or even a nice dark green, but not, definitely not, scarlet velvet.

On that thought she fell happily asleep.

Ella spent the following day almost exclusively in Philip's company, though they returned to the house for tea at four. Laura had suggested accompanying them when Philip had said he meant to show Ella Manchester, but he had vetoed her suggestion on the grounds that she would want to go in and out of the department stores. There were a great many things besides shops that were worth visiting, he told his sister grandly: museums, art galleries and fine architecture for a start.

But in the event, Ella realised later, the day had been spent in getting to know one another and to appreciate each other's tastes. They visited the museums and found they both enjoyed browsing among the exhibits, and in the art gallery they both admired landscapes rather than portraits. They had lunch at Lyons Café on Victoria Street and then, rather to Ella's surprise, they did a good deal of window shopping, walking down a narrow little street in which there were a number of jewellery shops. Philip invented a game which consisted of his trying to guess which of the wonderful sparkling emerald, sapphire and diamond rings she would prefer. What was more, he scored high on her preferences, making her feel they had similar tastes in other matters than museums and galleries. Indeed, when she asked him why he did not consider rubies, he said at once that he thought them too flamboyant for her own particular style of beauty and had guessed that she would prefer sapphires or emeralds.

When they reached home it was to find the whole family, including Grandmama Grimshaw, seated around a roaring log fire in the drawing room, eating muffins and buttered toast, and drinking tea from delicate china cups.

The two of them sat down and enjoyed a hearty meal, for dinner would not be served until eight o'clock and so much walking had made Ella hungry as any hunter. Presently Philip excused himself on the grounds that he had some wrapping of presents to do in his room. Ella accepted this but suggested to Laura that they themselves might follow his example, since she had bought a few small presents that morning, which she had not yet wrapped or labelled. Standing up to leave the room, her eye was caught by a movement on the other side of the window glass and, to her surprise, she saw that it was Philip, coated and hatted, making his way down the steps and along the pavement. He had hunched his shoulders and sunk his head as low into his collar as he could, and Ella thought, with a pang of dismay, that he looked somehow furtive. She was forced to wonder whether he was off to visit an old friend and thought bitterly that if it was the horrible Emmeline Griffith, then he was welcome to her. She just hoped that Miss Griffith would show her true character by making some catty remark which would send Philip home disgusted with her. She half wished that she had told Philip what the older girl had said about her ball gown, then dismissed the idea. She was being as petty as Emmeline Griffith when she allowed herself to harbour such thoughts and anyway, it was far likelier that Philip had merely run out of paper or string and was going out to renew his supplies.

Being only human, however, Ella could not help thinking wistfully how nice it would have been to have Amy near at hand; for the past couple of years the two of them had discussed every aspect of their life and thoughts – and, indeed, their loves – with a frankness that would have astonished most of the people they knew. Now, in a strange house in a strange city, surrounded by people she had met for the first time the previous day, Ella knew once again the sharp pangs of loneliness which had assailed her when she had first come to Liverpool.

But Philip was her friend; he had brought her here and would make sure that she had a good Christmas, even if their relationship never became any closer than it was now.

Vaguely comforted by this thought, Ella continued to make her way up to her room.

It was a small house with a dusty track running along the front of it, dividing it from the river, which at this time of year was in full spate and noisy enough to keep Mary awake at night, although after the first day she was so tired that she could, she thought, have slept on a clothes line.

But hard though the work was, it was done with

such happiness and delighted anticipation that Mary would not have missed it for the world. What was more, she had been impressed by the small town of Mold, set in a cup in the hills which reared around it like inverted green pudding basins; these were not the mountains of Wales but the gentle foothills, grazed by placid sheep and bedecked on their lower slopes by mixed woodland. Mary, who had only known the Liverpool area and the great city of Manchester, thought she had never seen country so beautiful.

She and Haydn had returned to the small market town on the day before Christmas Eve and had spent the intervening time preparing for the Christmas holiday. The children were wildly excited and welcomed Mary with simple delight because she was their father's friend. They clearly wanted this beautiful golden girl to be their friend also and hung around her, asking questions, telling her of their lives, their school, their friends. Old Mrs Lloyd was equally delighted with her, particularly when she found that Mary meant to take full part in all the work of Christmas, as well as the festivities. Indeed, while they were washing up the dishes on that first evening, she had told Mary that much though she loved her grandsons, she was 'beginning to be too old to handle them, good though they were'.

When Haydn and Mary had arrived in Mold, the children and old Mrs Lloyd had been settled round the kitchen table with pots of flour-and-water paste, and strips of previously painted newspaper. Under their grandmother's tuition and with Mary's help, the strips had been made into garlands, which Haydn pinned to the picture rails, festooning the room. The boys, Emrys and Geraint, were five and six, attractive, rosy-faced children with identical round, dark-brown eyes, straight fringes of equally dark hair falling across their foreheads and sturdy young bodies. Because Emrys was tall for his age and Geraint rather shorter, Mary could scarcely tell them apart, but she realised that this was only because she did not yet know them very well. They both spoke Welsh as their first language – as, indeed, did Haydn and his mother – but they spoke English at school and courteously tried to speak it whenever they were in Mary's company. Geraint was fluent, Emrys slightly less so, but Haydn said that the English of both boys would improve over Christmas and since they must speak English in school this was a good thing.

The two small boys had been out in the woods the previous day, and had cut festive greenery and a good clump of mistletoe to decorate the house. Now, the brilliant holly and ivy were wreathed around pictures and door frames, while the mistletoe was tacked to the kitchen ceiling. Haydn kissed all his family beneath it and, when the children were in bed and his mother snoozing before the fire, he kissed Mary, too, with a gentleness which touched her heart.

Preparations for the Christmas feast were already well advanced by Christmas Eve. Mrs Lloyd had baked mince pies, sugar cakes and an apple tart. The Christmas pudding, ceremoniously stirred by one and all and wrapped in its white linen cloth, had been boiled for hours, so that on the following day only a further hour's cooking would see it ready for the table. The cockerel, which was to be the focus of the meal, had spent a year in a smallish run in the back garden, being fattened on grain gleaned from the fields, dandelion leaves from the hedgerows which the boys collected on their way home from school, and any leftover scraps from the Lloyds' table. Mary was grateful that the bird had been slain before her arrival, for she gathered that every year the little boys grew fond of their forthcoming meal and shed bitter tears over his demise.

'It was not as if it was a friendly bird,' Mrs Lloyd had grumbled to Mary in her stilted English. 'Take your finger off soon as look at you, if you poked it through the wire netting. But the boys dug worms for it and thought of it as a pet, so I got Mr Evans from up the road to wring its neck while they was in school; that way, the loss wasn't so personal, like.'

Mrs Lloyd had confided this news to Mary on her first night in Mold, when the two of them were sharing Mrs Lloyd's bed in the tiny room under the eaves. Haydn and the boys slept in the slightly larger room, but Mary, who had made such a fuss about sleeping with her own sisters, was happy to share with Haydn's mother. She would have been happy, she reflected, to sleep on the living room floor if it meant that she could become a part of this poor but happy family.

That night, before they went off to bed, the children had hung their stockings from the mantel-piece and had urged their father anxiously to make sure the fire was truly dead so that Father Christmas, in his descent down the chimney, did not set his boots or beard on fire. Mary did not think that either child truly expected the stockings to be bulging with presents next day, for they admitted that such a thing had never happened at Christmas before. There had been an orange one year and a tin whistle each, but not a great many gifts. This year, however, she and Haydn had worked hard either to make or to buy small gifts for the boys, and Mary found herself eagerly anticipating their pleasure on the morrow. There would be nothing expensive, of course, but she had got Albert to whittle her a couple of toy railway engines and had herself painted one green and one scarlet, so that each child would know his own. She had made toffee and coconut ice in the kitchen of a friend and had wrapped them enticingly, and she knew Haydn had visited the penny bazaar whenever he had money to spare. One way and another, therefore, this should be a good Christmas.

When planning for the holiday she had taken Haydn's advice and had bought Mrs Lloyd several skeins of wool; his mother, Haydn told her, was a great knitter and made all her own shawls, stockings and gloves. For Haydn himself Mary had bought two ounces of pipe tobacco and a clay pipe with a curly stem. She knew he liked to smoke occasionally, but seldom did so since tobacco was so expensive.

The fire was now beginning to die down and Haydn was carefully spreading the ash, so that it would be completely out by morning. The boys' stockings hung on either side of the fireplace, satisfyingly bulky, and in one corner of the large living kitchen a small Christmas tree stood in its pot, its branches hung with paper ornaments, tinsel and a few home-made crackers. The boys, who had made the crackers in school and therefore must know the contents, were still as excited as though they were a complete novelty and were already arguing over who should have first pick when the great day arrived.

'I think everything's ready,' Haydn said at last,

looking round the kitchen. Every surface gleamed and the lamplight reflected off the newly white-washed walls, and cast into strong relief the bunches of holly and ivy, and the mistletoe on the ceiling.

Mrs Lloyd had gone to bed an hour previously, so that she and Mary were not trying to undress at the same time in such cramped conditions, and after a last glance around her Mary stood up. 'Well, I'd best be off to bed myself, because tomorrow's going to be pretty busy,' she observed. 'If we take the bird down to the baker for cooking and then go to church, do you think it will be ready by the time the service is over?' She did not add, as she had been half tempted to do, that it might seem better if she were to stay at home and keep an eye on things, for the service would be in Welsh and would mean perhaps an hour, but probably longer, of extreme boredom, while the parson rabbited on and the congregation eyed this stranger among them with curiosity, if not antagonism. But she had realised that staying away from the service would lead to awkward questions, and for Haydn's sake she wanted the day to be one of complete pleasure, so she had agreed to attend.

Haydn put his head on one side and grinned at her. 'Cooked it will be in that time and probably overcooked,' he said wryly. 'You can't stop a Welshman from preaching, cariad, especially on Christmas Day. But never fear, Roasty Jones knows all about Christmas services and all about sermons as well. He'll put everyone's bird in at the same time – and there'll be a good few of 'em, so I tell you. That way they cooks slower . . .' he smacked his lips. '. . . but taste better,' he finished.

'Right you are, then,' Mary said.

She was turning towards the stairs when Haydn

caught hold of her arms and swung her to face him. 'You're a good girl, Mary,' he said. 'This Christmas would have been nothing but hard work and sad thoughts of past Christmases if it hadn't been for you. But I want you to know, my lovely girl, that it isn't of my dear Rhiannon that I've been thinking these past couple of days. I loved her very much, but she died soon after Emrys's birth, and now I've done with grieving and can turn back to making a life for myself and the boys. And ... well, and ...' He glanced up at the ceiling and Mary followed his eyes. They were standing directly beneath the bunch of mistletoe. 'Mary, fach, you're the sweetest person, the best thing that's happened in my life for several years,' he said softly, then turned slightly to look towards the clock on the mantel; it was a few minutes past midnight. 'Happy Christmas, cariad, and I pray to God we'll share more of 'em.'

This time the kiss was neither soft nor gentle, but held all the hunger and longing a passionate man feels for the woman of his choice. All in a moment Mary knew that he loved her and that she loved him, too. She returned the embrace with a fervour which astonished her, and as his strong arms closed round her the strangest thought entered her head. I need never be alone again, the thought ran – yet Mary had never thought of herself as lonely until this moment of wonderful shared warmth and affection.

'Mary? Do you ...? Can you ...? I know I'm a pretty ordinary sort of feller and you're a real little beauty, but I swear to you, you'll want for nothing I can provide, if only ... if only ...'

Mary moved back from him a little and then, taking his face between her hands, she studied it for several breathless seconds. He was right, he was a pretty ordinary sort of fellow and the only life he could offer her was likely to be a hard one, with a family to provide for before the banns were even called and an old mother dependent on him. Was she really considering marriage with him? Why, he was . . .

Slowly, with half-shut eyes, her mouth went to meet his and Haydn prolonged the kiss, stroking her back in comforting circles as though she had been a child. By the time she opened her eyes again and broke free of him, she knew that she would never see him as plain, let alone ordinary, again. He was her man, the one person in the world she thought she could never live without, and the fact that he came complete with responsibilities . . . well, what did that matter? What mattered most was that they loved one another.

'Mary? Oh, cariad, I want you . . . but properly, in marriage, not . . .'

'Dear Haydn,' Mary whispered, clinging. 'Oh, darling Haydn! Of course I'll marry you and as soon as you like.'

Haydn began to smile. He put both arms round her and lifted her off her feet, giving a subdued cheer as he did so. 'Oh, my lovely girl! What a Christmas this will be!'

'Amy! It's morning and you said when morning came . . . oh, Amy, *do* wake up!'

Amy struggled out of a deep and satisfying sleep to find something – or someone – sitting on her stomach while a voice, all the more imperative because it was whispering, bade her to 'wake up . . . you *promised*, so you did! As soon as it's morning, you said . . .'

Amy heaved up her middle to form a bridge and Becky, for it was undoubtedly she, rolled off her sister and landed with a plop on the cold linoleum. She also giggled, but then repeated obstinately, 'But you did promise, Amy, you know you did! As soon as it's day, you said, and there's light out there, I can see clouds ... oh, dear Amy, *do* wake up!'

From the far side of the bed, against the wall, another voice added itself to the monologue. 'For God's sweet sake tell that kid to shurrup and go back to sleep. It's the middle of the bleedin' night,' Minnie said in a sleep-blurred voice. 'Becky, if you want my present when it's really daytime then you'll shurrup now, like I said, and let honest folk sleep. Remember, your sister and meself didn't get home till gone ten, what wi' one thing and another.'

'Oh! But Minnie, there's day on t'other side o' the curtains, honest to God there is! Wait, I'll go and pull 'em back so's you can see.'

There was a brief struggle, then thin grey light invaded the room. Amy groaned and sat up. 'Look, Becky, any fool could tell you that it isn't daylight at all, it's just ... just that an overcast sky ... if I let you open one present now, will you go back to sleep until it really is morning? It gets properly light at about eight o'clock I suppose, so ...'

'Eight o'clock! But how can I open a present now, Amy? Me stockin' is downstairs, hung by the fire so's Father Christmas would find it as soon as he slid down the chimbley. I suppose I could go down on tiptoes, but like as not ...'

'If you go over to the washstand you'll see my spongebag on the window side. Open that and you'll find a little parcel ... wait, best light the candle or you won't know what you've got. Oh,

371

what a pest you are, Becky Logan!' Amy sat up in bed and reaching for the matches, lit the candle. By its light Becky ran across to the washstand, fumbled in her sister's spongebag, and presently returned to the bedside with a small parcel in one hand and an expression of great delight written large on her small fair face.

She struggled a moment with paper and string, then let out a squeak. 'Oh, Amy, you are kind to me! What a pretty, fat little dolly; I have never seen one like it! And it's so brightly painted ... I must not call you "it", though, my pretty darling. You shall be called Mabel, which is quite my favourite name at present.'

'If you unscrew Mabel, you may get a surprise,' Amy said, as her small sister squiggled back into bed and began to admire her present. 'Look!'

And presently she revealed that the fat little wooden doll contained another one, which in its turn contained yet another, until a whole line of fat little wooden dolls were ranged on the counterpane, while Becky squeaked with delight and excitement, and tried to name each doll as it emerged.

'Where on earth did you get them?' Minnie asked presently, thoroughly roused by the unfolding drama of the Russian dolls. 'I can't recall ever seeing anything like that – how pretty they are. It's enough to make you wish you was a kid again yourself!'

'A guest at the hotel showed me one ... oh, several months ago,' Amy told her friend. 'I asked him if he could possibly get me one for my little sister if I gave him the money and a few weeks ago he came back, complete with the Russian doll. Well, chuck,' she added, addressing her sister, 'I'm glad you like your present, but Minnie and me's still worn out, so you can just do as you promised and go back to sleep until daylight.'

'I don't mind at all ... I'll just fit the dolls back together again first, though,' Becky said, suiting action to words. 'Thank you *ever* so much, Amy – I do love you!'

Paddy was down before the rest of the family, helping Suzie to prepare breakfast. Because it was Christmas Day and the main meal would be eaten after they returned from morning service, Suzie usually did a simple breakfast – buttered toast for the females of the family and bacon sandwiches for the men, and today was no exception. Paddy sat before a blazing fire with a slice of bread on the end of a toasting fork held out to the flames, and as each slice cooked it was added to the pile on the plate which stood to one side of the fireplace.

Despite the dullness of the job, Paddy was secretly very excited, more excited than he had been over Christmas for many a long year. About a week earlier Amy had brought her friend, who was to spend Christmas with them, home for tea to meet the rest of the family. Paddy had braced himself to greet Philip with a warmth that he was far from feeling and was delighted to meet Minnie, especially when the girls, in conversation, revealed that Ella Morton was spending Christmas in Manchester with Philip Grimshaw.

At the time, Paddy had continued stolidly eating his tea and had not even looked up from his plate, though he had felt a little rush of excitement at the news. Later, however, when the girls had gone back to the city centre, he had questioned Suzie closely and had learned that Philip and Ella had been going about together ever since Ella's emergence from hospital. So I was wrong, Paddy told himself gleefully; Amy's still fancy free – or at least, if she's got a feller she's keeping him pretty dark. He remembered vaguely that there had been talk at one time of Amy going about with a friend of Philip's, but it had clearly come to nothing. And Christmas is a romantic time, Paddy had told himself, as he slogged up from the beach with his share of the latest catch. Surely I can do something over Christmas to make her think of me as a friend, if nothing warmer?

After much thought in a similar vein, Paddy decided that he would buy her a present and it would be one which would show in some way that he admired her and wanted, once and for all, to forget their past differences. He began to haunt the shops, department stores and markets around Bold Street, Church Street and Renshaw Street, looking for something – anything – which Amy would really like. He was beginning to despair, to think that there was no such gift in the world, when he happened upon a tiny, narrow shop, squeezed between two very much larger ones, in Upper Parliament Street. The word 'Curios' had been painted in wobbly white letters at the top of the small window, which was crammed with a wide variety of strange objects all, at first glance, of an oriental nature. Paddy stood before the display, totally fascinated. Richly caparisoned ebony elephants jostled with striped and snarling tigers, ivory warriors and tiny, delicate porcelain cups and saucers, eggshell thin. As Paddy stared a thin, yellow hand, with long, curved nails came into the window space and sought out a tiny porcelain half eggshell, in which lay a beautifully carved naked baby, complete to the last detail. Paddy took a deep breath, squared his shoulders and pushed the creaking door wide. Inside an ancient Chinese, with his hair in the traditional pigtail, was showing a young seaman the child in the egg and extolling its virtues in a cracked but musical voice. His English, to Paddy's secret amusement, was the English of the Liverpool docks, but he supposed that if the old fellow had been living here for many years a Liverpool accent would have come more naturally to him than standard English, or even the pidgin English spoken by so many of the Chinese seamen.

While the two at the counter argued amicably over the worth of the tiny object cupped in the Chinaman's hand, Paddy took a thorough look around. There were so many beautiful things here. He guessed they must all be expensive and also that a good many of them were old, and he also thought that any woman would be enchanted by the majority of the objects on display. He was contemplating a tray upon which lay quantities of ivory carvings, when his eye was caught by a flash of green in a display cabinet, just behind the old man's silk-clad shoulder. Paddy moved a little further along the counter, the better to see what had caught his eye and was immediately enchanted. The cabinet was filled with jade carvings; a tiny frog, jewel-bright, perched on a jade lily pad, an imposing stork, every feather delicately carved, stared malevolently down at the frog and lizards, fish and even tiny figurines, were displayed on the shelves. He was about to turn back to the counter once more, where the seaman had clearly completed his transaction, when he noticed that above the figurines hung a slender gold chain, upon which there were suspended, at regular intervals, droplets of jade. The droplets were minute by the clasp of the necklace, but grew in size until the one at the apex was the size of a little fingernail, and the whole thing was so delicately beautiful that he longed to hold it in his hand, if only for a moment. What was more, he knew without a shadow of doubt that the necklace would look wonderful round Amy's slender white throat. The jade would match the colour of those strange but brilliant eyes and the gold would echo the red-gold of her piled-up hair.

Even as Paddy turned towards the old Chinaman to ask the price of the necklace, the man had forestalled him. He produced a little key from a bunch which jangled at his waist and unlocked the cabinet door, throwing it wide and saying, in his high, cracked old voice, 'The gentleman wishes to admire my jade? What has caught your honour's fancy?'

'Oh! Oh ... er ... the necklace,' Paddy said, almost gasping in his eagerness. 'Can I just take a look at it?'

The Chinaman took the necklace reverently from its place and draped it across Paddy's hand. Seen close to, it was even lovelier than it had been in the showcase – and even more expensive, Paddy thought despairingly. Nevertheless, he knew that it was the very thing for Amy and he had been saving up, after all. 'How much?' he asked boldly. He knew that haggling was a way of life for the Chinese but suspected that he would be no good at it, still ...

'The chain is pure gold and the jade is old, very old,' the man said, naming a figure which made Paddy gasp. It was not that it was so expensive;

indeed, he thought it was probably quite reasonable, but it was more than he had ever spent on a present for anyone, even his mother. If he bought it at the asking price it would reduce his savings considerably. Quickly, before he lost courage, he suggested tentatively that the man might like to accept half the figure named, and after a good deal of wrangling they settled on a sum which Paddy felt he could just about afford. He fished out his money, carefully counted out the required amount and took the small white box which the Chinaman handed to him. Turning to leave the shop, he thought ruefully that the rest of the family would have to make do with inferior offerings this year. But there was no denying it, he had found the perfect present for difficult, disagreeable, adorable Amy Logan.

Paddy was brought abruptly back to the present when the slice of bread on his toasting fork burst into flame. The heat of it travelled along the fork, causing him to fling both toast and implement down on the floor, where he trampled it into Suzie's rag rug, causing his mother to give an indignant shriek.

'There now, Paddy Keagan, look what you've done to me lovely rag rug, let alone that piece of toast,' Suzie said, bringing a brush and dustpan across to sweep up the embers of both toast and rug. 'That's what comes of dreamin' when you should be concentratin'. And what's more, you've toasted enough bread for an army, so leave off and start butterin'.' Paddy, considerably chastened, did so and presently the family began to gather round the kitchen table, wishing each other the compliments of the season and eyeing the small pile of presents beneath the Christmas tree, which would be opened when they got back from church. Becky had come down for her stocking as soon as it was light, but the rest of them had to wait until later in the morning. It was a ritual with the Logan family to open their presents then, so Paddy, who was desperate to see Amy's reaction to his own gift, would have to wait, as everyone else did.

'It was a nice service, wasn't it?' Amy said to Minnie, as the two girls followed the rest of the family out of St Thomas's. 'But listening to the sermon and singing all those carols has given me a good appetite. Dad bought a goose from one of the stalls in St John's Market and Suzie took it down to the baker's early, so as to have it ready for one o'clock; that'll just give us time to open the presents before we eat.'

No one ever spent much on Christmas presents for adults, though they tried to make sure that children had as good a time as they could afford. Minnie had bought token presents for Bill and Suzie – pipe tobacco and chocolates – but had not attempted to buy for the boys, or for Charlie's new wife, a pleasant girl called Lottie, who was already six months gone with child. Amy herself had bought mufflers for her brothers, a pair of silk stockings for Suzie and a pile of little gifts for Becky, and she and Minnie had agreed not to exchange presents this year. Amy knew that Suzie and Bill were going to give Minnie two handkerchiefs and a bag of peppermints and guessed she herself would receive something similar from her father and stepmother. So it was without any particular excitement that she joined the family around the tree to open her presents.

Charlie and his wife opened their gifts first, as did

Gus, and then the three of them went off to the baker's to fetch back the goose while the rest unwrapped their packets and parcels. Amy, seeing the small white box with her name written neatly on the lid, picked it up and glanced thoughtfully around her; surely she had opened all the presents from her family? Who could this be from? There was only her own name upon the lid, but then it was a small box with little room for anything else.

The box was fastened with string and red sealing wax. Amy undid it and lifted the lid, then gave a gasp of pure delight. Reverently, she lifted the jade and gold necklace out of its bed of cotton wool and held it up so that it sparkled in the thin sunlight slanting through the window. 'Look!' she said, her voice clear and yet hushed. 'Oh, look at this! Isn't it just the most beautiful thing you've ever seen? But who ... ?'

For a moment there was total silence. Everyone stared at the delicate necklace swinging from Amy's forefinger and nobody spoke. Then Paddy cleared his throat. 'I gorrit in a curio shop on Upper Parly,' he said gruffly. 'I thought ... I thought it 'ud suit you.' Amy's eyes travelled doubtfully from the necklace to Paddy's face and then back to the necklace. For once in her life, perhaps for the first time, she found herself completely bereft of words. From anyone else, from any one of her brothers or friends, she would have greeted the gift with the pleasure it deserved, but coming from Paddy, who had always hated her ... or had he? For the first time it occurred to her that on several occasions lately, when he could have been rude or dismissive, he had been polite, almost friendly. She seemed to remember that at some point over the past few months he had more or less said they ought to forget the old antagonism and try, at least on the surface, to behave like civilised, rational people. He had not used those very words, of course, they were probably not part of Paddy's vocabulary, but that was what he had meant.

She looked up at Paddy through her lashes, realising abruptly that the silence had stretched for too long; if she did not speak soon ... 'You really shouldn't have, Paddy,' she said stiffly, trying to meet his eye, but he would not look at her, watching the necklace as it hung from her fingers with an intensity which she found more embarrassing than a glance exchange between them. 'It's the most beautiful thing I've ever seen, but it must have cost a great deal and ... I ... I shouldn't accept it from you.'

Paddy looked up at her; it was difficult to read the expression in his dark eyes, but at least he met her own as she made an attempt at a friendly smile. 'Are you sayin' you won't take it?' Paddy asked baldly. 'Are you sayin' I ain't even good enough to give you something pretty, as a Christmas present?'

Amy was still searching for a reply which would enable her to give back the gift without appearing downright hateful, when Bill spoke. 'Of course she ain't sayin' any such thing,' he said gruffly, 'no daughter of mine would be so bleedin' rude, let alone ungrateful.' He turned to Amy. 'Why, queen, next thing we know you'll be askin' young Becky for the money for them Russian dolls you give her this morning. Or offerin' to pay me so much a pound for the spuds what I grew for Christmas dinner.'

The rebuke, though thoroughly deserved, brought the hot colour flooding to Amy's cheeks. She clutched the necklace, crumpling it into the palm of her hand, suddenly wanting to hurl it in Paddy's face and walk out of the cottage for ever, never to return. It was all his fault! He had made her look a mean, ungracious beast, which was no doubt what he had intended. She had been right to hate him, he had always been against her and now he meant to turn the rest of the family against her, too. However, unless she kept her thoughts to herself she would ruin Christmas Day for everyone and she did not intend to do that. Slowly she released the necklace from a grip so tight that the gold chain had scored deep into the palm of her left hand. She glanced around the ring of faces; everyone except Paddy was staring at her with an expression of mixed shock and disappointment. Poor Minnie, who knew nothing of Amy's past suffering at Paddy's hands, was clearly horrified by her friend's strange and ungracious behaviour. It occurred suddenly to Amy that Minnie might not know that she and Paddy were step-brother and stepsister; certainly, she would be completely ignorant of their childhood antagonism.

Slowly and fumblingly, Amy put the necklace round her throat and tried to fasten the little gold clasp, but it was tiny and she could not quite manage it. For a moment she continued to struggle then looked across at Paddy. He was staring straight at her, round dark eyes eager, his mouth opening to form words. 'Can I ... shall I ... ?'

'Yes, please, Paddy, if you would be so kind,' Amy said, trying to make her voice sound friendly. 'I'm sorry I was so rude ... I didn't think ... I didn't realise ... it's just that it's so beautiful and must have been such a price ... would you do it up for me, please.'

She bent her head forward meekly and felt

Paddy's fingers against the nape of her neck. She was aware, as his fingers touched her skin, of a strange sensation in the pit of her stomach and knew, irritatingly, that she was blushing. Looking round beneath her long lashes, she saw the relief which swept like a tide across the faces, watched smiles come back as people turned towards one another and began to talk. The tension, which had been almost visible, had drained away and everyone was at ease once more. Except for me, Amy thought bitterly. I'm the only one who knows, bleedin' Paddy never does anything, except for his own ends. Well, I'll have to wear the necklace for today, but first thing tomorrow ... no, the next day, we'll still be here tomorrow ... I'll hand it to the first beggar I see.

The rest of the day passed very pleasantly. Amy and Minnie made an excuse in the afternoon to go out, and because Amy was well aware that no shops would be open for miles around she took Minnie round to Ruthie's house. Her friend was delighted to see them and asked them in, but went into a fit of the giggles when Amy explained her errand. 'Paddy Keagan gave you that beautiful necklace?' she gasped. 'And you come round here so as I can hand back the bag of bull's-eyes you give me for me little brothers and sisters? You've gorra be mad, chuck, they were ate afore breakfast. Still an' all, you're welcome to a box of chocolates what were give me – there's only two been took out.'

Despite herself, Amy giggled. 'No, but there must be *something* I can give him,' she said desperately, glancing around the room as though she expected a row of gift-wrapped parcels on every surface. 'Did anyone give your dad pipe tobacco? Or ... or thick woollen socks?'

Ruthie's dad, a large, red-faced man with a shock of grey hair, was sitting by the fire, toasting a round of bread, but he turned at Amy's words, grinning broadly. 'Why not give him a lock of your 'air, chuck?' he said. 'Or what about a pair of your frilly drawers? Reckon he'd value them!'

'Don't be so vulgar, our dad,' Ruthie said reprovingly, though she was still smiling. 'Don't you think it looks kind o' worse to give him a last-minute gift, like? He's bound to guess you didn't buy him nothin' – and why should you? He's never given you anything but hard words, as I recall.'

This downright partisanship made Amy feel a good deal better, though she voiced her earlier thought to the assembled company that, once back in Liverpool, she would give the bleedin' necklace to the first beggar she saw.

She also agreed with both girls – for Minnie had backed Ruthie up – that perhaps it was best to accept Paddy's gift gracefully for the time being and not try to return it. 'But I'll knit him a perishin' muffler, so's he can wrap it round his perishin' gob or tie it round his perishin' throttle,' she said crossly as she and Minnie made their way back to the house in Seafield Grove. 'If it's around his gob, p'raps he won't speak to me, and if he ties it tight enough ...'

'You are a horrible person, Amy Logan,' Minnie said, but she was smiling. 'Can't you see the feller likes you?'

Amy snorted. 'Like fun he does!' she said scornfully. 'He just wanted to show me up and he certainly did that.'

During the walk home, however, Minnie made

her point a little more forcibly. 'You want to use your eyes, queen,' she said earnestly. 'You should have seen the look on Paddy's face while you were unwrapping his present. He looked like little kids look on Christmas Day – all lit-up and excited, as though they expect something wonderful to happen. He bought that necklace to please you – it must have cost him a deal of money – and instead of throwing your arms round his neck and givin' him a big kiss, you looked like someone who's bit into a cream bun and found the cream's gone sour on you.'

'I didn't,' Amy said, half laughing, half horrified. 'I thought I'd put on a jolly good act ... but Minnie, he's never liked me I tell you. I can't understand why he bought the necklace in the first place, unless he meant it for some other girl who's been and gone and let him down.'

'Amy Logan, you're an ungrateful girl and don't deserve to have any beaux at all,' Minnie said roundly. 'Why do you think he bought jade, eh? It's 'cos you've got green eyes, that's why! Now how many girls around here do you know with green eyes?'

'I don't know any, but Paddy may know a dozen for all I know,' Amy pointed out. 'Oh, do leave off, Minnie, because even if Paddy can change his feelings overnight, I don't know that I can. Now, let's talk about something else if you please.'

But though Minnie's efforts at matchmaking appeared to be unsuccessful, they had made Amy think and by the time they reached Seafield Grove she was beginning to admit to herself that she could have been wrong. Paddy could have bought the necklace especially for her and it could be the first sign of a thaw in their previously frosty relationship.

Feeling strangely light-hearted at the thought, Amy ushered her friend into the warmth and brightness of the kitchen, and began to help Suzie to prepare the meal.

When they had finished tea and washed up, the furniture was pushed back and the kitchen table was carried into the scullery to give more room. The house had been converted, at Bill's request, by their landlord many years earlier. They had knocked down a wall, losing the parlour but gaining a double-sized kitchen, which the family much preferred. Albert had gone up to Ruth's to spend the evening with the Durrants but neighbours from the surrounding houses came in and a great many games were played in the Logans' large kitchen. Blind Man's Buff, charades, and Oranges and Lemons all proved great favourites, and when they were exhausted and seated themselves around the room on chairs, cushions and even upturned fishboxes, Paddy produced his mouth organ and played carols and popular songs – 'I'm Twenty-one Today' and various other hits. When he struck up 'Has Anybody Here Seen Kelly', Minnie jumped to her feet, grabbed Amy's hands and, whirling into the centre of the room, began a spirited polka. They were speedily followed on to the floor by other couples; Bill leading Becky round with great verve, while Gus danced with Suzie. In fact, they might have danced all night, had it not been for Paddy running out of breath and insisting that someone else should take over. Gus, who was quite good on the penny whistle, started to try to play the mouth organ, but threw it back to Paddy complaining that it was full of spit, which made everyone laugh.

Jim Price, from next door but one, nipped home

for a moment and came back, carrying a fiddle. He began to play *'Shine on Harvest Moon'* and Lottie melted into Charlie's arms and immediately began to dance, speedily followed by most of the younger members of the assembled company. Amy was about to suggest that she and Minnie should take to the floor when Gus unceremoniously seized both Minnie's hands and pulled her into the dance. Minnie was a tall girl, of Junoesque build, and now it occurred to Amy what a nice couple she and Gus made, with Gus's fair hair only overtopping Minnie's gleaming dark locks by a couple of inches.

She was still standing on the sidelines, laughing and clapping in time to the music, when someone caught her hands. 'Dance?' Paddy asked gruffly.

For a moment Amy felt all the old familiar irritation rising up in her; then she remembered the necklace. Damn, damn, damn, she thought furiously, allowing him to lead her on to the floor. I can't very well refuse to dance with him, having accepted his present. Oh, why did it have to happen? Why didn't I buy him something really small and mean, then I wouldn't have to feel beholden?

Jim Price was revealing a rare talent with the fiddle, playing the beautiful music so softly and seductively that Amy, who had intended to dance as stiffly as any poker, found herself relaxing into Paddy's embrace, following his lead as though they had danced with one another all their lives and almost – only almost – she found she was enjoying herself. When Jim Price slid into another tune, which she recognised, though could not immediately put a name to, she made no effort to free herself from Paddy's arms but continued to dance. Paddy held her lightly but firmly, his head a little bent, and though she kept her eyes averted from his she knew that he was looking at her face. Presently, almost absent-mindedly, he began to sing along to the music, in a soft, but rather pleasant tenor voice. '*I wonder who's kissing her now?*' he sang, '*I wonder who's teaching her how? I wonder who's looking into her eyes, sighing sighs, telling lies? I wonder if she has a boy? That girl who once filled me with joy. I wonder if she ever tells him of me? I wonder who's kissing her now.*'

As the tune ended, Amy tried to pull herself away from Paddy, suddenly aware of a rush of the strangest feelings; sensations so strange that they made her want to stay where she was within the circle of his arm. It's just the music, she told herself wildly, and the fact that he's a feller and dances better than anyone else I know. I still hate him, I do, I do! Only it's Christmas and the necklace is beautiful, and he's got a lovely singing voice and ... and ...

Jimmy Price was beginning to play again; this time Amy recognised it at once as '*Alexander's Ragtime Band*'. Paddy tried to continue holding her, one arm firmly round her waist, his left hand grasping Amy's right, but she pulled away, saying half jokingly, 'I mustn't be selfish, Paddy; give someone else a chance – why not have a whirl with Jimmy's sister Hettie for a change?'

Paddy said nothing, but he released Amy, who scuttled across the floor and into the scullery, where Suzie was setting out cups and plates, and putting round mince pies and slices of cold pudding. 'Let me give you a hand,' Amy said rather breathlessly, going over to the draining board where a number of cups stood ready for filling. She pressed her hands to her hot face, pushing damp locks of hair off her brow. 'Gracious, it's warm in here! We ought to open the back door, let some air in.'

'Oh, folk will be goin' home soon,' Suzie said easily. She hefted an enormous tin teapot, which one of the guests had lent them, and began to pour tea into the waiting cups. 'Your pal Minnie is gerrin' on awful well with our Gus. It's about time that young feller found hisself another girl, though he's been shy of trying his hand ever since that horrible Peggy Higgins behaved so badly last summer.' She turned to refill the teapot and gave Amy a shrewd glance. 'Saw you dancin' with our Paddy just now,' she observed, her eyes flicking all over Amy's flushed face. 'Enjoy it, didja? He's a good dancer, is our Paddy, got natural rhythm like his mam. You made a fine couple, danced as if you'd knowed each other all your lives.' She guffawed, clapping a hand to her mouth. 'Wharra fool I am – you *have* known each other all your lives, of course. You could ha' been brother and sister – you certainly fought like cat and dog when you was younger.' Eyes suddenly sly, she glanced across at Amy under her lashes. 'There weren't never no love lost atwixt the pair of you, so it seems strange to see you dancin' together.'

Amy, putting the filled cups and saucers on to a battered tin tray, ignored the remark. Indeed, her own feelings were far too complex and confused for her to want to discuss Paddy with anyone, let alone his mother. And presently, when the guests had eaten their cold supper and were beginning to depart, Amy picked Becky up from the chair in which she was slumbering and set off for the stairs, observing to Minnie that it was high time they were all in bed.

She had only reached the second stair, however,

when Paddy caught her arm. 'Aren't you going to say goodnight to your dancin' partner?' he said, his voice teasing but his eyes serious. 'I can't offer to walk you home like I would after an ordinary dance, but I'll carry Becky for you if you like.'

'It's all right, thanks,' Amy said rather breathlessly. She told herself it was the weight of the child which was affecting her breathing, but had a shrewd suspicion that Paddy's nearness and the hand on her wrist also had something to do with it. 'If you take her she'll wake and start grizzling, but thanks all the same, Paddy.'

Paddy grinned at her and rumpled her curls with one large hand, then slid the hand down under her chin, tilting her face up to his. Amy's heart began to pound as his face got nearer, but then a voice spoke from behind them. 'Gerrup them stairs, you daft girl, 'cos if I doesn't get to bed soon I'll sleep the clock round. If you're goin' up, Paddy, then pass the girl. Carting that great Becky, she'll be slow as a snail and I want me bed.'

It was Albert, grinning all over his face and beginning to push his way past Paddy. Not knowing whether to be glad or sorry Amy, with her heavy burden, hurried up the stairs and joined Minnie in their room. *Had* Paddy been going to kiss her? It was probably as well that Albert had come upon them before she had been forced to snub Paddy yet again. Whether or not she would actually have done so she did not honestly know, but was glad – or told herself she was glad – not to have been put to the test.

She began to get Becky ready for bed as Minnie said, sighing blissfully, 'It's been a grand day. I do like your brother Gus, Amy, he were ever so kind to me, got me supper, danced wi' me ... he even suggested we might take a walk in the moonlight on the beach aways, only when I peeked out through the door it were rainin'. Still, there's always tomorrow.'

Amy was pleased, she told herself, that Minnie was so taken up with Gus she did not so much as mention Paddy, nor the fact that he and Amy had danced together. Yet a part of her very much wanted to discuss what had happened that evening so that she could convince herself that the strong physical attraction she had felt for Paddy while they danced was a feeling she would have felt for any man in similar circumstances. The scene at the bottom of the stairs, she told herself, was probably not romantic at all; Paddy had merely offered to carry the child, after all, and whether he had meant to kiss her or not was something she would never know.

Since there was no apparent interest in her problem from Minnie, however, she had to content herself with thinking it over in her own mind and, since she was worn out, such thoughts speedily gave way to dreams.

Chapter Ten

Boxing Day dawned bright but cold, though few in the Logan household saw the dawn; they had played, sung and danced into the early hours and consequently slept late. Becky, Minnie and Amy did not so much as stir until they were awoken by Bill banging on their bedroom door. 'Gerrup you lazy lot,' he shouted cheerfully. 'I've been down and pulled the kettle over the flame and your mam's makin' porridge for everyone, so you'd best gerra move on.'

Amy groaned and sat up, stretched and yawned, then glanced towards the window. The curtains were thin cotton and had not been properly pulled across the night before, and through the gap she could see frost flowers obscuring the bottom half of the window, though the sun had melted the top half, showing the frosted rooftops of the houses opposite. A seagull perched on the roof must have seen the movement, for it cocked its head and looked hopefully across as though it expected the window to open and a shower of bread to come forth. Beside Amy, Becky gave a mutter of protest and tried to cuddle further down under the covers, but Amy, now properly awake, would have none of it. 'Wake up, our kid,' she said in a tone of resolute cheerfulness. 'Christmas Day is over, but we're on holiday still and it's a lovely day; the sun's shining fit to crack the paving stones, so what say we go for an early swim?'

Becky, still burrowing back into bed, gave a stifled giggle but Minnie, who had appeared to be sound asleep, groaned loudly. 'Even the thought of getting out of this warm bed makes me shudder,' she said plaintively. 'As for goin' outside ... Oh, I suppose you're right an' we'd best gerrup before the perishin' boys eat all your mam's porridge.'

'What about that swim, then?' Amy said mischievously, throwing back the cover. 'Some folk do swim at Christmas, I read about it in the newspaper once. Only I reckon it were down south somewhere, where they're all mad anyroad.'

She jumped out of bed as she spoke and began to pour water into the round tin bowl on the washstand – or rather she would have poured it had the water in the ewer not been ice for the top half-inch. Seizing her hairbrush, she bashed at the ice, then took pity on the shivering mortals in the bed behind her. Becky, whimpering a protest, had just begun to remark that she would not wash at all in water so cold when Amy remembered that Bill had said he had pulled the kettle over the flame. 'All right, all right, you delicate creatures,' she said, throwing her old shawl round her shoulders and going out on to the upper landing. 'I'll fetch up a jug of hot water from Dad's tea kettle and then we can wash in comfort, providing you're quick, of course, and get washing before it freezes up again.'

When she returned to the bedroom Minnie and Becky leapt, shivering, from their warm nest and a good deal of horseplay ensued as all three of them tried to wash simultaneously before the water grew cold. Amy dressed as rapidly as she could, then turned to help Becky, who was tugging on a disreputable jersey with unseemly haste; clearly Becky had had a 'cat's lick and a promise' instead of a proper wash. Minnie, meanwhile, was selecting a clean blue blouse to wear with her navy-blue serge skirt. The matching jacket was not new but she had trimmed the neck and sleeves with some fur remnants which she had got cheap in the pre-Christmas sale and Amy thought that, with her dark hair tied up with a length of blue ribbon and her cheeks flushed from the chill, Minnie looked really pretty. Checking her own reflection critically in the mirror on the washstand, Amy felt that she, too, looked presentable enough in a cinnamon-brown dress with chocolate-coloured trimmings and Becky, even in her play clothes, always looked sweet. Amy, brushing out the child's hair which had been confined in half a dozen small pigtails in the night, told her little sister that her hair rippled like corn in the sun and Becky, smiling self-consciously, danced ahead of the older girls down the stairs, calling out to her mother that they were on their way and were desperate anxious for porridge.

Despite Bill's waking shouts, the girls had finished their breakfast and were discussing what they should do for the rest of the morning before Gus put in an appearance. He plonked himself down at the table, yawning hugely and, accepting a large bowl of porridge and a mug of tea, told the world at large that Albert and Paddy would be down presently. 'Albert's goin' to Ruthie's for his dinner,' he told them rather thickly, spooning porridge into his mouth. 'But Charlie and Lottie will be here soon.'

Charlie and Lottie were staying with the Carpenters who, having no children of their own at home, had willingly agreed to put the young people up for a couple of nights.

'Let's go round to the Durrants' and see what they had for Christmas,' Becky said eagerly, bouncing up and down on her chair. 'Etty's me best pal and she were hopin' for a proper skippin' rope, the sort with red wooden handles.' She glanced across at her mother, cleaning vegetables over the sink. 'I wish *I* had a skipping rope with red wooden handles,' she ended wistfully.

'You've got most things, you spoilt little madam,' Amy remarked, just as Paddy and Albert came clattering down the stairs. Albert's hair stuck up like a hedgehog's, but he was wearing a clean white shirt and a blue tie – courting clothes, Amy thought, with an inward grin. It still seemed odd to her that her brother should be taking an interest in girls at last, particularly Ruthie, whom he had known all his life. Paddy, blessed with a mop of curls, had clearly managed to find time to drag a brush through them, though he was wearing a grey working shirt and navy trousers. *Not* courting clothes, Amy thought rather ruefully, and scolded herself for the thought. Since Paddy wasn't courting anyone, why on earth should he wear his best?

In the end, by mutual consent, the young people helped Suzie in the house all the morning. Dinner was cold goose, mashed potatoes and swede from Bill's allotment, followed by mince pies and custard. Albert, of course, did not share in this feast, since he had gone round to the Durrants' house, but the rest of them were all hungry, despite the excesses of Christmas Day, and the meal disappeared in record time. Amy, seated opposite Paddy, caught him taking covert glances at her several times and realised rather guiltily that she was not wearing his necklace. She had dressed in such a hurry that she had not thought to put it on, but determined to do so as soon as she could. It would seem ungracious not to wear it, although the cinnamon dress had a high, round neck and it wouldn't have been visible anyway.

When the meal was over and the washing-up and clearing away done Gus suggested, with a sideways glance at Minnie, that a walk along the shore would help to settle their dinners. 'It'll make room for our teas, what's more,' he said. 'Suzie's making pancake batter and if there's one thing I love it's pancakes.'

Although Bill and Suzie elected to stay by the fire and to prepare the tea for the rest of the family, everyone else decided a walk would be a good idea. Amy and Minnie ran upstairs to fetch coats and stout shoes, and Amy glanced quickly around her, looking for the necklace. She knew very well that she had left it on the washstand the previous night, but now there was no sign of it. Oh, well, it'll turn up, she told herself, putting on her thick coat and tying a scarf round her head. No one with a grain of sense would wear a hat on Seaforth Sands – unless they wanted to see it flying off to New Brighton of its own accord, that was, and presently she and Minnie went downstairs and joined the others.

Despite the cold and the strong wind, it was pleasant enough on the beach, although it very soon became apparent that poor Becky was not enjoying herself in the least. Among the dunes they were partially sheltered, but as soon as they came out upon the open shore the wind whipped loose sand at their legs with devastating force. The older ones, in long skirts or trousers, were able to bear this with equanimity but Becky, whose thin stockings were little protection and whose skirt was too short to offer any help at all, begged to be allowed to return home. 'I could go round to Etty's,' she shrieked against the wind, clutching Amy's hand and pressing close to her sister. 'Etty's mam is always glad to see me and we could have a go with her skipping rope in the backyard. Maybe they'll ask me to tea – they often do.'

'All right, darling, you'll probably be a deal better off with Etty than having your legs sandpapered by this perishin' wind,' Amy said cheerfully. 'I'll walk you round there, just make sure that everyone's in and they've not got a family party going.' She shrieked an explanation to the rest of the party, then turned back towards the town, Becky clinging grimly to her hand. They had only gone a few yards, however, before a figure, coat collar turned up and trousers tucked into boots, joined them, taking hold of Becky's other hand. It was Paddy.

'Oh, Paddy, there's no need for you to lose your walk,' Amy said as they gained the shelter of the dunes. 'I can take care of Becky; if there's no one at Etty's house we'll go on to the Durrants' and if there's no one there either we'll go back to Seafield Grove. By then the others will have turned back so all I'll have to do is walk to meet them.'

'Good try,' Paddy said, grinning. 'I suppose it doesn't occur to you that I don't fancy playin' gooseberry? Anyway, once we've dropped Becky off we can both catch up with the others if we've a mind.'

By the time they returned to Seafield Grove it was

growing dusk and Amy, to her own secret astonishment, had allowed Paddy to put his arm round her as they walked back along the shore. For the first time in her whole life, she realised, she and Paddy had talked seriously about their lives without either one sniping at the other. She had learned that Paddy's ambition extended beyond the fishing boat, that he was tempted to try his luck aboard a trawler or even to start out as a seaman on one of the transatlantic lines, which plied almost daily from the Liverpool docks.

'I've never told anyone this before, but I guess I ought to see the world before I settle down, get married and that,' he had told her. 'Liverpool's a grand city, so it is, but do you realise, Amy, I'm Irish yet I've never seen Dublin, let alone the rest of the country. As for the truly foreign parts, what chance has a chap of seeing the world from a shrimping boat? Oh aye, it'd be grand to see a bit of life before I settle down. I don't know about girls, but most fellers feel like I do.' He turned Amy so that he could look into her face. 'How about you, queen? Don't tell me you want to share a room with your pals and work in a hotel for the rest of your life?'

'I mean to marry one day and settle down and have kids, I suppose,' Amy said, having given the matter some thought. 'But I love my job and sharing is great fun – when you do it with good friends, that is. As for seeing the world, I doubt I'll ever do that – I'd like to see a bit more of England, though. And Wales, come to think of it. Oh, and I'd like to go to Ireland one of these days. You can catch a ferry from the Landing Stage.'

'What do you say to us going together?' Paddy suggested. 'It'd be much more fun wi' the two of us.

There's all sorts in Dublin, shops, museums and a huge park. We could go in the summer if you'd like it.'

Amy felt that this was going too far and too fast, and made some non-committal reply, and presently Paddy changed the subject, telling her that catches aboard the shrimping boat had been pretty good, considering the time of year. He was saving up, since as a single man he had few responsibilities and could afford to put money away each week. 'I wouldn't leave your brothers and your dad in the lurch,' he assured her. 'But quite honestly, queen, provided they could get themselves a lad, Gus and Albert could manage the boat and the nets easy. So one of these days . . .'

He had not finished the sentence but it did not need a mind reader, Amy thought, to realise that despite what she had believed, Paddy was as ambitious as she, perhaps more so. And as they made their way to Seafield Grove through the deepening dusk, she realised with a little pang that if he did go she would miss him.

The last evening of the holiday was spent by the entire family, with the addition of Ruthie Durrant and two of her small sisters – and Minnie of course – in playing quiet games around the fire. The children had played Musical Chairs, with Paddy on the mouth organ, but this, being far from a quiet game, was soon rejected in favour of 'Chinese Whispers', which caused great hilarity, especially among the younger members of the party whose interpretation of the ordinary whispered sentences had everyone in stitches.

Encouraged by this, other parlour games were

embarked on. They played 'The Moon Is Round . . .', and, 'I Went to Market . . .'. The boys wanted to play 'Postman's Knock', but at this point Suzie, Amy and Minnie disappeared into the scullery to serve the supper, which they had made earlier, so the game was abandoned whilst they ate scones and short-bread and drank tea or beer.

When supper had been cleared away Ruthie, looking at the flushed faces of her little sisters, suggested that perhaps she ought to be taking them home, but Albert said hastily that they would play a quiet game first to calm the kids down a bit. A discussion ensued, at the end of which Bill went to the kitchen dresser and, opening one of the long drawers, produced some sheets of lined paper and several stubs of pencil. He explained the game of 'Consequences' to the younger members of the group, handed each person present a piece of paper and a pencil, and the game began. Although this was a quiet game it produced almost as much hilarity as 'Chinese Whispers' had done. When the papers were collected up and first one person and then another read the results on the page he held there was a good deal of laughter.

At this point, Ruthie rose to her feet, saying firmly that no matter how they tempted her she must go home now, for by the time she had put her little sisters to bed she would be almost asleep on her feet. 'And tomorrow I'm back in the dining rooms, probably rushed off me feet from early morning till late evening,' she said. 'I'm fond of me job and don't want to lose it, so I've gorra be on the early tram 'cos it's not just a couple of stops to work like it is from Huskisson Street. It's a fair old trek from the Rimrose Bridge to the city centre.'

'You aren't the only one who'll be catching that tram,' Amy said ruefully, also getting to her feet. 'Minnie and me will be up at the crack of dawn as well.' She turned to Suzie. 'But thanks for a lovely day, Suzie – two lovely days – it's been the best Christmas I've had for years. You worked really hard and I'm sure we've all had a grand time.'

'It's been the best Christmas I've had since me mam died,' Minnie said shyly, smiling at Suzie and Bill. 'You've made me feel one of the family. I'll never forget your kindness. When Ella and Ruthie said they were going away for Christmas me heart sank, but then Amy said I could come home with her and I'm sure the Queen of England couldn't have had a better time.'

The party having broken up, Albert walked Ruthie and the girls home, Charlie and his Lottie went back to the Carpenters' house, and Gus and Paddy began to bring the furniture back into the kitchen, to set out the rugs and to fetch the fuel and water for the next day, while the girls tackled the washing up and clearing away. When this was done they all trooped off upstairs to bed, for the girls were not the only ones who would have to work in the morning. The boys would take the boat out to search for what fish there was and Bill would catch a tram to St John's Market where he would clean down the stall, buy in fresh ice and prepare to gut and clean whatever fish the boys caught.

Outside the door of the girls' room Paddy put a restraining hand on Amy's arm. 'It were nice of you to thank me mam for all her hard work,' he said quietly. 'I know she didn't say much, but she were really pleased. It were kind, Amy.'

'It was no more than the truth,' Amy said equally

quietly. 'Your mam's been rare good to my dad and to young Becky, and now that I'm older she seems to like me a bit better too; we get on pretty well, your mam and me.'

Paddy opened his mouth to say something more, but at that moment Bill came clumping up the stairs behind them and Paddy touched Amy's chin lightly with his forefinger, grinned and disappeared into the boys' room, while Amy joined Minnie and Becky, and the three of them began to get ready for bed.

'Amy, I were talkin' to Etty today when we were skippin' in the backyard, and *she* said she'd been talking to Annie Durrant, Ruthie's sister, and *she* said . . .'

'Not now, chuck,' Amy said sleepily, burrowing her head into the softness of her pillow. 'Me and Minnie's got an early start tomorrow and I'm almost asleep on my feet. Tell me in the morning.'

'You aren't on your feet, so how can you be asleep on them?' Becky said plaintively. 'You're lying flat on your back in a nice soft bed and it won't take a minute to tell you what Etty said Annie said . . .'

A tiny curling snore issuing from her sister's mouth, however, convinced Becky that further conversation would be a very one-sided affair. Sighing, for there are few more annoying things than being the possessor of information which one cannot pass on, Becky settled down and was soon asleep herself.

Next morning, despite the best of intentions, everyone overslept. Amy, indeed, was the first to wake and realised with dismay that the bright light of morning was showing through the curtains. She gave a yelp, shook Minnie hard and jumped out of bed tearing her nightgown over her head and

401

beginning to hurl her clothes on, not daring to stop for a wash in water which she knew would be ice-cold, if not actually iced. Minnie, waking, echoed Amy's yelp and jumped out of bed too, beginning to dress with equal haste, while Becky curled protectively beneath the blankets, an arm flung up to shield her eyes from the intrusive light.

Fortunately the girls had packed their few belongings the night before, so now all they had to do was to seize their bags and rush downstairs. A glance at the kitchen clock confirmed Amy's worst fears. They would have to run all the way to the Rimrose Bridge and even then they might not succeed in catching a tram.

'I've not had to run like this since I were a kid,' Minnie gasped, as they raced up Crosby Road. She reached into her pocket and produced a comb which she dragged through her tangled locks. 'I feel a real scarecrow and I 'spect I look like one too. Still, I don't suppose we will have many customers in first thing. Rich people lie in later than us on ordinary days, so at Christmas I reckon they won't get moving until around eleven o'clock. Oh, glory be to God, the tram's there, oh, wave Amy, shout at him to wait.'

Both girls shouted and waved and the tram, which was half empty but had begun to move, slowed and stopped, only starting up again when they were safe on board. The girls thanked the conductor breathlessly and collapsed on to one of the slatted wooden seats. 'Phew! But at least we shan't be late,' Amy said, as the vehicle gathered speed. 'Oh, my God, I meant to have another look for my necklace! I know it can't possibly be lost but I wouldn't be at all surprised if I had it on in bed, and it came off and got mixed up with the blankets. Damn, damn, damn! And I won't be going home again till the New Year, because having had time off over Christmas they're going to keep me hard at it so's other people can have a break. Oh, look, there's Ruthie sitting up the front. Shall we go and join her?'

Ruthie, who had turned at their approach, tutted at their dishevelled appearance and moved up to make room for them. 'Lucky old Ella, off work for another four whole days,' she remarked, as the tram jolted onwards. 'She'll have a lot to tell us when she gets back from Manchester. I bet she's had a grand time!'

Half an hour after the girls had left, Paddy came lurching down the stairs, still rubbing the sleep from his eyes. He looked around the kitchen, ran a hand through his dark curls and addressed his mother, who was desultorily pushing back chairs and tidying away the remnants of the party. She had already removed the paper chains and a good deal of tinsel and holly, and was throwing the berried branches on the fire where they crackled and spat, causing her to jerk back hastily from the sudden heat.

'Who'd ha' thought folk could make such a mess,' she grumbled, as her son entered the room. 'That there Consequences game – well, the consequence is a deal of paper and mess, if you ask me.' She giggled at her own joke, then swept a hand along the broad mantelpiece, sending a mass of papers, apple cores, sandwich crusts and other such detritus to falling into the hearth. 'Wharra you going to have for your breakfast, chuck? I could boil you a couple of eggs, or there's kippers, if you can face fish,' she added.

She turned towards Paddy as she spoke, her eyebrows rising. Paddy, taking his place at the table, said, 'No, I'll just have bread and jam. I ate enough yesterday to keep me goin' for a week,' and added, rather plaintively, 'Where's the girls, then? Don't say they're still in bed!'

Suzie, pouring tea from the big, brown pot into an enamel mug, shook her head. 'No, it ain't them what overslept this morning, it's you fellers,' she informed him, shuffling back across the room with the mug of tea in her hand. 'Bill's gone an' all, though he weren't so quick off the mark as the girls, but he reckons there won't be many customers early today – and he'll only have potted shrimps and salted fish and a few kippers to sell until you fellers bring your catch in.'

'Oh. Right,' Paddy said, scooping jam out of the jar with a knife and spreading it on his bread and marge. He thought, rather aggrievedly, that Bill might have woken them when he got up and wondered why the girls had not at least banged on the boys' bedroom door. It would have been nice, come to that, if Amy had seen fit to shout out cheerio at the head of the stairs, but she had clearly done no such thing. His heart, which had been high and full of hope, sank a little at this thought. Amy had been so friendly yesterday, they had laughed and joked and told each other things which, he imagined, neither of them normally ever gave voice to, yet she had not seen fit to shout a goodbye before she went off to work.

Suzie, sitting down opposite him at the table, gave him a shrewd look. 'Lost a quid and found a penny?' she enquired amiably. 'You look sour as a lemon. What's up?'

'No one called us,' Paddy mumbled. 'I'd ha' thought young Amy might have given the door a knock or even called out. Why, she never even said cheerio.'

'I doubt they had the time,' Suzie said judicially. 'I weren't up meself, but I heard 'em clattering down the stairs an' out the door, without stopping for so much as a bite of bread or a drink.'

'Oh,' Paddy said. 'So that's the way of it, was it? Well, I hope they caught their tram or all the rushing in the world wouldn't get them to work on time. I wonder whether Amy will come back home for New Year? I dare say she will. When we deliver the fish to the market I reckon I just might pop into the Adelphi, ask her what her plans are.'

Suzie looked thoughtfully across at her son and Paddy felt the heat rush to his cheeks, and hastily crammed more bread and marge into his mouth. Suzie was smiling now, looking quizzically at him and he wondered uneasily whether he had given himself away by suggesting a visit to the Adelphi.

'If I remember rightly, it were you who used to twit Amy over the smell of fish,' Suzie said thoughtfully. 'I don't know as a visit to that posh hotel in your fisherman's gear wi' scales all over you is likely to impress them as works there. If I were you I'd go round to Huskisson Street of an evening – you might take Gus an' all, once you've changed your shirt and kecks for something more . . . more suitable.'

'Less fishy, you mean,' Paddy said, grinning. 'I might take your advice an' all, Mam, because I do recall I used to rag young Amy now and then.'

'Well, you must do as you think fit,' Suzie said. She got to her feet. 'That young Becky don't do a hand's turn in this house if she can help it. She'll grow up a lazy little slut if I don't make her mind me more. Make up the fire before you go out, Paddy, while I go up and tear the bedclothes off of Becky. Do you think I ought to give Gus and Albert a knock? Only your dad wants fresh fish before the market closes, you know.'

'Yes, give 'em a shout,' Paddy agreed. His mother hastened up the stairs and Paddy guessed that she would help Becky to wash and dress, and would probably not be down again for some time. Becky was spoilt, he knew that, but thought it a good thing rather than a bad. He could still remember all too clearly how hard his mam had been on Amy and how it had affected her. He was glad that Becky at any rate would not grow up with the sort of chip on her shoulder Amy had had.

Paddy finished his bread, drained his mug and got up. He went over to the fire and began to riddle the ash. The coal bucket stood in the grate and he was about to select some lumps of coal, when his eye was caught by a crumpled ball of paper, lying between the coal bucket and the grate. It looked as though someone had aimed the ball of paper at either fire or coal bucket, but had missed. Paddy bent and picked it up, and was about to toss it into the fire when he realised that the paper bore his own name. Startled, he looked more closely, remembering the game of Consequences the previous evening. He did not immediately recall whether he himself had written his name on one of the sheets, or whether it had been added as an answer to one of the questions by somebody else, but he began to unwrap the paper, smiling to himself at the thought of the previous evening's fun.

As he unwrapped, something slithered out of the

paper and fell with a tiny *plink* on to the hearth stones. He glanced down at it and for a moment could only stare; it was a delicate gold necklace, interspersed with droplets of milky green jade.

For what seemed like ages Paddy could literally not have moved a muscle. His brain felt at first cold and sluggish and then pain and rage rushed over him. He clenched his hand round the necklace and drew back his fist to hurl it into the fire. How Amy must hate him. To write his name on a bit of paper, wrap it round his gift and simply chuck it down where he might never have found it seemed somehow to be the height of cruelty. But he would not throw the necklace into the fire; he thought confusedly that it had been bought and presented with love, and did not deserve such a fate. He would keep it and one day he would give it to someone special, someone who deserved it and could appreciate its fragile beauty.

He thrust the necklace into his trouser pocket and went across the kitchen rather blindly, dragging his duffle coat and muffler off the peg on the back of the door, and shoving his feet into his seamen's boots. He could hear Gus and Albert wrangling as they came out of their room and knew, suddenly, that he could not face them now. To his horror, as he shot out of the kitchen and into the cold of the December morning, he realised that there were tears in his eyes. Without pausing to wonder what he was about to do he turned up Crosby Road towards the tram terminus. He could not, would not, face Amy's brothers right now.

Pulling up the hood of his duffle-coat and pushing both hands deep into his pockets, he headed away from Seaforth towards the city and the docks.

Becky came down just after the boys did and wailed plaintively when she saw the empty bread and margarine plate, and realised that her mother had either used all the porridge or not made any that morning. 'Why didn't you wake me, fellers?' she whined, taking her place at the table. 'Oh, you are mean – as mean as Amy and Minnie. They woke me up and made me all cold when they gorrout of bed, but they never thought to tell me I were goin' to miss me breakfast.'

Gus leaned across the table and ruffled her silky blonde hair and Suzie, crossing the kitchen behind her daughter, began to cut more slices off the loaf. 'Don't worry, chuck, there's plenty for everyone,' she said breezily. 'The girls didn't have any breakfast at all, you know. They were so late they simply ran straight out the door and off to the tram stop.'

'Oh!' Becky said, clapping a hand to her mouth. 'I meant to see Amy before she went off but I dare say . . .' She jumped off her seat and went over to the mantel, peering up as if to discover what time it was. Then, with a sigh of satisfaction, she returned to her place at the table. 'It's awright,' she said rather obscurely. 'Can I have a cup of milk now, Mam?'

On 29 December Ella returned to Huskisson Street – but she was a different Ella from the one who had gone off to Manchester scarcely knowing how she would manage to spend the whole week in the company of Philip's grand family. She bounced into the room at eight o'clock that evening, to find her three friends making Welsh Rarebit and discussing what they should do for the New Year.

Ella came across the room in a series of twirls, threw her Gladstone bag on to her chair and advanced towards her friends, a hand dramatically held out to display her new possession – a sparkling diamond and sapphire ring encircling the third finger of her left hand. 'Philip and I are engaged,' she said rather needlessly, as the girls clustered round, admiring the ring. 'Oh, girls, it was ever so romantic – he asked me to marry him on Christmas morning after church, when he had taken me for a walk in the Square Gardens. There was snow on the flowerbeds and long icicles hanging from the trees overhead, but the sun was shining and the sky was blue and I was – am – the happiest, luckiest girl in the world.'

'I thought you'd probably come back engaged,' Amy said complacently, giving her friend a hug. 'When will you be getting married, queen? Where will you live, you and Philip? Don't say Manchester! I couldn't bear to lose you – oh, it will be awful at the Adelphi without me best pal.'

Ella laughed, but shook her head at her friend. 'What makes you think I'll move anywhere?' she enquired mischievously. 'Being engaged isn't the same as getting married, you know. Why, people wait two or three years sometimes, before they change their single state.'

'Yes, but you aren't going to,' Minnie observed shrewdly, eyeing her friend's flushed and excited countenance. 'It isn't as if young Philip's short of a bob or two, so there'll be no nonsense about saving up for a nice little house somewhere. I reckon you'll have a June wedding, probably from a very smart church. Can the three of us be bridesmaids?'

'She can't have me as a bridesmaid, because it isn't done to outshine the bride and I would,' Amy said grandly, gently easing the ring off Ella's finger and placing it upon her own. 'Does it suit me, girls? Because I'm thinking of getting married meself ... only I haven't told the lucky fella yet because I haven't met him.'

'Don't believe a word she says, girls,' Minnie advised them. 'Why, she were given the most beautiful gift by one of the fellers! You could see he were keen on her and all over Christmas they were carrying on with ...'

'*I* was?' Amy squeaked, diving at Minnie and clapping a hand across the older girl's mouth. 'Why, my brother Gus took such a fancy to our Min that he's been round here most evenings, pestering the life out of her to go to the theatre or to a dance, or just to go back to Seaforth for supper with him. If that isn't a sign of serious intentions I don't know what is.'

The rest of that evening passed, as Amy had guessed it would, with the girls hearing all about Ella's wonderful Christmas holiday and the other three recounting their own far less glamorous adventures. What Amy did not say – could not say – was how puzzled and upset she had been when Gus had arrived on their doorstep, either alone or accompanied only by Albert. She had been certain that Paddy would come to see her as soon as he was able to do so, but this had not happened. She had not liked to question Gus or Albert too closely about the third member of the fishing boat's crew and they had clearly not felt it incumbent upon them to comment on Paddy's absence. But I'll find out just what is happening when I go home for New Year, Amy told herself. I've never thought of Paddy as shy, but perhaps he is when it comes to girls. Maybe the thought of visiting the four of us, after how things have been in the past, simply scared him off.

But in her heart she did not believe it. Paddy had never been shy, so there must be some other reason for his not visiting her and, when New Year arrived and it was possible for her to catch a tram and go home, she discovered the reason almost as soon as she walked into the house.

The family were eating their supper around the kitchen table. Charlie and his wife had returned to the Midlands long since, but Gus, Albert, Bill, Suzie and Becky were all eating fish and fried potatoes, and greeted her cheerfully as she entered the room.

'Nice to see you, queen,' Bill said breezily. He turned to his wife. 'Is there any fish left, love? You can soon fry a few more spuds, 'cos there were a big bowl of cold 'uns in the fish scullery.'

There was a bustle as Suzie went over to the fire and Amy took off her outdoor things and hung them on the back of the door noticing, almost without realising it, that Paddy's duffle, muffler and seaboots were missing. 'Paddy's late,' she remarked, taking a seat at the table. 'Where's he gone?'

There was moment of embarrassed silence and then Bill said uneasily, 'Well, he's on his way to South America, I think he said. Didn't you know, queen? The day after Boxing Day he come in here and said he'd got a yearning for foreign parts and meant to be off as soon as he could find a lad to take his place on the shrimping boat, which I'm bound to say he did and young Ben is as likely a lad as you'll find in all Seaforth. Still, that's beside the point. Paddy's berthed as an ordinary seaman aboard the SS *Frederica*; he left us a letter tellin' us so. I thought he'd told you. The *Frederica* is one of them coasters

411

what go up and down the Americas for six months at a time, buying and selling, you might say. I reckon he'll see a deal of strange places afore we set eyes on him again.'

On New Year's Day, Amy sat in the office of the big hotel, typing away at her machine, but though she seemed to be concentrating on her work her mind was far from the task in hand. The previous evening, once she had got over the first shock of Paddy's abrupt departure, she had gone up to her room, stripped the bed and searched every inch of it. Suzie had not changed the bedding so there was no fear that the necklace might have got into the washing process and by the look of it, Amy thought disapprovingly, her stepmother had not brushed the linoleum nor shaken out the clothing which hung on hooks behind a piece of flowered curtain. But no matter how diligently she searched, the necklace was not to be found.

Once she was certain it was not in the room, Amy had descended the stairs, meeting Becky who was on her way up to fetch her sister down. 'It's near on time to start the first footing, Amy,' Becky had said excitedly. 'The neighbours are here and Mr Bulstrode has brought a barrel of punch; he says it ain't strong, so we can all have a drink.'

She took Amy's hand and turned to descend the stairs with her, but Amy drew her to a halt. 'Becky, do you remember the necklace Paddy gave me at Christmas? I wore it all Christmas Day but on Boxing Day I forgot. I had breakfast without it and then went upstairs to get it. Only it wasn't on the washstand, where I thought I'd left it. I didn't think of it any more until I was on the tram, heading for

Lime Street, but since I was sure it was somewhere in the house, I didn't worry too much. I thought it might have come off in the bed only I've searched the whole room and there's no sign of it. I suppose you haven't seen it, queen?'

'I saw it on Christmas Day,' Becky said immediately. 'Do you mind that you've lost it, Amy? Only you've always said you didn't like Paddy and Etty told Annie and Annie told me that you were goin' to chuck it away as soon as you got home.'

'Whatever made Etty ...?' Amy stopped short, remembering her hasty words to Ruthie on Christmas morning. She felt the heat rush to her cheeks and said defensively, 'Folks say things they don't mean sometimes, Becky. They say them and then they're sorry for them. I ... I'm afraid it might hurt Paddy's feelings to know that I've lost it – the necklace I mean. Not that he does know – does he?'

'I dunno,' Becky said, tugging Amy down the rest of the flight. 'Hurry up, Amy, Mam's made treacle tart to go with the punch when midnight comes, and Dad's hottin' up the poker and he says I can push it into the punch to make all the steam and sizzle.'

The rest of the evening had passed in a blur for Amy. She could not help wondering whether the loss of the necklace and Paddy's sudden departure were connected in some way. Since she was sure that she had lost it in the bedroom, she did not see how Paddy could possible realise that she no longer had it. However, just in case some other member of the family might have been involved, she waited until all the excitement of welcoming in the New Year was over and then asked Suzie, Bill, Gus and Albert bluntly whether they had seen her necklace.

No one had, but Amy thought that Suzie gave her

a rather strange look and presently, when they were clearing up and the men had gone to bed, Amy asked Suzie why she thought Paddy had suddenly decided to go to sea.

She half expected a snubbing reply, but instead Suzie dried her hands on a tea towel, sat herself down on a kitchen chair and gave the matter her full attention. 'I dunno for sure, queen,' she said slowly. 'In fact, I hoped you'd be able to tell us. Did you quarrel? Because I won't deny it seemed to me that Paddy was sweet on you and had been for a while, only of course you didn't feel the same about him. After he'd give you the necklace he were all lit up, like, happier than he's been – oh, for months, probably ever since Gran died. Then on Boxing Day the pair of you had your heads together, chattering away like magpies and laughing fit to bust, and Bill and I, I don't deny, we thought the old feud betwixt the two of you was over and a bleedin' good job too. We've wondered what could possibly have gone awry after that, because the day you left to go back to Huskisson Street Paddy didn't have a civil word for anyone. He went out without finishing his breakfast, and when he came home he just told us he'd signed on aboard the SS *Frederica* and wouldn't be home again for six months.'

She glanced across at Amy and suddenly Amy realised that it was a look quite without reservation; Suzie was as puzzled as Amy herself over Paddy's defection and was certainly not blaming Amy for one iota of it. Amy found herself warming to the older woman, now that they shared a common anxiety and affection for Paddy. She said musingly, 'I wondered if he thought I didn't value the necklace. I wondered if ... if someone might have found it

414

and handed it to him, telling him it meant I didn't value him either.'

Suzie gave a little cry and got to her feet. Clasping both Amy's hands in hers, she said roundly, 'There ain't one of us would do such a mean thing, not to you nor to our Paddy. I know I've been against you in the past – I were jealous of you, truth to tell – but I've learned your value now, queen, and I'd be a happy woman if I thought you and our Paddy might make a go of it. He went off very unhappy, there's no doubt of that, but he'll be home again and the two of you can talk it out face to face. He's goin' to write home, he said he would and Paddy's a man of his word, so there's no knowin' – you might get a letter an' all, explaining things.' She gave Amy's hands an encouraging little shake, then leaned forward and kissed her cheek. 'Cheer up, queen!' she said. 'There's worse things happen at sea. Oh, Gawd, that ain't what I meant to say at all – what I meant to say was it'll all come out in the wash. Now you go up to bed, because you've got a full day tomorrow.'

So now, Amy sat at her typewriter, working away automatically and trying to tell herself that she would not worry over Paddy. As soon as they had an address for him she would write to him herself and perhaps then he would write back and she could discover the reason for his flight. Until then she would just have to learn to live without him – something which she had done happily enough for a good many years.

Ella's wedding took place in June, as her friend had prophesied, and Minnie, Ruthie, Laura and Amy were all bridesmaids. Mrs Grimshaw had elegant gowns made for them in turquoise silk with matching accessories and hats of cream straw, lavishly decorated with artificial flowers. Ella looked radiant in a white gown with a long train; her veil held in place by a coronet of lilies of the valley, and her bouquet contained the same flowers, as well as the more traditional white roses and orange blossom.

Amy thoroughly enjoyed the wedding and the reception, which was held at the Adelphi, so that Ella's colleagues as well as her friends might enjoy the party. The only sadness Amy felt was for the loss of her friend, for Ella was to leave work and become a full-time housewife in a new house on the Wirral, which Philip's parents had bought for them as a wedding present.

Ella had tried at first to say that she wanted to continue working, but Philip had dealt with this in a masterly fashion. He had assured her that if time hung heavy on her hands or she was unhappy, she might take another job, either in the city of Liverpool or in one of the villages nearby, but first he maintained that she should give their home and marriage a chance.

So now the room in Huskisson Street only had three occupants and Amy suspected that there would soon be only two, for Gus and Minnie were planning a marriage of their own in the autumn, and even Albert and Ruthie, who still had a deal of saving up to do, meant to marry when they could afford it.

Amy had wondered if she and Mary might move in together, but that was before she had met Haydn. Having met him, she had been forced to acknowledge that he and Mary were deeply in love and would be marrying as soon as arrangements could be made for Haydn either to find work in Mold or to move his family to a house in Liverpool.

Amy, accepting any shifts, no matter how awkward, which the hotel had offered her, sometimes felt so lonely that she could have cried. In the six months that had elapsed since Paddy's flight from Seaforth she had been out with four different young men and had found each of them in turn insignificant and boring when compared with Paddy. A stranger might have thought she had not known Paddy well, but as the months had passed, Amy had realised she had known him very well indeed, but until Christmas had refused to think of him as anything but her enemy. Once the barriers had crumbled, however, she had begun to appreciate him for himself, even to love him, and though he was now far away she could not unlove him.

Letters had come from Paddy whenever he was in port long enough to dispatch an epistle, but none of them had been addressed to Amy and he had given no hint in any of them what had caused his sudden flight. What was more, he had never sent them a forwarding address, saying that his vessel's movements were uncertain so they had best save up all their news for when he returned in the summer.

'Amy, have you finished that report yet? Mr David sent me to fetch it as he needs to read it through before he speaks to Mr Frank.'

Miss Carew's small, bright face, poking round the edge of the door, made Amy jump, but she whipped the paper out of the machine and smiled at her colleague. 'Just finished it,' she said reassuringly, casting a quick glance over the four pages she had typed. 'I haven't had a chance to check it through,

417

though. Can Mr David wait another five minutes while I do that?'

'Oh, I'm sure he can,' Miss Carewe said easily, perching on the corner of Amy's desk. 'Have you heard, Amy? There's been an outbreak of measles – or was it whooping cough? – in Seaforth; ever so many kids have got it. Isn't that where you came from? Oh, I know you lodge in Huskisson Street, but don't your people live in Seaforth?'

'Yes, they do,' Amy said, trying to concentrate on the sheets of paper spread out on her desk. 'Do shut up for a moment, Miss Carewe, or I'll never get this finished.'

'All right, all right, don't snap my nose off,' Miss Carewe said without apparent rancour. 'I just thought you might know a bit more about it, you coming from there. Don't you have a sister still in school? Whooping cough is a nasty thing and measles can be pretty bad, though of course modern medicine does help.'

Amy agreed rather absently, finished reading through her work, pinned the four pages of the report together and handed them to Miss Carewe. Then she picked up her typewriter cover, fitted it over the machine and left the office. Her shift had been over half an hour ago, but she never grudged finishing off a job for Mr David, who was an easygoing, thoughtful employer. As she left the building and crossed Lime Street to catch her tram, she was debating whether to go straight home or whether to pop into Lyons Café for a cup of tea and a bite to eat, which would save her cooking when she got back. She had just decided on Lyons when someone tapped her shoulder, and turning, she saw her father, his face streaked with sweat and his blue eyes anxious. 'Amy! I were just about to go over to the hotel to see if you were there, when I spotted you crossin' the street. Me love, I've come straight from Seafield Grove – your mam's not herself and your sister's really bad. Can you come?'

'Yes, of course. What's the matter with them?' Amy asked, falling into step beside Bill. Once, she thought, she would have corrected the expression 'your mam' pretty sharply, but now she felt that this no longer reflected on Isobel. Suzie had been a good mam to Becky and the boys, and of late had been a good friend to Amy herself, so why not refer to her in future as mam?

But she said nothing of this as the two of them hurried to the nearest tram stop. Bill was explaining that Suzie had suspected Becky of having whooping cough and had put the child to bed, only to wake next morning with a sore throat, a burning head and a voice which sounded so hoarse that he had scarcely understood a word his wife had said. 'I've done me best to see to them both, but it's not easy for a feller,' he explained earnestly as they got on the tram. 'Becky's burning hot and calling for her mam, and poor Suzie keeps struggling out of bed to go to her . . . it all happened so suddenly, Amy. The boys went off to the boat and I meant to make your mam comfortable and then come in to the stall . . . only what with trying to keep Suzie in bed and telling Becky she'd be all right if she'd only keep under the covers . . . and we can't afford to let the fish go bad because there's only young Kenny on the stall to sell it . . .'

'It's all right, Dad,' Amy said soothingly. 'I'll spend the evening with you, make the boys a meal, get the invalids comfortable and then go back to

Huskisson Street. If they are no better by morning then we'll send for the doctor. Why didn't you send for him today, incidentally? One of the girls at work said there was whooping cough or measles, she didn't know which, in Seaforth. Did you notice if Becky had spots? I imagine Suzie probably had measles when she was a kid – perhaps she's got a nasty feverish cold, or influenza or something.'

'In June? Isn't that a winter illness? As for gettin' the doctor, there was no one to send,' Bill said, looking harassed. 'The truth is, Amy, that I've never had to deal with illness before. When your mam was ill there was you and Mary and the nurse always on hand, and the doctor coming in, and when you kids were young your mam saw to you. Last year, when Becky had the chicken pox all I had to do was pop me head round the door when I got home at night, ask her how she was feeling and give her any little treat I had managed to pick up. This ... this is different.'

How different it was Amy was able to judge for herself within moments of entering the house. The fire, which Bill must have been neglecting all day, was dead in the stove and though this scarcely mattered as far as warmth was concerned, for it had been a hot day, it meant that it was not possible for Amy to make the invalids a hot drink until it had been rekindled. What was more, the room was in great disarray, the table covered in dirty crockery and cutlery, the porridge pan on the draining board stiff with dried porridge and the dirty washing, which someone had carried downstairs, piled in an untidy heap before the low stone sink. There was also a stale and unpleasant smell in the room, which caused Amy to fling open both windows and the door before heading for the stairs.

Becky was in the girls' room, alone in the big feather bed. Her face was scarlet and she was breathing with difficulty. She had thrown off her bed covers but was sunk deep into the feather mattress. The bed itself was wet with Becky's sweat, as were her nightgown and her small, burningly hot body. She had appeared to be asleep when Amy had softly opened the door, but as Amy trod across the room towards her she opened large, fever-bright eyes and began to cry. 'Oh, Amy, I feel so ill, I does,' she said in a tiny, hoarse voice. 'Our dad gave me a drink before he left, only I knocked it over and now the bed's all sticky and horrible. I were sick on to the lino and I'd only taken two mouthfuls,' she added pathetically.

'So I see,' Amy said ruefully, gazing down at the sticky patch of vomit on the linoleum. 'Never mind, sweetheart, presently I'll come in and clean you up and change you into a fresh nightgown. I'll do something about that bed as well,' she added, eyeing the sticky, crumpled sheets with revulsion. 'But I must just go along and see how Mam is. She's ill as well as you – did our dad tell you?'

'She isn't as ill as me,' Becky wailed, scrubbing at her tear-filled eyes with small, grimy fists. 'She went downstairs to fetch up my dolly, only she forgot to bring her back. And she said we should have porridge, or a nice rice pudding, only that was *hours* ago and I've not had a thing to eat since yesterday.'

'Mam *is* ill, queen,' Amy said, heading for the door. 'Are you hungry then, Becky? Could you eat some porridge if I made it? Rice pudding takes ages to cook.'

'No, I'm not hungry, I'd be sick if I tried to eat porridge,' Becky whined. 'But I'm ever so thirsty, Amy, ever so ever so thirsty. I could drink a whole big jug of lemonade or even of water, if there weren't nothin' nicer.'

'I'll get you a drink when I've seen Mam,' Amy promised from the doorway. 'I'll be back in five minutes, don't you fret.' She left the child's room, passed the open door of the boys' room, glancing in and seeing with disfavour that it was a tip, the bed unmade and the floor covered with dirty clothing. She reached Suzie's room, tapped briefly on the door and went in. The bed was empty.

For one horrified moment Amy could only stare. Then she remembered Becky's remark about Suzie going downstairs to get the child's doll and a dish of porridge but Suzie, she knew very well, had not been in the kitchen when she passed through. She might, of course, have been in the fish scullery but had this been the case, surely Suzie would have called out or made some sign. Amy turned and was about to leave the room again when it occurred to her to look under the bed. The large chamber pot, wreathed in red roses, was missing. Straightening up with a relieved sigh, Amy realised that Suzie must have taken the pot downstairs to empty it and was probably even now coming back across the yard.

Accordingly she returned to Becky's room and was looking for a clean nightdress in the child's drawer when she heard a shout from below: 'Amy! Come and give us a hand, chuck. Your mam's come over all fainty like and I can't . . . I can't . . .'

Amy fairly flew across the room, down the stairs and into the kitchen, where she found Bill in the scullery doorway, struggling to get his wife off the floor. Suzie was a big woman and for the first time Amy realised that her father was no longer a big man. She was horrified that without her really noticing he had grown old. Now that she thought about it, she remembered that he was past sixty and the arms that clasped Suzie, though sinewy, were frail compared with her own.

'It's all right, Dad, I'm here,' Amy gasped, bending to heave Suzie up into her own arms. It was no light task, but between the two of them they managed to manoeuvre the unconscious woman to the sofa, where she lay with her head propped at a most uncomfortable angle and her limbs sprawled all anyhow. Amy felt her burning forehead and pointed to the open door. 'Fetch the doctor,' she said imperatively. 'I'll see to Mam and don't go running, because I can't have you ill on my hands as well and you're no chicken, Dad. If you meet the boys on your way, send Albert for the doctor and you come back here. And don't *worry*,' she added. 'It's still maybe only a feverish cold.'

By the time Bill arrived back with the doctor the situation was looking a good deal better. Suzie had recovered consciousness and was sitting up and drinking a cup of cold water, and the kitchen was much tidier, with the dirty crocks soaking in the sink and the washing out of sight in the scullery. Suzie was wearing a clean nightdress, and Amy had her own guess confirmed as soon as the doctor took a look at his patient, for when she changed Suzie's nightgown she had seen the faint beginnings of a rash all over her stepmother's neck and shoulders. 'Aye, you've got the measles all right, Mrs Logan,' the doctor said cheerfully. 'Only fancy a grown woman taking the measles – whatever were you thinking of? I can see we shall be off school for a day or two.'

Suzie smiled rather feebly at this gentle raillery, but Amy could see that she was relieved by the diagnosis, measles being a childish complaint from which the sufferer usually recovers without much difficulty. The fear of scarlet fever had been the first thing that had sprung to Suzie's mind when she had begun to feel so dreadfully ill and it would have meant weeks away from her family, imprisoned in the isolation hospital.

But when the doctor saw Becky he was less certain what ailed her. She had a sore throat, complained that her eyes were hurting her and had been sick twice, but as yet there was no rash. On the other hand when he sounded her chest he told her jokingly that there seemed to be a little orchestra playing down there, and when he and Amy returned to the kitchen he admitted it was possible that the child had somehow managed to contract more than one ailment. 'There's whooping cough about and with her mother having caught measles it's possible, though unlikely, that young Becky has a touch of both,' he said bluntly. 'However, I'll give you a prescription for something which will help the cough and bring the fever down, and you must keep her as clean, cool and comfortable as you can. If the weather weren't so hot I'd advise you to take Becky into her mother's room, but as it is, she's best with the bed to herself. Is it possible to change the feather mattress for a horsehair one? She would be a good deal cooler and very much easier to nurse.'

'Yes, I can manage that,' Amy said. She knew that the single bed in the boys' room which Paddy had once occupied had a horsehair mattress. 'But what about my mam, Doctor? Is she best upstairs? The trouble is if I nurse her in the kitchen I'll be spending all my time running up and down the stairs. And could you write me a note for my employer, please? I don't want to lose my job, but I can't see myself getting away from here for the next week or two.'

Nodding, the doctor pulled out a pad of paper and began to scribble, and presently handed her three notes, two for the chemist and one for the Adelphi Hotel. 'They'll maybe expect you to do without your salary for a few weeks, but I'm sure they won't dismiss you,' he said, indicating the explanatory note destined for the hotel. He looked at her over the top of his pince-nez. 'Have you had whooping cough, m'dear? I remember you and your brothers getting the measles but I can't recall any of you whooping when I came round. Because if you haven't had it, you might become infected yourself – and they're contagious diseases so no hotel will want you back until the three weeks' quarantine is over.'

'What a good thing you mentioned it,' Amy said. 'You're right about the measles, we all had them when I was five or six, but none of us ever had whooping cough, not even the boys. Oh, dear, does this mean they won't be able to go near Becky until she's completely clear?'

'I'm afraid so,' the doctor confirmed. He patted her cheek, then began to pack his stethoscope away into his case. 'Call me if you need me; send one of your brothers if they're at home,' he said over his shoulder, as he strode towards the door. 'Remember, plenty of cool drinks, a light diet and quiet. If you can give them that they'll be right as rain in no time.'

Despite the doctor's cheerful words, Amy had a tough couple of weeks trying to nurse her two patients, for Becky did indeed develop measles as well as whooping cough and had a miserable time of it. Unable to ask for help from the boys because of the fear of infection, she judged it more sensible to move her brothers out into lodgings temporarily, which left only herself and Bill to run the house and see to the invalids. Oddly enough, although Suzie was very sick indeed for ten days, she began to perk up quicker than Becky, whose temperature remained high for far longer. Bill went to the market each day to sell the fish and slept downstairs on the sofa, for he resolutely refused to go into lodgings with his sons. 'I had the measles when I were a young 'un and all us lads had whooping cough in our teens,' he told Amy gruffly when she mentioned the fear of infection. 'I know I'm an old feller and not much use in a sickroom, but at least I can do the messages, bring in wood and water, empty slop buckets and the like. You won't want to leave the house while Becky and her mam are so ill, so you'd best make the most of me. The lads would help, I'm sure, but they've not had the whooping cough.'

Amy was grateful to her father, particularly since he slept lightly and often heard Suzie call out before she herself did. It was hard enough nursing the invalids all day and looking after Becky all night without having to go to Suzie whenever she needed someone.

Amy did her best to obey the doctor's instructions but she reflected it was just her luck that her mam and sister should be ill during the hottest fortnight of the summer so far. When Bill came back from the fish market he carted with him a bucket of ice; Amy used it to freshen the home-made lemonade which her patients enjoyed, but nothing, not even the horsehair mattress, could keep Becky cool. Two or three times every day Amy gave her little sister a blanket bath in cool water and changed her sweat-soaked nightdress, and though Becky was patheti-cally grateful for the attention and always thanked Amy and said she felt much better now, within an hour she would be hot again, tossing and turning on her pillow, giving the whooping cough which Amy grew to dread and often vomiting into the bucket placed beside the bed for that purpose.

Gradually, however, as the days went by, both Suzie and Becky began to improve. After two weeks Suzie started to get up for an hour or two each day, though Amy flatly refused to let her go into Becky's room – Suzie had never had whooping cough. But if Amy peeled potatoes, gutted fish, or prepared vegetables for a stew, Suzie would put the pans over the flame and keep an eye on them until they were done. What was more, as she improved she began to do small tasks such as washing up, clearing away and laundering Becky's nightdresses and bed linen, both of which had to be changed frequently.

For many days Becky ate nothing at all and a good deal of what she drank came back, including the doctor's medicine, which she condemned roundly as being the nastiest stuff in the world. Then Bill came back with an egg custard, which the baker had made specially for Becky. It looked delicious; but Amy put a small helping into a dish and carried it up to her little sister without very much hope; Becky had turned down so many things with which they had tried to tempt her appetite. However, Amy told Becky how the baker had made it specially for her and how Bill said he had been followed by a group of little dogs, eagerly sniffing the air as he had brought it home, which made Becky laugh and consent to try a spoonful.

With Amy telling her jokes and trying to take her mind off the job in hand, the bowl was scraped clean before Becky fully realised that she had eaten it, and when the custard had not put in a reappearance twenty minutes later Amy dared to hope that the worst of the sickness was over at last.

There followed a few days when Becky was languid but far more comfortable, then she became demanding, wanting Amy to play games with her, to read to her and also to provide any food which she fancied. Bill remarked one evening, when Becky was in bed and asleep, that his older daughter was looking worn out and would, if she did not take care, end up ill herself. Amy pooh-poohed this, but Bill must have said something to Becky, because next day when Amy went to her sister's room with a bowl of warm bread and milk, Becky flung her arms round Amy's neck, kissing her warmly and telling her that she was the best sister in the world and that she, Becky, was a wicked child who did not deserve such kindness.

'Wicked? Well, I dare say you might have been a little naughty in your time,' Amy said, laughing. 'But I doubt very much if you've ever been wicked in your life.' She sat down on the bed and picked up the book she had been reading to Becky the previous day. 'Now you eat up your bread and milk, and I'll continue to tell you about Alice's adventures in Wonderland – won't that be nice?'

'Why, ye-es, only I can't talk and eat at the same time,' Becky objected. Nevertheless she began to spoon the sweetened bread and milk into her mouth with more enthusiasm than she had previously shown for a dish which she considered to be baby food. 'Only I *were* wicked once, Amy.' She looked up at Amy, her large blue eyes pleading. 'It were ages and ages ago – last Christmas, in fact. I did something naughty, something what I shouldn't have done, and then . . . and then I were afraid to tell you. Oh, Amy, it were me what took your necklace.'

Amy stared at her rosy, innocent face. 'You took my necklace?' she repeated incredulously. 'Oh, queen, whatever for?'

'To show me pals,' Becky said dolefully. 'I did try to tell you, Amy, but you said you was tired and I could tell you in the morning. Only you went off early next morning and I thought you'd took it, but when you came back for New Year you said it was still lost . . .'

'Hey, hang on a minute,' Amy said. She was still smiling but the smile was mostly to reassure her little sister. 'When you took it, did you lose it? I mean, did it fall off your neck while you were out in the road, queen? I'm afraid I don't understand.'

Becky heaved a deep sigh, as though Amy were the stupidest person in the world and cast her eyes up to the ceiling, but replied patiently, 'I *telled* you, Amy! I took the necklace on Boxing Day to show me pals – that were why I made you take me off the beach so's I could visit Etty – and then I brought it home with me and forgot all about it because we were playing such jolly games, weren't we? And I knew you'd take me up to bed and help me undress – then you'd have seen the necklace. So I wrapped it in paper and purrit on the mantelpiece.'

'But it wasn't on the mantelpiece; I turned the

whole house upside down,' Amy began, then remembered the haste with which she had left the house. 'No, no, I'm getting it wrong, aren't I? I left the house in such a hurry the day after Boxing Day that I didn't even remember I'd lost it. So go on, there it was on the mantelpiece . . .?'

'I don't know what happened to it after that,' Becky confessed, looking unhappy for the first time. 'I thought you'd taken it, which would have been all right. If you'd been there, Amy, I'd have give it you – I meant to tell you I'd found it on the floor, near where you'd been sitting when we was playing Consequences, only you went early, like you said. And when I came down for breakfast it were gone, honest to God it were.'

There was a pregnant pause while Amy's mind raced. She knew that no member of the family had taken it, but she supposed that wrapped in a piece of paper it might easily have been taken for rubbish and thrown into the fire. She was about to assume that this had happened when she suddenly remembered Paddy's abrupt departure. Was it possible that he had found it? But if so, why had he not simply returned it to her?

Because he thought you'd chucked it away, you blithering idiot, which is what anyone would have thought, a small voice said inside Amy's head. *Remember, you didn't tell him you'd mislaid it and were hunting for it, which any normal human being would have done. But you were too proud and you'd been pretty nasty about the necklace to start with, so you didn't want Paddy to know that you'd been careless enough to lose it. Oh, if he found it he will have been so hurt! And I can't get in touch with him, can't tell him what Becky's just told me. Whatever am I going to do?* She must have

430

spoken the last sentence out loud for Becky, looking puzzled, said, 'Do? Well, you said you'd read me from *Alice in Wonderland*, so you could do that.'

Amy laughed but picked up the book and began to read. Children are so single-minded, she thought. Becky had told her the story of the necklace and by doing so had cleared her own conscience of any suspicion of wickedness. It would not occur to the child that her action might have had repercussions. Once confessed, it could be forgotten, and Becky had done just that.

When Amy had finished her chapter and Becky her bread and milk, Amy put the book down on the side table and stood up. Casually, as though it were of no importance, she asked, 'Why didn't you put the necklace back on the washstand, queen? Why put it downstairs on the mantelpiece? If you had wanted me to find it, you might have known I'd look in the bedroom first.'

'Amy, I *telled* you,' Becky exclaimed. 'I slipped it off me neck while you were in the pantry helping Mam to get us suppers. I didn't think to take it upstairs, I just wanted to hide it so's no one could see. I had me paper from the game of Consequences, so I wrapped it in that and stood on the fender, so's it looked as if I were checking the clock to see how late it was. And I put the crumpled-up ball of paper with the necklace inside by the clock. I meant to come down early next morning, throw the paper in the fire, and put the necklace down by the chair you'd sat in to eat your supper. But when I got down the necklace was gone. *Now* do you understand?'

'Yes, I understand queen,' Amy told her gently. 'Paddy came down before you, didn't he?'

'Yes, 'cos I slept in,' Becky said readily, 'but I don't

see ... oh, Amy! Could that be why he were in such a mood? I mean, would it make him cross to find the necklace wrapped up in a bit of old paper? Why couldn't he have just give it back to you?'

Becky was bright, Amy thought, telling her sister soothingly that it didn't matter because if Paddy had picked it up no doubt he would keep it safe until he saw Amy again. But in her heart she thought that Paddy, if he really had found it, might well have chucked it into the fire and made up his mind to forget her and find a decent girl who would treat him with respect and cherish any gift he gave her.

But no matter what had been, it had happened over six long months ago and was best forgotten. So Amy picked up Becky's slop bucket and carried it and the dirty dish down to the kitchen, and began her day's work.

The SS *Frederica* came into the Crosby Channel and Paddy, leaning on the rail, could see even through the shimmer of the hot July air the Crosby lighthouse to his left and the Rock lighthouse on the New Brighton point to his right. He had told himself that he would not be affected by his first sight of the city of his birth; it had not occurred to him that passing along beside his old fishing ground would be so full of memories. Every inch of these waters he and the Logan boys had known like the backs of their hands and they had had good times out here, too. Clear, cool autumn days, when the nets had been so heavy that it had taken all three of them to heave the catch aboard; days in winter when they had fished in vain and had had to come home, frozen-fingered and depressed, with nothing to show for their hard work. Other people might not feel that they had come home until they saw the 'Liver Birds' looming out of the heat haze and though Paddy guessed that this would affect him too, it was these waters which had been his workplace for so long, and which he remembered now with a mixture of pride and nostalgia.

When the Liver Birds came in sight, however, half the ship's crew were beside him on the deck, already planning how they would spend their first day ashore. The *Frederica* would be in port for ten days, perhaps a fortnight, while her master sold the cargo he had carried across the wide Atlantic and cast around among those import/export companies who might give him an outgoing cargo for his next trip.

Many of the men, Paddy knew, had no longer got families or close friends living in the 'Pool, and would go straight to the sailors' home on Paradise Street and book in there for the duration of their time ashore. They would spend the first couple of days getting gloriously drunk and throwing around the money they had made on the voyage, picking up Liverpool judies, fighting with anyone who wanted a scrap and buying trifles for anyone who took their fancy. Several of the men, Paddy knew, had bought objects which they would sell on as soon as the city was reached. If they could find a curio shop, similar to the one on Upper Parliament Street where he had bought the necklace, they would find a ready sale for curiosities purchased from South America. And such deals would give them yet more cash to spend ashore.

The thought of the necklace immediately brought a picture of Amy's face into Paddy's mind. He could see her large, green-grey eyes fringed with dark lashes, and the glorious red-gold hair, which he had

433

once rudely called 'carroty', piled on top of her small head. But it did not do to think about Amy, because it brought the whole business back. He had already made up his mind that he would neither visit her in Huskisson Street, nor try to get in touch with her during his time ashore. For over six months he had concentrated on his job as a seaman while they were on board ship. When ashore, he had always chosen girls who were as different from Amy as they could possibly be. This had not been difficult, since South American beauties tended to black hair, glittering dark eyes and, rather too often for Paddy's taste, a dagger slipped into a stocking top. Being spirited was all very well, but Paddy had no desire to find himself on the wrong end of a stiletto and treated such ladies with considerable caution.

He had no doubt that the Liverpool judies who haunted the port, had their own method of keeping unwanted lovers at bay, but since he had no intention of embroiling himself with any local girl, no matter how pretty, he would be safe enough there.

Come to that, although he had mixed with the local girls when ashore in the Americas, he had always made it plain that he was not interested in either buying or otherwise obtaining their company. It was not, he told himself, that he was embittered by what had happened between him and Amy, but he acknowledged that at any rate he had been deeply hurt by it. He fully intended to get married one day and hoped that he would meet the right girl and be as happy with her as his mother had been with Bill, but he thought he would wait a while before taking such a giant step. Bill had been well past fifty before he married Suzie, which was a bit extreme – Paddy thought forty a more suitable age himself – but clearly it behoved one to move cautiously before committing oneself to marriage.

The clatter as the gangplank went down brought Paddy out of his reverie and sent him scuttling down the nearest companionway to pick up his ditty bag. He meant to go straight home to Seaforth, catching a number 17 tram from the Pier Head to the Rimrose Bridge and surprising the family by bursting in upon them just as they were sitting down to their main meal of the day. He imagined, since it was seven in the evening already, that the boys would be back from the fishing and Bill from the market, and he found himself greatly looking forward to seeing them all again. He had brought tobacco for the boys and Bill, a feather boa for Suzie and a hand-painted fan for Becky, depicting a man and a woman dancing flamenco, and a little tambourine made of chicken skin stretched over a frame with brass discs round the edge.

It was a fine evening and as Paddy climbed aboard the tram he had to fight a terrible urge to jump off again and make his way to Huskisson Street. He could make some excuse, he told himself, say he thought Becky might be visiting there . . . but he was firm. Such an action could only lead to more pain, more misunderstanding and was best totally banished from his mind. So he took his seat on the tram, choosing the open upper deck since it was such a warm evening, and watched with increasing pleasure as the vehicle rattled along Great Howard Street. The shops were doing a roaring trade and several times Paddy actually recognised someone, either from his school or a customer to whom he had sold shrimps.

He got off the tram at the terminus without having spoken to anyone and made his way along Crosby Road, whistling a tune beneath his breath and feeling the first stirrings of delighted anticipation. He told himself he couldn't wait to see the lads again, but knew his excitement lay in some strange way deeper than that. You can't be such a fool as to imagine you're going to have a second chance with Amy, he thought derisively, unwilling to acknowledge that the excitement could be caused by such an unlikely event. And presently he put the whole matter out of his mind as he began to recognise the houses of friends and Seafield Grove drew near.

Turning into the jigger which ran along the back of the houses made him think of Gran, and he felt a stab of regret that he would not be able to tell her how his life had changed and his horizons broadened. She would have been interested; the sights, smells and sounds he had experienced, the adventures which had come his way, the new friends he had made would have fascinated her. His mam, though she loved him, had her new family and would not have the sort of interest which Gran would have shown. The lads, Albert and Gus, had their own lives to lead and might even feel a little jealous, a little left out, when he began to tell his stories.

He crossed the yard and pushed open the kitchen door. He stepped across the threshold and glanced around him; the first person he saw was Amy. She was standing by the sink, her curly hair caught back into a knot at the nape of the neck, a large calico apron enveloping her slim figure. She was washing dishes but looked up as he entered and immediately dropped the bowl she held, which crashed to the floor and broke into a thousand pieces.

Paddy had meant to be cool to the point of coldness, should he be unfortunate enough to see Amy during his time ashore but somehow, as he saw the big green eyes slowly fill with tears and a pink flush creep into her cheeks, all his vengeful thoughts disappeared. Without at all meaning to do so, he held out his arms and Amy, with a choking little cry, flew into them.

For a long moment neither spoke nor moved, but then Amy, whose head had been nestled into the hollow of Paddy's shoulder, drew a little away from him so that she might look into his face. 'Paddy? What happened? Why did you go so quickly, without even saying goodbye? And it's been over six months – the longest six months in my life, I should think – without so much as a postcard. Oh, Paddy, I've been so unhappy!'

'I've been pretty unhappy meself,' Paddy admitted. 'But when you flung me necklace into the fire . . .'

'Oh, Paddy, I never did any such thing,' Amy gasped, snuggling close to him once more. 'It was all a horrible accident – have you had whooping cough? Or measles?'

'What's that got to do wi' anything?' Paddy asked, but his arms tightened round her. 'As it happens I've had both. But that doesn't explain why you tried to chuck me necklace . . .'

'It may not explain about the necklace exactly,' Amy said, detaching herself from his embrace and beginning to pull him towards the stairs. 'But poor old Becky's had both – she's still in quarantine – and she's the only person, just about, who can explain

437

what happened to the necklace after Christmas. Honest to God, Paddy, there's been so much unhappiness and misunderstanding caused by what happened – I take it you found the necklace on the mantelpiece? What made you think I'd chucked it in the fire? Not that it matters, because once you've spoken to Becky you'll understand everything.'

'Yes, but I don't want to speak to Becky, not right now,' Paddy said, holding her hand very tightly as they mounted the flight. 'If *you* explain, sweetheart, that will be just fine. Why does it have to be Becky?'

But Amy would not reply, merely dimpling up at him and shaking her head, and indeed, when she ushered him into Becky's bedroom she was glad she had not tried to untangle the web. Becky was leaning back against her pillows, playing rather listlessly with a jigsaw on a tray set out across her knees, but as soon as she saw Paddy she sat bolt upright, sending jigsaw and tray bouncing unheeded across the floor. 'Paddy!' she squeaked, scrambling on to her knees and flinging her arms around his neck in a suffocating hug. 'Oh, Paddy, don't be cross with Amy 'cos it were me that took the necklace. I only meant to show it to me pals ...'

The story came pouring out as Paddy sat down on the bed and settled Becky on his knee, telling her comfortingly that it was quite all right, he and Amy had sorted themselves out and now that he knew no one had intended to throw the necklace away he was quite happy. 'Why, if I weren't happy I wouldn't be going to marry the girl just as soon as I've found us a place to live,' he said, grinning up at Amy with a wicked twinkle in his dark eyes.

Amy took a deep breath to tell Paddy what she thought of him, then expelled it once more in a long, whistling sigh. After all, she already knew she wanted to be with Paddy for the rest of her life, so marriage seemed the obvious step. The fact that he had informed Becky of his intention before so much as mentioning it to her was just typical of him. 'Never take anything – or anyone – for granted, Paddy Keagan', Amy said with mock severity. 'There's a jug of fresh lemonade cooling in the sink, Becky, and just before Paddy arrived I'd taken a batch of scones out of the new oven. Could you do with a little snack, queen? Because I'm sure Paddy would like to have a bit of a wash and a mouthful to eat before the rest of the family arrive back.' She had not said anything about Suzie, but thought she would do so presently and would let Paddy take her the cup of tea, which she usually made for her stepmother at this time of day.

'Ooh, Amy, I love your home-made lemonade and I love scones with butter on as well,' Becky said eagerly. 'Can Paddy come and sit with me while I have me tea?'

'We'll see,' Amy said, crossing her fingers behind her back. 'Now get back into bed, queen, and I'll make you tidy.'

Presently, returning to the kitchen, she found Paddy had had a quick wash and was vigorously drying himself with the roller towel on the back of the door. Amy poured tea into four enamel mugs, sliced and buttered a plate of scones and turned to Paddy. 'I didn't tell you before because I thought you'd had enough news for a while,' she observed. 'But Paddy, my love, your mam is having her afternoon rest because she went and caught the measles and has been pretty ill herself. If you'd like to take her tea up . . .'

But Paddy, ignoring her words, had come round the table in a couple of long strides and caught hold of her by the shoulders, staring anxiously down into her face. 'Dearest Amy, I were so gobsmacked to find you here that I never wondered *why* you weren't at the Adelphi, or in Huskisson Street. Now I come to look at you, though, it's clear as crystal that you've been nursin' Becky and me mam, and you're fair worn out. Why, girl, you're as white as a cod's underbelly!'

Amy tried to pull away from him, but such maidenly shrinking was foiled by Paddy's fingers simply tightening their grip. 'Why couldn't you say my face was white as pear blossom?' she enquired aggrievedly. 'Why does it always have to be perishin' fish?'

Paddy laughed and dropped a kiss on the end of her nose. 'Well, I'm used to seeing you with cheeks as pink as a shrimp ...' he began and had to dodge the swipe which Amy aimed at him. 'Now, now, no violence, or you won't get the pretty present I've brought back for you from halfway across the world. Look, Amy, just because we're having a bit of a joke, that doesn't mean I'm not grateful for what you've done for me mam, who wasn't that good to you when you were small. Why, you must have risked losing your job to take care of mam and little Becky – you're one of the best, so you are.'

'Your mam and I have been getting on much better for some while and I must say she's done everything she could to help me, once she was well enough to get out of bed,' Amy told him. 'Besides, she's your mother, so I would have done all I could for your sake, old Paddy. As for my job, they've told me to stay away until I'm clear of quarantine, so *that's* all right. Now what was that about a present?'

Paddy dug a hand into his pocket, then held his clenched fist out enticingly. 'Are all our differences over, or shall I find another pretty lady to wear my gift?'

Amy smiled and held out her hand. The next moment she was gasping with surprise and pleasure as Paddy slowly opened his fingers, around which hung the necklace of gold and jade. 'You had it all the time!' she said, her eyes glowing. 'So you really did think I'd thrown it away, it didn't get knocked into the fire like I imagined. Oh, Paddy, you must've thought that I was the most ungrateful girl in the world. Only ... only why didn't you tell me you'd found it, confront me with what you thought I'd done?'

'I dunno,' Paddy said briefly. 'I guess I was a fool, but I thought you were trying to tell me you didn't want *anything* from me, not my presents, nor my kisses, nor the necklace. So I ... I berthed aboard the SS *Frederica* and tried to forget all about you.' His fingers were at her neck, fumbling to get the little catch done up and Amy took hold of his shoulders and stood on tiptoe to kiss his chin.

She began to tell him how sorry she had been and how very happy she was now, and how they must never let such a misunderstanding arise again, but she had barely got two words out when she realised that Paddy was lifting her into his arms and that his face was getting closer and closer ...

Presently they moved apart, both more than a little breathless. 'For a first kiss that was really something,' Amy murmured, gazing up at Paddy with shining eyes. 'All those wasted years, Paddy, years when we spent all our energy in hating one another when we could have been doing ... doing ...'

'First kiss?' Paddy said, grinning all over his face. 'It might have been your first kiss, queen, but I've been practising up and down the coast of South America. Just so that I'd do it properly when I came home to you, of course,' he added kindly.

'I meant the first kiss between us two,' Amy said with what dignity she could muster. 'I've had a feller or two since you went, you cocky Keagan! Oh, I suppose you don't know that one of our room shares, Ella, got married last month? She married Philip Grimshaw, you remember him. And Mary is marrying a Welshman with two little sons – Haydn Lloyd his name is. And Gus and Minnie's going steady, and Albert and Ruthie ...'

'My God, they'll have to call Huskisson Street the marriage mart,' Paddy said, taking the mug of tea and a scone and beginning to climb the stairs.

Amy, following him with Becky's tea, nodded. 'You're right there – and one more small piece of news. Peggy Higgins and that sailor she left our Gus for have split up, and Peggy came round here, sweet as sugar, to tell Gus she'd made an awful mistake and would he have her back? You can guess what Gus said to her.'

Paddy chuckled. 'Just about,' he agreed. He flung open the door of his mother's room and entered, the tray balanced precariously on one hand. 'Guess who's come home from the sea ...' he began and was interrupted by a shriek like a steam train's whistle, as his mother leapt from her bed and charged across the room to throw her arms round her son's neck. Amy stood and smiled as tea, tray

442

and plate of buttered scones flew in three different directions while Paddy, laughing, tried to greet his mother, get her back into bed and answer the questions she was firing at him all at the same time. Amy stole forward and closed Suzie's bedroom door quietly, then returned to Becky. Sitting on her sister's bed she reflected that it was only right Suzie should have her son to herself for a bit after his long absence. For Amy there would be plenty of time – a lifetime, in fact.

But Amy did not get Paddy to herself until quite late that night, for he had to go round to the lodgings, which Gus and Albert still shared, to tell them he was home. Back at the house in Seafield Grove Suzie had come down for the evening meal, as she did every day, and Bill had returned from the fish market. He greeted his stepson with real pleasure, especially when it was explained to him that Paddy and Amy meant to marry when they could afford to do so. 'I always thought you two hid your feelings for one another under all that sniping and disagreeableness,' Bill said sagely. 'What's more, I reckon you're like as two peas in a pod – sharp tongued, quick-witted, but soft as herring roes underneath.'

'Oh, Dad, herring roes!' Amy said, giggling. 'There was Paddy telling me I looked pale as a cod's underbelly when he first came home and now you're telling me I'm squishy as herring roe underneath my quick wits. Still, I know what you mean, and there's a good deal of truth in it. Only in future, Paddy and me are going to be a bit more careful of one another's feelings; isn't that right, chuck?'

Paddy had agreed and they had spent a comfortable family evening, while the prodigal son told them all his adventures and assured them that he would not again take a berth aboard a ship which came into the port so rarely. 'Now that I've had a bit of experience aboard ship, I thought I'd try for a berth on a transatlantic liner,' he said. 'I'd be away three weeks at a time, I grant you, but that isn't like six months. Anyway, that's all for the future. Right now I'm taking a holiday. Besides, Amy and I will want to talk about both our careers, because if I do get a liner then I don't see why she shouldn't try for a job aboard as well. The really big ships employ quite a number of women and Amy's so efficient . . .'

Amy had been enchanted by the idea and intended to look into the possibilities, but right now she wanted to enjoy Paddy's company and talk about their lives together rather than their careers.

So when at last Suzie and Bill had settled down before the hearth, clearly with the intention of making an evening of it, Paddy took Amy's hand and informed their parents that they meant to go for a walk along the beach.

Outside the air was balmy with the scents of summer and when they reached the beach the freshening breeze brought the evocative smell of the sea to their nostrils. Paddy put his arm round Amy and drew her gently down into the shelter of one of the dunes. 'Oh, Amy, Amy, you smell so sweet,' he murmured, smoothing his hand down her cheek.

Amy responded for one giddying moment, then pulled herself free to remark, 'What? You mean the smell of shrimps has faded at last?'

Paddy laughed and held her a little tighter. 'I reckon you never did smell of any sort of fish,' he mumbled into the side of her neck. 'I were just getting at you because you didn't seem to admire me the way I thought you should. But that's all water under the bridge, queen. Now we've sorted ourselves out we'd best get a ring, make it official. Oh, Amy, *how* I do love you.'

Around them the little breeze played in the marram grass and now and then a movement from one or other of them disturbed a tiny, chilly river of sand, which ran down the side of the dune and formed its own miniature mountain on the beach below. But Amy and Paddy never even noticed. Warmly, sweetly, they were beginning to understand what had brought them together. Locked in each other's arms, on the dark beach, with the round silver moon the only witness, Paddy and Amy began to kiss.